The Girl Who Rode Dolphins

by

Michael J. Ganas

authorHOUSE®

AuthorHouse™
1663 Liberty Drive, Suite 200
Bloomington, IN 47403
www.authorhouse.com
Phone: 1-800-839-8640

This book is a work of fiction. People, places, events, and situations are the product of the author's imagination. Any resemblance to actual persons, living or dead, or historical events, is purely coincidental.

© 2008 Michael J. Ganas. All rights reserved.

No part of this book may be reproduced, stored in a retrieval system, or transmitted by any means without the written permission of the author.

First published by AuthorHouse   7/8/2008

ISBN: 978-1-4343-9364-7 (e)
ISBN: 978-1-4343-9362-3 (sc)
ISBN: 978-1-4343-9363-0 (hc)

Printed in the United States of America
Bloomington, Indiana

This book is printed on acid-free paper.

This book is dedicated to my wife, Harriet, and my daughter, Melissa:

The former is the gemstone of my life, a fortress of bewitching comfort and encouragement, truly the strongest person I have ever known;

The latter is my mist of bliss, a mountain of joy any dad would be proud of.

Facts

Haiti is currently the poorest country in the Western Hemisphere, a Caribbean nation beleaguered by economic strife, dismal squalor, and political instability, a land of defoliation and ecological ruin. It is a place with a violent past, punctuated by a succession of bloody rebellions and previously governed by a long line of statesmen and dictators whose policies were either inept, ineffectual, unpopular, corrupt, or oppressive. The Duvalier dictatorships of father and son, however, proved to be the most corrupt, oppressive and violent, and under their brutal regimes Haiti suffered deeply.

Francois "Papa Doc" Duvalier ruled Haiti from 1963 until his death in 1971 when his son Jean-Claude "Baby Doc" Duvalier took over the reins of power. Under the Duvalier governments, the population was kept in a state of fear, terrorized by the regime's secret police force, the Tonton Makout. They were also known as the VNS, Volunteers of National Security, and Papa Doc referred to them as his "civilian" military, while the citizens called them "the bogeymen." They were recruited mostly from Haiti's slums and were used to crush all opposition, often imprisoning without trial, torturing and even killing individuals considered enemies of the state. An estimated 60,000 Haitians were murdered at the hands of the Tonton Makout, which had a standing force of roughly 10,000 loyalists. Papa Doc made sure his secret police outnumbered the Haitian army by a factor of 2 in order to assure that he did not get overthrown in a military coup.

Both Francois Duvalier and his son also took advantage of the people's strong belief in voodoo to control the population. Consequently, much of the citizenry believed them to be voodoo spirits. To this day, voodoo blended with Catholicism is the religion of choice embraced by most Haitians.

Misappropriation of government funds amounting to hundreds of millions of dollars was common practice under Baby Doc's tyrannical rule, and in the wake of intense political unrest and pressure from the United States to step down, he was finally forced from power in February of 1986, whereupon he fled to France.

A wealth of evidence shows various drug cartels to be firmly entrenched in present day Haiti, where the stormy political climate, endemic poverty and a breakdown in civil order makes it an ideal staging area for the transshipment of illegal contraband, where public officials are often threatened or corrupted by bribery to keep a blind eye to drug trafficking.

Navassa Island is a small, uninhabited island, which lies in the Caribbean Sea between Haiti and Jamaica. Jurisdiction of the island was originally disputed by Haiti before it was claimed in 1801 as an unorganized, unincorporated territory of the United States, which currently administers it through the U.S. Fish and Wildlife Service.

Malique is a fictitious fishing village that lies roughly midway between the real cities of Saint-Marc and Gonaives along Haiti's western coastline. It has been created solely for the purpose of this novel.

Osama Bin Laden and his Al Qaeda following constitute an actual present day organization of Islamic extremists bent on the destruction of the United States and its allies.

All mention of Haiti's former leadership and historical events, both past and modern day, are based on documented chronicles and are used as a backdrop for the writing of this novel. In this way, history and current world affairs have been merged with fiction. All characters, creatures and unusual settings that play a key role within the novel's plot are entirely fictitious and have been created solely for the reader's intrigue and entertainment.

—

Prologue

November 4th, 1985, Somewhere in the Caribbean Sea

The woman clung helplessly but with grim determination to the piece of flotsam, the final remnant of the sailboat that had borne her along the West Indies Archipelago over the last several weeks. The irate sea had become a brutal tormentor, lashing her face and eyes incessantly with brine that now burned like acid. She was exhausted, feeling her remaining strength rapidly ebbing by the constant buffeting. In spite of this, she stubbornly hung on, wondering how much longer the storm would last. If anything, it had gotten worse, much worse.

The pervading ebony blackness that had ravaged her throughout the night had now given way to a fierce mournful gray, and she knew that dawn had come. With wanton hands, the pounding gloom pressed itself upon her like a pillaging marauder caught in the throes of lust, every so often thrusting downward with a clumsy errant spike of searing white light and unleashing a harsh crackling outburst that merged with the cacophony of an excited sea. It tossed and jostled her violently, seemingly intent on ransacking her very will.

As another swell lifted her high, she pushed herself up as best she could from the meager panel of wood, careful not to unbalance it. The flotation it gave her was scant and she wanted to avoid upending it again. Craning her head and reducing her eyes to mere slits against the onslaught of wind and riven rain, she glanced hopefully about. The sea remained desolate, with neither watercraft nor land in sight. Only a bleak wash of huge marching whitecaps and foam, raging and turbulent, lay beneath a low-slung formation of angry dark clouds that clung to the ocean like an impenetrable blanket of destruction. The dreary view disappeared as the wave bearing her suddenly swept away, and as she dropped down into another churning canyon she felt her spirits plunge.

But she was not ready to give up. Withdrawing into herself once again, she sought to escape the immensity and loneliness of it all. It was an old trick she had learned during her days of competition, a way of distancing herself from the pain. And now she would use it to hold at bay the demons of despondency that sought to pull her hope of survival into the dismal depths. Bolstered by this state of mind, she hung on, unwilling to quit.

As if adding to her misery, the wind abruptly swirled, howling madly and whipping up a frothing spate that dashed her without warning. Temporarily blinded, she failed to prepare herself for the next towering wave that sought to devour. She became aware of the danger only at the last instant, and when she did, her pulse quickened. It was a white water monster of colossal size, far bigger than anything that had come before it. Cresting to a dizzying height, it hung momentarily as though it would swamp the earth. And then it descended, hammering down on her with such savageness that she thought she was being crushed. A torrent of water tore into her, viciously battering and tumultuous, seeking to find entrance into mouth, throat and lungs. Smothered to near suffocation, she was tumbled and pulled down yet again, much deeper this time. Inwardly, she screamed, but it was not a cry of panic, for she would not let herself yield to such primitive emotion. Rather it was a cry of defiance against the seemingly endless chain of crashing water that had pummeled her mercilessly and relentlessly throughout the night.

With gritty determination she somehow found the strength to kick her way free of the ocean's death grip, desperate to capture another morsel of life-sustaining breath amid the wild turbulence. Reaching atmosphere, she was immediately racked by a seizure of fractious coughing and gagging as she strained air into heaving lungs. Squinting through eyes swollen and scalded red, she caught fleeting glimpses of electrical discharges that danced in jagged streaks over the wind-whipped froth, contributing immeasurably to the hellish synergy of a sky and sea gone mad.

The wind suddenly shifted and intensified, coming around as if to challenge the very waves it had spawned, shrieking like an angry falcon set on drowning out the sea's pervasive roar. It slammed into the next rising swell, pushing back with a raw belligerency as though determined to destroy the wave's impetus. But the wave was not to be stopped, and it rose up mightily like a rearing warhorse, building upon itself in preparation to trample and crush all that opposed it. Caught in its grip, the woman felt her stomach lodge in her throat as the mountainous swell catapulted her upward with explosive force. Flung to a seemingly impossible height, she glimpsed the sheer precipice of water that fell away, a giddy drop that shocked her to the very core. She remembered to inhale only at the last possible moment, filling her lungs as a massive sheet of water licked out to take her. The wave curled sharply, and she found herself hurled roughly into the abysmal trough far below. The water felt like granite as she struck, and the panel of teak to which she clung bucked up into her like a rodeo bull, driving the wind from her lungs, and for one fleeting moment she had the sensation of being smitten by the hand of an angry god. Tons of water pushed her deep as the wave collapsed on top of her, and it took all her strength to battle her way back to the surface above. Almost losing her grip on the hatch cover, she kicked insanely to keep her head above the surge, giving succor to the floundering buoyancy of her makeshift float. The wind blasted her, digging its fingers into the rampaging sea, roiling and aerating the water into a foaming maelstrom, and it was only an act of will that made her fight on.

Once again she managed to find purchase in an atmosphere without pity, and she gulped greedily in an effort to trap air into starving lungs. Almost immediately, another furious jumble of white water engulfed her, tumbling and dragging her under like the claws of an avenging demon.

It was then that her will began to flag. She had been in the storm-tossed sea for what seemed like an eternity, although only fifteen hours had passed since her vessel had suddenly taken on water. Subsequent to a horrendous pounding lasting most of the previous day, the severely battered 50-foot sloop had finally succumbed to a watery grave despite its tenacious attempt to remain afloat.

For what was perhaps the thousandth time, she fought her way to the surface in the ragged buoyancy. The realization that she was no longer clutching the hatch cover only added to her torment, underscoring the utter hopelessness of her predicament. And for the first time since her nightmare had begun, she began to welcome the prospect of death. The fight within her was now gone, replaced by a budding eagerness for the sea to finally take her. It would be so easy. The ill-defined vortex that existed somewhere between a churning ocean and whirling wind seemed to suddenly diminish in its ferocity, and it beckoned her downward into the serene depths with a strange enfolding comfort. She hesitated, wondering why she had resisted the sea's promise so savagely and for so long.

With a detached awareness she puzzled over the luminescent oblates floating languidly below her, perhaps twenty in all pulsing in a silent synchronized dance as they bobbed in the surge, and she marveled at the multitude of iridescent strands that trailed behind each. She was familiar with all the known variations of such life forms, coelenterates that had flourished and evolved throughout the earth's oceans over the last 650 million years, but she had never seen a species such as this. She looked on, watching the silhouette of her physical body eclipse the soft glow of shimmering light. Vaguely she became aware of her own form, the outline of limbs, torso and bloated abdomen, and with it a surge of guilt.

Startled, she was reminded why she had fought so hard to survive and suddenly the depths were no longer inviting, the wavering iridescence now suffused with the burning embers of hell as thread-like wisps embraced her like vines of searing fire. Fully galvanized back to consciousness, she began to scream in response to the intense pain rapidly consuming her, but the crushing burden of sea would not allow this, threatening to inundate throat and lungs with liquid death. Steeling herself against the pain and the temptation to inhale, she fought back the rising panic that was like a convulsing rhino in her chest, one that was quickly gathering momentum in a headlong charge toward oblivion.

Trying to orient herself to the roiling surface, she glanced wildly about. It was the fading afterglow of lightning bolts acting like beacons from far above that gave her a sense of direction, but at the same time their remoteness drove home the overwhelming futility of her plight. With a feeling of total failure she realized she was now too deep and too exhausted to reach atmosphere before blacking out. As darkness began to flood the fringes of her consciousness she cursed her own weakness and the men who had brought this upon her. She would perish without a trace, lost at sea like the others who had accompanied her. Even worse, her potential offspring would be denied the life that awaited it, and instinctively she embraced her swollen womb protectively in an act of forlorn sympathy.

The movement increased her agony as more painful welts erupted along her belly, a severe reminder that she was still entangled among the strange life forms. But the pain also told her that she was still among the living, and it gave her a temporary respite against the blackness that was slowly eating its way toward the center of her awareness.

The pain became her universe, predominating all her other senses, and she did not notice the gentle nudge that came from behind. Looking up in a final farewell to the world above, she became mildly aware that the surface was much closer, the flickering discharges of electrical energy seemingly directly overhead. Perceiving she had transcended into a state of delirium she suddenly felt herself lifted into the explosive interface between sea and air, and she automatically inhaled deeply, simultaneously swallowing choking mouthfuls of water as an avalanching wave slammed into her. She didn't care, managing to get yet more air into aching lungs, coughing wildly in the process.

Encouraged, she could feel a residue of her former strength returning, and with it a shred of optimism. Something seemed to be keeping her up, stabilizing her against the turbulence. Yes, it was directly under her, alternately nudging and bumping her anatomy with a precision that was both gentle and yet strong enough to counter the violent surges that threatened to take her back under.

With considerable effort she managed to glance behind her and was immediately stricken with terror. A dorsal fin poked above the rolling foam. Abruptly, the small spark of hope that had touched her vanished with the speed of a tiny comet plummeting into a black hole. She stared in horror as the creature rose higher, continuing to nudge her. It's dark back glistened, aglow in the faint luminescence cast by the mass of thread-like tentacles draped over it.

In that moment of despair she lifted an arm inundated in the jelly-like strands towards the heavens and cried out to God to give her a quick and merciful ending. Almost instantly and in answer to her plea, the clouds responded with a crackling burst of light that streaked down upon her, sizzling the water with a flaring brightness so intense that she was certain the gates of paradise had opened to receive her. All at once, both her plight and misery dissolved, replaced by strange images and thoughts that thundered through her mind with the grace of stampeding elephants. Then all sense of consciousness deserted her.

—

May 23rd, 2008, Port-au-Prince, Haiti

The two men looked glum as they drank thirstily from frosty mugs in a dingy corner of the dimly lit bar, one of many such watering holes situated along the shabby harbor. Speaking in hushed, guarded tones, they glanced warily at the occasional patron that drifted into the grimy establishment. Though seated, one of the men appeared to be a hulking giant, possessing wide bulky shoulders that ballooned from his tightly fitting tank top and leaned over the table like massive obsidian cliffs. The bright red bandana that encircled his forehead seemed to be in a losing battle at stemming the flow of perspiration that emanated from the glistening dome of his cranium, an aftereffect of the muggy confines of the tavern, which provided little respite from the steaming tropical heat outside.

The black goliath listened intently to the quiet comments of his companion sitting across from him, a white man with riveting green eyes, intense and penetrating like those of a timber wolf on the hunt. Though physically dwarfed by his associate, he was by no means diminutive in size, displaying a hard lean torso to which his damp t-shirt clung and well-defined muscular arms that hinted of explosive strength and athletic prowess.

"It doesn't make sense. We should've found something by now," the smaller man whispered with exasperation.

The larger man gave a sympathetic nod. "Maybe so, but we have not yet completed all the possibilities. The area to the north may prove to be more fruitful. Perhaps tomorrow will bring us good fortune." Zimbola sipped the cold ale, his expression distant. "Perhaps some spiritual guidance from Bon Dieu will put us on the right track."

Jake eyed his partner with skepticism. "You're not going to start with that voodoo malarkey again, are you, Zimby?"

Zimbola scowled, a rather frightening visage to those unfamiliar with the man's quirks. Leaning his bulk farther forward, he hissed, "Tis Obeah. I've told you before, in the English speaking Caribbean we call it Obeah," pronouncing it "oh bee ah" and emphasizing the "ah."

Jake shifted closer. "Well, it was your oh bee ah," he mimicked, "that almost got me killed near Anse. Remember?"

The larger man's scowl vanished like a squall scudding over the horizon. Zimbola shrugged. "A dream spirit seduced me into believing we would find that for which we have been searching if we looked there. But the Loa was not an evil one, not an eater of men's souls."

Jake held up his left forearm, displaying the jagged puckered scar. "No, it was an eater of flesh... my flesh. That mako nearly had me for dinner."

"That mako got us the equivalent of fifteen hundred dollars U.S. at the Hilton in Anse," Zimbola countered. "At a dollar fifty a pound, it became dinner for the rich hotel guests who think they are eating swordfish."

"We didn't find anything, did we?" Jake reminded him.

"Loas come in many forms and their motives are not always understood by the living. Yes, it may have appeared to mislead us but it nevertheless brought us good fortune. Did it not?"

Jake waved a disparaging hand. Zimby, as he affectionately called his oversized friend, had grown up in Jamaica and had been indoctrinated into the islanders' beliefs from a very early age. Zimby's faith was unshakeable, and sometimes a nuisance. To Jake, the worship of voodoo was primitive and barbaric, based on superstition and spectacle that overlapped the realm of black magic and witchcraft. But he had no desire to offend Zimbola by telling him that, although he suspected his friend sensed this. Zimbola had often tried to explain the fundamentals of this animist religion in which objects and natural phenomena are believed to have holy significance, to possess a soul or Loa. The Loa formed a pantheon of deities that included hundreds of spirits. Although Jake had been raised in a Christian family, his convictions were inherently temporal-based, instinctively rooted in the pragmatic: if you couldn't see, hear, touch, taste or smell it, then it didn't exist. Unlike his Jamaican counterpart, Jake shied away from the notion that good fortune was the result of divine intervention, holding steadfast to the premise that you made your own luck. As of late, unfortunately, their luck had been anything but good.

As if reading his thoughts, Zimbola said, "We must take the necessary steps to turn the bad luck into good. I have heard of a most powerful Maman who lives on Tortuga Island." Zimbola ignored the frown that abruptly clouded Jake's face. A Maman was a high priestess of the Jamaican version of voodoo. "Perhaps if we went to her, she could provide us with the spiritual guidance to help with our search. If we sailed tomorrow, we-"

"Mr. Javolyn, I knew I'd find you here." The voice cut off Zimbola's discourse like a finely honed sword lopping off a head. The man behind it was short, dumpy, and walked with a pronounced limp. Chester Hennington hobbled over and sat down in the chair nearest Jake. Hennington claimed an eclectic lineage of English and Black African, with a smattering of French and other extractions introduced into his family tree at some point or other in generations past. Native to Port-au-Prince, he was a full-time broker by profession, typically intervening as agent to a variety of legitimate ventures but more often acting as a go-between for unsavory parties engaged in illicit activities. As usual, Hennington was clad in his customary three-piece suit of white linen which, although quite expensive by Haitian standards, never quite succeeded in producing the image of a successful businessman, a status he had actually achieved within both the rich and infamous circles of island culture. Beyond an air-conditioned environment, the ravages of oppressive heat and humidity were ever present throughout the sweltering city, causing even the most freshly laundered and pressed fabrics to hang limply on sweat-dampened bodies, particularly on individuals who were foolish enough to embellish themselves with formal attire that was further adorned with wide-brimmed white fedora and tightly cinched necktie of glossy white silk, as did Hennington.

"I trust you gentlemen are having a pleasant day," Hennington said in nearly flawless, unaccented English, displaying a smile fringed with crooked, tobacco-stained teeth.

Jake kept his expression somber. "We were until you got here."

"Oh, come now, Mr. Javolyn, you're not going to keep blaming me for that little mishap that occurred last month, are you?" Hennington objected wearily as he removed the fedora to expose a flattened mat of thinning silver-streaked hair. He placed the hat on the table and began to dab away at the sweat that beaded on his honey-colored but deeply furrowed brow with a handkerchief. The remnants of what must have been a nasty bruise marred his right cheek, and the flesh below his left eye appeared to have developed a line of scar tissue since the last time Jake had seen him.

Jake slugged down some more ale, taking the opportunity to take inventory of the three black men that had accompanied Hennington into the tavern and who were currently lingering at the bar, watching the conversation with quiet interest. They seemed to be paying special attention to Zimbola's imposing presence and the menacing scowl he focused in their direction.

Jake couldn't fault Hennington for his precautionary measures at self-preservation. In a country with a minimum wage of less than $2 a day, personal bodyguards were cheap. In Haiti, the Western Hemisphere's poorest nation, guys like Hennington were prime targets for roaming thugs, called *"zenglendoes"* in the native Creole, who mugged and killed for money. Rampant violent crime had been plaguing the country's capital, an overcrowded and crumbling city of two million inhabitants, for several decades now, and it seemed to be getting worse. Just last week, a well-known businessman was gunned down in broad daylight on a thoroughfare in one of Port-au-Prince's "safer" neighborhoods when three cars blocked his vehicle in traffic and an assailant shot him five times. In another recent incident at a local cockfight arena, a guy named Junior went into the ring to cash in on his winnings only to be gunned down. Stray bullets from the gunmen also killed two security guards and a bystander, while another innocent onlooker was severely injured. Political unrest accounted for a significant amount of the crime. A month earlier, four pipe bombs were thrown at the residence of a U.S. Embassy official. Jake recalled the rise in violence that seemed to accompany every presidential and legislative election, underscored by politically motivated killings and indiscriminate gunfire directed at pedestrians. All of these occurrences tended to create an overall environment of fear in which no citizen felt safe. With armed robberies and break-ins, murders and car hijackings becoming commonplace, criminals were operating with near impunity. Trying to impose law and order in the impoverished Caribbean nation was a challenging undertaking, particularly in light of the legal system that was both inefficient and infested with corruption. Understaffed with some 3,000 officers in a country of nearly nine million people, the Haitian National Police force was extremely limited in its enforcement capabilities, with bribery being epidemic among its constituents and some of the officers being worse than the vilest of criminals. The bottom line was that the more affluent members of Haitian society could ill afford not to pay the expense of personal security if they wanted to survive.

Jake slammed his stein onto the table with more force than intended and affixed Hennington with a hostile glare. Out of the corner of his eye, he spied the man's retinue stiffen in readiness. Hennington waved them off.

"You told me the Kingston run would be a cakewalk, that there'd be no risk. Just a simple load of bootleg CDs and DVDs, that's what you told me. Well somebody wanted that shipment pretty badly, enough to wager having a running gun battle at sea and shooting up my vessel."

Several customers at nearby tables were beginning to stare, and Jake realized he was starting to shout. He made a conscious effort to lower his voice and eyed Hennington intently. "Somehow we managed to get away, but I couldn't help being suspicious about what I was carrying so I decided to have a look inside those crates. And do you know what I found?" Jake paused for effect. "Military grade weapons. AK-47s, land mines, RPGs."

Hennington looked unperturbed. "You have to understand, I'm just a simple middleman. Clients come to me all the time seeking a runner and I arrange it. I'm rarely informed about the true nature of the contraband."

Javolyn wasn't convinced if this was true or not. He and Zimbola only occasionally resorted to smuggling, and only when they were in desperate need of cash. In conducting such work, it was a normal rule of the trade not to be too concerned about what one transported, only that you moved it from point A to point B, with no questions asked. With smuggling, there was always the risk of being boarded by authorities, or even worse, by being ambushed by pirates. Whenever a smuggler was captured by authorities, penalties were subject to the type of illegal cargo he was caught hauling. But more often than not, you could bribe your way out of such a predicament. When such an option failed to work, long-term incarceration was usually the inevitable result of being caught with shipments that involved drugs or weapons since such contraband invoked the most severe punishments. In the event one was unfortunate enough to be waylaid by pirates, however, you could easily find yourself thrown into the briny depths as shark bait. And many smugglers could not discount the possibility that a gunboat captain operating under the flag of an island nation would resort to piracy for personal gain. All in all, any self-respecting individual engaged in the clandestine trade of smuggling understood that the level of monetary compensation for services rendered should be based on the degree of risk one undertook.

"I should have been paid three times more than what I received," Jake snarled.

"I'm sorry, but the deal was consummated when you made the delivery. My client will not agree to dispersing additional compensation."

"Then I should have deep-sixed the cargo when I had the chance," Jake said with annoyance, fighting back a strong inclination to cinch the tie surrounding Hennington's bloated neck a few inches tighter. Unfortunately, he still needed the man, for better or worse, and had no desire to terminate the relationship as yet.

An uncomfortable silence followed before Hennington said, "I have another job for you, actually two…that is, if you're still interested," his tone conciliatory.

"What is it this time, nuclear bombs?" Jake replied hotly.

Hennington ignored the sarcasm. "I think I can get you $50,000 for the next run."

Even Zimbola, who had been keeping a wary eye on Hennington's entourage, turned to look at the broker. The most they had previously been paid was $15,000. The blatant anger that had characterized Jake's foul mood a moment earlier subsided into a mask of impassivity. Something extremely valuable had to be at stake to be offered a sum of that magnitude, but this time he would not be duped.

"I have to know what I'll actually be hauling before I can accept," Jake retorted stiffly.

"I'm not at liberty to divulge that."

Jake studied Hennington shrewdly. "Operating expenses have escalated considerably as of late and my boat sustained quite a bit of damage on that last run. The repairs were exceptionally expensive." In actuality, he and Zimby had patched all the bullet holes themselves with nothing more than epoxy, paint and gel coat. "On top of that, not knowing the disposition of the cargo will cost extra. Make it one hundred and you have a deal."

For the first time in their mutually beneficial relationship, a relationship that had up to now favored the fat businessman, Hennington failed to maintain a poker face. In fact, he appeared quite aghast. "If time were not of the essence in this matter, I'd take my business elsewhere," he bristled in outrage. "Seventy-five!"

Jake remained adamant, sensing he had the upper hand. "No way. It's one hundred or I pass on this one."

Hennington gathered in his dignity. "Very well. But don't expect me to throw any more work your way once you complete the run."

Jake ignored the threat. He was now convinced that the man needed his services more than he needed Hennington. "When and where do I make the pickup?" he asked.

"You'll be notified of that as soon as the client gives me that information," Hennington said, once again assuming a business-like demeanor.

Javolyn leaned back in his chair. "You mentioned two jobs?"

Hennington sighed. "I have a small party from the states that's looking to charter a dive boat – marine zoologists from the University of Miami. Their spokesman made a point of telling me how limited their funds are. Fellow by the name of Grahm." Hennington had arranged charters for Javolyn on numerous occasions in the past, most of them sport diving excursions in which Jake had played host to wealthy vacationers.

"By any chance, his first name didn't happen to be Franklin?"

"Why yes, I believe it was. Do you know him?"

Jake shook his head. "I never met the man, but I've read some of his work. He's an eminent scientist within his field. Can he afford twelve hundred a day?" Twelve hundred was his minimum going rate, otherwise he was losing money.

Hennington's fingers played with the brim of the fedora lying on the table. "One thousand dollars for each day's leasing of your boat was the most he was willing to offer. However, he did agree to pay the cost of any fuel expended that exceeded five hundred gallons during the trip. He mentioned he needed a vessel of sufficient size to accommodate three people on an outing lasting two, maybe three days."

"Did he have any particular destination in mind?"

"He said he'd disclose that once his party boarded your vessel. He'd like to sail tomorrow. Do you want the job?" Hennington seemed to be growing impatient.

Jake hesitated, strongly tempted to turn down such a meager offer. If he hadn't been so desperately strapped for cash, he would have. "Yeah, I'll take it," he said begrudgingly, casting morose eyes on the stein of ale in front of him. "Have him meet us at the usual place, oh six hundred." As an afterthought, he added, "I assume this trip will not conflict in any way with our first item of business."

"The shipment won't be ready for at least one week, that much I know," Hennington answered testily. "Please make sure you and your vessel are available at that time."

"You don't have to worry about that." Jake scrutinized the broker's face. "By the way, Hennington, you don't look so good. You have an accident or something?"

"I fell off a ladder," Hennington muttered. He stood up and placed the hat back on his head. "Gentlemen."

Zimbola watched as Chester Hennington's escort followed their benefactor from the premises. "You constantly surprise me, Jay Jay. First you agree to ferry cargo without knowing what we be carrying or where we be goin'. Then you go against your own policy of never taking a party sailing for less than your normal fee." He looked lugubrious. "My father used to say 'A fool is the man who sells himself too cheaply, but the biggest fool of all is the man who is easily lured by the promise of wealth, for he unwittingly takes the devil along for the ride.'"

Jake merely smiled at the metaphor. There would always be risks.

- 2 -

Almost four weeks prior to having met with Jake Javolyn and Zimbola in the waterfront tavern, Hennington sat meekly, hat in hand, before Colonel Henri Ternier at the Port-au-Prince Headquarters of the Haitian National Police. Ternier's office, though neat, orderly and modestly furnished, gave no hint of the brutality of the man, with the walls lined with a multitude of framed photographs predominantly depicting a smiling Ternier shaking the hand of various important government officials. The largest picture, strategically hung behind his desk so as not to be missed by anyone visiting him in his inner sanctum, showed Ternier standing tall and proud next to president-elect Rene Preval, the current leader of the Haitian government. Less obvious and positioned in a far corner of the room, another picture displayed the Colonel with Preval's predecessor, President Jean Bertrand Aristide, removed from power by the U.S. in February of 2004 in the midst of a rebellious uprising.

Henri Ternier had good reason to smile, Hennington thought grimly, having amassed a considerable amount of wealth in connection with narcotics and weapons trafficking over the last several years. Following the ouster of

Baby "Doc" Duvalier in 1986, Haiti's government had been notoriously unstable, drawing the attention of rich Colombian drug lords who had immediately taken advantage of the complete breakdown of bureaucratic institutions during that period. Haiti was particularly appealing because of its geographic location, offering the most direct route - barring transit of Cuba - from Colombia to the United States. In addition, the Island of Hispaniola on which Haiti is situated had a wide variety of harbors and inlets that provided ideal protection to drug smuggling vessels. Moreover, the Haitian Air Force had no radar facilities and did not routinely patrol Haitian airspace. Planes laden with drugs could take off and land freely at any of the island's numerous secondary airstrips. The country offered many ideal staging areas where large quantities of drugs from the cartels could be stored prior to shipment to the states. By first buying up legitimate businesses to serve as front companies for their smuggling operations and gaining access to local commerce, the Colombians then focused on recruiting and corrupting public officials to protect their interests. Key military officers such as Ternier were ideal candidates for recruitment since they were in a position to assure noninterference in drug operations.

Command of the Desallines Barracks had allowed Colonel Ternier to play a pivotal role in Haitian politics, mainly because his unit was responsible for safeguarding the Presidential Palace. One particularly powerful drug lord, Rafael Cardoza, had established a working relationship with Ternier by using Hennington as a go-between. Payoffs to the Colonel to look the other way were made on a shipment by shipment basis. As of late, unfortunately for Hennington, Colonel Ternier had been growing increasingly dissatisfied with the amount of money he had been receiving and seized a shipment of drugs in protest, re-selling the load through his personal connections at a substantial profit. When Cardoza investigated the impoundment, he discovered that Hennington had been pocketing most of what should have gone to Ternier. Hennington's left kneecap still throbbed painfully at the memory of the beating he had received at the hands of Cardoza's ruffians for his transgression.

Cardoza had sent his chief lieutenant, Sebastian Ortega, with two other hooligans to administer the punishment and to make sure Hennington was to right the wrongs he had committed against Ternier. Ortega let it be known in no uncertain terms what the outcome would be if Hennington did not get back in the good graces of the Colonel. Ternier was too valuable a resource to lose at this point in time and they had an aggressive schedule of shipments to maintain, most of which would make their way through Haitian territory. Upon being kicked and punched just short of having severe bodily damage inflicted on him, Hennington was given a final reminder. The heavy blow to the kneecap had left him a hobbling cripple during the last month, and walking had been especially painful.

Hennington remembered the intense agony of the baseball bat bashing his patella as he lay crumpled on the floor and the final instruction mouthed by a snarling Ortega standing over him. He was to meet with Ternier as soon as possible. He was to get back into the Colonel's good graces by making concessions with his own funds. The Colonel would be expecting him.

Ternier appeared to be concluding some paperwork as he sat behind his desk, completely ignoring Hennington ever since he had limped painfully into the office and been offered a chair by one of the Colonel's adjutants. After what seemed like several minutes of prolonged, unbearable silence following the aide's exit from the room, the barracks commander finally looked up, locking dark baleful eyes onto him. The abysmal loathing lurking deep within those hellish orbs was hypnotic, like vicious monsters rising to the surface to devour prey, and Hennington suddenly found himself paralyzed with fear. Unlike the congenially smiling man in the photographs decorating the office walls, the feral grin displayed on Ternier's face was so far removed from a state of benignity that it could only be described as malevolent and foreboding. Here was a side to the man he hadn't seen before. Hennington felt a chill knife through his body, realizing that up to now he had severely misjudged the true nature of the man seated across from him. The amiable benevolence Ternier had shown him on previous occasions had been a skillfully erected façade, designed to deceive by masking the intrinsic profundity of underlying cruelty that was now revealed in one fleeting moment, mainly through those terrifying eyes. Clearly Ternier was not a man to be trifled with.

"So, Mr. Hennington, I am told you have been cheating me," Ternier said in mock joviality, speaking in the native Creole.

Hennington swallowed hard, unable to conceal his growing fright. "It was all a misunderstanding, I can assure you." He was aware of his own quavering voice.

"Yes, I'm sure it was," Ternier said softly, rising from his chair and calmly walking around the side of the desk. "How foolish of me for thinking a man such as yourself would let greed get the better of him."

Ternier began a slow circuit of the room, hands clasped behind his back, his bearing rigid and aristocratic. He was a tall man, clean-shaven and possessing a light-brown complexion complemented by a closely trimmed mat of tightly curled black hair capping his head. Sporting a crisply starched and pressed uniform that molded snugly to a brawny, evenly proportioned body, Ternier presented a striking figure.

Stopping with his back to Hennington, he stared at the wall as if looking through it. "How despicable of me for considering the supposition that you were withholding the remainder of my gratuities for yourself when I should have known all along that you were merely keeping those monies in escrow on my behalf," he said evenly, reverting to English that held a slight French accent.

Hennington sat transfixed, galvanized with dread. "Yes, yes, I was going to turn it all over to you at the conclusion of the next shipment...as a token of my, uh, appreciation," his reply coming out in a sputter.

Henri turned around, directing rabid eyes at the fat broker. "I am too cynical to be worthy of your friendship," almost sighing as he said it. He walked behind Hennington who sat as if electrified.

"Can you ever forgive a man like me for his lack of good faith."

Hennington nodded vigorously, too fearful to speak or look behind him.

Ternier eyed the back of Hennington's head, a myriad of gruesome possibilities flashing through his psychotic brain. "You do me honor," he said. "But perhaps I can atone for my mistake by giving you a tour of our humble facilities here."

Ternier nearly crept as he came around the chair to loom over Hennington, who appeared as if he were on the verge of a stroke. "Come," Ternier murmured in a barely audible whisper, smiling without humor. "I have some things you may be interested in seeing."

Fifteen minutes later, Chester Hennington, escorted by Colonel Henri Ternier and three policemen, was led down a poorly lit, squalid corridor, one of many such hallways in the National Penitentiary adjoining the Desalines Barracks. The three plainclothes police officers worked directly for Ternier and were the same three men that Jake Javolyn would later assume to be Hennington's personal bodyguards. In a way they were, for they had been assigned the ardous task of keeping Hennington alive and safe on the crime-ridden streets of the city. This arrangement had come about shortly after Ternier was contacted by Cardoza's chief lieutenant. Ortega had apologized for Hennington's greed. He had also informed the Colonel about the nature of the punishment Hennington had received and that the broker had some amends to make. Restitution would be forthcoming. Greenbacks previously pocketed by the broker were to be immediately turned over to Ternier. Ortega further told Ternier that in Hennington's present condition, however, the broker would fall easy victim to the "zenglendoes" prowling the waterfront since that was where Hennington conducted most of his business. Upon hearing this, Ternier had quickly dispatched the three undercover policemen, making it clear that while they were to protect him, they were also to obey the broker's directives until further notice.

As the five men proceeded down the corridor, the air became rank with the smell of unwashed bodies. Human sweat and excrement seemed to hang in the air, making Hennington almost gag. As they came around a bend, a holding cell reminiscent of a slave ship appeared before them. Within the cell's dark confines, Hennington could just make out a horde of black bodies crammed into a space no more than twelve by fifteen feet. The overpowering stench of biodegrading urine assaulted his nostrils like a heavy blow, and he nearly collapsed from dizziness in the 105 degree Fahreheit temperature.

About forty-five men sat on the cement floor, one behind the other in tight rows, knees to chins. Most were scrawny, and a profusion of interminable sweat plastered their tattered, soiled clothing to their bodies. Beyond the bars there was no toilet or sink with running water. The entire floor was jammed with inmates, with no room available to lie down anywhere. Even worse, there were no fans, air-conditioning, or ventilation of any kind to reduce the buildup of stifling heat and foul odors. Such amenities would have required electricity to power them, a relatively expensive commodity in the poverty-stricken nation. The broker was appalled at the sight of a communal bucket caked with feces sitting in one corner of the cell where prisoners could defecate or urinate. To Hennington, the overall scene was horrifying. He had heard rumors about these conditions, but one had to actually see it to believe that such an environment of human misery existed.

Ternier broke the spell of revulsion. "These men are criminal detainees. They get one meal a day, and it is not very much. Malnutrition is common here because we can only afford to feed our prisoners 1,300 calories per day. Most people require 2,000 calories if they are to survive. As a result, a few of these men will ultimately die of starvation before they are released." The Colonel was speaking English again. He seemed to be enjoying himself immensely at the sight of such abject suffering. The wretched conditions did not seem to invoke any repugnance from him whatsoever.

Ternier continued with his rhetoric. "These men are kept here in pretrial detention. They have not yet had the opportunity to go before a judge. With our inefficient judicial system and without the posting of bail, some of these detainees will be here for years, even if their offenses are very minor."

The Colonel directed the beam of the flashlight he carried at a pathetic, emaciated wreck of a human being at the rear of the cell. "That one there has been in here for nearly three years awaiting trial for the theft of a tape recorder. Such an offense would normally get him a maximum sentence of thirty days jail time, but he will most likely starve to death before he goes to trial."

At that moment, Hennington could no longer restrain the rising nausea overwhelming him. He let fly, grabbing hold of the holding cell's slime-ridden bars to keep from collapsing, vomiting copiously onto the filthy floor. When he finally lifted his head, he appeared quite sick.

Ternier and the three officers laughed loudly at this. "Surely the sight of these inmates does not make you ill," he chortled. "But I do not advise touching these bars. Fungus and parasitic infections are very common down here."

With a start, Hennington let go of the bars and wiped his hands vigorously against his trousers.

"And unfortunately, nothing can be done for these poor souls if they should get an infection. You see, there are no doctors available to diagnose or treat sick detainees. There is no medicine at this facility." Ternier spoke without sympathy, once again exhibiting that insane grin of his. "Come now, we have more to see."

A tremulous Hennington was led to a heavy steel doorway where two uniformed guards armed with shotguns were stationed. At seeing Ternier, they came to rigid attention and saluted. The Colonel did not reciprocate, flouting the military custom. Obsequiously, one of the guards pulled open the bolt on the door to let Ternier and the others pass. They came into a hallway where the lighting was much better. A succession of rooms with wire-reinforced glass windows lined one side of the corridor.

"It is inside this sector of the building where detainees who cause trouble are brought," Ternier said as he walked past the first two rooms, both of which were unoccupied. He stopped at the third cell and looked inside. Beyond the window, two guards were pummeling an inmate with batons while the man was strapped helplessly to a chair. Although the man was bloodied from a heavy gash in his forehead and appeared to be unconscious, the guards continued to enthusiastically beat him about the shoulders, arms and knees.

Ternier turned to Hennington. "This man complained too much about the length of his pretrial incarceration."

At the next window, two other guards were casually inflicting serious pain on another inmate. One guard wielded a cattle prod while the other held a lit cigar. They took turns, alternately electro-shocking and burning the victim, targeting various places on his naked black body while he hung upside down, suspended from the ankles by a chain attached to a ceiling hook. A slow trickle of blood oozed from a deep abrasion where the chain, wrapped tightly about the man's ankles, had chafed the flesh raw. The guards seemed to focus most of their efforts on the man's genitals. A mass of ugly blisters covered the man's body, giving him the look of a diseased leper. The man's agonized suffering must have been going on for some time now from the way some of the blisters were beginning to suppurate. With his hands cuffed behind his back and a cloth hood tied over his head, the detainee was totally defenseless.

Though somewhat muffled by the hood, the man's piercing screams could be heard quite loudly through the glass window, eliciting a wave of involuntary shivering in Hennington.

Hennington could not bear to watch such torture and glanced over at Ternier who took in the scene with glazed eyes. "This man struck a guard yesterday," the Colonel said slowly. "He will be subjected to this kind of punishment continuously for the remainder of the day. I have seen only two criminals survive such disciplinary action over a prolonged session such as you see here. But they are like walking dead men now."

Ternier savored the fact prisoners under his control perished on a frequent basis. He had established a fairly thriving business in the sale of Haitian cadavers to foreign medical schools. He had originally been indoctrinated about the merits of such an enterprise during the reign of Jean-Claude Duvalier, popularly called "Baby Doc" by the masses, when he had functioned as one of Duvalier's secret police. During that period, Jean-Claude's wife, Michele Bennet, had indulged in such a practice, which was found to be repugnant by many high-ranking officials in the Duvalier administration. In keeping such a gloulish tradition alive, Ternier had no doubts that this side venture would continue to bring in ballooning revenues as time went on. Periodic uprisings and revolts among the oppressed minions meant a growing supply of dissenters against government authority would be available for arrest and detention. Growing crime and increased political unrest were the progeny of abject poverty, and both were the main driving forces of an escalating detainee population, which had quadrupled in the last six years in the face of a virtually unchanged prison budget.

The new government was making extremely slow headway in implementing reforms, and little had changed in the ways of incarceration and the treatment of prisoners in spite of the outcries from human activists. Truth be told, most of the day to day power rested in the hands of ranking police officials such as the Colonel. Such thoughts gave Ternier much pleasure. But he had much bigger plans than the mere sale of corpses.

The Colonel gazed fixedly at Hennington. The fear written on the broker's face was as palpable as the wounds being wreaked on the man hanging inverted in the room before them. Fear was a viable and most effective method of control. Like a weapon, it could be pointed at any target of choice. It provided a perverted type of incentive for bending people to one's will. Instinctively, Ternier knew that every ounce of human activity could be traced back to this common denominator of all human emotions. Fear equated to survival. Primordial to human nature, it could govern anything as minute as a thought or as cumbersome as a choice. Fear could knock the person down who allows it or destroy the individual who forgets it. All modern dictators used fear as a mechanism for motivating the actions of the people they ruled. Lenin, Stalin, Hitler, Mao, Pol Pot, Idi Amin, and Saddam Hussein – Ternier had studied them all – had created a climate of fear through killing, torture and imprisonment of enough of the masses to convince the others that submission was the most efficient technique of survival. By terrifying the population of a country, the ruling government could do as it pleased.

Ternier smiled at Hennington's emotional state. The tour of the prison was having the desired effect. Only one more stop was necessary to ensure unwavering cooperation from the man. Leading him to an unguarded but battered steel door located at the far end of the hallway, Ternier stopped short of the closed entrance. His face revealed a dark, rancorous smirk that seemed to harbor knowledge of something even more frightening than the horrors to which the broker had already been shown.

The other members of the party stood frozen and the Colonel sensed their uneasiness. They had all been here before, but even they could not get used to the secret that lurked on the other side of the doorway.

Creaking on rusted hinges, the door swung slowly outward until it clanged with finality against the sidewall, the sound of the contact echoing dully down the corridor and unnerving everyone except Ternier. The entrance was vacant. Watching Hennington closely, Ternier could see the confusion registering on his persona, the result of wondering who had opened the door.

With a firm grip on Hennington's elbow, the Colonel guided him into the room beyond. The glow of burning candles danced eerily along the back wall, doing little to penetrate the darkness that dominated the closer reaches of the low-ceilinged chamber. Hennington looked sharply to each side of the entrance but failed to detect anyone standing in the shadows. Glancing apprehensively behind him, he realized the other three men in his escort were holding back, refraining from entering the poorly lit room. A chill raced up his spine. From the look on their faces and the way they fidgeted, he knew that whatever the chamber held could not be good.

As Ternier continued to lead him forward, Hennington felt the dark presence even before discerning its form, a tenebrous malevolence that blended in with the flickering candlelight as if it consisted of inky mist. A cloaked figure sat quietly, a hood concealing its head.

It was then that Hennington became aware of the multitude of human skulls grinning hideously at him from behind the silent figure, hundreds of them stacked one upon the other and lining the rear wall of the chamber. As if anticipating Hennington's reaction, Ternier tightened his grip on the broker's forearm and drew him still closer to the hooded apparition. Hennington's legs began to tremble uncontrollably, and it was all he could do to prevent his bladder from emptying at that moment. The evil that emanated from the personage before him was almost tangible, like the stench of a decaying corpse.

All at once, the figure rose, lifting the cowl from its head. A pair of eyes glimmered in the semi-darkness, mesmeric orbs that held the same ominous stare as did Ternier. Even before the old woman opened her mouth to speak, Hennington somehow sensed who she was.

The woman set her gaze momentarily on Ternier. "I am pleased you have come, my son," she rasped before bringing those crazed, penetrating eyes to bear on Hennington once again. "Do you wish this man to receive the punishment he deserves?"

Staring at Hennington, Ternier knew the man was now his, another addition to his already substantial cadre of acolytes who would be useful in helping him attain his ultimate goal. Yes, he thought, the dysfunctional mud hole known as Haiti was possibly a step closer to changing forever.

- 3 -

The reddish-gold afterglow of sunset cast the avenue in eerie shadow as Phillipe made his way toward the pub known as Dante's Cavern, one of the classier dives lining Port-au-Prince's waterfront. Dark complexioned and slight of build, some might easily have confused him for one of the city's countless street waifs if not for the state of his apparel. In sharp contrast to the other orphans who went about barefoot and barely clad in the remnants of grimy rags that passed for clothing, Phillipe appeared relatively clean and unscathed by the hardships the streets presented. And for that reason alone, his safety was always at risk, a fact that he well understood.

Garbed in unsullied shorts and t-shirt complemented by a pair of fairly new sneakers made in Taiwan, he knew he was a tempting target to the other urchins who infested the back alleyways, having been one of them during the first fifteen of his sixteen year life. Extremely astute in the ways of the street, he moved along with an outward confidence that belied his inner caution, a trait inherent to him. In the dismal slums, peril hung inexorably like the sharp blade of a guillotine, always ready to descend, and constant vigilance was key to keeping one's neck clear of it. With nightfall now upon him, the potential dangers he sensed lurking about were made all the more palpable and he quickened his pace.

The door of a nearby tavern unexpectedly flew open, throwing a feeble light from within onto the darkened pavement. A sudden burst of rhythmic reggae, blaring and laced with the sound of laughter, assaulted Phillipe's ears as it poured from the entrance like a gust of wind, wafting off into the placid night air as if to cleanse it of all iniquities. Phillipe kept walking as four men trooped out, their silhouettes eclipsing the pub's lit interior.

As the tavern door slammed shut behind the trailing member of the group, the din of festive gaiety abated abruptly, allowing the dispirited pall of Haiti to come flooding back like a dark, towering tsunami surging over a headland, turbulent and irrepressible. A vague sense of foreboding presentiment suddenly blossomed within Phillipe, making him shudder involuntarily.

"A donde vas mi cachorito?" one of the men called loudly, his tone guttural and ostensibly slurred.

Phillipe stopped momentarily, realizing he was being addressed. The man staggered forward in the classic reel of the drunk, repeating the question even louder than before. Phillipe spoke French, English and the native Creole fluently, including smidgens of several other languages, and knew the man's utterance was an idiom of Spanish, the kind typically spoken by Colombians and Venezuelans who were often seen along the waterfront. Although he rarely conversed in such a dialect, he clearly understood the words. *Where are you going, my young pup?*

One of the other men guffawed rambunctiously, throwing a bantering taunt in the same tongue as his inebriated associate. Phillipe translated the implication of the shouted jest. "You walk like you fly, Pedro…all over the place!"

With the exception of Pedro, an eruption of howling mirth ensued.

Pedro advanced on unsteady legs, ignoring his companion's gibe or the jeering repartee of the other two. "Come here, my young tuna," he grunted, his glazed eyes fixed implacably on Phillipe like those of a drugged cobra. "I'm going to carve a fillet from you."

As the man drew closer, Phillipe recognized him as a crewmember of the *San Carlo*, a Colombian tuna trawler currently berthed in the harbor. The men that worked aboard her were notorious bullies, having gained a reputation among the locals for inflicting excessive brutality and cruelty on anyone unfortunate to cross their path. Colombian fishermen, he knew, always had money in their pockets, enough to easily convince any policeman chancing upon their forays of violence to look the other way. After all, another orphan lying dead in the street, mutilated and discarded like so much trash, was actually acceptable to most Haitian police patrolling the area. They looked upon such deeds not as a crime but as a solution to eliminating the street rabble, a growing problem within the Haitian capital where petty thefts, robberies and muggings flourished with a growing frequency.

The man approaching him was perhaps the worst of the Colombian lot, having left at least one dead Haitian in his wake whenever his ship was in port. A sadistic killer by nature, he used the waterfront as if it were his own personal hunting ground, a place where he could satisfy his lust for blood with impunity.

Phillipe cursed himself for having hesitated and turned to leave, but the possibility of escape dimmed as the other three men scurried with surprising speed to cut off all retreat, surrounding him like a pack of hyena closing in on prey.

Not liking the manner in which his situation was developing, Phillipe tried darting between two of the bullies and would have succeeded if not for a foot extended by one of the men. He went sprawling chest-first onto the hard pavement as his assailants hooted loudly. Phillipe knew these hooligans were seeking some form of entertainment, and for the time being he was to be the center of their amusement.

Looking behind him, Phillipe caught the glint of metal in the hand of the one called Pedro. He had seen how alcohol consumed in quantity could cause even intrinsically good-natured people to become ignoble, but he perceived the man hovering above him to be the foulest type of drunk, ruthlessly dangerous and capable of any heinous act. Once the effects of his liquor-induced fugue wore off, such an individual would remember little of any atrocity he carried out. Even in sobriety, the man would likely harbor a nasty mean streak.

Phillipe endeavored to scramble to his feet, but a booted foot caught him in the side of the temple, knocking him onto his back.

"Hold the little tuna down so I can gut him!" Pedro ordered, lurching above Phillipe like a malicious beast.

Panic-stricken, Phillipe brought knees to chest and kicked upward, slamming his heels squarely into Pedro's stomach. The big man let out a grunt, teetering backward but managing to keep his feet.

"The tuna has spirit," one of the ruffians snarled as Pedro stumbled forward again. "Perhaps he is too much for Pedro to reel in."

"Shut your fucking mouth, Vargas!" Pedro screamed, brandishing the knife threateningly. "Maybe you'd like some of this."

A charged silence descended. The jovial mood of Pedro's companions dissipated like windswept fog, a capitulation born of fear rather than respect. That Pedro was the recognized leader of the group, Phillipe had no doubts, and his apprehension increased.

Getting his legs under him, Phillipe dodged beyond the grasp of the closest man, only to be seized from behind by two others.

"You little street scum!" Pedro bellowed. "I'm going to cut you good."

Mortified, Phillipe recoiled as though bitten by a snake. The blade wielded by Pedro gleamed malevolently in the moonlight as the big man swayed drunkenly before him. Phillipe stared dully, now unable to move or cry out.

A hand suddenly appeared out of the gloom and latched onto Pedro's wrist, immobilizing any further movement of the weapon it guided. Another hand girded Pedro's throat, easily enfolding it like a black python. The Colombian's eyes bulged in disbelieving shock as his body was lifted from the ground, feet dangling like those of a man hung from a gallows.

"I don't think you want to do that, mon," Zimbola hissed, his massive frame dwarfing the suspended man.

Phillipe gaped in amazement as something thumped heavily from behind. No longer restrained, he turned in bafflement as several more thuds resounded. One of Pedro's cohorts lay motionless at his feet while another was in the process of pitching face-first toward the ground in the aftermath of a vicious right cross that collided with authority against the man's jaw.

In comparison to the swiftly moving interloper who had delivered the knockout punches, the last of Phillipe's standing attackers moved sluggishly, launching a desperate but lackluster blow at the intruder's head. Gracefully and almost too quick to follow by eye, the intruder ducked under the punch, digging a hard left into the bully's ribs and following it up with a powerful right that nearly dislodged head from torso. Phillipe could not help but wince as the man's head snapped back from the impact, his body slumping in a heap as if his legs had been abruptly chopped off at the knee.

Phillipe glanced back over his shoulder. Pedro was still held aloft, his legs doing a crazy jig as they kicked wildly in the air. An expression of intense pain mingled with fear began to register on the Columbian's face as Zimbola gradually increased the pressure to both neck and wrist, cords of muscle slowly rising like heated dough in his forearms. All at once, the knife dropped silently from Pedro's hand to go clattering on the pavement.

Still clutching the man by the throat with his left hand, Zimbola raised his right, balling his huge fist and dropping it like a club. As if it were a sledgehammer striking an anvil, it slammed into the top of Pedro's skull. The Colombian's body immediately went slack, drooping like a wet dishrag, and Zimbola lowered him to the ground.

With the threat eradicated, Phillipe let out a long, slow breath, viewing his rescuers with a detached surrealistic awareness.

"I thought I told you to stay off the streets at night," Jay Jay scolded. "Had we not happened along when we did, you'd be fish chum."

The anger displayed by Jay Jay caused Phillipe to look away. "I-," he started to say.

"They clocked you pretty good," Jay Jay said, his ire replaced by concern. He stepped forward and, with a finger, gently explored the region behind Phillipe's right eye. The skin was noticeably swollen and Phillipe grimaced when Jay Jay touched it. His head suddenly throbbed miserably.

Zimbola stood over the fallen men, eyeing them with disdain. He spat contemptuously. His expression suddenly clouded and he looked around searchingly, his large, flat nostrils flaring wide like that of a bloodhound on the trail of a scent. He lifted his hands and sniffed them carefully, contemplatively.

Jake could not help but notice his companion's behavior. He had seen him do this before. "What? What is it?"

"These men, they have the reek of albacore rotting in the sun."

Jake tested the air. The usual blend of odors that pervaded Port-au-Prince's waterfront were all there, some of them quite pungent, including the unpleasant smell of decaying fish flesh. But Jake could not discern any trace aroma that would indicate tuna. He didn't have the finely tuned olfactory equipment that Zimby possessed.

"So? What of it?"

"They are tuna fishermen. Colombians."

Jake studied Zimbola questioningly. "How do you know that?"

"There is only one tuna trawler in the harbor, and it flies the Colombian flag."

"He is right," Phillipe chirped in. He pointed to Pedro's inert form. "That one there, he is an evil man. He has murdered many of the orphans who live in the streets. Killing gives him pleasure."

"All the more reason to keep off the street at night," Jake fumed.

"I had to come," Phillipe protested. "That boat that attacked us at sea, it came nosing around the Angel. Hector thought you should know right away."

"Are you sure it was the same vessel?"

"I am sure."

Zimbola took stock of the area all around them. "It would be wise for us not to remain here any longer," the black giant urged. "Come! Let us return to the Angel."

Jake nodded in agreement. And with the possibility of both zenglendoes and corrupt Haitian police lurking about, or even worse, the shipmates of the unconscious men coming upon them, it would be prudent on their part to vacate the vicinity as quickly as possible.

- 4 -

The moon hung peacefully in the star-rich heavens, bright and full, casting pale beams through the window of a simple thatched cottage. Small wavelets from a calm sea lapped softly like caressing fingers on the white sandy beach of the cove, no more than seventy feet from the modest structure which overlooked the water. Every so often, the tranquil atmosphere was punctuated by a low moan, a sound discordant with the pervading serenity. The noise grew more strident, more persistent, rising in volume. Within the cottage, a young woman tossed in troubled sleep, her forehead glistening with sweat in the subdued light, her wails of anguish incoherent and reaching a fever pitch.

Suddenly she sat bolt upright. "No!" she cried shrilly, her scream piercing the night with all the potency of a dagger thrust into living flesh.

A cacophony of chirps and twitters reverberated from somewhere nearby, as if in empathic response to the girl's distress.

With her eyes now fully open, the vision in the nightmare continued to haunt her much like the ache of a recent injury that, although mostly healed, keeps its victim in lingering pain, a pain which fades all too slowly. Restless, the girl shook off the final tendrils of sleep and arose to stare out the window.

The water shimmered quietly, its surface broken by several forms drifting languidly near the shoreline. As if aware of the girl's presence, the forms stirred in animated salutation, beckoning to her in a comforting lilt of low chittering. They were always there for her, affectionate companions whose very lives seemed to vacillate around the core of her existence. Their trust in her was implicit and unwavering. Whereas she hardly knew herself, they appeared to understand her completely.

She perceived that an outsider witnessing such interplay would have considered it to be nothing more than the equivalent of puppies displaying fawning adoration toward a revered master. But the bond went way beyond that. In stark contrast to a puppy, which had little insight about the world around it, the wisdom of the creatures in the cove transcended anything on a human scale.

In a convoluted way she was their nurturing sister, dispersing emotional nourishment, which they readily consumed and then channeled back to her many times magnified. Diametrically counter to the condemning nature that was indigenous to her own species, the creatures roaming the cove evinced an infinite capacity for compassion, and with it, unconditional forgiveness. Such noble qualities would normally preclude any desire for retribution, but she now sensed a subtle change in their attitudes. Whereas they were still averse to acts of reprisal, they were no longer willing to remain completely pacifistic, forever predisposed to accept the abuses cast upon them. This new perspective, she was certain, did not hinge on a desire for vengeance. Rather it was born of a need to defend, to survive. She could not fault them for it, for she, too, was changing.

She could no longer sit idle. Passivity, she realized, was a philosophical dead end, a path which was becoming increasingly illogical to follow if she wanted to see her friends flourish and propagate. There was so much to be learned from the new breed, newcomers to an already evolved species that viewed the universe around them with an awareness that differed markedly from humanity's. They were smarter than their genetic predecessors, possessing an elevated clarity of thought. Their numbers, however, were dwindling and they urged her to act, to lend them the assistance they so desperately required of her.

Again the vision tugged at her, pulling her spirits into a quagmire of despondency into which she was slowly sinking. She knew the creatures would have seen the vision. They always saw through her eyes, through her mind, and she through theirs. They were forever psychically linked to her, heart and soul.

The girl looked up at the moon, as if seeking an answer to her dilemma, wiping away the tears that flowed down alabaster cheeks. But she already knew what she must do. Jacob would help her. He always did. Mother, on the other hand, would not approve.

There were forces at work, ominous and powerful, of magnitudes far-reaching and which she could not fully fathom, but she knew that destinies would change monumentally for the worse as a result of them. A sense of urgency overcame her as the inner voices beckoned like strands of silk gossamer, pulling gently but firmly. If she went to Jacob now and they sailed within the hour, it was still possible they could prevent a terrible calamity from occurring.

The girl dressed quickly and left the cottage, her dark glossy hair streaming behind her and reflecting moonlight like polished ebony as she ran along the sandy beach.

- 5 -

Lights flickered over the water beyond the shipping berths, indicating the presence of various watercraft floating at anchor within the harbor. From the shadows, Jake, Zimbola and Phillipe studied a particular vessel no more than 300 feet distant, noting another boat that was tied up alongside.

"I smell trouble!" Jake whispered.

Zimbola glanced up at the sky and scowled. "I do not advise rowing the skiff out under such a moonlit night."

Jake was already slipping off his shoes. "Give me ten minutes, then follow me out in the skiff."

Zimbola grabbed Jake's arm. "We do this together."

Jake hesitated, looking solemnly at his friend for several seconds, then nodded. He turned to Phillipe who stood impassively, handing the boy his shoes. "Hold onto these and wait here. If we need you, we'll signal you by turning the deck lights on and off three times."

Zimbola shed his bulky clodhoppers and also left them with the boy. Both men crept out onto a nearby pier, darting behind pilings and keeping to the shadows. It was late and the immediate area was absent of any pedestrians. Jake spied a mooring line hanging loosely from a deck cleat and latched onto it, lowering himself effortlessly until he was fully immersed in the brine without making a splash. Less graceful than his companion, Zimbola followed.

A sudden bout of luck aided the men's stealth as the umbra of a cloud cluster slid across the lunar disk, shrouding the harbor in a tenebrous gloom. Abruptly, the silvery iridescence of the water fell into darkness. Jake kicked smoothly along in a silent breaststroke with Zimbola dog paddling beside him like a ponderous black walrus, each man careful not to swash the water's surface lest they be heard as they approached the tethered vessels.

As both men got closer, Jake noticed the abutting boat to be at least 20 feet shorter in length than his own 65-foot, 70-ton North Sea trawler. With the moon still obscured in cloud, it was difficult for him to detect any movement along the deck of the intruding craft, which was positioned with its starboard side against the trawler's larboard. He could just make out the outline of a dive platform jutting from the intruder's stern.

Fifty feet from the intruder, the vessel closest to them, Jake stopped and, treading water, faced Zimbola. Keeping his voice low, he said, "Let's split up! See if you can get aboard their boat, whoever they are." He turned and indicated the back end of the vessel. "Climb onto that stern platform. I'll go up the Angel's anchor line. Keep low until you hear something."

Zimbola acknowledged Jake's rudimentary plan with a nod, then swam away. It took Jake another two minutes before his hands clasped the coarse hemp of the trawler's anchor line, and he began his hand over hand ascent toward the Angel's bow looming 40 feet away.

Displaying the agility and supple strength of a spider monkey, Jake traversed the length of taut rope in a matter of moments. At the top he hooked a hand over the bow rail and with a final powerful heave, launched himself up and over the bar to land in a catlike crouch on the deck. As if sculpted in stone he remained in that position, watching and listening, until he was satisfied that he went unobserved. All was quiet except for the normal creak and groan of the hull timbers resounding softly through the vessel as it rocked gently in the slight tropical breeze, giving Jake the impression the trawler was deserted.

He crept forward on bare feet, peering up at the wheelhouse in anticipation of discovering trespassers, but there was nothing to suggest the presence of a boarding party other than the strange vessel reeved to the trawler. As Jake skulked along the starboard walkway adjacent to the galley, the faint sound of voices drifted over to him. Cautiously he moved forward.

The voices were coming from the aft deck house which served as a salon. Leaning with his back against the outer wall of the cabin, he sidled along it until he was even with the edge of its forward window. Someone was talking, the tone unmistakably accusatory.

"-arms to terrorists jeopardizes the security of the United States." The speaker sounded gruff, masculine.

"The captain did not sell military weapons to terrorists!" a second voice replied angrily. The voice was Hector's. "This vessel does not smuggle arms."

"You and the rest of the crew can be classified as enemy combatants by virtue of aiding and abetting Islamic extremists."

Jake listened in astonishment. *What the hell!?*

"This vessel can be impounded and its crew shipped off to Guantanamo Bay for indefinite detention and interrogation," the same speaker went on. "Unless you cooperate, that's what you can look forward to."

Something stirred in Jake's memory, vague and fleeting, then vanished just as quickly. He pivoted his head enough to peek through the plexiglass. Hector was seated at the teak dining table looking more recalcitrant than cowed. Four men stood hovering over him in a belligerent phalanx, the spokesman with his back to Jake. He could see that all of them had handguns strapped snugly in shoulder harnesses and that one of the men held a shotgun pointing idly at the deck. The faces of the strangers visible to him had the gravity of authority etched onto them.

Hector spoke defiantly. "You have no jurisdiction here. Haiti is a sovereign nation."

"This vessel flies the American flag, and as such is under the official registry of the United States government. The Haitian government is lending their full cooperation in countering any potential threats by terrorists."

Jake listened intently to the man's words, a sharp twinge of anxiety gnawing away at the pit of his stomach like a rodent scavenging for food. He hated terrorists and all they stood for. The very thought that he may have inadvertently assisted in the political objectives of Islamic radicals made his head reel.

The speaker of the boarding party continued to press Hector. "I ask you again, where is the captain of this vessel?"

Hector folded his thick arms stubbornly. "And I tell you once more, I do not know!"

"You don't know or you aren't saying?"

Hector remained mute.

Strangely, the inflection of the man's speech triggered some distant memento of past experience, but Jake had no time to mull over its significance. Before he even realized what he was doing, he walked through the open cabin door.

Jake kept his voice calm and level. "He doesn't know."

All four men were clearly startled, the shotgun wielder raising the weapon sharply to bear on Jake while the other two reached for their side arms. The leader of the group, however, reacted the fastest, spinning in a lightning manner to face the sudden intrusion, his gun drawn and leveled with the quickness of a mamba prepared to strike. A look of stunned amazement slowly flooded his expression as he regarded Jake.

Jake was equally stunned, and he stared at the man dazedly. "Mat? Is that really you?"

The weapon in the man's hand was instantly lowered. "By all that's holy, I can't believe what I'm seeing," he said jubilantly as he holstered the gun.

The two men came towards one another and embraced like long lost brothers, and in a way it wasn't far from the truth. Mat Daniels had been a brother in arms along with Jake in the U.S. Navy Seals. They had worked closely together on numerous missions with Seal Team Six, most of them classified and highly dangerous. Jake had saved Mat's life on more than one occasion when they had made intelligence-gathering excursions into Somalia, Afghanistan, Pakistan and Iraq. They had been together during several firefights during the toppling of Saddam Hussein's regime, and Jake remembered vividly how he had slung Mat over his shoulder, all 195 pounds of him, and carried him for more than two miles along the banks of the Tigris River in southern Iraq in order to avoid capture. An errant artillery round from an Iraqi tank had left Mat with a jagged 4-inch chunk of shrapnel lodged just above his right knee, reducing him to a hobbling cripple during the mission.

"You're a sight for sore eyes, buddy," Mat effused breathlessly, the air driven from his chest by Jake's powerful hug.

Ignoring the bewilderment of Daniels' companions, Jake broke from his friend's embrace and asked, "So what's this all about, Mat?"

Daniels suddenly appeared embarrassed and he looked away, avoiding Jake's eyes. "I think we have some talking to do," he said, obviously flustered.

Composing himself swiftly, Mat glanced at his associates. "Guys, meet Jake Javolyn, the most incorrigible bad ass this side of damnation."

The men continued to look befuddled, fidgeting nervously.

"He's all right, trust me. Jake hates terrorists more than I do."

Daniels turned back to Jake. "I have some things to discuss with Mr. Javolyn. Why don't the three of you go back aboard our boat and wait for me there." The men still looked uncertain, and in a placating tone, Mat added, "Don't worry, I'll explain later."

All three men filed past Jake, measuring him with appraising eyes and shaking their heads in exasperation.

Jake grinned back like a sated falcon that had just had its fill of carrion. "Oh, and by the way, guys, I strongly advise you to keep clear of the big black man sitting on your stern platform," he said, tongue in cheek. "He gets awful crotchety when he hasn't eaten."

Mat rolled his eyes, shaking his head. "Always the comedian."

Jake faced Hector. The Cuban seemed unperturbed by his recent ordeal, and not the least surprised by this fresh turn of events. With Jake, nothing ever seemed to surprise him. "Hector, let Zimby know what's going on and that I'll be indisposed for awhile."

Hector remained stoic, closing the door behind him as he stepped from the room. He was a short, blocky man, a head smaller in stature than Jake.

Taking a seat at the teak table, Jake scrutinized his old friend. All previous traces of humor on Mat's face were now replaced by a weighty graveness.

"So that was you a month ago," Daniels declared. It was more of a statement than a question.

Jake nodded slowly. "I had no idea it was you. At the time, I assumed I was being dogged by pirates looking to take the Angel."

Mat sucked in a prolonged breath. "I'm with the Department of Homeland Security now. Those men with me, we're part of a special counterterrorism task force assigned to the Caribbean."

"I couldn't help overhear you grilling Hector," Jake said. "Did I understand you to say Islamic extremists are operating here in Haiti?"

Mat hesitated, deciding how much information he should reveal. "Yes!" he finally offered. "Our intelligence gatherers have intercepted an inordinate amount of chatter emanating from terror cells affiliated with Al Qaeda. Much of that chatter alludes to this region. We don't as yet know precisely what, but it appears something big is coming down."

To Jake, such a possibility made little sense. As far as he could gauge, Haiti, one of the poorest nations on earth, presented few, if any targets that would attract terrorists. While it was true that the more radical elements of Islam had fanned the flames of an intense anti-Western hatred within the Middle East, particularly against Americans, they sought to disrupt such cultures in any way that would impact those economies in a negative way. Haiti, however, was far beyond the mainstream of Western economic well-being.

The number of Muslim fundamentalists joining the ranks of Islamic militants had grown dramatically over the last decade and was now reaching epidemic proportions, threatening Westerners on a global scale with their radical religious views. What had originally been confined to the Middle East had now spilled over to the rest of the world, spearheaded by overzealous and frenzied fanatics who used terror to further their goals.

Jake had lost one of his closest friends to Islamic fanaticism during the destruction of the World Trade Towers and had come to hate extremists. To Jake's way of thinking, religious fanatics mistakenly saw themselves as the spokesmen for mankind, stubbornly shoving their dogma down humanity's gullet. Islam, in particular, seemed to be more prone to violent fanaticism than other faiths with its extreme intolerance of non-Muslim cultures and viewpoints, often targeting Westerners for death in the form of spectacular strikes such as what occurred on 9-11.

Deep down, Jake did not buy the chief justification used by Islamic militants for such mayhem against Americans, and that was his country's support of Israel. He considered such rationality to be nothing more than a sham, a moral guise behind which they hid. Intuitively, he believed that abject poverty was the primary driving force behind their attacks, the actual mechanism that fueled their hatred. Although rich in oil, the wealth of Middle Eastern nations was predominantly controlled by the royal families who lived in lavish comfort in stark contrast to the overwhelming majority of their countrymen. Within such cultures, amenities produced by petroleum-induced wealth rarely made its way to the common man whose standard of living was far below that of the West. And with mushrooming Muslim populations spiraling out of control in combination with limited and continually strained resources, it was only natural that the poorer classes would turn to Islam as if it were a precious asset.

As Jake saw it, the present religious strife between Muslims and non-Muslims was simply a belated replay of the religious wars that had plagued the tail end of the European Middle Ages. Unfortunately he knew that conflict prolonged over an extended period tended to be self-perpetuating, often plunging out of control and overshadowing all sense of reason. And with fanaticism, the original tenets of the religion itself would somehow get lost in the midst of the rabid fervor that was rapidly taking hold.

The bottom line was that militant radicals within the Muslim culture were abusing their faith for religious and national causes. Members of the ultra-extremist Wahhabi sect of Islam were breeding the next generation of mass murderers through clandestine funding in conjunction with an international network of mosques and religious schools located not only in the Middle East, but in Asia and Africa, as well.

And although the more moderate constituents of Islam claimed that their religion was essentially gentle and non-violent at its core, Islamic fundamentalists continually urged their brothers to align themselves against nonbelievers of the Muslim faith, claiming it was their religious obligation. Regardless of whether their political goals were justified, to extinguish all Western influences in the Middle East and to exterminate Israel, their means of accomplishing those objectives were certainly not. Political suicide bombers, being trained by Hamas, Hezbollah and other groups on an on-going basis, were being taught that success would grant them a special place in heaven. Jake abhorred such acts. The horror of blowing up a busload of children could not, and should not, be rationalized under any agenda.

Far worse than the Third Reich had been, and much more dangerous in their potentially destructive capability, Islamic militancy advocates sought to destroy any last vestige of any culture or religion other than that which they practiced. Their ultimate goal was to establish a theocratic dictatorship throughout the world, much like the rule of the Taliban, which flourished in Afghanistan for a short period before the U.S. toppled the cruelest of all governments ever known to exist.

Jake assessed many of the Islamic states to essentially be loathocracies, with their faiths based on an extreme hatred of anything non-Muslim, most particularly Western cultures. And while he understood that you could not condemn a people or faith simply on the actions of its more extreme elements, history had shown that men never carried out evil so completely and cheerfully as when they did it out of religious conviction. In fact, more wars were fought in the name of religion than for any other cause throughout human history.

While in the Seals, both Jake and Mat had received extensive training in counterterrorism, not only learning techniques aimed at thwarting the ambitions of terrorists, but getting insight into their way of thinking and their underlying motives as well. Islamic fundamentalism was a subject they were well acquainted with and a topic on which they had had ample time to discuss on many occasions. Mat had often listened with rapt attentiveness as Jake espoused his philosophical views regarding religious extremists and knew that Jake had only one solution for dealing with such people. And that was to contain them at every opportunity. As Jake had often said, religious militants were unreachable on a rational level, for such individuals harbored deeply rooted and twisted ideologies that deviated substantially from the true tenets of their faith. Focused on killing and destroying in an effort to maximize body counts, their mind-set was of a single purpose and they would not be denied their fixation. And Jake well knew that it was so much easier to destroy than to create or construct. Overall, such religious fanaticism presented enormous setbacks to the advancement of the human race.

Jake had nothing personal against practitioners of Islam, nor the true doctrines of the religion itself. In fact, direct experience with most Muslims he had come across during assignments in predominantly Islamic countries had shown the people to be warm and courteous toward foreigners, providing hospitality to strangers whenever it was warranted.

Choosing his words carefully, Mat said, "Look, Jake, for whatever it's worth, I think you've been pulled into something much bigger than you bargained for. Knowing you the way I do, you probably had no idea what you were hauling at the time." Mat eyed his friend shrewdly. "Can I assume that to be the case?"

Jake weighed the question conscientiously. In a way he couldn't explain, he felt like a traitor, not only to his country of origin but to himself as well. "Yes…yes you can," he answered slowly.

Both men understood that if Jake admitted outright knowledge of the cargo, Mat's position as a United States counterterrorism agent would not only be compromised, but potentially put in jeopardy if Mat did not carry out his responsibilities by arresting his long time pal. And Jake knew that was something Mat would never do, no matter what the circumstances. The bond of trust that had developed between them was strong enough to outweigh any sense of duty on Mat's part, and he was certain Mat would never betray that trust. Mat owed Jake his life, plain and simple. It was basically a thing of honor and obligation.

"We've been tracking the people who received that shipment," Mat proclaimed. "It turns out the contraband ultimately reached a Yemeni national who runs an import-export business here in the city."

"And no doubt a Muslim!" Jake interposed without speculation. He had already done business with that same Yemeni, giving him cause to examine his dealings with the man under a new light.

Mat smiled, measuring Jake with a knowing look. "His business is relatively new, established within the last six months."

Jake found himself growing uneasy with the turn the conversation had taken. "So what's your take on all this? Why would Muslim extremists be interested in the Caribbean Basin? This region offers no economic importance of any significance worth disrupting, no target-rich environment."

Mat shrugged tiredly. "Maybe they see it as a useful staging area from which to launch attacks, a place within striking distance of American soil."

Jake thought this over. It made sense. Haiti reeked with political turmoil. While the new government was currently receptive to aiding the U.S. in curtailing the ever-present drug trade which was firmly entrenched in Haitian affairs, the fledgling regime had by no means given stability to the island nation. And although such cooperation was proving to be a thorn in the side of Colombian drug lords, making it much more difficult for them to conduct their operations and eroding their influence on the country, the cartels had counterattacked with resiliency. Battling back in a desperate bid to reassert indirect control of the nation, they deliberately incited various political factions in an effort to keep the region unstable. Political unrest equated to easier drug trafficking. One major drawback in creating such an environment, however, was that it inadvertently provided an inviting haven for terrorists, allowing them to go relatively unnoticed.

"You look like you could use some shut-eye," Jake commented, suddenly aware of Mat's weariness. It was apparent Mat had gotten little sleep in the past several days as evidenced by a dark growth of stubble dominating his lower face in concert with bag-ridden, bloodshot eyes. "This assignment wearing you down, old buddy? You always were one who never knew when to stop and rest."

Mat scrutinized Jake oddly. "That sounds rather strange coming from you. I've often wondered how you managed to carry my sorry ass all that distance back in Iraq. The doctors pried more steel out of you than they did me. You took down seven of Saddam's Elite Guard firing from the hip as you ran with me like a sack of useless baggage slung over your shoulder."

"Strong body, weak mind," Jake replied flippantly. "I've told you before, pain doesn't register on a small brain like mine." As soon as he uttered the words he grew serious. "The way I remember it, you were far from useless. You held onto your weapon and waxed at least three others yourself as I carried you."

"There's a subtle difference between compulsive valor and unavoidable discretion," Mat countered. "And it's usually fatal."

"So you've often said."

The grin on Mat's face fell away abruptly like a load of stone into a ravine. "You always enjoyed walking the edge, the thrill of the chase. To you, it never mattered much whether you were the pursuer or the pursued, the hunter or the hunted. Unnecessary risk and danger are like aphrodisiacs to you. You eat them like candy. But some day they're gonna be your undoing. You keep prodding the devil and he's gonna stick that pitchfork of his where the sun don't shine."

"I'll keep that in mind."

Mat's expression remained stony. "Same old Jake. I should have known that was you when our paths crossed a month ago. I must say, your use of that waverunner was admirable, the kind of tactics only you would think of employing. Very innovative and enlightening."

Jake could not help but chortle. "I would rather you use the word 'effective.'"

Jake recalled the incident lucidly. He always made it a practice to conceal his vessel's identity during a smuggling gig, flying a false flag to indicate a bogus country of origin and draping the boat's name and serial numbers with canvas. Such precautions made it difficult for potential boarders to trace the registry of his craft.

The pickup had gone fairly smooth. Jake and his crew had just completed stowing the contraband after having made the rendezvous at the designated transfer point at the east end of Montego Bay. The five large crates that had come off the beat up fishing boat were bulky and heavy, and it had taken the combined strength of the Angel's four crew members with the help of the five nondescript occupants of the transfer vessel to move the cargo aboard the North Sea trawler.

It was less than a minute after the two boats had pulled apart and the Angel was steering a course back to Haiti when Jake realized something was amiss. The intruder had been spotted on radar long before it got near enough to hear, a shadowy wraith closing rapidly on an intercept course as it sped over the dark, moonless ocean. Four times Jake had altered the trawler's direction, and each time the intruder had changed course to follow, dogging the Angel with the tenacious intent of a rapacious shark on the hunt and eliminating any possibility that they were not being pursued.

That was when Jake had resorted to a Code One. Hector and Phillipe immediately sprang into action and began prepping the waverunner, a Kawasaki STX-12F. The small craft sat perched above the vessel's fantail on the aft-most section of the Angel's superstructure, all portions of its surface painted a non-reflective charcoal black. At a distance of 20 meters on a moonless night at sea, even Phillipe's sharp young eyes could not discern it after it was launched.

A customized heavy-duty inflatable chute assisted in the launching and could be rapidly unfurled with the flip of an air valve, causing it to extend at an angle to the water directly astern of the trawler. An air-filled tube, 18 inches in diameter, formed each side of the chute, providing it with a certain amount of rigidity. The device was similar in construction to those used by commercial airlines for fast exiting of passengers following emergency landings. Four lengths of stainless steel cable-rail connected the air tubes to an elevated boom, two per tube, giving additional support to the structure, much like the cables supporting a suspension bridge. The chute was made all the more accommodating for launching the waverunner by a stream of water flowing down its surface. Water was supplied by a centrifugal pump, which automatically kicked in upon extension of the ramp, turning the chute into a veritable water slide. Incorporated into the system were two vacuum pumps devoted to sucking air from each tube. The pumps were automatically engaged by dual hydraulically driven reels mounted to the superstructure on opposite sides of the chute. The reels provided the means to retract the makeshift ramp and had the capacity to furl the contrivance within 20 seconds after full deployment. The entire setup had been rigged months earlier, primarily for discouraging pirates and other unsavory parties from attempting to hijack the Angel on the open sea. So far, this was the first opportunity Jake had had to use it.

Jake had carried out at least a dozen drills with the ship's crew in launching the STX-12F, springing the procedure on them without warning at randomly chosen intervals, day or night. Each man in the crew had a specific assignment to carry out during the operation. Flaws in the procedure had been discovered and perfected, and gradually their response times had improved to the point where Jake would be hitting the water within 58 seconds of a Code One alert. This did not include the time it took for Jake to don his shorty wetsuit with the Farmer John top which left his muscular arms exposed, nor the effort of securing the additional gear strapped to his body. Jake had made it standard operating procedure to be fully outfitted in such dress at the start of each smuggling run. He was a firm believer in preparedness, something drummed into him while in the Seals, and the *Seven Ps* were solidly engrained into his thinking: *Prior Proper Planning Prevented Piss Poor Performance.*

With ship's radar showing the intruder to be lagging just beyond one nautical mile astern of the Angel, Zimbola had laid back on the variable pitch control lever in the pilothouse, feathering the trawler's three propeller blades into a near-neutral angle of attack. Such a feature caused the vessel's forward speed to drop off quickly from its previous 22 knots in spite of the constant engine rpm.

Jake bounded rearward from the pilothouse and leapt onto the waverunner, now fully prepped and armed, as the launching ramp cascaded open to touch the sea 12-feet below him. In unison, Hector, Phillipe and Zimbola gave the tiny craft a mighty shove and the Kawasaki lurched forward like a bull out of a rodeo gate, sliding onto the chute's nylon surface. Strands of muscle stood out in Jake's shoulders and forearms as he gripped the craft's handlebars tightly, bracing himself in anticipation of the impending impact as the waverunner gained momentum on the slippery ramp. The Kawasaki rushed down and slammed into the ocean with all the ferocity of an orca looking to feed, and it was all Jake could do to keep himself from being catapulted forward. A curtain of spray immediately erupted as the craft's nose momentarily submerged and struggled to assert buoyancy. The Kawasaki wallowed crazily, teetering to one side as the trawler's wake caught it, but then righted itself and quickly stabilized.

Jake turned to watch as the Angel picked up speed again, its hulking silhouette shrinking as it receded into the night. The thrum of the trawler's Swedish Penta MD-96 diesel engine began to fade with distance as he engaged the Kawasaki's ignition and felt the 1,199cc, 4-stroke marine motor come alive in a quiet purr. He turned the throttle halfway and veered laterally away from the Angel's course, bumping lightly over the leading edge of the trawler's portside wake and skimming perhaps 200 meters before shutting down the craft's engine.

Checking the luminous dial on his Caravel dive watch, Jake confirmed that approximately 110 seconds, give or take a second, had elapsed since he had initiated the Code One. *Not bad.* The STX-12F was perfectly suited for the course of action he planned to undertake. With a vertical profile extending no more than 36-inches above the water, the small craft would be nearly undetectable on radar. And that included the special accessories Jake had retrofitted to the body of the Kawasaki just forward of the console. Most of the time, the unique accoutrements were kept hidden in a secret compartment aboard the trawler and could readily be retrieved and snapped into place on the waverunner in a matter of moments. In addition, the engine that powered the craft was one of the quietest in its class and would be almost impossible to hear over the drone of most powerboats plowing the sea.

Jake glanced around, trying to get his bearings. Except for the stars glittering overhead like bright jewels scattered over a black carpet, the ocean was a mass of gently heaving darkness, ominous and foreboding to those less familiar with it. Polaris, the North Star, winked like a comforting beacon, low in the darkness and directly forward of the tiny craft. A quick check of the console-mounted compass told Jake he was indeed facing north when looking over the handlebars.

The Angel's familiar but slowly dwindling thrum finally abated completely and Jake sat still, listening intently as the Kawasaki pitched sluggishly among the low, silent swells. All was quiet, black and lonely, as if Jake had been cast into deep space between galaxies. Several moments passed before the faint sound of another vessel reached his ears, progressively growing louder as it approached.

The intruder was running without lights and remained virtually invisible within the cloak of darkness as it swept along the same course as the Angel. The noise level grew rapidly in intensity, reaching a deafening roar that dominated all Jake's senses, and for one fleeting instant, with heart pounding and pulse racing, Jake expected to be crushed by the passing boat. But then a noticeable shift in the frequency of the sound suddenly occurred, the telltale sign of the Doppler effect, indicating the vessel was now traveling away from his position.

With great relief, Jake expelled the lungful of air he hadn't realized he'd been holding and strained his eyes in a futile attempt to locate the intruder. An indistinct eidolon seemed to momentarily materialize before him, then vanish just as quickly, a dark shadow on an even blacker backdrop, but he couldn't be sure. He rotated on the seat he straddled and pulled the combination earpiece-lip mike from the Kawasaki's rear storage compartment, plugging it into the waterproof Motorola radio attached to the console.

"This is Arrow," Jake said calmly. "You read me, Goliath."

Zimbola's deep voice rumbled back in Jake's ear. "This is Goliath. I read you loud and clear, Arrow."

By prearrangement, Jake had instructed Zimbola to keep radio chatter to a minimum lest their pursuers intercept their transmission. He knew, however, that such a possibility was quite remote.

Satisfied, Jake reached behind him again, this time retrieving the AN/PVS-7 night vision goggles which he hurriedly strapped on. Both shock resistant and sealed from the environment, the unit was indispensable to the task at hand.

The ocean surface abruptly blossomed into view before him, the intruder charging away at what he perceived to be nearly twice the speed of the Angel. Jake started the 140 horsepower engine and engaged the drive, accelerating rapidly over the calm sea and steering a course parallel to the pursuing vessel. He estimated the intruder to be a half-mile behind the Angel. Pulling to within 100 meters of the intruder, he let up on the throttle by a quarter turn and kept pace with the pursuing boat, maintaining a fixed position relative to the craft while holding the Kawasaki astern and to its port side just beyond its wake.

Jake decided to refrain from any action until he was certain of the intruder's intentions. The vessel chasing the Angel did not possess the classical lines of a U.S. Coast Guard Cutter. He studied it carefully, the NV goggles revealing it to have the configuration of a modern-type cabin cruiser, the kind with a swept-back, streamlined bridge. The vessel was sleek and fast and was swiftly overtaking the Angel dead ahead of it.

"Arrow, here!" Jake blurted. "I'm fixed on the tango. Let's see what he wants."

"I hear you, Arrow. Goliath out!"

Jake kept the NV goggles trained on the intruder, looking closely for signs of potential hostility as it bore down on the Angel. He reached forward with his left hand and groped the two securely fastened objects centered directly over the bow of the Kawasaki, an over-under weapons combination. They were locked, loaded and, if need be, ready to strike with the deadliness of poisonous serpents. But Jake's primary objective was not to wound or kill, only to defend and dishearten. Given a choice, he would much rather prefer to strike fear into possible assailants instead of injure. And though it was true that he had killed on several prior occasions in the midst of fierce firefights while in the Seals, he was not a killer by nature.

The lower weapon was an M-60 machine gun, the kind that could be side-mounted to light military helicopters, particularly LOHs, and aimed by lining up the aircraft with a target during a strafing run. A box-like magazine configured to the gun currently held 1000 rounds of belted 7.62mm ammunition, with every fifth round a tracer. The M-60 could spit 550 rounds per minute and had an effective range of 1100 meters.

Fixed in place above the sixty was an MK-23 Stoner, another rapid-fire weapon that had been popular with the Seals during the Vietnam War. Manufactured by Cadillac Gage, its magazine could hold 150 rounds of 5.56mm ammo that belt-fed at a rate of 850 per minute. Praised by the Vietnam-era Seals for its overwhelming suppressive firepower, the weapon had one major drawback, and that was its proneness to jamming unless kept immaculately clean. Mounted immovably to a special rack, each weapon could be brought to bear on a chosen object by aligning the longitudinal axis of the Kawasaki toward the target.

Jake controlled the elevation of the guns by changing the pitch orientation of the waverunner. By shifting his weight forward or backward and either gunning or laying back on the throttle, the nose of the craft could be elevated or lowered at will. Accuracy of the guns was a matter of skill and dexterity on the part of the driver.

The actual arming and firing of each weapon, however, was another matter. The sixty had an electronic safety and could only be armed by lifting a swivel-guard cap located on the lower console and flicking a toggle switch housed beneath it. A thumb button situated on the left handlebar of the craft could then be depressed to fire the gun.

Operation of the Stoner, by contrast, was all manual. A cable guide connecting a lever at the left hand grip to a sleeve on the Stoner's trigger provided the mechanism by which the lighter machine gun was able to discharge. The lever was similar to the braking device used on multi-speed bicycles and, in fact, was actually taken from one. By squeezing the lever against the Kawasaki handle grip, the Stoner could be fired.

Both machine guns and ammunition had been purchased illicitly through a bootleg weapons dealer operating within the heart of Port-au-Prince, the same Yemeni national Mat had mentioned. While perusing the dealer's extensive inventory, Jake had come upon the Stoner and had been immediately drawn to it like a moth to a lit candle. Unlike the stockless, aviation-version sixty which was not intended for use by the foot soldier, the Stoner could be quickly detached from its mount and hand-held, allowing its wielder to fire it from the shoulder or hip. And although the Stoner could be a most effective weapon because of its extraordinary discharge rate, its magazine could be expended in slightly over 10 seconds if fired continuously.

The Kawasaki STX-12F carried one more customized feature, which further enhanced its formidable disposition. It packed two 40mm torpedoes, also compliments of the Port-au-Prince arms dealer. Jake had learned that the dealer had obtained the torpedoes discretely from Rosoboronexport, a maker of Small Class submarines. The torpedoes could be launched from firing tubes retrofitted to each side of the Kawasaki hull.

The torpedoes were armed and fired via an electronic system similar to the sixty. Two pre-launch swivel guards protected arming toggle switches, one for each firing tube. The guards were essential in preventing accidental arming during rough, bumpy rides over an uncooperative sea. Another thumb button just to the left of the right hand throttle triggered the designated torpedo, depending on which toggle switch happened to be in the on position. If both switches were activated, then both the right and left side torpedoes could be launched simultaneously. To ensure that no significant deviation occurred along a torpedo's alignment path following launch, the manufacturer recommended the water-based projectile be fired from no more than 60 meters away from its intended target, and never in a choppy sea when launched from the surface.

Although Jake had previously test-fired both machine guns at floating targets during practice drills and was confident in his skill at hitting any object within their immediate range, the torpedoes were as yet untested.

Other than a sheathed survival knife secured to his calf, one additional weapon resided with Jake. A suppressed Heckler & Koch USP-9 semi-automatic submachine pistol rode his right thigh, held firmly in place by a ballistic nylon holster that descended from a tactical pistol belt and strapped snugly to his leg. The belt held five spare 15-round magazines. Jake had grown accustomed to such a weapon from his days in the Seals, and the feel of it always gave him great comfort whenever he was subjected to potentially dangerous situations. The USP-9 along with its associated ammunition had also been supplied by the same Haitian arms dealer.

Jake watched as the intruder got to within 50 meters of the Angel, then was nearly blinded as a brilliant flash of light, greatly intensified by the night vision goggles, lit up the night like a miniature sun. He quickly lifted the goggles to his forehead and blinked away the spots dancing before his eyes.

A marine flare arced lazily high above, its dazzling glare giving definition to the two vessels churning the water beyond him. As the flare descended, two figures could be seen scurrying out onto the bow of the pursuing craft, and in their hands the protruding muzzles of assault weapons coming to bear upon the Angel.

All at once, Jake lifted the swivel guard from the M-60's arming switch and flicked the toggle, steering wide of the intruder's prow before angling in on it. Leaning back in his seat, he maxed out the throttle so that the Kawasaki's nose rose up. At the correct moment, he thumbed the firing button. The waverunner vibrated in protest as the sixty chattered deafeningly under the short 12-round burst suddenly unleashed, then settled back into an easy glide as Jake eased off the trigger. Several tracers defined the trajectory of the enfilade, streaking over the heads of the individuals perched on the intruder's bow and sizzling off into the distance like tiny shooting stars, red and fiery. The men immediately hunkered down in confusion, completely caught off guard by this unexpected threat.

Jake leaned the Kawasaki over sharply, veering back toward the intruder's stern and building distance from it. With all surfaces of his craft and weaponry cloaked in a non-reflective coating of black, his wetsuit and accessories black, and all of his exposed skin smeared in lampblack, Jake was certain the crewmembers aboard the intruder would have trouble spotting him on the dark ocean. That is, unless they possessed night vision equipment as he did. It was a consideration he didn't have time to worry about, however.

Jake spoke curtly into his lip mike. "Arrow to Goliath. Please give our uninvited guests the welcome they deserve."

Zimbola's voice reverberated in Jake's ears like a bass drum. "It shall be my pleasure, Arrow. Goliath out."

Several seconds passed before a flight of red tracers erupted from the Angel's stern, spewing angrily above the intruder like a swath of broken laser beams. As pre-arranged, Hector was giving his pursuers something to think about.

The ocean receded into darkness once again as the flare faded and finally winked out. Jake's last glimpse of the armed men showed them to be sprawled face down on the bow of their vessel, now thoroughly discouraged from rising into a possible fusillade of shots coming from nearly opposing directions.

Lowering the NV unit to his eyes once more, Jake noted the relative positions of the pursued and pursuing vessels, careful to keep clear of the Angel's field of fire. Like Jake, both Zimbola and Hector were currently outfitted with similar night vision capability and were also tracking the movements of the intruder within the veil of darkness.

A sudden burst of return fire ensued from the pursuing vessel as the weapon bearers aboard her overcame their surprise. Muzzle flashes from their guns flickered brightly, stabbing into the surrounding pall of night with the urgency of a blind man poking away attackers with a cane.

Something pinged loudly in Jake's ear and Zimbola's voice came back at him in a bellow of surprise. "Jeez mon, that was close! Arrow, we are taking fire! We are being hit!"

"You don't have to be nice anymore, Goliath," Jake growled testily. "Give 'em hell!"

Zimbola did not bother to answer, and within moments the Angel sent a stream of tracers swarming low over the water. Through the NV goggles, Jake could just make out the barrel of the infantry-version M-60 aboard the Angel as it swiveled on its mount, its muzzle belching spurts of reddish-orange hell while it protruded menacingly from the opening in the inch-thick bulletproof plexiglass behind which Hector stood. The intense exchange of gunfire persisted as the intruder's gunmen homed in on the tracers' origination point at the Angel's stern, the occasional glint of ricochets caroming off Hector's shield attesting to the accuracy of their marksmanship.

It was becoming apparent to Jake that the intruder had no intention of backing off as it continued to dog the Angel like a hound on the scent. In spite of Hector's withering spray, the pursuing vessel kept coming, and Jake surmised that it was only a matter of time before a well-placed round found its way through the opening in Hector's plexiglass shield. And he could only imagine what the sporadic peppering of incoming automatic small arms fire was doing to his beloved vessel.

Circling back into the fray, Jake made the decision to end the conflict. As a measure of damage control, he had to disable the intruder as quickly as possible. Reaching down, he activated his right-side torpedo. Several days earlier, he had tampered with the weapon, unscrewing the nose cap and reducing the amount of explosive powder within by two-thirds. The torpedo he was about to launch was now limited in its destructive capability, presently rigged only to blow a hole of sufficient size at the waterline of an unsuspecting watercraft to possibly sink it. If the vessel before him was equipped with a heavy-duty bilge pump, then it might possibly be able to limp into the nearest port to effect repairs.

Jake opened the throttle all the way. The Kawasaki picked up speed rapidly as another discharge from the Angel's M-60 lanced out over the water and reached for the intruder. From Jake's perspective, it appeared as if the pursuing vessel was taking more than it was giving, but he couldn't be sure. The intruder was running a zigzag course, challenging Hector's skill, which was marginal at best.

Once again Jake charged in on the intruder's port side, quickly converging on it like a guided missile. Leaning the Kawasaki precariously to the right, he steered for a point seven feet forward from amidships on the vessel. He would make a sincere effort to avoid hitting the intruder's left fuel tank, which would normally be stationed more toward the stern on most modern cabin cruisers.

In its bid to remain elusive from the Angel's machine gun fire, the intruder unexpectedly veered back in Jake's direction and the gap between their relative positions closed even faster. In moments he was eighty meters from his target, then seventy. As he closed within sixty meters, the intruder shifted away abruptly, almost as if the boat driver was aware of Jake's presence. Muzzle flashes continuing to thrust forward toward the Angel from the intruder's bow told Jake otherwise, however, and he tilted the Kawasaki to starboard to match the course change of his target, gambling that the gunfire would not be diverted in his direction.

In less than a second, Jake adjusted his attack run and quickly homed in on the pursuing vessel until he was certain he couldn't miss. He thumbed the launch button and the Kawasaki yawed slightly to the right in reaction to the 40mm torpedo that shot away. Partially submerged, it raced across the gap of water separating the two watercraft.

Turning the waverunner hard to port, Jake angled off on a course parallel to the intruder with no more than thirty meters between them. When nothing immediately happened, he thought the projectile had either gone wide of its target or failed to detonate. But then an orange coruscation of fire flared up briefly from the intruder's side as the small missle punched through its hull. A plume of water flew skyward a half second ahead of the hydrostatic pressure wave that radiated outward from the small explosion and caught up to the Kawasaki. The force of it jolted the STX-12F and Jake had to hold on tight as it passed.

The effect of the blast was almost instantaneous. As if suddenly dragging a huge anchor, the pursuing vessel rapidly slowed, its bow rising sharply as its hull came off plane. The flicker of discharging weapons immediately ceased as those aboard her were rocked by the impact.

Jake knew the torpedo had done its job. With the integrity of the vessel's hull compromised, the bilge pump would be taxed to its limit. The rampant inflow of seawater gushing into the vessel would substantially add to its weight and pull the hull deeper, increasing its drag characteristics. With such a condition, the craft's powerful engines could not possibly propel it with the same impressive speed as before, and further pursuit would only exacerbate the rate at which water entered through the hole in its side.

As Jake sped away from the damaged vessel, he noticed it was beginning to take on a slight list as its gun bearers scrambled belowdeck to investigate the cause of the problem. He smiled knowingly, self-assured that its crew would be occupied with stemming the rush of seawater into the hold.

Speaking into his lip mike, Jake summoned the Angel. "Arrow to Goliath."

"Goliath here." There was an edge to Zimbola's voice.

"Cease fire! It's over!"

Relief showed in the black giant's tone. "I am most happy to hear that, Arrow. We will forever be in Agwe's debt."

Jake rolled his eyes. It seemed that whenever they survived a tight situation, Zimby never failed to credit some divinity within the pantheon of voodoo spirits. From what Zimbola had told him, he knew that Agwe was the spirit responsible for the sea, including organisms and other things residing in and above it. Water-based flora, fauna, ships and even hurricanes fell into its domain.

"Lower the ramp, Goliath. Arrow is now inbound for docking."

"I read you Arrow."

Less than a minute later, Jake gave the Kawasaki just enough throttle to make it back up the launching ramp. The maneuver never ceased to exhilarate him. With too little speed, the waverunner would fall short of its cradle immediately beyond the ramp's apex, only to slide listlessly backwards into the ocean like a salmon failing to make the next level in a steep cataract. With too much momentum, the STX-12F would invariably rocket up the ramp and slam into the cushioned bumpers within its crib like a runaway train, more often than not jettisoning Jake over the handlebars and into the padded backstop. The docking procedure was best carried out under mild sea conditions, and always with the Angel cruising along into the wind at the same constant speed - 12 knots - which allowed Jake to perfect his skill. Strong gusting winds and choppy or rolling seas always compounded the difficulty, and if too severe, made such a maneuver nearly impossible to execute. On this particular occasion, though, the Kawasaki slid smoothly into the awaiting cradle with nary a jolt.

A grumbling voice pulled Jake from his reverie. "We barely made it back to Kingston that night. You almost sank us."

The vivid memory melted away like ice over a hot stove as Jake suddenly became aware of his friend studying him intently. "You gave me little choice. My crew and I tried to discourage you, but you refused to back off. You should've followed your own advice." He sighed, then cracked a smile. "What was that you said about discretion?"

Mat remained somber. "Tell me, Jake, why are you here in this shit hole?"

Jake continued to smile but kept silent.

"I've looked this vessel over," Mat went on. "With it, you could probably make yourself a nice lucrative, and I might add, honest living in the more upscale tourist havens that abound in the Caribbean." He paused for effect. "But not in this godforsaken place. Something's keeping you here, Jake, and it ain't the smuggling trade. You're too smart for that. Care to tell your old pal what it is?"

A full ten seconds elapsed before Jake responded. "When the time is right, you'll be the first to know."

Exasperation scudded across Mat's face like a storm cloud. "God damn you, Jake! You're putting me in a very awkward position."

"I don't recall asking for any favors."

An uncomfortable quiescence began filling the room like fog sweeping in from the sea, and Jake thought it best to change the subject. "Tell me, Mat, why did you try stopping me that night without any backup? It doesn't fit your style."

"I did have backup, but they went after the vessel you rendezvoused with," Mat replied brusquely.

Jake nodded. He could see that Mat was under a lot of stress.

"Listen, Jake, why don't you join the DHS. They need guys like you. I can pull a few strings and have you on their payroll within a week."

When Jake did not immediately reply, Mat sweetened the pot further. "Your crew also. Hell, I'll even get them to lease this vessel at a more than fair price. It can be your base of operations. We've always worked great together, you and me. Whaddaya say?"

Jake sighed deeply. "I appreciate the offer, it's most generous. But I just can't do that at this time."

A volatile mixture of disappointment, frustration and annoyance sparked fleetingly in Mat's eyes, but he managed to hold back the flood of invectives that rose in his throat like superheated magma seeking escape. Jake had always been stubborn.

For a long moment Mat just stared back, perplexed by Jake's answer. "Not at this time?" he echoed in a pained tone, his bearing suddenly growing stiff. "Does that mean you'll reconsider it later on?"

"Yeah...I just may take you up on it, but not right now," Jake said, trying his best to mollify his friend.

This seemed to satisfy Mat and his manner loosened a bit. He reached into a pocket and scribbled on the back of a card. "This is my mobile phone number. You should be able to reach me most hours of the day. Call me if you change your mind. I'll keep the offer open long as I'm able to."

Jake took the proffered business card, his eyes roaming over the emblazoned bold letters: Mat Daniels, Director of Special Operations, Caribbean Counterterrorism Task Force, Department of Homeland Security.

"Impressive!" Jake said, taking in the information.

Mat appeared a trifle chagrined, shrugging disparagingly over the importance of his post. "Don't let the title fool you, titles mean nothing out here. Stopping the bad guys is the only thing that counts for anything."

"I assume your superiors have given you a certain amount of latitude in how you use your budget," Jake speculated. He was thinking back to his days in the Seals when constraining budgets could sometimes negatively impact the outcome of a mission.

Mat shook his head dismally. "Unfortunately, I have to account for every dime spent. Formal requisitioning is a way of life in the DHS."

Jake found it hard to keep the bitterness out of his tone. "Some things never change when you work for Uncle Sam."

"You can say that again," Mat agreed. "It was like pulling teeth getting the funds approved to have my boat repaired. The damage you caused *Relentless* was quite costly."

His expression hardened again. "Thanks to you I've been filling out forms for the last month."

"Sorry about that, old friend, but you should know better than to drop in on someone unannounced the way you did. One can never be too careful when sailing these waters, especially at night. We live in dangerous times."

"Just one more reason to consider joining up with me. Between us, we could do some serious ass-kicking keeping terrorists and the people who aid them off balance. Together we just might make a difference."

"Forever the idealist, the visionary."

"If we're going to win this war, we need hard-nosed warriors, men like yourself who are both tough and devious. You were one of the best to ever serve in the Seals. You owe it to your country."

The words hit a sensitive spot and Jake suddenly snarled. "Don't lay that patriotic rhetoric on me! I think I did more than my share for god and country. Unfortunately, there's too many so-called leaders who ultimately control the destinies of men like us, many of them either so incompetent that they are truly dangerous or so dishonest that they should be dismissed."

The severity of Jake's contempt stunned Mat as if he were forcefully slapped. "You're still stewing over Myers, aren't you?" he said softly.

"Yeah."

Mat well understood Jake's pain. He felt it too. It was like a persistent virus that wouldn't go away. Continuing to keep his voice gentle, he said, "Myers knew the risks same as us. You've got to let it go, Jake…let it go."

"I can't."

Dave Myers had also been a Navy Seal, a comrade-in-arms along with Mat and Jake, but had been killed in Afghanistan, the victim of an abominable betrayal within Jake's unit. A soldier turned traitor by the name of Yeslam Omar Raduyev had murdered him, shooting him in the back just before bolting off like a thief in the night.

Jake had first run into Raduyev during BUD/S training. BUD/S was a Navy acronym that stood for Basic Underwater Demolition/SEAL (Sea, Air, Land), and much of the training had taken place at the U.S. Naval Amphibious Base in Coronado, California. A Chechen by birth, Raduyev had immigrated to the United States in 1992 at the age of sixteen to attend college. Four years later, after having received a Bachelor of Science in Nuclear Engineering from Cornell University, he had enlisted in the U.S. Navy as a pre-condition for achieving American citizenship. Upon attaining the rank of ensign, he had applied for admission to BUD/S and was accepted.

From the onset, Raduyev had been a loner, absorbing all aspects of the training with ardent eagerness despite the brutality of the indoctrination. So physically and emotionally demanding was the six-month program that by the end of Hell Week, the third week of training, the original class of 180 physically fit young men had been pared down to 56. While all of them had been driven well beyond the endurance limits of even gifted athletes, three standouts began to emerge as the most promising of the elite warrior force – Jake Javolyn, Mat Daniels and Yeslam Omar Raduyev. Time and again, however, Jake had proven himself to be the toughest of the three, consistently besting his closest challengers as the training wore on and intensified.

To Jake the intense training rigors had been perversely enjoyable. Hard fought competition was nothing new to him. For most of his life he had thrived on it. In high school he had been the New Jersey State wrestling champ in his weight class during his junior and senior years. Such outstanding performance had won him an athletic scholarship to the University of Michigan where he had distinguished himself as a fierce competitor not only on the wrestling mat, but also on the football field as a defensive safety. In his third year at Michigan, he had led the nation in tackles, pass interceptions and return touchdowns, causing him to come under heavy scrutiny by professional football scouts who sought solid prospects. By his final year, he had captured the NCAA wrestling crown in the 189-pound weight class and was considered an Olympic hopeful. In the midst of his athletic prominence at Michigan, Jake had managed to earn himself a degree in mechanical engineering. But upon graduation, he had declined his invite to the Olympic tryouts and had opted for the military instead. The lore of mortal combat had always fascinated him and there was something that automatically drew him to the Seals, considered to be the world's toughest soldiers.

During his indoctrination at BUD/S, Mat had never let his rivalry with Jake get out of hand, always accepting lost battles with good grace. They soon became close friends and had been paired up as swim buddies during the grueling drills. Yeslam, on the other hand, quickly became embittered when he failed to outperform Jake during the training exercises, seeming to take it as a personal affront.

Early in the training Raduyev had kept a low profile, drawing little attention to himself. Whenever Jake would glance in his direction, he could not help but notice the Chechen's beady dark eyes darting about like those of a pernicious serpent, deceptively cunning and cruel, always seeming to search for signs of weakness in the other trainees. And like a serpent, Raduyev somehow gave Jake the eerie impression that the Chechen was gauging the ideal time to strike venom into some unsuspecting victim. Nonetheless, as the program advanced, the drill instructors began to take notice of Raduyev's physical attributes. He was exceptionally strong and only seemed to tire under the most taxing hardships. His body was lean, hard and muscular, exhibiting wide flat pectorals, chiseled abs and broad shoulders. At six feet two inches, he was a fairly large man, standing an inch taller than Jake and outweighing him by a good fifteen pounds. Whenever Raduyev would outdistance his classmates in a grueling long distance run or swim, his dark eyebrows would arch triumphantly over malicious eyes, giving him a malevolent, satanic look. But this only occurred when Jake was not immediately involved in such competition. Jake was the one man among the trainees who always seemed to outlast or finish ahead of the pack, including Raduyev, no matter what the exercise entailed. Jake particularly thrived on obstacle courses, blowing through them with relative ease. For all of Raduyev's speed and quickness, Jake was always faster. For all of Raduyev's exceptional stamina, Jake's endurance proved better.

As the weeks of training continued, Raduyev's bitterness towards Jake mushroomed into full-blown hatred, and the Chechen's quiet aloofness gradually transformed into overt contempt. The drill instructors noted Yeslam's growing discontent and his intense desire to be the top trainee among his peers. They saw the heated rivalry as a useful tool in raising the performance of the other students to new heights, and as a result both Jake and Raduyev were each designated as a team leader. With the entire trainee class divided into teams, a battle of wills quickly evolved between groups as to which one would be the best.

Mat Daniels was assigned to Jake's team, and it was Mat who put things in perspective one day during a brief respite between exercises. "I think Yeslam sees this as a contest between Islam and infidels," Mat muttered jokingly.

Jake looked surprised. He stared over at the Chechen and took stock of the way Raduyev glared back at him. "You think he's turning this into some kind of holy crusade?"

"Absolutely! There's six other trainees here that are Muslims and they're all in his crew. The drill instructors set it up this way to add fuel to the competition between teams. I overheard them talking about it."

Jake almost laughed. "So he wants to use this training program to make a religious statement."

"Yep." Mat spoke glibly. "And if his team succeeds in being the best under his leadership, then he'll prove that God is on his side and the rest of us infidels just can't cut the mustard."

Jake grinned fiendishly, setting his shoulders and thrusting out his jaw. "Well, we'll just see about that."

Shortly after, each team was issued an IBS – Inflatable Boat Small – and made to race one another over distances covering anywhere from five to twenty miles or more. The courses varied and spanned stretches of sandy beach and open water, with lots of obstacles in between. Boat crews were forced to alternately carry the heavy boats over deep sand and paddle through rough seas, frequently having to lift the bulky vessels over fences and other obstructing barriers and launch them in rough surf. Capsizes were commonplace, and very often crews had to beach their ponderous IBS while bucking awesome riptides. The races were always physically draining and the instructors did their utmost to ensure that crew members suffered as much discomfort as possible, keeping them constantly cold, wet, sandy, blistered, bruised and, most of all, exhausted. But Jake's calming presence and iron will to keep plodding along in the face of brutal conditions became a rallying point of inspiration for team members, and his crew easily succeeded in winning each race. There was a payoff to winning those competitions, too. The first crew to finish ahead of the others got to rest while awaiting the remaining crews to complete the course before the start of the next exercise. And nearly every time the boat crews concluded the final leg of a five, eight or ten-mile trek, they'd be instructed to carry the IBS back to the starting point where the instructors often made them fight their way back through the surf, only to repeat the course.

With each new race the intensity of competition would climb to a new height, and each time Raduyev's crew managed to come in a close second. Although the instructors hollered incessantly at the trainees that they were slow, worthless pukes, they were inwardly pleased. They realized they were witnessing the best times ever recorded in the history of the Coronado training facility. Even boat crews finishing third and fourth had faster times than those of top crews in years past. Those who were making it through the training walked proud. They were being tempered by extreme hardship and persevering. As they continued to be put through the fires of hell their confidence in themselves grew, and they started to believe there was virtually no physical demand they couldn't overcome.

It didn't take long for everyone, both trainees and instructors, to comprehend that Jake's determination to set the standard was ultimately responsible for elevating everyone's performance in the spirit of competition. As a result, a reluctant admiration towards him began to unfold from all the members of his training class – that is, all except Raduyev. With each loss to Jake's team, Raduyev's frustration continued to mount and fester. He began to grow increasingly irritable with other members of his team over their inability to win a single race. It did not take very long for him to become abusive and bullying, and the respect his crew had shown him early on began to dwindle. Near the end of the IBS exercises, a breakdown in the morale of his team caused them to lag behind the other crews, and a short time thereafter the instructors replaced Raduyev as team leader.

During a forced hasty meal at the facility's mess hall one afternoon, Raduyev's anger could be contained no longer. It boiled over into a silent, seething rage and he leered unwaveringly at Jake from two tables away with murder in his eyes. Several other trainees noticed the simmering hostility, and a member of Yeslam's crew sitting opposite from the Chechen, a trainee by the name of Myers, glared at Yeslam reproachfully. "What'd you want him to do, throw a race just to appease your bloated ego?" he openly admonished, his Kentuckian twang just loud enough for those closest to overhear.

Slowly, Raduyev turned his head and set his gaze on Myers, his face contorted grotesquely as if he was seeing something repugnant. His rancor suddenly faded into a harsh grin, though it clung to his face precariously. Keeping his voice low, he said, "Ah, the Jew speaks, the little pig-swine who caused us to lose all the races."

Mat grabbed Jake's arm to keep him from interceding. It was not considered acceptable practice in the Seals to interfere in the disputes of others. Such a breach of etiquette could bring disgrace to the one you were attempting to defend. It was an unwritten code of honor. In the Seals a man took care of his own problems. Seals were expected to be tough enough to settle their own quarrels man to man without anyone's assistance.

"I should smash your face for that remark," Myers snapped between clenched teeth, managing to hold his voice to a whisper.

Raduyev's expression changed again, this time to bemusement. "Ha, I will give you this opportunity," he shot back, continuing with the whispered exchange. He glanced surreptitiously at two of the instructors who were out of earshot and busy in conversation. "Tonight, behind the barracks just after dark…you can try to smash my face there. From what I have seen of you so far, it would not surprise me if you failed to show, little pig-swine."

At a wiry 140-pounds, Myers was no match for the much larger Chechen, but he had spunk and there was no way he'd even consider backing down. "Screw you, maggot. You can bet I'll be there."

Word of the impending fight spread rapidly, and immediately following sunset the majority of Seal candidates were gathered behind the barracks to bear witness. For the most part, the soft-spoken, perpetually calm Myers was well liked among his peers. Though he was one of the smallest men currently undergoing training, he was one of the most cheerful, never complaining about the exhaustive regimen he was subjected to, always making a joke of something even to the point of collapse.

As the crowd gathered, Myers stood stone-faced, his features revealing no emotion as he awaited the arrival of Raduyev. Finally the Chechen showed up, an arrogant smile plastered on his face as he stepped through the mass of trainees. He swaggered up to Myers and stared scornfully down on him as though the smaller man were some repulsive life form that had just crawled out of a sewer. The size disparity between the two men was suddenly apparent to everyone watching.

"Come, my little pig-swine," Raduyev growled. "Try smashing my face now. I will even let you take the first punch."

Myers met his stare evenly, his face breaking into a rueful grin. "I never touch pig shit unless I get it on me first."

The Chechen's eyes flared at the insult and his right fist shot out in a blur. Myers was ready for it and he slipped the intended blow with surprising speed, catching his opponent with a lightning counter punch that caught Raduyev just below the right eye. Yeslam staggered back, bringing a hand to his cheek. Astonishment flooded his expression as he pulled the hand away and noticed a heavy smear of blood. Those closest to him could clearly see the flesh below his eye laid open to the bone.

Yeslam scowled back at his opponent in disbelief, the hate pent up like a keg of dynamite about to ignite. Instantly, his eyes turned red, and within them was the look of murder. With the grace of a seasoned matador, Myers sidestepped as the bigger man charged straight at him, landing a solid roundhouse kick to Raduyev's ribcage as he stormed past. The Chechen spun and charged again, seeking to land a blow of his own but missing. Myers landed two more punches to Raduyev's body before sliding smoothly away, making his adversary appear clumsy. It quickly became evident that Myers was an accomplished martial artist. Nevertheless, Raduyev kept pursuing with unabated intensity. Myers' blows were more humiliating than incapacitating, only serving to enrage the bigger man all the more.

Then it happened. The Chechen managed to wrap an arm around the much lighter man and, in spite of taking three more blows to the head, pulled Myers into a crushing bear hug. Myers was then flung down savagely in a crunching body slam, and before he could scramble away Raduyev used his superior weight and strength to pin him to the ground. Sadistic pleasure gleamed in the Chechen's eyes as Yeslam clutched Myers' throat in a vice-like grip with his left hand. Jake watched helplessly as Raduyev raised his right into a balled fist, ready to strike.

"What in blazes is going on here?" a stern authoritative voice suddenly bellowed. "I don't recall giving anyone permission to play."

Startled, Raduyev froze as if splashed with liquid nitrogen.

Instructor Cunningham pushed his way through the throng and glared menacingly at the two combatants. From the look on his face, both men were already in the brig doing hard time. "Raduyev and Myers, get your sorry asses off the ground!" he yelled belligerently. Stonily, he spun to address the onlookers. "Everyone drop and give me fifty."

Other instructors seemed to materialize out of nowhere, and following set after set of agonizing pushups, the entire class was ordered to get their worthless, no load, good-for-nothing carcasses back to the beach. As expected, they had been hollered back into the cold surf fully clothed for the sixth time that day, unceremoniously forced to endure the Pacific's chilling turbulence for the next fifteen minutes.

"You want entertainment," Cunningham excoriated, "let's see how much fun you have rolling around in the sand again." Plastered with sand and grit, the class was taken on another four mile run along the beach, water slogging in their boots as always. Covering that distance in anything less than 32 minutes was unacceptable, and any trainee taking longer than that to complete the run was ordered back into the surf.

Jake and Mat would eventually learn that the drill instructors had gotten wind of the impending fight and decided to let it take place, at least in part, before breaking it up. Raduyev had ended up in the infirmary with eight stitches and ultimately a prominent scar that memorialized the incident. His classmates would always remember him as the one who had gotten the worst of the encounter. His esteem rapidly plummeted and he became the butt of mocking jokes.

By contrast, Myers' popularity had risen sharply. He was the ideal representation of what a true Seal should be, fearless under any circumstances, no matter what the odds. In the Seals the fortitude of a man mattered most. Physical size and strength were always secondary. Jake knew from firsthand experience that Seals came in all sizes and shapes, and that those who completed the training were all equally deadly under combat conditions.

He also learned that Raduyev would have been drummed out of BUD/S altogether except for one redeeming quality, one the military considered to be highly valuable – he spoke fluent Arabic. Such an asset would prove indispensable on missions in the Middle East, which were becoming more and more frequent as of late.

Shortly after the fight, Raduyev's attitude changed markedly. As the stitched laceration on his cheek began to heal, his mannerism became more tolerant and less hostile. Even the drill instructors noticed the metamorphosis. But as Jake and Mat would learn, it was all a sham.

For the next several months, Jake and the rest of the surviving trainees had learned how to dive, plant and detonate explosives, and make parachute jumps from altitude. High altitude parachute openings, commonly referred to as HAHOs in military jargon, became commonplace, with the skill of the men quickly escalating. Jake discovered that HAHOs were routinely used in infiltrating enemy territory covertly. A Seal team could deploy their chutes and glide in formation over a distance of twenty or more miles undetected to reach an objective.

As the jump training advanced, the Seals were then taught how to properly execute the more dangerous HALO, or High Altitude Low Opening maneuver. These took even greater skill to effectively carry out, not to mention nerves of steel, for a trainee would experience free falling for 35,000 feet or more before initiating a chute opening, often less than a thousand feet above land or sea. HALOs were designed for dropping in rapidly and silently on an unsuspecting enemy, giving a foe only a very limited time in which to spot you, and even less of an opportunity in which to pick you off while still in the air. A soldier was less of a target free falling than while drifting lazily over someone with gun sights locked on you. In completing the jump portion of his training, Jake became expert in packing a chute and the intricacies of plotting a jump so that he could account for wind shear, thermals and downdrafts and still land exactly where he wanted.

After several weeks of intensive jump training, it was during a practice HALO that Jake had almost bought the farm. He had leapt from a Hercules C-130 from an altitude of 26,000 feet, fully equipped for underwater diving exercises. Along with a dozen other trainees, including Mat, Myers and Yeslam, everyone had been instructed to open their chutes 2,500 feet above the Pacific, then drift down to the sea and regroup. Spread-eagled and reaching velocities of 120 miles per hour, the team had fallen swiftly toward the deployment zone.

Having been the last of the group to depart the aircraft, Jake watched the canopies of the others mushroom open below him, one after the other. His heart seemed to skip a beat when he noticed one of the jumpers continuing to plummet. It was Myers. Horror-stricken, he looked on as Myers tugged frantically on his ripcord, but nothing happened.

Without even realizing what he was doing, Jake withdrew his hand from his own ripcord and, holding his arms stiffly at his sides, arrowed his body headlong towards the waiting sea below. The maneuver minimized air resistance and accelerated his rate of fall. Within seconds he was gaining rapidly on the struggling Myers. By the time he had caught up to his classmate, he was less than a thousand feet above the water, and in that moment Jake knew this would be a one-shot attempt at saving his friend's life.

With perfect timing he changed the attitude of his body as he was about to hurtle past. Letting the air cushion his glide, he changed his angle of attack through atmosphere. Myers was suddenly before him, and steering himself closer, he drifted in on his target. In some respects, the maneuver wasn't much different than trying to close on an offensive running back on the football field, and he threw his arms wide a split second before making the tackle. Like a colliding meteor, Jake slammed into Myers with jarring impact, feeling the wind knocked from the smaller man. Managing to clamp both arms, then legs around his dazed friend, he groped for his own ripcord and found it. Yanking hard, he heard the familiar sound of his chute ruffle, then pop just before the ocean rushed up to meet them.

Both he and Myers had hit the water with jolting force, but miraculously the two of them had survived without sustaining any serious injury. Later on, a close examination of Myers' primary and reserve chute showed both had been tampered with.

Even though Raduyev showed concern over the incident, Jake refused to let the man's air of innocence fool him. Contrary to his nature, he had taken his suspicions to the commanding officer of the training facility, a captain by the name of Walter McPherson.

"Do you have any proof of this?" McPherson asked sternly.

"None sir, but I think Raduyev is the only one among us who would want Myers dead." Jake knew McPherson was privy to the fight that had taken place between the two men.

An angry scowl creased McPherson's face as Jake stood at attention before him. "Here at Coronado, Seal candidates do not accuse their classmates of anything unless they have actual proof to support it. Mere speculation is not sufficient grounds to incriminate someone. Do I make myself clear, Mr. Javolyn?"

"Yes sir."

"Up to now, your training record has been quite admirable. Don't blow it with any unfounded accusations." The captain pulled his glare from Jake and fixed his attention on some papers sitting atop his desk. "Dismissed!"

Jake didn't like McPherson. His initial impression of the base commander was not a good one, but having stood before him had only served to reinforce this opinion. He considered himself a pretty sharp judge of people, and McPherson in his judgement lacked the character and qualities befitting a captain in the U.S. Navy. It was not so much that McPherson refused to do something about Raduyev. The captain was correct in telling him he needed concrete proof in order to incriminate the Chechen. No, Jake couldn't fault him for that. And although he would be the first to agree that one shouldn't evaluate a book by its cover, McPherson just didn't exemplify the kind of attributes a person in charge of an elite combat training facility should project.

For one thing, the captain appeared flabby and out of shape, looking nothing like a warrior. But even worse, he could sense that McPherson was not remotely the warrior-type and would always lack the heart of one. No matter how hard the captain was to train, and that would be never, he could not be considered a warrior by any stretch of the imagination. In fact, he was certain the man would fold under the slightest physical hardship. Jake just could not picture McPherson ever leading a combat mission.

Based on what he had heard about the captain, he knew that McPherson was highly ambitious, having advanced relatively quickly through the Navy's ranks. It was primarily political clout that had advanced him, though to a lesser degree the man was also responsible for bringing innovative ideas to the attention of the Navy high command. It was McPherson who had pressed to have more Third World Muslims seeking U.S. citizenship go through Seal training, considering those with fluency in Arabic and in-depth understandings of Islamic cultures to be military assets. After all, it stood to reason that such individuals, with the proper training, would be extremely useful on missions in the Middle East, Northern Africa and Western Asia where Muslim cultures predominated and where an American presence was growing more and more these days. McPherson saw such men not so much as elite fighting soldiers but as diplomats to the U.S. cause. Because of McPherson's relentless efforts and his father's connections with several rear admirals in Washington, he had pushed such a concept up through the chain of command where his vision had gained the support of influential Pentagon officials. Eventually it came under the scrutiny of the Joint Chiefs of Staff who had endorsed this fresh new perspective, rewarding McPherson with a promotion to the rank of captain and installing him as the current Coronado facility commander to oversee the training of Muslims into Seals.

In view of this, Jake had anticipated that McPherson would be unduly biased and unyielding to his concerns about Raduyev, but he felt it necessary to bring the matter before him anyway. It was quite clear now where Jake stood. No way was McPherson going to let his program get undermined by this upstart lieutenant. The captain was a stuffed-shirt bureaucrat, a bean counter, completely out of sync with anything remotely connected with war. The man hadn't been aboard a ship in ten years and surrounded himself with several lower-grade officers essentially made in his own image because true warriors made him uncomfortable. Jake could see it in his eyes. This was how the military seemed to operate these days, led by a bloated, top-heavy bureaucracy of flag-rank officers like McPherson who were armchair commanders at best, incapable of leading from the front and earning the respect of the men who usually did the dying under their inept commands.

Jake had learned that McPherson came from a wealthy affluent family. In fact, McPherson's father was a retired rear admiral. And like his dad before him, McPherson was an Annapolis graduate. The Naval Academy class ring adorning one of his fingers had laid stark testament to this, an insignia for success within the Navy's caste system, reputed to be one of the most inflexible in the world.

Although incredibly stimulating and always challenging, the remainder of Jake's training passed without further incident. By the time graduation arrived, a strong camaraderie had developed between Daniels, Myers and Jake, and the three of them were nearly inseparable. Each of them knew they had formed a lasting friendship, something they would share for the rest of their lives. There was something about sweating, bleeding and hurting together when striving for the same goal, a bond forged in the fires of physical pain between men.

Because the three of them worked well together and were exceptionally adroit at the special tasks they had been trained to carry out, one of the power brokers up the chain of command had recognized the wisdom in teaming them on one particular clandestine mission. That assignment had taken them into the remote reaches of Afghanistan. By that time, Jake, Mat and Myers had more than half a dozen missions under their belts, and each of them had been decorated for combat valor several times over. Jake alone had already distinguished himself with a Navy Cross, two Silver Stars, three Bronze Stars, and two Purple Hearts. Four other Seals, including Yeslam Raduyev, had formed the remainder of the team, with three of the others being older warriors with considerably more experience under their belts.

Executing a HAHO from a Hercules C-130 at an altitude of 32,000 feet on a moonless night, they had glided in single file behind their team leader over a distance of 22 miles, sighting in on the infrared strobe lights strapped to his ankles. The jump had taken them into the craggy ravines and obscure trails bordering the Hindu Kush mountain range, a fortress-like maze of geography better known as Tora Bora. As the team homed in on the designated rendezvous point using their Magellan GPS modules, the flashing blue strobe of a portable beacon winked up at them from below, and they spiraled in one by one in a corkscrew descent. The ground was reasonably level and relatively clear of boulders and ankle-twisting rubble at the small landing site, and each man floated in without mishap in the windless air.

They had met with a Pashtun local by the name of Gullu Sherkhan, an Afghan militiaman and spymaster on the CIA payroll. Sherkhan had identified himself with the appropriate password. The team's objective had been a formidable one, to gather as much information as possible about the Al Qaeda presence in the immediate area, including the whereabouts of their exulted leader, Osama Bin Laden.

With an AK-47 held at the ready in his right hand, Sherkhan had led them silently up a boulder-strewn hill. The team had followed him over the darkened landscape, each man wearing a set of NV goggles to make the going less perilous over the rugged terrain. Carefully skirting a bomb crater fifteen feet deep without the use of such modern gadgetry, Sherkhan had groped his way through the darkness, eventually bringing the team to the mouth of a cave. Well back from the entrance, the interior of the cavern had been dimly lit by a series of lanterns strung out at intervals into the recesses of the chamber. The cave had twisted back into the hillside where it branched off into an array of honeycombed mazes. The memory was clearly etched in Jake's mind, and as he recalled it, he began to relive every facet of the experience.

Deep within one of the tunnels, Sherkhan felt it safe enough to address the team leader, Captain Jim Sheridan. "It was here among these hills and caves that we fought the Arabs for several weeks in the snow," Sherkhan said in near perfect, unaccented English. He was a sad-eyed man with a soft lulling voice. White-turbaned and wearing a ragged tan coat over U.S. Army-issue camouflage trousers, Gullu's manner was balanced between equal doses of battle-hardened bravado and guarded trepidation. His striking blue eyes took in every member of the team with mild interest, as if trying to gauge the true grit of each individual. Jake noticed that his gaze lingered a full second longer on Raduyev than on the others.

"Osama, himself, had holed up in this very cave," Sherkhan continued, his eyes taking on an awe-inspired glint under the glow of the lanterns. "All the caves in the immediate area are empty now. It is rumored that the Kuchis have taken Bin Laden under their protection."

Prior to the mission, Jake and the others had been briefed about the inhabitants of the region and their customs. The Kuchis were Pashtun nomads who drifted around Afghanistan and Pakistan and occasionally into Iran. More than a million strong in numbers and spread out over numerous tribes, they were reputed to have a spy network that was the envy of any Western intelligence agency. With their herds of sheep, goats and camels, these wanderers generally avoided towns and villages as they followed timeworn footpaths through the hills and deserts.

If passed on from tribe to tribe, it would be easy for Bin Laden and his cadre to remain hidden, particularly in view of the ancient but strange Pashtun code of honor called *nanawateh*. Translated into its English equivalent, nanawateh meant sanctuary, an often troublesome and paradoxical tenet to the hunters of Bin Laden. Along the Afghanistan-Pakistan border, the custom was almost never violated among the bewildering array of clans and tribes that inhabited the region. Collectively known as the Pashtun, the people were duty-bound to assist anyone who came knocking on their door seeking refuge, and that could include total strangers or even their worst enemies. A Pashtun was expected to defend his guest with his life if the situation demanded it. For any fugitive or outlaw, the part of the world where the Pashtun lived presented the perfect hiding place.

"Do the Kuchis know of the twenty-five million dollar bounty the U.S. has placed on Bin Laden's head?" Captain Sheridan asked.

Sherkhan stroked the close-cropped beard darkening his chin and upper lip, reflecting on Sheridan's question as if trying to make sense of it. "The Kuchis are aware of such a reward, yes. They are a treacherous lot and can often be untrustworthy, especially to outsiders to whom they look upon with deep suspicion. But once they give someone sanctuary they will fight to their last breath in protecting that person rather than betray him for the mere sake of money. To do so would bring disgrace to their tribe, one that would hang over them for many generations to come."

Sheridan nodded at this. "It seems that Bin Laden and his constituents have taken full advantage of such unique hospitality."

"We must not remain here too long," Sherkhan advised. "The night before, some Taliban led by a few Arab fighters attacked the nearby Afghan militia with rocket-propelled grenades and light machine guns. They are probably still lurking in these hills and watching for infiltrators. I am told that they have spies everywhere." His voice was so dull and devoid of emotion that he might have been warning them about the weather.

"Is it true that the enemy comes from the Pakistani side of these mountains?" Sheridan questioned.

"Yes. The Taliban and their Al Qaeda mentors move along trails that were once used by the mujahideen when they had fought against the Soviets. Several times each month they launch cross-border raids against American-led coalition forces, then retreat back into Pakistan's tribal region beyond the reach of U.S. warplanes."

Sheridan studied Sherkhan for several moments, then said, "Can you take us to Noor Ghani?" Noor Ghani was a local Wazir chieftain that the Seal team had been instructed to contact.

From the look on Sherkhan's face, the request did not sit well with him. "The man is not to be trusted. There is talk that he has been consorting with the Arabs. I must advise against it."

Sheridan was adamant. "Can you take us there?" he hissed.

Sherkhan sighed with deep resignation. "Yes, but we must move quickly. Dawn will be upon us in four hours and it is a long trip on foot."

Before leaving the cave, Sherkhan provided each member of the team with clothing typifying Pashtun dress, insisting that they would be less noticed and better received by the locals if they wore such garb. Various articles of clothing were stored in one corner of the cavern, some of the items in fairly good condition while others were worn, faded and stained with what Jake perceived to be dried blood. Sherkhan indicated that some of the garments had been taken from the bodies of Taliban and Al Qaeda warriors killed in battle. At first Captain Sheridan resisted Sherkhan's ardent recommendation, but after examining the clothing he decided it might be a good idea. With deft sweeps of his arms, Sherkhan wrapped a long, broad flag of ash-colored cloth in the Wazir fashion around the head of each Seal, all except Raduyev who was already skilled in the rudiments of donning a turban. After each man had finished dressing, Sherkhan gave a final inspection of the complete attire, looking over the baggy *shalwar* or *kameez* of each individual with a critical eye and making some final adjustments. Hidden beneath the loose clothing the men would still carry their utility belts and other Seal accoutrements, weapons and ammunition. In addition, each man would continue to carry his bulky backpack.

Upon leaving the cave, Sherkhan guided the team in single file through the dark unlit hills as if he had built-in radar. Several times during the journey, Jake could not shake the feeling they were being watched, and with senses heightened he had scanned the surrounding terrain through the NV goggles he had strapped firmly over his eyes.

After several hours of trekking along antediluvian goat trails, Sherkhan brought the team to a village just before sunup. As Jake looked around him in the rapidly advancing twilight of dawn, he noticed that almost every house was built on steeples of rock. The silhouettes of turbaned men with rifles strapped to their backs could be seen beginning their morning chores in an adjacent poppy field. As soon as they became aware of the approach of the eight-man party they unslung their weapons. Half a dozen Wazirs strode forward with Kalashnikov AK-47s nonchalantly aimed at Jake and the others. Out of the corner of his mouth, Sherkhan told Captain Sheridan to keep his team's weapons lowered and to remain where they now stood. With a hand raised high in a universal gesture of peace, Sherkhan walked calmly toward the armed group, greeting them in Pashtu, their spoken tongue.

A lengthy parley ensued during which one of the Wazirs turned and ran in the direction of the largest nearby dwelling, a castle-like structure with high watchtowers and twenty-foot walls. Sherkhan continued his discussion, which from a distance seemed to grow heated at times. Finally the man who had run off earlier returned to the group and more words were exchanged, upon which Sherkhan nodded and walked back to the Seal team.

"It is all arranged. Noor Ghani invites us to his home for lunch," Sherkhan stated, looking somewhat uncomfortable.

Later that afternoon, Jake and four of his teammates rested leisurely on rope-strung cots set out in a courtyard under the shade of a thriving grapevine pergola, having had their fill of roasted goat and okra. Apparently the hospitality accorded by nanawateh still applied, and Noor Ghani proved to be a most polite and convivial host. Sitting cross-legged in conversation with Captain Sheridan and Gulu Sherkhan, Noor Ghani was a gaunt man with searching pale eyes and a bush of a beard that had the texture of steel wool.

With bees droning lazily above him, Jake rose and stretched his legs, moving close enough to overhear tidbits of the conversation. Like most Pashtuns, Noor Ghani could speak several languages. As a courtesy to his guests, he spoke to Sheridan in English.

Sipping green tea, Sheridan looked over his cup and said, "You have to understand, Osama Bin Laden is responsible for killing over three thousand innocent American civilians. By committing such an act, he has declared war on the United States."

"I am told you Americans hate Muslims," Noor Ghani replied, taking another sip of tea and glancing over at Jake offhandedly. Twelve of Noor Ghani's men sitting nearby along a stonewall situated to one side of the courtyard eyed Jake coldly, and Jake had to force a congenial smile as he looked their way. Noor Ghani turned back to face Sheridan. "Is this true?"

"The American presence here has nothing to do with religion," Sheridan answered, a tinge of frustration evident in his tone. "We are not in your land to fight some kind of holy war the way Bin Laden makes it out to be. No, Americans do not hate Muslims."

"Then perhaps your government does."

Sheridan shook his head. "My government only seeks to protect its citizens from further attacks by Al Qaeda. By taking offensive measures, we are able to contain him."

"Ah," Noor Ghani said, smiling broadly. "You do not demand *badal*?"

Sheridan looked confused and Sherkhan translated. "Our host is asking if you want to exact vengeance."

The Seal team leader thought this over carefully, then gazed back at Noor Ghani and nodded. "Yes. Bin Laden and his followers must pay for one of the greatest mass murders in history. Do you have any knowledge of his whereabouts?"

Noor Ghani's expression darkened and a stony silence fell over the courtyard. Something made Jake turn in Raduyev's direction at that moment. The Chechen's expression was left unguarded as he looked over at Sheridan, and in his eyes Jake was certain he saw the fire of pure hatred. Raduyev suddenly became aware of Jake's penetrating stare and abruptly glanced away, quickly hiding his emotions behind an exaggerated yawn and stretch.

Sheridan's frustration became more apparent. Though only a gap of less than four feet separated him and Noor Ghani, it might as well have been as wide as the gulf between galaxies and as deep as the chasm of hell. In spite of the rift, Sheridan was not about to give up. "You seem like a reasonable man," he said, "a man of intelligence and compassion who is not fearful of speaking out. Yet I find it difficult to believe you would protect a man who seeks to brutalize people in the name of religion, an enemy of human rights and a threat to all those who do not agree with his philosophies. This man believes its righteous to use any weapon at his disposal to kill anyone he sees as not following his distorted view of Islam. He has meticulously woven an elaborate curtain of deceit behind which he hides in order to create a climate of fear, chaos and death. He is a man who expects others to do his bidding and, even worse, dying. Is he not a man who has boasted on numerous occasions that he looks forward to martyrdom, that he seeks a noble and honorable death during a head to head fight with American forces? If this is so, why does he continue to run and hide while he encourages others to do the dying for him?"

Sheridan eyed Noor Ghani coldly, waiting for him to respond, but the Wazir chief sat in brooding silence. "Bin Laden hopes to destroy people of different religions," Sheridan went on, "or even those Muslims who cling to divergent theological interpretations of Islam. His primary targets are all nations that are free in government, mind and religion. Surely you must see the divisiveness he represents."

The darkness faded from Noor Ghani's demeanor, replaced slowly by a budding smile. He seemed to be enjoying this exchange of views. "Many Muslims see Bin Laden as a cohesive force, keeping people united in situations where they would otherwise fall apart. They believe he and his followers are virtuous, devout men, holy warriors who have offered their money, blood and very lives to the almighty Allah in fighting for the downtrodden Islamic nations against the western cultures, which they perceive as being obscene and contradictory to the tenets of Islam. Most Muslims are likely to support Bin Laden."

Sheridan appeared bemused. "Until they feel the heel of oppression grinding into their necks, hearts and dignity," he countered. Pausing, he assessed Noor Ghani carefully. "Do you share this belief? Are you a supporter of Bin Laden?"

Noor Ghani's smile vanished. "What I believe holds little value in this part of the world. Most Westerners have great difficulty understanding Pashtun customs. The Pastun have a complex weave of loyalties and vendettas that goes well beyond politics and religion. Our people are divided into dozens of tribes and hundreds of clans. Disagreements between neighbors are common and often escalate into wars. Outsiders to our land are usually looked upon with deep suspicion. The presence of an invader has a tendency to unite the people, but as soon as the invader is driven out the tribes will go back to feuding among themselves. It is said that war against a common enemy is the only time the Pashtun are truly at peace with each other."

Captain Sheridan narrowed his eyes, trying to size up Noor Ghani as the Pashtun warlord went back to sipping tea. "I assume you are referring to the Soviet invasion of Afghanistan."

Noor Ghani lowered his cup and nodded mildly. "That was one such enemy, yes. But other would-be conquerors also learned about the Pastun resolve the hard way. Alexander the Great and the British were other invaders who tried to subdue this land, ultimately finding the Pashtun to be ungovernable."

"The U.S. helped your people expel the Soviets," Sheridan pointed out. "With the aid of the Pakistani intelligence services, my government secretly supplied Afghan rebels with guns and Stinger missiles, valuable weapons which contributed immeasurably to the expulsion of the Soviets from your land."

An ironic smirk formed on Noor Ghani's lips, partially hidden under his heavy growth of beard. "That is true. But so did the Arabs who saw the struggle with the Soviets as a jihad, a holy war. Many Arabs came into the Pashtun tribal regions during that time to join our cause, including Bin Laden, volunteering to fight the Soviets. But such an alliance created problems within our tribes. Pakistani intelligence wanted to disrupt the Pashtun social order by assassinating Afghan leaders who resisted Pakistani control of the war. Various elements within the Pakistani government supported the Muslim clerics from Saudi Arabia who established numerous religious schools in Pakistan. These schools were funded entirely by the Saudis and were used to indoctrinate many Pashtuns with Islamic fundamentalism. The students of these schools became the Taliban and seized control of the Afghan government five years ago."

"Yeah, brainwashed zealots who were taught to hate," Sheridan retorted, finding it difficult not to let his anger show. "Puppets of Bin Laden who saw justification in brutalizing people by imposing a barbaric, if not moronic, code of conduct on those Afghans that were not caught up in such extreme fanaticism. Under Taliban rule, the views of Bin Laden were propagated and enforced. Torture and public executions for even petty infractions became commonplace. The way I see it, Bin Laden hijacked both a religion and then a nation to serve him in reaching his perverted goals. Establishing such a sovereign regime made it convenient for him to plan attacks against America with near impunity. In Afghanistan, he could openly recruit people into Al Qaeda, set up terrorist training camps and experiment in developing chemical and biological weapons. Through covert affiliations with Pakistani scientists sympathetic to his cause he could garner the necessary resources to produce a nuclear capability."

"Yet he underestimated the resolve of your president," Noor Ghani interposed calmly, smiling at Sheridan's show of surprise over such a comment. "Bin Laden never expected your government to respond the way it did to the threat he posed. I think he was even more amazed when the Pakistani government allied itself with the U.S. against him. Within the protective curtain of Afghanistan, Bin Laden felt he was beyond the reach of foreign governments who were out to get him, safe and untouchable and surrounded by the Taliban who continue to see him as an exulted hero of Islam."

"Yeah, his colossal arrogance led to the downfall of the Taliban government," Sheridan agreed. "The Taliban would still be in power if not for him. Had they heeded the U.S. demand to turn him over they would have avoided much bloodshed. I seem to recall one of the Taliban mullahs claiming that Allah would protect the Taliban from attack by the U.S. It was as if they were goading us to invade and fight a drawn out war similar to what the Soviets endured. That was just before we blew all their military installations to dust from the air. As observers, we had learned much about the way the Soviets had handled their war, and because of it we were not about to make the same mistakes. With the Taliban now ousted from power, Bin Laden has been uprooted from his Afghan stronghold and forced to flee from cave to cave. He is a man who appears to avoid a fight with American troops at all costs, a man who is obviously fearful of getting caught."

Sheridan stopped talking momentarily to study Noor Ghani's reaction, but the Wazir leader only continued to wear a congenial smile. "If you give us information leading to Bin Laden's capture, you will be twenty-five million richer in American greenbacks," Sheridan stressed.

Noor Ghani looked down and poured himself some more green tea, his expression suddenly pensive. "You have to understand," he said regretfully, "such a large sum of money would be useless to me. My life and the lives of everyone in this village wouldn't be worth a goat's eye if I did what you ask. The disgrace would hang over the Wazir for many generations to come."

Sheridan gave Noor Ghani an icy stare. "You have given Bin Laden refuge?"

Noor Ghani ignored the question. "I would be accountable to the *jirga* if I accommodated your offer. They would see it as a violation of the Pashtun code and gather a *lashkar* to destroy our homes, kill our livestock and burn our crops."

From where Jake stood, he could read the confusion on Sheridan's face. There was something in what Noor Ghani just said that the Seal team commander hadn't been briefed on.

Sherkhan saw the look too and took the initiative. "The *jirga* are the supreme interpreters of *Pashtunwali*, the Pashtun ancient code of honor. The name refers to a tribal counsel of elders who are chosen by their respective clans. They are very wise men and their collective judgements are final and binding. They are the only men that a Pastun will accept as his superior. They have been known to settle blood vendettas and land disputes. They are particularly harsh with violators of *nanawateh* and will assemble an army or *lashkar* from the other tribes and clans to punish anyone breaking the code."

Sheridan nodded with sudden understanding as he mulled the impasse thwarting him. From his expression, the cultural divide was stark and difficult for him to negotiate. "I gather this has nothing to do with Islam then."

Sherkhan looked solemnly at Noor Ghani before placing his gaze back on Sheridan. "Our host is bound by a strict code of honor which prevents him from helping you."

"We hold no particular allegiance to Bin Laden, nor the Taliban, for that matter," Noor Ghani stated glibly. "While it is true that Al Qaeda has been recruiting many Pashtuns to their cause by offering them large sums of money, the Arabs are still regarded as foreigners here even though their religion gives them a common bond with the people of this region. But I must admit there have been times when the Wazirs have sided with the Arabs or the Taliban if only to use them to fight against the Kharotis, a neighboring tribe with whom we have been warring for many years now. It is the Kharotis who are our real enemy."

"Why do you fight them?" Sheridan asked.

Noor Ghani shrugged, letting out a small laugh. "What is the cause of most wars? Land. For centuries, we Wazirs have been locked in a struggle over land with the Kharotis. They are treacherous rascals and will even betray their own fathers if it meant putting more money in their pockets. They cleverly sided with you Americans when you first came here, handing over a

Uzbek terrorist to curry favor with your military. The Kharotis then coaxed the Americans into believing all Wazirs were allied with the Arabs, using your troops to harass and attack my people who resent being searched for weapons. When this happened, we had no choice but to side with the Arabs and the Taliban. They gave us weapons to fight against the Kharotis, but in so doing they wanted us to kill U.S. soldiers as well."

"It seems to me that both Al Qaeda and the Taliban have taken full advantage of your hospitality, what you call *nanawateh*," Sheridan said sourly.

Noor Ghani shrugged again. "It is our way."

Sheridan appeared uncomfortable. "You realize your people will remain in harm's way as long as Bin Laden or his followers stay holed up in this region."

A sly grin crept onto Noor Ghani's face, his eyes glinting diabolically. "Perhaps there is a way for me to help you without breaking the code."

This sudden shift in dialogue made Sheridan sit up straighter. "What might that be?"

"My daughter was kidnapped by the Kharotis," Noor Ghani said, his manner suddenly sullen. "This happened four days ago. She is the reason I have arranged this meeting." He fell into a gloomy silence and looked expectantly at Sheridan.

Sheridan was nearly speechless as he pondered the implications of this new development. "You want us to get her back for you, is that it?" he uttered in disbelief.

Noor Ghani nodded slowly, almost as if embarrassed by the unusual request. "Yes."

"And if we were to do you this favor, you would help us?" Sheridan pressed, folding his arms adamantly.

Sherkhan jumped to Noor Ghani's defense, seemingly grasping what the Wazir leader was offering. "He has already told us he cannot break *nanawateh*." Looking at Noor Ghani for his concurrence, he turned back to Sheridan and articulated what had been left unsaid. "Perhaps you will find the answers you are looking for if you rescue his daughter. Perhaps the whereabouts of Bin Laden will become apparent through such an attempt."

Sheridan dropped his gaze from Sherkhan and searched Noor Ghani's face to see if this was the actual offer. "Is this a pretext for shifting alliances?"

Noor Ghani smiled coyly. "While it is true my people resent an American presence in our land, there are some among us who have come to dislike the Arabs even more," he conceded. "They have brought us nothing but problems."

"What kind of problems?"

"By various unscrupulous means, they are slowly gaining control of our poppy trade."

Jake was well aware of Sheridan's deepseated revulsion over heroin trafficking. It was an indisputable fact that the production of heroin was a cornerstone of the Afghan and Pakistan economies, and growing poppy was the first step in producing the addictive drug. He was therefore amazed when the Seal captain managed to keep his disgust from showing on his face.

"Would ransom be one of those means?" Sheridan asked dryly.

Noor Ghani drew back almost imperceptively and stared at Sheridan in admiration. "You Americans are very perceptive."

"I'll accept that as a compliment," Sheridan muttered without humor. "But wasn't it the Kharotis who kidnapped your daughter?"

"Yes."

"And are they demanding a ransom for her?"

"They will only release her in exchange for a third of our farm land," Noor Ghani spat.

Sheridan remained silent for a long moment, tacitly inviting Noor Ghani to elaborate further. Something between confusion and exasperation began to manifest itself in his expression when the Wazir chieftain failed to offer additional information. "So where do the Arabs fit into all of this?" he coaxed, trying hard to keep his tone calm.

"For some time now, Bin Laden has been recruiting some Kharotis to be used as spies against American troops, bribing them with money and weapons. Through spies of our own, it has come to my attention that a neighboring Kharotis warlord by the name of Guz Khalil has taken them up on this offer. Khalil has been promised a portion of all the profits arising from the sale of poppy harvested on land controlled by Al Qaeda. It was Khalil who had my daughter kidnapped."

"Can I assume it was the Arabs who planted the idea of kidnapping your daughter in Khalil's head in order to gain control of your land?"

When Noor Ghani shrugged noncommittally, Sheridan's growing frustration became more evident. "Yeah, I know, *nanawateh*." Lapsing into silent contemplation for several seconds, he finally recapped the rudiments of the discussion. "So through our intervention, you feel you can kill two birds with one stone. If we succeed in rescuing your daughter, you keep your land. In the process an opportunity may arise that pinpoints the location of Bin Laden and his cohorts, allowing us to remove Al Qaeda from this region. Is all of this correct?"

A shrewd smile sprouted on Noor Ghani's face. "You will do it?"

"You'll tell me where I can find this Khalil character?"

"I believe Sherkhan knows the way," Noor Ghani said, looking to the Seal team guide.

"Just one other thing," Sheridan said, seemingly eager to end the discussion.

"Yes."

"What's your daughter's name and what does she look like?"

"She is called Tesha. She is a beautiful child, just short of her thirteenth year. Sherkhan knows her by sight."

The Seal team rested for the remainder of the day, planning a night excursion that would take them to a remote location near Dandar Kili, a small Pakistani village situated close to the Afghanistan border. Sitting in the shade, Daniels, Myers and Jake lounged comfortably, enjoying their special comaraderie and entertaining each other by exchanging stories about their lives before the Seals. It was Myers who had spun the most unusual tale between the three of them.

"Haiti, you say," Daniels said. "Sounds very exotic. How long were you there?"

"Just long enough to get a taste of extreme poverty," Myers replied. "My grandfather, Mercades Myers, was a treasure hunter who ran a boat in the Caribbean. I spent a few summers with him salvaging what we could from sunken vessels."

"I take it that's where you developed your love of diving," Jake speculated.

Myers grinned enthusiastically. "Yep. Learned a lot from the old man. Taught me things you don't learn in the Seals."

"So how'd you end up in Haiti?" Daniels asked.

Myers looked away, shifting his gaze to some distant mountains, his manner suddenly remote and reflective. "The last summer I spent with my grandfather was in Haiti, a place called Saint-Marc. I was sixteen years old." Pausing briefly, he seemed to explore something in the back of his memory before continuing. "Each day we'd take the boat outside the harbor, working the remains of an old Spanish galleon."

Jake's interest immediately perked. "You find anything of value?" The thought of finding sunken treasure had always intrigued him.

"Not at first," Myers said. "But towards the end of the summer, we started bringing up gold doubloons dating back to the sixteenth century. Let me tell you, it was one hell of a rush."

Jake had trouble containing himself. "So how much did you find?"

"Maybe a hundred coins. September was practically upon us by the time the venture began to pay off and, unfortunately for me, I had to get back to the states to finish my senior year of high school."

Still fascinated, Jake asked, "So was your grandfather still pulling up gold after you left?"

"Oh, yeah. About a week after I flew back, he hit the mother lode."

"You mean more coins."

"Coins and a lot of other things. Ingots were found, silver as well as gold, several tons of it. Jewelry and other types of valuable artifacts too, but mostly coins. Mercades called me a month after I got home to let me know the extent of the find. Claimed he had brought up close to twenty thousand doubloons. Said the haul was valued at somewhere between eighty and one hundred million dollars."

Daniels let out a loud whistle, prompting several Wazirs to look in their direction. "Good god, I had no idea we were speaking to the heir of a vast fortune."

"Hardly," Myers intoned, his demeanor suddenly turning rueful. "That phone call was the last time I ever spoke to my grandfather. He disappeared shortly after that."

The glint of something in Myers' eyes caused Jake and Mat to study him a little more closely. Lingering within them was a deep pool of anguish time had failed to erase.

Myers took hold of himself and forced a smile, realizing how melancholy he'd become. "Sorry about going wuss on you guys," he apologized, "but Mercades was special to me. I think I was closer to him than my own father."

"Did you ever learn what happened to him?" Jake prodded gently.

"Not right away, but give me a minute and I'll get to that. The whole time we were working that galleon, I had the feeling we were always being watched. Haiti is a poor, unstable country where government officials and the police are especially prone to corruption. I suppose there were a lot of people who would have happily slit our throats if they knew what we were bringing up."

"I don't claim to know much about treasure salvaging," Mat interjected delicately, "but doesn't one have to petition the local government to get salvage rights in waters under their jurisdiction? Wouldn't Haitian officials have known in advance what your grandfather was doing?"

Myers elicited an impish smile. "My grandfather was never one to follow the rules. Mercades had his own way of doing things, always skirting the law. He was always slipping money under the table to manipulate the system."

"So you think he bribed some of the local authorities to look the other way and leave his operation alone, no questions asked?" Mat pressed.

A short laugh left Myers lips. "This I know for a fact."

"So what did you do when you didn't hear from him again?" Jake asked.

"About a month after I spoke to him, I received another phone call. One of Mercades' crew, a sidekick of his, notified me that the treasure had been impounded by the Haitian government and that Mercades and a partner of his, a man by the name of Frank Jameison, had vanished. He had called from Kingston, Jamaica, telling me my grandfather's boat was berthed there at the time and that I should come pick it up. Said he'd managed to get the boat out of Haiti before the authorities could impound it."

"So what did you do?"

"Against the wishes of my parents, I left school and hopped a flight to Jamaica."

"You sailed his boat back to the states?"

Myers shook his head. "No. I ended up leaving the boat in Kingston with my grandfather's friend. We had an understanding that he'd take care of the vessel while I was gone."

A cynical frown formed on Mat's face. "Did it ever cross your mind that he might have done away with your grandfather and his partner in order to keep the treasure for himself?"

"Never. He had been with Mercades for a good ten years and was a trusted friend. He's Jamaican, a giant of a man with a normally gentle nature…well, that is if you don't piss him off. My grandfather had often told me not to judge a man solely by his outward appearance because sometimes a huge heart lay hidden beneath a rough exterior, and that this particular man was a perfect example of that. I had come to know this individual pretty well during the summers I had spent with Mercades. If you knew this man the way I do, you would know that such a thing was not possible. He's probably the most loyal person I've ever known, the kind you'd like standing behind you in a bad situation. As a matter of fact, this fellow gave me an envelope containing one hundred thousand dollars, saying Mercades wanted me to have it if anything ever happened to him."

Mat was astounded. "Wow! Now that's trust."

Jake wanted to know more. "Did you ever go back to Haiti to find out what happened?"

"Yes I did. Before I got there I informed the U.S. State Department about what had happened. They said they'd get back to me but they never did. Haiti was in turmoil at the time, with rebellions and anarchy the law of the land. The year was 1985, just before Haiti's dictator, Baby Doc Duvalier, was ousted under pressure from our government. At great risk, Mercades' friend and I along with another man sailed the boat back to Haiti and slipped quietly into Saint-Marc harbor one night. He insisted on coming ashore with me, refusing to let me go alone. That was the type of guy he was, always protecting your back. Anyway, we touched bases with some of the locals we knew, trying to gather information on what had become of my grandfather. There was a girl there I had taken up with that last summer. Her name was Veresa. Her uncle owned a tavern in Saint-Marc. Through him she had heard rumors that Mercades and Jameison had been tortured and killed by members of Baby Doc's secret police."

Myers' voice stiffened as he uttered the last sentence, unable to speak for the moment. Mat gave him a few seconds to gather himself before pushing the conversation further. "I'd heard about the kind of men that worked for the Duvalier regime. They were mean bastards. Were you able to get any names?"

Myers' eyes narrowed darkly. "Only one name, but one I'll never forget. A man called Henri Ternier murdered my grandfather." He paused momentarily to take a deep breath. "When my stint in the Seals is over, I have a debt to settle."

Jake thought he caught something in the way Myers said this. "Is that why you joined the Seals, Flash?" he asked curiously, using the nickname Myers had acquired during Seal training. "You wanted to learn how to kill in order to even the score?"

The question seemed to catch Myers off guard for one brief moment. Apparently he hadn't expected such frank probing from his best friend. "Does that surprise you?"

It was Mat who broke the interlude of stunned silence that followed. "Revenge won't bring your grandfather back," he said softly.

Myers' gave Mat a wry look. "You're throwing an overused cliché at me, something we've all heard in too many movies. This goes much deeper than vengeance. Justice has to be served. You think I should just forget about such a cowardly, despicable act? Isn't this very mission aimed at serving justice?"

"You're talking about going into a foreign country and executing a man you've never seen based on mere scuttlebutt," Mat argued. "To begin with, how do you know the rumor is true? How do you know that such a person even exists?"

"That's what I plan to find out," Myers insisted. His manner seemed to lighten as he leaned back, locking his hands behind his head as if to nap. "In any event, I'll be going back to Haiti, one way or the other." He expelled a deep sigh. "I have a son there."

"You're putting us on," Mat shot back.

"Nope."

"I take it you put Veresa in a family way," Jake deduced, smiling as he said it. "If my guess is correct, your son would be about sixteen or seventeen by now."

"He's almost eleven," Myers corrected. "But you're right about Veresa being the mother."

"So I take it you made other trips to Haiti."

"Yes. My last visit occurred in 1991, twelve years ago."

"When did you find out you had a son?" Mat asked. "I mean did you know Veresa was pregnant the last time you were in Haiti?"

Myers continued to loll reflectively. "It wasn't until two months ago I found out," he said. "Although Veresa and I kept in touch by mail, she never told me she had my kid. In the beginning, we wrote often, but then about seven years ago I stopped hearing from her."

"So how'd you find this out?"

"I received a letter from Veresa's aunt. In the letter she informed me Veresa had been killed some years earlier while visiting her in Port-au-Prince. She thought I should know I had a son."

"But how do you know it's your kid?" Mat reasoned.

"Oh, its my kid, all right," Mat answered. Reaching under his *kameez*, he pulled a photo from a pocket and handed it to Mat. The photo was not recent, depicting a boy that was perhaps eight years old at most. "His name is Phillipe."

Mat scrutinized the photo carefully before handing it over to Jake. "Sorry for doubting you, old buddy, but having another with your DNA running loose on this planet is more than this world can bear, I'm afraid."

"Ha ha, very funny. You're a regular riot, Alice."

There was no mistaking the resemblance as Jake inspected the photograph. Though the boy's skin was a few shades darker than Myers', the facial features were a close enough match to suppress any doubts that the child was his friend's genetic offspring.

"Once I'm finished with the Seals, I'm going back to find him," Myers vowed, taking back the photo from Jake's outstretched hand.

Jake's eyebrows rose up. "You mean you don't know where he's living?"

"Unfortunately, no. Veresa's aunt was very ill when she wrote the letter. She told me she'd been shot and was trying to recover. She caught a bullet while crossing the street in one of Port-au-Prince's slums, an innocent victim of a gun battle between rival factions. In the letter, she indicated she might not survive the wound and that she feared for Phillipe's safety because there was no one else to take care of him. From the gist of the letter, outbreaks of violence are common on the streets, with crime spiraling out of control there mainly due to squalor and political unrest. That's how Veresa died. She, too, was a victim of such violence, caught up in a deadly crossfire in the wrong place at the wrong time. Anyway, since receiving that letter I've tried writing the aunt, but so far she hasn't answered my letters."

"She most likely expired," Jake proposed.

"It's a strong possibility. I-"

Captain Sheridan suddenly loomed above all three men. "We'll be saddling up just before sundown," he informed them. "Be ready to move out as soon as it's dark." He glanced at Mat. "Would you mind taking a look at my Magellan unit, Mr. Daniels. I don't think it's currently functional." Each member of the team had unique skills, and Mat was the designated expert when it came to portable GPS systems.

After Mat got up and moved away, Myers looked at Jake strangely. "There's this thing I've been wanting to discuss with you," he confided softly, his tone oddly somber.

Jake had never seen his friend so serious. He immediately understood that whatever was sitting on Myers mind, it was a private matter meant for him, and him alone. "I'm ready to listen," he said, shifting closer in a show of confidence.

For the next five minutes, Myers went on to disclose something that had left Jake stunned, something that would ultimately determine the course of his life. By the time the team had set out in the direction of Dandar Kili, Jake was still sifting over the unusual disclosure Myers had revealed to him, all of it hinging on a promise he hadn't yet made, one he wasn't sure he could keep.

With Sherkhan leading the way, they traveled half the night through a mélange of ravines, ridges and nameless trails. Two hours before dawn, they came upon the glow of campfires in a valley below them. It was then that Sherkhan called a halt to the expedition. Turning to Sheridan, he stepped close to the captain, keeping his voice low. "For us to proceed any farther would be unwise until we learn who burns those fires. I suggest you and your team remain here while I go on ahead to investigate."

Jake was close enough to the team leader to hear what was being said. Though each member of the team wore a radio with wire lip mikes and earpieces so they could communicate quietly and securely, Sheridan had insisted on maintaining strict radio silence during the mission unless it was absolutely necessary to break it. It was a standard precautionary measure used by Seal teams. From experience, Jake knew that radios had a tendency to develop static, sometimes spouting loud feedback and crackling at the most inappropriate times. And if the enemy happened to be close by and was similarly equipped with radios, a transmission had the potential of printing on another unit and giving your presence away.

Still wearing his NV goggles, Sheridan was able to locate Myers crouching further back behind him in the unlit terrain. Motioning the smaller man to his side through established hand signals, he redirected his gaze at Sherkhan's dark form. "This man will accompany you."

A moment of hesitation ensued before Sherkhan said anything. "Perhaps the soldier who speaks fluent Arabic should go with me. I do not speak the Arab language. If those fires belong to the Arabs, then such a man might overhear conversations that may prove valuable."

"That assumes you can get within earshot of their campsite," Sheridan whispered back skeptically. "It's probable they have sentries posted."

"I know this valley well," Sherkhan replied. "With the moon below the ridgeline, the darkness is our friend. It will give me enough cover to practically reach out and touch them. They will not even know I am there. Your Arabic translator will be very useful under such conditions."

Sheridan hesitated with indecision. "Okay," he finally muttered. Though his tone was kept barely audible, Jake detected a faint trace of irritibiltiy in the captain's voice. "You can have both Raduyev and Myers, but I want you back here in twenty minutes. If you're not back by then, I'll assume all three of you have been captured."

Sheridan motioned Raduyev to join them before giving final instructions. "Twenty minutes is all I'm giving the three of you, otherwise the remainder of this team will be moving in on the people down there." He shifted his gaze between Myers and Raduyev. "One other thing," he stressed. "Unless you get into trouble or all hell breaks loose, I want you to continue maintaining radio silence. Is that understood?"

"Yes, sir," both men replied.

Sheridan set the timer on his luminous wristwatch. "Mark your watches starting…now!"

In the darkness, Jake could see Sherkhan nod in acceptance. "We will be back before then," Sherkhan murmured calmly. "You have my word."

"I hope so," Sheridan mumbled. "Now get moving!"

Within moments, all three men disappeared into the night.

This change of circumstance made Jake extremely uneasy. Sheridan's selection of Myers to accompany Sherkhan was a good one from a logical perspective. Myers was the smallest team member and probably the lightest on his feet among them, a man well suited for carrying out stealthy encroachments on an unsuspecting enemy. If any of them could breach the perimeter of an enemy basecamp undetected, it was Myers. But he didn't trust Raduyev, plain and simple. With the Chechen at Myers back under the cloak of darkness, various possibilities came to mind, all of them iniquitous in nature. Certain that nothing good could come of this, a premonition of disaster began to take hold of him, escalating his anxiety with each passing minute. Unable to sit still any longer, he found himself sidling up to Sheridan.

"Permission to speak privately, captain?" Jake whispered.

Sheridan continued to keep his eyes trained on the fires below, but shifted away from the nearest man in consideration of Jake's request. "What's on your mind, lieutenant?"

"Begging your pardon, sir, but I have a bad feeling about this."

"Your concerns are duly noted, but we have a job to do."

From the captain's tone, Jake could tell he was annoyed, that he didn't want this operation complicated any more than it now was. "You don't understand, sir. I believe Raduyev has a vendetta against Myers. If they run into trouble, I don't think he'd go out of his way to protect Myers' back. Out there anything can happen. I'd like your permission to go on ahead as an added measure of safety."

"Permission denied," Sheridan hissed angrily. "You'll remain right here with the rest of the team. Now get back to your position."

Frustrated close to the point of desperation, Jake moved away from the team leader and joined Mat once again, hunkering down next to him. Although there was no way Mat could have heard Jake's verbal exchange with the captain, his friend nevertheless placed a consoling hand on his shoulder as if he had heard it all.

"Myers is tough," Mat whispered. "He can take-"

Both men jumped as the din of small arms fire suddenly erupted in the valley below. "Move out!" Sheridan bellowed. "We're going in."

Jake and Mat scrambled to their feet, following their leader down the slope along with the two other team members. With no need for radio silence any longer, Jake heard Sheridan speak into his lip mike. "What's your sit-rep, Six?" Six was Myers call sign. When no response ensued, the captain spoke again. "God damn it, Six, speak to me. Anybody down?"

Jake winced involuntarily as a sudden crackle of gunfire resonated harshly in his earpiece. Myers' voice suddenly cut in. "I'd love to chat with you, One, but I think we've got our hands full at the moment." A short pause ensued before Myers replied again, the cacophonous clatter of a firefight continuing to hang in the background. "Hold your position, One. We're coming back at you with a small package in tow."

Sheridan brought the team to a halt. "Come back to me, Six! Did you say you have a package?"

There was amusement in Myers' tone. "That's affirmative. Be ready to neutralize the hostiles climbing up our ass."

As Jake held his ground with the other Seals, he could have sworn Myers was actually having fun with this. Sighting over the barrel of his weapon through the NV goggles, he peered downslope and awaited the arrival of his teammates. Another minute passed before running footsteps could be heard.

"Hold your fire!" Sheridan ordered. "If that's you, Six, give me the password."

Almost immediately, the word "Copenhagen" blurted in Jake's earpiece. "Let them pass!"

Jake watched as three forms burst into view on the terrain just below his position, the largest among them carrying something slung over his shoulder. The moment of anxiety passed as the threesome ducked down behind the temporary skirmish line formed by the team. Jake's relief was shortlived as a staccato of close range gunfire cut the night air, sending a horde of rounds caroming angrily off some nearby rocks. In response, the team opened up on the muzzle flashes downslope of them, peppering the area with a withering storm of return fire.

Sheridan barked another command over the radio. "Grenades!"

Jake grabbed one of the four baseball grenades he carried and pulled the pin, letting the spoon spring off. Grenades like these had a four second delay, and he held it for a count of two before lobbing it in a high arc meant to shower the hostiles with an airburst of lethal shrapnel. Putting his head to the ground, he felt both the air and ground quake as five asynchronous explosions reeked havoc on the pursuers. A prolonged scream echoed across the hills as someone cried out in pain, only to be followed by a pulsating silence.

Over the radio, Jake heard Sheridan mouth another order. "Pull back!"

With further pursuit discouraged, the team rose up and took off rapidly in the direction from which they had come. By the time they stopped to rest behind a mound of fallen boulders, they had traveled close to a thousand meters. With a steep cliff at their backs and a protective barrier of rock at their front, Sheridan posted two of the veteran Seals as lookouts to each side of their natural hideaway and once again implemented radio silence.

It was then that Raduyev set down the package he carried. Thoroughly winded from bearing such a load over the difficult terrain, he pulled back the heavy blanket that had covered what lay beneath. Through the NV goggles, Jake discerned the face of a young girl. The girl did not move, as though in deep slumber.

Sheridan kept his voice low as he addressed Sherkhan. "Are you sure this is the girl called Tesha?"

"There is no mistaking Noor Ghani's daughter. She has red hair and blue-gray eyes."

Sheridan placed a small penlight next to the girl's face, lifting one of her eyelids to confirm Sherkhan's claim. "Why is she unconscious?" Continuing with the examination, he answered his own question. "I think this girl's been drugged." He looked up sharply at the Pashtun and turned off the penlight. "What's going on here, Gullu?" he demanded.

Sherkhan shrugged as if mystified. "I am not sure. We found her in this condition."

Sheridan stared icily, awaiting something to sink his teeth into, something that would shed light on the mystery confronting him. When Sherkhan failed to offer more, Sheridan shifted his line of questioning. "How were you able to locate and make off with her so easily?" His manner was interrogative, his tone carrying the cutting edge of a machete.

Sheepishly, Sherkhan shrugged again. "Noor Ghani has a spy among the Kharotis. This man had informed him in advance when and where his daughter could be found. That is where I led your men."

With the aid of the night vision lenses, Jake was able to distinguish the imposing scowl that materialized in the captain's expression. "Why was I not told of this?" Sheridan growled. "Do you take me for a fool, Gullu?"

"Noor Ghani requested that I withhold such information. He considered it unimportant to this mission." The bland tone that had so far characterized Sherkhan was suddenly gone, his voice taking on a tenseness Jake hadn't heard before.

Jake sensed something altogether wrong with the current situation. Strange undercurrents were going on here that just didn't feel right.

The captain turned his attention to Raduyev. "Were you able to overhear anyone speaking Arabic back there, Seven?"

"I only heard two men speaking in the local Pashtu language."

Sheridan looked to Myers. "What about you, Six? Do you have anything pertinent to report?"

"It's pretty much like Gullu says. Slipping into that camp was fairly easy. Gullu seemed to know its exact layout, leading us to where the girl could be found. She was unguarded, almost as if she were a package set out for pickup by Parcel Post delivery. We didn't meet any resistance until we were on our way out."

"Who fired the first shot?" Sheridan asked.

"They did," Myers said.

"You're sure of that?"

"Yes."

"And did any of you return fire?"

Myers looked over at Sherkhan. "Gullu was the first to shoot back. Then we all began firing behind us as we ran."

The team leader nodded pensively. "Did the three of you remain in visual contact at all times?"

Myers gave the question some thought before replying. "That's affirmative, captain. We never lost sight of each other."

Sheridan let out a sigh of discontent. "What-"

One of the lookouts suddenly crowded up close to the captain, interrupting him. "We have a posse on our tail," Three blurted. "I counted twenty-six heads."

"How close?"

"About four minutes back. I could see their silhouettes coming up the rise."

From Three's vantage point, Jake knew the lookout would have had an unobstructed view of one area below them where the trail emerged over a ridgeline. With the team currently positioned along higher ground, they held a sizeable tactical advantage over the men presently trailing them.

An old hand at this sort of thing, Three stared questioningly at his team leader, calmly awaiting a response. "What's your plan, sir? Do we stand and fight or do we keep moving?"

Sheridan turned his head, acknowledging Jake. "You feeling strong enough to carry the girl for the time being, Four?"

Jake knew the trail that lay before them would continue to wind its way considerably higher. What the captain was asking would challenge the limits of physical endurance of even the best-conditioned athletes, perhaps even reduce most of them to whimpering quitters as they gasped for air. The climb would be brutal under the harsh load he was forced to bear. "I think I can handle it, captain," Jake said stiffly, still unable to shake the uneasiness plaguing him.

The captain placed a hand on Mat's shoulder. "You'll be relieving Four of his burden, Five, once we reach the plateau above.

"Yes sir."

As the team prepared for a hasty departure, Jake reached down and, with little effort, hoisted the girl from the ground and gently draped her over his right shoulder. She was light, probably weighing no more than one hundred pounds in his estimation. But with the grueling ascent that lay before him, the girl's weight in combination with the equipment and weapons he carried would grow progressively heavier.

With Sherkhan walking point and Three acting as rear guard, the team moved quickly up the rocky trail. They were strung out pretty good, making it difficult for an unseen enemy to take down more than one of them at one time should they walk into an ambush. Gradually they gained higher ground, and before long Jake's legs began to burn from the exertion. Forcing himself not to dwell on the pain, he ran other things through his mind. In a subtle way, the team had been steered away from its primary mission, and that was to locate the whereabouts of Bin Laden in these mountains. In helping Noor Ghani get his daughter back, they were led to believe an Al Qaeda presence might exist along the way. But so far, there was no evidence of such a connection.

As he thought about this, Sherkhan brought the team to a halt, motioning Captain Sheridan to his side. Though Jake was beyond earshot of what was being said, he sensed the team leader was being confronted with yet another decision. Standing fast, he saw Mat join the two men, and after another moment of discussion Mat came back to where he stood.

"What's going on?" Jake asked.

"The trail forks just ahead. Gullu recommends we take the branch we hadn't used before. The going will be longer, but he says there's less chance of an ambush if we go in that direction."

Mat scurried off toward the rear of the column where he conveyed this change in plans to the others. By the time the team began moving again, Jake's apprehension over impending danger had escalated several more degrees, and he kept his M4 assault rifle in low ready as he maintained a constant surveillance of the trail to each side.

The alternate footpath had less of a gradient than its predecessor, providing a more circuitous route around a cluster of nearby hills. With the uphill trek now less demanding, Jake found his legs rebounding and his strength quickly returned. The team trudged on for almost another twenty minutes before their Pashtun point man stopped the column's advance once again. Another short discussion ensued before Mat scampered back to Jake.

"Gullu's gonna take us through a cave that comes out the other side of the ridge," he said, holding his voice to a whisper. "We'll be able to pick up the original trail from there. The captain wants everyone to have their combat lights at the ready once we're inside. We're only to use them unless we absolutely have to."

As Mat moved back to inform the men to the rear, Jake checked the flashlight attached to his rifle. The device would be useful in probing the total darkness of a cave environment, illuminating any potential targets aligned with the barrel of the weapon. It would also come in handy if the NV goggles became ineffective. Unless there were sources of thermal emissions deep within the recesses of a subterranean cavern, infrared light would be minimal, rendering the night vision gear all but useless. But since all living creatures produced light in the infrared range, each member of the team would be able to see the thermal aura of the man directly in front of him, that is, all but Sherkhan.

To ensure visual contact with each other, the men stacked up closer together, one behind the other, before entering the dark maw set back in the hillside. Looking through his goggles, Jake followed Mat's glowing silhouette with no more than five feet separating them. About fifty feet beyond the entrance, Three's voice suddenly broke from Jake's earpiece, imparting a tone that dispelled any need for radio silence.

"We've got tangos coming up our rear, One. I'm still at the entrance looking back at them."

"Hold your position, Three, and keep them out of here!" Sheridan ordered, the words hissing harshly with static. "You know what to do."

"Indeed I do," Three remarked enthusiastically. "I'll catch up to you after I finish playing."

"We'll wait for you just outside the other end of the tunnel. Happy hunting, Three."

As Jake stayed on Mat's heels with the aid of his NV goggles, he wondered how Sherkhan was able to guide them through such ebony darkness without the use of such technology. The rocky passageway was not a straight run, consisting of numerous twists, turns and deadends. Even lit, the cave would have been difficult to wend. In spite of this, the Pashtun appeared to have no problems with the pitch-blackness, almost as if he had an intimate knowledge of the tunnel's precise layout. Navigating it without sight hinged on a complex sequence of memorized course adjustments, with each subsequent leg taking on a new heading followed by a specific number of paces. To do it by memory would have required making many practice runs through the dark confines with the use of a flashlight before doing it without one.

Turning left by almost ninety degrees to stay on Mat's tail, Jake felt the girl suddenly stir. He knew this was not a good thing, for if she regained consciousness in such a disorienting environment the consequences could be disasterous to the team, particularly if she cried out in panic. Her scream might carry down the length of the tunnel, alerting any unfriendlies to their presence. Much to his relief, though, the girl settled back down again, hanging listlessly across his shoulder like a wet dishrag.

Jake's relief was shortlived as the muffled sound of small arms fire from somewhere farther back brought all his senses on full alert. Sheridan was immediately on the radio. "What just happened, Three? Report!"

The question was answered with a brief burst of static, but an actual reply failed to come. Sheridan spoke again, his voice coming through Jake's earpiece hurried and tense this time. "Speak to me, Three! What's your sit-rep?"

A discomfiting silence seemed to saturate the air before all hell broke loose. The echo of sporadic gunfire resounded sharply as it was funneled through the tunnel. Sheridan's voice abruptly reverberated over the radio again, his tone ringing with confusion. "Does anyone see Gullu? Our guide is missing."

When no one responded, the captain's voice came back even more tense than before. "Somebody say something. I need answers, pe-"

Further communication was instantly cut off by a jarring blast that suddenly rocked the tunnel. Knocked off his feet, Jake lay dazed, his ears ringing like cathedral bells gone wild. Fighting his way through the cobwebs that muddled his brain, he managed to remove the night vision goggles and flick on his combat light. The air was thick with smoke and dust, and he groped blindly around him in an effort to orientate himself. The inert forms of Mat and the girl he had been carrying lay nearby.

Mat suddenly stirred, letting out a low groan, and Jake lifted the NV goggles from his friend's face.

"What the hell hit us?" Mat moaned.

Jake probed the beam of his light through the dust-laden air, playing it against a mound of rock and rubble clogging the tunnel. "An explosion collapsed the cave in front of us," Jake rasped. His throat was now raw from the airborne grit he was forced to breath. "My guess is the only way out of here is back the way we-"

Jake pivoted his head at the sound of movement coming from behind them, and an instant later his eyes fell on another light bobbing toward him. Behind the light, a ghostly form materialized from the dust.

"Don't shoot!" a familiar voice blurted, causing Jake to ease up on his trigger-finger.

Myers crouched down between Jake and Mat and coughed lightly, his gaze finding the wall of collapsed rock blocking their way. "Oh, shit!" he exclaimed dismally.

"Where's Raduyev?" Jake asked.

"Gone!" Myers snarled. "I got suspicious when he started to lag too far behind me, and I followed him when he backtracked. That bastard snuck back near the cave entrance and killed Three. Shot him in the back. Sent a few rounds my way, but missed, then disappeared down a side passage."

"I knew that prick couldn't be trusted," Mat grumbled disdainfully.

Jake looked grimly from Mat to Myers. "My friends, it appears we've been set up."

Mat stared back. "You think Sherkhan led us into a trap?"

"Yeah, and Yeslam was in on it." Shifting his eyes to the girl, Jake said, "Somehow I get the feeling this girl is not Noor Ghani's daughter."

"How do you figure?" Myers asked.

Jake aimed his combat light on the girl's face. "Take a good look at her. Noor Ghani told us his daughter was thirteen years old. Does this girl look like she's thirteen?"

Under the light, the girl appeared considerably older, perhaps closer to the age of eighteen or nineteen. Unhampered by the NV goggles, Jake was able to scrutinize the girl's features more fully. Even with the dust coating her face, a serene attractiveness was all too evident. But then again, Jake recalled Noor Ghani having said his daughter was very beautiful.

"Looks can be deceiving," Mat offered. "Maybe she looks much older than she really is."

Just as Mat said this, the girl roused, opening her large eyes and squinting into the light's harsh glare. Almost immediately she sat up and shielded her face, still groggy but clearly frightened.

Jake pulled the light away from her face and positioned it near his own so she could see him more clearly. "Don't be afraid," he whispered softly, unsure if the girl understood him. "No one is going to hurt you. Do you speak English?"

The girl nodded vigorously, her big eyes widening fearfully at the other two men hunkered next to Jake.

Jake kept his tone gentle. "Is your name Tesha?"

The girl nodded again, slower this time. "Where am I?" she said weakly, swiveling her head around apprehensively to assess the darkness beyond the light.

"You're in a cave several kilometers from Dandar Kili. I'll try to answer all your questions, but I'd appreciate it if you'd answer mine first."

The affright on Tesha's face slowly waned as she studied Jake's eyes, and again she nodded, her manner now calmer.

"Are you the daughter of a Wazir chieftain called Noor Ghani?"

A look of insult immediately gathered in Tesha's expression. "The Kharotis are my clan," she said, spewing the words out in anger. "Noor Ghani is a snake."

Jake shot a look at both Mat and Myers, noting the surprise on their faces before bringing his attention back to Tesha. "What's your father's name?"

"Guz Khalil is my father. He is a powerful Kharotis warlord."

Jake let out a dejected sigh, his throat and eyes continuing to burn from the dust still hanging in the air. He couldn't blame Sheridan for falling into the Wazir's deception, for Noor Ghani had seemed quite sincere. But the ruse had cost the Seal team dearly, and he had to assume three of his teammates were now dead, including his team leader. So far, the girl had given him enough information to conclude they had been severely tricked.

"Tesha, I'm sorry to say you have been drugged and abducted from your people," Jake said regretfully, deciding he at least owed the girl an explanation for her current situation. Though there was still a mystery to be sorted out, he knew that sooner or later he'd get to the bottom of it provided they didn't fall victim to any more of Sherkhan's treachery. "A man who calls himself Gullu Sherkhan was responsible for your abduction. Do you know him?"

The name seemed to strike a nerve within the girl, for her large eyes suddenly narrowed, pulled tight with petulance. "Sherkhan is another snake.

Some say he works for Osama Bin Laden who is trying to gain control of land belonging to my people."

"What about Noor Ghani? Does he work for Bin Laden?"

"Noor Ghani has often provided sanctuary to Bin Laden and the Arabs that follow him."

Mat touched Jake's shoulder. "We better get moving, buddy. Otherwise the posse coming after us is gonna have us trapped like rats."

"Good idea," Jake agreed, still looking at the girl. "Can you walk, Tesha?"

Wary concern crossed the girl's face. "Where are you taking me?"

"We have people after us that want us dead," Jake explained hurriedly, rising to his feet. "I'll try to get you back to your clan, but if we don't get out of here, the people pursuing us will get their wish."

The girl tried standing but faltered on unsteady legs, and Jake had to grab hold of her to keep her from falling back down. He pulled the NV goggles down over his eyes and turned off his combat light. "Lean up against me and try walking as best you can," he instructed the girl.

Tesha did as she was told and the group began backtracking the way they had come. With Myers leading the way and Mat following up the rear, they moved through the cave's ebony blackness using their night vision units to navigate. Between the weak thermal emissions left behind from the Seal team's prior passage and the heat from the explosion, there was sufficient residual infrared radiation for the NV goggles to pick up on. Jake was amazed, however, when they failed to encounter any hostiles waiting in ambush.

Five meters back from the entrance, Myers stopped, listening intently to the sound of movement coming from the rocky terrain just beyond. Turning, he moved close to Jake and pointed off to one side. "This is the passage Yeslam took," he whispered. "Whadda ya think?"

"I think we better use it before those tangos decide to send an RPG in here," Jake whispered back. "Sounds like they're preparing for a frontal assault. Either that or they're getting ready to blow the entrance."

Myers nodded in agreement, then slipped quickly into the side passage as Jake and Tesha stayed close behind. It wasn't long before Myers stopped again. "My NV unit's practically useless," he informed Jake. "I'm walking like a blind man. If we're gonna get out of here, I've got to use my light."

Jake pulled his own goggles to his forehead. "Alright," he concurred. "We'll follow your light, but Mat and I will keep ours off."

The group plodded on cautiously, aware that Raduyev could be lying in wait somewhere ahead of them. They had gone another 75 meters when an explosion rocked the tunnel some distance behind them. Immediately in its wake was a prolonged volley of gunfire, after which the muffled shouts of men could be heard. And then all was quiet again.

With Myers leading them higher through a seemingly endless succession of twists and turns, they finally reached a place where the passageway branched off in opposite directions.

Once again Myers stopped and looked back. "Do I flip a coin?"

Jake eyed the darkened maws, unsure which way to go.

"I know this cave," Tesha said, continuing to let Jake support most of her weight. "When I was younger I used to play with my brothers in here. If we go to the right, it will take us to the top of the rise."

"What about the left?" Jake asked.

"About fifty meters from here it becomes very narrow. Only a small child can fit through. It leads to the top of a cliff that faces the valley to the west."

Jake turned his eyes back to Myers. "You heard the girl, Flash. We go to the right."

It was ten minutes later by the time they emerged into the night air. Huddling low behind an outcropping of boulders, they were able to get a fix on their current location using the GPS coordinates provided by Mat's Magellan unit.

"I guess we better discuss our next move," Jake suggested.

"I think payback's in order," Myers announced angrily, holding his voice to a whisper. "I say we make a little visit to Noor Ghani and pay our respects."

Jake shifted his eyes to Mat. "What about you?"

"If Sheridan were still alive, he would've radioed us by now, assuming his radio is still working. I'm not sure the three of us can take on Noor Ghani's entire village by ourselves."

Jake sat silently for several seconds, taking the time to mull over these opposing viewpoints. "I think our next course of business should be getting Tesha back to her people." He glanced at the girl sitting quietly next to him. "We owe her that much."

"I don't think we'd be well received after what we did to them," Mat disagreed. "Perhaps dropping her off in Dandar Kili would be a wiser move. It's only a few klicks from here."

Jake brought his attention back to the girl. She was practically curled up against him, as if trusting his protection completely. "Do you have anything to say about this, Tesha?"

"If you please, I would like you to take me to Dandar Kili. There are people there that will send word to my father. He will come and get me."

Jake gazed stoically at Myers. "I'm also in favor of Kili." Sighing wearily, he added, "Sorry, Flash, but I guess you're outvoted three to one."

Myers nodded without complaint. "Then let's get to it. We can rehash the merits of payback once we drop Tesha off."

"Perhaps my father will help you once he learns what Noor Ghani has done," Tesha offered.

"We can always keep such an option open," Mat muttered. He rose to his feet and looked down at Myers. "I'll take point this time."

"To hell you will!" Myers shot back, standing to block his way. "A big lummox like you is too easy a target."

Mat gaped in surprise, words momentarily failing him. The lead man was always the most likely to catch a bullet, even under the veil of darkness, and Myers' more compact profile presented a smaller target.

Jake quickly interceded. "Oh, let the little man have his way if he's so eager to get shot."

"Besides," Myers added, his voice showing an overtone of cheerfulness. "Speed and grace always takes precedence over slow and clumsy."

Jake could see that Myers was trying to lighten the situation. With three of their comrades now presumed dead and a fourth member of the team defecting, it was hard for any of them to project anything but a dark mood. Yet Myers, true to form, was doing just that, boosting their morale.

Mat finally found his tongue. "Forget about Noor Ghani, buddy. My first priority for payback has just shifted to you."

As they set off in single file again, Jake mulled the events leading up to their present circumstances. Gullu Sherkhan was obviously a double agent whose loyalties resided with Bin Laden. Noor Ghani was another Bin Laden sympathizer, and between them they had been able to pull off a ruse that had systematically led Sheridan into a trap. The Seal team had fallen victim to a scheme clearly hatched well in advance by unscrupulous minds, and now they were paying the price for failing to see through the deception. He was now convinced Raduyev was a mole, a one-man cell sent by Islamic radicals to acquire Seal training. With such training under his belt, he could teach others how to employ Seal tactics against American forces. And by coming here on this mission, he was able to abet a prearranged plot aimed at turning the Kharotis against their U.S. ally. What better way to do this than by making Guz Khalil think his daughter had been kidnapped by American troops?

Jake had to admit the ploy had been well thought out, a brilliant stroke of master planning. But for the plan to work, it had required the cooperation of a traitor among those who served the Kharoti warlord, a trusted follower of Khalil. Trust was needed to get close enough to the girl in order to drug her, thus preparing her for abduction. Sherkhan had not lied when he said Noor Ghani had a spy planted in the camp they had raided. And now that he analyzed it, it was highly probable that the people hot on their trail would be members of Khalil's clan rather than men aligned with Noor Ghani. That would explain why the rear entrance to the cave had not been sealed off with explosives as the front had been. With the forward exit now blocked and the Kharotis coming up behind them, they would be trapped. Noor Ghani and his cohorts wanted the Kharotis to find Tesha in the clutches of the Seal team. But the Wazir chieftan had miscalculated. He had failed to block the alternate escape route out of the cave.

An eerie chill suddenly raced up Jake's spine as he continued to dwell on Noor Ghani's blunder. *No!* Instinctually he realized the Wazir had not slipped up at all, and he now knew with certainty that an ambush was imminent.

"Everyone down!" Jake yelled. But even as the warning escaped his lips, he knew it was too late. Muzzle flashes lanced out of the darkness. At close range, the staccato clatter of automatic fire assaulted his ears as he pulled the girl down to shield her with his body.

Tesha let out a horrid scream as several rounds tore through her petite form, and as they hit the ground, Jake felt her body go limp.

Jake stared dully as tracer rounds zipped overhead. With the girl so close to him, he found it hard to accept she was the one hit while he remained untouched. Reaching for the girl's carotid artery at the side of her neck, he could not detect a pulse. As if to confirm this, he became aware of the heavy smear of blood soaking the girl's chest, and he knew at once that Tesha's innocent life had been instantly snuffed out with a bullet through the heart.

A rush of adrenaline welled up deep within him as he looked down at the girl's lifeless body, and with it a wild surge of pained outrage. *You bastards!*

Catching sight of the muzzle flashes, Jake opened up, raking the nearby area with a savage hail from his M4. A short distance behind him, he sensed Mat doing the same. But up ahead, he heard no return fire coming from Myers' position.

Jake let up on the trigger and rolled to his left. Something seemed to brush his clothing, and he saw sparks fly from several rounds ricocheting off the rocky ground next to him. Arming a grenade, he held it for the count of two before flinging it. A heavy thump jolted the earth as the grenade detonated, and Jake had to hug the ground to avoid the spray of shrapnel slashing the air.

Jake lifted his head, searching out the shrieks that followed. His NV lenses were slightly askew, and he readjusted them as he scanned for movement. Rising to his feet, he spotted two distinct forms stumble and reel from behind some rocks. Drunkenly, they staggered forward, their silhouettes aglow in the greenish aura imparted by the lenses. Firing from the hip, he finished them off quickly.

Another glowing shadow materialized, rushing at him from the side, and Jake had to lean back to evade the point of the bayonet jabbed at him from the end of a Kalashnikov. Reflexively, he whipped his M4 around viciously, hewing his attacker squarely in the throat and almost taking his head off. Clotheslined, the man's feet left the ground and a dull thud resounded as he landed hard on his back. With his larynx crushed, the man let out a choking wheeze as he writhed snake-like on the ground, futilely trying to suck in breath. Unable to get air into hungry lungs, he clutched his throat with shaking hands.

"I've got your six covered, Jake." The voice was Mat's.

Jake hunkered down, unsure if any more threats were currently lurking in the dark. He glanced sharply in all directions before backpedaling toward Mat. "They killed Tesha," he hissed murderously, his rage almost pushing his voice above a whisper as he reached his friend's side. "Where's Flash?"

As if in answer, another voice rose from somewhere close by. "I finally got the little Jew." The tone was gruff and gloating, breaking off in a gush of laughter that chafed and goaded Jake with infuriating coldness.

"Show yourself, you fucking coward!" Jake bellowed.

More laughter came back at him. "I don't think so," the voice taunted delightedly. "Some visitors will be coming your way very shortly, and I am sure Guz Khalil will want to know why you killed his daughter."

Jake scanned the darkness, searching out Raduyev's position. He began reaching for another grenade, but before he could remove it, he heard Myers cry out.

"Ja…Jay…Jay!" The cry came to Jake's ears in a strained, whimpering gasp, as though uttering it required great effort.

Jake low-crawled in the direction of the sound, Mat right behind him. Myers lay on his back, one arm raised limply in the air, his head turned toward him. "Over…here!"

In seconds, Jake was on one knee cradling Myers' head and torso in his arms. Mat was beside him, lending support.

The light in Myers' eyes was fading fast, now faint as a flow of blood, black as ebony in the pale moonlight, welled up from his open mouth. "You…won't forget…our deal?" he croaked.

Jake nodded dumbly, suddenly remembering what Mat was asking of him. He had never considered it might come to this.

"Promise me!" Myers gasped, choking up more blood and focusing glazed eyes on the man holding him.

Jake could only nod, not trusting how he would sound if he spoke.

Myers groped for one of Jake's hands and squeezed, the grip surprisingly hard. "Say it!" he gurgled. "Promise me!"

For one fleeting moment, Jake forgot about Raduyev. "I...I promise," he vowed, afraid his tone would falter, but his voice suddenly firmed. "You have my word, good buddy."

The words seemed to satisfy Myers, for a smile came to his face. "You are the big brother I never had," he uttered weakly. And with that his grip went slack.

Jake gawked dazedly as Myers' head lolled to one side, the rage simmering within him like a pressure cooker about to explode.

"Jake..." Something nudged Jake's arm.

"Come on back to me, Jake."

Suddenly pulled back to the present, it took Jake a moment to realize where he was. "It never did work out quite the way that bastard planned it," he said acidly.

Mat sighed tiredly. "Cowards always run and hide." He was reminding Jake how Raduyev had scurried off into the night, disappearing completely. "But sooner or later fate catches up with them."

"Noor Ghani didn't hide."

"He'd probably still be alive had he done so."

Mat's reference evoked more memories to flash forward in Jake's mind. Leaving Tesha where she lay, they had moved as quickly as possible to elude the people chasing them. This had not been easy, for Jake would not leave without Myers. It was a Seal credo never to leave a fallen comrade behind, and in spite of Khalil's clan hot on their trail, there was no way he'd even consider it. There was nothing he could do for Sheridan and the other MIAs. In all probability, his team leader was buried under tons of rock back in the cave. But he could at least do something for Myers. Taking turns, he and Mat had carried Myers' along a winding trail for several miles, eventually finding a place where they could hide his body, noting the location with Mat's Magellan unit. It had taken another five days before a Seal team was dispatched to the site, retrieving the body and sending it back stateside for full military honors.

Seeking retribution, Jake and Mat had made their way back to Noor Ghani's village just before dawn. Catching the Wazirs by surprise, they had succeeded in killing more than half of Noor Ghani's men while they slept, after which a fierce but swift fire fight had ensued. In the end, Noor Ghani and his followers all lay dead.

He and Mat had been severely reprimanded by their superiors for these actions, and they had narrowly escaped being court-martialed for going against the latest ROE protocol – Rules of Engagement. Fearful of being excoriated by a biased liberal press for the conduct of one of its Seal teams, the Naval high command had been harsh in its chastisement, practically throwing them under a bus. After all, innocent civilians in a peaceful Afghan village had been needlessly massacred without any provocation. Deeply embittered by this, Jake had promptly resigned his commission.

Both men reflected a moment longer before Mat broke the silence. "Well, good buddy," he said, scrutinizing his wristwatch as if suddenly aware of the time, "I've got work to do."

"I'll try staying in touch, Mat."

Mat grinned. "Yeah. Maybe we'll have a beer together later on. Don't forget about my offer. With us teamed up again, the bad guys won't stand a chance."

Jake returned the grin. "Like I said, maybe I'll just take you up on it."

Just before sailing away, Mat disappeared into the main cabin of Relentless, returning several moments later with something in his hands. Casually, he tossed it over to Jake, who stood leaning against the Angel's rail to see him off.

Jake hefted the small canvas satchel. "What's this?"

Mat stared back, smiling shrewdly. "It's a satellite phone, my insurance that you'll stay in contact. You can reach me at any time with that little gizmo. It's supposed to be encryption-secure, but then again, one can never be sure if that's actually the case seeing its government issue. Give me a call in a couple a days, okay."

Jake looked back. "Nag, nag, nag."

- 6 -

The first rays of dawn filtered through the clear gray sky, outlining the mountains sitting in shadow to the east with brilliant hues of silver and orange radiance. A green Ford pickup, battered and belching wispy fumes of dark exhaust, made its way slowly up to the head of the wharf located in Port-au-Prince Harbor. Of the three men who got out, only one was smiling, displaying a shaggy mane of thick white hair that ran to his shoulders. He stepped forward toward a trim tanned and muscular individual who stood casually aloof with sinewy arms folded at the chest as if in challenge. With feet idly crossed at the ankles, the much younger man leaned up against a timber post, watching the approach of the grinning chap with the alert, intense look of a predator.

"Mister Javolyn, I presume?"

The younger man nodded.

"I'm Doctor Franklin Grahm," the older man said, extending a hand and continuing to smile disarmingly as if a frown would be impossible to achieve on so open a face.

Jake Javolyn disengaged himself from the post and clasped the offered hand. Grahm's grip was surprisingly firm and dry in spite of the early morning humidity, producing more strength than Jake would have expected from the aging zoologist.

Grahm turned and indicated his companions. "These are my assistants, Jeffrey Parker and Nicolas Henderson."

Jake assessed the others as additional handshakes ensued. Parker was short, stocky and stoic, while Henderson, a thin, bespectacled scholarly type, appeared somewhat brooding and pensive when measured against his amiable mentor. Both men were in their mid twenties, most likely graduate students, he surmised. He immediately took to the older gent, automatically drawn to the man's intrinsic cheerfulness. For the time being he would withhold judgement toward the other two.

A moment of silence prevailed as all three men stared beyond Jake to the large vessel floating lazily beside the wharf, as if trying to gauge its suitability and seaworthiness.

"She doesn't look like much," Jake stated dryly, "but I'm sure she'll be able to help you fulfill any objectives you hope to accomplish on this trip."

The doctor's assistants looked skeptical, but Grahm remained enthusiastic, his deep-set jovial eyes appraising the vessel's stern. "An interesting name," he remarked. "*Avenging Angel.* I rather like the sound of it."

Jake smiled inwardly, remembering his first glimpse of the vessel. With Zimbola insisting it would be bad luck to change her previous designation, he had instead assuaged the Jamaican's superstitions by adding a prefix to the original name.

"She's a sturdy old gal and can take almost anything the sea can throw at her," Jake said, acknowledging his vessel proudly. "Her and I have been through a lot together. To me, she is an angel."

The reverent affection in Jake's tone did not go unnoticed by Grahm. "Mr. Hennington informed me you have all the necessary dive gear, that you could provide the three of us with complete scuba rigs," Grahm said zestfully.

A broad smile blossomed on Jake's face, imparting a salient handsomeness to his features. All traces of his previous aloofness dissolved into an accommodating congeniality. "Everything you'll need is aboard this vessel. She's even equipped with surface-supplied air, complete with diver-to-surface communication and real-time underwater video recording capability. If you want to undertake especially deep dives, we also have various arrays of mixed gas available to extend your bottom time and reduce the duration of in-water decompression you would normally need on compressed air."

Parker's forehead wrinkled in interest. "I assume you mean nitrox."

"Both nitrox and heliox," Jake declared, taking pleasure at Parker's surprise.

Henderson frowned. The use of nitrox was rapidly gaining acceptance among members of sport and scientific diving communities who liked the challenge of going deep. But having heliox - a gas mixture of helium and oxygen - at their disposal was quite unexpected since it was primarily applicable to exceptionally deep salvage work or ocean-based oil wells where saturation dives were routinely carried out. "I don't think we'll have any need of helium in our breathing mixtures," he said, his tone supercilious. "We-"

Grahm cut his protégé off. "It seems you're better equipped than we had expected, Mr. Javolyn."

"You can call me Jake." He would reserve his preferred name once he knew Grahm better.

"As you wish, Jake. We had to pack rather hastily, so we only brought along the most essential gear. Is it all right if we bring these items aboard your boat?" Grahm pointed to an assortment of cases and luggage resting on the bed of the pickup.

"No need for you or your assistants to move them," Jake said. "I'll have Phillipe and Hector, two of my crew, bring it all aboard."

Fifty minutes later, the Avenging Angel was well underway, winding a course through one of the most difficult harbor entrances on the planet. Having safely stowed the gear of the passengers, Hector had remained up on deck with Grahm's two assistants while Phillipe stayed busy in the equipment locker preparing gear.

Parker and Henderson seemed content to linger in the mild sea breeze, glad to get some relief from the intense heat and humidity of Port-au-Prince's sweltering weather. Such conditions were palpable forces, causing every movement to take far more effort than they were accustomed to.

With Zimbola at the helm in the pilothouse, Jake and Dr. Grahm remained in the vessel's forward cabin. Jake followed the path Dr. Grahm's finger traced over the nautical chart laid before them.

"This is where I'd like to start," Grahm said. He pointed to a tiny teardrop-shape lying in the Windward Passage some 40 miles west of Haiti.

Jake nodded knowingly. "Navassa Island. I'm familiar with it. It's a desolate hunk of limestone."

"Yes, but it's also a marine scientist's dream. The submerged coral shelf is one of the most intact and thriving ecosystems in the Caribbean."

There was something in Grahm's voice that made Jake look up. "Mind clueing me in on what you plan to do there."

The doctor remained silent for several seconds, seeming to weigh something of great significance. "Before I get to that, I think I should fill you in on a few things."

Jake didn't bother to divulge what he already knew about the man's work.

"Tursiops truncatus, better known as the bottlenose dolphin, is one of the most interesting creatures on the face of the earth," Grahm said. "The bottlenose has the second largest brain to body size ratio of any animal, topped only by human beings."

A smile crept onto Jake's face. "I've had more than a few encounters with the species."

"Then you know that they live in social groups that are highly structured in the way they function. Although there is major disagreement in scientific circles as to how intelligent dolphins are, particularly since it's difficult to define just what intelligence is, the collective opinion is that dolphins are exceptionally intelligent creatures. To survive in their groups, more precisely called pods, they must behave and communicate according to complex rules. A few scientists, myself included, have theorized that the complexity of this group interaction is the actual reason behind their highly evolved state of intelligence."

Grahm hesitated, collecting his thoughts. At that moment, the boat's intercom buzzed and Jake toggled a nearby switch. "What is it, Zimby?"

A disembodied voice filled the cabin. "We'll be clearing the harbor soon. What heading you want me to take?"

"Steer a course of two-seven-zero," Jake instructed. "We're going to Navassa Island."

"Two-seven-zero it is, Jay Jay."

"How long before we reach the eastern side of the island?" Grahm asked, seeming anxious to get there.

Scrutinizing the chart, Jake did a mental calculation. "Sea is relatively calm. ETA will be roughly oh eight three oh, give or take several minutes."

Grahm nodded and continued with his lecture. "Did you know that the bottlenose has a cerebral cortex about forty percent larger than a human's? Their cortex is stratified in much the same way as ours, with their frontal lobe developed to a level comparable to man's. However, their parietal lobe, the part of their brain which interprets the senses, is larger than the human frontal and parietal lobes combined."

The marine zoologist paused to study the puzzlement on Jake's face and grinned out of sympathy. "In other words, the dolphin brain has evolved to analyze sensory information to a much greater degree than our own. In addition, they have a higher neural density in some parts of their brain than humans, especially those areas that deal with such things as emotional control, objectivity, reality orientation, logically consistent abstract thought, humor, and creativity. This seems to be correlated with a dolphin's ability to maintain a healthy emotional state while in captivity. Humans in similar situations often don't fare as well emotionally."

Jake listened attentively. He had always been fascinated with dolphins. There was something about those amazing creatures that struck a resonant chord deep within him. He remembered quite vividly his first up-close encounter with these streamlined marine mammals while on maneuvers with Seal Team Six off Bermuda. The pod had been large, foraging and chittering away quite noisily just beyond his visual range as he flippered along at a depth of roughly 30 feet in the clear pristine water. Two bottlenose had suddenly burst into view, apparently inquisitive about his presence. They had darted and swooped in close, making a succession of rapid passes, emitting a series of clicks, whistles and beeps as they did so. Finally, the larger of the pair had overcome its caution and swam to within arms reach of him, remaining almost stationary as it surveyed him with that peculiar perpetual smile characteristic of the species. As Jake had stared into its black inscrutable orbs, something had moved deep within his soul, something akin to peace and bliss. In that instant of time, he had somehow perceived that he was gazing upon an evolved spiritual entity, and a profound though inexplicable connection transpired. An eternal bond had been born, not specifically with the creature floating before him, but a link that embraced the species and all its closely related cousins. From then on, he would forever be incapable of seeing any harm come to such beings, and instinctually he knew they would never bring harm to him.

Following that mystical experience, Jake had gotten the opportunity to work directly with a team of five specially trained bottlenose dolphins during a mine clearing exercise in the Iraqi port of Umm Qasr following the fall of Saddam Hussein. During that period, he had been loaned out to assist the Navy's Special Clearance Team One, a mine-clearing unit out of San Diego, California. He had been assigned to the unit in order to replace one of the unit's human divers who had impaled a leg on a sharp shard of metal jutting above the mudline in the area where the diver had been working. Jake had quickly learned about the astounding echolocation capabilities of these creatures, a kind of biological radar used for assessing their surroundings. By using both high and low clicking vocalizations, objects hidden from sight such as mines are revealed once the emitted sound waves are bounced back in the dolphin's direction. Developed over 50 million years of evolution, dolphin sonar was incredibly precise for locating mines or other objects in cluttered shallow-water harbors where electronic military hardware is rendered virtually useless.

Jake remembered the words of Lieutenant Gary Watson, the officer in charge of the M-7 series of mine-clearing dolphins. *"They can distinguish and pick out objects like you wouldn't believe under the murkiest conditions, even down to detecting different types of metal."* The memory of an M-7 bottlenose named Reno stuck with him. Upon locating a mine, the animal would return to its handler to be given a transponder, which was then dropped near the ship-destroying device in order for divers like Jake, skilled in explosive demolition, to home in on and detonate with an explosive charge.

Based on that experience, Jake understood one thing for certain, that a dolphin's built-in sonar far surpassed the performance of any state-of-the art equipment produced by man. Not only could it clearly discern the size, shape and texture of a submerged object, it could also gauge its density. Furthermore, according to Lieutenant Watson, no one had yet been able to jam or distort a dolphin's sonar. The lieutenant had demonstrated some of these remarkable abilities when he tossed a single air rifle BB shot a distance of perhaps 70 feet from their Zodiac. It had taken Reno less than 30 seconds to locate, retrieve and return it to Watson's hand. *"They are exceptionally adept at directionalizing their sonar beams",* Watson had explained.

"Are you with me, lad?" Grahm asked, bringing Jake back to the present. "You seem like you're a million miles away."

Jake suppressed his embarrassment. "So that big brain of theirs is designed to make sense of acoustic signals in such a way that they're able to see with their ears."

Grahm looked pleased. "Very good, Jake my lad. A dolphin gets the same input from its ears that we get from our eyes. Since their brain is much more acoustically oriented than ours, they are able to generate visual images based on auditory input, paralleling our own subjective experience of visual models. The neurological pathways and the brain area devoted to auditory processing in dolphins matches quite closely with that of the visual processing mechanism in humans. By means of its emitted sonar signals, a dolphin constructs a three-dimensional visual world around itself exactly as humans do with electromagnetic light waves reflected off their surroundings. Because of the reversal in the sizes of the human and dolphin visual and auditory brain cortices, one might say that the dolphin is able to hear as well as we can see and see as well as we can hear, or perhaps better on both counts.

Grahm glanced out a starboard window at the gentle heave of the sea as the trawler pursued a westerly course, then turned back to Jake. "Now here comes the interesting part, the part about how dolphins communicate with each other. Up until recently, most researchers attempting to analyze the sounds dolphins make have erroneously assumed that they communicate auditory information in the same linear, analytical form as humans do. Such an assumption, unfortunately, keeps leading to the same dead-end. A better approach to understanding their means of communication would be to assume that dolphins can reproduce or mimic the sounds they hear, or actually see. Let's call the process of a dolphin sending out sonar waves to see its environment as *speak-see*. In addition, let's refer to what they perceive through the signals bounced back to them as *hear-see*. By recreating the hear-see sounds, dolphins are then able to relate events from distant or remote time-space coordinates to other dolphins. Let's call this mimicking or recreating process *picture-speak*. Based on this, a complete communication cycle or loop between dolphins would be something like the following. One dolphin performs a reconnaissance of its environment by speak-seeing. It then mimics the sounds reflected back from its surroundings by picture-speaking. A second dolphin hear-sees the message from its immediate environment and remembers it. That dolphin, in turn, picture-speaks these same arrangements of noise to other dolphins, ultimately creating a kind of virtual reality around its neighboring dolphins."

"Has such a hypothesis been proven?" Jake asked.

Grahm let out a great sigh. "Not conclusively. But there's a wealth of supporting evidence which makes such a theory plausible."

"For instance?"

"Well, the best example involves a pod of orcas swimming among a flotilla of fishing vessels. Orcas, better known as killer whales as I'm sure you know, are another type of dolphin. Anyway, when one of the harpooners killed a member of the pod, the remaining whales began to avoid only those boats rigged with harpoon guns, continuing to approach the other vessels lacking such a killing device. With the exception of the harpoon guns, those other vessels presented the same exact overall configuration as the killing vessels. Yet the whales correctly perceived the non-harpoon vessels as no threat. That a verbal, linear analytical description of the potential killing vessels would suffice as an effective form of communication to keep the entire pod clear of just those particular vessels seems highly unlikely since the descriptions of the harpoon guns would have required a high degree of exactness for the whales to differentiate between boats. But by transmitting a visual image of the harpooning itself, the whales receiving the image would have no trouble distinguishing the harpoon vessels from the fishing boats that didn't have them. Such an acoustically sent message would be analogous to a holistic pictorial movie reel or TV news report."

"This is all very interesting," Jake said. "So, whereas one of us spinning a tale in words will cause our audience to conjure up images in their minds, a dolphin telling a story has the ability to bypass verbiage because it can project those images directly to its listeners."

Grahm appeared to be pleasantly satisfied with Jake's understanding of his discourse. "Yes, but whereas in humans the conjured images are internally visual, the images the dolphin receives will be externally visual."

"I see what you mean," Jake remarked thoughtfully, digesting this information and searching for flaws in such a postulate. "But how does a dolphin distinguish the virtual presentation of a spoken picture from the actual picture of its current environment?"

"A good question," the scientist admitted, "and one that I haven't been able to provide an explanation for as yet. All I can tell you is there must exist some perceptual clues which would allow a dolphin to distinguish a spoken environment from a real one. A human can watch the comedian Rich Little impersonate Sean Connery and still know its not Sean Connery. With dolphins, its probably possible for them to become so enraptured in an unreal, virtual environment, one transmitted by a skilled picture-speaking member of their own or a neighboring pod, that they actually tune out their real surroundings for a time. Such a scenario, however, could be potentially detrimental to their safety. In safeguarding against this, their basic survival instincts would most likely cause some portion of their awareness to be attentive to the approach of predators or food."

Jake smiled in understanding. "So if we put an anthropomorphic spin on what you've just described, it would be like you or I watching and listening to a videotape and an actual speaker at the same time. In such a situation, we would alternately pay attention to one and then focus in on the other."

"That's a very good analogy, lad. Like humans, the architecture of the dolphin brain shows two distinct hemispheres. But unlike humans, each half has its own separate blood supply, a trait exclusive to dolphins. This may account for their independent eye movement, which has led many scientists to believe they are capable of sleeping one of the hemispheres while the other hemisphere remains conscious and vigilant. In any case, there is strong evidence to show they use the two hemispheres completely separately. This allows them to produce clicks with one side of the brain while the other side can simultaneously produce whistling. Because dolphins have a right and left nasal passage, with each passage containing a separate phonation apparatus, a given dolphin can have each hemisphere of its brain carry on an isolated conversation completely out of phase with the opposite hemisphere. Thus if the left half of the brain is having a whistle conversation, the right side can be having a clicking conversation, with each half acting completely independent of the other. The reverse of this can also occur, but the two halves cannot both be whistling or clicking at exactly the same time. Such a dual communication mode is very efficient when two dolphins converse since it permits them to simultaneously speak-see and picture-speak, therefore letting each to see the other dolphin and to communicate with it all at once. The two kinds of sonic exchanges, that is, clicking and whistling, do not occur at the same time and there is a politeness involved on the part of the dolphins whereby the one receiving or listening will not interrupt the one sending or transmitting. If one dolphin transmits a click train, the other will listen and refrain from clicking, although it may emit whistles while it is receiving the clicks."

Jake suppressed a laugh. "No wonder it sounds so noisy when a school of dolphins is in the vicinity of a dive. I guess what you're saying is that one pair of dolphins communicating will actually sound like two pairs talking, one pair exchanging clickings, the other pair exchanging whistles."

Grahm gave an encouraging nod. "The need to take turns seeing and to take turns talking makes a pod sound much larger than it actually is even though the seeing and talking proceed concurrently."

"It kind of makes sense for them to be polite and take turns speaking," Jake agreed. "With each dolphin creating a picture-speak virtual reality, it would be rude to modify that picture while they were talking."

The marine scientist seemed to appreciate Jake's grasp of the subject. With a twinkle in his eyes, he went on to explain that the two phonation mechanisms in the dolphin's nasal passages can be linked to each other to produce a stereo-location process during execution of the speak-see channel. Dolphins also had a third sonar emitter in the larynx especially constructed for the projection of an ultrasonic beam. Grahm further indicated that if the speak-see process is, in fact, a stereo-location operation and the picture-speak process is a non-stereo operation, such a difference would allow dolphins to distinguish between the virtual and non-virtual realities. He pointed out that whereas in humans the process of seeing is an input operation only, with human eyes acting strictly as receptacles for visualizing the world around us, a dolphin's ears and phonation apparatuses, by comparison, provided it with both receptacles and transmitters of visual information.

Jake studied the garrulous doctor for an extended moment before replying. "This is all very intriguing, but what's your objective in telling me all this?"

The expression on Grahm's face seemed to indicate he had been anticipating such a question and he smiled effusively. "Don't you see," he gushed, "the processes by which a dolphin receives and communicates information are perfectly suited for computer modeling. Such a model would bridge the gap between the two most complex biocomputers on the planet, the mind of man and the mind of the dolphin."

Jake became solemn. "Somehow I get the feeling you've made some progress in this direction."

Grahm's face lit up like that of a child in a candy store. "Yes we have. Up until about eighteen months ago, progress had been exceedingly slow, moving at a snail's pace, you might say. Initially there were some major hurdles to overcome, primarily because we were dealing with a species that is acoustically oriented, as opposed to humans who are visually oriented. While a dolphin's visual system operates at one-tenth the speed of ours, their sonic and acoustic systems more than compensate for such a weakness by functioning at a rate ten times faster than our own. In other words, dolphins can absorb through their ears the same amount of information in the same amount of time that we are capable of taking in through our eyes. This presented my team with the problem of developing some highly complex algorithms that could solve the sonic picture language of the dolphin, algorithms that had the capacity to decipher various arrangements of acoustical noise by training a computer neural network to recreate those signals and convert them to recognizable visual images that we could understand. The process was incrementally tedious, to say the least, much like decoding the Rosetta stone. By reversing the process via the use of ultrasonic transducers with similar operating characteristics as the dolphin's, we could use the neural net to picture-speak back to the dolphins. Henderson pretty much took care of the monumental task of programming a Mac OS X and Macromedia Director on a Mac G4 with Velocity Engine that would allow us to do this."

"You're getting a bit ahead of me, doc. You mentioned something about eighteen months ago?"

"That was when we found Natalie."

"Natalie?"

"An injured female bottlenose dolphin. We found her stranded on a desolate stretch of beach on the island of Jamaica during a previous research expedition. Seven others of her species had also beached themselves, but they were already dead. As best we could tell, the injuries sustained by Natalie and the others were consistent with those caused by a concussion-type pressure wave that results from detonating an explosive charge underwater. She was in pretty bad shape when we discovered her, but we were able to get her aboard our research vessel and bring her back to Miami. Somehow she survived the trip and once we got her back to our facility, we were able to nurse her back to good health rather quickly. As we would soon discover, finding Natalie was an unbelievable stroke of good fortune for us, for she not only proved to be exceptionally intelligent relative to her species, she became the key to greatly accelerating our program. In human terms, her intellect was comparable to that of an Einstein. Almost immediately, she seemed to figure out what we were trying to achieve, and within one month we had learned the equivalent picture-speak vocalizations of several hundred concepts which had meaning to both humans and dolphins alike, concepts such as *food, help, up, shark*. In short order we learned how to effectively communicate with dolphins."

"That's incredible!"

"In more ways than you'd believe possible. Our database is now quite extensive, filled with numerous combinations of clicks and whistles. These are used as a baseline of comparison for sound recognition. The computer can then convert the sound trains into visual images and, in most cases, accompanying English language, making it fairly easy for us to understand. If we choose, we can reverse the process, using English syntax as a means of conveying a certain concept and having the computer convert that concept into a delphine sound. This allows us to project a picture-speak sound train back to the dolphin."

"Have you been able to carry on an actual conversation using this method?"

Grahm's brow bunched like two white beetles, making the frown look out of place on his normally upbeat demeanor. "With the exception of only a few instances where the exchange consists essentially of a simple query followed by a snap reply, we haven't yet figured out when to pause our side of the conversation in order to be polite. And in spite of the super speed of the computer system we use, it's unable to process the signals fast enough to keep up with a dolphin's rapid fire emission of complex picture-speak sonar which will convey multiple concepts during a conversation."

"It sounds like your system operates on the same principles as mechanical sonar."

The marine zoologist flashed another smile. "Lad, with that inquisitive mind of yours, you should have been a scientist." He drew a deep breath before continuing. "This system is far superior to the type of sonar found aboard most submarines. It can emit complex signals in the same way a dolphin does to assess its surroundings. But its true value lies in the way it can convert the reflected sounds into a holographic picture on a detailed level."

"So what you're saying is it can both speak-see and hear-see.

"Thanks to Natalie, we've made great strides in that direction, but only on a very basic, rudimentary level. By rudimentary, I'm alluding to what a dolphin would probably consider it. But I believe most members of our own species would deem it a marvelous technological breakthrough. We've built our first stand-alone working prototype that houses such technology. It's considerably smaller and has far less capacity than the computer system back home, but it's portable and diver friendly. Henderson was instrumental in developing it. He's a brilliant electronics engineer."

Jake leaned back, glasping his hands behind his head in a lazy manner. "So that's what this trip is all about. Testing this unit of yours."

Grahm shook his head, and for the first time since meeting the man, Jake noticed a lugubrious sadness come over him. For several seconds the scientist stared dismally out the starboard window before turning back to Jake.

"The purpose of this trip is twofold. To investigate an anomaly we've discovered, but most important, to find Natalie," Grahm corrected.

"You lost her?"

"In a manner of speaking, yes." The words were spoken very softly. "We felt it necessary to get her back to her natural habitat and monitor how she communicated with other dolphins outside the artificial laboratory environment, so we radio-tagged her."

Grahm noticed Jake's puzzlement. "Dolphins have no prehensile extremities for manipulating their environment, and contrary to the human preoccupation with controlling the world around us, the dolphin's intelligence, it seems, has gone in a direction counter to ours. Their thoughts are quite different from ours and have been left to develop inwardly over more than fifty million years of evolution. Compare this to the paltry two million years during which the hominid mind has grown outward. Overall, dolphins appear to display an emotional stability that easily surpasses that of humans and, unlike us, rely heavily on one another for their survival. That their culture is totally different from our own cannot be denied. But I am even more convinced that they have an intelligence at least equal to our own, if not greater. As I've already indicated, Natalie is very unusual for a bottlenose dolphin. Among other things, her skin tone is albino, completely white over her entire body, a rare occurrence among her kind. She also has a long scarification along her left flank. But her most distinguishing feature-" Grahm hesitated and watched Jake closely. "Her most distinguishing feature was the prehensile extensions that jutted from beneath her pectoral fins."

At first Jake thought the doctor was putting him on, but something subliminal stirred in a back corner of his mind, and a troubling memory suddenly came to life.

"Hands!" The word leapt from Jake's mouth in a flash, and a sense of hopeful relief began to circulate within his brain. "You're telling me she had hands?" he pressed.

The doctor let out a small laugh, amused by Jake's enthusiastic outburst. "Oh, yes. Natalie had the equivalent of hands. The amazing thing was she could actually grasp and manipulate objects with them."

"A mutation?" Jake asked, finding it difficult to restrain his interest.

"I would call it more of an evolutionary jump," Grahm surmised. "What I didn't tell you earlier was that all of the other beached dolphins we found near Natalie exhibited the same set of appendages. Natalie, however, was the only albino among them."

Jake mulled this over. The memory lodged at the back of his mind continued to haunt him like a shadowy wraith.

"Surprisingly," Grahm went on, "all of the appendages were retractable, forelimbs that folded up and came in tight against their bodies much the way the wings of a bird fold upon landing. They could be pulled in so as not to induce any drag on the pectoral fins. In this way, Natalie and her cousins were able to maintain a streamlined configuration when swimming fast. Anyway, scientific curiosity got the better of me and I thought if we released Natalie back into the wild, we might be able to track her back to her pod and possibly find more like her. Since most Caribbean bottlenose travel in relatively small groups, its unlikely Natalie's pod would have exceeded more than twenty-five in number. And with seven of them already dead, it was doubtful we'd locate surviving members possessing those same anatomical irregularities. But it was worth a try. So about three months ago, we brought Natalie back near the beach where she was found and attached a satellite-linked radio transmitter to her. Radio telemetry linked to satellites is a marvelous tool for tracking a dolphin's movements, particularly when the unit is augmented with a microchip transponder that can record sequences of dolphin biosonar and then send it back to us in the form of compressed sound trains."

Once again, Grahm brought his signature smile to bear on Jake, searching for comprehension.

"So you could communicate with her from far away," Jake acknowledged.

"The communication was only one-way, from her to us. Although we couldn't communicate with her, we could actually see what Natalie's reflected sonar pulses brought back to her, the hear-see mode of her reflected transmissions once the Mac G4 did the processing. No matter what Natalie's position was in terms of latitude and longitude, her sonar transmissions could be received back in Miami for visual interpretation by the computer. The two-dimensional image could then be redirected back to the vessel we were aboard."

"Extraordinary!" Jake muttered, deep in thought. "Could this device also record and send pictures of what Natalie was seeing above the water?"

"Unfortunately, no. The Delphine Biosonar Transmitter, or Dee Bee Tee as I like to call it, was designed to record water-based sounds only. For the device to work correctly, it was essential that it be immersed in a hydrous medium to receive signals."

"So what happened with Natalie?"

"For seven straight days we were able to keep track of Natalie's movements, catching glimpses of her surroundings even though we couldn't keep up with her. On the open sea, she was an incredibly fast swimmer. Even among normal bottlenose dolphin, she would have been considered to be exceptionally fast, and unfortunately the vessel we were using had a top speed of only nineteen knots. So within a span of only two days, more than fifty miles separated us."

An intense sadness overcame the doctor once more. "Natalie was near the Haitian coast when we lost her signal."

Jake eyed the scientist intently. "And that was about three months ago, you say."

"Yes."

"And where precisely was Natalie when you lost her signal?"

"Well, I'd have to consult my notes to give you the exact global position, but I recall it was near the coastal town of Anse. Why do you ask?"

Now it was Jake's turn to smile. "Because I think I had an impromptu meeting with your dolphin."

- 7 -

Grahm listened with enraptured attentiveness as Jake related his encounter with Natalie. The Avenging Angel had been sitting at anchor, quietly bobbing in the gentle swells that slowly rolled seaward above a coral reef of jagged, irregular topography, approximately one mile from the Haitian coastal town of Anse.

At a depth of 60 feet and hovering another 10 feet above an outcropping of mostly dead coral covered in fleshy algae, Jake had been caught totally off guard as something grabbed hold of his left arm from behind and tugged with shocking, startling power, jerking him sideways. At first he thought it was Zimbola who had latched onto him and who had entered the water with him some ten minutes earlier to reconnoiter another section of reef, for Jake had heard no telltale clicks or whistles to herald the approach of a nearby dolphin. With pounding heart and adrenaline surging, Jake could not mistake the torpedo-like shape that shot past and disappeared in the subaqueous gloom. Underwater visibility had not been particularly good during the dive, limiting his field of vision to perhaps 40 feet at most in a water column that held considerable amounts of particulate matter moving laterally with the mild current. So close to shore, such organic pollution was not uncommon with a nation of 9 million people having no sewage treatment facilities, nor sanitary landfills. Such human waste contributed significantly to the growth of fleshy algae, which tended to smother and kill off delicate corals and sponges.

Confusion engulfed Jake as he realized something still continued to clutch his arm. He spun and stared with disbelief at the ghostly apparition floating beside him. With the exception of an elongated indentation running along its left side, the skin was smooth, white and pliable as it brushed up against him. He glanced at the pectoral fin that overlapped his arm and wondered how it could grip with such vice-like strength, then abruptly became aware of the finger-like appendages protruding from the base of the flipper. At least that's what he thought he saw a split second before the claw released him. In an instant, the creature turned to face him. The bottlenose dolphin let out a series of chirps as it peered through Jake's facemask, its permanent smile somehow giving Jake solace in the midst of his bewilderment. Jake looked again to the base of the mammal's pectoral fins to confirm the impossible, but nothing jutted from the underside of the creature's lateral rudders. He must have been hallucinating. Then Jake noticed a small mechanical object strapped behind the dolphin's dorsal fin.

The dolphin suddenly let out with a loud piercing squeal, galvanizing Jake. He failed to spot the returning short-finned mako until it was almost upon him. Possessing a length of 12 feet and a girth that suggested at least half a ton, the shark was about as big as a mako gets and a good 3 feet longer than the white dolphin next to Jake. The large predator streaked to within arms length before veering off, flashing a band of silver that separated a rich ultramarine dorsal surface and snowy underbelly as it shot past. Classically opportunistic feeders, this particular mako radiated a mean-tempered aggressiveness, probably driven by hunger. This was understandable since overfishing in the vicinity of the island had greatly reduced fish populations. And although fishing permits were required by law, the number of active fishing boats dramatically exceeded the number with permits, causing fishing to become so intense that few fish reached reproductive size. Jake also knew that in warm tropical oceans, makos notoriously liked to swim deep, preferring the cooler water below 650 feet. The fact that this one was hunting relatively shallow attested to its hunger and it was not to be denied its meal.

Propelling itself stiffly through the water with short strokes from a thick, powerful tail, the mako turned and swooped in again with muscular efficiency, its pointed conical snout rushing forward with the effortless thrust of a guided missile. Jake recognized the severity of danger confronting him and instinctively pulled the short bang stick from the scabbard strapped to a thigh. He had no doubt that he was in deep trouble.

Makos were the fastest of all sharks, let alone most fish in the sea. Although some shark experts maintained the isurus oxyrinchus was capable of speeds bordering on 60 miles per hour, more conservative estimates held them to top speeds of 22. Short-finned makos were known to leap as high as 15 to 20 feet above the sea, making them the most spectacular game fish on the planet. And with their lower teeth always erect, makos appeared as one of the meanest looking animals on earth. The teeth of a big mako are huge in comparison to the more rounded pearly whites of smaller specimens. Resembling curved knives set in the jaw, they are flattened on the forward surface. When not in use, the teeth of most sharks remain in a laid-back position. Only when the mouth is opened do the teeth assume a vertical attitude. This phenomenon occurs to a limited extent with the mako, but its lower teeth are perpetually bolt upright, serving to give such a shark a snaggletoothed and fearsome visage, the kind of which nightmares are made.

Time seemed to expand as Jake watched the big shark bore down on him, as if the monster moved in slow motion. With his right hand, he held the 12-inch bang stick straight out, arm fully extended as the shark's jaws gaped wide to display its full arsenal of frightening weaponry. At the last second, a white blur slammed with crunching force into the side of the beast, deflecting its charge. The collision tumbled Jake backwards and when he regained his senses, he realized he still possessed the bang stick, its 12-gauge shotgun cartridge still not discharged. An inky cloud billowed around him, and he noticed the welling of blood emanating from the grisly gash in his left forearm where the mako's teeth had raked him. Stunned and confused, the shark turned sluggishly. Almost too quick to follow by eye, the white bottlenose streaked in once more, ramming its rigid beak into the long gill slits of the monster. Jake saw his opportunity and kicked wildly toward the stricken predator wavering dazedly no more than 15 feet from him. He readjusted his grip on the bang stick in preparation for an overhand strike. With the killing tip pointing downward, he jammed the cartridge into the head of the beast, between its black malevolent eyes. The stick bucked with brutal shock as the round exploded, causing Jake's hand to go numb. The fired slug tore through cartilage and brain matter, a killing thrust that rendered the shark a drifting hulk in an instant. Jake watched the creature slowly capsize, twitching and jerking spasmodically as it tumbled lazily toward the bottom. The shark finally came to rest between two mounds of bleached brain coral where it remained motionless.

Jake looked around for his savior, but the albino dolphin was nowhere to be seen. A glint of metal near the dead mako grabbed his attention, and upon swimming closer, discerned it to be the same mechanical device he had observed strapped to the bottlenose. He glanced hopefully about once more and, disappointed at not spotting his benefactor, retrieved the fallen object.

"A most interesting story," muttered Grahm. The scientist's words pulled Jake back to the present. "That certainly explains why we lost the signal. Do you still have the unit?"

Jake nodded somberly and opened a nearby cabinet. He pulled out an oblong object that fit snugly into the palm of his hand, gleaming with the characteristic shine of stainless steel. A length of nylon strap hung loosely from an intact clip on one side of the device, but it was obvious that the opposing clip had been sheared away.

Grahm examined it thoughtfully before lifting it from Jake's hand, then said, "If the microchip isn't damaged, Natalie's perception of the episode you just described will be stored in its data bank."

The statement surprised Jake. "Wouldn't you already have seen it?"

Grahm lifted his face from the contraption to acknowledge Jake. "This unit can only relay information when above the ocean surface. When submerged, the water greatly attenuates the signal."

Jake's expression flooded with understanding. "I get it. Natalie never breached the surface during the shark attack, so you wouldn't have received a transmission."

"That's correct. But the device has limited storage capacity. Once its bank is full, it will broadcast a compressed signal at the first opportunity in order to free up space for new information, and that would require the dolphin to come up for air."

Jake's eyes narrowed. "Wouldn't it have transmitted when I pulled it from the water?" he countered.

"It should have, but apparently it did not," the scientist puzzled, retrieving a small kit of Allen wrenches from an accessory waistband and pulling one out. "I suspect the micro-transmitter may have been damaged from the impact." He began to unscrew the housing.

Jake eyed Grahm appraisingly. "There's just one other thing, doc."

Grahm raised an eyebrow, continuing to putter with the unit. "Yes, lad, what is it?"

A short silence followed, just long enough for Jake to give his question special significance. "Could Natalie speak English?"

The scientist looked up sharply and locked eyes with Jake. "Why do you ask?"

"Because I could have sworn your dolphin yelled out a warning just before the mako made a second run at me," Jake said, his voice conveying both skepticism and certainty all at once.

Grahm held his gaze, staring expectantly. "What do you think you heard her say?"

Jake sighed, feeling foolish in repeating something that should have been impossible. He realized if he uttered them, the professor might deem him an idiot. Yet the words he had distinctly heard suddenly reverberated within him with tenacious stubbornness, echoing inside the dome of his cranium with a furor that demanded a way out. But when he did voice them, they came out in a meek whisper. "She said 'Look out.'"

- 8 -

Jake Javolyn was quite relieved when Dr. Franklin Grahm confirmed that Natalie could indeed speak English, for he had been doubting his own sanity ever since the female bottlenose had alerted him about the approach of the shark. When he had mentioned this fact to Zimbola shortly after the incident, the large Jamaican had looked at him as if he were crazy. Upon further describing the white dolphin's grasping appendages, Zimby's eyes went wide as he said, "Either one of Damballah's loas has taken over your brain, mon, or you been hittin' a little too much of that fine Jamaican rum behind my back."

"So you taught her to speak in our tongue," Jake surmised.

Grahm produced an enigmatic grin. "Hardly," he chortled. "She already knew how to converse in English when we found her."

Jake's mind floundered, leaving him momentarily speechless. "But… how's that possible?"

Grahm shrugged resignedly. "How is it possible she grew prehensile extensions? Both are mysteries I'm still trying to unravel." The scientist fell silent.

Jake was not about to give up so easily and came at the marine zoologist from another angle. "Didn't you tell me her appendages were caused by an evolutionary jump?"

"It's just a theory, pure speculation!"

"Then you must have a theory as to why she could speak English."

Grahm cleared his throat at the young man's persistence. "The fact that Natalie can speak is not so surprising when you consider that dolphins are capable of producing a seemingly endless variety of audible airborne noises, including a mimicry of humanoid sounds. In the wild, they primarily use water as a medium of exchange when communicating and rarely, if ever, resort to an airborne mode. Even dolphins in human captivity will initially attempt to communicate with us through waterborne whistles and various complex clicking patterns, the same as they do with one another, trying to induce us to use hydrosound. However, our consistent use of air-based sounds over a fairly long period of close, kindly contact with them seems to cause a voluntary though radical shift in their behavior, prompting them to accommodate us in our own medium. When the shift occurs, they will mimic or at least try to approximate the sounds we make. Unfortunately, the noises they emit tend to get distorted by the limitations of their phonation apparatus and blowholes. The way they hear the airborne sound is also distorted since their hearing mechanism is much more attuned to a subaqueous medium. If they hear a sound differently from the way we perceive it, their reproduction of that sound may deviate markedly from the way it should actually be pronounced. They can easily enunciate vowels but have great difficulty producing consonants. Such a phenomenon is not unlike a deaf person learning to speak. In any event, when we speak to dolphins from above the water, they will lift their blowhole into the air and answer us. If we attempt to talk to them underwater, they will revert back to hydrosound emissions in response."

Jake was growing impatient and interjected. "Yes, but those dolphins are just trying to imitate the way we talk. While I admit Natalie's words were garbled and high pitched, they were clear enough to convey the meaning that she intended me to understand."

A contemplative, far off look was evident on Grahm's face. "She could articulate speech much more clearly out of the water," the scientist rejoined. "It was as if she had experienced human companionship for most of her life. She was familiar with many human concepts."

"Such as?"

Grahm reflected on this for several seconds. "Love…if she liked a person, she could be very affectionate, very loving…she…" The scientist searched for the appropriate word. "She could be very empathic," he said at last. "She frequently spoke of others, all of whom she deeply missed."

"Dolphins?"

Grahm shook his head slowly, remorsefully. "I just don't know. Natalie never distinguished between people and cetaceans, even when asked to specify what type of being she was referring to."

"Did she have names for the others?"

The scientist nodded. "The names she mentioned the most were *Apollo* and *Artemis.*" He paused momentarily. "But there were others she talked about. *Aphrodite, Hermes, Hercules, Athena and Amphitrite* were other entities she often referred to by name."

"Correct me if I'm wrong, doctor, but aren't those names from Greek mythology?"

A strange smile crossed Grahm's face. "Yes. With the exception of Hercules and Amphitrite, the others are the names of five of the twelve gods the ancient Greeks called the *Olympians.* If you're familiar with Greek mythology, and it seems you are, you'll know the Olympians were the deities that overthrew the Titans. All of the Olympians were related in some way. They were so named because of the place where they dwelt, and that was Mount Olympus."

The Girl Who Rode Dolphins

"Did she mention any other names?"

Grahm thought some more. "As I recall, she referred to another called *Jacob*. She also kept mentioning *Coral* and *Reef*, but I assume she was alluding to generics."

Jake's forehead wrinkled in confusion.

"You know, the animals that build submerged calcareous structures and the resulting formations." Grahm suddenly took on a distant look, then frowned. "One thing she frequently said was that the future of her kind was in the hands of destiny."

Jake pondered this before replying. "So you believe Natalie must've had considerable human contact to be able to speak English the way she did."

Grahm drew in a deep breath. "Yes."

"And the computer system you developed to communicate with dolphins... you didn't need that at all to talk to Natalie. She just helped provide you with a reference for talking to other dolphins...dolphins unlike her, dolphins without finger-like projections and an ability to speak English."

"Again, yes."

Jake thought some more. "Underwater visibility was not particularly good when I ran into Natalie...or I should say when she ran into me. Why didn't I hear any of her echo-locating sonar before she grabbed me? Shouldn't I have heard a series of clicks for her to find me so easily?"

The doctor scratched his chin pensively. "She probably emitted sound pulses above your hearing range."

"Okay, but why did the shark come straight for me? Natalie pulled me out of the way just before I became lunch. Most sharks will circle before striking."

" My guess is the mako had been stalking Natalie for some time before your paths crossed. Because you were smaller and slower than Natalie, the shark perceived you as easier prey. You became a target of opportunity."

"Makes sense."

Jake stared silently out to sea as Grahm went back to puttering with the telemetric device. Without the transmitter strapped to her body, the likelihood of finding Natalie was extremely remote.

As an afterthought, Jake said, "Aside from trying to locate Natalie, you had mentioned a second item on your agenda."

Without looking up, the scientist continued to disassemble the unit. "The anomaly?"

"Yeah."

"Two days after we released Natalie, we received a rather startling transmission." Grahm fell mute as he detached the casing housing the unit, exposing a tight knot of electronic circuitry. "Just as I thought," he murmured distractedly. Lifting the device for Jake to see, he delicately prodded a tiny strand of loose wire within the mishmash of microchips and resistors with the tip of the Allen wrench. "There's the problem. A little solder and it'll be good as new."

Jake nodded. "What was so startling?"

With great care, Grahm gingerly placed the transmitter on the table and fixed his eyes on Jake. "As we tracked Natalie, she passed near Navassa Island. One sequence of transmitted signals we received showed a sunken boat."

Jake shrugged. "The seafloor throughout these waters is littered with sunken wrecks. What's so unusual about that?"

Grahm paused, suddenly appearing very solemn. "I was quite familiar with this particular vessel. My wife had been aboard it just before she disappeared."

The lingering hurt on Grahm's face made Jake look away. "Uh...I'm sorry for your loss," was all he could think to say.

"It happened a long time ago," Grahm added morosely.

An uncomfortable silence ensued. Grahm sat mutely, seemingly recollecting some deep memories, and Jake stood quiet, not wanting to intrude.

"*Tursiops* was a fifty foot sloop owned by my wife and me," Grahm finally offered, taking control of his grief. "My wife...she was a heck of a sailor, better than most men. She loved the sea, sailing the Caribbean at every opportunity." He abruptly stifled a choke. "I should have been with her, but I was already committed to attend a conference in Chicago."

Grahm hesitated, once again composing himself before continuing. "Harriet was an extremely strong-willed woman, uncommonly independent and self-reliant. She was one of the strongest individuals I've ever known. So it was no surprise when she insisted on taking the voyage without me...at least the initial leg of the voyage. We finally agreed that I'd meet up with her in Kingston, Jamaica."

Jake tried to phrase a question as tactfully as possible, but the words he chose seemed to betray any attempt at sensitivity as soon as he uttered them. "Did your wife sail alone?"

Grahm shook his head. "While she might have been called stubborn by some, by no means was she a foolish woman. She was five months pregnant at the time. Another scientist and two grad students made the trip with her. Like me, she was a marine zoologist. She had planned to do some field research during the outing, hoping to catalogue new species of coelenterates."

Jake's face clouded. "Coelenterates?"

Grahm looked bemused. "Jellyfish...that was her area of expertise."

Jake could not help but ask, "How long ago was it when she sailed?"

Grahm inhaled sharply. "Roughly twenty-two years has transpired since I last saw my wife or the people who made the trip with her."

"Are you certain the boat you saw was yours?" Jake prodded gently. "A lot can happen to a sunken vessel over time. In a tropical sea like this, they often become encased in coral and other marine growth. Their appearance can change drastically."

A deep introspection manifested itself on Grahm's face before he answered. "When I initially viewed the transmission, I didn't place much significance on it. Natalie's sonar reflections had revealed at least a dozen sunken vessels while we tracked her. She was a curious dolphin and always seemed to take special interest in objects not indigenous to the ocean bottom, typically making numerous passes to investigate them. The data containing the echo signature of that particular vessel ultimately became filed in my archives back in Miami. Believe it or not, it wasn't until a week ago that I had a most disturbing dream. In the dream I saw the wreck again, exactly as I had first seen it on the monitor during the transmission. I guess it was my subconscious alerting me to something I had previously missed. And like you said, a profusion of sponges and coral blanketed a good portion of the boat's hull and superstructure, effectively distorting its true configuration, but not enough to conceal the boat's distinctive bowsprit. You see, the *Tursiops* was uniquely outfitted with a six-foot bottlenose sculpted in bronze. Although the bowsprit I saw in the dream was covered in heavy growth, I was able to see beneath it, as if I had x-ray vision, and the image of the bowsprit the way I remembered it shone clearly through. When I awoke, I retrieved the stored electronic file and subjected it to a more thorough computer analysis, scanning the secondary sonar pulses echoing back at an ultra frequency and culling them out."

Jake's expression clouded with puzzlement once again and Grahm quickly explained. "The use of this technique is analogous to that of using a real x-ray, and as we know, dolphins are able to penetrate objects with their tight beam laryngeal emitters which can produce sonar emissions at a much lower wavelength. They can turn this beam on any object and examine it in detail, and to a degree, see inside it. Once these particular wavelengths were converted to a visual, they not only revealed an underlying image of a dolphin, they also confirmed that it was composed of bronze. This discovery prompted me to make this trip."

Grahm paused momentarily. "I have no doubts that the vessel in question is the *Tursiops*. Maybe-"

The scientist realized he was raising his voice. "Maybe I'll learn what happened to my wife," he said softly.

Jake sat down, nodding slowly. "Do you have the precise coordinates of the vessel?"

"Yes. She lies near the southeast side of the island."

"Have you given any thought as to why your boat sank?"

A pained expression darkened Grahm's features and he sighed with the effort of answering. "Following the convention, I was to catch a flight from Chicago directly to Kingston, but a force-three hurricane near Jamaica delayed my departure for three days. When I finally got to Kingston, there was no record of Harriet ever having reached port. I notified the Coast Guard and a search was immediately undertaken. I remained in Jamaica for two weeks, hoping for the best, but the *Tursiops* never arrived, neither there or anyplace else. Eventually, the Coast Guard abandoned the search."

"Was there any record of the Coast Guard or anyone else receiving an S.O.S.?" Jake pressed.

"None. The sloop vanished without a trace. My wife…she and the rest of the crew were never seen or heard from again. In those days, it was very hard for me to accept this. It still is. Harriet was a very resourceful woman, a true survivor. It wouldn't have been the first time she was caught at sea in a violent storm, especially one of hurricane strength. She was about as tough as they come, with a will of iron."

A wistful smile broke out on Grahm's face. "She was an exceptionally strong swimmer. Did you know that she was a member of the 1976 U.S. Olympic Swimming Team? In Montreal she competed in the five thousand meter crawl stroke. She had come in ahead of the rest of the field in all the preliminary heats, setting the best times. If not for a severe groin pull sustained in her pre-final heat, she probably would have taken home the gold going away. With such an injury, she could have easily opted to withdraw from the medal round and none of her teammates would have faulted her for doing so. Instead, she chose to race anyway, never once considering the prospect of dropping out and quitting. In spite of such a painful injury, she still managed to win the bronze."

Jake could not help but admire such a person, drawing from personal experience the full measure of such an injury. While with Seal Team Six, a groin pull had temporarily crippled him, making in-water mobility extremely painful and difficult. The fact that Grahm's wife had endured such suffering over 5000 meters – more than 3 miles - while giving it all she had in order to medal bespoke volumes about the woman's grit.

"Sounds like she was a most courageous individual," Jake said, his voice tinged with both reverence and respect.

Grahm's expression suddenly brightened and he looked at Jake with appreciation in his eyes. "She was, lad…believe me when I tell you, she was."

-9-

With dark sunglasses shielding his eyes from the intense sun glare, Sebastian Ortega's focused stare in combination with his hooked beak of a nose gave him the look of an avian predator preparing to dive down on unsuspecting prey. Shifting his gaze forward, he continued to scan the ocean below, a vast expanse of indigo that stretched toward the horizon where a lone island jutted from the sea. Turning his head, a concentration of white lacy foam suddenly caught his attention.

"*Ahi!*" he barked, pointing furiously. *There!*

The pilot seated to his left noted the disturbance and tilted the cyclic stick hard to starboard, causing the Bell Ranger to swing rapidly in the direction Ortega had indicated.

"Lower! Bring us lower!" Ortega instructed in Spanish, speaking exuberantly into the microphone that protruded from his headset.

The pilot lowered the collective and the helicopter dropped to within 100 feet of the ocean surface where a huge shoal of fish congregated in agitated confusion.

Ortega smiled as the pilot hovered the chopper. The water was alive with the glimmer of scales extending in all directions just below the surface. "Alert the fleet!" he ordered. "Tell them we've got the mother of all tuna conventions."

With his side door having been removed before the flight, it was easy for Ortega to lean his torso out to get a better view. "Looks like a mix of blackfin and skipjack," he added.

Fascinated, he continued to watch the frothing turmoil as three vessels in the distance began to close the gap on his position. His smile turned to perplexity as he realized something must be herding the tuna into such a congested and stationary grouping. He scrutinized the water closely, finally spotting the sleek gray bodies moving along the outer perimeter of the mass, their dorsal fins slicing the waves as they encircled the multitude of entrapped fish.

Dolphins! He hated dolphins.

His lips curled in a savage sneer. Never taking his eyes from the darting forms, he groped behind him. From a box on the fuselage floor, he withdrew a cylindrical concussion grenade and pulled the pin. Extending his right arm out laterally, he released the spoon and let the grenade fall freely into the sea below. Several seconds passed before a tall geyser of white spray shot from the water, nearly reaching the height of the aircraft. Almost immediately, the dense pack of fish bolted en masse, the water thrashed white in frenzied havoc as the shoal sped rapidly away.

Ortega cursed. "Stay with them!" he screamed, reaching for another grenade.

This was nothing new to the pilot. A veteran of many similar events, he kept pace above the heaviest concentration of churning pandemonium. Driven by the mayhem he was causing, Ortega dropped a second grenade, then another. Within a span of one minute, he detonated seven more concussion canisters into the fleeing throng. The explosions quickly took their toll and the water became littered with thousands of tuna floating sideways or belly up on the surface. Among their ranks, perhaps a dozen dolphins floundered lethargically, either stunned or dying.

Ortega laughed hysterically as he surveyed the scene. While spotting tuna was not his function within the Cardoza organization, he did it whenever he had the opportunity, taking immense pleasure in the thrill of blowing things up. And although the objective was to incapacitate as many tuna as possible for the fishing vessels to haul in, the fact that he got a few dolphins in the process only added to his enjoyment.

Like other Columbian and Mexican drug cartels, the Cardoza enterprise had invested heavily in a fleet of tuna vessels as a means of illegally transporting vast amounts of cocaine and other drugs. Hidden under huge loads of fish, hundreds of tons of cocaine could be smuggled with relative ease into the U.S. and Europe. And as a front for drug trafficking, the business became a legitimate vehicle for effectively laundering hundreds of millions of dollars in illicitly gained revenues.

One major pitfall in commercial tuna fishing, however, was the inadvertent killing of dolphins, which tended to get trapped in the huge seine nets of the fishing trawlers. When the U.S., Canada, and the European Union banned imports of dolphin-deadly tuna in the early 1990s, they literally crippled the major drug-smuggling pipeline of the crime syndicates. Cardoza's organization was particularly hard hit, and Ortega's percentage of the take had dropped considerably. With intense loathing, the Cardoza underboss recalled the costly bust of the 160-foot tuna trawler *Don Miguel*, boarded by the U.S. Coast Guard near Puerto Rico. A total of 9.5 tons of pure cocaine was found hidden in special compartments under tons of albacore. With a street value of nearly $500 million, the loss was staggering. The impounded vessel, valued at another $15 million, presented an additional financial setback to the organization. And all because of some overzealous passengers on a passing yacht. They had witnessed a number of dolphins being hauled aboard the trawler in its enormous seine nets and alerted the Coast Guard. The captain of the USCG cutter that was dispatched to investigate the incident just happened to be a dolphin lover. To Ortega, personally killing dolphins was payback for all the trouble they had caused him.

Continued reflection on the matter caused Ortega's upper lip to flare with outrage. On top of the lost profits dolphin-safety regulations had cost him, large amounts of money had also flowed from the cartel in an effort to overturn those mandates. One major coup was persuading the World Trade Organization to rule that the U.S. embargo was an illegal restraint of free trade. Additional bribes aimed at corrupting American, Mexican and European officials were slowly weakening the International Dolphin Conservation Act, originally enacted in 1997. Dubbed the Dolphin Death Act, its original intent to invoke strict standards for the Dolphin Safe label on American tuna cans was being systematically undermined, making the labels a farce.

Ortega had made substantial payouts to several high-ranking politicians within the U.S. government to downplay the tuna-drug connection and to allay public outcries over dolphin deaths, attempting to kill two birds with one stone. Such avaricious individuals were key to getting an observer program implemented that would pacify environmentally conscious citizens. Using their considerable influence, the officials had pushed through legislation which implied that the IATTC, the Inter-American Tropical Tuna Commission, could effectively be used to deter drug smugglers while simultaneously insuring the safety of dolphins by placing observers aboard tuna boats. Ortega smiled inwardly at the knowledge that the IATTC had never once levied a fine against a single member nation for killing dolphins. In fact, tuna imported from dolphin-killing countries could now be labeled dolphin-safe even if dolphins were chased, netted, injured or even killed in the pursuit of tuna. But only as long as on-board observers were willing to claim that no dolphins were seriously harmed.

The ruse had given Ortega some satisfaction. Intimidation was a most useful tool in coercing observers to falsify dolphin mortality records when bribery failed to work. The image of one uncooperative observer came to mind. The obstinate dolphin lover had been dragged behind the *San Carlo*, another Cardoza-owned vessel, as a pack of maddened sharks induced to frenzy by the scent of blood in the water tore his body to pieces. Even now, the memory of the man's intense screams of terror continued to gratify, producing a perverted arousal within Ortega. Reported as an unfortunate case of a man falling overboard in a shark infested sea, the incident had accomplished the desired result. When word of it had gotten out, no further problems had emerged within the ranks of IATTC observers.

Environmental blackmail also had its uses. The governments of Columbia, Venezuela and Mexico all but threatened that their fishing fleets would go out and intentionally slaughter more dolphins unless the U.S. changed its laws and redefined the dolphin-safe label.

That was all well and fine with Ortega. He would certainly continue to do his part in swaying the U.S. stance. But right now he had another important matter to attend to.

"Head for the island!" he ordered.

Glancing sideways, the pilot acknowledged the command with mild stoicism before banking the aircraft hard in the direction that would take them to the massive outcropping of rock and green vegetation jutting above the sea.

- 10 -

Even at a distance of several miles, the girl could sense the physical distress and suffering of the creatures. Impatient to reach them, she conveyed her intent to Jacob merely by pointing. At the moment, there was no need for words. Without hesitation, she slipped the goggles over her eyes and launched herself gracefully from the side of the small boat as it continued its slow plod, its single antiquated engine laboring in a steady, coughing chug. Her plunge was clean and precise, hardly making a splash as she disappeared beneath the surface with the deftness of a seabird diving for fish.

Jacob well knew there was no need to be concerned as the girl was joined by one of her companions. In moments she was quickly carried away from him. He would follow, eventually catching up and doing whatever he could. The girl had known him her entire life and had come to depend on him in the familiar way a child might come to depend on a parent. Inherently inclined toward the philosophic, he lived simply, never requiring much and possessing only those things that gave him sufficient shelter and the means to eke out an existence. Yet he was a happy man by nature, but more so because the girl gave him endless joy.

He lifted his eyes to the indistinct band of what appeared to be white mist squatting low on the horizon, judging it to be no more than five miles distant. Both he and the girl had visited it countless times in the past, but never with the urgency that consumed them now. The girl was currently far ahead, her escort of six surrounding both her and the one she rode in a symmetric formation, their coordinated movements in synchronous harmony so precise that from afar they appeared as a single entity.

The bond that existed between Jacob and the girl was strong, almost as strong as the bonds she had formed with her companions, and he was continually elated with the knowledge that his face was one of the very first the girl saw when she came into the world. Though he was biologically unrelated to her, he smiled the way a proud father would as he watched the ebony sheen of the girl's wetted mane glimmer in the early morning sunlight as she distanced herself from him. Exhibiting extraordinary abilities shortly after her exit from her mother's womb, the girl had kept him in a constant state of wonder as he witnessed those abilities develop and mature over the succeeding years. A Christian by conviction, Jacob truly believed the girl's special gift had a divine purpose, one that had come about not by chance but by the will of God, and it gladdened him that he was able to convene routinely with so unique a person, for it imparted meaning to his life as well.

Jacob listened to the monotonous chug of the diesel as it struggled to push his dilapidated pinnace forward, the sound of it giving the misguided impression that the pistons were always on the verge of missing a stroke. But they never did. The pitch of the motor had changed little since the girl's birth some twenty-two years earlier, and lulled by it, his mind drifted back to that strange milestone in his life.

He had lived alone, preferring the solitude of the cove rather than the nearby village. Serene and beautiful, the place was enclosed by rugged, heavily vegetated outcroppings of limestone. The craggy terrain rose steeply in a series of steps from the thin strip of white sandy beach that skirted its base. It was more of a narrow chasm that had been gradually carved out of the rock over eons of time. On one side high above, a natural spring sent an endless torrent of freshwater cascading down the rock walls until it joined the normally crystal-clear water of the cove in a tumultuous spray.

There had been no gray in his beard in those days and his body, at age thirty-six, still retained the lean hard lines of youth before the ravages of unrelenting sun and wind in unison with the passage of time would slowly take their toll.

The storm had been exceptionally brutal, the worst one he had ever seen. All the warning signs heralding its approach had been there, the peculiar tufts of cloud, the subtle change of wind, the unusual behavior of the songbirds seeking refuge in the rocky crags above his home, and the reddest dawn he had ever gazed upon just hours before it hit.

And though it held no significance that he could correlate to the impending storm, he also remembered the twin-engine seaplane as it raced out over the ocean on that morning, no more than two hundred feet above the water. Had it been another precursor of the storm to come? Why such an event would stay indelibly ingrained in his memory, he had no inkling. Perhaps it was the odd drone of its engines that struck a subliminal chord within him, subtly reminding him of the imperfect engine that powered his own craft. But somehow he had detected an abnormal tempo within them as they strained to keep the fixed-wing aircraft aloft as it disappeared over the western horizon.

Sadly he remembered the other fishermen from the nearby village who had ventured out to sea, never to return. He had given them ample warning of what was to come, virtually pleading with them not to go, but they just laughed and told him how foolish he was. For some inexplicable reason during that period in his life, weather reports were inaccessible to the locals as radio and television transmissions in the area were always garbled, incessantly distorted by static. Everyone assumed it was because of the steep terrain hugging the coastline that blocked the signals. Then again, most villagers had no electricity available to power such devices anyway, although several of the more affluent, as he recalled, did have generators at the time. And batteries had been very expensive and hard to get.

The hurricane had struck like a colossal demon, vengefully pummeling the coast with merciless wind and lashing rain, pushing monstrous waves before it. Miraculously, the small cove where Jacob lived provided just enough lee to allow both his boat and rundown abode to remain relatively undamaged as the pernicious cyclone tore past unabated.

It was nearly two days later while pulling tree branches from the roof of his shack that something had caught his eye. It had entered the cove on a low roller, floating torpidly along the surface of the turbid water. From his elevated vantage point, it looked like a thick tree trunk that had been ripped free by the recent blow. At first he gave it no more than a passing glance and went back to removing sprigs lodged in the crown of his home. Moments later, movement drew his attention back to the object and he suddenly became aware of the person clinging to it. By the time he had climbed down, he knew that what he was seeing was a dolphin with a woman hugging its back, a white woman, her head barely above the water and draped to one side of the dolphin's dorsal fin.

The unusual event in all its detail would stay lucently etched in his mind for the remainder of his days. After the dolphin had beached itself, Jacob was amazed to discover that both beings were not only female but pregnant, their midriffs swollen in the latter stages of procreation. The extreme exhaustion of the strange pair was evident, however, and the profusion of crisscrossed angry raw welts blistering both bodies jarred his senses. Relieved of its burden, the dolphin had managed to squirm off the sandy shore in the creaming backwash of a diminutive breaker, swimming sluggishly out to the center of the cove where it lingered idly, as if awaiting how the woman fared.

The woman was rather small and scantily clad, wearing baggy Bermuda shorts and a bikini top. With the exception of her protruding belly, she was thin and appeared to be badly dehydrated. She groaned in agony as Jacob gently lifted her from the light surf foaming around his ankles, carrying her to his home nestled against the rock wall of the cove where it overlooked the beach. And although she initially seemed conscious of his presence, she soon became delirious and lapsed into coma, remaining in that condition for two days as he periodically administered his own specially prepared salve to her wounds. He recognized the welts to be the nasty by-product of severe jellyfish stings and knew his home remedy would speed up the healing process and ease the pain. Every so often, he lifted the woman's head from the pillow as she lay on his bed, squeezing drinking water out of a dampened cloth so that it trickled into her mouth.

By the third day, the unconscious woman was beginning to show signs of improvement. Her breathing became less labored and the severity of her burns appeared to be subsiding. As Jacob was applying more of the soothing embrocation to her arms, she abruptly opened her eyes. Though seemingly alert, she stared at him in confusion.

"Who are you?" she croaked weakly, her question spoken in English.

"My name is Jacob," he answered cheerfully, producing a warm smile in an attempt to show the woman she was in safe hands. He rarely conversed in any language other than Creole since leaving the university where he had studied philosophy. The locals from the nearby village were the only people he spoke with these days, and that was only occasionally, but the Christian Bible he possessed was the King James version and most of his books were written in English, all of which he read regularly.

The woman's eyes darted about the small room in alarm, as if searching for some sign of familiarity. "Where am I?"

"You are just south of the tiny village of Malique."

"Where is that?"

"It lies midway between the cities of Gonaives in the north and Saint-Marc to the south. You are in Haiti."

She tried to rise, but flinched from the effort, shrinking back in obvious pain.

"It would be unwise to sit up just yet," Jacob advised tenderly. "Your body is still not healed." He scooped some more of the ointment from the jar he held, a concoction of various herbs he had gathered from plants growing in the narrow gorge that towered above his home.

The woman lay momentarily still, then asked, "How did I get here?"

"A most gracious and concerned friend carried you here." He watched her face closely. "You do not remember?"

Slowly, the woman shook her head.

"She still waits outside. You are very fortunate to have such a devoted friend. Most people are not so lucky."

Jacob stopped spreading the ointment. "You have not told me your name."

A blank stare fell across the woman's face and suddenly her eyes went wide. "I...I don't know." There was the residue of panic in her voice.

"You are still very weak," Jacob said sympathetically. "Perhaps your memory will return after more rest and some nourishment."

He reached behind him and lifted a jug of water laced with more medicinal herbs, pouring the water into a glass. "Please drink, it will speed up your recovery." He placed a hand under the woman's head, helping her to sip from the glass. Gulping greedily and breathing hard, she coughed and nearly choked as she quaffed down the liquid. After a second glass, her thirst seemed to abate and she lay back wearily as if to sleep. But when Jacob brought a tray full of baked grouper fillets and various tropical fruit, the aroma of the food seemed to reawaken her, and she hungrily ate every hand-fed morsel given her. After that, the woman dropped off into a deep slumber.

Jacob stepped outside and scanned the water. He quickly located the female dolphin, her dorsal fin poking above the water on the far side of the cove. On impulse, he hefted the bucket containing the remaining portions of the twenty-pound Nassau grouper and strode down to the beach, placing the bucket in the tiny dory he had set back from the water. Dragging the dory across the sand, he pulled it out through the low surf until the water was at knee level, then stepped over the aluminum gunwale. As he rowed toward deeper water, the dolphin swam in his direction until it came alongside the small boat. The permanently smiling face rose to scrutinize him.

Jacob stopped rowing and smiled back. "Good deeds deserve good rewards," he said as he lifted a chunk from the bucket.

The dolphin's head rose higher, as if in anticipation of Jacob's intentions. She was a big female, longer than the eight-foot dory he sat in. When the creature was within a foot of the boat, Jacob extended his arm out over the gunwale and dropped the chunk into the waiting jaws. The food was immediately swallowed and the animal looked expectantly for more. Jacob was happy to comply. Hefting another four-pound chunk, he brought his hand to within inches of the dolphin's powerful beak, unconcerned about the potential danger to which he was exposing himself. He had been around the sea all his life and understood the bite of a rumbustious dolphin was something to be avoided, but he made no attempt to pull his hand back. As ravenous as she was, the female plucked the morsel from Jacob's grasp with the delicate precision of a surgeon before gulping it down. The process was repeated several more times until the pail was emptied of its contents.

Feeling a close kinship with the animal, Jacob reached out and gently rubbed the female's forehead. Like the woman, the welts on its skin had diminished considerably, but to a much greater degree. He had often heard about the remarkable ability of these creatures to rapidly heal themselves following an injury and had previously dismissed such talk as the idle exaggerations of over-imaginative minds. But as he studied the docile female, he was now convinced that such outlandish assertions were actually true.

"I am very sorry, my sweet girl, but I have no more food for you right now," Jacob said, keeping his voice soothing as he continued to stroke the dolphin's head and snout. "Perhaps I can catch you some more fish to eat."

There was appraisal in those dark, mysterious eyes, almost as if the creature had understood his words, and as he stared into them he suddenly sensed an unfathomable intelligence. In that instant he was certain the animal trusted him and that an accord had been struck. There was something else.

Jacob's smile quickly gave way to comprehension. "If you are wondering about your friend, she is slowly regaining her strength." With those words, the dolphin nuzzled his hand affectionately before gliding away toward the far end of the cove.

In the days that followed, Jacob had a succession of moderate successes in netting fish whenever he sailed his pinnace out into the open sea. Each time he brought back the catch, the dolphin ate most of it, devouring each fish given it with insatiable intensity.

Just before sunup on the fifth day since discovering the woman, Jacob awoke to find her missing. Upon arising from his bedside vigil, he soon located her standing motionless on the sandy shore with her back to him, tiny wavelets washing around her feet. Something held her attention, and as his eyes adjusted to the dawn twilight he discerned the head of the dolphin staring back at her from the water. As he watched with growing fascination, both woman and dolphin continued to contemplate each other with the eternal reverie of statues frozen in time. Then as if a silent signal had passed between them, the woman suddenly waded into the nearly flat surf. When she was waist deep she pushed off in an overhead stroke that brought her to within arm's length of the marine mammal. For a few moments she tread water before grabbing hold of the dolphin's dorsal fin. As the light grew stronger, the strange pair moved out across the water, slowly at first, then with increasing speed.

For the next several hours, the dolphin circled the cove with the woman in tow, most of the time along the water's surface, and Jacob became uneasy whenever the duo would disappear into the depths, now pristine and clear, only to reemerge at some other corner of the cove. The duration of each submergence seemed longer than the last, and yet the woman's face glowed with unrestrained elation each time the pair came up for air.

Later that morning after the woman strode briskly ashore, her spirits seemed to flag when she still failed to remember her past. "I don't know who I am," she stated morosely as Jacob prepared the morning meal. Sighing with frustration, she sat on a boulder fronting Jacob's tiny dwelling and surveyed her surroundings with a critical eye. After a few minutes, her manner brightened. "I love this place, Jacob. It's like a tiny little paradise, a microcosm of all the good things life has to offer."

Jacob nodded in agreement. "I have always been able to think clearly in this cove. It is the reason I have chosen to live here and not closer to the village."

The woman peered in awe at the kaleidoscope of pigmentation highlighting the vegetation lining the craggy rock walls rising steeply above her. Various species of wildflowers, predominantly hibiscus, bloomed everywhere, their multi-hued effect spanning the entire spectrum of a rainbow. Palm trees and jumbled arrays of fruit-bearing trees further added to the hodgepodge of living matter growing from the tiered ledges. The thriving plant life teemed with brilliantly tinted butterflies and brightly plumed tropical birds flitting and nesting among the dense flora. The proliferation of biota with its explosion of pigmentation dazzled the eye. "Nature wears many colors," she said offhandedly.

Jacob smiled. "A noted philosopher and poet once wrote something very much like that. Did you ever read the work of Ralph Waldo Emerson?"

From the expression on the woman's face, Jacob could tell he had dislodged some shred of memory from the woman's previous life. "Didn't he say that nature always wears the colors of the spirit, that a person laboring under calamity will know sadness from the heat of their own fire?"

"Yes. And do you know what he meant by that?"

Something registered with sudden clarity in the woman's eyes. "Nature is the symbol of the spirit. We are connected to the landscape and as we turn, so does it. As our moods change, so too do our perceptions of the hues and shapes of nature."

"I see you have obviously studied Emerson." Jacob looked thoughtful. "It is very likely you are an educated woman. Maybe you had attended a university at one time," he hypothesized encouragingly. "You seem to have a bit of the philosopher in you."

"Do you think?"

"Another wise man once wrote 'Nature is the art of God' when he attempted to reconcile religion and science. If you were truly a scholar of philosophy, you would surely remember his name."

The answer came easily. "Sir Thomas Browne said that in 1635 in his *Religio Medici*."

Jacob grinned again, pleased with the answer. He thought some more. "The famous Greek scientist and philosopher, Aristotle, gave philosophy a definition. Any student of philosophy would remember it."

The words were out of the woman's mouth before she realized she had uttered them. "Philosophy is the science which considers truth."

Jacob was enjoying the woman's company. "I think we have taken the first step in unraveling who you are."

The woman looked up at the profusion of colorful plant and avian life overlooking the water, seemingly mesmerized by the magnificent panorama. Like the dolphin, the unsightly blemishes that had marred her skin when he had found her were now gone, with no trace of scarring anywhere. Her complexion was now beginning to take on a smooth, robust glow, further enhanced by her developing pregnancy. Still slightly damp from her earlier swim in the cove, her dark brown hair hung limply to the middle of her back. He knew that when it dried completely, it would be thick and wavy, much like a lion's mane, tinged with streaks of reddish-gold that gave it a lustrous sheen when the sun reflected off it. He judged her to be somewhere in her late twenties. She was a petite, pretty woman, with large and expressive dark brown eyes that seemed to take in everything with measured interest. If not for her jutting belly, he could tell she would normally be athletically trim and lithe, and when she walked along the beach she carried herself in the determined posture of the achiever, the type of person that seemed to constantly strive for purpose.

Jacob handed the woman a plate of exotic fruit consisting of sliced mangos, apricots and papayas and glanced out over the water. "Does your friend have a name?" he asked, indicating the dolphin floating lazily near the base of the waterfall.

The woman broke from her reflective mood. "I have decided to call her Athena."

Jacob ran his fingers through his beard, crinkling his eyes with amusement. "Ah, yes, from Greek mythology. The daughter of Zeus." He popped a piece of mango into his mouth. "She sprang full grown in armor from his forehead and therefore has no mother. She is fierce and brave in battle, but fights only to protect the state and home from outside enemies. She invented the bridle, which allowed man to tame horses. Other things like the ship and chariot were created by her. She is the embodiment of wisdom, purity and reason. Among his children, Zeus considered her his favorite and allowed her to use his weapons, including his thunderbolt."

"You seem like a very learned man," the woman said between bites. "Your little house is stuffed with books."

"I have a hunger for knowledge. Many things interest me. I enjoy reading."

"Yet you live very simply."

"I do not require anything more than what you see all around us. I am very happy here." Jacob studied the woman thoughtfully. "Would you mind if I gave you a name to call you by…at least until your memory returns?"

"That depends on what it is."

"Amphitrite. I would like to call you Amphitrite."

"Wasn't she another Greek goddess?" It was more of a statement than a question.

"Yes. The circumstances that brought you here parallel to a certain degree the story of Amphitrite. She was the queen of the sea, variously given as the daughter of Oceanus and Tethys or of Nereus and Doris. The sea god Poseidon-" He abruptly hesitated and lowered his eyes, trying to conceal his sudden embarrassment by stuffing more fruit into his mouth but nearly choking.

The woman looked at him expectantly. "Yes, go on. What about Poseidon?"

Jacob found himself tongue-tied as he realized the faux pas of using such a comparison. "He, ah…he wanted her as his bride, but she declined from the honor and hid from him in the Atlantic Ocean," he said, unable to hide the fluster in his voice. "A dolphin not only located her, but also brought her back to him and he married her. As a reward, the dolphin was granted a place in heaven."

The woman laughed. He could tell she was not offended.

Jacob quickly recovered his poise but avoided looking at the woman's belly. "Thereafter, Amphitrite gave birth to Triton, the fish-man."

The woman kept smiling. "That's an interesting story."

"Greek amphoras often depict Amphitrite riding a sea creature surrounded by Tritons. Like the queen she is, she is shown decorated with her waving hair covered with a net, and sometimes with the pincers of a lobster attached to her temples."

"How do you remember all these things?"

"For some unknown reason, God has given me an eidetic memory. Whenever I see, hear or read something, I never forget it, down to the most minute detail."

The woman eyed Jacob with envy. "Such a talent must be a blessing."

Jacob shook his head. "It is more of a curse. Never being able to forget anything can sometimes be cumbersome. The more I learn, the more things I realize I don't know. This makes me hunger to gain more knowledge, and because of it my head gets filled with all types of information and correlations."

Jacob sighed wearily. "Sometimes I wonder if knowing less would make life so much simpler."

The woman listened with interest, but consumed her food as though she had not eaten in several days. "Didn't someone once say knowledge is power," she said between mouthfuls. "Such a statement leads one to the conclusion that most people who strive for knowledge are either consciously or unconsciously seeking power in some form. With what you know, you could probably be a rich man within Haitian society, yet you live the life of a simple man."

"I have no desire for power or riches. Didn't you ever hear the phrase 'Power corrupts?' Most of the ills of this world seem to be caused by those who seek power." Jacob let out another sigh, deeper than before. "Anyway, I am very happy to live here in this cove and read my books. It has been my observation that most people of ambition who succeed in achieving power and wealth ultimately yearn for communion with nature. They buy country estates with gardens and luxury yachts, looking for a place that offers peace and tranquility. I have all of that right here."

The woman gazed at Jacob with undisguised admiration. "You're an unusual man, Jacob. I guess I'm very fortunate that you found me." She continued to eat, seeming to ponder something, then said, "Your choice of name for me...Amphitrite will do just fine for the time being."

For a long moment, Jacob remained silent and withdrawn, caught up in the midst of a heavy decision. "The American Embassy in Port-au-Prince may be able to pinpoint your identity. You have the look and speech of an American. A bus comes by the village each week bound for the capital. I can take you there if you like," he offered unenthusiastically.

The suggestion seemed to startle Amphitrite. She glanced apprehensively in the direction of the dolphin. "If it's all the same to you, I'd like to stay here a while longer." She turned back to Jacob, her eyes revealing both a profound confusion and a plea. "You've been very kind to me, and it isn't my intention to impose on your gracious hospitality by overextending my stay, but..."

"Yes."

"Athena needs me right now and I can't leave her after what she's done for me, not just yet."

The vibrant smile that blossomed on Jacob's face was not unlike one of the hibiscus flowers adorning the cove. "Both you and your friend are welcome here as long as you wish to stay."

The next week went by quickly. Early every morning Amphitrite took a long swim in the cove with Athena, frolicking playfully for hours at a time. Jacob noticed that on each of these occasions before Amphitrite entered the water, the same strange ritual would occur. As had happened the first time he had witnessed it, Amphitrite and her dolphin friend would stare fixedly at one another for several minutes, as if some covert communication transpired between them on an unknown level. Each time the woman would stand immobile on the sandy beach, her face frozen with the inscrutable expression of a statue sculpted from marble. And each time Athena would float nearly motionless, with unfathomable anthracite eyes locked on Amphitrite. Then without a word uttered, Amphitrite would wade out into the water with the vacant gaze of a sleepwalker.

Sometimes Jacob would sit on the sand and watch the interplay with the fascination of a child seeing something new and unusual unfold before its eyes. At other times he felt distantly removed from the abysmal bond the woman and dolphin shared and would turn away to attend some chore or sail beyond the cove to net more fish.

Later each day, Amphitrite would return from her swim refreshed and exuberant, always eager to engage in conversation with Jacob. In spite of her memory loss, she soon revealed an intelligent, sagacious mind, seeming to be well versed in a surprisingly broad range of subjects. While she failed to remember any portion of her former life, she was able to draw upon substantial blocks of both general and specialized knowledge retained in her brain. This tended to support Jacob's initial supposition that she was educated. Often their confabulations were intellectually stimulating, and Jacob quickly found himself appreciating the woman's company more and more.

When not swimming with the dolphin, the woman was now spending most of her waking hours with Jacob, opting to accompany him whenever he went fishing or brought Athena food.

One day while feeding the dolphin a particularly meager catch of fish, he looked soulfully into the creature's eyes and apologized for not having more. Amphitrite appeared momentarily distant as if listening to some inner voice, then said, "There is no need to explain yourself. Athena knows you do the best you can."

"Is that your assessment or Athena's?"

"It's what she told me." Amphitrite noted Jacob's skepticism. "She knows only that you're a kind man and that you are truly concerned about her welfare. That is all she needs to know."

The following day as Jacob prepared his pinnace for another bout of fishing, Amphitrite displayed an enigmatic grin. "I think there's a sizeable school of striped mullet that awaits your net today," she announced happily.

Jacob smiled back politely, enjoying her jovial mood but keeping the absurdity of such a proclamation to himself. He knew that striped mullet were not commonly found in the Caribbean. Either she was grossly naïve or jesting, particularly in light of the fact that overfishing in Haitian coastal waters had decimated populations of mullet decades earlier.

"I do not think that is possible," he said seriously. "Such fish vanished from these waters long ago."

Amphitrite retained her cheerful smile. "Athena and I are going to show you they're still around," she replied optimistically.

As the pinnace chugged from the protection of the cove, Jacob was surprised to note Athena knifing through the low swells on the craft's port side. As far as he knew, this was the first time the dolphin had ventured beyond the cove's rocky confines since he had discovered her.

After the pinnace had cleared the narrow channel through the reef, Jacob began steering a wide arc that would take them on a northerly course to the spot he deemed the most promising for harvesting fish.

"South will prove to be the better choice today," Amphitrite recommended. To Jacob's puzzlement she still wore that strange enigmatic smile.

"Why do you say that?" questioned Jacob. "The better fishing has always been north of here."

Amphitrite directed her gaze behind Jacob. "See that promontory jutting out into the ocean." Jacob turned around and noted the headland she was looking at three miles distant. "If you take this boat just off that point of land, good fortune will befall you."

Bemused, Jacob laughed aloud. "Translated into its English equivalent, the place you are referring is called the Devil's Horn. The currents near the Horn are unpredictable and the fishing has always been a disappointment to all the fishermen who have tried their luck there. No one fishes the Horn anymore."

Amphitrite remained unmoved by Jacob's lack of faith. "If you go there, I promise your luck will change."

"It will be a waste of fuel," Jacob objected wearily.

Amphitrite just kept smiling encouragingly, and his resolve began to waver. Against his better judgement he turned the boat around. "Okay," he conceded, "but only for a short time. If no fish come into my net within one hour, then we will go to the place of my choosing with no arguments. Agreed?"

"Fair enough."

With Athena leading the way, they were soon positioned off the Devil's Horn and drifting with the current. "Here!" Amphitrite cried jubilantly. "Drop your net here. Athena will herd the fish into it."

Begrudgingly, Jacob flung the net and Athena disappeared beneath the surface. Within seconds he felt a heavy resistance on the drag lines, and as he began to pull, the effort of hauling in the net took all his strength. As he heaved the net to the surface, it became obvious it was filled with a squirming mass of fish, most of them averaging one foot in length. Mouth agape, he stared at Amphitrite strangely. The net was glutted with striped mullet.

With Athena's assistance, Jacob swiftly succeeded in hauling aboard eight more loads of fish. Each time the net bulged voluminously with hundreds of striped mullet.

Jacob had outfitted the pinnace with several large holding tanks a few years earlier, but it had been quite some time since they had been used. Now the tanks were filled to capacity with the sudden windfall, and with the aeration pumps keeping the catch alive and the gunwales substantially lower in the water, Jacob put the boat on a heading that would take them back to the cove. Along the way he tossed Athena fish after fish until she was sated and could eat no more. With her belly gorged almost to the point of bursting, she swam sluggishly as she re-entered the rocky domain that served as Jacob's home.

In one corner of the cove Jacob had installed a fish pen, and he filled it with most of the captured mullet. There would be enough live fish on hand to keep Athena well fed for several weeks to come.

Sunset was always a wondrous sight in the cove from October through March. Framed by the steep sides of the chasm, the red solar disk provided a surrealistic vista as it dipped below the rim of the rock wall towering above the cove's west side like a molten ball of magma.

"It was a beautiful day," Amphitrite remarked blithely as the light began to fade. "It's been many months since Athena has eaten so well."

Jacob mulled this and frowned. "So you are starting to remember events prior to coming here?"

Amphitrite held his gaze momentarily and shook her head. "Athena told me this. She wanted me to thank you and tell you she'll try to reciprocate your act of kindness."

Jacob sat still, looking out over the water as darkness descended to engulf them. He knew that darkness fell much more rapidly the closer one got to the equator. "How did you know?" he asked. He kept his tone casual.

"Know what?"

"How did you know where to find the fish?" Like a pesky gnat buzzing relentlessly about his head, the riddle had plagued him most of the day.

Amphitrite pondered the question as if examining some hidden truth from several different angles. "I know it sounds crazy," she said at last, "but I saw it in a dream. Just as it happened today, I saw it in a dream last night. It seemed so real that I knew it would actually happen, and it did."

Jacob's mind raced. Even as a young boy, his grandmother, now deceased, had instilled in him never to ignore events which unfolded in dreams. Because of it, he had made it a priority to read up on any information that dealt with the subject whenever he could find it.

"You experienced precognition," he said, trying to restrain his excitement and succeeding. "It occurs predominantly in dreams for most people who experience it, although it can also take the form of a waking vision, flashing thoughts entering the mind, or a sense of just knowing. There is much scientific evidence to support that some people are able to see certain future events, although there is currently no accepted explanation as to how or why it occurs. It may be possible you have such a psychic ability, one that enables you to have visions of things to come."

Amphitrite appeared stymied. "I have no memory of having experienced visions before the one in my dream last night," she replied stiffly. "Try as I might, I can't seem to picture any past at all. It's as if I never existed anywhere else other than in this cove."

There was a profound sadness in her words, and Jacob placed a consoling hand on her shoulder, a gesture of sympathetic understanding. "It may be that your inability to remember your past has somehow given you the power to glimpse the future...at least some portion of it." He thought about it some more. "In a way, what you saw became a self-fulfilling prophecy."

"Does that make me some kind of freak?" There was the hint of weary resignation in her voice.

"Hardly! Precognitive dreams are quite common. Many people have them without realizing it, perhaps because they do not recall the details or fail to properly interpret the symbols within the dream."

"There were no symbols in my dream. I saw the future exactly as it occurred this morning."

"What you experienced was a prophetic dream. It predicted the future with a high degree of accuracy, what some might call an unchangeable future. Prophetic dreams are much rarer than most other forms of precognition. By definition, all prophecy is considered to be precognition. However, not all precognition can be classified as prophecy."

"Why is that?"

Jacob found himself regurgitating some of the things he had read on the subject. "There are basically two types of precognitive dreams. One involves a perception of the future that cannot be altered. That is what you saw. It predicted what would happen and was therefore unchangeable. Whatever happened in the dream occurred because it was already etched in the great cosmic plan, what most people would call destiny or fate. The other type of precognitive dream involves a look into a possible future, but one that can be changed. Such a dream allows someone to change the future outcome. This apparent ability to alter the perceived future makes precognition difficult to understand since if it is truly a look into the future, then the effects are witnessed before the causes. Such conditions do occur in quantum physics, however."

"I'm not very familiar with quantum physics," Amphitrite said, tilting her head to survey the velvet tapestry of the heavens that had so rapidly replaced the last glimmers of daylight. The stars twinkled spectacularly with remote indifference.

A look of intense satisfaction broke out on Jacob's face. He was in his element. Maybe he should have become a teacher, he thought. He was a veritable storehouse of information and he enjoyed disseminating it. "It is one of the foundations of modern science. Quantum physics focuses on studying matter at the subatomic level. It was developed to explain various anomalies observed in classical physics. At its core, classical physics is a flawed theory, but only dramatically flawed when dealing with very small particles on the atomic scale or exceptionally fast velocities that get close to the speed of light where relativity takes over. For everyday things, which are much larger than atoms and much slower than the speed of light, classical physics does an excellent job at predicting what will happen, at least with a high degree of approximation. Plus it is much easier to use than either quantum mechanics or relativity, each of which requires a more extensive amount of mathematics to compute the end result. Recent discoveries in quantum physics and also in cosmology, the branch of astronomy that deals with the universe taken as a whole, have shed much light on how the mind interacts with the universe. These findings compel acceptance of the idea that there is far more than one universe and that we constantly, but unconsciously, interact with other unseen or hidden universes and higher dimensions. Unfortunately, most books on quantum cosmology are written in mathematical language that few people understand."

Amphitrite remained quiet, intent on listening, and Jacob elaborated further. "Anyway, to avoid digressing on the nuances of quantum mechanics, I will simply say that some scientists believe it holds the key to revealing the precise process by which precognition works."

Jacob inhaled deeply, savoring the sweet aroma of hibiscus before continuing. "To date, two theories have emerged which may explain it, but they are rather general in nature. The most popular theory holds that precognition is a glimpse of a possible future that is based upon present conditions and existing information, and which may be altered depending on acts of free will. Such a theory implies that the future can cause the past, a phenomenon called backward causality or retro-causality. However, a different and much more controversial theory contends that the precognitive experience itself unleashes a powerful psychokinetic energy, which directly influences the state of matter. This then brings the envisioned future to pass, and therefore your self-fulfilling prophecy."

A heavy cloud of introspection seemed to wash over Amphitrite. "It was a marvelous vision, my prophetic dream. Only good came of it." She hesitated briefly. "But what does one do if the dream were to contain something horrible. Having such an ability to prophesize something bad like that would be a terrible thing, would it not?"

The happy air that had accompanied Jacob's lecture a moment earlier vanished abruptly. "Only if the final outcome could not be altered to result in something beneficial or benign," he stated solemnly.

Late that night Jacob stirred groggily from a sound sleep. Something had awakened him and as he sat up he became aware of cries coming from Amphitrite's bunk. The woman thrashed about wildly in the throes of some nightmare, her face glistening with sweat in the dim moonlight. He immediately rose and gently prodded her. With a start she jerked awake, letting out several short gasps.

"It is all right," Jacob said comfortingly. "You are safe here." Amphitrite looked about dazedly. "You were having a bad dream."

Teetering on the verge of panic, Amphitrite stared at him with wide, fearful eyes. "The village! How far is the village?" she demanded.

"Not far," Jacob said calmly. "Maybe a thirty minute walk through the hills. The climb out of this cove is difficult and treacherous. By boat it takes a little longer, but the journey is much safer and less strenuous." Jacob was perplexed. "Why do you want to know?"

The answer came back in a barely audible whisper as Amphitrite trembled uncontrollably. "There is no time to explain." As if in empathic synchrony with Amphitrite's despondency, Athena chittered mournfully from the nearby water.

Jacob's soothing presence did little to alleviate Amphitrite's fright. He lit a candle to bring more illumination inside the dwelling. With tears trickling down her cheeks, Amphitrite's face was a waxen mask, her eyes clouded with misty shadows that foretold of chilling horrors lurking in her mind. "We must hurry!" she implored, rising hastily from the bed and slipping on the sandals Jacob had made for her. "Please take me to the village by the quickest route." There was a latent tension in her voice.

Jacob studied her expression intimately a moment longer. He sensed something dark and terrifying to the spirit, something that was all too real to the woman. He pressed the matter no further, springing to his feet and striding to the door of the dwelling. "Follow me!" he blurted. If there was an explanation for Amphitrite's request, he was certain she would tell him on the way to the village.

Under a gibbous moon, Jacob led Amphitrite up the escarpment, steep in areas and shelved in others. Although faint, there was just enough light to distinguish the nuances in topography they had to negotiate, and Jacob was thoroughly familiar with all of them. Years earlier, he had set about making the climb out of the cove easier when he had planted various types of flowering plants and fruit-bearing trees along the broader ledges where sufficient topsoil existed. A series of strategically placed guide ropes, railings and handholds allowed them to pull themselves along those rocky pathways which were less precipitously sloped, while wooden ladders fastened along fissures in the limestone provided the means to scale the worst portions of the chasm. As they made their way up, Jacob kept close to Amphitrite, reaching out from time to time to hold her arm. Her gravid condition made him nervous and he focused on keeping her safe. Near the uppermost region of the ascent, a narrow trail opened up and wound its way through a dense thicket of thorns and underbrush. The ground underfoot was still soggy from the recent storm and their feet became mired in mud at intervals as they trudged along the path.

"Does a man by the name of Emmanuel Baptiste live in the village?" Amphitrite suddenly asked, huffing heavily from the climb.

Jacob almost stopped in his tracks, but then decided to keep going. "Yes," he said. "There is such a person with that name." The mention of Baptiste was strangely disturbing to him, for he knew that the man was a fierce and outspoken opponent of the current dictator that ruled the population.

"His life is in terrible danger," Amphitrite uttered hoarsely, gasping for breath as she tried to keep up with Jacob. "Some men are coming this very night to kill him. We must warn him before they get there."

Jacob stopped and turned sharply. "You saw this in a dream?" Dreams that involved death could not be ignored under any circumstances. His thoughts scurried ahead, suddenly filled with foreboding apprehension. *And if it was a precognitive dream, could murder be averted?*

"It was another of those dreams," Amphitrite answered, her voice shaking. "It was so real, so terribly evil."

Prodded by her words, Jacob resumed walking again, his legs moving more hastily this time. "How can you be sure it was a precognitive dream?"

"I can't explain it, I just know." Though still shaken, her tone held a trace of indignation. Jacob had no desire to offend the woman and he offered no argument.

After moving another twenty paces Amphitrite asked, "What does the phrase 'Tonton Makout' mean?"

Yes, Jacob thought, it made sense. "It is a Creole term that translates to bogeymen in English. The Tonton Makout are the bully boys of "Baby Doc" Duvalier, the president of Haiti. They are very evil men."

When Jacob was a young boy, Baby Doc's father, Francois Duvalier, had ruled Haiti with an iron fist. A physician by profession, he came to power in 1957 with the full support of the Haitian army behind him. "Papa Doc", as he came to be called, was overwhelmingly reelected president in 1961 in a military-controlled sham election. And in 1964 he declared himself dictator for life. His regime, the longest in Haiti's history, was a brutal reign of terror in which all political opponents were either jailed or summarily executed. Under Papa Doc, the populace was kept in a constant state of abject fear by his personal secret police force, the notorious Tonton Makout. These were unpaid volunteers who were directly responsible only to Duvalier and who were given a virtual license to torture, kill and extort in order to achieve Papa Doc's political objectives. Under Francois Duvalier's administration, the Tonton Makout had murdered hundreds, maybe thousands, of opponents, sometimes publicly hanging the corpses as warnings to the rest of the citizenry. While the economy of Haiti had been slowly declining prior to Duvalier's succession to power, it continued to deteriorate under his rule, and the illiteracy rate of the nation remained at about ninety percent. Papa Doc nevertheless maintained control over the nation, and his practice of voodooism encouraged rumors among the people that he possessed supernatural powers. Before his death in 1971, he arranged for his son, Jean-Claude, to succeed him.

Jacob recalled that the first few years of John-Claude's installation as Haiti's ninth president-for-life were a largely uneventful extension of his father's rule. Baby Doc, however, did change the name of the Tonton Makout to the Volunteer Security Nationals, though they continued to terrorize the citizenry. To most of the population the VSN were still referred to as the Tonton Makout. Under Baby Doc, the balance between the VSN and the armed forces changed. He realigned these competing power bases, if only to ensure control over Haiti's security apparatus.

In a half-hearted attempt to open Haiti to the outside world and to secure renewed foreign assistance from the United States, Baby Doc initially curbed the abuses of the VSN. Unfortunately for the nation, Jean-Claude limited his interest in government to various fraudulent schemes and to outright misappropriations of government funds for which no balance sheets were ever kept. Baby Doc's kleptocracy, along with his failure to back with actions his rhetoric endorsing economic and public-health reform, left the regime vulnerable to unanticipated crises that were exacerbated by endemic poverty. With public services already minimal, the ineptness of government further deteriorated as Jean-Claude and his ruling clique continued to abscond with funds from the national treasury.

Jacob remembered the widespread discontent that began to manifest itself in March of 1983 when Pope John Paul II visited Haiti. During the visit, the pontiff had openly declared that the economic and social climate within the poverty-stricken nation needed change. He called for a more equitable distribution of wealth, a more egalitarian social structure, more concern among the elite for the well-being of the masses, and increased participation by the ruling party in public life. The message had revitalized both laymen and clergy, and it contributed heavily to a sudden rise in political and social activism.

A short time after the Pope's visit, the Haitian Bishops Conference launched a nationwide but short-lived literacy program in the midst of mushrooming discontent with the Duvalier regime. Anti-government riots quickly ensued and the VSN stepped in to quell the disturbances. Two hundred peasants were massacred at Jean-Rabeau after demonstrating for more land. A revolt began in the provinces two years later. Raids on food-distribution warehouses occurred in the coastal city of Gonaives and quickly expanded in a sequence of riots that spread to six other cities. As his power began to wane, brutal excesses by the increasingly desperate VSN further eroded Duvalier's position. With the military no longer supporting him, he relied heavily on the VSN and on limited local police capabilities to restore order, but to no avail.

Jacob had heard rumors that altogether as many as 60,000 people had been killed and tortured by the VSN during Baby Doc's reign in order for him to retain his dictatorship. But he also knew that it was only a matter of time before the government collapsed completely and Baby Doc was forced to flee the country, particularly if the Haitian army wanted Duvalier ousted. So far, though, Duvalier was stubbornly hanging on to the reins of power and was even resisting pressure from the United States government to step down.

As he brought Amphitrite along the path that led to Malique, Jacob well understood the consequences of what they were trying to do. He made a decision and abruptly stopped, turning to face Amphitrite and speaking gravely. "If the men you saw in your dream are truly Tonton Makout, then we will be killed if they catch us trying to warn Baptiste. He is a potent adversary of Duvalier and has been inflaming the local citizenry to revolt against the government. Baptiste commands a great amount of respect and support from the population."

Amphitrite's face was an indistinct shadow against the backdrop of subdued moonlight. "It isn't just Baptiste I'm trying to save. These men are coming to kill everyone in the village, even the women and children. We must do whatever we can to keep that from happening."

Jacob was momentarily at a loss for words. He had lived a simple existence for most of his life, generally keeping to himself and doing his best to prevent the rest of the world, with all its problems, crises and miseries, from touching him. Rarely, if ever, had he been confronted with a situation that placed him in extreme peril.

"You will be putting both yourself and your unborn child in unnecessary danger," said Jacob. "There is no reason for you to come. I will go on ahead and alert the villagers. You will do much to ease my mind if you return to the cove and wait for me there."

When Jacob turned to leave, Amphitrite grabbed his arm. Her grip was surprisingly strong and tenacious. "It's crucial that I go with you."

Jacob shook his head stubbornly. "No!"

Amphitrite maintained her hold on Jacob, her voice urgent. "You don't understand. I see it clearly now. I think I know how we can stop these men, how we can keep them away from the village."

"How?"

"Is there not a road that leads to Malique from the south?"

"Yes. This trail overlooks that road on the other side of the village."

"The Makout will be taking that road, Jacob. They will be coming in a convoy of four trucks led by a jeep."

"I still do not see-"

"This trail runs by an ancient stone wall. The wall is crescent-shaped and stands to one side of a huge tree high above the road. The slope there is steep and barren of other trees. Isn't this so?" There was resolute conviction in her words.

The hair rose on the nape of Jacob's neck and a chill crept down his spine. The place Amphitrite described was a voodoo shrine, established two generations earlier by the locals. Candles, carvings of wood, and the blood and bones of sacrificed animals were scattered in the immediate vicinity of the towering tree. The villagers believed the tree was protected by the *maitre du grand bois* – the master spirit of the great woods.

"Yes, there is such a place," Jacob acquiesced. "Some of the villagers go there to get drinking water. There is a well near the tree. The tree you speak of is a giant mapou tree. It draws precious spring water to the surface from deep underground."

Amphitrite rushed on hastily. Lives were at stake. "The ground, Jacob. The ground that slopes toward the road is very unstable. If we can cause a mudslide, we can block the road."

Jacob had some understanding of soil mechanics and had once read a book on the subject. What Amphitrite was suggesting meant that the torrential rains brought by the recent hurricane had saturated the soil to the point where the load of elevated overburden started to exceed the shear strength capacity of the underlying earth and rock. If inordinate amounts of rainwater collected on top of a slope before it was able to drain, the substratum could no longer support the added weight by frictional resistance. Eventually the instability would cause the overlying mass of earth and rock to shear away and plunge to lower ground. Mudslides were common on the Island of Hispaniola and were often attributable to the deforestation of hillsides by locals who needed the wood from trees for cooking and building.

"And how do you propose to accomplish this?" Jacob asked. He tried his best to keep any trace of skepticism from his voice.

"If we can collapse the rock wall, the ensuing avalanche will do the rest," Amphitrite stated with certainty. "The hill will slide down."

Jacob hesitated a moment longer. "You saw the hill come down in the dream? You saw a landslide?" He needed confirmation. He had to know if the dream was prophetic in nature.

The question seemed to discombobulate her, and she wavered with uncertainty before ascertaining the full meaning of his query. "No! I did not see a landslide," she countered in agitation. "But I believe the dream contained a clue how we can save the village."

"What? What did you hear? What did you see?" Jacob demanded, refusing to go another step. "I will not take you to the tree unless you describe the contents of the dream exactly."

Exasperated, Amphitrite spoke quickly. "There was a man, the one in charge of the convoy. He rode in a jeep leading four trucks. In his left hand was a sickle, in his right a machete. In the dream his face turned into a skull, and the skull yelled the words, '*The Tonton Makout has come to harvest Emmanuel Baptiste and all of Malique, and only a river of mud can stop the slaughter.*' Then the skull smiled horribly and turned to stare up at a steep hill. Except for one enormous tree that stood at the top of the hill, the slope was barren. A partially collapsed stone wall stood in front of the tree. I heard the screams of women and children in the background and the machete and sickle held by the skull began to drip with blood. The screams turned to thunder as the skull changed back into the face of the Makout leader. The man opened his mouth and said, '*If the wall fell, so would the hill, but now we are free to do what we will. The maitre du grand bois has no power over us.*'"

Amphitrite drew breath before going on. "As soon as he said it, the convoy entered the village just as a tidal wave of blood swept in from the sea to engulf everything, including the mapou tree."

Amphitrite stopped and stared at Jacob, as if the weight of what she was telling him was too much to bear. Her lips quivered and she spoke again in a low, subdued voice. "When the sea of blood receded, the tree and village were gone. There were bodies scattered everywhere along the shore."

"If the dream was prophetic, then we cannot stop it from happening," Jacob said despondently.

"No! There still may be a chance."

"What do you mean?"

"There was more. The dead suddenly disappeared and Malique was whole again. I saw the mapou tree firmly rooted in the center of the village."

Jacob stood as if mesmerized and Amphitrite had to push him hard to jar him from the grip of horror she had just described. "We are running out of time!" she screamed.

Even though Jacob had grown up in the midst of a society dominated by superstition and a fear of the unknown, he rarely let himself become influenced by such things. He was a learned man and left such nonsense to the illiterate masses that clung steadfastly to such beliefs. Yet Amphitrite's precognition of future events was something that bordered on the supernatural. Somehow he trusted her, sensing there was at least an inkling of truth to the things she had foreseen. Two questions hung heavily on his mind. *Could they reach the mapou tree in time? And how would they collapse the wall?*

In that moment Jacob made a decision. "I will take you to the mapou tree," he said, turning to follow the trail.

They continued along the path, gradually gaining higher ground as it wound through rock outcroppings and thorn scrub. Eventually the moderate upward grade gave way to more level terrain, and as they walked around a bend the dark mass of the ocean came into view like a vast sheet of polished slate. Under the glow of a crescent moon, the village of Malique hugged the hillside of an inlet. A dense cluster of houses and shacks nestled above a rocky beach where several piers jutted obtrusively into the sea. A fleet of small fishing boats abutted the piers, perhaps thirty in all, with several larger vessels dominating the group. With the exception of a few lighted windows, it appeared that most of the citizenry was asleep. A heavy silence pervaded the air, belying the possibility of any impending calamity that might befall the slumbering community.

As they moved on a little further, the trail abruptly forked. Jacob halted and faced Amphitrite. "The path to the left leads down to the village," he said. "The one to the right will take us to the mapou tree."

"How much farther?" Amphitrite asked in a strained voice.

"Almost two kilometers."

Even in the semi-darkness Jacob could discern the toll their journey was taking on Amphitrite. Her face glistened with sweat and it was becoming increasingly difficult for her to maintain the pace she had set earlier. Jacob intentionally slowed to accommodate her growing fatigue. "Perhaps we should rest a minute," he suggested.

"There is no time for that!" she protested breathlessly, plodding past Jacob and taking the trail to the right.

As they trudged on, the trail began a rapid descent through a rugged landscape, falling away steeply in a few places. Jacob kept a firm grip on Amphitrite in areas such as these lest she stumble and fall. Within minutes the trail meandered down to a narrow dirt road and traversed it.

"This is the road that leads to Malique," Jacob said.

Immediately beyond the road, the trail rose quickly and Amphitrite began to gasp for breath. They ascended higher. Amphitrite's step began to falter but she refused to quit. Suddenly she stopped and doubled over. A stifled cry revealed her agony. In the midst of her spasm, something flashed in her mind.

"You must rest!" Jacob ordered. "Think of your baby!"

"I can't!" she groaned.

"The mapou tree is not much farther. I will go on ahead and topple the wall. I can do that by myself. I do not need your help."

Amphitrite's face relaxed as the pain eased. She straightened up, but her speech was labored. "You will need me to show you the weak spot on the wall. There is one stone that will bring down the others. If it is moved even a little, the rest of the wall will collapse."

"You saw this?"

"Yes. It came to me a moment ago."

"Tell me where it is and I will find it," Jacob pleaded.

Amphitrite began walking again. "The location is indistinct. I'll know it when I see it."

A short time later, the immense bulk of the mapou tree loomed over them like an ominous shadow, its trunk rising to a dizzying height and blocking out the stars overhead as it reached for the heavens. A jumbled semicircular formation stood to one side of the tree, the stones comprising it leaning precariously over the incline of the hill. The formation was the remains of an antediluvian well, its wall becoming exposed as the hill eroded away from deforestation. Stones that had once comprised the portion of the well closest to the hillside littered the slope below. The dark shapes of various objects could be discerned scattered near the outer rim of the wall or hanging from the branches of the tree. Jacob knew that daylight would reveal them to be symbolic wood-carvings and the bones of sacrificed animals. The ancient voodoo shrine had always made Jacob feel uneasy whenever he had ventured near the site, and because of it, he generally avoided the place.

As they approached the wall, Amphitrite let out a gasp, a sound born of surprise rather than pain. "They're coming, Jacob!" she blurted apprehensively. "I can feel them."

Jacob took several steps back to command a better view of the base of the slope to the south. He knew the closest portion of road that led to Malique was roughly 300 meters southwest of the old well and almost 120 meters below their position vertically. The location where the road would be showed nothing in the scant moonlight.

"I do not see anything," replied Jacob in frustration, but he somehow trusted her senses. He scampered back near the wall. "Show me the spot where the wall is weakest," he instructed.

The silhouette of Amphitrite's darkened form seemed unreal in the dimness of night. "I need light, Jacob. I cannot point out something I can't see."

Jacob noted the wall's convex side. Shielded from the dull light cast by a waning moon, it was obscured in shadow. An idea came upon him and he strode cautiously to the crude altar fronting the tree. He knew that a cluster of candles was usually placed there, and as he drew closer to it an involuntary shudder coursed through him like a jolt of electricity. He shrugged aside the feeling and groped beneath the dais in a sheltered alcove hewn from coarse wood until his fingers located a small box. As a small boy he had witnessed a few of the ceremonial voodoo rituals venerating the master spirit purportedly residing in the great mapou tree. From experience he knew the box would contain matches with which to light the candles, but there was an implied warning to his trespass. No one ever took any of the artifacts surrounding the tree. Although religious custom forbade the tampering or removal of any objects from the site, it was actually superstitious dread that prevented it. If the custom were violated, the wrath of the master spirit would descend upon and devour the offender. Only a *mambo* or *houngan* was allowed to touch the tree or the ornaments adorning the holy site.

Jacob hurriedly opened the matchbox and struck a match. The sudden burst of light illuminated a row of candles in various states of deformed consumption, their waxy bases bonded with the altar's wooden surface. Jacob lit the largest candle and broke it from its perch, then walked swiftly back to the rock wall.

"Hurry, Jacob!" Amphitrite shouted anxiously. "I can see them."

Jacob craned his head around the wall, careful to keep the candlelight concealed behind the rock formation so as not to alert anyone of their presence. Five pairs of headlights pierced the night, strung out in a single column at the far end of the valley below them. Like the implacable yellow orbs of nocturnal predators, they crept slowly forward with leisurely patience, as if there was no doubt that quarry would soon be snatched between serrated jaws.

Ducking back behind the convex side of the rock formation, he looked up at its highest section standing nearly four meters above the uneven ground. Some of the boulders comprising the stack were huge, judging them to weigh as much as half a ton. Raising the candle to illuminate the wall more clearly, he surveyed the interlaced chunks of rock intently. What remained of the stonework appeared quite stable and immovable.

He glanced at Amphitrite questioningly. "Where?"

Under the candle's flickering glow, her eyes flittered over the structure like hummingbirds in search of nectar. Jacob could see a growing alarm in them. "I don't see it!" she cried. "I can't visualize it anymore."

Jacob moved the candle further along the wall, changing the way the light reflected off the stones. "Maybe you are trying too hard," he suggested soothingly. "Visions cannot be forced, nor a remembrance of all their details." Everything he had ever read about precognition pointed to such a fact. He shifted the candle some more, as if it might help her recall the key to toppling the wall. On an impulse he told her, "Touch the stones! Touch them and clear your mind of any thoughts, as if it were an empty vessel." Based on what he had read on the subject, the human mind had little control invoking precognitive events. Conscious effort rarely worked.

The wildness in Amphitrite's eyes steadied as she comprehended Jacob's words. She nodded and reached out to place a hand on the stonework, then closed her eyes. She remained still for many seconds before stirring. She opened her eyes again and stared at Jacob, her expression resounding with hopelessness.

Jacob lowered the candle to the ground and peered around the wall. The headlights were much closer now, bobbing erratically as the vehicles bounced along the pothole-ridden road. Turning, he took Amphitrite by the hand and led her to the mapou tree. The trunk was enormous, at least 23 feet in circumference. Jacob envisioned the way it looked during the day. Under a bright tropical sun the trunk was a startling pale gray, rising straight up and branching only near the top where it unfurled a broadleaf canopy.

Coming to within arms-length of the tree, he stopped. Never had he come this close to the mapou. That he still retained a shred of his ancestral beliefs revolted him. As learned and rational-minded as he was, it was difficult for him to discard completely the last vestiges of superstitious dogma that had been so thoroughly ingrained in his people and passed on to him. Black magic and mysticism were for the illiterate and weak-minded, he often chided himself. But as he stood before the tree, he could not help but sense its awesome energy.

Esmerelda's essence abounded in that tree, at least some vestige of her spirit. That was what his grandmother had once told him. *There will come a day, Jacob, when you must cast aside your fear, for within this tree lies the salvation you will surely need.* Esmerelda had read the expression on his face and smiled. *Do not impede yourself with logic, Jacob. To do so will only discourage you from drawing on that which I leave behind.*" With his mind teetering on the cliff of doubt, he had watched as his grandmother had placed her palms upon the mapou's trunk.

Jacob pulled Amphitrite beside him. She came docilely, seeming distant and preoccupied with her own dismal failure. "Put your hand on the tree!" he urged. His voice was tight, betraying the fear that was inbred within him.

The proximity of the tree seemed to polarize Amphitrite's awareness. She stepped closer as if drawn to some unseen force and extended a hand. Jacob blinked. He could have sworn he saw sparks fly as her fingers made contact with the mapou's bark. Abruptly her body stiffened and she let out a small, startled cry. His instincts were right. The tree was a reservoir of mysterious energy and had triggered something in Amphitrite.

Jacob avoided touching the tree himself. He rose up on tiptoes instead to look beyond a rift in the hill's crest. The ground elevation at the tree was higher than the top of the wall, and it afforded him a view of the valley floor from where the convoy approached. He could see the lights of the lead vehicle were almost even with the base of the hill closest to their position. In another minute Duvalier's thugs would be beyond the reach of any possible avalanche.

Jacob turned his head back to Amphitrite. She suddenly flinched, drawing in a sharp intake of breath as if something stabbed deeply into her flesh. She cried out again, letting a prolonged scream escape her lips, a scream that grew in shrillness and conveyed intense pain. In panic, Jacob tried to pull her away from the tree, but it was as if her body was a rigid extension of the wood comprising it. He could not budge her. In disbelief he used both his hands to grip the wrist of her lone hand making contact with the mapou and tugged hard. He could not free it. Her palm remained flattened up against the trunk as if fused with the timber at the molecular level.

A strange rhythmic humming seemed to flow beneath his fingers as they clutched her wrist, and as he puzzled over it, a gentle rumbling could be felt underfoot. The rumble escalated rapidly, moving like rolling thunder through the soil until the earth trembled and shook violently. The sound of splintering rock drew his attention back to the wall. Fragments of stone caromed into the air as the exposed remnants of the ancient well crumbled away and toppled down the incline of the hill. Like an approaching earthquake, the rumble became a deafening roar. The ground pitched and vibrated and a jagged split in the earth began to materialize all at once, not more than five meters from where they stood. The rift widened swiftly like the hideous jaws of some titanic beast gaping wide to swallow anything near it.

Jacob stared in awe as the outer edge of the hill trundled away, breaking up and tumbling in a cataclysmic cascade of rock and muddy soil. The view down the hill broadened as the slope collapsed, and the headlights of the approaching convoy came fully before his eyes, its occupants unsuspecting and oblivious of the danger hurtling down to meet them. Jacob could not bring himself to look away, enthralled by the magnitude and ferocity of the spectacle. The immense mass of mud and debris surged on and gathered momentum, its leading edge a barrier of impending destruction, and it tore into the column with devastating force. One of the trucks flared, erupting in flames and sending a churning, expanding fireball soaring high above. A swath of fire spewed forth, trailing away on top of the moving wall of mud.

The inferno lit the night in vivid clarity, and Jacob knew that it was the severe impact and heat of collision that had caused the truck's fuel tank to rupture and ignite. The powerful rush of mud and rock bent and twisted the metal frames of the trucks as if they were flimsy paper toys. Under the deadly press, men and steel disappeared, crushed and buried as the pull of gravity compressed the onslaught of flowing rubble into a tightly compacted hodgepodge that was fast becoming a graveyard.

The lead vehicle was more fortunate. As the tsunami of earth swept over the road, it carried the smaller transport with it like a kayak caught in a surge of foaming whitewater. The beams emitted from its headlights rotated skyward as the wave of mud pulled it along, partially engulfing it. Within seconds the torrent of debris slowed, finally coming to rest on the far side of where the road used to be, the rear-half of the remaining vehicle embedded in a thick slurry of earthen matter, its lights pointing vertically at the stars as though they were signal beacons.

Almost immediately, the ground ceased shaking and the train-like rumble abruptly abated. The patter of a few pebbles trickling down the newly carved slope was the only sound to mark the aftermath of the impossible event. Sometime during the avalanche, Amphitrite's cries had died away, and as Jacob tore his eyes from the scene of destruction, her hand came free of the tree. Illuminated by both the distant flames and modest moonlight, her face was ashen and glazed. Released from her ordeal, she was now drained and exhausted, no longer possessing the strength to remain standing. She slumped backward listlessly and Jacob extended his arms, cradling her body before it hit the ground.

He stared back at the rearranged landscape below the mapou tree, his mind speeding along in analytical amazement. Somehow he and the woman had stumbled upon a hidden portal of the mind and spirit where few people ever journeyed.

- 11 -

The buzz of the trawler's intercom jolted Jake from his focused reverie with the piercing acuteness of a pistol shot. He had been mulling over all the things Grahm had told him, and one item troubled him deeply. He had turned that item over and over, examining it minutely from every angle much the way a jeweler might examine a rare gemstone for crystalline flaws under a magnifying glass. Reaching for the intercom, he toggled the switch and put aside the thought.

"What is it, Zimby?"

"I think you better get up here, Jay Jay. I want to hear you tell me Damballah is not playing tricks with my eyes." Zimbola's deep voice seemed to quake with awe.

Dr. Grahm looked up sharply from fiddling with the electronic gadgetry in his hands.

"Excuse me, Doctor," Jake apologized, hiding his annoyance, "but I better see what's troubling my overgrown friend."

Jake made his way forward and climbed the ladder leading to the pilothouse. "What?" he questioned with more than a little testiness. He hated it whenever Zimby made reference to the voodoo snake god. It often meant that strange or unwanted events were about to befall them.

Zimbola extended a huge arm and pointed off the starboard bow. "There! Are you seeing what I am seeing?"

It took several seconds for Jake's vision to adjust to the sun glare reflecting off the sea before he spotted it. His initial perception was that he was looking at some gigantic but unknown sea monster. As his brain continued to process the sight, he realized what he was actually seeing. A small group of bottlenose dolphins clove their way through the water on nearly the same heading as the Angel, no more than forty feet from the side of his vessel. All were albino…all except for the one in the center of the pack. That one also displayed white skin, but something was astride its back.

Jake closed his eyes, then opened them again, only to witness the same thing. A human female clung to the dorsal area of the creature at the pod's hub. Sunlight shimmered off a mane of long flowing hair with the consistency of burnished anthracite as it trailed down her back in the wash of waves.

As Jake watched, the dolphins began to pull away, switch-backing swiftly through the sea in perfect unified synchronization, the speed of the group much greater than anything the Angel was capable of. From what he could discern, the dolphin on which the female rode appeared to be the largest of the pack, its dorsal fin jutting higher than the others. For one brief moment the human female turned her head to glance in Jake's direction, seeming to look directly at him. A set of goggles was strapped firmly over her eyes, effectively concealing the full extent of her facial features. With the exception of her head, neck and hands, her body was completely clad in a one-piece, form-fitting wet suit, its color precisely matching the skin tone of the creature she rode. Her body was lithe and tiny, exhibiting the feminine lines indigenous of a healthy young woman. The girl swung her head forward again as the group raced hurriedly away toward some obscure destination, and Jake could not help but sense a measured purpose emanating from the pack.

The entire episode left Jake reeling in amazement. As if he had suddenly lost his voice, he stared mutely at Zimbola who stood frozen at the helm gazing at the rapidly fading pod with the glazed look of a sleepwalker. For several more seconds neither man spoke. Only then did Jake become aware of Grahm standing behind him. Apparently the scientist had followed him up to the bridge out of curiosity and had witnessed it all, for his eyes continued to track the strange procession of creatures in the distance.

Jake was the first to break the silence. "As I live and breathe, I've never seen anything like that."

Grahm's introspective manner suddenly changed gears and he became animated with excitement. "I think we've just seen some of Natalie's cousins," he said effusively.

Jake noted the faint outline of white limestone cliffs floating on the horizon, appearing insubstantial and ethereal rather than something comprised of rock and earth. Navassa Island was dead ahead. "Seems their destination may be the same as ours," he uttered. The way the group had surrounded the girl reminded him of a military escort, the kind assigned to guarding an important dignitary. "Those creatures appeared to be very protective of that girl, whoever she is." He looked inquiringly at Grahm. "You don't suppose she's the person who taught Natalie to master human speech?"

"Who is Natalie?" Zimbola asked in bewilderment.

A subtle smile broke out on Grahm's lips and he turned to address Jake, his eyes alive with the implications of the discovery. "Possibly!" He stared back thoughtfully toward the receding pod as it seemed to merge and then blend in with the misty bluffs in the distance. "The only way we'll know for sure is to speak to her."

"Who is Natalie?" Zimbola repeated.

Looking up at him, Jake said, "I'll explain it all to you later, but right now I need you to follow that pack!"

- 12 -

The small helicopter set down on the southwest side of the island like a falcon coming to roost, its skids finding purchase on the only available patch of flat terrain clear of scrub and jagged bedrock within the immediate area. All around it low-growing poisonwood trees predominated in dense clusters, with scattered cactus and thorn scrub adding to a hodgepodge of vegetation capping the island's broad plateau. With the throttle eased, the main rotor blades slowed rapidly, swishing through the air in a mild but deadly whisper. Hopping down from the co-pilot's side of the cockpit, Sebastian Ortega ducked his head and ambled over to the lone individual who stood watching him.

As Ortega drew closer, he took careful stock of the man awaiting him. The man was large and trim, exuding an air of haughty arrogance. A neatly trimmed shock of coarse, dirty blonde hair carpeted the lower half of his youthful face, the skin the color of unpolished bronze. His brow was wide and deep, his gaze dark and penetrating like that of a mesmeric cobra, cold as obsidian. Taking in the full measure of the persona before him, Ortega had difficulty tearing his eyes from the prominent scar marring the skin just above the man's right cheekbone. Somehow such a blemish seemed in character with the underlying savageness the man represented. Though subtle in nature, he thought he recognized the disconcerting gleam of the fanatic burning within the depths of the man's pupils, much the way hot embers might continue to smolder beneath spent ashes in a seemingly extinguished hearth. He looked at the shoulders and arms and saw the telltale signs of muscular development underlying the sweat-stained long-sleeved shirt that clung snugly to a lean but powerful torso. The dark haft of a long-bladed Bowie knife jutted from a sheath of black leather strapped firmly to his right thigh, and a shoulder holster containing a 9mm Browning P35 rode under his left armpit, both weapons appearing as if they were permanent bodily fixtures. In many ways, here was a man much like himself, tough, ruthless, and when circumstances called for it, cruel and without mercy. He had no doubts the man was exactly what he appeared to be, a warrior.

"Allahu akhbar!" the man greeted him in Arabic.

When a look of incomprehension manifested itself on Ortega's face, the man quickly reverted to English. "God is great, is he not?" he said, then added, "I trust your flight went well."

Although Ortega possessed little patience for idle small talk, nor religious convictions of any significance to acknowledge such pious reverence, the fact that he was now face to face with a supposed ranking member of the Afghan drug trade caused him to curb any impulse toward sarcasm. With the exception of divergent ideologies governing each of them, and that was only speculation on his part, he instinctually sensed a similarity in their core natures. For the time being he would refrain from sardonic replies or mocking comments, something he normally had no compulsions against directing at most people with whom he did business. While a show of sarcasm would generally indicate a total lack of trepidation on his part, it often conveyed a disrespect or contempt of that same person. Such self-styled interaction had a way of invoking fear, and fear made others subservient and eager to please, discouraging the temptation to swindle or deceive.

Though Ortega had a history of doling out insults, his reputation was such that he did not handle barbs well when on the receiving end. Habitually bad-tempered, there had been times when he was in a particularly foul mood, which was often, that he had been known to eradicate an offender for even a misperceived slight, and in a most brutal manner. For some strange reason, he was certain the man standing before him had a violence of temper akin to his own and could not be intimidated. But because he valued the man's affiliation as potentially useful, he preferred keeping him an ally rather than an adversary through unwarranted offense. After all, an Afghan connection would ultimately prove rewarding and most profitable to the Cardoza organization, assuming the man was who he professed to be.

In studying the fierce individual standing before him, Ortega wondered if the fat little broker had purposely withheld any other relevant information. According to Hennington, this meeting had been arranged at the request of the Colonel, who claimed the man to be a representative of an international drug consortium controlling a multi-billion pound supply of heroin stockpiled in Afghanistan. From what he had been told, the man had come to Haiti seeking to provide exclusive rights to the enterprising Colombian drug lord willing to take on the task of distributing huge amounts of *white* heroin, a type of narcotic that is 80 percent pure. Going by the name of Omar, he was looking to do business with only serious-minded people having the available resources to effectively handle vast quantities of such a drug.

Ortega had concurred with Hennington's assessment that only Al Qaeda operatives had enough clout in that part of the world to keep a firm grip on such an enormous stockpile. Smelling rich profits to be had, Ortega readily agreed to meet with Omar at the prescribed place and time, not even bothering to notify his boss, Rafael Cardoza, about the planned rendezvous. Before apprising the drug lord about the meeting, he wanted to ferret out the legitimacy of the offer. For reasons known only to Omar, the man had chosen this desolate chunk of rock.

Ortega realized Omar was studying him intently, expecting some kind of courteous reply to his greeting. "My flights are always enjoyable whenever I am able to mix business with pleasure," he remarked in English, thinking back to his recent grenade-dropping escapade. He beamed with genuine heartfelt delight at the memory. "But tell me," he questioned, continuing to keep his manner cordial, "what is the nature of this meeting?"

Omar seemed a little taken back. "Did your good friend, Mr. Hennington, not inform you?"

Ortega feigned ignorance. "My schedule was such that I was unable to get any details. Perhaps you can elaborate on what you had told Mr. Hennington."

A cloud of suspicion suddenly arose from Omar, and he surveyed his surroundings with the wary, alert eyes of a man expecting an attack from any quarter before focusing his gaze on three ships many miles away along the southwest horizon. "Those ships, they belong to you?"

"To my organization, yes."

"I understand them to be tuna vessels. Is this not so?"

Maintaining his patience, Ortega nodded.

"Your boats, their holds are large enough to accommodate sizeable cargoes?"

"Yes."

"They are outfitted with heavy duty winches capable of lifting ten tons or more?"

Ortega's brows furrowed with impatience. "Yes."

A deep somberness overcame Omar as he seemed to digest this information with the analytical demeanor of a billionaire deciding where to invest his wealth. His black serpentine eyes flicked over to the helicopter pilot who sat alertly at the controls while keeping the engine idling, the aircraft's main rotor continuing to slice the air in a low whooshing pitch. Though Omar's right hand hung loosely, seemingly casually near the haft of the Bowie knife riding his leg, it was all too evident to Ortega that he was prepared to draw it at the slightest hint of danger. Ortega could tell he preferred the use of the blade over the pistol he carried, making him think of Pedro, Cardoza's truculent and all too often fractious nephew. Here was an individual who lived always on the edge, a risk taker. An existence based on subterfuge was a natural way of life to the man.

Satisfied with the answers for the moment, Omar appeared to make a decision. "I represent an Asian group that maintains control of most of the poppy fields in that part of the world. As I am sure you know, processed correctly, poppies can be converted into opium and heroin."

Omar paused to observe Ortega's reaction to his words, but the Colombian remained stolid. "A recent bout of bumper crops during the past several years and improvements in the way the poppies are processed have allowed us to produce excessive amounts of high grade Heroin Number Four, what you might call white heroin."

Omar's eyes never left Ortega's face as he spoke. "My people are looking for a buyer that can undertake the distribution of substantial amounts of this drug." He let the last sentence hang in the air, awaiting a response.

The corners of Ortega's mouth rose in a shrewd grin. Normally he was exceptionally adept at reading people, but it was still possible Omar's proposition was not authentic, that he could very likely be an agent working undercover for the U.S. Drug Enforcement Administration or the ATF. It would not be the first time such agents attempted to entrap him. His instincts, however, told him otherwise, and although he felt he could trust what the man had told him so far to be valid, he would refrain from tipping his hand just yet. "Mr. Hennington may have misled you. I am in the business of catching and exporting tuna, a legitimate enterprise that keeps within the boundaries of international law governing commercial fishing and trade, nothing more."

As if perceiving the preposterousness of Ortega's declaration, Omar did not look the least bit perturbed or disappointed. He reached into a pants pocket and produced a small plastic bag containing a white powdery substance, then held it before him as if dangling an apple before an obstinate donkey. "Perhaps you would be willing to change your mind once you sample the product."

Narrowing his eyes, Ortega stared at the packet with fascination, then abruptly met Omar's penetrating gaze. The man was practically leering at him. "I would think drug trafficking would go against the teachings of Islam," he tested.

The statement seemed to catch Omar off guard and he flushed with irritation, a crazed glint in his eyes.

Emboldened, Ortega decided to probe deeper. "Why would your spiritual leader, Bin Laden, resort to what most Muslims would call a vulgar display of unholiness?"

From the look on Omar's face, he could see that Hennington's assessment had been right on the money. Omar seemed to have great difficulty composing himself and Ortega half expected him to draw the blade at his side out of frustration. Surprisingly, the denial of such an affiliation never left Omar's lips. "Yes, it is true that our great leader has had to advocate the use of such a blasphemous activity, but it is a necessary evil that can only help us achieve our goals."

"And they are?" Ortega pumped.

A humorless smile materialized across Omar's countenance. "Why to raise money to fund our operations. Ridding Muslim lands of Americans and Jews is our primary aim."

"You mean Westerners, don't you? All those you consider to be infidels?" Ortega tested him further. "What makes you think an infidel such as myself would be foolish enough to consider doing business with the organization you represent?"

"Non-Muslims who aid our cause will not be harmed. The will of Allah forbids it."

The way the words were uttered made Omar appear ostentatiously pompous and Ortega almost burst out laughing, but caught himself. Instead, he reached for the bag still clutched by the Islamist. The bag was already open and he dabbed a tiny portion of its contents on his tongue. Although extremely bitter in taste, he suddenly smiled as if assessing a sweet succulent fruit.

Omar did not return Ortega's smile. Ortega could still detect the faint glimmer of the religious zealot emanating from the man's eyes, making the Colombian feel uneasy. It was becoming increasingly difficult for him to remain outwardly affable.

Glancing briefly around him, Ortega wondered how the man had gained access to the higher inland plateau. On the flight in he had ordered the pilot to make one complete low-altitude pass along the fortress-like cliffs skirting the island's 8-kilometer perimeter. There were no sandy beaches and the cliffs, ranging in height from six to twenty meters, dropped directly into the sea and were often undercut, making landings by water impossible in most places. He had not seen any boats near the shoreline or any signs of human habitation, judging the place to be deserted. With the exception of transient Haitian fishermen occasionally using the island as a camping stopover, or a fact-finding scientific expedition, visitors to the island were far and few in between and the place generally remained unoccupied.

The island was actually the remains of an ancient coral reef, a clump of irregular karst protruding above the sea and covering an area slightly over five square kilometers in the shape of a teardrop. Extensive stretches of undulating topography defined by dogtooth limestone made the island inhospitable and perilous to walk along in many locations. Above the encircling escarpments was a lower terrace that had once been mined for phosphates back in the latter half of the nineteenth century, giving the terrain there a crater-pocked landscape, hosting only meager vegetation in the bottoms of the pits. Farther upland there was another set of cliffs that defined an upper terrace, and within the upper terrace dense stands of poisonwood trees predominated.

While reconning the island, Ortega had instructed the pilot to make one low-level pass over the interior, and he was certain he had spotted a footpath that wound its way through the vegetation. The path seemed to run from east to west along the southern side of the upper terrace, terminating in the clearing where he now stood. Only in one area was there a relatively gradual slope between the upper and lower terraces, and that dropped down to the old landing spot where the phosphate ore had once been loaded onto boats, a place designated as Lulu Bay on nautical charts of the island. The name was a misnomer, for it did not resemble a bay at all. From the air Ortega had noticed the ruins of the abandoned workers' settlement at the base of the slope below him, the only location where a determined individual could make their way up a deteriorated ladder consisting of rusted steel and weathered rope in order to reach the higher elevations. If anything, the island seemed uniquely equipped to repel human visitors.

Before this trip, Ortega had taken the liberty of familiarizing himself with the island's past. Its recorded history began in 1504 when Christopher Columbus, stranded on Jamaica, sent some crew members to Hispaniola by canoe for help. Along the way, the men had stumbled upon the island and stopped in search of fresh water. Finding none, they resumed their journey and for the next 350 years mariners avoided the place.

It wasn't until 1857 when the United States claimed the island under the Guano Act. Prized as a powerful fertilizer, guano was actually petrified bird dung, which was in big demand by agriculture before the advent of artificial fertilizers. The Guano Islands Act had been intended to spur American entrepreneurs to seek out and exploit sources of guano. At the time of its enactment, American agriculture was clamoring for this new and much sought fertilizer, particularly Maryland and Virginia farmers whose soil had been decimated by decades of rapacious tobacco and cotton production. This congressional wisdom dictated that any uninhabited, unclaimed island on which a U.S. citizen mined guano would automatically become U.S. property. Under the Act, mining rights could be awarded to any explorer who discovered guano on an uninhabited and otherwise unclaimed island. In other words, once some procedural paperwork had been completed, one could essentially hoist the Stars and Stripes over any desolate island, cay, atoll, key or reef covered in bird droppings.

The Haitian government had protested the U.S. claim, sending a pair of vessels a year later to proclaim that the island and its guano belonged to Haiti, especially since it was located only 40 miles west of Hispaniola's southern peninsula. Upon such encroachment, several U.S. naval vessels were summoned to chase them away. Up to the present day, Haiti still continued to claim sovereignty over the island. The thought that both the wealthiest and poorest nations on the planet would contest an island with its only worth being tons of petrified bird shit had made Ortega laugh aloud when he had first researched it. The fish-filled waters near the island had attracted vast flocks of seabirds, mainly Redfooted Boobies, which roosted and defecated for tens of thousands of years to ultimately produce rich layers of solidified bird dung more than one hundred feet deep in places along the island's perimeter.

Looking eastward, Ortega caught sight of the highest point on the island, an aged lighthouse towering 46 meters above its base and slightly over 120 meters above sea level. Two circular turrets were visible near the top of the structure, the lower one a walk-around observation deck. Built in 1917 by the U.S. Lighthouse Service in response to the opening of the Panama Canal three years earlier, the tall concrete and glass spire had remained essentially unmanned since the time of its automation in 1929. Prior to the automation, a keeper and two assistants had lived on the island in quarters adjacent to the tall structure. Situated in the Windward Passage between Cuba and Haiti, the island presented a hazard to ships plying the waters from the American eastern seaboard to the Canal; thus the installation of a lighthouse had been necessary to warn shipping away. The U.S. Coast Guard had serviced the automatic beacon twice each year since taking it over from the U.S. Lighthouse Service in 1939. During World War II, the U.S. Navy had established an observation post in the lighthouse, but since then the facility had remained essentially unoccupied with the exception of occasional Haitian fishermen passing through.

In 1996 the U.S. Coast Guard had decommissioned the lighthouse in the face of widespread usage of global positioning systems which rendered the beacon obsolete, and a year later the U.S. Department of the Interior assumed control of the island and placed it under its Office of Insular Affairs. Ortega well knew that while the OIA still retained direct authority for the island's political affairs, it was in 1999 that the U.S. Fish and Wildlife Service assumed administrative responsibility for the island, which then became a National Wildlife Refuge. Technically, he was violating the jurisdictional laws of the United States by trespassing on it without the explicit permission of the Fish and Wildlife Service.

Ortega knew the U.S. Coast Guard paid little attention to the waters in the immediate vicinity of the island, patrolling them only infrequently. And when it did, a well paid informant embedded within its ranks always gave him sufficient advance warning as to when and from what direction one of its cutters or aircraft would be coming. Several other high-ranking individuals representing a few other branches of the United States military were also on the Cardoza payroll, greatly reducing the risk of having their activities compromised. Such knowledge made Ortega dizzy with pleasure, for it allowed him to operate in this region of the Caribbean with near impunity.

Shifting his gaze to the broad expanse of sea below him, he could not help but wonder why the fishing near Navassa was so good. From experience he knew that this had not always been the case. Over the last several decades, the great shoals of edible fish within the Caribbean Basin had been decimated by overfishing, forcing the large commercial tuna enterprises to venture into both the Pacific and Atlantic in search of more fruitful fishing grounds. To Ortega, more fish meant increased amounts of legitimate product that was crucial in concealing large quantities of illegal drugs. Greater tonnages of harvested tuna equated to being able to transport vaster amounts of heroin and cocaine more quickly. In Ortega's estimation, he would require huge catches of tuna to effectively hide the magnitude of white heroin that Omar was offering for sale. The record hauls he had seen of late gave him a certain degree of assurance that he could undertake the distribution of such huge drug shipments. For some unknown reason, the local environment abounded with enormous schools of tuna, the largest he had ever seen. Somehow this discovery had eluded competing fishing fleets which were busy elsewhere, thereby giving his organization a monopoly over what the adjacent waters could produce.

Aside from the abundance of tuna plying the immediate sea, Ortega puzzled over another peculiarity he had stumbled upon close to Navassa. It had occurred during a fishing excursion near the island almost six months ago. Just as he had done earlier on this day, he had resorted to the use of concussion grenades during that trip, dropping them into swarming masses of yellowfin and skipjack. Upon hauling in its net, the San Carlo had brought aboard three dead bottlenose dolphins, their gray-toned carcasses intermingled with an incredibly large catch of tuna. The strange thing was, they were unlike any bottlenose he had ever seen before. From all outward appearances they seemed to exhibit all the traits characteristic of their species, with the exception of one striking anomaly. All of them displayed finger-like appendages protruding from the underside of their pectoral flukes. A close examination of those appendages had shown them to be retractable. The significance of the find had stunned him and, never one to miss the smell of potential profits, he had carefully measured and photographed the creatures, documenting details of the odd protuberances from every angle before storing the bodies in deep freeze within the San Carlo's hold.

The unusual find had taken place just before he had decided to dispose of the stubborn IATTC observer stationed aboard his vessel. As of yet the

IATTC had failed to provide a replacement for the murdered observer, which was quite all right with Ortega, and the San Carlo was still without one.

Considering it important that he keep the San Carlo's participation in the discovery of the freak dolphins anonymous, he had given the photos of the creatures to Hennington, instructing the broker to find a buyer for their frozen remains. Amazingly, and to Ortega's intense satisfaction, Hennington had succeeded.

Standing before Omar, Ortega stifled a grin thinking about how quickly Hennington had found a prospective purchaser, an individual that went by the name of McPherson. According to Hennington, the man was willing to offer the equivalent of a king's ransom for a live and fully intact specimen of this new type of dolphin. McPherson was a high-ranking U.S. Naval officer. Yes, Ortega thought, things were going exceptionally well lately.

And if he could capture just one of those creatures alive, he might have a most useful bargaining chip for further and more lucrative transactions.

As Ortega pondered all this, he became aware of Omar's penetrating stare. The Islamist was awaiting an answer.

"Perhaps we can do business," Ortega said, managing to suppress his excitement by keeping his manner and tone neutral.

- 13 -

The small pod of white dolphin slowed as it came to within three miles of the squat mount jutting above the sea, the lone human female riding its center fully sensing the pain of the pod's injured cousins. Like a homing beacon, the distress of the wounded was easy to follow, emanating steadily from a point directly ahead. As though they were of one mind, the girl and the pack attuned their thoughts further, thus reducing the possibility of missing their intended target in so vast an ocean. Fleeting visual images continued to impinge on their consciousness, intertwined with intermittent twinges of suffering and panic that rose and fell like the ebb and flow of a rapidly moving tide, pulsing stronger as they neared their destination. While the sensation greatly dispirited the group, they pushed on with tenacious resolution.

Within a short interlude a sonic holographic picture was sent their way from one being in particular, its familiar signature whistle identifying itself and providing the pod with additional information on the calamity that had befallen its comrades. Although unnecessary, the pod answered back in kind, millions of years of evolutionary conditioning causing instinct to override and frequently conflict with newly developed abilities. A sudden burst of rapid-fire speak-see clicks triggered at frequencies approximating 160,000 hertz was suddenly sent forth in a tightly directed beam by the laryngeal emitters of every member of the group ringing the girl. Almost instantaneously, the returning echoes were processed by highly sophisticated brains. Deciphering the complex sounds into symbols and pictures, they confirmed the presence of seven other bottlenose dolphin, five males and two females. Among these creatures, four were physically impaired, two severely. All were adults except for a juvenile male which remained unharmed.

Once again, the use of such old fashioned biophysical processing was unnecessary. The girl and every member of her pod would have seen and felt the plight of their laboring cousins anyway.

On a microscopic structural level, the brain of each animal in the pack was at least as advanced as the human brain, with cell counts just as high per cubic millimeter and the number of layers in their brain cortex equally as great. However, in the last four generations of this new breed of dolphin, the number of cells interconnected to one another had increased by one-third over the average human brain, giving them extraordinary powers of the mind. Strangely, the girl's brain also manifested this same anomaly, something passed onto her from her mother, providing her with a telepathic link not only to the creatures surrounding her, but to others with similar genetic traits. Such an attribute had made it possible for her and her companions to align their thoughts and emotions into harmonic resonance, allowing them to achieve a mental synergy well beyond the grasp of scientific explanation.

As the other dolphins came into visual range, two paired teams of adults could be seen supporting the two most injured, each team using their heads and snouts to buoy up one of the badly wounded creatures high enough so that its blowhole remained clear of the water. If they failed to do this, the creatures would drown.

Both of the succored dolphins were grays. Each of the assisting pairs contained one albino dolphin. Although one of the albinos was mildly injured, the other was unscathed. Altogether, the adults consisted of two albinos and four grays, all bottlenose. One of the assisting grays displayed a lacerated pectoral fluke and was teamed with an uninjured albino. The injured albino was teamed with an uninjured gray. The girl could sense that both dolphins being supported were fending off unconsciousness from internal trauma. Her heart went out to the juvenile albino, little more than four years old, flitting among the adults in confusion and panic.

The girl opened her mind to the eddies in time and space swirling about her, currents caused by past events and events yet to come. A powerful malevolence had passed this way and would soon come again, and she intuitively knew they had little time with which to lend assistance.

Breaking formation, the two dolphins leading the girl's pod shot forward to help. Hermes was a male, Aphrodite a female. Both grays being kept afloat were in critical condition, and like all cetaceans, their respiratory mechanisms were totally voluntary. Unlike most land-based mammals whose breathing systems were automatic and involuntary when unconscious, dolphins could not afford to have such a mechanism. If they did it would cause them to breathe water while submerged in an unconscious state. For a cetacean, passing out for any reason in the open sea was dangerous and usually fatal if left unattended. They needed to be awake to breathe. And because of it, a voluntary breathing system created an interdependency among dolphins and among whales if they were to survive. A seriously incapacitated cetacean had to rely on his fellow creatures to bring him to the surface and keep him awake in order that he inhale, otherwise he dies.

The girl watched the rescue unfold as Hercules, the abnormally big male she rode, dipped below the surface in the crystal-clear water. One of the endangered grays, a female, appeared to be slipping into coma. Hercules' fine beam sonar verified that the gray had ceased breathing. Inconsolable, her young calf shot back and forth close by, squealing forlornly at the physical distress of its mother.

Continuing her mind meld with those of her companions, the girl sensed the parlous condition almost as quickly as did the albinos. Ultrasonic scans of both supported creatures revealed significant hemorrhaging among their internal organs, particularly in the lungs, and every so often, a fine pink mist would spew forth from blowholes bubbling with red froth. But now nothing emanated from the nostrils of the female. Hastily, Aphrodite squeezed deftly between the two dolphins supporting the unconscious gray, raking her dorsal fin across the anal region of the comatose creature. The contact caused an involuntary reflex contraction of the gray's pectoral flukes and seemed to revive her. Persisting in keeping the ailing dolphin conscious, Aphrodite kept nudging the female with her rostrum.

Something further out caught the girl's attention, just a faint nudge on her consciousness. Coral and Reef had detected it, a miniscule trace of unpropitious presentiment wafting in like the aroma of rotting flesh. Apollo and Artemis were the first to assess its significance. Several large tiger sharks were being drawn inexorably to the scene by the scent of blood and the physical distress. Though they were still several hundred meters off, she sensed them as if they were within arms reach. Abruptly, Apollo and Artemis, the brother-sister twins forming the rear guard of the albino pod, veered off sharply in opposite directions to discourage and divert the advancement of the pelagic predators.

The girl was not concerned about the safety of the duo as they disappeared from sight into the submarine murk. From firsthand experience she knew they and the rest of the albinos displayed exceptional athletic abilities that surpassed those of the common bottlenose strain. Superior muscular development and greater natural speed coupled with enhanced cerebral intelligence and a heightened physical endurance over and above their gray cousins made them a formidable match for any large and ferocious oceanic carnivore. According to Jacob, if not for the environmental abuses proliferated by man, and barring any cataclysmic natural disasters, the new breed would, in all likelihood, survive and continue to proliferate under any other circumstances.

The beings that comprised the girl's pod were implausible creations of nature. Superbly sleek and marvelously agile, Hermes was the fastest of the lot and could explode through the sea with an acceleration unequaled by his companions. It was not unusual for him to leap to a height of twenty meters above the sea when frolicking exuberantly with the others of the group or when seeking a bird's eye view of the sea around them. His graceful and energetic displays of aerial acrobatics were fantastic sights to behold, and the girl never tired of watching, always awed by each performance. Whereas Hermes was the personification of blazing speed and unparalleled agility, his twin sister, Aphrodite, was the embodiment of empathic clairvoyance and psychic healing. Her extraordinarily loving and compassionate nature gave her a distinct aura that resonated to all members of the pod like a lambent jewel, and the girl constantly delighted in the gentle and disparate caress of her astral presence, which was always the most soothing among any of her kind.

The youngest members of the pack, Apollo and Artemis, were the most analytical and calculating among them, and their healing prowess was only surpassed by that of Aphrodite. They were always the quickest to interpret the meaning of psychic anomalies that occasionally permeated the fabric of four-dimensional space surrounding them and which drifted just beyond the boundaries of physical awareness.

Coral and Reef, the flanking members of the pod's traveling formation, were the holistic thinkers within their ranks, providing philosophical guidance to the clan whenever it was confronted with a moral dilemma. They were always the backdrop of reason and wisdom to those of their ilk. The two of them were the only ones that could read Jacob's thoughts with any degree of consistency. They were the oldest of the three pairs of twins comprising the immediate group and the most adept at being able to sense impending danger. Coral was the female of the pair and Reef her brother.

The most prodigious among them, Hercules, was the manifestation of awesome strength and raw power, exhibiting inordinately thick muscular development throughout the length of his massive body. Incredibly, the albino bull was considerably larger than his counterparts and stronger than any orca having a body size twice his length and thrice his weight, measuring slightly over five and a half meters from the tip of his beak to the end of his tail fluke. The extra drag the girl caused him was no more than an afterthought. Known as the gentle giant of the pod, his characteristically mild temperament would transform radically to one of cold, measured belligerence at the slightest threat confronting the group, most particularly one directed at the girl.

The girl had hoped the rescue would go unimpeded, but all her senses told her otherwise. Jacob still lagged far behind and the pinnace would be needed to bring the incapacitated dolphins to safety. She felt deep compassion for her ailing friends, understanding completely their fear and revulsion of drowning at sea or becoming a meal for the predators that abounded in it because they were too weak to escape or defend themselves. When sick or significantly injured, or when death was inevitable, a deep-seated primeval calling always drew them unrelentingly to the land, the place of their primordial origins where their ancient ancestors once flourished. They would much prefer to perish under the light of the sun or moon on a remote sandy shore rather than in the cold, dark depths of the ocean. The land always beckoned under such circumstances and accounted for the beaching of untold numbers of dolphin ever since they first ventured into antediluvian seas in aeons past. By beaching themselves or entering the very shallow water of a protected estuary or lagoon, they at least had a chance to recover from their illness, secure from the threat of sharks and other predators. But out here in these waters she knew there was no immediate safe haven where they could bring the enervated dolphins. She was quite familiar with the nearby island, knowing that its surrounding cliffs rising directly from the sea provided no shelves, beaches or inlets. What the island did hold, however, was the key to the ultimate salvation of the dolphins. That it might also benefit the future welfare of the human race was also a strong possibility, for the secret it held was truly a blessing.

As Hercules breached, the girl looked around hopefully. Although she could feel Jacob's presence, there was still no sight of him. The outline of another vessel in the distance caught her eye. Different in configuration from the pinnace and much larger in size, she realized it was the same vessel the pod had overtaken a short time earlier. Although the proximity of a strange vessel would typically make her feel uneasy, she sensed that it posed no threat. Under normal circumstances, the pod would have exercised caution and steered clear of marine traffic, knowing that a human observer might consider the sight of it highly unusual considering a human female rode one of the creatures in its midst. Such an event might induce a curious sailor to pursue the pack for a closer look, something Jacob had warned her about. According to him, one could never be fully sure of the intentions of strangers since they might potentially bring harm to members of the pod. Therefore it would be prudent to avoid contact with unknown humans at sea altogether. But this was an emergency, and the pod had felt it necessary to take a direct route to its stricken cousins if they were to have any chance at all of saving them. Although passing in full view of the boat's crew had been a risk, it had nevertheless been one worth taking.

A strange feeling had come over her when the pod had come close to the other boat. She remembered the name painted on its stern. It was an odd name, a contradiction. *Angels* were supposed to be endowed with goodness, perfect spiritual beings that were kind and loving. *Avenging* implied a retaliatory punishment or payback for harm received, an act of evil, of wickedness. How could an angel harbor such a malicious trait? Wouldn't it be incongruous with a morally pure nature? Didn't Jesus tell everyone to turn the other cheek? Wasn't he the one who promoted the golden rule: Do unto others as you would have them do unto you? She momentarily puzzled over these fleeting thoughts, vaguely aware that her musing didn't go unnoticed by the other members of the clan. Her mind was still linked synchronously with them and she sensed their confusion over the diametrically opposed and conflicting concepts, particularly the latter idea. Such turpitude went against the grain of their inherent makeup.

She recalled that there had been six men aboard the Avenging Angel, three of them gawking oddly at her from the open doorway of the pilothouse. Other than her mother, Jacob and the villagers of Malique, she had seldom run into others of her kind. Jacob had instilled in her that most of the world's ills were caused by human greed. Was it not man who was slowly but methodically killing off the dolphins and whales, he had often reminded her. Were not humans responsible for overfishing the oceans with vast nets and poisoning the waters with toxic wastes, garbage and organic pollution. Man was an out of control virus that, if left to his own vices and thoughtless actions, would eventually consume the earth, ultimately destroying all its beautiful wonders.

During her young life, the girl had seen many of her aquatic friends injured and killed by the abuses of man, most often due to carelessness and ignorance, but sometimes because of a thing Jacob referred to as sadism. Although it was a trait indigenous to some human beings, it was something she was ill prepared to conceive of, a notion totally alien to her. Jacob had tried to explain it to her but it was a concept that escaped her like water slipping through her fingers. The idea that a person could experience pleasure by deliberately inflicting pain or death on another living creature was a notion she had trouble grasping. But as she glanced over at her debilitated comrades, a dawning comprehension took hold of her and she suddenly knew they had been disabled by such an act.

As the girl watched the approach of the strange vessel, Jacob's words rang clearly in her head. *We humans are still fighting each other, destroying more than we are creating. There are some people who want to gain, not only at the expense of other humans, but other living organisms, as well. Mankind has evolved to the point where it has made great strides in many things. It has sent men to the moon and the deepest part of the ocean, it has made tremendous breakthroughs in physics and medicine, yet it has failed miserably in mastering its own human nature. Humanity is using its abilities incorrectly and causing terrible damage to our planet and all its inhabitants in the process. Man is still insufficiently developed to protect and care for the world we live in.* She was only six years old when he told her this, but the words stayed with her as if he had uttered them yesterday.

She vividly remembered the place where he had given her this moralization. She had been sitting in the pinnace as it chugged along the coast many miles south of the cove. She had looked questioningly at Jacob. "What is that?" Jacob had shielded his eyes from the sun and followed her gaze. A vast quantity of plastic containers and garbage littered the nearby beach, most of it washed in with the tide. A look of distaste crossed Jacob's features as he eyed the waste. "This is Haiti, little one. If the land could speak it would tell of tragedy and abuse, of power and greed, violence and bloodshed." She realized then how ugly the world could be beyond the beautiful sanctity of the cove.

It was shortly thereafter that her real education had begun, but it wasn't until she turned ten that they had initiated the project. "You and your playmates were put on this earth to fulfill a profound and far reaching purpose," Jacob had told her solemnly on her birthday. "Mother Nature is a wise old lady. Perhaps in her infinite wisdom she has seen fit to place the care of this planet in the hands of more responsible creatures." He had paused and let out a great sigh. "And I believe she has chosen you and your friends. The time for intervention has arrived." Even then, at so young an age, she had instinctively comprehended what he had meant.

With the exception of her mother, she was certain she was the only human on the planet that truly understood the mind and soul of the dolphin, to revel in the joy of simply being. She was completely aware of their dual existence, knowing that these incredible creatures simultaneously dwelt within two realms, one of the mind and one of the spirit. For some inexplicable reason, this duality was also indelibly ingrained in her, and like her companions, she understood the multifaceted light of love, the most powerful force in creation.

She fathomed its pure energy that was capable of transcending all barriers, both material and ethereal, perceiving its endless flow from an eternal, infinite waterfall. It was a ceaseless, all encompassing radiance that set no conditions or boundaries, streaming forth unconfined and without limits. And it was firmly rooted in who she was, integrated into her soul, her very essence.

She could feel this same energy, its purity and simplicity, emanating outward from all the pod members, blanketing and imbuing the stricken dolphins, and she added that which was a part of her astral being into the discharge. On a spiritual level, unconditional love radiated forth and intensified, becoming greater than the combined total of their individual outputs. But on a physical level, the biosonar wave emissions originating from those closest to the wounded creatures created a cavitation, a rippling effect in the matter comprising the damaged flesh. The resonance of the impaired tissue changed and healing suddenly accelerated. Even Jacob could not provide a satisfactory scientific explanation as to why it worked, but she knew it did.

On both planes of existence, spiritual and physical, the girl and her clan avoided absorbing the greater portion of the pain of the injured, for a requisite amount of detachment on their part had to be exercised if their ministrations were going to be effective. She knew the danger of integrating too much pain and suffering into the minds and souls of the healers. Doing so could easily overwhelm, pulling the potential healer under tumultuous emotions that should not be their own to bear. This was a lesson carried down and expanded upon over the ages among cetaceans, and then further refined by the new breed. She understood that neither the healer's soul nor the one for whom they are absorbing the pain is ultimately served by such actions, for no soul can do this for another since we are all here to journey our own path. If this tenet were overlooked or ignored, then the assisting soul risks being pulled down and drowned in a quagmire of suffering, and the one they desire to assist is denied the life lessons they were sent here to learn. Thus the need for an adequate level of restraint to take on the full brunt of the pain of another.

The girl was proud of her relationship with these noble beings. She knew it was unique, that a special bond existed between them that transcended time and space. Their boundless sensitivity and awareness continually amazed her. Her companions were fully awakened creatures who knew themselves to be one with all things and they experienced this through the power of love at all times. Their minds transported them into unlimited consciousness, carrying them beyond earthly restraints. Their physical bodies resonated with unconditional love and limitless energy, filling them with ecstasy and unconstrained joy. They understood the key to oneness and harmony. They shared love at all times and held no judgements. Their use of sound went well beyond current medical technology, making them able to alter frequencies to create the most appropriate healing actions for the sick and injured in the water with them, seeing inside the being and manipulating the required energies perfectly. She knew without a doubt their blissful presence and loving nature was capable of healing wounds of the heart and opening the spirit to portals of boundless freedom. On spiritual planes, they were powerful and creative guides, using geometry, sound and light to inspire higher awareness, clear consciousness, and pure wisdom.

The girl's awareness was suddenly brought back to the strange vessel as it neared, and she studied it with a mix of uncertainty and …something else. A transference of psychic warning echoed from Coral and Reef simultaneously. Hercules turned sharply and the girl looked below her. A dark shadow glided through the depths far below, holding to a course bearing directly at the island. Too deep for the sunlight filtering into the void of inky hydrospace to provide definition to the object, it remained indistinct to her human eyes as it traveled on a straight and level heading. Her current position was a significant distance from the island and the underlying water was still quite deep.

Biosonar emissions from her companions were quickly directed at the strange object and an image of the thing suddenly flashed in her mind. It was large, very large, having an overall length almost as great as that of a fully-grown blue whale and a configuration just as streamlined. But it lacked the characteristics consistent with living flesh. Rather than being soft and pliant in texture, the object was rigid and metallic, a thing fabricated by human hands, a submarine. The girl had never seen one before and wondered what such a machine was doing out in these waters. A thought suddenly galvanized her. *What if the people piloting the strange craft were to find the undersea cavern and discover its secret?* A feeling of dread began to engulf her and she quickly shook it off. Her eyes followed the shadow a few moments longer before all traces of it vanished into the dark blue murk.

By the time Hercules again breached, the girl found herself looking up into the faces of several men leaning over the side of the surface vessel that had followed her pod. Sensing no menace from them, she stared silently back, not knowing what to do next.

"I believe you and your friends can use some help," the man in the middle called to her, a thick shock of white hair cascading down to his shoulders from beneath a baseball cap and a smile parting his lips.

Something about the man struck a chord deep within her, perhaps the lilt of his voice. Somehow it conveyed solace, reassurance. Without immediately realizing what she was doing, however, her gaze was drawn to the face of the man standing to the left of the older gent. She found it difficult to pull her eyes away from those penetrating green orbs.

"Are you a friend of Natalie?" the white-haired man asked.

The question stunned the girl and she stared back intently at the elderly man, sitting up straighter as Hercules floated docilely beneath her. Only a handful of people knew the names of her friends, including the man who had saved Natalie.

"Are you the man who rescued Natalie and tended her injuries?" the girl queried in a mellifluous voice. The man fit the description Natalie had given her and she studied him with newfound respect.

"Yes. My name is Franklin Grahm...Doctor Franklin Grahm," the scientist said exuberantly, looking hopefully to the other creatures floating close by. "Is Natalie with you now?"

Pivoting her head, the girl took inventory of the other men perched on the deck above her, her eyes flitting from one face to the next, seeming to gain some insight as to the true essence of each persona aboard the vessel. Her gaze came back to linger on Grahm for several more seconds before settling on Jake once again. "Natalie is not among this group," she said at last, her voice containing an unmistakable sadness.

It was then that she lifted the goggles from her eyes, letting them rest on her forehead. Jake noticed that the goggles were actually a low-volume facemask with a nosepiece that allowed the wearer to equalize the air pressure behind the two separate eye plates with the surrounding water pressure. He also noted that even after prolonged immersion in the sea, there was a healthy glow to the girl's creamy complexion, which was smooth and unblemished. Amazingly, the goggles left no temporary imprint on the skin surrounding a large pair of doe-like eyes that glistened a sparkling brown and which stared back serenely as if regarding the world beyond from a strange and alien perspective. Gazing into them was like focusing on a revolving prism subjected to the light, mesmerizing the beholder with a variegated spectrum of endless mystery. On the whole, however, it was her eyes that gave definition to a face of protracted innocence and limitless compassion, uncorrupted by cynicism or the darker side of man's nature.

Silence hung heavily in the air a moment longer before Grahm spoke again. "If you'll allow us, my dear, we can bring your injured friends aboard and treat their wounds."

The girl continued to stare steadfastly at Jake, appearing inattentive to the offer. "Thank you, but that will not be necessary. Help will be here shortly." As if to emphasize this, she withdrew her eyes from Jake and glanced over her shoulder.

In unison, Jake, Grahm and Zimbola looked in the direction of the girl's gaze. A tiny white dot sat on the eastern horizon, still a considerable distance away.

"Is there anything we can do for you?" Grahm persisted, disappointment apparent in both his tone and manner.

The girl shook her head, her eyes now fixed on the approaching boat.

"What is your name?" Grahm continued to press.

The girl brought those doe-like eyes to bear on Grahm once again. "My name is of no importance." Her voice was soft and melodious, almost childlike in timbre.

Grahm smiled warmly. "Sometimes names can be very important," he said tactfully, touching Jake's shoulder. "This gentleman, here, goes by the name of Jake Javolyn. He is the captain of this vessel." He looked to his left. "This rather large fellow is Zimbola, Captain Javolyn's first mate." Looking aft, Grahm indicated the other members of the crew, introducing Hector, Phillipe, and his two assistants. Turning back to face the girl, Grahm's manner became imbued with alacrity. "Now that I've introduced everyone, good social etiquette can only be satisfied if you introduce yourself, as well."

The girl studied Grahm with renewed interest before replying. "I'm called Destiny."

The name did not surprise Jake. As a matter of fact, it provided the missing piece of the puzzle he had been mulling over concerning Grahm's conversations with Natalie. *The future of her kind was in the hands of Destiny,* Natalie had told Grahm. This had not gone over Jake's head and he had not ruled out the possibility that the reference to destiny might involve a person. With mild amusement, Jake watched the expression on the doctor's face unfold. The false assumption Grahm had previously harbored lifted like a curtain on a Broadway stage to reveal a hidden truth, and the doctor nodded at the girl with sudden understanding.

Grahm let his eyes drift over the other nearby sea mammals. "Tell me, my dear, did you teach all of these dolphins to speak English as fluently as Natalie?"

Destiny's face turned passive. "I didn't teach them anything."

A cloud of confusion swept across the scientist's countenance. "Then how did Natalie acquire this ability?"

"She-," the girl started to say, but stopped abruptly. Her eyes seemed to glaze over in that instant, as if listening to an inner voice. Although she continued to stare directly at Grahm, the doctor had the impression she was not seeing him at all, that she was looking right through him.

"Natalie's in trouble," she said suddenly, her voice carrying an edge of urgency. "I must go to her."

As Jake and the others watched, the large white dolphin the girl rode began to turn away, but Destiny glanced back at the three men grouped together next to the pilothouse. "A man will be here shortly. His name is

Jacob," she cried out, her tone almost pleading. "Please help him recover my injured friends." Her eyes singled Jake out as she said this, as if speaking to him alone. Refitting the facemask over her eyes, she hunched forward and reached down on each side of Hercules broad body to grasp a rein looped over the base of each pectoral fin. She quickly sped away on a southwest heading, unattended by her previous retinue.

Jake ducked into the pilothouse and retrieved a pair of binoculars, bringing them to his eyes and aligning them with several objects far away. He didn't need the spyglasses to distinguish the outlines of the three ships hanging on the horizon, estimating the nearest one to be only two miles distant. The binoculars, however, confirmed something else. Satisfied, he lowered the glasses, handing them over to Zimbola while continuing to keep his gaze locked on the closest vessel. "You recognize anything about that ship?" he asked.

Zimbola lifted the binoculars to his eyes and scanned the vessel, the instrument looking ridiculously small in his huge paw. The big man nodded. "It is the Colombian tuna trawler we saw in the harbor yesterday. Her crew is just beginning to drop her net."

Without wasting another second, Jake craned his head over the gunwale and shouted aft, calling to Hector and Phillipe. Both men stood gawking at Destiny's receding form. "Prepare the Kawasaki," Jake ordered.

"With everything?" Hector shot back, clearly perplexed. The crew knew that Jake only used the Kawasaki during a Code One which, based on experience, always occurred at night. Code One implied fully armed.

"Everything!" Jake growled. "I want it fully locked and loaded."

Zimbola appeared taken back, and he stared down at Jake questioningly.

"What are you doing?" Grahm asked.

Jake halted in mid stride. "I don't know what's going on, but something tells me I better help that girl before she buys herself a whole heap of trouble she's not ready to take on." As an afterthought, he turned back toward Zimbola. "After I launch, stay here on station."

Eyebrows rose up on the big man. "You do not want me to follow?"

"You heard the girl," Jake bellowed. "She wants us to assist a guy called Jacob."

- 14 -

As the pinnace crept closer to the distant island, Jacob's thoughts continued to drift back to earlier times. Subsequent to the landslide that had thwarted the Tonton Makout raid on Malique and Amphitrite's ensuing collapse at the ancient mapou tree, he had been confronted with carrying her limp body to safety. At first he had sought to move her back to the cove but then realized her gravid state ruled out such an endeavor. Attempting to move her by himself down the ladders anchored to the cove's steep walls would have been too risky for her and her baby.

Having lifted her from the ground and cradled her in his arms, he knew the only logical place to bring her would be the nearby village. Trudging along with her inert form up and down the hilly trail had been an undertaking that had taken him to the absolute limits of his endurance, and every so often he had to stop to rest, lowering her body gently to the ground. The last thing he wanted was to stumble and drop her. Wearily, with biceps, shoulders and back burning with fatigue, he had eventually made it to the village. Staggering with his burden to the front door of Baptiste's humble abode, he had kicked at it loudly with his foot. A good ten seconds of hushed silence had prevailed before Jacob was forced to repeat the action, and then he had heard movement inside.

"Who comes to my home in the middle of the night?" a groggy but wary voice had questioned in French from the other side of the door.

"It is me, your cousin Jacob," he had answered in the same language, his tone faltering and all his reserves nearly gone.

Baptiste had opened the door a crack and peeked outside. Seeing Jacob with the comatose white woman, his eyes had widened with surprise and he had hastily ushered them inside. Baptiste's wife, Lucette, had been at Jacob's side in a flash and, with her and her husband assisting, they quickly had Amphitrite lying comfortably in a cot.

So vibrant was the memory that Jacob became lost in the full range of its scope, and he was suddenly reliving it once again and correlating the experience with other items of significance. Baptiste turned his full attention back to Jacob. "Who is this woman, Jacob? What has happened to her?"

Jacob found a chair and seated himself, too exhausted to speak as yet. He was still breathing hard from his physical ordeal.

"Have you no eyes, Emmanuel?" Lucette interceded. "Can you not see your cousin is trying to catch his breath?" She ran from the room and returned several moments later, handing Jacob a tall glass of water. Greedily, he quaffed it down.

Both Emmanuel and Lucette eyed him expectantly, their gazes implacable as owls in an aviary waiting to be fed succulent mice by the keeper. "Your village has been targeted by Duvalier's thugs," Jacob wheezed, his speech barely understandable. "This woman managed to stop them."

Baptiste and his wife looked at one another, their expressions muddled.

Jacob felt his strength returning and he found his voice again. "The hill where the sacred mapou tree sits has partially collapsed and blocked the road leading to this village. It triggered a mudslide that prevented the Tonton Makout from coming here."

Baptiste still appeared confused. "A moment ago you said this woman stopped them." He turned to glance at Amphitrite's still form. She seemed to be sleeping peacefully. He swiveled his head back and his mouth took on the shape of a silly smile. "Did she cause the mudslide?" his query saturated with doubt.

The directness and simplicity of the question rocked Jacob. Both he and his cousin were analytical thinkers. Growing up in a society characterized by superstition and antiquated beliefs, the two of them had refused to accept such indoctrination at fairly early ages, considering such credence to exceed the bounds of reason and belonging to another time and place. Emmanuel had long ago cast off the shackles of such dogma, proclaiming that such thinking belonged to the ignorant.

Jacob was suddenly at a loss for words. Here he was, about to describe something inexplicable, something seemingly miraculous. How did he explain that Amphitrite had simply placed her hand on the tree and caused the hill to come down? Was it mere coincidence? How improbable was such a two-sided happening. In this case logic was ambivalent towards supporting a relationship between the two distinct and what could be considered mutually exclusive incidents. On the one hand Emmanuel could argue that the recent heavy rains wrought by the hurricane had made the hill unstable, thus setting the stage for the inevitable mudslide, a condition that would remain unconnected in any way with Amphitrite's contact with the mapou. He wondered what the odds were for such a confluence of supposedly unrelated actions, the touching of the tree and the collapse of the hill, to occur at nearly the same time. Jacob was certain Emmanuel would reject any suggestion of causality. In an orderly universe, logic dictated that an interrelationship between both events was contrary to nature, a cause and effect duality that defied the impossible. But he had seen it with his own eyes and could not refute it. The woman's precognition he could accept as lying within the realm of possibility and therefore would have no difficulty elucidating upon. There was a wealth of scientific evidence to support it. In retrospect, there was no satisfactory explanation for initiating a mudslide by placing one's hand upon a tree…unless. He looked sharply at the unconscious woman. Unless one accepted the premise that Amphitrite was endowed with telekinetic powers. From experience, he knew Emmanuel would consider such a possibility as being absurd.

Jacob found himself nodding slowly in reply to Emmanuel's question, a gesture laden with diffidence. He was not fully prepared to shrug off the skepticism his words were sure to prompt. "How she was able to do it, I cannot account for," was all he offered, his tone betraying the reticence he felt.

Emmanuel absorbed this information quietly, peering owlishly over his glasses at Jacob. "Who is this woman, Jacob?" he finally asked. "She is unfamiliar to me."

Jacob's mind changed gears. "A dolphin brought her to the cove where I live. She-"

A stifled cry left Lucette's lips and she brought a hand to her mouth, her eyes huge and penetrating, staring at Jacob as if he were a ghostly apparition.

Agitated, Emmanuel turned to face her. "What is wrong, woman?"

"Esmerelda's prophecy!"

"What are you talking about?"

Lucette pulled her eyes from Jacob and took hold of her husband's arm, glancing behind her at the sleeping woman. "It is just as Esmerelda prophesied."

Emmanuel's expression went blank. "I do not understand."

Swallowing hard, Lucette said excitedly, "The day before your grandmother's death, she told me a white woman would come from the sea riding a dolphin. She said that once this woman arrived upon our shore, life as we knew it would change forever."

Jacob was stunned. This was a revelation that caught him totally by surprise. But he was sure Lucette would not mislead Emmanuel with such a story for she had been very close with Esmerelda and would have been privy to many of her thoughts.

Emmanuel suddenly appeared angry. "My grandmother was both the practitioner and victim of archaic cultural beliefs rooted in witchcraft. Her predictions of the future rarely amounted to anything more than generalizations that could be applied to any situation under most circumstances."

Jacob listened to the diatribe with analytical interest, understanding Emmanuel well enough to know that his words lacked sufficient conviction.

Emmanuel refocused his attention back on Jacob. His countenance remained clouded. "Please go on. Pay no mind to the ravings of my wife who still insists upon holding onto primitive tenets and outmoded consuetude. The prognostications of Esmerelda held no significant meaning."

A play of emotion rippled across Lucette's face. "How can you say such a horrible thing?" she decried. "Your grandmother loved you." Her gaze swept back to Jacob, her eyes glistening with moisture and foreshadowing tears. "She loved all of us." She spread out her arms. "She loved this village. She protected Malique with her vaudun."

Emmanuel's petulance turned to exasperation. "Did her vaudun warn of the storm that nearly wrecked our village?" he countered, the sting in his voice abating a notch. "Did it save five of our fishermen that perished in it?" Pausing for effect, Emmanuel brought more venom back into his tone, slamming home a final point like a hammer blow. "Did it save her?"

The first tears trickled down Lucette's cheeks. "Her magic spared us from Duvalier's assassins when others were not so fortunate. Even now we are still protected. Did not your cousin just tell you the Tonton Makout were stopped from reaching this place?"

Emmanuel threw his arms up in frustration. "Why must you be so bullheaded, woman?" Abruptly he turned back to Jacob. "Are you sure the Tonton were coming here?"

A wave of heat surged up the back of Jacob's neck, its flame threatening to climb onto his face. An intense feeling of discomfort washed over him and he looked away to conceal the chagrin that was rapidly eating away at his composure. "I can not substantiate that," was all he could bring himself to say.

"Then how can you be certain this village was in any danger?" Emmanuel grumbled with annoyance.

"She saw it in a dream," Jacob riposted, gesturing toward the still unconscious Amphitrite.

Two years Jacob's senior, Emmanuel grew momentarily quiet, his eyes filled with reprobation, magnified further by his owlish spectacles. His reply was cold and harsh. "I would have thought that you of all people would have known better. You-"

"Her dream was precognitive in nature," Jacob interrupted, spitting out the words in protest. "This woman never met you or had any previous knowledge of you, yet she heard your name in a dream, a dream that told her the Tonton Makout were coming to kill you this very night."

"Most dreams never equate to reality. Their contents rarely transpire in the real world, and hardly ever the way we remember them when they do. Nightmares are especially unlikely to play out the way they were dreamt. Could it be that you had mentioned my name in conversation and it reemerged in her nightmare? How can you be sure Duvalier's assassins were coming here at all?"

Too tired to become argumentative, Jacob kept his voice level. "Would you have preferred me to ignore her vision altogether and do nothing. The value I place on your life and this village is too high for me not to have taken any action at all."

Jacob paused, letting the full impact of his words sink in. "No, your name was never brought up in conversation prior to her dream. You know as well as

I that dreams can often foretell the future. Sometimes they are prophetic. But sometimes they act as a warning against approaching danger, often providing us with a course of action to follow in order to avoid the threat. Earlier on this night, the white woman awoke from a sound sleep in a highly emotional state. She was very concerned for your safety and the safety of this village. She saw the men and the trucks traveling along the road that leads here and described them to me. She referred to them as the Tonton Makout and asked me what the name meant. She even described the sacred mapou tree as well as the remnants of the old well next to it."

A scowl broke out on Emmanuel's face. "There is nothing sacred about that tree."

Jacob disregarded the remark, noting Lucette's dismay before continuing. "Though she had never laid eyes on the tree nor had any awareness of its existence before the dream, she knew the hill from which it grew was unstable enough to cause a mudslide capable of destroying the convoy of trucks."

"You saw this convoy?"

"Yes. Even before we reached the hill, she told me four trucks led by a jeep would be coming. My own eyes confirmed her description to be accurate."

Emmanuel pursed his lips and nodded, a slow, almost imperceptible acknowledgement of Jacob's story. Although his cousin's previous testiness was rapidly evaporating, Jacob could tell he was not entirely convinced about the dream's accuracy or validity. "Then tell me, cousin," Emmanuel continued to probe, a shrewd gleam in his eyes, "how this woman was able to cause the mudslide at just the right moment?"

Jacob mentally winced. Emmanuel was a master at locating the pivotal point in any argument. Like a bloodhound, he always seemed to sniff out the possible flaws in the fabric of truth, the areas where the subtle scent of controversy was strongest and could be exploited.

Remaining steadfast, Jacob refused to alter what he had witnessed. "Just before the convoy passed the hill, the woman reached out and placed a hand on the mapou tree. It was then that part of the hill tumbled away and buried the trucks."

A broad smirk suddenly spread across Emmanuel's face, compounded further by a rumbling laugh that burst forth from deep down in his belly. "Forgive me, my cousin, but I find such an assertion to be highly amusing," he cackled. "Either you were hallucinating or that exceptionally bright mind of yours is starting to revert back to ancient beliefs." Abruptly, he stopped hooting, seeming to consider something. "I just hope this alleged mudslide did not injure or kill any innocents. Maybe we should go there to see if anyone is still alive," he ridiculed.

"Attempting to provide any aid would not be a wise course of action," Jacob objected wearily. "If there are any survivors, only misfortune can result in trying to render assistance." A vision of the lead vehicle remaining only partially buried came to mind, its headlights aimed at the firmament.

Emmanuel sobered markedly. "How can you be so certain of this?" he challenged, looking closely for any signs of doubt in Jacob's face. "It is unlike you to accept such a supposition without absolute proof. I would think it is quite possible that the people trapped in this mudslide of yours are not members of the Tonton Makout at all."

Jacob remained unwavering. "Everything points to the premise that the men in that convoy are Duvalier's assassins. Who else would be traveling toward this village in the middle of the night in a military-type convoy? That road ends here and goes no farther." He shook his head. "No, cousin, any survivors you find will, in all probability, be armed and dangerous. As a precautionary measure, I strongly recommend you post some villagers with weapons in concealment along the trail leading here."

Emmanuel absorbed this logic thoughtfully for several moments. His demeanor slowly changed, and a look of deep-seated respect seeped into his eyes. "Tell me about this woman, Jacob," he requested, turning to view the sleeping woman on the cot.

"She was delirious and in poor physical condition when I found her. She was suffering from a combination of severe jellyfish stings, dehydration and exhaustion. As of now, she is afflicted with an extreme case of amnesia. Because she has no recollection of who she is or where she came from, I have taken the liberty of naming her Amphitrite until her memory returns."

"When did you find her?"

"Almost eleven days ago."

Like Jacob, Emmanuel Baptiste was one of the few locals to have received a college education. Both men had graduated the university in Port-au-Prince together in 1975. Gaunt and scholarly-looking by virtue of a set of tiny spectacles clinging precariously to the bridge of his nose, Emmanuel had distinguished himself at the university as an outspoken proponent of environmentalism. "Haiti is an ecological disaster," he had often said. "If all our citizens banded together, it is within our power to make Haiti a more beautiful country, not the garbage ridden eyesore the rest of the world sees. The land is ours, and if we fail to give it the respect it deserves, we should not expect other people to love and respect it for us."

Both men shared the same but now deceased grandmother, Esmerelda Brisson, a renowned priestess of *vaudun*, the branch of voodoo considered to be white magic. Widely venerated for the potency of her powers, she had become a formidable adversary of both the Papa Doc and Baby Doc regimes.

Many believed that she, and she alone, had been able to invoke a spell that had allowed Malique and its inhabitants to escape the brutal reign of terror perpetuated by the Duvalier government. In fact, some of her staunchest followers had credited her with causing the death of the senior Duvalier in 1971 at the age of 64.

It was Papa Doc who had initiated the use of *voudun*, the evil branch of voodoo, to sustain his regime over the peasant culture that dominated the nation. His practice of black magic and sorcery encouraged rumors among the people that he possessed dark mystical powers, further bolstering the abject fear he spread as a means to controlling the populace. Often seen dressed in a black top hat and coat reminiscent of the outfit worn by *Baron Samedi*, the powerful spirit of the cemeteries, Papa Doc had recruited many practitioners of the black occult into his network of spies and informants.

Although Catholicism was made the official religion of Haiti in 1860, the majority of people, living as peasant farmers and fishermen, had developed a system of beliefs drawing on African traditions. While ninety-five percent of all Haitians were Roman Catholics, voodoo was considered the country's national religion, which most voodooists believed could coexist with other religions. Through personal experience with his grandmother, Jacob well understood that adherents of voodoo did not perceive themselves as members of a separate belief. Paradoxically, most Haitians had conjoined the two religions, claiming that you could not serve the spirits unless you were Catholic.

As a means of self-defense against outright opposition to its practice, most predominantly by those of the Protestant faith and to a lesser extent by the Catholic Church, voodoo had come to be shrouded in mystery and secrecy. It existed as a semi-underground religion, with ceremonies taking place at night and its temples hidden away. Unlike structured formal religions, voodoo had never been codified in writing, lacking a fixed theology or organized hierarchy, making it extremely difficult to pin down exactly what it was. As did Esmerelda, Jacob knew each practitioner developed his or her own reputation for either helping people or causing harm to others.

Although he had deeply loved his grandmother, both he and Emmanuel could never bring themselves to embrace her beliefs, considering them to fly in the face of reason. Born with superior intellect, their minds were encumbered by too much rational and analytical thinking, as Esmerelda had put it, to fully grasp the dimensions of spirituality that plainly existed just beyond the constricting boundaries of reality as they perceived it. *We are mirrors of each others' souls,* she had preached. *The universe is all one. No event has a life of its own, and each thing affects something else. Nature knows this.* A strange visceral smile would further broaden Esmerelda's characteristically wide face whenever she sensed Jacob's struggle to accept her teachings, for she had implied that deep rational thinking was not conducive to understanding such concepts. *Since we all serve as parts of one,* she had said, *what you do unto another, you also do unto yourself, because you are the other. Voo doo, view you. The creator is manifest through the spirits of ancestors who can bring good or harm and must be honored in ceremonies. Do not strangle your mind with limitations,* she had frequently warned. *Do not question everything. The mysteries voodoo holds have no room for ambivalence or skepticism. You must open yourself and let your mind soar to untold heights if you are to achieve divine wisdom.*

Esmerelda Brisson had been the most powerful mambo in the land, able to diagnose illnesses with the touch of a hand, frequently revealing the origins of another's misfortune. An accomplished herbalist who had successfully treated a wide variety of ailments and injuries over her lifetime, she had imparted some of this specialized knowledge to Jacob.

When Jacob had attended the university, he had been a quiet and reserved student in stark contrast to his outspoken cousin, who did not go unnoticed by those within Baby Doc Duvalier's administration. Emmanuel had frequently ridiculed the government for its unrestrained corruption and its dismal failing to implement environmental policies that would improve the country. A gifted orator and skilled debater, Emmanuel had rapidly garnered a following, and because of it, the junior Duvalier saw him as a potential threat. But fearful that he might provoke the wrath of Esmerelda if he attempted to silence the voice of this rising star, Baby Doc refrained from dispatching his henchmen. Instead, he had his acolytes search the land high and low for the most powerful adept of voudun, hoping to counter any spell invoked by the powerful Esmerelda through such a person. It did not take them long to find such an individual, a woman that called herself *Erzulie,* so named after the mistress of Damballah. In order to strengthen his hold on the population, Baby Doc had brought the woman into his inner circle, often showcasing her by his side during public appearances. It soon became evident that the woman was the epitome of pure evil. Dissidents of Duvalier's dictatorship began to mysteriously disappear.

Not long thereafter, Esmerelda had been summoned by several Malique fishermen to improve the fishing in the waters close to the village. While she was performing an incantation, the sky suddenly darkened and a black ominous cloud scudded low over the water belching thunder and bolts of lightning and unleashing a torrential downpour. A towering wave had abruptly risen up and swept over the vessel upon which Esmerelda stood, upending the boat and washing overboard all those riding it. Eyewitnesses who had been closest to the event swore they had seen the jaws of a monstrous shark close over Esmerelda's body as she thrashed about in the water. Her remains still had not been found.

That ill-fated event had taken place little more than two weeks earlier, and it had left the village of Malique bereft of its beloved mambo. Lucette had taken Esmerelda's death especially hard, and much to her husband's revulsion, it was she who had tried to fill the void left behind by the parting of Emmanuel's grandmother. As Esmerelda's apprentice, it was only natural that she do so, but unfortunately she was greatly lacking in the powers or insights of her highly regarded predecessor.

A sudden loud rapping jarred Jacob from his fleeting thoughts. Someone was knocking on the front door.

Emmanuel visibly paled at the intrusion but quickly overcame his unease and stepped close to the door. "Who comes to my door at this hour of the night?" he said with annoyance.

"It is Jimenez," a disembodied voice answered.

Cautiously, Emmanuel opened the door a crack, then peeked through the gap. Satisfied at the identity of the intruder, he allowed the man entrance.

Middle-aged and of medium build, Jimenez displayed a face with the weathered consistency of mahogany subjected to excessive amounts of sun, wind and sea. Having spent his entire life hauling in fishing nets from the local waters, his forearms gave the appearance of fluted black stone.

"What is it?" Emmanuel asked.

Jimenez looked grave. "Two boats have entered the harbor."

"So."

"I am unfamiliar with these boats. They have made no attempt as yet to come ashore and appear to be holding to positions a stone's throw from our docks."

Emmanuel abruptly stiffened and glanced apprehensively at Jacob before turning back to Jimenez. "Who—"

A sharp obtrusive gasp cut Emmanuel off. Amphitrite was now awake and standing on unsteady feet. Her eyes were wide and unfocused, as if seeing something beyond the room. Her mouth parted in an attempt to speak but no words escaped her lips.

In an instant, Jacob was at her side and lending support. "You must rest," he said.

Amphitrite's eyes rolled back, then focused. All at once she became aware of the others occupying the room. "The people aboard those boats are intent upon doing this village much harm," she said in a voice low and trembling.

"Who are they?" Jacob questioned.

"More Tonton Makout." Amphitrite seemed to look inwardly again. "But there is one among them who is much more dangerous than the rest. The only way I can describe this person is that she pulses with pure evil."

"Erzulie! Erzulie is with them!" Lucette screeched hysterically. "Esmerelda warned me about her. She is the most evil witch in all of Haiti. Black magic is her source of power. She will put a vile curse on us all." Lucette immediately made the sign of the crucifixion, but from the look of her Jacob thought she was on the verge of fainting.

"Stop your gibbering at once, woman," Emmanuel scolded. "How can you let yourself believe such nonsense?"

"We will all die!" Lucette wailed. "Without Esmerelda we are doomed."

Jacob scrutinized Emmanuel's reaction carefully. In his cousin's manner he could sense the glowing embers of both confusion and indecision. And though subtle, there was something else...a growing sign of fear. He could tell Emmanuel was truly fearful of this sudden turn of events.

"Do you not see what is going on?" Jacob blurted. "Duvalier wanted to hit this village from two sides simultaneously, one by land and the other by sea. Those vessels floating idly out there await a land-side attack. They are positioned to stop and destroy anyone from attempting to escape by sea."

"Maybe you are assuming too much," Emmanuel said hastily. "You have no way of being certain of this."

Jacob glowered angrily at his cousin. He was beginning to lose patience with such ridiculous obstinacy. "Do you think so? Baby Doc views you as one of the few people in our land capable of garnering widespread rebellion. He sees the seeds of insurrection firmly rooted in those loyal to your cause, which is essentially everyone in this village. He perceives Malique as a bastion of resistance and prefers that all its inhabitants permanently disappear. When Esmerelda was alive he was too caught up in his own superstitious convictions to believe it possible that this village could be wiped out, a prisoner of the very tool he has consistently used to keep political unrest at bay. With our grandmother now gone, he is convinced Malique is now vulnerable to attack, no longer under the protection of a once powerful mambo. Do you not see that Duvalier believes a retaliatory strike or spell invoked by Esmerelda against him is no longer possible?"

"Erzulie would never have come here when Esmerelda was alive," Lucette chimed in meekly, giving support to Jacob's argument. She now seemed ashamed of her previous craven outburst. Staring demurely at Emmanuel, she added, "Even Erzulie knew she would be no match for your grandmother, not against what Esmerelda possessed."

"Esmerelda's untimely death is not common knowledge," Emmanuel countered. "Only the people of this village know about it. How would Duvalier have learned of this recent circumstance?"

"Perhaps you have a spy within your midst," Jacob offered. He threw his hands up in the air. "What does it matter now anyway? Apparently Duvalier is fully aware of Esmerelda's demise and seeks to put an end to the threat you pose."

Jacob paused as another thought struck him. He looked at Jimenez. "These strange boats in the harbor. Were you able to estimate their size?"

"Each has a length of about nine meters. Under the moonlight their shapes were nearly identical."

Jacob nodded reflectively. "Taking an informed guess, I would venture those are government gunboats, most likely Montauk motor vessels. The Haitian Navy has only five such gunboats and most of the time they are in a state of disrepair. They are rarely seen because they are frequently inoperable. However, they all possess a fifty-caliber machine gun. Such a weapon has the capacity to wreak much damage on anything within range."

Jacob noted a stubborn trace of skepticism still lingering on his cousin's face and quickly added, "I know this because I once read a block of material that provided facts about Haiti's limited navy. The article was published by the Combined Arms Research Library, an institution located in Fort Leavenworth in the American state of Kansas. You know as well as I do that I am able to retain and regurgitate any such trivia."

Emmanuel's expression appeared to give ground, and Jacob could tell his cousin was close to being won over, but not just yet. "If, as you contend, these boats are armed with such firepower, why have they not already destroyed our fishing fleet and eliminated any possible escape by sea?"

"Because the only incentive Duvalier's secret police have for carrying out his orders is the looting they can partake in. Remember, rumor has it that Baby Doc does not pay the Tonton Makout. They do not enjoy monetary recompense for their services, that is, other than what they can plunder and ransack. They see the fishing vessels of this village as valuable assets and will avoid damaging them unless they absolutely have to."

Emmanuel sagged heavily into a nearby chair, seemingly caving to Jacob's logic. "What do you suggest we do?" he muttered helplessly.

Jacob gave the question careful consideration, then looked to Amphitrite. "This woman you spoke of, you are sure she is on one of those boats?"

Amphitrite produced a weak nod. She was still wobbly and Jacob kept his arm firmly around her waist until he had her seated. Kneeling down beside her, he held her gaze for several seconds before addressing her in a quiet comforting voice. "I am not sure what powers, if any, this woman you described possesses, but somehow I believe you have a profound purpose in all of this."

Jacob's mind was speeding along, continually searching for answers to the situation confronting them. It didn't make sense for Erzulie to accompany

Duvalier's thugs in raiding the village…unless. He stared at Amphitrite curiously. "Do you sense any motive this woman has for being here?"

"She seeks to gain possession of a valuable but ancient artifact, a charm she perceives as having great power." The exhaustion in her speech and manner made Jacob nervous.

Lucette drew in a sharp intake of breath. "Esmerelda's amulet. She wants Esmerelda's amulet."

Jacob visualized the trinket Lucette spoke of, a garish pendant about the size of a U.S. silver dollar that had often been worn around Esmerelda's neck. His grandmother had greatly cherished the object, claiming that it had been handed down from generation to generation from a long line of ancestors. This extensive ancestry dated all the way back to the pharaohs of Egypt where one of her Nubian forebears had been a slave to a high-ranking priestess in the Temple of Hathor. The amulet was a bronze disc with a symmetrical, exquisitely cut crystal of blue quartz embedded in its center and seven slivers of yellowed ivory radiating outward from the central gem, a relic from a bygone era of human history. According to Esmerelda, the amulet had been originally worn by the priestess as a symbolic ornament during religious rites, but had been given to the slave as a tribute for many years of faithful service. For the next three thousand years, the ancient heirloom had made its way through the heart of the African continent, moving among various tribes where it had been frequently used in rituals and religious ceremonies.

"There is a wealth of untold history and power in this charm", his grandmother had once told him. *"The spirits of all your ancestors have left some of their essence in it. In the hands of a true believer in whose veins flows the blood of our ancestors, it can be used to invoke much good or great harm."*

At the time, he had dismissed her allegation as utter nonsense. And although the amulet held substantial historical value, to him it was just a worthless piece of timeworn junk.

"Esmerelda's amulet was lost at sea with her," Jacob reminded Emmanuel's wife.

Lucette shook her head vigorously. "No. You are mistaken. Your grandmother gave it to me for safekeeping." A gloomy sadness crept into her eyes. "For some unknown reason she refrained from wearing it on the day of her demise. She told me if anything happened to her, I was to hold onto it until the day came when I would know what to do with it."

"That day may have already arrived," Jacob muttered grimly. "But how does this woman know of the amulet?"

An icy dread seemed to take hold of Lucette's persona. "I do not know."

"Esmerelda and this woman come from the same African lineage," Amphitrite suddenly explained, her voice reduced to a dull monotone.

Everyone's gaze fell on her in disbelief. Oblivious of the stares, she seemed to search inwardly as if trying to grasp some elusive shred of knowledge before continuing. "They both descended from common family roots, but their genealogy separated four generations ago. They share the same great great grandmother. Knowledge of the amulet has been passed onto this woman by traditional family lore."

Emmanuel scowled, staring at Amphitrite as if she were insane. "How can you possibly know this?" he challenged.

Amphitrite did not look at him. "I have no explanation for it." Her manner appeared distant, almost trance-like.

"If this is true, it is little wonder Erzulie never openly tried to match her power against Esmerelda's," Lucette interposed. "Because she shares a common origin with Esmerelda, she felt the older spirits of her African ancestors, the *rada*, would favor the descendant that possessed the amulet. Erzulie was afraid she would displease them if she attempted any confrontation with your grandmother. If she had done so, she would have risked bringing great harm to herself. With Esmerelda now gone, she has no such fear."

"But you are now the possessor of the amulet," Jacob pointed out.

"I am a family member only by marriage, not bloodline. The loa of Esmerelda's ancestors can not protect me."

Jacob well understood that voodoo was a family oriented belief, revolving around ancestral spirits who were inherited through maternal and paternal lines. Voodoo was actually a derivative of the world's oldest known religions that originated in different parts of Africa long before the Europeans started the slave trade in the Americas. It was the enforced immigration of enslaved Africans from different tribes and ethnic groups that provided the setting for the birth of present day voodoo in Haiti. In the abject misery of slavery, various transplanted Africans began to integrate and fuse differing beliefs until a new religious structure evolved.

"She comes ashore," Amphitrite announced dully.

"Erzulie?" Jacob asked.

"If that is her name, yes."

"Are there others with her?"

"Yes, there are two others."

"Are they armed?" Jacob pressed.

"It is difficult to determine."

"Do you see them in a vision, a waking dream?"

"No. It is what Athena tells me."

This revelation surprised Jacob. "Athena is in the harbor?"

"Yes."

Jacob had completely forgotten about the dolphin. The fact that Athena was currently conveying information to Amphitrite about the interlopers in the harbor only further substantiated the mysterious communication that existed between them. It suddenly struck him that the dolphin would have little or no concept of what a weapon was and therefore would be unable to identify one as such.

From the way the others in the room looked at him, it was understandable that they would be confused, but he had no time to explain. Even he was mystified. There was something going on here that defied reason, extending way beyond the boundaries of what should actually occur in a logical, orderly universe. In any case, either Athena had sensed the present danger on her own and swam up the coast to Malique by choice or Amphitrite had summoned her earlier on. *Was it possible Amphitrite had glimpsed the woman and her two-man escort through the eyes of the dolphin?*

Rising from his chair, Emmanuel said, "If, as you say, this planned landside raid has been neutralized, then perhaps the people aboard those supposed gunboats will eventually leave when-" His words were abruptly cut off and he sank to his knees clutching his throat.

Lucette jumped to her husband's side, grabbing him by the shoulders. "What is wrong?"

Emmanuel looked up into her face, his eyes filled with a strange mix of shock and panic.

"He cannot breathe! He is choking!" Lucette shrieked. She looked to Jacob for help. "Do something!"

"The witch senses the proximity of her distant relative," Amphitrite stated, speaking with a detached air. "She has conjured a spell and will not release it until the amulet is brought to her."

Like a man being slowly strangled, Emmanuel's tongue lolled from between convulsing lips and his eyes began to bulge in terror. "Do not let her do this to you!" Lucette cried, hugging him fiercely.

Jacob put a hand on Lucette's shoulder to get her attention. "You must give me the amulet," he instructed, urgency in his voice. He was desperately trying to keep the alarm he felt from showing in his tone. "I will bring it to this woman."

Lucette hesitated for one brief moment, then beheld Emmanuel's dreadful expression once again. He was close to suffocation. "Yes, yes," she suddenly agreed. She bolted quickly from the room, returning several seconds later with the ancient charm and handing it over to Jacob. "Please hurry!" she begged. "Give the witch what she wants so that my husband may live. There is little time to lose."

Emmanuel let out a strained, quavering wheeze, holding out his arm in a futile bid for Jacob not to go.

Jacob ignored the gesture, running past a stunned Jimenez and throwing the door wide to expedite his departure. He sprinted rapidly toward the docks, expecting to see Erzulie and her escort at any moment, but the witch failed to appear. Continuing on, he ran out onto the main pier, noting the dark shapes of the vessels described by Jimenez floating about fifty meters further out to sea on each side of the structure. A varied array of local fishing craft lined both sides of the aging wooden platform, their differing sizes and configurations contrasting sharply in the moonlight. Puzzled that no one stood before him he slowed his pace, then stopped altogether. In the late night breeze, the sound of creaking timbers and the chafing rustle of mooring lines seemed to charge the air with a foreboding energy. Jacob advanced a little farther along the deck planks, now fully wary and anticipating the worst.

"You will give the amulet to me!" a voice suddenly said, hissing out the command like red-hot steel being plunged into cool water. Spoken in Creole, the words came from behind him.

Jacob spun and immediately froze. Not more than three meters away a dark figure stood in the center of the pier, its features hidden under a hooded cloak. The unexpected appearance made Jacob take a step backward, and as he did so, the figure seemed to float closer.

"Give me the amulet!" the figure repeated in the same serpentine hiss.

As if to comply, Jacob extended the hand holding the amulet, but was not ready to relinquish it just yet. "You will first release my cousin from whatever dark power you have unleashed upon him."

"You will give me the amulet now!" the figure ordered shrilly. "I have waited all my life for what you hold in your hand and I will not be denied it now."

Jacob felt his throat constricting. It was as if a cord had been looped around his neck and tightened. He gasped for air as the witch appeared to hover still closer. She dangled something conspicuously before him.

"Do you remember this?" she cackled gleefully.

Jacob studied the object as he strained for more breath. A small black doll hung from an ascot cinched snugly around its neck. In the faint glow of moonlight he recognized the tie almost immediately. He had worn it during his graduation ceremony at the university in Port-au-Prince, a delicate hand-stitched strip of cloth made by his grandmother and given to him as a gift shortly before he had earned his college degree. The design depicted a pod of white dolphin embroidered on a cobalt-blue backdrop. The focal point of the artistic layout, however, was unusual and automatically drew the eye. It was an ivory-skinned girl with long-flowing black hair streaming behind her. The girl sat astride the largest dolphin positioned at the center of the pack.

As Jacob looked on, the witch fumbled briefly under her cloak and produced another strip of cloth knotted tightly around the throat of a second doll. It was another of Esmerelda's beautifully handcrafted ascots, but this one portrayed a mix of colorful yet odd-looking jellyfish interspersed among a group of sea cucumbers. The second ascot was similar to the first in that it displayed the same cobalt-blue background. Both neckties had turned up missing subsequent to the graduation of the cousins. Someone had broken into their dormitory room and taken not only the ties, but several other items of clothing.

In spite of his pain, Jacob tightened his grip on the bronze medallion. If the witch could do this to him with such seemingly insignificant objects, he wondered what horrors she would be capable once she had the primordial charm in her possession.

"You and your cousin have always amused me with your pitiful rejection of ancient beliefs," the witch continued in that sibilating hiss of hers. She lifted the doll representing Jacob so that it dangled only inches from his face. "And yet the strangulation you are experiencing would not work unless some part of you, whether you are consciously aware of it or not, actually did accept what you have so insistently refuted as being nothing more than ineffectual sorcery." She suddenly cinched the dolphin necktie tighter.

Jacob began to reel dizzily as he felt himself beginning to black out. Managing to keep his feet under him, he backpedaled drunkenly away from the woman as he clutched his throat. He tried to speak but no words were able to escape his larynx.

Erzulie shadowed him, keeping close. "Your grandmother was a worthy adversary, a powerful practitioner of vaudun, but only because she possessed what you presently hold in your hand."

Jacob continued to stagger backward with Erzulie following. "With Esmerelda now gone, it is I, Erzulie, who is the natural heir of the amulet, the one most deserving of it. The rada must have foreseen the merit in helping me invoke the forces of nature that took your grandmother from this world so that someone more worthy should take charge of it." Erzulie cackled raucously at Jacob's futile stubbornness.

An intense feeling of torpidity was beginning to consume Jacob. His previous steadfast belief in a world based on rationality and logic was being severely challenged on this night. Aside from his physical distress, he felt like a man viewing a lush oasis from afar in the midst of a hot sandy desert, only to discover that what was assumed to be a sanctuary of life-giving sustenance was nothing more than a mirage. For the closer he got to it, the more the vision crumbled away to reveal only more of the same desolate hellhole in which he now found himself stranded, a place devoid of the beauty and harmony which he so dearly cherished, a realm where only evil and misery flourished. He was a man fast sinking in the quicksand of self-doubt. It was only at this moment as he was inexorably being drawn toward death that he was now beginning to grasp the true essence of reality and he suddenly understood that the three-dimensional space of ordinary experience was simply an illusion, a thing created by the mind. But try as he might, the forces assailing him were much too powerful for even his superb intellect to fight, let alone comprehend. He felt himself rapidly weakening, buckling under the witch's onslaught.

He realized he had collapsed onto the wooden deck of the pier, and as he looked up, the witch loomed over him. Too weak to resist any longer, he watched listlessly as Erzulie abruptly stopped cackling, her fingers prepared to impart a final wrench on the necktie's knot. He knew she was about to terminate his life.

"You will now learn of the ultimate penalty that others who have defied me have wrought upon themselves," Erzulie said, her words dripping with contempt and hatred.

Even with the prospect of death now imminent, Jacob continued to withhold the amulet. The witch would have to take it from his inert corpse. With an abruptness he did not immediately perceive, the pressure on his throat relaxed and, reflexively, he inhaled deeply, inundating his lungs with sweet Haitian air.

A piercing howl suddenly knifed its way through the night as Erzulie inspected the doll representing Jacob. The doll had somehow fallen away from the necktie's noose.

"My spell has been broken," she squawked incredulously. "How can this be?"

"You cannot bring harm to the people of this village," a familiar voice said.

Though Jacob knew who had spoken the words, there was a strange new quality in the way they were uttered, a calm authority behind them. Freed from his painful stupor, he watched Erzulie's dark form go rigid before turning to face the unanticipated intrusion behind her.

"I have felt your presence earlier," the witch hissed venomously. She cocked her head, remaining still for several seconds as if listening for something in the air. "You are an outsider…yet I sense something familiar about you."

"You were never meant to possess the amulet," Amphitrite said. "Even if you hold it in your hand you will be unable to draw on its power."

"That is not possible," Erzulie countered angrily. "The rada have already chosen me to take charge of it."

Amphitrite looked beyond the witch to Jacob. "Give her what she wants, Jacob. Let her see for herself."

The remaining traces of Jacob's incapacitating suffocation fell away, leaving him clear-minded and alert. Although stunned by Amphitrite's directive, he instinctively trusted her. He nevertheless hesitated. "My cousin, Emmanuel…he is alright?"

"He has been released from the spell," Amphitrite assured him.

Erzulie gasped loudly, realizing the necktie had fallen off the doll representing Emmanuel. "You will pay for your insolence," she screamed.

Jacob thrust the amulet in front of the witch, letting it dangle invitingly before her. Though Erzulie's face still remained hidden within the shadow of her cowl, he could tell she was working herself into a maddening rage. "Here! Take it and leave us in peace, witch," he spat irritably.

Erzulie's hand snaked out and snagged the talisman, clutching it tightly. Seemingly pacified for the moment, she caressed the charm lovingly with her fingertips, enjoying the feel of it. "Without this ancient artifact, Esmerelda would never have been able to protect this village from me. I find it most strange she chose not to wear it at the time of her death. Had she done so, it is possible she would still be alive and this village spared from the wrath it is about to suffer."

"Your plan has failed," Amphitrite said. There was an unconquerable confidence in her voice. "The motor convoy you have sent to attack this village has been crushed in a mudslide. There is nothing else you can do here."

As Amphitrite addressed the witch, Erzulie appeared to concentrate her attention briefly on the small gathering of villagers led by Emmanuel and Lucette that was beginning to congregate at the foot of the pier. Her cowled head swiveled back toward Amphitrite. "The fate of Duvalier's main force is of little consequence now that I possess this," she intoned in a sibilating hiss, indicating the amulet. "I have no need of an army to destroy all those who live here. Malique is about to be bathed in its own blood."

With those words, Erzulie's cloaked visage seemed to swell, looming closer to Amphitrite. "I will start with you."

The witch began to recite a low rambling chant, repeating the litany over and over, each redundancy rising in volume and fervor. Though the phrases did not conform to any language in which Jacob was fluent, their meaning was all too clear. All at once the mild breeze changed into a swirling turbulence and whitecaps began to form in the water on both sides of the pier, the disturbances gaining more violence with each rendition of the mantra.

Jacob looked on, overcome with alarm as lightning flashed overhead and the sky rumbled in protest. The witch threw her arms wide, slowly raising them to the heavens as her incantation reached a fever pitch, then abruptly stabbed the fist holding the amulet toward Amphitrite who held her ground with impassive defiance. Erzulie held that position for a short interlude, then let out a sharp guttural cry.

In unison, the swiftly forming vortex of wind quickly died away and the churning sea rapidly subsided. Erzulie held her hands stiffly before her in the now intensified moonlight, standing with the rigidity of a mountaineer frozen in the icy grip of a Himalayan gale. Her gaze lingered on the dark liquid oozing from both palms before letting the blood-drenched talisman slip from her fingers. The ancient charm hit the wooden platform with a dull clunk, then disappeared between two of the deck planks, dragging its chain with it.

"I told you the amulet would be useless in your hands," Amphitrite reminded the witch. "In attempting to use it to destroy others, you have only managed to bring injury upon yourself."

Erzulie's bloody hands clenched, then shook uncontrollably. Jacob watched the spectacle with amazement, noticing the witch's dark form was quaking violently as if in seizure. He had the distinct impression that the paroxysm was caused by colossal humiliation rather than pain.

"You will pay for this," Erzulie screamed as she studied the blood dripping from her palms. She was beside herself with rage, swearing profane obscenities and gruesome vengeance on all those nearest her.

"You will be unable to hurt any of us," Amphitrite insisted, cutting into the witch's ravings. "Your power has been neutralized."

Erzulie suddenly sobered. Appearing to gain some semblance of control over her emotions, the witch lifted her gaze to Amphitrite. "You think you have won," she said, hissing out the words like a cornered reptile. "But you are wrong. You and all these people will die anyway." She looked behind her and called loudly. "Antoine! Dervin! Show yourselves."

From opposite sides of the pier, two figures emerged from hidden positions aboard the nearest berthed fishing vessels. They hopped quickly onto the dock and stood shoulder to shoulder, staring implacably at those before them. Erzulie scrambled to meet them, taking refuge behind the men. It was then that Jacob became aware of the assault rifle each man wielded.

"Kill them all!" Erzulie shrieked. "I want them all dead."

At the witch's command, each man chambered a round, bringing his gun barrel to bear on Amphitrite and the villagers grouped behind her. Jacob looked on in horror at this sudden turn of events, but before a single round could be unleashed, a large glistening object flew from the water on one side of the pier. With blinding speed it cleared the tethered boat immediately in front of it and rose still higher, following a low parabolic trajectory. Awestruck, Jacob tracked its flight as it turned sideways in mid-air, closing in on its intended targets. Erzulie and her cohorts became aware of it only a split second before it struck. But by then it was too late. The tail of the hurtling object flicked laterally, slamming into the three assassins with uncanny precision and sweeping them from the pier. With arms and legs flailing crazily, the witch and her accomplices hit the water with a resounding splash.

Side by side, Jacob and Amphitrite stepped to the edge of the deck and looked down. Their would-be attackers floundered in agitated confusion. Athena surfaced moments later off to one side, then submerged again.

"It appears Athena has saved us for the moment," Jacob praised in admiration. He made no attempt to hide the affection he felt for the dolphin. "But those gunboats standing by out there are another matter we must concern ourselves with."

Amphitrite glanced seaward. "The village will be spared," she said, her tone carrying unbridled conviction. She lowered her gaze to the water below the pier and her expression hardened as she watched Erzulie and her cohorts struggle to stay afloat. "You must leave this place at once," she cautioned the witch. "Should you direct any further aggression toward the people of this village, that aggression will only flow back at you tenfold."

Erzulie appeared to heed the warning, for within moments her companions were towing her toward the nearest gunboat coming forward to meet them.

As Jacob observed their departure, Athena suddenly popped her snout above the water. Something glinted in the moonlight. Curious, Jacob jumped down onto the deck of the adjacent fishing boat for a closer look. Esmerelda's amulet was clutched gently between Athena's jaws. The dolphin raised herself higher out of the water and tossed him the charm with a flip of her head. Jacob caught it, then climbed back onto the dock.

"I think you should hold onto this," Jacob told Lucette, handing the trinket over to her.

Lucette took possession of the ancient medallion with undisguised reverence, cradling it so gently in her outstretched hands that one would think it was comprised of fragile glass rather than hard metal. She studied the charm intently, periodically gazing over at Amphitrite, her eyes harboring a far off look as if something weighed heavily on her mind.

Emmanuel joined Jacob, watching Erzulie and the two men assisting her being pulled from the sea by the gunboat's crew. "Power held by a ruthless dictator through the use of violence is an aberration and will only last as long as people are willing to obey him," he said off-handedly. "With political unrest now widespread in our land, Duvalier's reign may be coming to an end."

Jacob kept his eyes fixed on the gunboat. Now less then twenty meters away, he could clearly hear Erzulie's rantings. The witch berated the men aboard with a steady stream of rabid scolding, venting her frustration and rage on them and every so often threatening some grisly form of mayhem. Within a short time the second gunboat joined the first, after which the two vessels slowly turned away, following the coastline on a southerly heading. The sound of Erzulie's ceaseless tirade gradually tapered off as the boats gained distance from the village.

Glancing around him, Jacob noticed the way the villagers closest to Amphitrite gawked at her. It was as if they were witnessing some strange yet benevolent white goddess that had suddenly come into their midst without warning, and in a way it was not far from the truth. To most Haitians, whites were regarded with suspicion, a carryover from Haiti's violent past when the black population rose up and liberated itself from its chains of bondage. But for reasons unknown to Jacob, it was apparent the locals were accepting her.

With a look of genuine awe on her face, Lucette walked over to Amphitrite and held the amulet before her in offering. "Esmerelda told me I would know what to do with this when the time came. Although you are not of her ancestry, I think she would have wanted you to have it." Other villagers standing behind Lucette nodded their agreement.

Amphitrite stared at the amulet as if recognizing an old friend, and as Jacob watched, he could have sworn something had changed in the white woman's manner, some profound transformation that somehow imparted a regal aura to her persona. A heavy silence seemed to hang in the air when Amphitrite did not immediately respond. She continued to contemplate the amulet in quiet consideration for a full ten seconds before lifting her eyes to Lucette, whereupon she gave a slight nod and lowered her head. Smiling broadly, Lucette draped the chain holding the artifact around Amphitrite's neck, letting the charm settle gently above her breasts as if it belonged there.

The moment passed swiftly. Amphitrite stared vacantly off into space, then abruptly turned to Jacob and sighed deeply. "I am tired, Jacob. Please take me back to the cove."

The recent events had taken a tremendous toll on her, both physically and emotionally, and it was now showing in the way she carried herself.

Jacob could still feel the effects of the adrenaline that had driven him on since the collapse of the hill at the mapou tree and he was willing to make the journey, if only to satisfy Amphitrite's request. She had done Emmanuel and the people of the village a huge service on this fateful night and he felt indebted to repay her for her sacrifice in whatever manner he could.

Emmanuel, however, would hear none of this. "The two of you are welcome to spend the remainder of the night with Lucette and me," he offered jubilantly. He looked at Amphitrite with renewed interest, his expression inquisitive and searching. "Forgive me for not introducing myself earlier. I have been extremely impolite. I am Emmanuel Baptiste, Jacob's cousin."

He hesitated momentarily, pulling Lucette to his side. "And this is my wife, Lucette. Both you and Jacob have endured through much in the last several hours. Perhaps a good rest will revitalize you before you go back to Jacob's home."

Amphitrite eyed him tiredly. "That is most gracious of you, but I don't wish to impose on your hospitality."

"It is no imposition at all," Emmanuel replied. He regarded the white woman appraisingly with an owlish stare. "Jacob tells me you have no recollection of your previous identity, that you suffer from amnesia. Your accent leads me to believe you are an American, but I find it strange you can speak Creole. Visitors to this land generally have great difficulty in learning such a dialect, particularly when it is much more practical to communicate in French. Oddly, you seem to be fluent in both tongues."

It suddenly dawned on Jacob that Amphitrite had spoken both French and Creole ever since she had regained consciousness in the village. He frequently alternated between the two languages without any forethought, and with the threat of Erzulie and the gunboats confronting them, he had failed to notice Amphitrite's use of colloquial French in Emmanuel's home and her subsequent withdrawal into the more common Haitian pidgin during her encounter with the witch. Because his very first conversation with her had been in English, he had made the foolish assumption she was monolingual.

As Jacob listened he noted that his cousin was speaking to Amphitrite in French. He knew that Emmanuel generally avoided the use of pidgin, considering such an idiom to be too simplified to adequately express oneself in a rich, stylistic manner.

Amphitrite nodded wearily. "If I knew where I learned these languages, I would know who I am," she murmured weakly, replying in Emmanuel's tongue. She suddenly swooned.

Jacob had been standing ready for such a possibility and caught her as she collapsed, cradling her in his arms once again. The villagers that had crowded out onto the pier parted to open a path as Jacob carried her forward. With the throng following, Emmanuel and Lucette took up a position on each side of him as he moved in the direction of his cousin's abode.

"This woman is in need of rest," Jacob huffed, turning his head to face Emmanuel as he walked with his burden. "If you have not noticed, she is with child."

"Forgive me, cousin, for being so inconsiderate," Emmanuel apologized. "I should have been more observant."

No further words were exchanged until Jacob had Amphitrite gently positioned back on the cot in his cousin's house.

"She seems to be sleeping peacefully," Emmanuel said. Jacob detected a subtle trace of contrition in his tone. He knew Emmanuel only too well, sensing that his cousin was ashamed of his earlier skepticism over Jacob's mudslide story, particularly after witnessing something he would have otherwise deemed impossible.

Lucette laid a hand on Jacob's arm. "You should get some rest yourself. I will watch over this woman while you sleep."

Jacob suddenly had great difficulty keeping his eyes open as an overpowering drowsiness crept over him. Whatever reservations he had against Lucette's offer quickly faded and he let Lucette lead him to the bed she shared with Emmanuel. Within seconds he dropped off into a deep slumber and did not awaken until late the next morning. As he opened his eyes, a vague remembrance of the nightmares that had haunted his dreams continued to swirl in his head, visions of dark demonic figures relentlessly chasing him down winding passageways. The pursuit terminated at the end of a dank, dismal hallway where, seemingly by itself, a corroded steel door abruptly swung open to admit him. Within the room beyond, a cloaked shadowy creature awaited, rising up at him with malicious intent and pulsing with pure evil. He had no doubt that the creature was Erzulie.

Rising from the bed, it soon became apparent to Jacob that the house was deserted. Rubbing the sleep from his eyes, he left the lodgings and wandered out along the waterfront.

A small crowd was assembled on the beach, and as Jacob got closer he could see that all faces were enchanted by something out on the water. Amphitrite was riding Athena again, and as he looked on, it was plain that the twosome were following a course that would take them down the coast. Perplexed, he kept his gaze riveted on them until they disappeared from sight around a rocky promontory jutting from the shoreline south of the village.

Emmanuel separated himself from the onlookers and approached Jacob with a spring in his step. "You have missed much here this morning, my cousin." There was a rare gleam of appreciation in his eyes as he said this, something Emmanuel seldom exhibited as far back as Jacob could remember. "Your woman and that dolphin of hers are a strange pair, indeed."

"She is not my woman," Jacob corrected, desperately fighting back the offense he felt. The loose comment implied a sexual relationship. And although he was almost certain Emmanuel had not meant it that way, the unintended innuendo somehow diminished Amphitrite's rectitude. He stared back toward the promontory, anxiously wondering where the woman and dolphin were going.

Emmanuel stopped in his tracks and studied Jacob carefully for several seconds. "What is the name you have given her? I have forgotten it already."

"Amphitrite." Mouthing the word, it sounded appropriate, a befitting designation to a most unique woman.

"Amphitrite awoke early and left the house while Lucette was still asleep," Emmanuel informed him. "Jimenez and several others discovered her and the dolphin swimming together near the docks. It would appear that the white woman takes great pleasure in riding that dolphin. Being that Jimenez was preparing to get underway to go fishing anyway, he followed the two of them out to sea. They led him to a bonanza of fish. His boat came back filled with striped mullet."

Jacob nodded distractedly. This did not surprise him at all.

"Two other fishermen also came back with full boatloads after the woman and dolphin showed them where to cast their nets," Emmanuel said, his voice light and cheerful. "Amphitrite rode the dolphin back to the beach after the boats returned. Louwanda happened to be there with her son. The white woman led the boy out into the water until he was chest deep, whereupon the dolphin circled him several times before nuzzling up against him. It was then that the woman placed a hand on the boy's head."

Emmanuel hesitated and a small laugh left his lips, causing Jacob to turn back and face him. He was suddenly intrigued. "And?"

Emmanuel broadened his smile. "Samuel can see again. His sight has returned."

To Jacob, the implications of such a revelation astounded him. Two years ago, Samuel had struck his head on a submerged rock while spear fishing. A freak wave had swept him into an outcropping of jagged coral. The boy had been blind ever since.

As Jacob recounted the history of Samuel's catastrophic injury, Louwanda strolled up to him with the twelve-year old boy next to her. "God bless you, Jacob," she sobbed, hugging him with a rapturous fervor and planting a huge kiss on his cheek. "May the spirits of your ancestors bestow good fortune upon you." Tears of joy streamed down her face. "Thanks to you my boy is able to see the beauty of the world around him once again."

Jacob was nearly speechless. "I...I did nothing for Samuel," he stammered awkwardly.

"You brought the dolphin woman to our village. That is enough."

Jacob continued to stare in amazement as Louwanda led Samuel away. The boy turned his head, looking back at him with hero worship evident in his eyes. The ugly scar Samuel had carried on his forehead ever since the tragic accident was now almost gone. Jacob suddenly became aware of others regarding him with similar looks. Glancing around, he found himself to be a focal point of attention.

Emmanuel's manner sobered. "Earlier this morning I visited the moupou tree and confirmed everything you had told me to be true," he confessed. "All the trucks were crushed, mostly buried under tons of mud and rubble, but the jeep was only partially covered."

Such verification made Jacob feel better, for he had begun to question his own sanity. "Did you find any survivors?"

"None. I had several others from the village accompany me and we found the soil to be very soft in many places. It was easy for us to become bogged down up to our knees. Next to and leading away from the jeep, it was evident that two people had struggled through the mire trying to reach firmer ground. They left a trail of sunken footprints heading west toward the coast. We followed their tracks into the hills where their spoor vanished on the exposed bedrock."

Jacob absorbed this information thoughtfully. "Perhaps it is better that you did not encounter these people. As I told you before, it is likely that they carry firearms."

Emmanuel nodded gravely. "That is probably true. And with the safety of our people possibly at risk with armed assassins running loose around the countryside, it is necessary that we be equally armed. Fortunately for us, the two men who assisted the witch lost their weapons in the water when they were knocked from the dock." Emmanuel paused, suddenly displaying a broad smile. "Those weapons were recovered earlier this morning and are now in our custody. We dried them off and oiled them. The cartridges appeared to be watertight, but just to make sure, we test fired one round from each gun and they seem to function perfectly. I have given your prior suggestion careful consideration and decided to post two sentries in concealment with those weapons along the trail leading here as a precautionary measure."

"That may prove to be a wise course of action," Jacob agreed, growing increasingly uncomfortable as more of the locals began to stare in his direction. An introvert by nature, he had always been regarded as a recluse by his neighbors. In the past, they had normally taken little notice of him during his infrequent visits to the village. But the scrutiny he was now drawing was becoming disconcerting and he found himself suddenly yearning for the cove's solitude.

"Did Amphitrite say where she was going?" Jacob asked, struggling hard to keep the anxiety he felt out of his voice.

Emmanuel peered at him owlishly before replying. "No, cousin, she gave no indication as to where she was going."

Lucette made her way through the crowd of onlookers and came up to Jacob. "This belongs to you," she said, placing something in his hand. Jacob stared dumbly at the ascot depicting the ivory-skinned girl amid the pack of white dolphins. She held his gaze with solemn reverence. "There was purpose in everything your grandmother did. Maybe time will reveal what this tie signifies."

Jacob folded the tie carefully and slowly turned away.

"Where are you going?" Emmanuel wanted to know.

"Home," Jacob muttered. "I wish to go home."

Emmanuel was aghast. "Did we not just discuss the possibility of Duvalier's assassins roaming the nearby hills?" He shook his head in horror. "I do not want you walking the trail by yourself. I will take you back by boat."

Jacob hesitated. He desperately needed to get away from the village and its people, to be alone to mull over all the extraordinary things he had seen and heard over the past ten hours. He needed to rationalize past events, to put everything in perspective. A long walk by himself, undisturbed, would give him the time he needed for such reflection. But his cousin was right. Traveling back to the cove on foot had potentially dangerous consequences. He turned fully and met Emmanuel's eyes. "As you wish," he acquiesced.

The boat ride down the coast was slow and uneventful. Emmanuel's vessel was similar in construction to Jacob's, pushed along by a listless diesel far past its prime, a mechanical conglomeration of cannibalized parts that, if pushed too hard, protested with a hammering chorus of ear-splitting pings as it coughed occasional wisps of black smoke. Lucette had accompanied both men for the short trip, taking up a position near the bow and sitting quietly as she stared directly ahead.

Emmanuel seemed to sense Jacob's need for reflection, refraining from conversation and piloting the pinnace with a steady hand. With eyes squinted behind spectacles that rode low on the bridge of his nose, he periodically shifted his gaze, alternately scanning the open sea and the waters adjoining the coastline.

Gaining access to the cove was a difficult undertaking, even for a skilled seaman like Emmanuel, and if he did not pay careful attention he could easily miss the narrow break in the reef. With the tide now low, it was the only place within several miles that would allow passage for even a shallow draft boat to the leeward side of the coral barrier. As Emmanuel guided the craft through, imposing but perilous fangs of calcareous growth loomed up on each side of the hull only inches from the water's surface. Once through the treacherous opening, Emmanuel swung the vessel sharply back on a heading opposite the way they had come down the coastline, paralleling the rocky shoreline for nearly a hundred meters.

From the seaward side of the reef the entrance to the cove was almost impossible to spot. The natural topography of eclipsing rock formations rising steeply from the water presented an optical illusion that kept the gorge well hidden. Angled into a jagged bluff of bedrock, the cove entrance was deceptive to the naked eye even at close range.

As they entered the narrow opening, a feeling that something was amiss suddenly engulfed Jacob like a tsunami crashing down on a calm shoreline without warning. Emmanuel steered the boat past the last outcropping in the confined inlet, giving Jacob an unobstructed view of the small structure that served as his home. Amphitrite stood in the doorway with her back facing him, seemingly preoccupied with something in the cabin. Close to the beach, Athena could be seen knifing rapidly through the water and throwing out a wake. She seemed to be in a highly agitated state. As the pinnace glided closer to the beach, Athena began to slap the water violently with her tail. Up to now, he had not seen this type of behavior in the dolphin.

Emmanuel reversed the throttle and slid the bow of the craft gently onto the sandy shore, whereupon Jacob jumped out. Amphitrite was still facing away from him, but as he moved closer she backed out of the entrance to his home.

Jacob abruptly froze as two men emerged from the doorway. Each was clad in blue denim with a red necktie, the typical dress of Duvalier's private militia, the Tonton Makout. One man carried a revolver holstered at his hip while the other brandished an assault rifle. Jacob recognized the rifle to be similar to the weapons carried by the men Athena had swept from the pier, and from photographs he had seen of such firearms, knew them to be Kalashnikov AK-47s. He immediately presumed the men to be the mudslide survivors Emmanuel had talked about. The dried mud covering much of their clothing further supported this presumption.

The man sporting the rifle darted past Amphitrite and came on at Jacob, his eyes filled with malevolence. "Do not attempt to flee," he grunted in Creole. He prodded Jacob forcefully with the muzzle of the weapon. "Lie face down in the sand with your hands behind your head and do not move or speak, otherwise I will kill you."

Jacob considered resisting but quickly abandoned the idea upon studying the man's face. A hair trigger temperament clearly manifested itself there. If irked even slightly, he was certain the assassin would have no compunctions about squeezing off a few rounds.

Lying chest down in the sand, Jacob heard the man order Emmanuel and Lucette from the boat and, in a harsh, belligerent tone, force them to lay prone next to him in the same manner he had been instructed to assume.

Jacob lifted his head and looked forward. The other man grabbed Amphitrite roughly by the arm and walked her over to where he lay. Shoving her down into a sitting position next to Jacob, the man strutted slowly off to one side with his hands clasped stiffly behind his back in a smug, authoritative manner. He was a solidly built individual and from all outward appearances seemed to be the leader of the two-man squad.

"Tell me," he said, "have any of you noticed any unusual flotsam drifting in the local waters?" The man spoke in crisp, impeccable French. He turned around and swaggered back toward Jacob and the others, raising an eyebrow. "Is it possible you might have seen some odd wreckage wash up on the shoreline, what could be identified as the remains of a seaplane or sailboat?"

The man halted and leveled his gaze at Jacob, expecting some kind of response. When Jacob did not answer, the man shifted his eyes to Emmanuel. "You…you are a fisherman. Perhaps you have observed some of these things."

Jacob had not seen any plane wreckage, nor did he anticipate that Emmanuel had, either. He was surprised, however, when his cousin chose to respond. "We have had many sightings of debris and wreckage. It is common after a powerful storm like the one that recently passed through here."

The man stared hard at Emmanuel. "You did not answer the question to my satisfaction. I will ask you again. Did you see what might be considered the wreckage from a seaplane?"

"I have seen no such objects," Emmanuel said.

The man riveted Emmanuel with a baleful glare, punctuated by crazed, chilling eyes. He turned suddenly, his hands still clasped firmly behind him. He held that position for a prolonged period before spinning back around and displaying a shrewd smile. "A rumor has reached my ears that some wreckage from an airplane was discovered near here." He looked once again to Emmanuel for an answer.

"As I already told you, we have found no plane wreckage," Emmanuel spat with annoyance. "What significance does a wrecked seaplane hold for you?"

"You will address me as Captain Henri Ternier, a soldier in the service of President Jean-Claude Duvalier, the leader of our country." The man gave Emmanuel a few seconds to digest the name, then went on speaking. "I should think you would remember my name. Like you and your cousin, I had attended the university in Port-au-Prince during the same period when both of you were students there."

Yes, of course, Jacob thought. The memory of the man came flooding back with brutal clarity. During his studies, two factions had comprised the student body at the university: pro-Duvalier and anti-Duvalier, with those against the current regime predominating by a ratio of three to one. Ternier had been the leader of the group supporting the policies of Baby Doc.

As Jacob scrutinized Ternier he understood why he had failed to immediately recognize him. The man's features had changed considerably. No longer the gangly youth, Ternier's physique had filled out substantially, his shoulders broadening to an impressive width and his frame gaining solid muscle in all the right places. The transformation gave him an imposing bearing of strength and power. Even the structure of his face had changed, maturing into a stately, almost handsome countenance. It was the eyes of the man that had remained the same, however. When Ternier was irked, they burned with a wild intensity that tended to unhinge anyone unfortunate enough to look into them. Jacob also knew the man harbored an exceptional intellect, for Ternier had been one of the top students at the university while he was in attendance there.

Jacob swiveled his eyes and read his cousin's face, seeing the outrage about to erupt. Emmanuel arched his head up in a bold show of defiance, unable to contain his anger. "Duvalier is a murderer and a thief," he spat furiously. "He has plundered the national treasury and stolen most of the government assets. He holds power at the end of a gun. Instead of seeking change and positive ends, he seeks to destroy the very fabric of Haitian society. He-"

Emmanuel's outburst was abruptly silenced as the man with the Kalashnikov slammed the butt of the weapon forcefully into the back of his head. Lucette let out a terrified scream as Emmanuel's body instantly went slack, his face slumping into the sand.

"Do not attempt to try my patience again," Ternier warned ominously, his demented eyes flaring and falling back on Jacob. "The consequences will be most unpleasant."

Ternier tilted his head and looked at Lucette who sobbed quietly, then turned his gaze on Amphitrite. "Your survival amazes me," he said. "It appears the sea has not taken you, after all. I applaud you for having beaten tremendous odds." He shook his head in a mendacious display of commiseration. "What a pity you have endured the worst the storm could throw at you, only to fall into my hands a second time."

Ternier's words threw Jacob off balance and he shifted his head in an effort to gauge Amphitrite's reaction. Bewilderment blossomed in her expression. He could see that she was having great difficulty trying to make light of what Ternier was saying. As he continued to watch, the water thrashed wildly behind him, and droplets of water began to rain down on all of them. The disturbance seemed to escalate in direct proportion to Amphitrite's growing frustration at failing to remember past events.

The sound of the commotion drew Ternier's attention and he smiled with wry amusement. "I have to assume the dolphin over there is the reason you did not drown. Too bad it cannot save you now."

Amphitrite stared at Ternier, her face revealing intense inner confusion.

"The woman has no recollection of what you speak," Jacob found himself saying. "She has lost her memory." He heard Ternier's underling move behind him, half expecting to be clouted in the same manner as his cousin.

Ternier held out a hand, keeping the other man at bay. Studying Amphitrite intently, he said, "You do not remember our previous encounter?"

Amphitrite did not acknowledge the question. She seemed to be lost in a quagmire of deep introspection.

Ternier grew angry. "Answer me, woman! Do you remember what happened?"

"I have no remembrance of my life prior to coming here," Amphitrite stated. "I draw only a blank when I attempt to recall it."

"Then I will refresh your memory," Ternier snapped back, his face contorting into a twisted, sadistic grin. He seemed to glean some perverted joy in what he was about to divulge. "Several weeks ago I had been given the responsibility of delivering a valuable cargo for President Duvalier. With a small contingent of men under my command, the cargo was loaded aboard a seaplane about thirty kilometers south of this location. The flight was bound for Grand Cayman Island. The cargo was quite sizeable, and unfortunately, may have put too much of a strain on the aircraft engines. As a result, the plane lost power and the pilot had to execute an emergency landing into the sea. While descending, the pilot spotted a sailboat in the water below and he was able to land the plane safely near the boat's position."

Ternier paused, fixating widened, unnerving eyes on Amphitrite, watching her closely to assess the effect his words were having. "You were aboard that boat, you and three companions. In your eagerness to provide assistance, I commandeered your vessel. It was my intention to remove all of the cargo from the plane and load it aboard your boat, then complete my assignment by sailing on to the Caymans. The pilot of the seaplane had received weather reports that a hurricane was on the way and informed me that we had precious little time to transfer all the cargo. To expedite the process, we managed to lash the plane and boat together."

Ternier stopped talking, waiting for some kind of reaction. When Amphitrite failed to respond, he continued. "As it turned out, you were not very cooperative and proved to be a constant thorn in my side, consorting with your friends to thwart my mission at every turn. Because of you, I found it necessary to put an end to the resistance your companions posed by shooting each of them and throwing their bodies overboard. You were spared because you were needed to operate the boat and navigate it to my planned destination. Your boat was equipped with a state-of-the-art global positioning system, which neither the plane's pilot nor myself knew how to operate. As a precautionary measure, I ordered my men to bind you to a chair in the boat's main cabin. While my men were transferring the cargo, the sea began to build, eventually making it impossible for us to complete the transfer to your vessel. Only a few items still remained aboard the seaplane, but this nevertheless created a most serious dilemma for me. You see, Duvalier is a most unforgiving individual. Had I lost even a small portion of the cargo, he would have been very displeased. Therefore, the only available course of action for me was to attempt to ride out the storm, keeping the plane and boat tied together. As it turned out, the ferocity of the storm surpassed my expectations, and the boat and plane began to slam together with such force that I was afraid both would eventually sink. At that point, I had no alternative but to cut the plane loose. I attached a towline to it and trailed it behind the boat, leaving the pilot and two of my men aboard the aircraft to do what they could to keep it afloat. That plan also failed. After playing out the entire length of towline, a large wave flipped the plane upside down, snapping off one of the wings. Within moments it took on water and began to submerge. Had I not cut the towline, the weight of the plane would have pulled the boat under as well. Unfortunately, three of my men went down with it."

Ternier lifted his gaze from Amphitrite and glanced out over the water, his expression remote as if reliving the incident. Jacob still had his hands clasped tightly behind his head, not wanting to provoke the man holding the rifle. His neck and upper back began to burn painfully with the effort of keeping his eyes trained on Ternier's face. To relieve the discomfort, he rested his chin in the sand and watched Ternier's booted feet as they took several paces beyond where Emmanuel lay. His cousin was still unconscious, the glasses on his face askew and partially buried in the sand.

"It was most dispiriting, seeing that plane go down like that," Ternier said. "But at least I had instructed the pilot to record the plane's last known position just before we landed in the sea. Our geodetic coordinates were written down on a scrap of paper and placed within a waterproof briefcase which I carried with me. After hijacking your boat, I noted the water to be less than a hundred meters deep, as indicated by the depth sounder aboard the vessel. With such information I was confident I could return to the area and, with a little luck and the right equipment, locate the plane again. The cargo aboard it could then be recovered. Misfortune, however, has a way of continuing once it comes your way. I soon learned that the boat was taking on water at a rate greater than the bilge pump could handle. An inspection of the inside hull revealed a jagged hole with seawater pouring in. My guess was that one of seaplane pontoons had punctured the hull. The intensity of wind and sea had reached dangerous levels, and with the waves surging, the sailboat had taken a terrible pounding from the seaplane while the two had been tied together. It was inevitable we were going to sink. I quickly realized I had to abandon the vessel if I was to survive. The boat was equipped with an inflatable life raft, the type that is enclosed and provides shelter from the elements. Launching it was exceptionally difficult, particularly since I had only one man left to help me carry out such a task."

A muffled groan suddenly interrupted Ternier's recount as Emmanuel stirred. Powerless to do anything, Jacob watched with dismay as one of Ternier's booted feet abruptly pivoted and impacted viciously against the side of Emmanuel's temple. Lucette wailed loudly once more as Emmanuel lapsed back into silence a second time. Jacob tensed and peered upward, straining hard to catch a glimpse of the intense hatred that flamed in the countenance hovering above him.

Ternier cast cruel, accusing eyes on Amphitrite. The promise of depravity-ridden reprisals for all his ill-gained misfortune flowed from him like searing heat from a furnace. Paradoxically, his voice remained calm.

"You proved yourself to be a most resourceful woman. You managed to free yourself from your bonds and arm yourself with a spear gun while the life raft was being launched. I had just climbed aboard it and had reached back to take possession of my briefcase handed me by my assistant. This was no simple task because the raft was bouncing wildly in the surge. While my assistant was handing me the case, you fired a spear into his back. He fell into the sea and disappeared from sight."

There was a moment's hesitation as Ternier let Amphitrite absorb this last bit of information. Athena was now slapping the water with a renewed frenzy and Jacob felt another spray of water, heavier than before, rain down on him. He could see some of the droplets fall on Ternier, but the man seemed not to notice.

Amphitrite stared up at Ternier stolidly. "What happened after that?"

A brooding scowl materialized on Ternier's features. "The force of the wind pulled the life raft away, and as I looked back, your boat was beginning to flounder. It was awash in whitewater and began listing to one side. You stood at the railing, watching me. I found it rather strange that you showed no fear."

The frown Ternier wore changed into a twisted smile at the memory. "Until today, that was the last glimpse I had of you just before a large wave took your vessel." He scanned Amphitrite's face closely. "Has the event I just described caused your memory to return?"

Amphitrite's features remained devoid of all emotion. "I remember none of this."

Ternier went rigid, the whites of his eyes suddenly appearing bloodshot and bulging grotesquely. The sight made Jacob think of stories told by his grandmother about zombies risen from the dead. Clearly this was not the answer Ternier wanted to hear. Jacob had seen this same reaction in the man during his days at the university and knew Ternier was on the verge of bloodlust. He remembered an incident in which Ternier had suddenly attacked another student without warning, exhibiting the same behavior just before plunging a knife into the chest of his victim. Even though the other student had died, Ternier had not been charged with any wrongdoing. It was his political clout with Duvalier that had exonerated him of the crime. Even back then, rumor had it that Ternier was a spy for the Haitian dictator.

"I must have the geodetic coordinates of the area where the seaplane went down," Ternier said calmly, his tone belying the madness consuming his face. "You will search your memory and give me the position of your vessel when you first saw the plane."

Amphitrite met his frightening gaze, appearing unfrazzled and sitting mute.

Ternier suddenly reached out, grabbing Amphitrite's shirt and tugging hard. "Do you hear me, woman? You-" A metamorphosis seemed to take hold of his expression as he became aware of the amulet that popped out from under the shirt. In one swift motion, his hand shot out and yanked the medallion from Amphitrite's neck, snapping the chain from which it dangled. "Where did you get this?"

Amphitrite's eyes narrowed and she rose up from the sand. "It is ill advised for a man such as yourself to hold what is in your hand. Only pain can come of it."

Something sizzled and Ternier flinched, letting out a thunderous bellow. He dropped the amulet as if it were a burning chunk of coal. His eyes widened again, but this time out of shock and awe. "You are a witch of the vaudun, a white mambo!" he roared accusingly. "How is such a thing possible?"

Amphitrite reached down and retrieved the amulet from the sand. Jacob perceived the crystal at its center emitting vivid bursts of blue fire as she stepped close to Ternier. "You cannot hurt any of us anymore," she said, holding the charm in such a way that the light emanating from its jewel danced up into Ternier's face. To Jacob, her tone matched her expression, a countenance in which all traces of emotion were absent.

Ternier took a step backward. "How can such a thing be?" he languished, his voice lowered to almost a whisper. "Whites have no knowledge of the secrets voodoo holds." He stared down at the amulet, then gazed back at

Amphitrite in disbelief. "No. You are a *cheval*. A loa has taken possession of your soul," he bayed. "It is the only explanation why you are here now, why the storm did not take you."

"You cannot hurt any of us anymore," Amphitrite repeated.

"You have already died," Ternier insisted, his voice rising into a frantic shout. "It explains why your memory fails you, why you have no recollection of your former life. You are not alive. You cannot be."

"You will leave this place at once and never return," Amphitrite commanded, crowding closer to Ternier and holding the amulet near his face.

Ternier drew back, reaching for the revolver at his hip and drawing it from the holster. "You are an accursed thing, a vile corpse with the spirit of a loa inside you," he raved, bringing the barrel of the pistol to bear directly between her eyes.

Jacob sprang to his feet, no longer mindful of the man at his rear. He was by no means an athletic individual, but he nevertheless summoned all the strength and speed he could muster and channeled it into one fleeting movement, slamming into Ternier's blind side with jarring force. The collision drove the hand gripping the gun off its intended alignment a split second before the weapon discharged, the sound cracking the air as if caused by a whip. Jacob felt his shoulder go numb from the impact as both men went sprawling. Ternier was a big powerfully built man and Jacob felt as though he had tackled a tree.

As Jacob wrestled with the larger man, Ternier glanced over at his accomplice. "Shoot her!" he howled. "Shoot her before she uses any more of her magic against us."

Knowing he could not stop the inevitable, Jacob looked up in horror at the sight of the man wielding the assault rifle. Preoccupied with this, he suddenly became airborne as Ternier placed a foot against his chest and pushed hard. He felt the wind knocked from him as he landed on his back near the water's edge, a good twelve feet from where Ternier had launched him. With dazed vision, he watched the nightmare unfold as if in a dream.

The man with the rifle stood frozen for several moments, refraining from pointing the weapon. His eyes were filled with fear and indecision as he faced Amphitrite. "It is unwise to provoke a loa," the man gasped tremulously, an obvious slave to superstitious dogma. Keeping his gaze trained on the amulet in Amphitrite's hand, he added, "We invite great misfortune upon ourselves by doing so."

"Then you are a fool," Ternier spat venomously, rising from the ground. He still retained custody of the pistol, but the gun was now covered with a coating of damp sand. He cocked the hammer, bringing a sickening smile to his face.

Jacob quickly gathered his wits about him. He had a gambit to play that just might drive the wedge of controversy still further into the opposing views. "It was this woman who caused the mudslide that destroyed your truck convoy," he announced, spitting out the words in time to make Ternier look over at him before the pistol was fired. "She was able to invoke such an event simply by willing it. She does not want to harm you, she just wants you to go away and leave us in peace. If you try to hurt her or any one of us, the repercussions will be disastrous for you."

"I will take my chances," Ternier snarled, bug-eyed once again. He turned back in Amphitrite's direction.

Jacob played one more card. "Her powers are greater than you can imagine. She defeated Erzulie last night."

Ternier froze in his tracks. He turned back fully to face Jacob. "Such a feat is not possible. Only one mambo was powerful enough to oppose Erzulie and she is dead. You are a liar!"

Jacob forced himself to laugh. "I have been called many things by people who truly know me, but never a liar. The amulet held by this woman was taken from the hand of Erzulie in the same manner by which she took it from you."

For the moment, it was becoming clear that Jacob's revelation was keeping the situation temporarily in check, for Ternier's expression became contorted with an equal mix of caution and the need for retribution. "That is impossible," he persisted uncertainly. "Erzulie has likely laid waste to Malique by now."

"Erzulie has left Malique undamaged and all its citizens alive," Jacob chuckled. "She has already fled down the coast, fearful of what this woman can do to her." The words spoken by Amphitrite during her confrontation with the witch suddenly came to mind and he grasped at them in desperation, hoping to neutralize Ternier's thirst for vengeance. "If you direct any further aggression against any one of us, that aggression will only flow back at you and your companion tenfold."

Ternier continued to vacillate for several seconds longer before scowling darkly. "You are lying!" he growled savagely. He raised the revolver and aimed it at Jacob. "Tell me you are lying!"

Jacob ignored the threat and looked over at the second man. "Only an idiot would fail to heed my warning. This woman was able to destroy your assault force because of what they intended to do to the nearby villagers." He brought a measure of sternness to his voice and manner. "Either leave us in peace or the loa inside this woman will bring an agonizing end to you. Harm us and you gamble with the lives of your children as well. Incessant misfortune and suffering will plague your families for generations to come."

A contemptuous laugh sprang from Ternier as he took careful aim at Jacob's head. "I have no children," he sneered.

"Stop!" the other man screamed, suddenly pointing the barrel of his assault weapon at Ternier. "Do not do it. I do not wish to have the wrath of a powerful loa befall me or my descendents."

Ternier glanced back in surprise at the lone soldier under his command. "Do you presume to question the judgement of your commanding officer?"

The man remained insubordinate. "Anger has clouded your judgement. You do not see what you are doing. I have a wife and three children and will not risk bestowing a life of torment and misery on them by offending a goddess of the underworld."

Ternier's eyes bore into the man. "You will lower your weapon at once, sergeant," he ordered.

The sergeant shook his head lugubriously. "I cannot, I have my family to consider."

Ternier's brow bunched questioningly over this sudden turn of events. "You would shoot me?"

"If I must, yes."

"Very well," Ternier said, seeming to concede the argument. He sighed deeply and extended his arms wide in a show of compliance. "Maybe you are right." He turned away from his mutinous subordinate, lifting the flap on his holster and appearing to slide the handgun back into its leather case.

"Begging your forgiveness, sir, but you gave me no choice," the sergeant lamented apologetically. He dropped the muzzle of his weapon so that it pointed at the ground. "You know I have never before hesitated to carry out your orders without question, but this woman has shown us powerful magic. She-"

Two sharp reports suddenly cut through the air, startling Jacob. The sergeant's mouth hung open in a silent 'O' of shocked amazement as he looked down at the merging twin stains spreading rapidly across the front of his shirt. Slowly, he lifted glazed eyes to bear dully on Ternier, taking an unsteady step forward and dragging the tip of the assault rifle through the sand before letting it slip from his fingers. Taking another step, his left knee gave way under him, causing him to totter sideways to the ground where he rolled onto his back and stared sightlessly at the sky.

To Jacob, the moment was surrealistic. Ternier stood immobile, his dark pupils contracted to the size of pinpricks within the swollen white orbs surrounding them. His gun arm was still fully extended, gray tendrils of smoke drifting lazily upward from the barrel of the pistol gripped tightly in his hand.

Ternier looked down at the fallen man, his demeanor suddenly changing and exhibiting infatuation over the spectacle of death sprawled before him. "A pity he feared the cheval more than me," he mumbled as though talking to himself. He glanced quickly at Jacob, but tilted his head to keep a wary eye on Amphitrite as well. "Had he not challenged my authority, he would have seen the absurdity of your story, though it seems the woman here is able to exert some small measure of magical power."

Ternier took several paces to his left until both Amphitrite and Jacob were within his line of sight, keeping Amphitrite closest to him. "But now I must end the threat you pose, whatever you are." Thumbing back the hammer on the revolver, he pointed the gun at Amphitrite and squeezed the trigger.

Nothing happened!

Though the firing pin clicked with an audible sharpness, the pistol failed to fire. As if in panic, Ternier depressed the trigger several more times with the same result. His composure seemed to be disintegrating rapidly. Hurriedly, he examined the weapon, bringing it close to his face, then opened the cylinder for an inspection of the cartridges. With practiced hands, he removed the four dud .38 caliber bullets plus the two spent casings, replacing them with spare rounds from his belt. Expertly, he spun the reloaded cylinder and clicked it shut.

Amphitrite remained standing before Ternier, not attempting to move during the reloading process. "The weapon will not work," she said calmly.

Ternier's lips curled into a sadistic smile. "We shall see," he replied, the words coming out in a sick, demented laugh. Once again he targeted Amphitrite and pulled back on the trigger.

Still nothing!

Ternier let out a string of profanity. Thoroughly enraged, he hurled the pistol away and reached down, snatching from the sand the Kalashnikov that lay near the dead sergeant. Examining the weapon's safety, he flicked it to semi-automatic firing mode. Satisfied, he brought the stock of the weapon to his shoulder and sighted over the barrel, aligning it on Amphitrite.

"The weapon is useless in your hands," Amphitrite maintained doggedly, displaying not the slightest bit of fear.

Ternier growled insanely before squeezing back on the trigger. A single earsplitting clap resounded, sending out a shock wave that reverberated off the confining cove walls before fading away into a throbbing silence. Ternier staggered back, stunned and bleeding, the assault rifle torn from his hands, its barrel ripped asunder and laying in shattered pieces on the ground in front of him. Falling to his knees, he moaned lethargically, his arms drooped pitifully at his sides. A gush of blood flowed profusely from an open gash along his cheekbone and lower jaw where the stock of the weapon had abutted the side of his face just before exploding. Dazedly, he stared up at Amphitrite with glazed, uncomprehending eyes as she stepped close to him.

Amphitrite placed a hand on his injury. "You were forewarned, but you did not listen," she said softly. "Your hatred has come back at you full circle."

Ternier opened his mouth to speak but abruptly collapsed into the sand, now unconscious.

Jacob was immediately at Amphitrite's side, trying to make light of what he had just witnessed. Intrigued, he reached for the remains of the gun barrel, discovering the wet sand clogging the muzzle. Enlightened with understanding, he looked questioningly at Amphitrite. "You knew the rifle barrel was blocked and would explode?"

Amphitrite stared back with soulful eyes. "I only knew we could not be harmed." She looked over at Emmanuel, still out cold, his head resting in Lucette's lap. Lucette was stroking the side of his head soothingly where blood had congealed from the vicious kick Ternier had delivered.

"We must heal Emmanuel's injury before there is permanent damage," Amphitrite advised. "Help me pull him out into the water, Jacob."

A minute later, Jacob, Amphitrite and Lucette had Emmanuel in waist deep water, careful to keep his head propped above the surface. Athena swam in close and nuzzled her beak against the nape of Emmanuel's neck, emitting strange sounding creaks as she did so. Jacob noted the severity of Emmanuel's injury, an ugly laceration in his cousin's left temple.

Holding the amulet in her left hand and placing her right over the wound, Amphitrite closed her eyes, appearing to focus her full concentration on some image of the mind. Almost immediately, the quartz jewel at the center of the talisman began to pulse slowly with an eerie blue light, dimly at first and then growing in brightness as it blinked with escalating rapidity. Reflexively, Jacob closed his eyes at the blinding flash that suddenly erupted from the jewel, a light so intense that it seemed to penetrate to the very core of his being.

As Jacob opened his eyes, a multitude of spots danced before them, and several moments passed before he was able to see clearly again. Emmanuel abruptly stirred and his eyelids fluttered wide to full awareness. "What has happened?" he asked weakly.

Lucette let out a small joyful cry and a cascade of tears flowed down her cheeks as she clung to her husband.

"You were hurt and Amphitrite revived you," Jacob said, awed by the sight of Emmanuel's almost fully healed wound.

Jacob shifted his gaze to the white woman's face, amazed at her strange abilities, but his manner changed swiftly to one of concern as he studied her.

Amphitrite appeared physically drained and paler than usual. Athena drifted to her side, letting the woman clutch her dorsal fin for support.

"You must rest!" Jacob found himself saying. "You have been subjected to more than any woman in your condition should be put through." He reached out and placed a hand on her shoulder. "Come! I will help you from the water."

Within minutes, everyone was settled into Jacob's small cottage. Unsure if Ternier was alive or dead, Jacob decided to go back outside and check on the man. Ternier was still out cold, but his pulse was steady and the open wound on the side of his face had ceased hemorrhaging. He wondered if Amphitrite had been responsible for stopping the bleeding when she had laid a hand on the injury.

Not wanting to take any more chances, however, Jacob retrieved some spare rope from his boat and hog-tied Ternier, binding his arms and legs behind him while the man still remained unconscious and leaving him where he lay. He would let the Tonton Makout captain stay in that position for the time being, still considering the man to be extremely dangerous despite Amphitrite's belief that he could not hurt any of them. Though it went against his core nature to treat another human being this way, he would rather be harsh than foolhardy, and besides, he was just too damned tired to attempt to move the big man at this time.

Rising from the prostrate form, Jacob looked over at Ternier's dead underling. He would bury the man a little later, but right now other things weighed heavily on his mind.

Distractedly, he wandered along the beach, and as he did so his eyes fell upon the discarded handgun lying in the sand directly in front of him. On impulse he picked it up, carefully inspecting the weapon and determining that the muzzle was free of any sand or debris and that the firing pin was intact. Thumbing the cylinder open, he removed the cartridges one by one, examining each round carefully for any flaws before placing it back in its chamber. Puzzled, he aimed the gun at the opposite side of the cove and pulled the trigger, expecting the firearm to remain dormant. The weapon abruptly jumped in his hand as a shot rang out. Even at a distance, he could discern a burst of rock fragments where the bullet had struck, a stark testament to the gun's lethal power.

Dumbfounded, he examined the pistol again. The recent string of events he had been witness to were rife with phenomena that could not adequately be explained in the universe he had come to know and understand, a place where certain proven physical laws supposedly governed and could not be violated. Yet here he was again, observing still another paradox that slipped through the net of reasonable explanation.

Thoroughly confused, he tossed the gun aside as though it were some repugnant, hideous thing. Wearily, he sat down in the sand and stared long and hard out over the water, his mind churning with a myriad of previously uncharted possibilities. Like a tangled mass of worms, they swarmed and ceaselessly intertwined, each segment in constant motion, interminably disappearing and reemerging. One thought in particular kept rising to prominence within their midst, however. *Was it conceivable that Ternier had been correct about Amphitrite? Was she a cheval, possessed by the spirit of a loa? And even more importantly, if this were somehow true, did this sufficiently rationalize all the improbable happenings he had observed?*

Jacob continued to sit and meditate deeply on these matters for such a prolonged period that by the time he arose, the sun had set, replaced by the grandeur of countless pinpricks of light twinkling majestically above on a velvet carpet of night.

- 15 -

Skimming over the ocean at full throttle, Jake had no idea what he was going to do next. What he did know, however, was that the crew of the closest tuna trawler were not the type of people that would act kindly towards the girl, assuming that was where she had gone. And if Natalie was truly in trouble as Destiny had said, then he had a debt to repay. He owed the female dolphin that much. The girl was another enigma. There was something about her that automatically made him want to protect her, some intangible arcane quality that was too elusive to grasp.

As Jake approached the fishing vessel floating ponderously before him, he could clearly see its immense net being deployed. A small workboat was working in concert with the vessel and currently in the process of hauling the purse seine back to the ship to complete the entrapment circle. Weighted at the bottom and having a continuous series of floatation buoys strung together along its upper edge, the purse seine was like a gargantuan drape that was moved along an invisible circular curtain rod, ultimately positioned to close off a huge volume of ocean. Once fully deployed, a set of cables acting as draw strings were used to pull the bottom of the net together much like the jaws of an enormous purse, thus closing off any possible escape to fish and other creatures trapped within its confines.

Through the binoculars aboard the Angel he had noted the ship's name. The *San Carlo* was a modern tuna trawler, the majority of its hull and superstructure standing out a bright white in stark contrast to the dark blue sea upon which it rode. Angled so that its bow was nearer to Jake than its stern, the ship's orientation was such that its port side faced him, a hulking barrier of steel that seemed to portend an aura of extreme menace the closer he got to it. A sixteen-foot runabout with a lone driver cruised further out from both the ship and workboat. Jake was familiar with the tactics being used in such an operation, knowing the noise from the runabout's engine would tend to keep shoals of fish herded toward the net until the circle was completed.

Judging the trawler to be just over 280 feet in length, Jake understood that a vast amount of fish could be stored in its refrigerated holds and that it carried enormously powerful winches. He also knew that once the catch was trapped and the seine drawn into a tighter circle, the crew would remove captured fish from the net's confines by dipping a large collecting basket into the squirming mass, then dropping the catch into a chute leading to a freezer compartment. Organisms unfortunate enough to remain entangled in the net's mesh would be ripped apart once the winches hauled the net through the elevated power block, which was suspended from a gantry straddling the ship's rear superstructure. If left in the net, remnants of shredded and crushed fish would decompose and produce the unpleasant smell of rot and decay.

As if confirming this, a slight breeze sprang up, blowing off the ship directly into Jake's face and bringing with it a sickening stench. The loathsome odor did not surprise him. In fact, he had expected it. He knew that many Colombian fishing vessels were used as drug runners. True fishermen generally took pride in their vessel, often taking the time to keep their ship free of rotting organic matter following a catch. A vigilant power block operator was responsible for monitoring the net as it was being hauled back aboard, often stopping the net to remove fish caught up in the mesh. On the other hand, putrefying organic matter would make the vessel particularly offensive to approach, thus discouraging shipboard searches by crews of the U.S. Coast Guard.

Jake continued to scan the water between him and the ship but failed to spot the girl or the giant bottlenose that carried her. He had lost sight of Destiny and her mount shortly after she had left the vicinity of the Angel, and since she had seemed to be holding to a course aimed straight at the San Carlo, he had naturally assumed that was where she had gone. He suddenly wondered if she had purposely decoyed him in the wrong direction in order to avoid being pursued. Although he couldn't rule out such a possibility, he still trusted his instincts that she had headed toward the Colombian ship.

Coming closer to the vessel, Jake discerned seven crewmembers on the trawler's stern and three more individuals aboard the workboat. He could see that the ends of the net were being drawn inexorably closer together. Acting as a small tug, the workboat only had to travel perhaps another six hundred feet in a clockwise direction before the leading edge of the net was brought back to the ship. The net was immense, encompassing an area which he estimated to be at least fifteen hundred feet across.

As yet, the trawler's crew had not taken any notice of him. Nearing the vessel, he could see that something else had grabbed their attention. All heads on both ship and workboat appeared to be drawn to the same focal point, which was out near the center of the area girded by the net's floatation boom. Whatever it was, it seemed to distract all hands from their assigned tasks, creating a mild confusion among their ranks. Mouths agape, men on the ship's deck ran to the rails to get a better look, while the crew of the tug ceased all activity as they too sought a more distinct view of something in the water.

The diversion was short-lived. One of the men on the trawler's stern began gesticulating wildly and shouting orders. Within moments all hands were scrambling back to their stations. The workboat abruptly ceased its aimless drift and immediately resumed its bid to complete the enclosure. With renewed and fervid energy, the entire crew went back to work, but now with the objective of keeping the thing they had seen from escaping. Harvesting tuna was now secondary.

With all eyes continuing to stay riveted on the object, Jake was able to slip to within a hundred feet of the ship's stern before bringing attention to himself. The rear of the ship no longer blocked his view and he could now see the cause of the uproar. Off to one side of the ringed enclosure, Destiny's petite form sat astride the huge albino bull. The bull was assisting a smaller white dolphin in keeping a gray bottlenose afloat, both albinos nudging the creature toward the slowly diminishing gap in the net.

Leaning his weight to starboard, Jake brought the waverunner on a new heading, streaking toward the opening separating the tug from the ship's aft section, the area the net had not yet closed off. As he raced past the trawler's stern, one of the crewmen looked his way, the same individual who moments earlier had been shouting at everyone. Jake recognized the man immediately. It was the one called Pedro, the vicious Colombian fisherman Zimbola had knocked unconscious outside the Port-au-Prince tavern the night before. Even at a distance of thirty meters, Jake could make out the heavy bruises on the man's face and neck. Sporting two ugly black eyes and a huge purple contusion where Zimbola's banana-size fingers had gripped his throat, it was a wonder Pedro was standing on his feet at all, let alone moving about.

As Jake shot past, it was apparent that Pedro did not know what to make of Jake's presence, evidenced by the unmistakable surprise etched on the Colombian's face. Jake was certain the man could not possibly have noticed him while in the grasp of a crushing stranglehold applied by Zimbola.

A moment later, the Kawasaki roared through the gap in the net, still three hundred feet wide, but shrinking ever smaller with each passing second. His first impulse was to steer directly for the girl, but a sudden idea made him swerve toward the tug.

Having an open deck that lacked any kind of pilothouse or cabin, the workboat was outfitted with two powerful diesel engines capable of towing the massive purse seine. Possessing a raked bow with a slight taper, the craft was wide and squat, with an overall length of approximately thirty feet and a fourteen-foot beam. Bearing down on the vessel, Jake let off the throttle, letting the Kawasaki coast into the path of the on-coming tugboat. The three men working its deck stared back at him as if dumbstruck. Drifting at idle, Jake drew his fingers across his throat, gesturing that he wanted the tug operator to cut his engines.

Instead of reducing power, however, the workboat kept coming on at a relatively slow, steady pace. Either the tug operator had failed to read the sign or Jake was being ignored. If Jake failed to move, the Kawasaki would be overrun and swept back into the tug's churning propeller blades where he would be torn to pieces.

Jake decided it was time for a little persuasion. Up to now he had kept the Kawasaki's guns concealed under a small tarp tied down snugly over the weapons. Yanking on the slipknot that held the tarp in place, he lifted the canvas covering from the guns, bunching it quickly and stowing it in the rear compartment. With a flick of the throttle, he turned the waverunner sideways so that the crewmen aboard the workboat were given a broadside glimpse of the automatic weapons, then swung the small craft towards the on-coming vessel, both gun barrels trained on it.

With a broad smile on his face, Jake yelled the word, *"Pare!"* He knew little Spanish and doubted the workboat's crew would hear the command to stop above the din of the tug's diesels. But the gun barrels turned out to be a most effective communicator, and the eyes of the tug operator went wide at the threat they posed. Cowed for the moment, the man abruptly put the engines into neutral, staring back at Jake, his face bloated with fear and uncertainty.

Unfortunately for Jake, the driver of the small runabout had seen the situation unfold and apparently had other ideas. With reckless abandon, he swept past the ship's stern, racing toward Jake's rear as if to ram him. Coming to within sixty feet of the Kawasaki, the boat veered sharply and began to speed away, but not before the driver tossed something into the air. As if in slow motion, the object flew end over end in a lazy arc, following a trajectory that sought the Kawasaki.

As the small cylinder reached its apex, the blood in Jake's veins turned to ice as he realized what it was. Reflexively, he twisted the throttle gripped in his hand with such savageness that he was afraid it would shear away. Like a thoroughbred racehorse bolting from a starting gate, the Kawasaki leapt forward, but to Jake's now heightened awareness it accelerated with all the sluggish inertia of a thousand ton barge.

Glancing over his shoulder, he caught a final glimpse of the thing as it fell into the sea. As if attesting to the skill of the man who had hurled it, the object hit the spot where he had been only an instant earlier with chilling accuracy. He was nearly flung from the waverunner as the sea erupted violently behind him, lifting the small craft clear of the water for one brief moment. Falling back into the sea, the craft slammed down with bone jarring force. Dazed, Jake had the vague impression the Kawasaki had been severely damaged, but the familiar vibration of the engine beneath him seemed to contradict this. Still managing to clutch the throttle, Jake felt the waverunner race forward as a tumultuous spray washed over him. With a detached lucidity, he noticed a tall geyser mushroom overhead, then plummet to rejoin the sea. By the time he fully regained his senses, the remnants of the water column began to dissipate into a fine mist, dispersing rapidly on the wind. It was then that the tug loomed up at him and he had to lean the Kawasaki heavily on its larboard side to avoid a head-on collision.

Missing the tug's bow by mere inches, Jake righted the waverunner, bringing it back on an even keel and scanning the sea for his assailant. He caught sight of the motorboat racing away rapidly in the direction of the girl. He quickly realized he had a dilemma on his hands, one that offered only two options to choose from, neither of which would do much to remedy the present situation. Deeming the driver of the runabout to be the more immediate threat, he tore after him. He had no idea what these men would do to the girl and her companions should they be captured, but knowing what he did of their cruel natures he could only assume the worse. As far as he was concerned, the girl and the dolphins were in big trouble if he did not intercede at once.

With the modified STX-12F engine now running wide open, he began to overtake the runabout like a cheetah running down a rabbit. As he closed in, the driver glanced back at him in obvious surprise, alarmed at how fast the Kawasaki was closing the distance separating them. The man suddenly turned and reached for something as the craft under him bounced over the waves. Hunching his shoulders, the man looked back again, tracking Jake's approach. Without warning, the driver lobbed another canister behind him. This time Jake was ready and he swung the waverunner wide of the grenade's path, veering away almost laterally. Once again the water erupted in a towering geyser, but Jake was well clear of the blast.

Putting the Kawasaki into a steep bank, Jake angled the small craft back to head off the runabout, giving it full throttle. He literally exploded across the water and quickly outflanked the driver, effectively cutting him off from the girl. All at once, the runabout veered away and Jake pulled in behind him, much the way a fighter pilot might come up behind an enemy aircraft during a dogfight. He had all he was going to take from the man in front of him. Without taking his eyes from his quarry, he thumbed aside the safety guard on the M-60's arming switch and flicked the toggle. He had the advantage now, and as he closed in on the driver he could see the man stare back into the gun barrels mounted atop the Kawasaki, the expression on his face seeming to quail at the deadly power they represented. The man was swarthy, burned dark from too much time spent in the sun, but his skin seemed to suddenly pale and in his demeanor Jake sensed the panic of a routed foe.

In an attempt to shake Jake off his tail, the man took the boat into a sharp right turn, sliding out from under the sixty's sights. Jake had anticipated the move and reacted with the swiftness of a mongoose taking down a cobra, sticking to the runabout's tail like a Louisiana tick. The driver was now running a zigzag course, but one that was taking the racing pair ever closer to the purse seine's floatation boom.

With sudden abruptness the driver veered acutely, tracking back in the opposite direction. Jake mimicked the maneuver, pulling to within thirty feet of the runabout's stern and lining up the sixty on the Evinrude outboard engine that powered the craft. Looking beyond the runabout, Jake made sure the girl and her companions were currently out of his line of fire. Satisfied, he triggered the machine gun. A shudder swept through the Kawasaki as a burst of rounds poured from the weapon and tore through the Evinrude. His spirit lifted as the outboard cowling flew apart a brief nanosecond before the cylinders flared into a fireball. The explosion sent the driver hurtling through the air and into the sea as the boat spun sharply toward the floatation boom defining the net's boundary. Continuing on with unspent momentum, the boat plowed into the boom, nearly gliding over it before the remnants of its outdrive got hung up in the mesh. It was then that it's fuel tank ignited, setting off a monstrous secondary blast that sent a huge fireball swirling skyward. The concussion from the explosion nearly toppled Jake from the Kawasaki, forcing him to turn his face away from the ensuing heat. He realized he had initiated a chain reaction that had triggered the unused grenades aboard the runabout.

Jake looked back at the boat driver. Shaken up and a little scorched but otherwise none the less for wear, the man floundered aimlessly about, kept afloat by an orange life vest strapped to his chest. Shifting his gaze in the direction of the runabout, Jake realized it had sunk from sight, pulling a small portion of the net below the surface. Steering closer to the breach, he stared down into the clear water. The boat was caught up on the seine, no more than fifteen feet below him, a gaping hole in its keel. The weight of it had compromised the positive buoyancy of the floats in the immediate area, causing the edge of the net to sag downward.

To Jake, this was an enormous stroke of good fortune. With adrenaline still coursing through him, he located the tug. As expected, its operator had recommenced towing the net and was now only moments away from reaching the ship. His pursuit of the runabout had almost taken him to the far side of the entrapment circle where he presently sat, a good twelve hundred feet from the ship's stern. As his eyes continued to survey the enclosure, he spied the girl's form bobbing midway between his position and the ship. He quickly fathomed she was moving away from him, albeit slowly.

Twisting the throttle, he pivoted the Kawasaki and raced over the open water like a man possessed. The driver of the runabout glared up at him as Jake flew by, a look of intense hatred screwing up his features. Jake ignored him, leaving the man in his wake and steering directly toward Destiny and the three dolphins. He couldn't help but notice clumps of dead fish littering the water, the bulk of the carnage seeming to be tuna.

The Kawasaki covered the distance to the girl in less than ten seconds, and as Jake throttled the craft down, the girl glanced up at him distractedly. Though her facemask was still strapped firmly in place, he detected the faint glimmer of sadness in her eyes as they gazed back at him from behind the lenses.

Jake shouted stridently. "You've got to stay away from that ship. The-"

A spray of water suddenly sprang up twenty feet away, cutting off Jake's warning. They were taking fire from the direction of the ship. In spite of it he kept his outward demeanor calm, locking his gaze more fixedly on Destiny's face.

"There's an opening in the net," he yelled, pointing to the distant break in the white line delimiting the net's periphery, some five hundred feet away. "You must go there at once!"

Jake turned and indicated the ship as the water erupted again in a series of mini-geysers, this time several feet closer. "The men aboard that vessel will do great harm to you and your friends if you don't get out of here now." He swung the waverunner around, positioning himself between the girl and the ship, shielding her from the deadly salvos.

"Go!" he bellowed.

Destiny studied him for a brief moment longer before the giant bottlenose bearing her began to move away, nudging and pushing the incapacitated gray in unison with its small albino partner. Through the pristine water, Jake could discern the lengthy lateral scar running along the flank of the shorter albino.

Water continued to kick up in sporadic bursts in front of Jake, and he knew it was only a matter of time before the shooter zeroed in on him. In response, he turned the throttle lightly, causing the Kawasaki's nose to rise in alignment with the level of the deck at the ship's stern. The sixty was still armed and he sent a short burst of 7.62mm rounds streaking toward it.

Another storm of gunfire roiled the sea, this time impinging simultaneously on opposite sides of the Kawasaki. Staying low behind the console, Jake spotted gunmen. He was now being targeted by more than one shooter. Giving the engine more gas, he answered the in-coming salvo with another burst. Heads aboard the vessel abruptly hunkered down as the glint of steel sparked briefly along the ship's railing. For several seconds there was no return fire, and Jake glanced behind him quickly, taking the momentary respite to track the girl's progress.

She still had the length of a football field to cover in order to reach the area where the boom sagged. Although he was certain that the albinos were capable of leaping over the barrier at any point along the net's perimeter, he also knew it was unlikely the pair would leave the stricken gray, which was too weak to perform such a feat. Thus it was crucial the group reach the opening if they were going to escape.

Jake snapped his head back, taking in the ship before him. A few gun barrels began to poke out from above the bulwark lining the deck. Gunning the throttle, he brought the nose of the craft higher above the water, leaning the Kawasaki to larboard and peppering the upper edge of the trawler's hull as he did so. The effect was almost instantaneous. Gun muzzles were suddenly withdrawn, disappearing behind the bulwark as he unleashed a withering enfilade of suppressive fire. He kept his strafing run short, letting off the trigger and veering sharply to his left. As he raced away, a curtain of water suddenly rose up on his starboard side. Something zinged close to his scalp a split second before he felt a hot sting on his left triceps. A trickle of blood running down his forearm told him he had been hit, possibly a graze, but he had no time to assess the wound.

Leaning the Kawasaki hard left, he shot away from the ship, building distance between himself and the weapons tracking him. Circling in a wide arc, something caught his eye and, reflexively, he turned his head to see what had drawn his attention. Another runabout, almost identical to the first one, was skirting clockwise along the outside perimeter of the net. Jake chastised himself for not anticipating such a possibility. When he had initially approached the trawler, he had taken note of the small boat suspended from davits situated on the ship's forward port side.

Sometime during the firefight, members of the fishing crew had launched the second runabout covertly from the opposite side of the ship, driving it along the vessel's portside hull, completely hidden from Jake's view. By the time he had spotted it, the boat was way beyond the ship's bow, having already circumvented one-third of the floatation boom. Four men could be seen occupying the boat, three of them bearing firearms. As the runabout raced along the outside edge of the net, it suddenly dawned on him that its passengers were seeking to block the opening in the seine. If they succeeded, Destiny and her retinue would be trapped.

Seeing this, Jake hastily adjusted his course. Though he was still within range of the ship's weaponry, the marksmanship of the gunners was too inept to be effective, and the gunfire quickly abated. The girl was still plainly visible before him, and he estimated her group had only another hundred feet to go before gaining access to the open sea. Unfortunately, the burden of the injured dolphin was making progress exceedingly slow and cumbersome, making it possible for the men in the boat to reach the breach in the net ahead of them.

Only moments elapsed before Jake overtook the three dolphins, and as he sped by he could see Destiny watching him. Rocketing through the gap in the net, he leaned the Kawasaki hard left, nearly laying the craft on its side before cutting the throttle and facing the on-coming boat head on. A steely resolve took hold of his emotions. It was all consuming, pushing against his gut like the icy thrust of an arctic glacier, relentless and unstoppable. He recognized the danger of it, a total disregard for self-preservation. He had experienced it many times in the past, each occurrence transpiring while on dangerous Seal missions. When it swept over him like this, he felt omnipotent and invincible, but a surviving thread of rationality within him understood the utter recklessness of being in such a state. It was as if a portion of his being stepped aside, a neutral observer that was both amazed at his stupidity and powerless to stop it as the feeling came on with all the momentum of a runaway freight train. Helpless in its grip, he threw aside all caution to the wind.

Less than two hundred feet away, the runabout's crew opened up on him, sending a hail of bullets screaming past the waverunner and kicking up the sea behind it. Undaunted, Jake watched the rapidly approaching threat with cold, unflinching eyes, any thoughts of personal safety as remote as the far reaches of the cosmos. He was immune from harm, invulnerable, his body cast from some unknown, indestructible metal forged from the deep interior of a distant star.

As the boat continued to come on, weapons blazing, Jake armed the starboard torpedo a split second before triggering the sixty. The sixty belched, spewing a storm of rounds directly into the bow of the runabout. Abruptly the boat veered sharply to port, no longer firing. As it swung wide of him,

Jake could see the gunners aboard it holding on desperately to keep from being flung overboard with the sudden course change. Flicking the throttle slightly and leaning his weight, he gave the Kawasaki just enough power for the STX-12F to pivot, allowing the torpedo launch tube to lead the bow of the passing boat by ten feet. With the runabout's broadside now totally exposed, Jake depressed the firing button. The Kawasaki kicked, yawing slightly right as the torpedo leapt away, a streaking blur just beneath the water.

A half-second elapsed before the missile and runabout converged in a horrendous explosion. Hurled skyward, the boat somersaulted end over end, savagely ejecting the men aboard before plummeting upside down into the sea where it abruptly sank. Fortunately, all four men were wearing life vests, allowing them to remain afloat. Surveying the damage, Jake realized how potent these torpedoes could be when allowed to retain their full charge.

Jake looked behind him. Destiny and the dolphins had finally succeeded in reaching the net's breach and were now clear of the enclosure. He half expected them to immediately head off in the direction of the Angel, but was surprised when the girl and her mount suddenly veered toward him, leaving the smaller albino to support the disabled gray. As the twosome came upon the nearest floating casualty of Jake's attack, the girl leaned her torso sideways, reaching out laterally with one arm and grabbing hold of the injured man bobbing listlessly in the water. Maintaining a tight grip, she held on as her mount towed its newfound burden to the seine's buoyed perimeter where she dismounted and floated beside the stricken individual. The large bull turned, whereupon it gently nudged the comatose man with its snout as Destiny placed a hand on the man's forehead. A few seconds elapsed before the man stirred, awakening with a start and appearing unnerved by the proximity of the huge albino.

Seemingly satisfied with the man's condition, the girl pulled herself onto the dolphin's back and headed to the next victim, leaving the revived man holding onto the net's boom. Jake looked on with interest at the girl's show of compassion, watching her repeat the procedure three more times as she resuscitated each man in silence. Occasionally she would glance in his direction, her eyes peering stoically at him from behind the facemask before refocusing her attention back on the task at hand.

Within a short period, all four Colombians were left floating together as Destiny rejoined the smaller albino and its charge. Mystification flooded the expressions of the revived men as the girl and her mount departed, but Jake noted the lingering hatred on several faces whenever they stared his way. As he studied the men, however, he sensed no ill will emanating from the youngest among them. He could now hear the thrum of the trawler's winches in the distance, causing the stranded men to recede more quickly behind him as the powerful machinery began to haul in the seine.

Jake removed the headset from the Kawasaki's rear compartment, jacking it into the waterproof Motorola before folding it over his cranium. "Arrow to Goliath." Several seconds passed as he awaited a reply. When none came, he repeated the call, but this time a response came back almost immediately.

"This is Goliath," Zimbola answered, the static garbling his tone unable to hide the concern it harbored. "Where you been, Arrow? We beginning to worry."

Jake's countenance eased into a smile. "Arrow back to you. Seems our Colombian friends wanted to throw a little farewell party in my honor. Tell you all about it later. Has the girl's friend arrived yet, over?"

"His boat is tied alongside. He wants to know if you found the girl."

"Affirmative. She's got two more friends with her, one of them in pretty bad shape. I'm on her six and following her back now, but the going is slow. ETA will probably be another hour. See you then. Arrow out."

- 16 -

A nefarious smile lit Ortega's face. An informal accord had been struck. All the rudiments of a loosely knit working arrangement had been made with the man called Omar. The initial terms of the transaction had been laid out and agreed upon with minimal negotiation. Sitting cross-legged in the shade of a poisonwood tree, the two men had parlayed for almost an hour.

From Ortega's perspective, it had all seemed easy, so natural that the two men would do business. And though he made it a habit never to trust anyone, he instinctively sensed that Omar was cut from the same ilk as he himself, a man whose very existence was characterized by violence, a man not to be crossed. Omar seemed to sense a similar trait in Ortega, and because of it, a common bond of begrudging respect had quickly developed between them.

Ortega was more than satisfied with the terms of the deal, and he wondered if Omar had any business sense at all. From his perspective, it seemed that the Islamist had been far too accommodating, seemingly giving away far more than what he would receive. Initially, no money would change hands. For starters, Omar would provide Ortega with three tons of white heroin. *Three tons!*

The amount staggered the Colombian, and he found it difficult to believe he was in a position to become the Caribbean's sole distributor of such a highly prized narcotic. In exchange, Ortega would place one of the Cardoza tuna trawlers at Omar's disposal for a period of one day, to be used for the retrieval and delivery of a cargo whose nature was to remain undisclosed. One other stipulation was placed on Ortega to cement the deal, and the requirement caused the Colombian to grin even more wickedly than before. As far as he was concerned, satisfying that end of the bargain would be exceptionally simple, particularly since he had at least a dozen crewmembers aboard the San Carlo who would take great pleasure in following through on it.

Ortega was suddenly pulled from these thoughts, summoned by the voice erupting from the walkie-talkie clipped to his belt. Fernando was calling him. Swiveling his head, he looked back at his pilot sitting at the controls within the helicopter cockpit twenty meters away. He knew there were no Coast Guard reconnaissance flights scheduled over the island today, but he had made it a standing practice to keep his pilot stationed in the aircraft, prepared for a rapid takeoff during times like this.

Holding back his annoyance over the interruption, he brought the walkie-talkie to his mouth, making an effort to keep his tone bland. "What is it?"

Fernando's voice was urgent. "A call has come in from the San Carlo. Pedro tells me the ship has come under attack. Both runabouts have been destroyed and several crewmembers injured."

Omar noted the way Ortega's face abruptly clouded. "There is a problem?"

Ortega did not answer as he jumped to his feet, raising a set of binoculars to his eyes and aiming the instrument seaward. Although the lenses were powerful, the San Carlo was still too distant for him to discern anything amiss, though he could tell that most of the seine had been hauled in. The net's white boom had a tendency to stand out even at great distance, contrasting sharply with the blue-gray mantel of sea upon which it floated.

Scanning the ocean between the ship and the island, Ortega's eyes were suddenly drawn to a tiny black speck slowly traversing the water. He was able to track it for a few seconds before losing sight of the object. Realizing a nearby rise in the land was blocking his view, he moved to a better vantage point and looked through the glasses again. He cursed silently when the lenses revealed an empty sea. He had to shift the binoculars around before locating the strange object a second time, but as he studied it he could only conclude that it was too insignificant in size to have any type of attack capability.

Ortega lowered the spyglasses in frustration and lifted the portable radio to his mouth. "Hail the San Carlo, Fernando, and ask Pedro what attacked them."

While Ortega waited for a response, he continued to scan the ocean surrounding the trawler. With the exception of the other two Cardoza fishing vessels floating much further out to sea, the waters proved to be devoid of any other watercraft within striking distance of his flagship. Failing to find any other boats, he checked the sky for signs of aircraft.

The radio blurted again, alive with Fernando's voice. "Pedro informs me that a man on a waverunner attacked them. He said it had a machine gun mounted on it and that it was able to maneuver at a high rate of speed. He is not certain, but he thinks one of our boats was hit by a torpedo."

Fernando started to say something else, but Ortega cut him off. "Does Pedro have any idea why this man attacked us?" he roared, unable to control his temper, yet aware that Omar was watching him closely.

Ortega looked through the binoculars once more, locating the distant black speck again. The object was now closer. Straining his eyes, he could see it was trailing behind something in the water…no, there were other objects out there, a small cluster of them grouped tightly together. Estimating the group's direction of travel, he moved a few paces closer to the edge of the island's upper terrace and traversed the glasses slowly across the vast panorama of ocean, following a projected heading of east by southeast. Another vessel suddenly came into view within the circle of magnification. Focusing the lenses, he was able to distinguish not one but two boats tethered together, one much smaller than the other. Compared to the distant black speck, the vessels were close enough for him to discern the anchor line angling away from the bigger boat. As he studied the scene, it became evident that a fairly large floatation device was being used to support something on the water's surface, but the larger vessel partially blocked his view. Even without the aid of the binoculars, he could see the boats clearly.

"Pedro said several dolphins were trapped within the net," Fernando's disembodied voice came back, his speech buzzing with radio static. "A girl was riding one of them. It seems this man was trying to protect the girl and the dolphins."

Ortega lifted the glasses to his eyes again. He could now see what was taking place.

"Crank up the bird," he yelled into the radio, now totally enraged. "We have some business to attend to." He met Omar's eyes. "Care to go for a ride?"

Omar hesitated only briefly before nodding. Intrigued by the situation rapidly developing before him, he would be a fool not to accept the offer. A bird's eye view of the island might prove useful down the road, particularly since the place was to become his primary base of operations in the Caribbean.

- 17 -

Volunteering himself as acting rear guard to the small contingent of dolphins, Jake pondered the strange girl riding the freakishly oversized bottlenose. To him, the sight was totally alien to anything he had ever previously seen, and Jake had seen plenty of odd things during the past twenty-nine years of his life.

As he drove the STX-12F behind the slowly plodding group, he could not help but wonder how such a partnership had evolved. The girl seemed completely at home in the ocean, somehow giving the impression that she could easily survive out in the open sea, far removed from the proximity of land. Yes, he concluded, as long as she had her dolphin friends to accompany her, she would remain immune to the hazards indigenous of an ocean environment. The presence of man, however, complicated that picture. With the introduction of man into the equation, both the girl and her dolphin companions would be defenseless against the dangers man represented, vulnerable to perils not typically associated with the briny depths. Humanity, plain and simple, was an interdicting element, a careless constraining blight within the hydrosphere, posing a lurking threat to the girl and these strange albino mammals.

Studying the group before him, Jake realized he was witnessing a symbiosis of completely dissimilar but highly evolved organisms, a psychological connection of spirits that appeared to harmonize in a way that benefited both species.

Jake continued to dwell on this seemingly mystical alliance, noting the girl's concern for the injured dolphin the other two creatures were supporting and pushing along. He was certain she would have ridden the huge bull hundreds of sea miles in the harshest weather if it meant saving just one of these amazing creations of nature.

Jake was glad he had helped this odd union of beings, deriving pleasure in the way the girl would glance over her shoulder to stare back at him every so often, but uncertain whether she was condemning him for his aggressive actions toward the trawler crew. He was beginning to relax, enjoying this small journey back to the Angel in spite of the painfully slow progress the group was making.

Jake suddenly tensed. His awareness shifted to full alert at the sight of the girl lifting her head to gaze skyward. The drone of the approaching aircraft over the purr of the Kawasaki caused his pulse to quicken, and he knew immediately that it had been a mistake to assume they were out of danger.

Scanning the haze above him, Jake spotted the helicopter as it swooped rapidly toward them like an angry bee intent on stinging. Though there was no overt sign of a threat, all his instincts told him otherwise, that they were being pursued by people hell-bent on doing them harm.

Leaning the waverunner hard to port, Jake swung the nose of the Kawasaki less than ninety degrees so that its guns aligned with the oncoming aircraft. Better to be cautious than sorry, he thought. He had to be prepared to counter any hostile moves the aircraft might make.

Searching his memory, he didn't recall seeing a helicopter aboard the tuna trawler he had recently opposed, but now that he thought about it he remembered the vessel had a raised platform nestled among its superstructure, what could easily qualify as a helicopter landing pad. A vision of the throngs of dead fish floating belly-up within the perimeter of the seine net abruptly came to mind, and he suddenly understood how the dolphins had been injured.

Almost instantly, a cold rage swept over him like a blast of arctic wind, besieging him with an intense desire for retribution. Automatically, his fingers found the arming toggle to the sixty as he cast frigid eyes on the swiftly approaching target, still too distant to bring down. Here was an opportunity to wipe some of the slate clean of the wrongs man had wreaked on dolphins. If he were to have any chance of hitting the aircraft at all, it would have to descend still lower. As if his mind had been read, the helicopter suddenly veered right, gaining altitude rapidly and presenting a target that was currently above the maximum elevation his guns could achieve. And with the fixed mounting of his weaponry, he knew that his guns would only be effective against a moving target at fairly close range. Beyond that it would be a waste of ammunition.

Jake followed the helicopter's flight path, keeping the nose of the waverunner aimed in the general direction of the aircraft as it began to circle cautiously some distance away. He was familiar with many types of helicopters from his days in the military, and he recognized this one to be a Bell Ranger. Uneasily, he watched as it began to climb, taking on a new heading until it was several hundred feet almost directly above him. With the aircraft in such a position, the people aboard it would be able to exploit the current limitations of his weaponry. It was then that he had an inkling of what was in store for him, and a moment later that thought was confirmed.

The sight of the tiny object hurtling down from the sky caused him to gun the Kawasaki to get clear of its path. Keeping his gaze locked on the object, he calculated that it would land a tad wide of him and the girl, but close enough for concern. Even before it reached the water it detonated sharply, quaking the air with a deafening boom and dusting him with a thin cloud of gray smoke.

Jake craned his head around, reliefed that the girl and dolphins remained unscathed as they continued to maintain a heading toward the Angel, now less than half a mile away. Reaching out in front of him, he removed two locking pins and a cable fixture from the upper weapon emplacement, quickly disengaging the Stoner from its mounting and taking it off safety mode. Looking above him, he sighted the gun on the whirlybird hovering high overhead and squeezed off a quick burst, bracing himself against the hard recoil of the weapon. Several red tracers streaked away, disappearing rapidly from sight as they merged with the aircraft.

The figure of a man leaning out of the cockpit withdrew sharply back into the open cabin. Like a frightened pigeon, the helicopter abruptly broke from its near hover as its pilot realized he was being fired upon. Breaking right, the pilot dipped the rotor blades low, taking the Bell Ranger into a shallow dive in an effort to gain air speed.

Jake sighted the Stoner again and let off another short burst, giving the pilot little respite in eluding the unexpected counterattack. With the Stoner having only a limited supply of ammunition within its magazine, Jake would have to maintain a strict firing discipline. One hundred fifty rounds were all that had been available for the rapid-fire weapon prior to using it. Already he was likely down by thirty rounds in his estimation. And if the temperamental weapon ended up jamming, he always had the Heckler and Koch USP-9 submachine pistol riding his thigh to fall back on as a last resort.

As Jake tracked the aircraft, it seemed like the people aboard it were uncertain about what they were going to do next, for the helicopter withdrew to a safe distance where it proceeded to turn several circles in the sky. Then, all at once, it leaned over in a steep bank before heading off in the direction of the Angel.

Jake gripped the Motorola headset and spoke rapidly, literally yelling into the lip mike. "Arrow to Goliath."

Zimbola's reply was almost instant, the natural rumble of his tone higher than usual. "Jeez mon, you tryin' to make Zimby go deaf, Arrow?"

"A Code One is headed your way, Goliath," Jake warned, his tone brisk and conveying the urgency the situation warranted. "That bird coming straight at you from the west is not a friendly. Break out the firearms and be prepared to fend it off. It's armed with concussion grenades."

Zimbola's voice was all business. "I read you, Arrow. Goliath Out."

A sense of dread took hold of Jake as he watched the Bell Ranger grow smaller as it shot for the Angel. Thinking quickly, he weighed his limited options, redirecting his gaze to Destiny as he did so. The girl stared off in the direction of the helicopter, seemingly aware of the lethal capability it posed but, as far as he could tell, appearing calm and unperturbed about its presence. Her tranquil disposition somehow galvanized him further, and suddenly he knew what he must do. Clenching the Stoner firmly between his upper arm and right side, he managed to clutch the Kawasaki handgrips awkwardly before bracing himself for the rough ride ahead. Gunning the engine to full throttle, he took off in pursuit of the whirlybird, leaving the girl and dolphins behind.

- 18 -

Ortega had not anticipated the man on the waverunner to be capable of firing straight up at him. Such an erroneous expectation had been based solely on information conveyed to him by Pedro, who had indicated the machine guns carried by the small watercraft were fix-mounted and could only fire straight ahead. Supposedly they would be unable to line up on an aircraft flying high above. He should have known better, he thought. Pedro had the judgement of an idiot. Unfortunately, he was stuck with Cardoza's irksome nephew for better or worse, although it was the latter case which seemed to prevail most of the time.

Lifting his eyes to the roof of the cockpit, he surveyed the two diminutive holes where small caliber bullets had punched through, narrowly missing him in the process. The sight of the perforations maddened him to the brink of insanity, causing him to envision the various heinous tortures he would dole out on the man below if ever he got his hands on him.

Upon instructing Fernando to keep out of range of the unknown sharpshooter, he was relieved to find that the Bell Ranger had not sustained any critical damage. Apparently nothing vital had been hit. A quick scan of the gauges fronting the aircraft's instrument console told him that all mechanical and electrical systems were functioning normally and that there was no immediate danger of an ensuing malfunction. Carefully assessing the sound of the engine, he neither heard nor felt any unusual noises or vibrations, certainly a telltale sign of no serious impairment to the power train.

Checking the rear fuselage behind him, Ortega was also relieved to find his passenger unhurt and none the less for wear. Omar appeared not the least bit unhinged by the close encounter, providing further proof that Ortega's original assessment of the militant Islamist was correct, that the man was used to close brushes with death.

The state of Omar's health was now very important to Ortega. From his point of view, Omar represented a potential windfall of newfound wealth. The fact that Omar had not been killed meant that their budding business relationship would now be able to grow and prosper. A dealing of such magnitude would allow him to be able to skim some of the immense profits right out from under Cardoza's nose, something he had managed to get away with from time to time in the past. Perhaps he would eventually be able to stash away enough cash to buy the right loyalties. Then he could usurp Cardoza and take over the organization. But right now he had other business that demanded his attention.

Assessing the situation at hand, he knew it would be too risky to attack the rider of the waverunner again, particularly since the helicopter presently lacked the necessary firepower he would need to attempt such a stunt. Aside from the ineffective short range of the handguns both he and Omar carried, the grenades were all he had available in seeking retribution. And unfortunately, he would have to place the aircraft in too compromising a position in order to use them. If anything, the foe below was a skilled marksman, having hit the airframe with his opening volley. With this in mind, the Colombian could not help but wonder what other damage the Ranger might have taken.

Just before he had dropped the grenade, Ortega had gotten a good look at the other objects in the water. The sight of the white dolphins had astounded him, one so big that at first he thought he was looking at an albino pilot whale or small orca. At seeing a human riding the back of the larger creature, he was reminded of what Pedro had said about a girl. Something most strange was going on here.

Recalling the odd scene, he pulled the binoculars he carried to his face and trained them on the water in front of the waverunner, steadying the spyglasses as best he could. Focusing binoculars on even a stationary target from a moving aircraft was not easy to do, and because the objects below him were on the move, the task was made all the more difficult. As he stared through the lenses though, he realized Pedro had been correct. There was a girl down there. Continuing to study the creatures, he discovered that there were actually three dolphins and that two of them did indeed possess a white skin tone.

Lowering the glasses, an image of the mutant bottlenose dolphins he had previously discovered suddenly came to mind, their carcasses still in deep freeze aboard the San Carlo. He was scheduled to deliver them to Hennington during his next stopover in Port-au-Prince. While they were not albinos like the ones below him, they had nevertheless been caught in these waters. Dwelling on it, he began to see a weird connection between the two, a link that could not possibly be coincidental in nature as far as he was concerned.

Ortega continued to seethe as he mulled over the state of affairs confronting him. The present situation was a personal effrontery and demanded some form of retaliatory action, something that would give him satisfaction. Yet he dared not get too close to the rider of the waverunner who seemed to be protecting both the girl and the strange dolphins.

There was, however, another course of action open to him. Looking east, he eyed the two vessels sitting at anchor less than a mile distant. Yes, he thought, a feral grin suddenly replacing the dour expression that had dominated his features only an instant earlier. Revenge was a most pleasant undertaking if you went about it the right way.

- 19 -

Jacob had nearly completed deploying the specially fabricated floatation devices that buoyed up the two most seriously injured dolphins, getting assistance from several people aboard the vessel called Avenging Angel. When he had first spotted the boat from afar, his initial inclination was to steer clear of it. But a subtle inner flicker had beckoned him on, causing him to hold to a course directly toward the unfamiliar vessel.

Over the years, Jacob had grown accustomed to such flickers infringing on his consciousness, and these days they seemed to be stronger than ever, coming upon him at the oddest times. Sometimes they gave him a fleeting glimpse of something felt or seen by the creatures, even when they were far removed from him. In any event, he had learned to trust such inward stirrings whenever they invaded his awareness or, as happened today, whenever they interrupted his daydreams. Even before he had become mindful of the vessel, it was one of those strange flickers that had pulled him from his deep reminiscence over events that had taken place years earlier, bringing him back to reality.

The people aboard the vessel had been awaiting his arrival, forewarned by Destiny that he would be coming to attend the injured dolphins. While all the other albinos in her escort were on hand to meet him, the girl, much to his surprise, had gone off somewhere with Hercules and was still missing. According to one of the people assisting him, the white-haired individual called Doctor Grahm, Destiny had left to find Natalie who she said was in trouble, but that the captain of the Avenging Angel had followed shortly thereafter her departure to help.

About ten minutes after his arrival, Jacob was relieved to learn that Captain Javolyn had radioed the Angel, reporting that he was currently on his way back with Destiny and three dolphins. But now, another radio transmission had just come in, this one seemingly urgent and blaring, causing the black giant presently in charge to shout orders at two others of the crew. All at once he sensed an orderly panic as these crewmembers scrambled forward to retrieve what he distinctly heard to be guns.

Trying to fathom exactly what was going on, Jacob was suddenly struck by another flicker, making him heedful of a growing buzz. Looking toward the sound, he lifted his eyes to the west to observe a helicopter bearing straight at them, the aircraft rapidly slowing and descending quickly as it approached.

At that moment, Jacob knew they were vulnerable. Coral and Reef were currently maneuvering the floatation mat into place beneath the second incapacitated gray, each albino grasping a side with their unique appendages. Once the mat was positioned correctly, Jacob would throw the valve that would inflate it, thus raising the injured mammal above the water. The oldest and wisest among the new breed, Coral and Reef would not leave their posts until the task was completed.

Out of the corner of his eye, Jacob vaguely perceived that no weapons capable of repelling the aircraft were currently on deck. Knowing that it was now too late to avoid an attack, he turned to face the on-coming helicopter just as it flared into a near hover almost directly over the Avenging Angel. Something small glinted in the sunlight on the right side of the whirlybird for one brief moment, then fell.

Something much larger exploded from the water in that same instant, rising on an intercept course with the falling thing. Spellbound, Jacob realized that something was Hermes. Leaping to a height of fifteen meters, the athletic albino snagged the object in midair with its beak, seeming to hang suspended in defiance of gravity. With a deft flick of his head, Hermes whipped the object skyward, launching it back the way it had come just before he fell off into a lazy seaward plunge. Jacob stared in amazement as the albino clove the water cleanly a split second before the surrounding atmosphere was shaken by a powerful air-burst.

Buffeted by the blast, the helicopter yawed violently, sliding sideways overhead as its pilot fought to regain control. Jacob kept his gaze fixed on it as it fluttered upwind and abruptly stabilized. He could see three men aboard it, two of them poking their heads from the aircraft's open doorways as they looked back at the scene below. It was then that the loud stutter of a machine gun assaulted his ears, causing the aircraft to veer rapidly away.

Turning his head, Jacob spied the black giant firing an assault rifle from the hip, the weapon appearing like a toy in his hands. Another sound caught his attention above the staccato din, adding to the cacophony. As he turned to investigate the source, he noted a small watercraft racing around the side of the larger vessel, its driver unleashing intermittent bursts from another rapid-fire weapon snuggled tightly to his side by one arm. As Jacob took in the spectacle, the driver of the watercraft tore off in pursuit of the helicopter, chasing it across the water and continuing to fire upon it with sporadic volleys.

With the heavy barrage put out by the two weapons, Jacob was certain one of the shooters had scored a hit, for a thin plume of gray smoke suddenly streamed away from the aircraft. The helicopter made a wide turn, swinging low over the water and heading off in the direction from which it had come. Seeming to have difficulty maintaining its air speed, it labored on, all the while with the small watercraft tenaciously dogging it. From his perspective, it appeared that the helicopter was making for the distant white ship. As he watched, the two foes began to recede into the distance.

With the threat now gone, Jacob went back to finishing the job he had started. He noticed that Coral and Reef had completed their task, and he could see that the injured gray was ready for lifting. With a turn of the valve, he sent a stream of compressed air into the floatation device. With relief, he watched the mat inflate, buoying the dolphin cradled within its cushioning folds. Satisfied, he pivoted his head to study the other injured gray and the air mat upon which it lay. In tandem, both floatation rigs would be towed behind the pinnace for the long trip back to the cove. But right now he had to await the arrival of Destiny before he headed back.

- 20 -

The Bell Ranger set down heavily on the landing pad aboard the San Carlo, and not a second too soon. Fernando immediately shut down the overheating turbine, hoping the engine was not too extensively damaged. He had been monitoring the temperature gauge for the last several minutes of flight, cringing when it had gone into the red. The turbine had taken on a vibration and he had avoided putting any more strain on it than was necessary, shunning the temptation to put more pitch into the main rotor blades and climb higher for fear that the power train would come apart.

The unknown assailant chasing after them on the waverunner had been relentless, continuing to fire upon the helicopter every so often as it struggled to stay aloft. They had been lucky, he knew, for their air speed had begun to drop enough for their attacker to gain on them. Had the man not decided to break off the attack, he would have nailed them for sure.

Fernando was eager to exit the aircraft, wanting to effect whatever repairs were necessary to get the helicopter back up and flying again. Within the holds of the tuna trawler, they had enough spare parts to practically build a second helicopter. Of greater urgency, however, was a need to keep busy and out of Ortega's way. The Cardoza lieutenant was one step away from a neurotic outburst that might seriously injure or even kill one of the crewmen.

Fernando had been witness to Ortega's homicidal rages, and anyone within striking distance of him was potential game. That is, anyone except for Pedro. As always, Ortega would refrain from harming a single hair on the head of Cardoza's favorite nephew.

Far as Fernando could tell, the only thing presently keeping Ortega's fury in check was the presence of the passenger who had accompanied the flight and who was, by necessity, still with them. Fernando had worked under the Cardoza lieutenant long enough to know that only one thing would supplant Ortega's need for vengeance, and that thing was greed. Though Fernando hadn't been privy to the discussion that had taken place between Ortega and the other man, he had seen the plastic bag containing the white powder and was confident the meeting was the initiation of a drug deal. Ortega, he was certain, would keep a tight rein on himself if he thought a display of temper would turn the stranger off to doing any further business. Side ventures outside normal business channels indigenous of the Cardoza monopolies gave Ortega the opportunity to siphon off additional profits into his own pockets.

And while Fernando feared Ortega, the stranger made him feel even more uneasy, much like the way he felt when he had gotten a glimpse of Cardoza's pet tiger back at the drug lord's compound in Colombia. Though the tiger appeared to be well fed, there was that lurking yet unmistakable measure of uncertainty about one's own safety hanging in the air like the promise of death should one get too close to the creature. Fernando had made eye contact with the man only once, just before the stranger had stepped aboard the helicopter, but it was enough to make him avoid looking directly into that face again. Like the tiger, there was the ready challenge of the predator that lay within the man's eyes...and something else. Yes, it was a deep-seated streak of maliciousness, cold and unyielding to any influence not within the man's sphere of belief.

As the main rotor came to a stop, Fernando climbed up onto the airframe, noting the two bullet holes in the engine cowling and several others in the main rotor. Removing the cowling, he winced when he saw the damage to the turbine.

Ortega scowled up at him. "How long before you have this bird flying again?" The tone of his voice was strained and curt, as if he were having great difficulty holding back the temper tantrum building behind the stiff exterior he presented. The fact that Ortega's composure hadn't cracked already was something new to Fernando, but he nevertheless expected the man to erupt at any moment. He likened Ortega to an ocean dike that gave no indication it was ready to burst, structurally unsuitable to hold back the pressure pushing against it.

Fernando did not like having to disappoint his boss, knowing the potential consequences of such negative news, but he had no choice. "It doesn't look good," he croaked, shaking his head disconsolately and trying to mask the nervousness he felt. "At least a day."

Ortega spun and stared out to sea, letting his gaze linger hatefully in the direction of the waverunner. The unknown rider was still within sight, heading toward the two vessels positioned near the southeast side of the island. Grumbling to himself, he turned his eyes to Pedro who had just come up the steps to the heliport.

Pedro opened his mouth to say something but stopped short when he saw the blond stranger standing off to one side.

"What is it?" Ortega said irritably.

"I have called both the *San Diablo* and the *San Pinto* and told each of them to send a runabout this way," Pedro informed him, his eyes shifting to the distant waverunner. "We will catch that bastard before the day is out."

"You idiot!" Ortega bellowed scornfully, unable to contain himself any longer. "Small motorboats will be useless against our attacker." Walking to the edge of the landing pad, he pointed disgustedly at the remains of one of the destroyed runabouts. The ruined boat hung suspended from the trawler's power block, still caught up in the seine net. "Look at what he's already done. Do you want the rest of our boats wrecked as well?"

Pedro frowned darkly at the insult, but said nothing.

"Get back on the radio and tell the other vessels not to send any boats," Ortega growled. "I'll not have any more of our equipment damaged."

Pedro hesitated momentarily as if to question the order, then nodded. Briefly, he cast curious eyes on the stranger once again before climbing back down the steps leading from the landing pad.

"I have a suggestion," Omar said quietly, speaking for the first time since arriving at the San Carlo, prompting Ortega to turn and face him. "Is there someplace we can go to talk privately?"

- 21 -

The girl and the three dolphins rendezvoused at the Angel only a minute ahead of Jake. Leery of another attack, Jake felt it prudent to keep the Kawasaki tied alongside the Angel rather than stow it back aboard the vessel. As an added precaution, he made sure the other weaponry was at the ready, including the second M-60, which was left mounted on its pedestal at the Angel's stern. Stationing Hector behind the special plexiglass shield that was brought up from below deck, he posted him as lookout for the approach of any other unwanted guests.

With these measures now in place, Jake was able to feel more relaxed. Focusing his attention back on the marine mammals, he observed how the last of the severely impaired dolphins was being assisted. The sight of two of the albinos employing those remarkable appendages of theirs drew his interest as the creatures used them to position an inflatable mat under the third stricken gray. The man called Jacob gave him a brief smile just before injecting the mat with air. Within moments the mat expanded, then bobbed to the surface with its burden secured and cushioned atop it. Almost immediately, the closest albino extended one of its claw-like appendages and removed the air hose from its quick disconnect fitting attached to the side of the mat. With this accomplished, Jake watched Jacob tie a tow rope to the float, attaching it to one of the other floatation devices. The three mats would form a line towed behind the pinnace.

Gathered at the swim platform of the Angel, Jake noted Grahm and his two assistants taking in the proceedings with scientific curiosity. When Jake had first arrived back at the Angel, he had seen the way Grahm had been preoccupied with one albino dolphin in particular, leaning over the water in greeting. "Good to see you again, old girl," Grahm had said close to tears, stroking the mammal's snout affectionately in the manner of old friends. "You don't know how much I missed you."

To Jake, the reunion was touching. And although he had been forewarned about it, he was astounded when he heard the dolphin reply, *"I, too, have missed you."* Distorted by the medium of air, Natalie's speech had sounded garbled and close to incomprehensible, but the words were enunciated clearly enough for him to decipher their meaning.

As he ran such a seemingly implausible exchange over in his mind again, he had the vague impression he was being watched. Turning his head, he spied the girl studying him intently as she continued to sit astride her mount less than twenty feet away, her facemask now resting against her forehead. Jake found himself staring back as the girl drifted closer on the huge albino.

"You have been injured," she said softly, her voice dulcet and enchanting. She pointed at the coagulating blood dribbling slowly down his left arm. "If you let me, I can stop the bleeding."

Jake had completely forgotten about the wound, lifting his arm to scrutinize the extent of the injury. It was more than a graze. A bullet had sliced deep enough to furrow the flesh across his triceps, leaving it bloody and swollen. In the tropics, infection would set in rapidly if such a wound were left untreated for too long.

"Come into the water," the girl invited in that soothing mellifluous voice. "I will heal your injury."

Jake remembered the way the girl had revived the men he had routed back near the tuna trawler and knew there might be a shred of truth in what she was offering. Nevertheless, he found it difficult to stop the sardonic grin that crossed his face. "I think it will take more than good intentions to fix this little inconvenience," he replied matter-of-factly. "More likely a good antiseptic and a few stitches."

Jacob looked up from the pinnace berthed alongside the Angel. "Good intentions are not what the girl is proposing," he interposed, smiling wryly. "If you let her treat the wound, the result may surprise you."

Grahm wandered to Jake's side, motivated by curiosity. "My lad, why don't you take her up on the offer," he suggested solemnly. "Perhaps she can do what she says."

Jake eyed Grahm in surprise. "I would think a true scientist like yourself would doubt such a thing is possible."

Grahm suddenly chuckled. "One must always keep an open mind when it concerns scientific inquiry." He stared at Jake a moment longer, coaxing him with an encouraging smile. "Go on lad, you've nothing to lose."

Jake looked back at Jacob. Though the man was grizzled and weather-beaten, his eyes danced with a warmness not altogether different from Grahm's. As he searched the man's face, he sensed a deep reservoir of underlying intelligence that seemed totally at odds with the simple outward appearance the man exhibited. Jacob was a contradiction. There was more to the man than met the eye, as if he and he alone were privy to some cryptic cosmic joke humanity was in the dark about.

Jake found himself suddenly laughing, deciding to play along with this absurd notion, if only to get closer to the girl. "Oh, what the hell," he muttered, removing the submachine pistol strapped to his thigh and tossing it to Phillipe who stood nearby. Grabbing hold of the boat's railing, he vaulted over it into the sea.

Not sure what to expect, he treaded water as the giant bottlenose brought Destiny abreast of him. The girl seemed ready to dismount from the huge bull but stopped just short of doing so, suddenly appearing shy and confused. She clung to the dolphin for several more seconds before sliding off, then floated beside Jake. Three more albinos abruptly broke the surface near the girl and crowded in close, surrounding Jake and brushing him lightly with their rostrums. Reaching out, Destiny placed a hand on the injury.

A strange sensation suddenly took hold of Jake. He was abruptly suffused with a feeling of immense happiness, simultaneously taken to glimmering oceanic depths and the farthest reaches of the cosmos, the vastness of both making him feel insignificant. All at once an ineffable peace swept over him, nearly taking his breath away. Images danced before him, some lucid, others vague. It was as though he were being borne by a gentle breeze to a distant place, another dimension. He was not a religious man by nature, but if God truly existed he was being held in the palm of his hand. Spellbound, he glanced sideways into the orbs of the unique creatures surrounding him, then fell into the eyes of the girl at the far end of the universe. There was no discernable difference. It seemed he was looking into their very souls. The girl and her companions were unified by swirling threads of energy, bound together as tightly as the matter comprising a neutron star, matter that was paradoxically as lose as the wind. A profound wisdom shone within each of those dark orbs, transcending the barriers of flesh and form. He could feel their rhythmic breathing, deep inhalations that seemed to draw from the wellspring of time and space, followed by exhalations that fell in crashing crescendos like waves against craggy rocks and sandy beaches, purifying everything they touched. And then he understood. All life was to be nurtured and loved.

Lacy patterns of sunlight shimmered on the water's surface as Jake found himself back in the sea, immensely refreshed as if awakening from a deep, satisfying sleep. The adult albinos had pulled away and the girl had remounted the large bull. Looking up, Jake found Grahm staring down at him from the Angel, his expression inquisitive.

Jake was about to climb back aboard the vessel when the water erupted next to him. An albino juvenile bounded from the sea, turning slightly in midflight to make eye contact just before disappearing with a tail flip. The smaller bottlenose leapt from the water several more times, spiraling and pirouetting before splashing down less than two feet away.

"I think he likes you."

Jake turned in the direction of the pinnace, realizing it was Jacob who had spoken.

The Haitian exuded a wry grin. "Achilles usually keeps his distance from humans."

Jake took in the words distractedly, still marveling over the incredible rush he had just experienced. He spun in the water to look at Destiny again. The pensive expression she had previously worn had now changed over into a shy smile. He studied her for several more seconds, awed by the girl's loveliness. There was a radiance to her that went way beyond physical beauty, an elusive mystique all too alluring that made him want to reach out for her. Moments ago he had only gotten a brief glimpse of it and yet he was still confused. She had made a connection with something deep inside him, though he wasn't quite sure what it was. The girl was an enigma, harboring some unknown quality that was obscure and esoteric in nature. Not knowing who she was triggered a fountain of curiosity within him.

Jake's reflective mood was suddenly interrupted, and he became aware of Zimbola calling out to him. He pulled his eyes from Destiny and turned his gaze to the black giant who stood next to Grahm on the Angel's deck.

"A boat approaches from the direction of the ship," Zimbola grunted.

Jake followed the giant's gaze. A small vessel appeared to be making for the island. Quickly, he propelled himself to the side of the Angel using a few powerful overhand strokes. Zimbola reached over and grabbed his hand, pulling him up onto the deck with little effort.

Taking the spyglasses from the Jamaican's other hand, Jake stared through the powerful lenses. The vessel presented a low profile.

"It's the tug that pulls the net," Jake commented. "Probably the only vessel they have left besides the ship." He continued to study the tug, able to discern four men aboard it. Even with the binoculars, the distance was too great to clearly make out their features. As Jake watched, the tug continued on a slow steady course toward the island.

Jake handed the spyglasses back to Zimbola. "They don't appear to be a threat at the moment, but keep your eye on them. I'd like to know what they're up to."

Casting a sideways glance in the direction of the girl, Jake noticed she had climbed aboard the pinnace and was standing next to Jacob. He couldn't help but wonder about the relationship between the two.

"Your wound!" Grahm uttered in astonishment. "It's almost fully healed!" His tone was racked with emotion.

Jake had completely forgotten why he had gone in the water. Reflexively, he ran his fingers over the injury. Feeling no pain and only smooth skin, he craned his head over the area that had been lacerated. All the blood had washed away, revealing only pink scar tissue in the final stages of healing. Awestruck, he looked back at Destiny. *How was such a thing possible?*

"We'll be on our way now," Jacob said, throwing a knowing smile in Jake's direction. "We thank you for your assistance."

"Wait," Grahm shouted, his expression rife with consternation. "There's so much we have to discuss, so many questions that need answers. My life's work has revolved around dolphins. You…you can't just leave."

Sympathy showed on Jacob's face. "I'm sorry, my friend, but I must get these injured creatures to a place where we can better take care of them."

"Let us go with you," Grahm persisted. "I'll help you any way I can."

Jacob fidgeted uncomfortably before turning to the girl beside him, looking to see how she was reacting to all this. Destiny stared at Grahm searchingly before shifting her gaze to Jake. A strained silence hung in the air as Grahm waited for an answer. The silence was finally broken when Achilles suddenly bolted from the water, executing a spectacular triple somersault and reaching a height of at least eight meters above the surface. Reentering the water in a perfect dive, the juvenile disappeared from sight. As if responding to the antics of the young bottlenose, Destiny turned to Jacob with an approving smile and nodded.

"Your offer is accepted," Jacob said gravely, looking to Grahm. "But I must warn you, the trip will be slow and time consuming. The maximum speed this old boat will give me is about seven knots and we have about forty-five nautical miles to travel. You can follow if you like, but we will take no offense if you should decide to leave us during the trip."

Grahm could not hold back his excitement, his expression overflowing with joyous exuberance. "You don't have to worry about that, we'll be right behind you every step of the way," he gushed, looking to Jake for his concurrence.

Without even realizing it, Jake found himself nodding in agreement.

Two hours had gone by since pulling anchor. To Jake, the voyage was agonizingly slow and tedious as the Avenging Angel continued to hang behind the pinnace as it plodded along directly ahead. At Grahm's request, Jacob had allowed the scientist to board the smaller vessel where he could better utilize the time to carry on discussions and ask questions of the girl and her companion.

Jake had consulted his charts. Based on their heading, he knew they were running a course that would take them just south of the tiny village of Malique on the Haitian coast. The Kawasaki had been brought back aboard the Angel and secured. Not wanting to leave his rear unprotected, however, he continued to keep the auxiliary M-60 mounted at its rear station with Hector manning it. His days in the military had thoroughly honed the importance of vigilance into him, and every so often he would scan the surrounding sea to look for the approach of any other vessels or aircraft.

Just before their departure near the island he had observed the tug from the tuna trawler through his binoculars. According to a chart of Navassa Island, the tug had made landfall at a place designated as Lulu Bay. A lone individual had been dropped off and had quickly disappeared, vanishing into the rugged terrain rising up from the shoreline. After that the tug had chugged back the way it had come. As of now, both the tug and its mother ship were long gone from sight, having been left over the horizon more than an hour ago.

To busy himself, Jake had disassembled both machine guns carried by the Kawasaki, wiping away the saltwater residue and oiling all the parts before reassembling them. He had expended all 150 rounds from the Stoner and was diligent in replacing the missing ammunition, refilling the gun's magazine to maximum capacity. The Kawasaki's remaining torpedo was then removed from its tube and also wiped down and oiled. This accomplished, he stowed each of the weapons in their concealed hiding place belowdeck. In these waters he had to be prepared for a fight at all times. It was ingrained in him, an integral part of who he was.

Jake came back out on deck and stretched, then climbed up to the pilothouse. Zimbola was at the helm, and as Jake entered the cabin his first mate eyed him oddly.

"What?" Jake asked, somewhat taken back by Zimbola's strange manner. There was something on his friend's mind.

Zimbola opened his mouth as if to say something, then abruptly shut it and cast his eyes on the smaller vessel leading the way. His expression was somber.

"What's going on?" Jake pressed.

Zimbola turned and looked down at Jake's left arm. "Your wound…it appears to have healed completely."

Jake ran his fingers over the area, then scrutinized the remaining thin line of pink scar tissue in amazement. It was hardly noticeable. "This is a bad thing? Why should this bother you?"

"The way your injury has healed is not what concerns me."

"Then what's bugging you?"

The black giant shook his head dismally. "There is evil lurking about… very powerful evil."

Jake let out a laugh. "We chased away the bad guys, didn't we?" He glanced at the pinnace in front of them. "We helped these people. Whatever evil you feel is far behind us now."

Zimbola's expression remained bleak. "The girl…she is a witch."

"A witch, huh." Jake was starting to get annoyed. Here he was again, listening to his first mate spouting off on superstitious belief. "You're telling me she's evil?"

"No!" The Jamaican shook his head emphatically. "The girl has the power of white magic within her. She is not evil. Only a white witch can heal such a wound so quickly."

Jake was floundering in confusion. He threw his arms up in frustration. "Well if you don't think she's evil, then just what are you getting at?"

"White witches are like magnets. They have a way of attracting evil. The forces of evil are always at odds with goodness. Evil will always challenge virtue."

"So by being around these people you feel we're placing ourselves in great danger?"

"It is what I sense, a premonition of things to come."

"You were never one to shy away from danger, to show fear. I've never seen you run from anything."

"It is not myself I fear for," Zimbola said, bringing doleful eyes to bear on Jake.

"Who then?"

Zimbola's expression hardened. "You should not trouble yourself with the worries of an overly cautious black man."

Jake punched Zimbola lightly on the arm. "I've never considered you overly cautious, big guy. Perhaps a bit headstrong, but never too cautious." With that said, he wandered out onto the deck, not wanting to press his oversized friend any further. He was glad to end the discussion. He hated it whenever Zimby indulged in island cultural beliefs. It sometimes tended to put the man in an emotional funk as it did now.

Climbing down from the pilothouse, Jake walked forward to the bow and made a surveillance of the sea all around him. Satisfied that they were not being followed, he studied the scene immediately in front of the Angel. Trailing behind the pinnace, eleven bottlenose dolphins knifed their way slowly through the sea on each side of the floatation mats being towed, nine of them albinos.

Jake abruptly frowned. Two albinos were missing from the pack. Keeping his eyes glued to the procession for several more minutes, he performed a mental recount five additional times to see if he had overlooked any. When no others breached the surface, he was certain he had not miscounted. He ran over in his mind the number of bottlenose he had witnessed earlier on. When he had first spotted the girl, seven albinos were in her escort, including the giant upon which she rode. Destiny's pod had joined up with seven more dolphins, three of them proving to be this new breed of white bottlenose with the claw-like appendages. That brought the count to fourteen dolphins, with only four in the mix being the more common grays. Two additional bottlenose were later discovered within the tuna trawler's seine net, one of them Natalie. Altogether, that added up to sixteen dolphins, including five grays. With three injured grays towed along on the mats, a total of thirteen bottlenose should have been in the water, eleven of them albinos. And yet all he could see were eleven, nine of which were this new breed. Two albinos were missing.

Jake couldn't help but wonder what had become of the two white dolphins. He looked over at the girl, attempting to get a read on her, trying to determine if she was aware of this. She was sitting at the stern of the pinnace, withdrawn and contemplative, monitoring the incapacitated creatures being towed on the mats. Every so often she would glance his way, resting her eyes on him for several seconds before bringing her attention back to the injured dolphins.

The swimming dolphins remained close to the floats, periodically splashing water onto their wounded cousins. It soon became obvious to Jake why they were doing this. Although Jacob had secured blankets over the injured creatures in order to shield their skin from the intense tropical sun, the protective fabric had to be kept both damp and cool to prevent the blanketed dolphins from overheating and their skin from dehydrating.

As Jake continued to watch, he could see Grahm and Jacob in deep discussion. From where Jake stood, Grahm's manner differed sharply with that of Jacob's. The scientist appeared quite animated and jovial, seeming to throw a non-stop series of questions at the islander, whose attitude looked to be pensive and guarded by contrast.

Jake let his gaze fall on the girl once again. In his mind, he revisited the moment Destiny had climbed aboard the pinnace. From where he had stood aboard the Angel he had had an unobstructed view of her. It was the first time he had not seen her hunkered forward astride the huge bottlenose or treading water. He had noted how slim the girl was and how graceful she walked. She was so young and lovely, so pure and innocent. The skintight wetsuit clinging to her body only tended to emphasize the long coltish legs, the small buttocks and the subtle feminine curves she possessed. She was tiny, barely five feet in stature and probably well under ninety pounds. Were it not for the thrust of her breasts, which were full and round, and her long black hair fluttering in the breeze, she might have been taken for a boy at a distance.

As Jake pondered this, he couldn't help but dwell on the words Zimbola had used in assessing the girl. *White witch.* He couldn't refute the girl's unusual ability, having had a firsthand taste of it. And while it was true she had a mysterious bond with the most incredible creatures he had ever come across, the word witch just didn't seem quite appropriate. No, he decided. Destiny was anything but a witch. Continuing to dwell on it, he concluded that only one word seemed befitting enough to describe her.

Angel!

Jake had a special fondness for the word. After all, didn't his own vessel go by such a name, at least in part? Angels, he knew, were selfless spiritual beings that looked out for the welfare of others. They were protectors, altruistic to the core.

Destiny met his eyes as he stared over at her. Yes, he suddenly realized. He had no doubts, no doubts whatsoever that he was looking at an angel.

- 22 -

The Haitian coastline rose up like a distant storm cloud looming over the eastern horizon, dark and towering as the sun began its final descent toward the sea. Sunset was less than two hours away. The pinnace continued on its slow trek until it was less than three hundred meters from the craggy escarpments lining the shore before it turned ninety degrees and headed south, skirting an outer barrier reef. The Avenging Angel kept pace behind it until the operator of the smaller vessel suddenly threw the engine into idle, letting the craft drift lazily in the gentle swells.

Jake could see Grahm nodding in acknowledgement to something Jacob was pointing at in the water. The scientist exchanged a few more words with the man before turning and signaling the larger vessel to come abreast of the pinnace's starboard gunwale. Jake stepped to the Angel's port railing as Zimbola steered them alongside and reversed the prop.

"Jacob tells me there's a break in the reef here, but that it's too narrow for your boat to get through," Grahm shouted. "He wants you to anchor your vessel farther out and come in by dory. One of the dolphins will guide you in. I'll be going on ahead with these people."

Grahm turned back to Jacob again, attentive to something else the Haitian was telling him. Jacob pointed to the water south of where the pinnace now drifted, seeming to be deeply concerned about the seabed directly under his craft. At the conclusion of the brief discussion, Grahm pivoted his head around to face Jake once more. "Jacob says to make sure you set your anchor at least one hundred meters south of this location. He'll explain why later."

Jake scanned the nearby bluffs and nodded, then climbed up into the pilothouse to give Zimbola instructions. Monitoring the depth sounder, he could see the bottom was dropping off quickly as they moved away from the barrier reef. When they were in sixty feet of water, he had Phillipe drop the Dansforth. Turning, Jake caught a glimpse of the pinnace just as it disappeared from sight behind a rocky outcropping north of the channel through the reef. He blinked in surprise at the deceptiveness of the coastline here. From his position, no inlets, bays or openings in the craggy escarpments were visible, giving him the impression that the shoreline was impenetrable.

Jake looked back at Zimbola. "I'll make sure we're hooked onto something solid," he said. "I don't want our sweet girl slipping her anchor in the middle of the night and ending up on the reef. That coral comes too close to the surface for my taste."

Zimbola nodded in agreement as Jake headed below to grab a mask, fins and snorkel.

Less than a minute later, Jake jumped from the Angel's prow and began to follow the anchor line to the ocean floor. Underwater visibility was close to a hundred feet, and as he dipped under the surface he was astounded at what he saw. In place of the dead zones he had grown accustomed to seeing when diving close to the Haitian coastline, the seafloor was rife with life. Interspersed over a sandy bottom, a wide assortment of corals bloomed in thick clusters where various species of small tropical fish hovered in dense clouds.

As he descended, the longer wavelengths of the visible spectrum were quickly filtered out, causing the majority of colors exhibited by the different flora and fauna to be suppressed. Red tinctures were the first to get absorbed by the water, followed by a sequence of other rainbow gradations the deeper the remaining light traveled. At a depth of ten fathoms, such a condition tended to give most of the sea life a pale blue or pale green tinge with the reduced amount of sunlight penetrating to the seabed. Some dull yellows were also in evidence. He knew, however, that the place was actually abounding with an explosion of color, a fact that could easily be confirmed if the corals and fish were to be exposed to artificial light at close range. Such a thriving environment was not typical of the local waters where heavy pollution and excessive runoff from deforestation had devastated marine ecosystems immediately adjacent to the land. As Jake pulled himself deeper along the line, he wondered what had caused such a startling rebound in the ecology at this particular place.

Reaching the bottom, he removed the anchor from where it had snagged onto an outgrowth of healthy brain coral. Locating a nearby stand of dead coral barely protruding from the sand, he repositioned the anchor flukes so that they hooked under the lip of one of the outcroppings. He tugged hard on the line to test it, making sure the anchor held fast. Satisfied that it would not come loose, he spun around and inspected the first cluster of coral he had come upon. While the upper portion was alive and robust, its base displayed patches of dull calcareous growth long dead. As best he could surmise, the coral had begun to revive and bounce back within the last ten or fifteen years.

Lingering longer than originally intended, Jake could feel the strain on his lungs as the urge to breathe started to grow stronger. At that moment, a dark shadow glided over him, making him look up sharply. With relief, he realized the huge albino Destiny had ridden was nearby and watching him intently.

Another torpedo shape, substantially smaller than the giant bottlenose, shot out from behind a nearby coral head and began to circle Jake. Achilles greeted him with that peculiar plastered on smile so typical of his species. Although the juvenile was perhaps only a few inches longer than him, Jake knew it still had a ways to grow judging from the size of the adult albinos.

Upon orbiting Jake a few times, Achilles suddenly came to a hover less than a foot away. On impulse, Jake reached out and grabbed hold of the albino's dorsal fin, certain it was being proffered. He had the strange notion the dolphin understood his growing need for air and wanted to hasten his ascent to the world above.

With a flick of its tail, the juvenile took off for the surface with Jake in tow. In that instant, Jake got a sense of the raw power typical of these creatures as the young albino pulled him along with relative ease. Suddenly filled with euphoria, he stared ahead as the boundary separating hydrosphere from atmosphere rushed closer, its surface dancing like quicksilver under the glowing light of the evening sun. No more than a few arm lengths away, the giant albino matched Achilles' speed, holding to a parallel course. In unison, both creatures breached the surface at exactly the same time, giving Jake the opportunity to refill his aching lungs.

Not wanting to overstay the courtesy of the ride given him, Jake released his hold on the smaller dolphin. Abruptly, Achilles spun around and faced him. The juvenile's mouth opened slightly as the creature emitted a high-pitched chirp. Jake looked back in confusion as the dolphin repeated the sound, an odd, almost rhythmic lilt. Then remembering what Grahm had told him about this incredible new breed, he realized the creature was trying to communicate with him. Listening carefully, he was able to cut through the poorly spoken diction, isolating each syllable and word and getting to the gist of what the young dolphin was telling him. *"Hold on, Jake Javolyn,"* it said. *"To Destiny and Jacob I will take you."*

Though Jake had already witnessed Natalie speak in such a human-based tongue, the albino's utterance of such words flabbergasted him nevertheless. The fact that it even knew his name also astonished him. But then he realized that Grahm had previously introduced him and other members of the Angel's crew to Destiny when they had provided assistance to the girl back near Navassa Island. Either the girl had disseminated this tidbit of information to the rest of the pod or the dolphins had heard his name mentioned during the introduction.

Finally overcoming his awe, Jake removed the snorkel from his mouth, then looked into Achilles' dark liquid eyes. "I'll go with you," he responded. "But first I must give instructions to the people aboard my boat."

Achilles replied with more garbled speech, but Jake quickly found meaning in the prosody of words as he translated the lilt of the inflections. *"I will take you when you are ready."*

Jake turned in the water and found the Angel at anchor less than twenty meters away, its starboard stern closest to where he now floated. Zimbola was hugging the railing, watching his interaction with the dolphin.

Jake called out to him. "I'll be going on ahead, Zimby. Have Hector and Phillipe stay aboard and mind the store. You and the others can come on in when you're ready."

As an afterthought, Jake turned to the larger albino floating next to him. "What's your name?" he asked curiously, placing a hand on the dolphin's huge beak. He was clueless about the creature's name, remembering that neither Destiny nor Jacob had mentioned it.

The giant bottlenose regarded him with black inscrutable eyes before speaking. *"I am called Hercules."*

To Jake, the words of the larger dolphin were more clearly enunciated than those of its smaller counterpart. As he reflected on this, he realized it made sense that Hercules would articulate air-based speech better than the younger dolphin. Hercules was an adult of this marvelous new species, or so he assumed. Being much older than the juvenile, the huge albino would have had many more years in which to develop such a skill. Even human children had trouble pronouncing certain words.

Jake addressed the giant bottlenose again. "Hercules, will you stay here and wait for my friends? They'll need you to guide them through the opening in the reef."

"That is why I am here," Hercules said, appearing to nod his head in an almost human-like manner.

Satisfied with the albino's reply, Jake was about to reach out for Achilles when another thought struck him. "Tell me, Hercules, how old are you?"

"My essence has existed since the beginning," Hercules answered.

The statement confused Jake. Wondering if he had understood the words correctly, he tried another question. "No...I mean how many years have passed since the time of your physical birth?"

When Hercules did not immediately respond, Jake had the impression the dolphin did not understand the query. He was about to restate the question differently, but before he could do so, Hercules spoke. *"This planet has completed fifteen point three four orbits around its star since the time of my physical conception."* The permanent smile etched on the dolphin's face seemed ridiculously incongruous with the depth of intelligence the statement implied.

Jake took in the words, continuing to ponder the creature's unique affiliation with the girl. Something Grahm had told him suddenly came to mind. Making sure to phrase the question precisely, he queried Hercules again. "Tell me, Hercules, what do you believe your fate will be?"

Hercules did not hesitate. *"The ultimate course of my life has already been predetermined."*

"By whom?" Jake pressed. He was getting good at how quickly he was able to understand the dolphin's garbled singsong speech.

"By the great creator."

Jake tried another approach. "Does your fate reside in the hands of the girl who you carry on your back?"

Hercules exhaled sharply before refilling his lungs. The albino bull seemed to turn the question over and over before providing Jake with the information he sought. When the answer finally came, though, it was more than Jake had expected. *"Up until today, all those of my pod believed that Destiny held the key to our proliferation. But now we are certain this world cannot survive without her."*

Jake found it difficult to comprehend the full measure of what this strange creature was telling him. He had to keep reminding himself he wasn't dreaming, that the conversation he was having was not some surrealistic figment of his imagination. "What exactly do you mean when you say this world cannot survive without her?" he found himself asking.

"Without Destiny, all life on this planet will perish."

A feeling of uneasiness began to take hold of Jake. Under normal circumstances he would shrug off such a doomsday comment. He had heard this type of claim before, usually entwined in the rhetoric of a noted scientist or acclaimed ecologist. But there was nothing normal about the creature he was conversing with. To ease his mind, he decided to get additional clarification. "Does that include humans…mankind?"

"Humans are a part of this planet's biosphere. Humankind would also perish."

Jake was dumbstruck. Dazed by the context of the words, he found himself groping for something appropriate to say. "We will speak again, Hercules. I have enjoyed your company immensely."

"And I have enjoyed yours as well, Jake Javolyn."

Like a man in a stupor, Jake refitted the mask to his face and placed the snorkel in his mouth. Absently, he reached out and grabbed hold of Achilles' dorsal fin. The juvenile gathered speed quickly, moving north along the water's surface. Using only one hand to maintain his grip, Jake lowered his face into the water to observe the seabed as it swept past.

The break in the reef soon came into view, and as they approached it he noticed thick vine-like strands that wound their way through the sand and stands of coral. They littered the bottom haphazardly, many of them crisscrossing and appearing to extend from the deeper water toward the barrier reef. He could see no beginning and no end to them, each strand seeming continuous in length. In all the dives he had made throughout his relatively young life, he had never seen anything like them before. Greatly puzzled, he kept his eyes riveted on the strange rope-like growths as Achilles pulled him through the narrow channel.

Once through the reef, Achilles turned to his left by almost ninety degrees, paralleling the cliffs looming high above them. Along the inside of the reef and less than twenty feet down, a white sandy bottom predominated the seascape adjacent to the shoreline. As Jake hung on he was surprised to find the strange vine-like growths still beneath him. Stationary and intertwined, they continued to wend their way along the sand like cables strung out on the seabed. From Jake's perspective, it seemed as if Achilles was following the trail they made. The odd organic strands appeared to be segmented, forming a chain, and as best he could tell, each segment was about eight to twelve inches long and roughly two inches in diameter. In the shallower water they appeared bright green in color.

With the organic chains now much closer to him, he became aware of something he hadn't noticed before. *They pulsed.* Though subtle to the naked eye, each segment comprising the chain billowed incessantly, swelling and contracting at a rate slightly out of sync with its immediate neighbor. The way the chainlike strands rhythmically palpitated reminded him of arteries pumping blood. Scrutinizing one of the strands carefully, he could see the pulsations go rippling along its length, each pulsation separated by approximately one second and heading off in Achilles' direction of travel.

Achilles suddenly veered hard right, following the path formed by the vine-like projections. Jake took the opportunity to get his bearings. Looking above him, he noted the escarpments jutting high overhead on each side. They were entering a wide cleft in one of the rock walls lining the shoreline, actually a crevasse that was perhaps thirty feet across. As the juvenile tugged him along he observed a slight dogleg to the rocky inlet. Within moments they traveled down the length of it before it opened into a large cove, and as he glanced around he was amazed at what he saw.

The place was a veritable Garden of Eden.

Aside from a lush and healthy coral reef, it was one of the most beautiful places he had ever seen. The cove was set in a chasm with steeply tiered sides that funneled down to the water from high above, giving it the shape of a crude amphitheater. Off to one side and farther back, a waterfall threaded its way down from a natural spring located at the highest section of the gorge, cascading in a series of cataracts before making its longest and final plunge to the pristine water trapped within the basin.

With the sun now low on the western horizon, much of the vista was bathed in shadow, but where sunlight did fall it revealed an eruption of color. Along the tiered sides, various types of fruit trees abounded along with flowering bushes in full bloom. The slopes were alive with flora, and flitting among the lush vegetation Jake could see substantial throngs of multihued songbirds and butterflies representing a variety of species. At the base of the gorge, a white sandy beach ringed the cove by about two-thirds of its perimeter, providing balance to the strange but breathtaking vista. The place had an unreal quality to it, as if constructed by the brush strokes of some gifted painter who had seen such a panorama on another world at the far end of the galaxy.

As Achilles pulled Jake across the placid water, the scene before him was made all the more surrealistic by the two thatched structures that adorned the opposite shore. Though crude and set back from the beach, their rustic appearance seemed to harmonize well with the setting. It was the pod of white dolphin milling near the beach, however, that instilled a profound depth to the picture, the eye-drawing focal point that gave the backdrop a dimension like something out of a fairytale.

Out of curiosity, Jake dipped his head below the surface again, wondering if his gaze would fall on any other unusual sights. The green organic chains were still under him, twisting around one another in a thick concentrated bundle, throbbing with ceaseless micro-pulsations that shot forward toward the shore.

No more than thirty feet from the beach, Jake's expectation of seeing something else strange was suddenly met. The dense cluster of vine-like strands abruptly terminated in a huge bulbous node lying on the bottom, a squat mound of living matter that rose and fell at regular intervals as if periodically inflated and deflated. As Jake studied it, he realized it was pulsing at a frequency roughly equal to the rate at which the segmented strands palpitated. It reminded him of a beating heart. The mass of organic tissue had the approximate shape of a pumpkin and swirled with a mix of contrasting colors, mostly deep reds, rich greens and vivid yellows. He judged it to be nearly twelve feet in diameter.

Knowing the way the tide had been running, Jake was almost certain the water level had reached its lowest point for the day. Where the beating node presently sat, he estimated the water depth to be no more than ten feet. Fully expanded, the highest portion of the organism came to within two feet of the water surface. Emanating from the top of it, a continuous stream of bubbles rose upward.

It was then that Jake noticed the inverted metal funnel positioned directly over the unusual mass. Flaring wide, the funnel currently dipped a foot below the water, held firmly in place by a cantilever steel frame connected to several pipes embedded vertically in the bottom and located closer to the shoreline. The pipes also supported a hose that attached to the apex of the funnel and extended horizontally over the water to the beach where it eventually became buried in the sand. Though the exact purpose of the rudimentary setup was a mystery to Jake, he knew the system had been designed to collect the gas streaming forth from the pumpkin-like node.

As Jake took in the odd sights, he realized Achilles had been hovering close to the strange organism for several seconds. Dropping his face back into the water again, Jake scrutinized the colorful object once more. At its base, a thick carpet of glittering material, granular in texture, caught his eye. It sparkled and shimmered with a dazzling radiance as it reflected rays from the fading sunlight, nearly hypnotizing him with a mix of yellowish and grayish-white lusters.

Not quite believing what he thought he was looking at, he released his hold on Achilles and dove down to examine it more carefully. Scooping up a heaping handful of the stuff, his suspicions were quickly confirmed as he brought it close to his face.

The material was composed of metallic grains, a rich mixture of gold and platinum.

Jake was stupefied. Letting the grains slip from his hand, he rose to the surface with his mind reeling. The weird occurrences he had been exposed to on this day were too much for any sane man to be subjected to in so short a time. As he thought about it, he knew he had to be either dreaming or hallucinating. *This couldn't be real.* Sometime during the voyage to the Haitian coast he had crossed the boundary of reality and fallen asleep. There was no other explanation. He was currently having a lucid dream. And in a dream you could do anything, maybe even fly. In a dream there were no limits as to what was possible.

Staring at the throbbing organic mass before him, he reached out to touch it, but before his fingers made contact, Achilles interceded and nudged him away. Somewhat taken back, Jake raised his head above the water and looked questioningly at the juvenile albino.

Achilles phonated a string of garbled speech, sounds to which Jake was rapidly growing accustomed. "*Touching the thurentra is not advised, Jake Javolyn. To do so may injure your anatomy.*"

Jake thought he heard Achilles pronounce the word *thurentra*, whatever that meant. "What is a thurentra?" he found himself asking, having some difficulty rolling the sound off his tongue. He thought it rather distracting to carry on a conversation with a creature that continually smiled back at him. He wondered what it was truly thinking.

"*It is a hybrid life form, genetically related to both holothuroidea and coelenterates,*" Achilles stated.

Based on the lesson Grahm had given him, Jake knew what a coelenterate was. He was unfamiliar with the other word, however. Rather than attempt to pronounce it, he simply nodded his head as if in understanding. "I see," he said. "What does it do?"

"*The primary function of the thurentra is to produce hydrogen gas. Other byproducts come from it as well.*"

"I assume gold and platinum are some of these other byproducts," Jake replied, finding it difficult to restrain the smile working its way onto his features. "Are you aware of the worth and benefits such metals bring to whoever is fortunate enough to possess them?"

"The thurentra produces the substances you speak of, yes, but no true benefit is derived from the production of such elements."

Jake eyed the juvenile in confusion. "Platinum and gold are considered to be some of the most valuable metals on earth," he intoned, practically gasping out the words. "Things of great value are always beneficial."

"Jacob has taught us such elements have been the cause of many wars among mankind."

Such a simple yet irrefutable statement caught Jake momentarily off balance. How could he possibly debate the concept of precious metals as a medium of exchange with a creature that had no use for such commodities? He looked around the cove in frustration, searching his surroundings for the people who had led him here. Jacob had moored his vessel off to one side of the cove's center and was still aboard it along with Grahm. Both men appeared to be awaiting the arrival of an aluminum dory currently being towed over to them by one of the albinos. The floatation mats carrying the ailing dolphins were no longer tied behind the pinnace. As Jake took in the scene, he couldn't help but assess the condition of the Haitian's boat. To Jake it just didn't add up. The pinnace was in a deplorable state, exceedingly rundown and in need of repairs. With the amount of wealth lying on the cove floor, Jacob could be the owner of a modern mega-yacht.

Turning his head, Jake located Destiny and the remainder of the pod. They were still attending to the injured dolphins at the north end of the cove. Several of the albinos were currently slapping the surface with their tail flukes, sending a heavy spray of water onto the stricken grays still cradled on the floatation mats. Apparently, periodic dousing was still necessary.

Lifting his eyes to the lush slopes forming the gorge, he was suddenly struck by the contradicting nature of the place. There was a luxurious poverty here, a majestic splendor that somehow seemed to be in conflict with an underlying privation. There were riches to be had, substantial accumulations of gold and platinum that had the potential of greatly improving the lifestyle of the mysterious people living here. Yet those riches went unheeded, completely ignored as if such wealth had no meaning. To his way of thinking it just didn't seem logical that Jacob would consider precious metals to offer no benefit.

Jake returned his attention to the juvenile. "Achilles, if Jacob were to collect some of the precious metals below us, he could use it to buy himself a new boat." Shifting his gaze to the two structures set back from the shore, he added, "He could also repair the cottages on the beach. Aren't such things beneficial?"

Though Achilles had no control over the grin permanently cemented on his features, to Jake it seemed absurdly out of place with the juvenile's response. *"To use these elements in the manner you speak of would only bring harm to Gaia."*

"Who is Gaia?" Jake asked, greatly perplexed.

"Gaia is the name of this place."

Jake surveyed his surroundings again. "Gaia, you say." Although the name had an oddly familiar ring to it, he couldn't quite remember where he had heard it before. Strangely enough, though, it seemed quite appropriate.

- 23 -

The red dusk heralding the setting sun was soon replaced by an inky blanket sprinkled with a spectacular array of twinkling dots. A yellow lunar disk hung high overhead within their midst, bathing most of the gorge in a gentle wash of pale golden light that shimmered off the calm waters. In close proximity to one of the structures fronting the beach, a stone grill of sorts glowed brightly with a steady flame as fillets of grouper sizzled softly at its center. Between the grill and the abode, six men clustered, some sitting on boulders while others stood, the combination of light cast from the heavens and the nearby flame causing their features to undergo weird transformations as they intermittently turned faces in conversation.

"…a most amazing place," Grahm said, lifting another morsel of grilled fish to his mouth. "Having a perpetual supply of free energy is something most people only dream about. When and where did you first discover this strange new organism?"

Jacob turned another slab of grouper over the flame. "It was many years ago. The thurentra came into being right here in Gaia."

One of the other men turned his head toward Grahm, light flickering off his eyeglasses as they reflected the flame from the grill. "Are we to accept this man's claim that this so called thurentra is a crossbreed between a sea cucumber and a jellyfish?" Nick Henderson interjected sarcastically. Pivoting his head, he looked back at Jacob. "How can you be so sure of this? You're not a marine biologist."

Jake turned his head sharply to look over at Grahm's upstart computer whiz. The scientist's assistant had a definite tendency to annoy.

Jacob smiled back, ignoring the barb. "The thurentra did not just spring into existence by the natural processes that drive evolution." He hesitated briefly, apparently deciding what he was willing to divulge about the organism. "Rather it was the result of an experiment."

Henderson's eyebrows shot up questioningly behind his glasses. "Then you do profess to be a marine biologist?"

A small laugh escaped Jacob's lips. "Hardly. But I am well read and can tell you many things about the biota contained within these waters."

"So what led you to perform this so called experiment?" Henderson continued to press, his tone exceeding the bounds of politeness.

Henderson's rude manner was beginning to piss Jake off, but before he could set the man straight on what constituted good manners, Jacob expounded further.

"Whether you are aware of it or not, Haitian waters abound with holothuroidea, more commonly referred to as sea cucumbers outside scientific circles."

"Exactly just what is a sea cucumber?" Grahm's other assistant asked, giving Henderson a look that suggested he better stem his abrasiveness. Jeff Parker seemed much more friendly than his peer, displaying an infinitely calmer temperament and better social graces than Henderson.

"A sea cucumber is a type of animal that most often resembles its namesake, but it is best described as a slug with warts," Jacob answered. "It lives on the sea floor. Over fourteen hundred varieties have been classified worldwide, with various species inhabiting nearly every marine environment known to man. They are most diverse in the tropics where shallow-water coral reefs are in abundance, but they also have been discovered at the bottom of the deepest oceanic trenches. Their body sizes range from two to two hundred centimeters in length, attaining a thickness of between one and twenty centimeters. Their colors vary, with many species exhibiting a dark green or dark red-brown pigmentation." Jacob halted his discourse to remove some more cooked grouper from the grill.

Jake noted the metal hood situated above the brazier, paying particular attention to the tubing that rose from the top of the contrivance and extended to one side where it dropped back down in a series of spirals. The tubing ended in a large flask.

"I've seen them," Parker blurted. "They're usually scattered over the sand or lying under boulders." A frown seemed to materialize on Parker's face in the semi-darkness, partially revealed by the fire dancing on the grill. His eyes were suddenly concealed in shadow as he turned his head to gaze out over the water. He seemed to be searching for something. "But don't they also like to burrow down into the sea floor?"

"They especially like rich organic mud," Jacob said. "Here in Haiti, they like to graze on the bountiful organic snow that drifts down from above. This probably explains why they are so plentiful off our coast. There is an abundance of food to sustain them. As I think you are aware, the ecosphere in and around Haiti has been severely damaged by runaway pollution. To a small degree, these scavengers tend to counter the effects of nutrient pollutants on our environment. The fact that they consume organic waste helps to cleanse our waters, but unfortunately, not enough to overcome the vast amount of garbage and toxins that is rapidly overwhelming the marine habitats adjacent to our coastline."

Jake looked over at Grahm to get a read on how the scientist was reacting to all of this. As far as he could gather, the man appeared content to just sit back and listen, letting his assistants do the talking. On impulse, he scanned the cove, wondering what had become of Destiny. The last he had seen of her, she had been at the north end of the cove with the dolphins, occupied with the injured grays. Though the moon was full, there was insufficient light for him to see any activity in that direction. He assumed she was still out there.

"The reef outside this cove looked healthy enough to me," Parker countered. "On our way in I could see no damage to the corals. As a matter of fact, the habitat appeared to be thriving."

"Yes, that is true," Jacob agreed. "What you saw, however, is not typical of what you will find farther along the coast. The teeming marine habitat here is an anomaly, not characteristic of the overall marine environment that exists around Haiti."

"You mentioned an experiment," Henderson interrupted, his tone slightly less abrasive now.

"Ah, yes, the experiment," Jacob said. He sighed deeply and glanced out over the water. "Over the years, the excessive pollution in our waters has caused a huge bloom in the number of jellyfish, causing them to flourish and propagate. Currently, there is sufficient scientific evidence to support such a correlation, but that is another subject I will forego for the time being. With the proliferation of such huge numbers, it is hypothesized that some mutations will occur, causing new varieties to emerge. There are still a lot of species out there that we have no knowledge of. Some of the first organisms to appear on the planet at the beginning of animal evolution were jellyfish and corals. Jellyfish and corals are closely related and are both classified as coelenterates."

Jacob took a ponderous breath as if preparing for a lengthy discussion. "Anyway, about twenty years ago one of my associates, a person very knowledgeable on the subject of coelenterates, began to notice an influx of a type of jellyfish she had never seen before."

"A mutation?" Parker asked.

"If it was a mutation, she had no way of proving it. But she was certain it was a new species, something never previously cataloged in scientific journals."

"Most of the things I've read on mutations show them to offer no favorable benefit to the new species," Henderson stated. His tone was testy again.

Grahm, who had previously chosen to remain silent, suddenly chimed in. "Pardon the interruption of this old scientist," he said apologetically, directing his gaze at Jacob, "but I'd like to offer my two cents on what I know of the subject… that is, for what it's worth."

Jacob nodded. "Please go on."

"There are four primary things I know about mutations. Number one, mutations happen. Number two, they happen with great frequency. Three, almost all mutations are neutral; that is, they offer no benefit or harm to the species or the environment. And four, of the mutations that aren't neutral, the benefit or harm they offer depends on circumstances."

"How can you tell if the mutation is favorable?" Henderson queried.

"Normally you can't," Grahm said. "But it's important to realize that mutations do not as a rule occur in response to the environment. They simply happen. A mutation is a change in the genetic material that controls heredity. The average human being has between fifty and one hundred mutations occurring in his body over the course of a lifetime, primarily because most cells are constantly being regenerated. If the typical mutation were harmful, life would go extinct in short order. The more reproductions of a species that occur, the greater the chance a mutation will take place. Bacteria evolve very rapidly, mainly because they reproduce at a rate many times greater than other organisms. This increases the chance for mutations. Because of this, it is not surprising that they often develop a resistance to antibiotics over many successive generations."

"So what do you mean when you say the benefit or harm of a mutation depends on circumstances?" Parker asked.

In the flickering light of the fire, it was hard to tell if Grahm was smiling when he answered the question. "The English peppered moth provides a perfect example of how circumstances come into play. English moths come in two varieties, light and dark. Prior to the Industrial Revolution, dark moths were very rare, mainly because birds eat the kind of moth they can see most easily, and that was the dark moth. During that period, light moths were more difficult to see since they blended in better with the light colored lichens that often covered the trees in England. However, during the worst years of the Industrial Revolution, the air became very sooty, causing the trees to become darker from the soot. This resulted in a reversal of the circumstances, which had previously favored the light moths. The environment had changed. Now it was the dark moths that had become more difficult for the birds to see against the darker background, whereas the light moths stood out like sore thumbs. This situation ultimately led to the dark moths becoming more common, while the light moths became rare."

Parker was the first to respond. "I get it. What you're telling us pretty much coincides with Darwin's theory on natural selection, something I'm somewhat familiar with. As I remember, Darwin postulated that any trait which allowed a member of a species to survive more easily in a particular environment would give that member an edge, allowing its progeny to proliferate and multiply. Conversely, the ones lacking such a trait would gradually die off or have their numbers greatly diminished." In the flickering light, Parker looked down as if in deep thought, then looked back at Grahm. "But something you said just doesn't seem logical to me."

"What's that, my boy?"

"You said that mutations do not occur in response to the environment. Has this been proven conclusively? Isn't it true that plants exposed to nuclear radiation will undergo abrupt mutations?"

"Hmmm, that's true. Such mutations are usually deleterious to the organism. Rarely does it survive for very long following such an event. But I see your point."

Henderson suddenly fidgeted uncomfortably as if being pestered by some unseen insect. Turning his head, he stared condescendingly at Parker. "Aren't we beginning to stray from the original topic of discussion?" he said in annoyance. He glanced over at Jacob. "This man was telling us about an experiment."

Henderson's words hung in the air like noxiously gas from a sewer, leaving everyone momentarily speechless in the way one might avoid opening their mouth for fear of breathing in the bad air.

Jacob broke the silence by first clearing his throat. "As I was saying, about twenty-two years ago, an unknown type of jellyfish started appearing in the waters just beyond this cove. While they were small in numbers, they began to have a strange impact on the local marine habitat."

"What kind of impact?" Parker wanted to know.

"Every living organism they came in contact with would be injured, but shortly thereafter the organism would rebound and function in a more robust state. During that time, most of the corals that were still alive out on the reef here were in very bad shape, and there were very few fish. But I started to notice little subtle changes in the immediate marine environment that made me wonder about what was taking place. Within several months, the reef began to teem with life. Fish populations began to soar and numerous corals started to bloom in lush, heavy growths."

"So you attributed these changes with the arrival of these strange jellyfish?" queried Parker.

"That is correct. It was too coincidental not to postulate some sort of correlation between the positive changes to the ecosystem and this unknown organism. It was my associate who suggested we expose other life forms to one of these jellyfish to see what would result."

Jacob stopped talking to retrieve several chunks of grilled fish from the brazier. Placing them on a dish, he handed it over to Zimbola who had been standing nearby listening to the conversation.

"So what happened?" Parker asked eagerly, unable to contain his interest.

"The organism that lives in this cove is what happened." Jacob let the statement hang, suddenly becoming quiet.

Henderson jumped back in, his tone now fully chafing. "Would you mind elaborating on that? We'd all like to know exactly how that thing out there came about?"

Jacob kept his eyes on the fillets cooking on the grill, as if deciding to continue. Finally he said, "Six of these unknown jellyfish entered the cove on a day much like today, coming in with the tide in a tight group. They were very large oblate organisms, heavily covered with stinging tentacles. On average, they were about two meters in length and one and a half meters in width. They floated just below the surface of the water. My associate suggested we drop an injured grouper from the fish pen on top of one of them to see what would happen. We also had a yellowfin tuna that was barely alive. Attaching both specimens to a fishing line, we lowered them into the water. Each fish was stung and quickly became paralytic. Following that, we retrieved them and placed them back in separate bins within the holding pen."

Jacob plucked additional morsels from the brazier, then turned to Jake. Handing him a plateful of grilled tuna, he regarded the former Seal with appraising, curious eyes, as if up close he might see something he hadn't seen before.

"Thank you," Jake said appreciatively. "The fish smells great."

Jacob acknowledged the comment with a nod before turning to meet the cold stare Henderson gave him. "Upon penning the two fish, my associate gathered some sea cucumbers from the floor of the cove, leathery muscular specimens with spines jutting from their skin. These we simply dropped on top of one of the oblates. Although the specimens became caught up in the tentacles, nothing unusual occurred. For the rest of the day, we gave little thought to the experiment, leaving the cove for a day of fishing at sea. It was not until the following day that a huge surprise awaited us. The strange oblates had vanished from the cove, that is, all but one. It had undergone a startling change. The texture of its body had transformed, becoming less gelatinous. It had also become anchored to the sandy bottom in much the same manner holothuroidea do. The sea cucumbers were still visible, but they had also changed…and grown. They became elongated, extending outward in segmented ropelike growths, working their way slowly toward the cove's entrance. These extensions were also doing something else unusual. They were undulating with pulsations. In researching holothuroidea, I found that they breathe by pumping seawater in and out of an internal organ called a respiratory tree, but under normal circumstances such a process is not very pronounced and therefore not usually noticeable. These new coils, however, were alive with what appeared to be visible pulsations. Each day that went by, the extensions became longer, gradually making their way out of the inlet. For reasons unknown to my associate or me, the extensions followed the inside of the barrier reef, continuing to grow still longer. Once they had reached the break in the reef, they altered their direction, winding their way through the opening. Beyond the outer reef, they began to spread out more, snaking and coiling their way among clusters of coral and working their way toward deeper water."

"How fast did they grow?" Parker asked.

"As time went on, the rate of growth began to accelerate," Jacob said. "For a while I monitored the coils on a daily basis, noting that the extensions were elongating by as much as twenty feet a day once they had reached twelve meters of water."

"When did the organism begin to produce hydrogen gas?" Grahm asked.

"Six months went by before the main part of the organism began to vent off the gas."

"A most interesting story," Grahm said.

"So for the past twenty-two years you've been using the gas from the thurentra to cook with," Parker added.

Jacob nodded. "Yes."

Grahm suddenly arose from the boulder he had been sitting on. "You seem to believe this thurentra is one new organism, but have you considered it may actually be comprised of two new mutated organisms that exist in a symbiotic relationship?"

"Such a possibility has occurred to my associate. Although she has not been able to substantiate such a relationship, she believes an exchange of DNA between the two organisms occurred to cause the mutations."

"I assume she was referring to what is known as a horizontal transfer of portions of the genome," Grahm said.

Parker looked puzzled. "I'm not following you."

Grahm scratched his head. "Well, most mutations take place through vertical transfer. These occur when the genome is copied during reproduction and transferred from ancestor to descendent through vertical lines of descent. In the original work on population genetics, it was assumed that all mutations were propagated through vertical transfer. But then it was discovered that genes could be propagated much more quickly through horizontal transfer. If evolution were to be represented by a tree, vertical genetic movement is the transmission of genes along branches as opposed to horizontal genetic movement, which is the transmission of genes between branches."

Parker looked to Jacob for confirmation. "So your associate surmised that a horizontal transmission of DNA material took place between the jellyfish and sea cucumbers?"

Jacob again nodded. "She did."

Grahm appeared thoughtful as light from the brazier flickered off his face. "Has your associate figured out how the organism is able to produce hydrogen?"

Jacob turned to stare out over the cove, then looked back at Grahm. "She has developed a hypothesis, but again, she has no way of verifying it conclusively."

When Jacob failed to elaborate further, Grahm prodded him gently. "And that is?"

"There is some kind of delicate interaction that she does not fully understand, but she believes the ropelike coils from the thurentra reach thousands of feet down to the deeper parts of the ocean where they become buried in the organic sediment. Within the sediment these coils somehow interact with microbes called archaea. Such microbes are found in the deep mud along cold seeps where methane gas bubbles up from faults and fissures covered in organic mud. The archaea actually govern the earth's methane cycle, which is really one loop of the planetwide carbon cycle. One form of archaea microbe living deeper down in the mud produces methane gas from hydrogen and carbon extracted from organic sediments. Other species of archaea in concert with other microbial partners consume the methane for energy and reduce the sulfate contained in the mud to hydrogen sulfide."

Jacob paused, taking another deep breath. "My associate has theorized that the thurentra extensions are able to free up the hydrogen within this compound through some kind of biochemical process."

Everyone remained silent for several seconds, trying to absorb Jacob's explanation. Henderson, however, was still intent on doing battle. "The whole thing sounds ridiculous to me. For one thing, your theory assumes the thurentra extends its tentacles for thousands of feet to reach the depths you speak of. It seems rather absurd that a living organism can grow to the incredible lengths you infer. Secondly, how would the organism be able to nourish so much body mass?"

"My associate believes that such a thing is possible," Jacob rejoined. "Jellyfish do not have much of a nutritional need and therefore do not require much in the way of food to survive. All they consist of is a nervous system and a gut that is bell-shaped in most species. They have tentacles with stinging cells that stun their prey. One percent of their body mass is made up of organic matter while the remainder is water. And even though the original organism has mutated, my associate contends that most of the basic protein structure has remained the same."

"Who is this associate you keep mentioning?" Henderson demanded testily. "And what are her credentials?"

"Nicolas!" Grahm chastened sharply. "I remind you that we are the guests of this man. How dare you show our host such disrespect?"

Grahm's chastisement was like a forceful slap in the face to his young assistant. Henderson's look of shock was quickly replaced by one of sullen withdrawal.

Jake thought it best to intercede. "Tell me, Jacob, why do you call this place Gaia?"

Jacob appeared eager to distance himself from the embarrassing scene. "Gaia is a term used by the ancient Greeks. It embodies the idea of a Mother Earth, the source of the living and non-living entities that make up this planet. The name was adopted by a renowned atmospheric chemist to describe a revolutionary hypothesis he originally developed over forty years ago known as the Gaia Hypothesis. Formulated by James Lovelock and published in a book in 1979, it has become one of the more controversial ideas of our time."

"I thought the name sounded familiar," offered Jake. "The hypothesis states that the Earth is alive, doesn't it?"

A happy smile crossed Jacob's face. "It seems you have read up on Lovelock's work, or at least some of the concepts spawned from it."

"Ah, yes," Grahm chirped in. "Lovelock saw our planet as a single living entity, an idea that has tended to rankle many noted scientists."

"The concept was really nothing new," Jacob amended. "In the latter portion of the eighteenth century, James Hutton, a man considered to be the father of geology, once described the Earth as a kind of superorganism. But the key point these men were trying to make was that the Earth acts as a single system, a coherent self-regulated assemblage of physical, chemical, geological and biological forces that interact to maintain a unified whole, balanced between the input of energy from the sun and the thermal sink of energy discharged from the planet into space."

"I've always been a fan of Lovelock's," Grahm said. "He viewed the Earth as a complex entity involving the interaction of the planet's biosphere, atmosphere, oceans and lithosphere, a totality that constituted a feedback or cybernetic system seeking to optimize a physical and chemical environment conducive for life."

"That is true," Jacob agreed. "Through Gaia, the Earth is able to sustain a kind of homeostasis, a maintenance of relatively constant conditions that would best support life. In its strongest form, the Gaia Hypothesis states that life creates conditions on Earth for its own purposes, basically to suit itself."

"There is a growing body of evidence that both supports and detracts the concept," Grahm said. "Overall, it appears to have gained a toehold in the scientific community. In its weakest form, the hypothesis still holds merit. The idea that life has an influence on planetary processes is now generally accepted."

Parker's head pivoted back and forth like a man watching a tennis match as he listened to the conversation. "Forgive my ignorance," he interjected apologetically, "but I'm not sure I completely understand how life can bring about a balance that is optimal to its own survival." He glanced at Grahm. "Can you provide an example?"

The marine zoologist looked to Jacob. "Is there any case you can think of that would enlighten this bright young mind?"

Jacob smiled, more than happy to comply. "To a large degree, phytoplankton, single-celled plants that are abundant in the world's oceans, contribute significantly to controlling the temperature of the earth."

"How?" Parker persisted.

"Given that the oceans cover more than seventy percent of the Earth's surface, it is relatively simple to conclude that anything that causes the formation of clouds over the water will have a major impact on the global temperature. The formation of clouds affects the amount of sunlight being reflected away from the earth. Solar energy is blocked and therefore cannot be absorbed by the oceanic thermal reservoir. The greater the cloud cover, the more solar energy is bounced back into space. This causes the planet to cool. With less clouds, the planet warms."

Parker's eyebrows rose up sharply in surprise. "So you're saying phytoplankton are responsible for producing clouds? I find that difficult to comprehend."

"Phytoplankton is only one of a number of factors that effect cloud formation," Jacob stressed. "The interaction between sea and atmosphere is another major factor. Weather fronts are another since they also contribute to cloud cover."

"So how do phytoplankton produce clouds?" Parker wanted to know.

"You have to examine the mechanism behind cloud formation to understand how these plants are able to do this," Jacob explained. "Clouds form when water vapor in the atmosphere condenses or freezes, but for this to happen a particle or nucleus must be present to collect the water into a droplet. Such particles are called cloud-condensation nuclei. Certain types of phytoplankton, particularly coccolithophoroids, are known to release trace quantities of dimethyl sulfide into the atmosphere. It is these particles of dimethyl sulfide that provide sufficient nuclei for clouds to form out over the ocean. When there is little cloud cover, phytoplankton will grow rapidly as do most plants when they receive an abundance of sunshine. This leads to the production of dimethyl sulfide and a corresponding increase in the amount of cloud cover. This increase blocks sunlight, causing less energy to be absorbed by the oceans and therefore a temperature reduction of the planet. With more cloud cover, the incidence of sunshine reaching the Earth's surface is lessened, causing the phytoplankton to grow more slowly and release lower amounts of dimethyl sulfide."

Jacob let out a satisfied sigh. "This self-regulating cycle continues to repeat in a balanced manner, tending to keep the temperature of the planet in a state of equilibrium."

"The type of phytoplankton you mentioned…coccolithop-," Parker stammered, having trouble pronouncing the name. "What did you call them?"

"Coccolithophoroids. England's White Cliffs of Dover are the fossilized remains of such organisms. Their beautiful calcareous skeletons are revealed under a microscope."

"I find this most amazing," Parker said in awe. "Imagine that! Tiny single-celled plants regulating the Earth's thermostat by maintaining non-equilibrium conditions in the atmosphere." He turned to Grahm, then pivoted his head back to Jacob. "But I see one major flaw in this so called Gaia Hypothesis."

"What is that?" Jacob asked.

"If the concept suggests that the Earth is alive, how come the planet lacks the ability to replicate itself like other living organisms? I was taught to believe that one of the hallmarks of life was its ability to pass on genetic information to succeeding generations. How does the Gaia Hypothesis account for this inability?"

"Your argument is nothing new," Jacob admitted. "Critics of Lovelock have used it to reject his idea, for if the Earth were truly alive it should be able to reproduce. Some proponents of the hypothesis, however, believe that man is the means by which the planet will reproduce."

"Huh?"

"It is inevitable that sooner or later, the dominant sentient species on Earth will develop the means to leave this world and colonize other planets. If the species is honorable and unselfish, if it is morally upright and respectful of life in all forms, we can assume that this species will only seek worlds where life has not yet begun to evolve or where life has long since died off. In doing this, all their technology and knowledge will be used to transform the dead planet into a place of beauty, a living, evolving entity which will have a self-regulating environment optimal for the survival of the life it will support."

Jacob looked as if he was seeing something far away. "Imagine... a place previously static and hostile to life as we know it slowly being changed forever, a place of frozen desolation and barren waste miraculously transmuted, blossoming. Healthy oceans and thriving forests will spring up in once sterile environments, places where life can flourish in a delicately balanced ecosystem undisturbed. No longer will nature be viewed as a primitive force to be subdued and conquered, stranded on a planet without purpose and endlessly traveling around an inner sun. This is indeed the power of Gaia, and one of the more compelling reasons to consider her existence and to speculate about the consequences of our own presence here."

"Why do you use the term '*dominant sentient species*'?" Parker puzzled. "The way you say it makes it sound like the species can be something other than man."

Jacob shrugged, his manner hinting frustration. "For those of us who believe the Gaia Hypothesis to be true, we can no longer think of the Earth as a thing with separate distinct components. We can no longer believe man's actions in one part of the planet will remain independent from some other part. Anything that occurs on the planet will ultimately affect the entire organism, whether it be an increase in the emissions of carbon dioxide, the pollution of the oceans, or the deforestation of the land. If the Earth is indeed self-regulating, then it will eventually adjust to the negative impacts of man... maybe-." Jacob abruptly looked away, suddenly appearing uncomfortable. He seemed reluctant to expound further.

"Yes," Parker encouraged. "Maybe what?"

Jacob took a deep breath. "Maybe introduce something completely new to counter man's destructive tendencies."

"I'm not sure I get your drift," Parker said slowly.

"If Gaia is going to achieve replication, she must first insure the survival of the home planet. She will require an agent to carry out such a task, an instrument of her choosing."

A small gush of flame licked up from the grill as Jacob flipped one of the filets, the sudden wash of light revealing Parker's deepening puzzlement. "Such as?"

Jacob lifted his gaze to study Parker's face momentarily before continuing. "Whether it be the Homo sapien or another evolved and clever species will only bear the test of time."

Jake noticed that Henderson had moved closer to the fire, and in his eyes Jake could see a lust for battle growing steadily in the flickering glow. "So you think man is too stupid to undertake such a burden?" Grahm's freckled assistant said. His tone was just short of outright ridicule.

"Are you familiar with the writings of Friedrich Nietzsche?" Jacob replied patiently.

"Wasn't he a nineteenth-century German philosopher?" Parker said quickly, cutting Henderson off before he could interject further.

Jacob nodded soberly. "Yes, a very wise philosopher who displayed a fondness for aphorism. But among his writings, one profound idea stands out." The Haitian paused introspectively, scanning the faces all about him. "Nietzsche saw mankind as something to be surpassed."

Jake searched his memory, remembering something he had once read. According to Nietzsche, man will travel through three stages of evolution: ape, present-day man, and...a strange feeling took hold of him as he reflected on the word...and destiny. He rolled the concept over in his mind with newfound understanding, shifting his gaze back in the direction where he had last seen the girl. Man was destined to be replaced by a higher intelligence, much the way the ape had been superseded by man's superior intellect.

Jacob surged on before anyone could interrupt, the rapidity of his words swiftly gaining momentum. "So far, man has shown himself to be an irresponsible life form, placing too many demands on too few resources. Food and energy are the primary commodities that support mankind. In obtaining these staples we have disrupted the ecological balance of our world, causing such problems as the greenhouse effect and the ozone hole. Once mankind made the transition from the nomadic wanderings of hunter-gatherers to creatures that used agriculture to increase food production, he began to extract a huge toll from the planetary ecosphere. To keep pace with our expanding population, agriculture demanded that we clear forests, subject grasslands to the plow, and appropriate vast tracts for grazing our herds. Human numbers surged exponentially, and with it a growing need for energy. Strip-mining of timber beyond its sustainable yield began to occur in many parts of the world, resulting in substantial clearing of forests and runaway erosion of landscapes. Over reliance on fossil fuels became our biggest problem, however. Burning coal and oil unleashed enormous amounts of carbon dioxide and acids into the atmosphere, doing untold harm. Accumulating buildups of carbon dioxide has created a potential for global warming that threatens to melt the polar ice caps. Already this is happening. Acid rain is increasingly killing off timberlands. Urban blight is another growing problem. Immense numbers of poor people in search of employment keep flocking to already over-congested cities that continue to expand like slime molds, spewing out mountains of garbage, sending torrents of toxins into our seas and casting an umbrella of smog into our skies. Overall, the rapacious demands of mankind is overtaxing the environment and bringing Gaia perilously close to the brink of extinction. If the human race is to be judged in its entirety, it is apparent that man has proven himself unfit to live in harmony with his environment. As such, we cannot rule out the possibility that Gaia will take proactive measures against the chief source of her problems, maybe introduce a species-specific plague to eradicate all of us and let another species evolve to take dominion over the Earth, a species that has the potential for a greater show of sapience than does the Homo sapien. But then again, maybe the human race will be given a chance to atone for its sins, to redeem itself for past mistakes by correcting the wrongs it has inflicted on the ecosphere. Either way, Gaia will have the opportunity to heal herself. Whose to say what options Gaia will choose?"

Parker seemed taken back by Jacob's rhetoric. "Assuming your argument were true, why would the planet follow a course of action that would eliminate man? If we adhere to the definition that Gaia is the sum total of all the things that comprise the Earth, why would it eradicate a portion of itself?"

"A logical question," Jacob said, "and one that deserves a logical answer. From Gaia's perspective, perhaps mankind is perceived as a tumor harmful to her health, a group of cells that have somehow gotten out of control and become an intrusive growth, cells that have malfunctioned and strayed from the purpose for which they were originally intended. Either the tumor must be removed entirely from her body, or it must be shrunken to a small enough size so that her bodily processes can attain a state of equilibrium once again. If she does this, her tissues will eventually be restored to a condition of vitality, allowing her to reproduce at some future point in time using an alternate group of cells to carry this out."

"This is preposterous," Henderson railed, unable to contain himself any longer. "You speak of the Earth as if it is some superorganism capable of making rational decisions."

"Whether it can be described as a cell, an organism, or a superorganism is merely a matter of semantics, a topic best left to the philosophically minded. I am not claiming the existence of a sentient intelligence behind Gaia, but then again I cannot refute it. But even organisms lacking a brain possess various defense mechanisms. Certain types of coelenterates such as fire corals have stinging cells with which to discourage attack in order to avoid being damaged. However, if in fact Gaia does harbor an intelligence of some kind, perhaps it resides in the conscience of man. After all, man is one of the organisms comprising the biosphere, and as such, is therefore a part of Gaia."

Henderson was beginning to seethe. "For better or worse, life has evolved man as the only species with the intelligence and digital extremities to build machines, the one species destined to make the jump into space. It is only a matter of time before he gets his act together and stops bringing harm to the environment."

Jacob gave him a lingering stare. "For all our sakes, I hope you are right. But time is the very thing working against Gaia. A recent report by the Millennium Ecosystem Assessment concluded that human activity is putting such a strain on the natural functions of the Earth that the ability of the planet's ecosystems to sustain future generations can no longer be taken for granted. According to this report, man has caused ecosystems to change more rapidly and extensively over the past fifty years than any comparable time in human history. This has resulted in two-thirds of the planet's resources being heavily polluted or depleted over this time period. This includes energy sources, fresh water and clean air. There is little doubt we are destroying the earth. If mankind fails to take immediate and assertive action, it may be too late for all of us, assuming it is not too late already. The longer we delay, the more inevitable it will become that the Earth's ability to rebound will reach a level that is irreversible. The way I see it, time is quickly running out."

"You're talking about one report," Henderson countered smugly, "the opinions of a few scientists."

"The report was prepared by thirteen hundred and sixty experts from ninety-five nations," Jacob shot back.

"Humans are the most successful species in the history of life on Earth," Henderson said in exasperation. "If anything, we are an ingenious, resilient, stubborn lot, without equals on the evolutionary scale. We'll figure out a way to avert disaster."

Jacob mulled this over for several seconds, his face suddenly hidden in shadow as he turned his head away from the fire to look up at the tiered precipice rising high above them. As if making up his mind about something, he swung back around and met Henderson's glare. In the dim flickering light cast by the brazier, Jake was certain he detected a strange, shrewd smile in the Haitian's expression.

"Perhaps it will be Gaia herself who will provide man with the way," Jacob finally said, his voice now carrying a mysterious cryptic quality.

- 24 -

The damp sand felt cool under Jake's bare feet as he strolled along the beach, making him revel in the comfort it gave him. There was something about wet sand between his toes that always seemed to give him a sense of serenity. *No, serenity was not quite right,* he thought, reflecting on the word. *Freedom.* Yes, that was the lemma that stuck in his mind now that he rolled it over introspectively.

Some distance behind him, the intermittent glow of a fire added enchantment to the fragrant night air, rich with the sweet scent of wild flowers and hibiscus. As he walked, he became aware of the cataracts pounding the water at the far end of the cove. At his present distance, the sound was reduced to a dull roar that hung in the background, ceaseless and soothing to the soul. Sometime in the last hour, spray from the falls had caused a cloud of vapor to go swirling across the cove, shrouding the waters in fine mist.

Continuing to follow the shoreline, Jake angled slightly left of where the brine met the sand, inexorably drawn beyond the juncture. He loved the water and hated being away from it for very long. Water was an elixir, invigorating and mind cleansing. As he entered it, tiny wavelets rife with moonbeams swashed a golden luminescence around his ankles. The strange place entranced Jake, blanketing him with a gentle yet powerful embrace, giving him a sense of unfathomable peace that reached down to the farthest recesses of his being. Filling his lungs, he took in more of the pervasive atmosphere, unable to get enough of it. Thoughts of *Shangri-la* raced through his mind, an imaginary idyllic hideaway depicted in James Hilton's classic novel, Lost Horizons. *If ever such a place existed, this was it,* he reckoned.

Though his spirits were greatly uplifted, there was something missing, an empty place within him that was unfulfilled and yearning for something more. He couldn't put his finger on it. Earlier on this evening he had become restless. Growing weary of the endless discussions and debates that continued to persist around the brazier, he had needed to get away. At least that was the excuse he had given himself.

Jake had deemed it best not to mention the gold he had seen lying at the bottom of the cove. He had heard stories about what gold could do to some men. Gold was an alluring temptress, a beckoning seductress that tended to twist and corrupt weaker souls. The abundance of wealth he had seen residing beneath the water was enough to make the man called Jacob one of the richest men in Haiti. Yet Jacob appeared to ignore the enormous potential it offered, preferring to live a simple existence here in this place. Jake had not allowed himself to be misled by Jacob's grizzled outward appearance. He had seen the stacks of books and periodicals piled high inside the man's cottage. The brief contact he had made with the Haitian had shown the man to be exceptionally intelligent, possibly one of the smartest individuals he had ever run into. Like the girl, Jacob was an enigma. The fact that Jacob saw value in the hydrogen gas rather than the gold only added to the mystery the Haitian posed. And though Jake could only speculate, he sensed that Jacob harbored some well-guarded secret, something that would make the thurentra's ability to produce gold and platinum appear insignificant by comparison.

The girl had failed to join the gathering, continuing to remain missing. He looked out over the water in the direction he had last seen her, wondering if she was still there. It was darker in that part of the cove, the moon's golden disk eclipsed by one of the chasm's towering walls. Where he now stood, the sandy shelf of the beach had ended, merging with some rock outcroppings.

Without giving it conscious thought, he waded out into the water and began to pull himself along in an easy sidestroke, trying to see through the veil of mist. Swimming out into deeper water, a soft chittering came to his ears, and as his eyes probed the shroud of darkness he could make out two wraithlike objects moving toward him.

A warbling gently cut the air, whistling softly like a hushed whisper being forced between the teeth. Jake immediately recognized the sound and the entity emitting it. *"We have been waiting for you, Jake Javolyn,"* Achilles said.

Jake stopped stroking, peering at the shapes before him. As his eyes adjusted to the dim light, he was able to discern the huge head of Hercules floating beside that of the juvenile albino. "Is Destiny still out here, Achilles?" Jake asked.

"Yes, Jake Javolyn," Achilles trilled back in that strange signature lilt, speaking more quietly than when Jake had first conversed with the young dolphin. *"Come, I will take you to her."* Achilles abruptly turned, presenting his dorsal fin. *"As before, I offer myself as an object of conveyance, Jake Javolyn,"* the juvenile added.

Jake latched onto the proffered fin, letting himself be whisked forward. Liquid tendrils tugged at him as the dolphin transported him across the water, and as he looked into the foggy dusk, the mist abruptly parted to reveal the outline of the floatation mats. Destiny was on one of the floats, her body stretched out horizontally beside the gray bottlenose lying adjacent to her. She was stroking the dolphin gently as the other dolphins hovered nearby, her head resting against the side of the injured creature. As Achilles pulled Jake abreast of the float, the girl continued to run her fingers gently along the gray's flank.

"Is there anything I can do to help?" Jake asked, keeping his voice low in the same manner as demonstrated by Achilles. He had no way of knowing it, but he was certain the young dolphin had not wanted to disturb the sanctity of this place.

Destiny shook her head slowly, turning her face slightly to acknowledge Jake's presence. "Thetis must decide to help herself. There is nothing more any of us can do for her. We have done all that is within our power."

Jake released his hold on Achilles and grabbed the float. "What's wrong with her?"

"She is unhappy and confused. She does not understand why humans would bring harm upon her and the others."

Jake himself was confused. "Then she is not ill?"

"Physical damage still resides within her, but it can be healed. She chooses to block our efforts."

"But why?" Jake asked, not knowing what else to say.

"She is not sure whether she belongs in this world any longer and feels that perhaps now is the time to make the spiritual transition to the next realm."

Jake recalled the scene when the Avenging Angel had first come upon the injured dolphins, remembering how distraught the juvenile albino was about one of the grays in particular. He posed another question. "Is Thetis the mother of Achilles?"

Destiny answered with a small nod.

"These dolphins...I've never seen anything like them," Jake said. "Are they all able to speak?"

The girl continued to stroke Thetis. "Only the white ones have developed such an ability. They are fluent in several languages."

"And do they all possess what some people would consider the equivalent of hands?"

"Thetis is the only gray here at Gaia who has such appendages, though all of the whites are endowed with them."

Jake looked over at the other two floats tethered to the one he was holding. "How're the others doing?"

"They are still weak but will recover." Destiny seemed preoccupied with something as she said this. "Thetis has been waiting for you. She would like you to place a hand on her."

Jake was perplexed. "She's never met me. Why would she be waiting for me?"

The girl peered intently at Jake, holding back a response. She suddenly sat up, letting her legs dip into the water. "Thetis wishes to discover who you are. Your touch will give her this knowledge."

Jake found the request unusual. "Getting to know someone takes time. How can a person's nature be perceived from a touch?"

"Thetis will know," the girl said softly.

Jake hesitated with uncertainty, but not wanting to refuse the girl he reached out and placed the palm of his right hand on Thetis' flank. Keeping it there for several seconds, he noticed that the creature's skin was smooth and rubbery.

As Jake did this, Destiny watched him closely, her eyes boring into him as if searching for something. "Thetis believes you are the one," she said at last.

Jake stared back, unable to discern her meaning. "I don't understand."

The girl turned her gaze to the heavens, then met Jake's eyes again. "Thetis had a dream, what some would call a vision. In it there was a man. She is now certain you are the man she saw, a person the pod can trust, the one to which her offspring will bond."

This was all getting to be too much for him to handle. "Offspring?" he uttered, a bit off balance. "Does she mean Achilles?"

"Yes."

Jake shifted his eyes to Thetis. The dolphin's right orb, the eye facing him, was scrutinizing him with a deep abiding interest. Taking in the moment, he turned back to the girl. "Thetis is not well," he reminded her. "Perhaps she's mistaking me for someone else."

Destiny was not to be dissuaded. "We have all experienced moments of inexplicable connection when events in a dream spill over into real life," she said. "There is an inner vision that exists in all of us that is often blurred, buried beneath daily stresses so that it is not readily apparent. Search yourself, Jake Javolyn. You must honor the wisdom of your inner voice, that part of yourself that knows what you are meant to do. If you deny it, you will destroy your spirit."

Jake was unsure as to what the girl alluded. The events that had taken him to this unusual place were strange enough. Attempting to make sense of the things Destiny was trying to communicate to him was like trying to unravel a riddle. And yet he had to admit there was a mysterious affinity that drew him to the juvenile albino, some genuine sense of connectedness that seemed to be awakening something deep within him.

Destiny came back at him with more words. "Thetis sees an inner conflict raging within you, an unfulfilled harmony between your conscious and subconscious states of awareness. If you are to reach the invisible worlds that lie just outside of ordinary reality, you must learn to access your own divinity and spiritual light to discover who you truly are beyond your own skin."

Though this bit of guidance continued to confound Jake, there was no need for him to dwell on it. He knew himself very well. He was a soldier of fortune, plain and simple, a person willing to accept whatever cards fate dealt him. And if per chance those cards threw hardship and suffering his way, he would meet such obstacles head on and without complaint. Whatever Thetis was seeing in him was clouded by her physical state, a condition that needed immediate rectification. "Thetis must overcome her fear of living and stop blocking your attempts to heal her," he snapped, surprised at the anger he felt. "She must engage in the direct experience of life regardless of how it may disappoint, frighten or pain her."

Destiny looked away, unable to meet Jake's choleric eyes. "Thetis is not afraid for herself," she said, her voice almost a whisper. "She fears for the survival of this world. She does not wish to see the pod perish with it."

"Some creatures choose to die because they are too cowardly to live," Jake argued, his words coming out harsher than intended. Realizing this, he softened his tone. "Thetis must learn to fight back against the men that did this to her."

"Fighting back is not in her nature," Destiny gently asserted. "Her species lacks a willingness for aggression. She is incapable of harming or destroying, of striking back in anger."

The girl went back to stroking the injured dolphin. In the subdued light, Jake could see a faint glistening on one of her cheeks. When she finally spoke again, her voice was close to a sob. "She will not let us heal her."

Jake tried a new line of reasoning. "If that's how she's going to repay you for risking your life for her, then I will forego bonding with her calf," he threatened.

Thetis visibly flinched over this sudden declaration, letting out a loud squeal of protest. "Thetis begs you to reconsider," Destiny implored, speaking for the dolphin. "Failing to bond with Achilles will place the pod in immediate danger, setting it on an irreversible course of imminent doom."

"Why should this trouble her?" Jake asked irritably. "She's already told us she doesn't want to stick around for fear of seeing her pod perish along with the rest of the world?"

Destiny stared at the gray as if listening to something. "She believes there is still hope, but only if you remain linked to Achilles. Without this link, the pod will cease to exist."

"Then the responsibility for such an outcome rests with her," Jake replied stubbornly. "I'll be leaving now." He pushed away from the float and began to swim toward the shore.

"Wait!" the girl called after him, her tone suddenly joyful. "Thetis will comply with your wish. She will allow us to heal her."

Jake stopped in mid-stroke. Turning, he stared back at the girl and her charge, the smile on his face concealed by the near darkness. "Then I will bond with her calf," he said, still unclear about what that meant.

Now that Thetis no longer blocked them, the combined efforts of Destiny and the eight albino dolphins quickly healed the internal injuries the gray had sustained. From Jake's perspective, the albinos formed a tight circle around the float, lifting their rostrums above the edge of the mat and making contact with Thetis' prone form. Less than a minute had gone by when the girl finally raised her head from the gray's back, appearing satisfied with the outcome of their ministrations.

"You haven't eaten anything all day," Jake said, feeling deep concern for the girl.

"Jacob will prepare something for me when I go ashore," Destiny replied wearily. "He always-," Stopping in mid-sentence, she spun around abruptly, directing her gaze to the cove's inlet. In that instant her manner changed, becoming tense and alert. "It approaches the reef," she stated sharply. "It nears your boat!"

Jake sensed an acute warning in her tone. "What nears my boat?"

"A submarine."

"How do you know this?" Jake asked incredulously, taken completely off guard by this sudden revelation.

"Apollo and Artemis are still out there watching it. It followed us most of the way from Navassa."

The two missing albinos, Jake thought. "Why didn't you tell me this before?" he demanded.

The girl read Jake's flash of anger, searching his eyes closely before answering. "The vessel stayed far enough away, presenting no danger at the time," she explained demurely. "But now the pod sees it as a threat."

With all the other strange things Jake had seen of late, the possibility of a mental link between the girl and the missing albinos did not surprise him at all. "Zimbola must be alerted to this," Jake said hurriedly. "Please go ashore and let him know what's going on. Tell him I'm on my way to the Angel." Jake knew that if Destiny followed through on this, Zimbola would give Hector a heads up about what was going on via the walkie-talkie he kept with him.

Jake turned and began to swim for the inlet leading from the cove, but before he had made more than half a dozen strokes, Achilles was at his side. The young albino squealed out in that odd warbling lilt of his. *"I will help you, Jake Javolyn. Grab hold."*

The speed at which the juvenile hauled Jake through the water amazed him. It was as if Achilles sensed Jake's immediate wishes and automatically responded to them. Without Jake even having to mention it, the young dolphin appeared to understand that, as of now, every second counted.

Jake needed to formulate a plan, and quickly. But before he could come up with one, he needed to know what he was up against. Unfortunately for him, he had left his mask, fins and snorkel on the beach and, as far as he was concerned, taking the time to retrieve them was not an option.

In less than a minute, Jake was transported across the cove to the inlet leading to the sea. Keeping his head above the water, he watched as the rock walls flashed by, sporadically illuminated where moonlight was reflected off the craggy surfaces. Hanging on by one hand, he looked behind him and spotted the brazier still glowing eerily on the other side of the water. To his relief, he could see the silhouette of a person emerging onto the beach and moving quickly toward the fire.

As Jake was towed along, he focused his thoughts on the problem at hand. *A submarine, the girl had said. What was a submarine doing here?* A string of questions began to race through his mind, none of them having answers. Managing to take a quick glance at his luminous wristwatch, he saw that it was a few minutes past midnight. He could only hope that either Hector or Phillipe was still up and keeping a vigilant watch to discourage possible intruders from boarding the Angel.

The moonlit panorama of the northern Caribbean Sea opened up before Jake as Achilles sped past the final outcropping of rock. A short distance to the southwest, the outline of his boat lay at anchor, undisturbed on the other side of the reef. Scanning the shimmering waters, he could see nothing that would indicate the presence of another vessel.

Jake was about to tell Achilles to stop swimming when the juvenile suddenly slowed and came to a halt. "Do you see any large objects under the water, Achilles?" Jake asked.

"I do not, Jake Javolyn," Achilles ululated back.

The albino's response made Jake wonder if Destiny had been wrong about the submarine. If no such vessel was currently lurking below them, he had to be sure. Perhaps he had not phrased the question correctly. "Does the reef block you from seeing what lies in the deeper water?"

"Yes, Jake Javolyn."

Jake felt like kicking himself for not initially considering something so obvious. If a large enough sub were skulking about, it could not possibly get through the reef. And the reef would interfere with dolphin biosonar, preventing speak-see signals from breaching it. "Are other members of your pod on the other side of the reef?" he continued to probe.

"Artemis and Apollo are there," Achilles squealed. *"They are watching a large metallic vessel below the water surface."*

Jake assimilated this. "Achilles, are you able to communicate with Artemis and Apollo right now?"

"Yes, Jake Javolyn," Achilles confirmed.

"Take me to my boat, Achi-"

Before Jake had even completed the sentence, the albino shot away like a torpedo rapidly accelerating toward a target, and it was all Jake could do to maintain his grip and hold on.

- 25 -

The bearded man lowered the periscope, the prominent scar marring the cheek just below his right eye giving him a sinister appearance in the console's greenish glow. He had not planned on crossing the body of water shown to be the Windward Passage on the nautical chart he carried. Troubled by his own rashness, he chastised himself for being so foolish, for letting his desire for revenge divert him from his primary mission. He had a rigid timetable to adhere to and he now ran the risk of messing it up. Normally he wouldn't have even considered helping the Colombian called Ortega, but he had seen something he had not expected, and a vendetta had to be satisfied.

When he had first spotted the individual riding the waverunner, there had been something vaguely familiar about him. It was when the helicopter had come within striking distance of the small watercraft that an old memory had re-surfaced, making him squint his eyes to get a better look at the man skimming the water below him. As luck would have it, he had been deprived of seeing the man clearly. The fusillade of tracer rounds screaming up at him had made him duck his head back into aircraft, but not before he had gotten a glimpse of the machine gun mounted on the small vessel. It was the way the waverunner had been configured with weaponry that had made him think of his old nemesis Jake Javolyn.

It was Javolyn who had come up with the idea of mounting machine guns and small torpedo launchers to waverunners, turning them into highly mobile attack vessels. He remembered how Javolyn had tried to sell the brass on developing such a concept. Yeslam recalled how happy it had made him when Javolyn's brainstorm had been brushed aside, scoffed at by Captain McPherson as being absurd. As far as he knew, Javolyn was the only man who would have followed through on the idea and taken the time to construct a working prototype.

Yeslam had gotten several more glimpses of the attacker shooting up at them during the ensuing skirmish, but never one that could positively confirm the identity of the man. By the time he had landed aboard the San Carlo, however, he had been certain their assailant could have been none other than Jake Javolyn. That was when he had decided to present Ortega with the offer.

If Ortega would ferry him over to the island, Yeslam would use his resources to follow the two boats to their ultimate destination. In exchange for providing the Colombian this information, Ortega would supply him with one hundred 55-gallon drums of diesel fuel. He had purposely refrained from mentioning the submarine he now rode in. For the time being, he would keep that a secret.

In the confined quarters, Yeslam Raduyev looked up at one of his subordinates crowding the sub's command console. Kalid was not smiling.

"Have you fixed the problem?" Raduyev asked testily in Arabic.

"The launch tubes continue to show an electrical problem and will not fire," Kalid said. "Perhaps Allah is giving you a sign. Perhaps he prefers you kill the infidels with your own hands."

Raduyev nodded slowly, studying the religious fervor burning deep in Kalid's eyes. Kalid's interpretation of the situation at hand gave him cause to reflect. "Yes…yes," he conceded begrudgingly, the irritability he felt towards his crew rapidly subsiding like a spent wave sliding back from shore. "Maybe you are right, maybe Allah must be satisfied another way."

Six other crewmembers turned to look at him as he gazed distractedly about the interior of the modified P-130 submarine. Although still fairly new, the sub had a few annoying bugs, one of them being the malfunctioning of the torpedo tubes. The 90-foot vessel had been purchased less than a year ago at a sum of $12,000,000 from Rosoboronexport, a huge Russian arms dealer. Other than the vessel's current inability to fire torpedoes, it had so far performed admirably. With a depth capability of 200 feet and a range of 2,000 miles, the diesel-electric powered submarine ran silently on batteries when submerged, making it virtually impossible to detect using passive acoustic measures. With a maximum underwater speed of 26 knots, the P-130 was designed to carry up to ten people, and as Raduyev had learned, had proved itself to be a most reliable vehicle for smuggling cargos and insurgents in and out of unfriendly coastlines.

After Ortega had ferried Raduyev back to Navassa Island, the Chechen had found his way back to the craggy fissure located inland among a concentrated cluster of poisonwood trees. The fissure lay well hidden within the thicket and led to a subterranean chamber deep under the island.

Raduyev and his crew had first discovered the chamber during their initial reconnaissance of Navassa in the hopes of finding a suitable base of operations. That had been six months earlier. Cruising the P-130 at a depth of 80 feet, he had spotted a huge gaping hole in the coral reef that ran along the island's southern perimeter. The reef had grown outward on both sides of the hole, cantilevers of calcareous rock precariously overhanging a deep vertical drop-off. As best he could judge, a massive buildup of coral had collapsed under its own weight, falling away into the depths to expose a dark yawning pocket beneath it. Intrigued by the possibilities it presented, he had brought the sub to a halt and swam out the airlock, accompanied by two of his men. Dressed out in diving gear and carrying powerful underwater flashlights, they had entered the opening in the reef, each of them riding a DPV. Letting the DPV headlights illuminate the way, they had discovered a wide tunnel that penetrated deep into the interior of the island. Following it back, they had eventually emerged into a spacious air-filled cavern of sufficient size to accommodate the sub. Shining their lights around the underground chamber, they had observed a profusion of sharp-pointed stalactites hanging down from a high-domed ceiling. It hadn't taken them long to discover a shelf of rock that provided enough space for fuel drums and other supplies to be stored.

Upon climbing from the water, they had shed their air tanks and knelt on the limestone floor between several stalagmites, giving thanks to almighty Allah for leading them to this hidden place. As far as Raduyev had been able to tell, it was the perfect staging area for carrying out their mission.

Subsequent explorations through a forest of stalagmites soon revealed several passageways extending through the bedrock forming the chamber's back wall. Upon following one of them, Raduyev noticed that it gradually wound its way upward. Squeezing himself through a few narrow places, he had ultimately gained access to the surface. In the ensuing weeks, he was to learn that the subterranean portions of Navassa Island was extensively honeycombed, literally riddled with what seemed like an intricate and endless labyrinth of tunnels and caves.

Through his Yemeni contact in Kingston, Raduyev had arranged several pickups at sea of various items and provisions to make the underground chamber more livable and better suited to carry out his mission. Generators and floodlights had been brought in, as well as thousands of feet of electrical cable and ventilation hose. In order to widen the passageways and to clear away stalagmites, compressors for powering pneumatic jackhammers and dynamite had also been mobilized. The magnitude of the work Raduyev and his crew had endured in carving and clearing hundreds of tons of rock had taken its toll, leaving them physically exhausted most of the time. Yet there was still a staggering amount of backbreaking work that remained. Though tracking down Javolyn had taken the Checken away from these labors, it was a welcome respite from the demanding toil that still lay ahead.

By the time Raduyev had met up with his crew in the underground cavern and launched the sub, the two-boat convoy had vanished over the horizon. Following what he had perceived to be their last known heading, he had steered the sub at full speed just below the ocean surface, every so often raising the periscope to scan the sea in all directions. Within an hour, he had spotted two vessels and, quickly closing the gap, confirmed the boats to be the ones he had been seeking. Keeping well to their rear, he had shadowed them for the remainder of the day, annoyed and bored at the snail-like pace they maintained. During that time, he had been tempted to sneak up closer to the trailing boat, hoping to get a clear look at the occupants aboard it. He needed to confirm once and for all if one of them was Javolyn. Such a move, however, would have been all too foolhardy, he finally reasoned. Knowing the ex-Navy Seal's proclivity for vigilance the way he did, the potential for compromising his position would have been too great a risk.

When they had eventually reached the Haitian coast, Raduyev had hung back at a distance and watched the smaller vessel disappear among the cliffs as the larger boat set its anchor. It was only after the sun had set that he had crept up close to where the anchored vessel now sat. From the air he had counted a total of nine people among the party he had pursued. In trailing the vessels, he had reconfirmed this count over and over through the sub's periscope, mostly out of boredom. Having observed most of the people go ashore, he was now certain that only two crewmembers remained aboard the boat that now floated before him. After weighing his options, he had originally decided to sink the moored vessel. But now that he thought about it, firing a torpedo into the boat's hull might alert authorities to the possibility of a rogue sub plying Caribbean waters, a fact that could jeopardize his mission. That his torpedo launch system was suddenly inoperable was surely a sign from Allah not to carry out such a foolhardy move.

Raduyev looked over at the Palestinian contingent of the sub's crew. Azzum and Bashir were watching him intently, awaiting his next command. He had trained both men as divers and found them to be marginally competent. And although they each had the desire to learn amphibious commando tactics, neither possessed the qualities or skills that came anywhere close to Navy Seal caliber, particularly Bashir who was the weakest of the two. Bashir, Raduyev knew, had a tendency to overestimate his abilities in the water, a man that would surely come apart at the seams if pushed too hard. Azzum, on the other hand, was easily distracted, unable to keep his attention focused on an objective for very long. As Raduyev studied the men, he was struck by the fact that they were the only divers he had available to him for the time being. But that would change in the near future. A group of highly skilled mujahideen fighters would be joining up with him by tomorrow, holy warriors that were cut from the same cloth as he, jihad crusaders that would form the backbone of an elite group of frogmen currently coming out of the Middle East. He was confident this little diversion of his would not offset his schedule, certain he could still reach the prearranged rendezvous point in time.

"Suit up," Raduyev ordered. "We will board the vessel."

"Are we to kill anyone encountered?" Azzum grunted, his eyes gleaming hungrily in the greenish light.

Raduyev weighed the question for several seconds before replying. "No. We will take prisoners for interrogation. I want to know who these people are and why they were near Navassa Island."

- 26-

Using both hands to grasp Achilles' dorsal fin, Jake's forearms ached miserably from the strain of holding on. The juvenile was all muscle and seemed tireless, cutting through the water with powerful, arm-wrenching flicks of its tail. Jake was sure the albino was capable of achieving a faster pace, but perceived Achilles was purposely holding back in an effort not to dislodge his rider, staying just short of exceeding Jake's physical limit.

Through eyes reduced to slits, Jake watched the outline of the Avenging Angel grow rapidly larger in the moonlight as the dolphin moved diagonally across the reef. The water had risen in the last several hours, allowing Achilles to stay above the razor-sharp coral that grew to within inches of the surface at low tide. As Jake neared his vessel, it became evident that none of the cabin or deck lights were on. Within the span of a minute, the juvenile had him at the side of the dive platform that jutted from the Angel's stern. As expected, the platform ladder that could be lowered into the water was in the up position.

As Jake let go of Achilles and reached for the platform, the marine mammal turned and faced him. *"Beware, Jake Javolyn,"* the juvenile ululated, keeping the vocalization just loud enough for Jake to hear. *"Others approach."*

Jake gave a quick scan of the darkened water all around him. Not seeing anything, he stared back at Achilles. "Do you mean people from the submarine?" he asked, careful to whisper out the question.

"Yes, they come from beneath the water and will be here shortly."

"How many?"

"Three."

Jake hauled himself from the water as quietly as possible, letting the platform support his weight. Leaning out over the edge, he placed a hand on the albino's beak. "Swim away from here, Achilles," he whispered. "If I need you, I'll call you."

Achilles complied with Jake's instruction, submerging quickly.

Rising into a standing position, Jake turned and silently climbed the three steps that ascended to the vessel's rear transom. Opting not to unlatch the gate, he hopped over the railing. Almost immediately, something loomed up out of the darkness and came straight at him. Instinctively he ducked, sensing the air being cleaved by an object swung in his direction a split second before it grazed his hair. Thrown off balance by the near miss, the assailant stumbled forward and collided heavily with Jake, the man's body having the rigidity of a block of wood.

"Easy, Hector," Jake blurted, clamping an immobilizing bear hug around the shorter man. "It's me, Jay Jay."

Hector let out a short, shallow breath. "You're crushin' the shit outta me," he wheezed painfully.

Jake released his python hold. "There are strangers coming to board us," he warned in a low voice. "You got the message from Zimby?"

Hector nodded, shifting the baseball bat he carried between hands and rubbing one of his biceps. "He called on the radio and told me about the sub."

Jake looked over Hector's shoulder. "Where's Phillipe?"

"Keeping watch up on the bow," Hector said.

"Go below and get me my backup mask, fins and snorkel," Jake ordered, reaching out and taking charge of the bat in Hector's hands. As Hector turned to retrieve the items, Jake grabbed him by the shoulder. "I'll also need my bang stick and MP-5."

Hector nodded again and scooted away. A moment later, Jake heard something bump lightly against the dive platform. He reached to his thigh, feeling the hilt of his K-Bar. Satisfied that it still rested firmly in its Kydex sheath strapped to his leg, he slipped the retaining ring off the knife's haft to make it readily available should he need it. Sidling up to the stern railing, he crouched behind it and peered through the crack in the gate.

The head of a diver suddenly poked above the platform and glanced furtively around. Jake held his breath and tightened his fingers on the handle of the bat. The diver looked back down at the water, appearing to gesture at someone else. As Jake watched, he could see two other hands grasp the upper edge of the platform. An instant later, the diver came to rest on the platform, boosted above the water by his as yet unseen comrades. A flag immediately went up in Jake's head. The maneuver involved teamwork and was similar to those practiced by Navy Seals when gaining access to overhanging structures without the aid of a ladder.

Jake remained motionless and well hidden in the semi-darkness, continuing to observe the scene as it unfolded. The dark figure on the platform removed his swim flippers and placed them aside, rising in a low crouch. Reaching back down, the interloper grabbed hold of something handed up to him from the water. In the dim moonlight, Jake could see the man remove an object from a sealed plastic bag. The outline of a submachine gun suddenly came into view as the man turned to climb the small stairway. Jake knew the man was seeking to secure the aft end of the Angel before he would give the all clear sign to his accomplices to come aboard. It was a standard commando tactic.

Thinking quickly, Jake groped behind him, feeling the lip of a bucket normally kept there. The bucket had lead weights in it, the kind that fitted to a diver's weight belt. Grabbing a three-pound weight, he waited until the intruder was almost to the top of the steps, then tossed the weight over the side as he kept his eyes locked on the man. The lead piece hit the water with a noticeable plop, making the man spin his head to investigate. Timing his move perfectly, Jake rose up at the exact instant the intruder looked away and swung for the bleachers, catching the man squarely on the side of the head with the sweet spot on the bat. With buckling knees, the man fell to one side of the steps, bounced off the platform and tumbled into the water with a loud splash.

His position of concealment now compromised, Jake slid back from the railing and faded into the darkness close to the Angel's rear cabin, keeping low. As he had anticipated, a bout of gunfire erupted a moment later as the felled man's companions realized what had happened and opened up with their weapons, raking the stern transom with small arms fire. Without having to look, Jake knew the remaining two interlopers were lifting their weapons over the dive platform and firing blindly, only putting their arms at risk. It was the type of move used by professional soldiers. Because the enfilade was coming up at an angle, none of the rounds had any chance of hitting Jake, who was now too far back to be in the line of fire.

In the midst of the din, Hector scurried back to Jake's side and handed him his Heckler and Koch MP-5 DPW. The other requested items were also in the shorter man's possession, including spare clips for the automatic weapon. Almost as quickly as it had started, the gunfire ceased. Jake removed the magazine from the submachine gun, checking to make sure the clip was full, then snapped it back into place. Grabbing the sleeve holding the bang stick, he strapped it to his left thigh. A moment later, he had the mask and fins strapped on.

Reaching out, Jake placed a hand behind Hector's head and pulled him close. "Stay right here and keep low," he instructed. "Be ready to take the gun and keep these guys from coming aboard."

With that said, Jake stood up and, now wearing the swim fins, frog-leaped to the railing where he unleashed several short bursts of suppressive fire into the sea. A heavy spray of water kicked up to one side of the dive platform, which remained vacant of any would-be boarders. Putting the gun's safety on, he tossed the weapon back to Hector and jumped over the side, keeping the dive mask pressed firmly against his forehead and removing the assault knife from its scabbard before hitting the water.

Plunging below the surface, Jake lowered the mask into place, cleared the water from it with a partial exhalation through his nose, and inserted the end of the snorkel into his mouth. He quickly oriented himself, directing his gaze aft along the Angel's hull. A subdued glimmer of moonlight penetrated into the depths, revealing little, if only shadows. Straining his eyes into the darkness, sudden movement caught his attention, then vanished. Glancing behind him, Jake made sure his six was clear before kicking off toward the stern. As he made his way below the swim platform, he peered around in search of the diver he had clouted but saw nothing.

Jake evaluated the present conditions. The tide had now gone slack, having reached its peak. With little current to carry the interloper away, the man should have floated close by, assuming that he was still unconscious or dead and that his dive equipment provided sufficient positive buoyancy to keep him afloat. As he analyzed the situation, only a few things were possible. Either the man had sunk to the bottom or he had regained consciousness and swum away. Jake dismissed these two suppositions and went with a third possibility, the one he deemed most likely. The other two intruders had taken their wounded comrade in tow and were now heading back to the sub.

Rising to the surface, Jake blew water from the snorkel and recharged his lungs. On instinct, he kept swimming forward, moving downstream of the Angel's stern. He was about to turn back to his vessel when a sudden flicker of light gleamed dully below him. A moment later it disappeared. Something was agitating the algae in the water, causing it to give off a phosphorescent glow.

Taking a huge gulp of air, Jake shot into the depths, descending upon the disturbance like a pelagic predator on the scent of prey. Again he perceived movement, and as he swam deeper he caught sight of a diver's flipper no more than five feet away. Kicking hard in an effort to catch up, his right swim-fin suddenly met resistance. Something was tearing at it, attempting to grab hold. Jake immediately spun, pulling his knees to his chest as he did so and preventing whatever it was from grasping his flippers. The silhouette of another diver was outlined in a wash of effulgent bioluminescence. Jake could distinguish the faceplate of the diver's mask as the man reached up for him. The glint of steel in one of the diver's hands galvanized Jake further and, reflexively, he smashed the heels of his feet into the oncoming face as it came within range, gratified by the solid impact. His assailant abruptly floundered, stunned from the blow, and Jake took advantage of the moment, sheathing his own knife before pulling the bang stick from its scabbard. The diver slashed out in agitated madness, unable to see through a flooded facemask. Swimming under the frenzied blade, Jake thrust upward with the bang stick, jabbing for the man's chest. As luck would have it, the man raked back with the knife in that instant, his forearm intercepting Jake's own weapon. The bang stick exploded with brutal force, and the gleam of polished metal fluttered before Jake's eyes as the blade spun away beneath him.

Jake was not about to take any chances, knowing the man could still be dangerous. He re-inserted the spent bang stick into its sleeve and pulled the K-Bar from its sheath once again. Reaching up, he ripped the regulator from the diver's mouth, his adrenaline flowing fast and furious. A split second later he severed the regulator air hose, cutting the line where it connected with the yoke mated to the scuba bottle valve. An explosion of air immediately erupted behind the diver's head and the man jerked around in desperation, fumbling with panicky hands in a futile bid to locate the gushing hose. Maintaining his advantage, Jake slammed his balled fist into the diver's midriff. Through the water, he heard a distinct grunt, and in the crepuscular light he could see a rush of air stream from between clenched teeth. Though greatly incapacitated, the man somehow found the strength to claw insanely for the surface. Maneuvering behind him, Jake remained clear of the man's flailing arms and tore free the dive mask sitting lopsided on his face.

Completely disarming the intruder was Jake's next priority. As the diver struggled for the surface, Jake stayed with him, looking for other weapons he knew the man carried. Re-sheathing his assault knife and groping with both hands, he located the submachine pistol holstered to the man's right thigh. Lifting the holster's Velcro flap, he pulled the gun free. From its feel, he recognized it to be a Colt 633HB 9mm. Based on the staccato din the weapon had made earlier, it did not surprise him that the gun's muzzle lacked a suppressor. Although the weapon was no longer protected in a watertight plastic wrapping, he knew it might still be capable of firing in the watery environment. Releasing his grip on the submachine pistol, he let it fall away. The gun left a sprinkling of phosphorescence trailing behind as it dropped harmlessly to the bottom.

Jake was amazed at how easy it had been to subdue the diver. The man was rather clumsy in the water, appearing insufficiently trained to attempt hand-to-hand combat in the open sea. Latching onto the neck of the scuba tank strapped to the man's back, he let himself be towed upward, riding his charge as if the man were a loggerhead sea turtle. Jake could sense the diver's escalating panic. It was apparent the man had become aware of the additional drag restraining his ascent, causing him to go completely over the edge, caught up in the throes of a maddening frenzy focused only on reaching atmosphere. The man coughed convulsively when he finally broke the surface, his body coming halfway out of the water and, as chance would have it, practically landing in the Angel's skiff recently taken ashore.

Jake was surprised to see Zimbola and Grahm looming above him as both men leaned over the boat's gunwale. "I'd appreciate you taking this guy off my hands," Jake huffed mightily upon spitting out the snorkel and steering his captive the short distance to the side of the skiff.

Zimbola reached down and hefted the man from the water, tank and all, careful not to upend the small boat as he did so. Bleeding profusely from an open wound on his right arm, the diver was now weak and lethargic, still gasping painfully for air and too physically exhausted to put up any fight.

Inhaling deeply to catch his breath and resting his chest on the opposite end of the skiff, Jake counterbalanced the additional weight being put aboard, watching Zimbola deposit the diver in the boat's stern. Grahm flicked on a flashlight, shining it in the man's face. Jake was immediately struck by the man's features, which suggested a Middle Eastern heritage. Though debilitated, the man looked over at him with smoldering, hateful eyes.

"I've taken away his gun and knife," Jake wheezed, seeing a deep frown form on the black giant's face in the faint moonlight, "but it wouldn't hurt to check him for other weapons."

"Who is this man?" Zimbola asked, kneeling down to search the diver.

"I'm not sure," Jake said hurriedly, getting his wind back. "But he's got a few companions roaming around below us, and they're not very friendly. I suggest you put him aboard the Angel and tie him up."

"This man needs medical treatment," Grahm stated, reaching for a length of rope lying on the floor of the skiff. He looped the rope around the man's injured arm and cinched it tight in an effort to stem the flow of blood.

"Where you going?" Zimbola questioned as Jake pushed away from the skiff.

"There's a sub lurking somewhere below us. I'm going to see if I can locate it."

Jake was about to dive down again when a sudden idea came to him. "Achilles!" he shouted. The name had barely left his lips when the juvenile albino appeared at his side as if by magic. "Achilles...the channel through the reef, the one Jacob uses to get his boat into the cove. I need the other members of your pod to position themselves along both sides of the channel," Jake petitioned. "I need them to show the Angel the way through the reef. Can they do this, Achilles?"

Achilles appeared to ponder the question, not making any detectable sounds and regarding Jake with that permanent, unwavering smile. *"They will do as you request, Jake Javolyn,"* the dolphin finally answered.

Jake turned back to the skiff, noticing the special interest both Zimbola and Grahm were taking in his exchange with the dolphin. "Get back to the Angel and pull her anchor fast as you can, Zimby," Jake ordered. "I want you to bring her through the reef and into the cove. The dolphins will show you the way."

"What you ask is too dangerous," Zimbola objected hotly. "We risk opening her hull."

"Better that than the sub holing her," Jake argued impatiently. "Do as I say or we won't have a boat at all."

Zimbola wavered, then gave a defeated shrug. "As you wish," he said gravely, engaging the skiff's tiny electric engine and grabbing hold of the tiller. As the big man headed off in the direction of their boat, it was clear that he did not relish the prospect of having to steer the Angel through so narrow a gap in the reef.

Jake reached for the juvenile's dorsal fin. "Take me to the sub, Achilles!" he instructed.

Achilles gave Jake just enough time to place the snorkel between his teeth and fill his lungs before submerging. The sea tugged hard against him as the dolphin accelerated quickly into the depths. Swallowing hard, Jake felt his ears pop in protest to the rapidly increasing pressure. A moment later, Achilles leveled off. Without a depth gauge, Jake had no way of knowing precisely how deep they had descended, but from the way his dive mask was pressing against his face he sensed he was now below fifty feet. Exhaling slightly through his nose, he equalized the pressure within the mask against that of the surrounding water. The discomfort the mask squeeze caused him abruptly vanished.

As his eyes adjusted to the reduced light, Jake suddenly caught sight of something huge and dark against the backdrop of hydrospace. Achilles raced along its entire length before turning and traversing its opposite side. Making yet another pass, the dolphin suddenly slowed and came to a stop near the object's midpoint, hovering within arm's length of it. The water's exceptional clarity in conjunction with the moonlight filtering into the depths made the object visible in the night sea. Through the murk, Jake perceived something sizeable protruding above the rest of the structure and immediately identified it to be a conning tower.

Looking into the near darkness, Jake's attention was drawn to a greenish lambent aura further back from the sub's tower. Something was stirring the water, causing the microscopic algae to flash like fireflies, an eerie sight in the surrounding black void. Jake knew such bioluminescence was common to marine environments, typically caused by single-celled dinoflagellates that emitted light when their cell walls were deformed by mechanical agitation.

And although it was a biochemical phenomenon he had grown used to, never before had he seen it so pronounced as he did now.

Jake released his hold on Achilles and kicked off toward the flickering radiance, feeling the first tinges of discomfort in his lungs. Checking the luminous dial on his dive watch, he saw that he had been submerged for nearly three minutes. If he didn't overtax himself, he might last another two before having to come up for air. He had been gifted with an exceptional pair of lungs and had the ability to stay underwater for prolonged periods when diving without the aid of scuba. Coming within ten feet of the glowing green pinpoints, he discerned movement. A diver had his back to him and was entering an airlock through a hatchway on the sub's deck, moving into the opening feet first.

Pulling his knife, Jack finned forward quickly, attempting to catch the diver off guard. But by the time he reached the opening, the diver was pulling the cover into a lockdown position. Jake caught the lid just before it sealed, getting the fingers of his free hand under the rim opposite the hinge and bracing both feet against the deck. Yanking hard, he rotated the hatch cover back up a quarter of the way before he met resistance. The diver pulled back furiously, attempting to batten down the hatch, and a tug of war instantly ensued, with each man trying to gain the upper hand. Effectively stalemated, Jake's lungs began to burn from the strain, but he was not yet ready to give up. Managing to reposition his feet and getting the fingertips of his knife hand under the lip of the cover, he threw his back into the task and applied more leverage. Now tugging with both hands, the lid began to come up again. In his current position, he knew he held the advantage, able to exert superior force over his opponent. Slowly, the lid continued to rise.

Jake was suddenly thrown backwards as resistance from the lid's opposing side abruptly ceased. The diver, carried upward by the motion of the hatch cover rotating on its hinges, rushed out of the airlock and came straight at him. Much less encumbered with equipment than his opponent, Jake recovered quickly, moving aside and just barely avoiding the tip of the blade thrust at him. Turning, the diver came at him again. Jake met the man's charge amid a swarm of sparking fireflies, parrying the blade that stabbed for his chest with the K-Bar and nicking the assailant's arm with a slashing riposte. The superficial wound seemed to freeze his adversary for one fleeting moment, giving Jake the opportunity to catch the wrist of the man's knife hand. Kicking hard with his flippers, he drove the diver backwards, reaching for the man's face with the other hand. The man seemed to anticipate the move, snaring Jake's free hand with a countermove of his own. Both men locked up, performing a strange undersea ballet, pirouetting and twirling and forming a pinwheel of bioluminescent radiance that spiraled away from the twosome as each vied for advantage.

Jake was surprised at the strength of his opponent. Unlike the diver's two accomplices, the man was proving himself to be a seasoned warrior. In the midst of the struggle, Jake discerned the conning tower looming above them and quickly changed tactics. He extended his legs laterally and kicked powerfully, spinning his opponent and driving the back of the man's head into the rigid metallic structure. Seemingly stunned, the man released his hold on Jake.

His lungs now screaming for air, Jake had no choice but to make a hasty retreat for the surface. Almost dizzy with a need for oxygen, he knew unconsciousness was not far away. With blackness rapidly eating away at the fringes of his awareness, he had trouble orienting himself, vaguely perceiving the nearby conning tower extending up from the submarine deck in the darkness. Using it as a guide to the surface, he swam above the structure and continued on, feeling his strength rapidly dwindling. In anticipation of gulping the sweet air he hungered for, he spat out the snorkel mouthpiece. He was certain he had been submerged for close to five minutes now, pushing himself to the max. The thought that he had stayed below too long and exceeded his physical limits crossed his mind, and though he could now discern the sea's upper boundary, the silvery sheen of moon glow upon it suddenly seemed unreachable, as if it were several light years away. He felt himself beginning to black out.

The sound of a diver's regulator hissed somewhere close, momentarily providing Jake with something to focus on, a point of reference for him to hold onto in the midst of his growing predicament. He looked below him, fighting off the fugue that was swiftly descending upon him like a dark cloak dropped from above. A swarm of air bubbles agitated the water just below his fins, highlighted by a twinkling of luminescence that somehow made him think of stardust. Through the expanding cloud, he could distinguish the aura of the diver dogging him, rising up to finish him off. He tried to kick away, unable to avoid swallowing water as he struggled for the surface. He had gone over the edge, way beyond the physical threshold of normal men. He had pushed himself too hard and desperately needed oxygen.

With delirium quickly enfolding him, Jake barely perceived something clutch both his armpits. He had the sensation of soaring, accelerating, rising swiftly like a gliding bird of prey caught in an updraft. An alpine breeze seemed to flow all around him, gently washing over him before finding a corridor to his soul, the center of his being.

And then reality spun back as he realized Destiny was hovering over him, her lips pressed firmly against his, her breath warm and sweet like the fragrant tropical flowers within the cove. Seeing his eyes flutter open, she pulled her mouth away and sat back astride Hercules, her expression showing deep concern and overlaid with a hint of disbelief. Strangely revitalized from the resuscitation he had just received, he began to clear his lungs, gagging up water and filling his chest with deep, satisfying gasps. He became aware of another creature behind him, propping him above the water's surface. Achilles was under him, floating on his back and using those strange grasping appendages to hold him snugly under both arms and elevate him.

Jake felt his strength returning as he continued to inhale greedily. "I'm okay, Achilles," he finally rasped. "You can release me."

The juvenile lowered him into the water and let go, spinning around to look him over. *"You are still weak, Jake Javolyn,"* Achilles ululated in that lilting speech characteristic of his unique species. *"You may rest your body on mine."*

Jake hooked an arm over the albino's back and stared back at the girl.

"The man chasing you has gone back to the submarine," Destiny informed him. The childlike timber of her voice was gone, replaced by a husky tightness that made him look at her more closely. In the soft wash of moonlight, her face appeared taut and her eyes slightly glazed.

The context of the girl's words suddenly registered, jarring him back to full awareness. *Yes, the submarine, he was reminded.* His recent encounter came flooding back all at once, making him spin his head to locate his vessel. The Angel had pulled her anchor and was now churning the water, heading in the direction of the nearby cliffs. Scanning the water forward of the vessel, he could just make out the dorsal fins of other dolphins leading the way. Already Destiny had moved off toward the pack, preparing to assist Zimbola in negotiating the reef. If the Angel could squeeze through the narrow channel she would be safe, beyond the reach of the sub. Having seen the size of the undersea vessel, Jake was certain it could not possibly follow his boat through such a constricted passageway where fangs of heavy coral lay in wait to tear open a passing hull.

But if the sub had a torpedo capability, it might very well launch such a projectile at the Angel, reef or no reef. Because the tide was up, a torpedo had the potential of traveling right over the coral, possibly clearing the highest calcareous projections by as much two feet.

"Where is the submarine, Achilles?" Jake asked anxiously.

"The metal vessel is coming to the surface as I speak, Jake Javolyn," the juvenile answered. Achilles turned almost ninety degrees. *"There!"*

The nose of the sub suddenly breached a short distance away, angling high above the sea before sending out a heavy spray as the rest of the vessel followed. In the pale moonlight, Jake had a broadside view of the thing, seeing that its overall length clearly exceeded the Angel's by at least twenty feet. As he looked on, a hatch opened atop the conning tower and the silhouette of a person poked out. Within moments the sub began to pick up speed, coming about quickly and pushing a bow wave before it.

Though the water was warm, a chill shot up Jake's spine as he realized where the sub was heading. "They're gonna ram the Angel," he yelled out in horror, feeling completely helpless for the first time since his stint in Afghanistan.

- 27 -

Raduyev's cheeks ticked with hatred as he kept a malicious gaze locked on the vessel plodding the water, its port broadside presented vulnerably to him as it made a run across his bow. Now that the sub was no longer hidden under the mantle of sea and was clearly on a heading that would intercept the watercraft, he was surprised that the boat before him did not waver from its present course. "Three degrees left!" he growled into the lip mike, speaking Arabic.

To confirm the order, a voice came back over his headphones, repeating the command in the same language. "Turning left by three degrees."

Raduyev listened to Kalid with annoyance. His second in command sounded a little too nervous for his taste. A brief moment elapsed before he sensed the P-130 swing slightly as the helm responded to his command.

As he closed the gap separating the two vessels, the other boat appeared to increase its speed. "Bring us left another three degrees!" he snarled. He would have his satisfaction with these infidels. By the grace of Allah, he would have it. The sub would be used in the manner it was intended. *Allah's Sword* would live up to its name.

"We have no more room to maneuver left," the helm warned, the voice in the headphones now urgent with a pleading edge to it. "We risk going aground on the reef if we do so."

Kalid's words fueled his growing rage. It was apparent the vessel before him was presently scrambling for the same passage through the reef taken earlier by the smaller boats. With the sub's diesel currently churning at maximum rpm, he could only hope to catch the wooden vessel before it made the channel, and that meant adjusting the sub's heading just a little more. Three more degrees would ensure that his prey did not escape. By his estimation, three more degrees was conservative enough not to put the sub in any danger. He knew exactly where the reef began to rise.

"Do not argue with me, Kalid," Raduyev screamed. "You will turn left by three more degrees. Do you think Allah will not protect one of his instruments?" Raduyev's words seemed to pacify his comrade-in-arms, for the sub turned to port a moment later, now perfectly aligned to intercept the vessel he was determined to destroy.

As Raduyev looked beyond the sub's bow, he became aware of the fins cleaving the water directly ahead of the target he was rapidly converging on. There were six of them. No, he suddenly corrected himself. He could now discern a person propped above the surface just forward of a seventh, much larger fin. He assumed it was that same girl he had seen earlier. The people the girl was associated with were an irritating lot. He could well understand Ortega's need for vengeance against these people. From all outward appearances the Colombian should have been able to crush them, and rather easily at that. But somehow they were proving to be an elusive, resourceful lot, having the means to block and foil both overt and covert attempts aimed at vanquishing them. And now these mysterious white creatures were adding to the mix of unforeseen factors, seeming to contribute to the problems he was experiencing. Perhaps there was more to these seagoing mammals than met the eye. The thought made him think back to Ortega. He remembered the unusual interest the Colombian had shown toward the strange albino dolphins, including the girl accompanying them.

Whoever the girl was, the sight of her made Raduyev's blood boil all the more violently. She had rendered aid to the man he had fought, her and one of the dolphins accompanying her, denying him his quarry. He had almost caught up to the man, perhaps a second away from stopping him from reaching the surface. His adversary had gone without air during their struggle, a most foolish yet extraordinary feat. The man had not only thwarted him from boarding and taking command of the vessel he was now pursuing, but had taken both his comrades out of the fight. Azzum was still out cold and Bashir had vanished without a trace. Plunging his knife between the man's ribs would have given him tremendous satisfaction, making his foolhardy and time-consuming voyage across the Windward Passage ultimately worthwhile despite the obstacles thrown in his path. His foe had been deprived of oxygen far too long and, from what Raduyev had been able to surmise, would have been easily defeated in such a weakened condition. Raduyev would have put an end to his adversary once and for all if not for one of those irksome white dolphins rushing in and carrying the man away beyond his reach. Driven on by the overpowering rage that had gripped him, he had nevertheless continued on and popped his head above the surface, only to witness the girl administering mouth-to-mouth resuscitation on the man no more than fifteen meters away. Running the incident over in his mind, Raduyev was convinced that only one man could have given him such a fight with such limited resources at his disposal, and that man was Jake Javolyn.

But now retribution was at hand. The sub's steel bow would crush the infidel vessel's flimsy wooden hull, staving through it with little effort. If the owner of the boat was indeed Javolyn, Raduyev would at least reap some gratification at knowing he had put a valuable possession of his long time nemesis on the bottom. And it was only befitting that Allah's Sword would deliver the lethal strike. A sense of elation began to build within him in anticipation of the moment of impact.

He tried to recall the name of the vessel converging with his own. *What was it called? Ah, yes, now he remembered. Avenging Angel. That was it.* When he had followed the watercraft he had elevated his periscope and gone to maximum magnification, getting close enough to read the words emblazoned on the boat's stern. It had struck him as blasphemous that an infidel would presume to identify his vessel with that of a spiritual entity created for smiting God's enemies. If there was avenging to be done, it would come through the power of Allah's Sword.

As Raduyev surveyed the scene unfurling before him, his eyes came to rest on the group of dolphins escorting the vessel he was about to turn into a mass of splinters. They had all stopped and were now spread out at even intervals from one another. Somewhat puzzled, he turned his attention back to the Avenging Angel, bracing himself for the impending collision. A malevolent giddiness began to take hold of him as the P-130 charged ahead, its bow about to smash amidships on the boat looming before him.

The expression on Raduyev's face instantly turned to shock as a screeching shudder reverberated through the sub's hull, and he gritted his teeth as his body was jarred sideways with unexpected violence. Suddenly slowed, Allah's Sword broke abruptly right from its intended target, deflected by some unseen obstruction. Dumbfounded, Raduyev could only watch as the sub's prow skirted past the Angel's stern, missing the vessel's dive platform by mere inches. Wide-eyed, he stared in disbelief as the Avenging Angel swept away from him unscathed, its hull plowing between the two lines of dolphins floating stationary on each side of it.

- 28 -

It was well past 1 a.m. by the time the Angel's crew had dropped anchor on the south side of the cove, well away from where the thurentra nestled. Miraculously, the North Sea trawler had made it through the confined opening in the reef without so much as a flake of bottom paint being scraped from her hull. What had made the feat even more remarkable was the fact that Zimbola had traversed the incommodious passage at full throttle, something the Jamaican would never have attempted had not the submarine sought to ram him. Jake knew, however, that had the dolphins not been so precise in their alignment or had the tide been so much as two inches lower, the outcome might have been far different. It was Achilles who had informed him of this, as conveyed to the juvenile by other members of the pod who, acting as channel guides, had perceived just how close the Angel had come to disaster.

Following the perilous episode, Zimbola had been able to squeeze the vessel through the second channel leading to the cove, clearing the rock walls on each side by less than a foot where the passageway was tightest. Not knowing what armaments the sub carried, Jake felt it prudent to bring the Angel into the safe haven the cove provided, certain that the sub could not follow. Even fully surfaced, the sub would have drafted too much water to clear the highest protuberances of coral lining each side of the reef channel. And while the sub had a beam approximating that of Jake's vessel, it lacked a hull tapered to the degree of the Angel's to adequately negotiate the narrow width the opening through the reef afforded. Though Jake had been relieved to learn the sub had left the area based on what the dolphins conveyed to him, he couldn't be sure it would not return. According to Achilles, the metal boat had sustained some damage, brushing up against a huge mass of brain coral on the outside portion of the reef. In the end, it had been the submarine captain's insane desire for retribution that had come back on him full circle, almost leading to the destruction of his own vessel.

Shortly after the incident, Jake had asked Achilles if members of his pod could follow the submarine to its next destination and report back this information. Upon communicating with the other albinos, the juvenile assured him that his request would be carried out. By arrangement, Hermes and Aphrodite would fulfill this task.

Although Jake's near drowning had left him with a severe headache, he deferred getting some rest until the man he had captured was properly treated and secured for the night. He had looked for Destiny to see if she could heal the man's wound, but the girl had vanished again. The last thing he needed was for the man to get free and become a danger to the Angel's crew or the other parties currently in the cove. Assuming his captive was willing to talk, he might learn something about the objective of the submarine crew. In the morning he would put in a call to Mat Daniels and apprise him of what was going on, but right now he was just too damned tired.

As he lay down in his bunk aboard the Angel, a jumble of snapshots depicting recent events danced through his mind. Tenaciously they followed him as he plunged through the barrier separating reality from the realm of dreams. Only one image seemed to dominate his thoughts, however, and that was of a raven-haired girl with doe-like eyes.

- 29 -

Colonel Ternier sat at his desk, idly scratching the scar marring his lower jaw. Omar's request puzzled him. If he followed through on it he risked reprisals from a host of human rights groups, and even worse, prosecution by the International Criminal Court at the Hague. But then again, a leak would have to occur within his network of acolytes and spies for him to get implicated, and that possibility was extremely remote. Fear and greed were the primary motivators he used to keep his people in check, and over the years he had come to realize the full magnitude of their effectiveness. Fear, however, worked best for him, and the use of such an incentive was much more to his liking.

Weighing his options, Ternier looked across the desktop at the fat little man sitting opposite him. It was already past three in the morning, an hour when his quarters would seem most ominous to anyone brought to such a place, a good time to conduct business. "Twenty able-bodied men, you say?"

Hennington appeared uncomfortable, dabbing the sweat streaming profusely from his brow with a handkerchief, a habit Ternier had grown used to seeing. "Ortega was very specific on that point. These men must be fit enough to withstand hard physical labor over a period of months."

Ternier got out of his chair and strolled around his desk, his hands clasped stiffly behind his back, his posture rigid. The Colonel knew the effect such a regal bearing had on people. He saw himself as a man destined to lead, and not just on the level he currently commanded. The winds of change were fast approaching and it was important he did not impede them.

"You may tell Ortega I will honor his request," he said, not bothering to look at the chubby broker. "How does he propose to take delivery of the merchandise?"

"He has arranged to have them put aboard the San Carlo when she makes port by week's end," Hennington said, his voice betraying the tenseness he felt.

Ternier stopped in mid-step, showing his surprise. "So, you have followed through on my suggestion. Good…very good."

Hennington fidgeted nervously in his chair as Ternier moved behind him. The Colonel enjoyed making the broker nervous. It only served to keep him in line, to make the man do his bidding.

Ternier glanced over at the wall behind his desk, his eyes singling out one photograph in particular, a scene showing a smiling Rene Preval, president-elect of Haiti, shaking Ternier's hand at a recent state function. As he stared at the picture, he had to remind himself that Preval was the current head of state of the strife-torn country. *So many leaders,* he thought amusedly. To him, they were all becoming a blur.

Scanning the wall further, Ternier located another photograph. Prior to Preval's national election victory in February of 2006, another man by the name of Gerard Latortue had provided interim leadership to Haiti, functioning as Acting Prime Minister during that period. Latortue had been one of the latest in a succession of Haitian leaders who had enjoyed U.S. backing, placed in power as a short-term remedy by United Nations mandate for quelling the chronic political unrest that afflicted the impoverished nation. Ternier knew that Latortue had been nothing more than an international business consultant who had previously served as Foreign Minister in 1988 under former President Leslie Manigat. Manigat had only lasted three months in office before being ousted by a military coup.

From Ternier's perspective, Latortue's appointment had been motivated primarily by U.S. and French interests assembling multilateral support for humanitarian intervention. A subtle sneer formed on Ternier's features as he mused over the politics that had always seemed to surface throughout the history of his nation. Restoring order in Haiti through the meddling of international economic giants like the United States was becoming commonplace these days. To Ternier, it was just another example of the rich imperialist countries exploiting the poor under the guise of nation building. In actuality, Latortue had manipulated his way to power, calling upon the Americans to remove President Aristide in the midst of mounting political strife that threatened the stability of the country. Sworn in under heavy security before a tiny gathering of only two hundred people, Latortue was simply another manifestation of illegitimate leadership thrust upon the Caribbean nation by outside influences who thought they knew what was best for Haiti. In essence, the interim government under Latortue had been a surrogate regime almost totally dependent on Washington for its survival. And from experience, Ternier had no misconceptions about what that meant. It had been a complete failure.

Being a student of modern history, the Colonel knew that, to date, no American-supported regime had ever made the full transition to democracy following the withdrawal of military support. Events since the fall of Baby

Doc had shown him that once U.S. or U.N. military forces withdrew from Haiti, the same problems that had previously plagued the country would resurface as they always did, and the transition to democracy would flounder yet again. From 1986 to 1991 the country had experienced as many as four military coups. Like his predecessors, Latortue had been forced to resort to repressive measures to maintain power, imposing martial law on the citizenry and relying on the Haitian National Police to enforce it. As in the past, this always led to some strongman rising to the forefront and seizing power to advance his personal ambitions. Botched nation building efforts historically produced undesirable consequences for the local population, with dictators always emerging from the wreckage. Ternier was convinced that the creation and maintenance of surrogate regimes always mutated into military dictatorships or corrupt autocracies, with the cycle endlessly perpetuating itself in the face of imperialist meddling.

Perhaps under the current president the country stood a chance at becoming more progressive, but Ternier strongly doubted it. Highly popular among the poorest members of Haitian society, Preval proclaimed himself to be a nonviolent anarchist, believing power should flow from the government to the people. A former Aristide protégé, Preval had shown less than stellar performance in the past when he had tenured as Haiti's president once before, serving from 1996 to 2001. Perhaps it was the never-ending array of internal problems that made stellar performance impossible to achieve. Preval had his hands full with Haiti's current state of affairs, incessantly facing a demanding schedule at resuscitating international assistance. Already many manufacturers within the country were closing up shop because of the growing gang violence. Shortly before being inaugurated as president for the second time over a year ago, Preval had addressed the U.N. Security council, citing the enormous challenges he faced in the form of widespread poverty, unemployment, dilapidated infrastructure, and chronic national insecurity. Preval, it seemed, appeared to be on a crusade at saving the land, proclaiming that Haiti needed more than just an influx of money to correct its problems. The country also needed expertise brought in from abroad in order to upgrade its electrical power generating facilities and improve its infrastructure, health, and education sectors, all of which were his top priorities. Preval had been careful to stress that even if the nation got both the finances and expertise it so desperately needed, it would take at least 25 years before real progress would be seen. Therefore his people should not have unrealistic expectations for an immediate solution to the critical woes afflicting the nation. With such a long timetable in the works, Ternier was certain that political unrest would soon boil over once again, manifesting itself in more riots and bloody rebellions.

And that kind of atmosphere was just fine by the Colonel. He loved political instability, a situation that allowed him to cultivate his own aspirations. Without it, he could not possibly enjoy the power he exerted. He was one of the true power wielders behind the scenes in Haitian society. But he would not allow himself to make the same mistakes all the others had made before him, lured by the desire for overt ascendancy over a nation only to be dethroned by American might shortly thereafter. No, he was too smart to make such a futile grab for power in the face of looming imperialism; that is, unless the time were ripe. Without some cataclysmic upheaval to divert its attentions, the United States was currently far too strong to let its core security and economic well-being go undefended.

Ternier held down the laugh beginning to take root his belly, for he knew the time was now very close for that upheaval.

At heart, Ternier was a true cynic, believing that the American goal of building democracy in Haiti was merely a pretext for advancing its economic interests. He was privy to much information and from what he could gather, the coup that had ousted Aristide in 1991 had been orchestrated by the U.S. Though Aristide had gotten sixty-seven percent of the popular vote in a democratic election, he had not been acceptable to Washington. With corruption and mismanagement of government funds by past Haitian leaders seemingly out of control, the U.S. had counted on Marc Bazin being elected, a man Washington deemed as having considerable integrity. Bazin was a former World Bank official who had been assigned to the post of Finance Minister in 1982 under the Baby Doc regime. Although Duvalier had officially appointed Bazin, Ternier knew that the arrangement had been a stipulation of the U.S. if Haiti was to continue receiving foreign aid. But Duvalier had not anticipated the extreme zealousness of his newly appointed Finance Minister, and Bazin had uncovered case after case of corruption. In the end, Bazin had determined that at least thirty-six percent of government revenue was embezzled, and as a consequence he had declared the country to be the most mismanaged in the region. And though Baby Doc had quickly replaced him, Bazin had given credence to the world that Duvalier had overstepped the traditional accepted boundaries of Haitian corruption where leaders had a history of self-enrichment.

The Colonel continued to reflect on those earlier years. Under intense internal as well as U.S. pressure, Baby Doc had fled the country on February 7, 1986, taking exile in France and absconding with millions in government funds. Back then, a real Haitian army had existed and although Ternier had been part of it, he had felt it prudent to keep a low profile, remaining in the background as the National Council of Government took charge of the country. After Aristide had been elected in 1991, it was General Raoul Cedras who had been responsible for deposing the people's choice of leadership. Rumor within the intelligence network had it that Cedras was a long-time agent of the U.S. Central Intelligence Agency. With Aristide temporarily out of the way, the U.S. had again pushed for a return to democracy in Haiti while supporting a half-baked embargo that exempted American-owned factories and demanding increasing concessions from the nation's government. If Haiti failed to comply, Washington would withhold badly needed economic aid to its beleaguered neighbor. Somewhere in the midst of political maneuvering, the U.S. had managed to weaken France's privileged position in Port-au-Prince politics and initiate sweetheart deals for American corporations. Even under Jean Claude Duvalier the U.S. had sought to make the Haitian economy more like an extension of its own. In implementing this, Haiti's tariffs had been cut, making the country a market for U.S. agricultural surpluses and a source of inexpensive tropical produce. Unable to compete with cheap American staples such as corn and beans, many peasant farmers failing to make ends meet began cutting down fruit trees to make charcoal, while others left their land and migrated to the burgeoning slums surrounding Port-au-Prince and the other cities, forming an immense pool of cheap manual labor for U.S. textile and electronics assembly plants. Already Haiti had become known as the *Taiwan of the Caribbean*. Whereas the nation was nearly self-sufficient in food in 1970, importing only ten percent of its needs, by 1993 that figure had risen to forty-two percent and was still rising.

Ternier suddenly thought of the rice trade. Haiti was currently the largest consumer of U.S. rice in the Caribbean, and the seventh largest in the world, importing well over two hundred thousand tons a year.

The Colonel felt no malice toward the U.S. or the de facto Haitian regimes that had favored American interests. That was the way the world worked. It was only natural for the strongest or smartest members of humanity to exploit the weak, either using them or pushing them aside for personal or national gain.

And as Ternier well knew, Haiti had fallen victim to exploitation throughout its turbulent history. Haiti had officially declared her independence in 1804 following the slave rebellions more than half a century earlier. Subsequent to much internal struggle to rid itself of slavery, the country saw Jean Jacques Dessalines, a black general, emerge as the new leader of the Haitian Revolution. But Dessalines' reign was short-lived. Two years after his crowning as Jacques the First, Dessalines was assassinated in an ambush. At first, the French government refused to recognize the new republic as an independent state. Through diplomacy, Louis XVIII tried in vain from 1814 to 1823 to regain Haiti as a colony. As a concession, Haiti's President Boyer signed an ordinance, agreeing to pay the French government an indemnity of 150 million francs to recognize the country's independence and to compensate for the loss of the plantations owned by the white colonists. Boyer's submission to that ordinance not only emptied the national treasury, but ultimately mortgaged the republic's future to the French. France did not recognize the country's independence until 1825, while the British did not accept it as a sovereign nation until 1833. Nevertheless, Haiti became the second republic in the Western Hemisphere and the first independent black nation in the world at a time when all the nations around it still resorted to slavery. The Spanish, French, English, Dutch, and Americans had all seen Haiti's successful revolution as a threat to their national interests and their status quo as slave owners, causing them to boycott, manipulate, isolate and refuse to recognize Haiti's independence until it was deemed that the small Caribbean nation was impoverished and made weak enough militarily so that it could not pose a threat to anyone.

The violent history of Haiti intrigued Ternier. Following Boyer's administration, the country went through twenty-two heads of state between 1843 and 1915, a period before occupation by the United States occurred. Of these, only one had been able to serve out his term in office. Among the others, three had died horribly while still serving. One was presumably poisoned, another was hacked to pieces by a mob, while a third was blown up with his palace. The Colonel refrained from laughing aloud as he thought about the fate of the others. Except for one who had prudently resigned from office, all were deposed by revolution after incumbencies ranging in length from three months to twelve years.

A sigh escaped Ternier's lips as he thought about Haiti's heyday, a bygone period in history when the land was surnamed the pearl of the Antilles because of its wealth in gold and other precious metals and stones, a place noted for its natural beauty. Unfortunately, too many occupations and interventions by outside nations had taken place since that time. He could not deny that Haiti was a country of seemingly unending turmoil, a land whose heritage and resources had been exploited and mismanaged by its sons, daughters and foes alike. But he had seen a dramatic change in world affairs as of late, something that, under the right circumstances, could be taken advantage of to restore the nation to its days of international prominence.

It was all proving to be so easy, he thought. The idea he had come up with was extremely simple at its core, in many ways not much different from that of a seed. In the right environment, a seed took root, tending to grow and flourish if properly nourished. In many ways, ideas mimicked seeds, often starting out as a tiny pip before germinating into something colossal, and with very little nurturing. As a small boy he had been quite fond of the fairytale *Jack and the Beanstalk*, liking how a very small bean had transformed itself overnight into a thing that stretched up into the clouds where a strange kingdom existed and where incredible riches abounded. Unaware of the power held in his hand, Jack had planted the bean only to find it towering into the heavens the next morning.

Unconsciously, a pompous little smile spread across the Colonel's face as he continued to stare at the framed picture on the wall, a vision of the giant falling to his death coming to mind, the ruler of the kingdom in the sky usurped by the diminutive Jack stealing the golden goose. His plan was rapidly gaining impetus, driven by forces requiring only a minimum of tweaking and tending on his part in order that a pathway to ultimate glory be paved for him. Yes, his beanstalk was now growing swiftly, sending out a multitude of shoots that spiraled and twisted about one another, each and all taking him ever closer to the realm of treasures and power he so desperately sought, a place where he would be the undisputed king, unchallenged by anyone.

Ternier did not perceive any aspects of the world about him as being evil. In much the same way, he did not see himself as being an evil man. It did not matter to him that philosophers and religious scholars alike denounced greed as a wicked human failing, an undesirable flaw in man's inherent makeup. The quest for power was the natural order of life, and wealth translated to power. Like energy and matter, the two were interchangeable and equivalent. Human nature being what it was, greed was a good thing. It tended to motivate humanity, advancing it toward bigger and grander stages of existence where it would otherwise remain stagnant. It was mankind's way, a standard the human race had no trouble conforming to. The fulfillment of greed often remained cloaked under the guise of demagoguery and altruism, false political posturing frequently used in placating the downtrodden. Humanitarian causes were popular these days among democratic superpowers with hidden agendas. From where Ternier stood, democracies were nothing more than hypocrisies, led by big business and the most affluent through the use of lobbyists and special interest groups to get what they wanted. He saw free elections as shams, designed to delude the masses into thinking they were somehow in control and guiding their own destinies. Things were rarely what they appeared to be. It all boiled down to survival of the fittest, nature's plan to discard the weak and ensure the proliferation of only the strongest among a species. This view was one of the cornerstones of Ternier's personality. If he refrained from going after the potential spoils he envisioned lying before him, there would always be another that would come along and seize what he could have taken himself. Timing was everything and he had to work quickly if his seed was to continue to sprout.

Ternier's smile abruptly disintegrated, turning into a frown as the thought of a seed taking root made him think back to that mysterious cove near Malique where he had almost lost his life many years ago. The place had teemed with plant life, providing a backdrop of beauty unlike any landscape he had ever seen. And it was there that he had his last and only glimpse of the ancient amulet, a treasure in itself. The power of that talisman was something that would have ensured his destiny.

Shortly after his encounter with the cheval in that strange place, he had lost contact with the one and only spy he had planted in Malique. Rumor had it that the man had died at sea, but he could never be sure. In any event, Erzulie had advised him against going back there, believing the cheval to be much too powerful for either of them to confront. Continuing to dwell on the subject, he could not dismiss the possibility that the cheval was now gone and would not return.

On impulse, Ternier took his eyes from the picture on the wall and lowered his gaze to the back of Hennington's head. "Perhaps you can do me a little favor," he said.

"Yes?" Hennington replied hurriedly, eager to please.

Ternier could not help but smile. Hennington's obsequious manner gladdened him to no end. "I would like you to take a trip for me." Pausing for effect, he added, "Have you ever heard of a fishing village called Malique?"

- 30 -

Jake was on one knee cradling Myers in his arms. The light in Myer's eyes was fading fast, now faint as a flow of blood black as ebony in the pale moonlight bubbled up from his open mouth. Mat was beside him lending support.

"Promise me!" Myers gasped, choking up more blood and focusing glazed eyes on Jake.

Jake could only nod, not trusting how his own voice would sound.

Myers groped for one of Jake's hands and squeezed, the grip surprisingly hard. "Say it!" he blurted, as if trying to speak from under a column of water. "Promise me!"

"I...I promise," Jake vowed, trying desperately to keep his tone strong. "You have my word."

Said aloud, the words seemed to satisfy Myers, for a smile transcended his face. "You are the big brother I never had," he uttered weakly. With that his grip went slack.

Jake stared dazedly as Myers' head lolled to one side. "No!" he found himself yelling. He glanced quickly at Mat. "We're losing him," he cried. Lowering Myers to the ground, the two men went to work, applying CPR to their fallen comrade. Jake was tenacious, refusing to give up, periodically blowing air into Myers' lungs and spitting away the blood that obstructed his effort.

After a while Mat clutched his shoulder. "He's gone, Jake," he said quietly. "There's nothing more we can do for him."

Extending a hand, Jake ran his fingers over Myers' eyelids, giving him the look of a man sleeping peacefully. Slowly, he became aware of the sporadic gunfire disturbing the night. His M4 lay on the ground next to him and he reached for it, beginning to rise in a semi-crouch.

A hand suddenly clutched his shoulder. "No, Jake!" Mat screamed. "You'll only get yourself killed.

Ignoring Mat's plea, Jake pushed his hand away and began to move forward. He could feel the tears streaming down his face, something he had never let show. *They would pay for this. By God, they would pay.* The hate he felt was overwhelming, taking on a life of its own and consuming him.

The hold on his shoulder was there again, restraining him, stopping him from doing what had to be done. "Jay Jay!" Mat persisted.

Jake shrugged the hand away a second time, vaguely aware of the name by which Mat addressed him. Mat never called him Jay Jay.

"Wake up, Jay Jay."

Jake reached up, grabbing the throat of the person jostling him and simultaneously pulling the K-Bar from its sheath.

"No, Jay Jay," the voice pleaded, the tone full of fright.

Reality slowly flooded Jake's consciousness as he became aware of Phillipe hovering over him, the boy's arms pulled back to fend off the blade. Lowering the knife, Jake removed his fingers from Phillipe's throat and sat up. Realizing his own cheeks were damp, he took a moment to wipe away the wetness, looking away to cover his embarrassment. "What is it?"

"You were yelling in your sleep," Phillipe said, rubbing his windpipe.

Something bumped the Angel's hull just below the bunk upon which Jake rested. Lifting the curtain that draped over the porthole overlooking his bed, Jake brought his face close to the plexiglass. The head of Achilles poked above the water and stared back at him. A quick peek at his watch told him it was a few minutes past 9 a.m., an hour of the morning he rarely slept past.

"Where is everybody?" Jake asked, trying to shake off the remaining grogginess that continued to cling to him like a cloud of mist.

"Zimbola is repairing the damage made by the men who tried to board us," Phillipe said. "Hector guards the man you captured, and the scientists are all ashore with Jacob and the white witch."

Phillipe's use of the last term made Jake look sharply at him. "She's not a witch," he countered in annoyance.

Phillipe appeared puzzled. "If she is not a white witch, then what is she?" the boy asked innocently. "Zimbola tells me only a witch of the vaudan possesses the power each of us saw her use."

"Zimbola is wrong," Jake said quickly, wanting to change the subject. He arose from the bed. "Has our uninvited guest given Hector any trouble?"

When Phillipe did not immediately answer, Jake scrutinized him closely. "Well has he?"

"The man says we are all dead men."

"Does he now?" Jake could not help but notice Phillipe crinkling his nose. "What?"

"You do not smell very good, Jay Jay."

Jake became aware of an unpleasant odor assaulting his nostrils. He was sweating profusely under the Farmer John wetsuit he still wore, realizing he had failed to remove it the night before. In the limited confines below the trawler's main deck there was little ventilation.

A wry little snicker escaped Jake's lips. "In the Seals, we drank in each others sweat all the time. It's part of being a soldier." Without warning he reached out and pulled the teenager to him, squeezing him in a bear hug. "Just think of this as part of your training."

Phillipe giggled mirthfully, trying to squirm away, and after a few seconds Jake released the boy. Jake knew Phillipe loved the show of affection he gave him. Growing up on the streets of Port-au-Prince, the Haitian lad had been starved for attention, learning to fend for himself for most of his young life. Jake had changed all that and had adopted the role of a protective older brother for the boy. In taking Phillipe under his wing, he had inadvertently rescued the boy from a life of despondency and crime. And without even realizing it, he had imparted solid core values to the former street urchin. In more ways than one, Jake had become someone Phillipe could look up to, a role model for him to emulate. Phillipe was now under his care and Jake took the responsibility seriously.

"What be all this ruckus?" a deep voice boomed. Zimbola's massive frame spilled into Jake's quarters. The big man rarely smiled, but from the look on his face Jake could tell he was amused by the horseplay that had just ensued.

"Just indoctrinating the lad in the way of the Seals," Jake stated glibly.

"I don't think this boat can handle more than one reekin' like that. What you trying to do, split open her keel?"

"Not the Angel, Zimby. Never."

"The good doctor called from the beach. He asks if you can come ashore to speak with him."

"Tell him I'll be there just as soon as I get cleaned up."

Jake took the better part of ten minutes to shower and shave, scrubbing himself down good using some of the Angel's limited fresh water supply and also taking the time to wash and rinse off the shorty wetsuit. He found it strange the suit stank the way it did, though he suspected it had something to do with the bioluminescent microorganisms that abounded locally. The suit had obviously picked up substantial amounts of plant and animal life that began to decompose once leaving the water.

As a rule, Jake was very conservative with the vessel's potable water reserves, particularly since uncontaminated drinking water was considered a commodity on the Haitian market, a substance in short supply. But the seemingly endless stream of fresh water cascading down the nearby falls afforded him the luxury of topping off his tanks. He would do that before he left the cove.

After freshening up, Jake used the satellite phone to put in a call to Mat Daniels. He was fortunate enough to get a signal, and Mat answered on the third ring.

"Daniels here."

"Any changes on the local front since I last saw you?"

"Is that you, Jake?"

"Last I looked in the mirror it was."

Mat laughed. "Always the jester. No, nothings changed, good buddy. What gives?"

"I've got a present for you."

"Oh!"

"Yeah. I think you'll like it. It's the kind of gift you've been looking for."

A moment of silence followed as Mat absorbed this. "Where can I pick it up?"

"Keep your phone handy, Mat. I'll call you later and let you know." With that said, Jake ended the call.

Jake's next course of business was to pay a visit to the man he had captured. Hector appeared bored with the MP-5 straddling his lap as he sat across from the prisoner who lay in a small bunk in the forward part of the vessel. One of the man's ankles was chained to an eyebolt jutting from a bulkhead at the foot of the bed. The man gave Jake a baleful glare as soon as he entered the compartment. In spite of his defiance, the man appeared pale and weak.

"Has our guest been behaving himself?" Jake asked.

Hector shook his head. "According to him, we'll all be dead by tomorrow. He has already promised at least ten different ways we'll be murdered, but I'll avoid elaborating on how he intends to do it."

Leaning on the edge of the bunk, Jake studied the man closely. He had the skin tone and features of a person indigenous to the southern Mediterranean.

A dark, close-cropped beard lined the lower part of his face. He was fairly young, no more than twenty-five in Jake's opinion.

"If I were a betting man," Jake said, "I'd lay a thousand to one that sub of yours is operated by Islamic extremists bent on hurting a lot of innocent people."

The words appeared to strike a cord, for the man's eyes flared subtly, just enough for Jake to confirm what he had suspected ever since encountering the submarine. "I suggest you avoid ever playing poker," Jake jeered, "though I doubt such a game would interest you."

The man turned his eyes away and stared at the ceiling in silence. Grahm had treated the man's injury, and from what Jake could see, the wad of gauze wrapped tightly around his right forearm was stained heavily with dried blood where it covered the wound. The man's wet suit jacket had been removed, leaving him bare-chested, and where the man's upper arm was exposed above the dressing, the skin was bloated severely and starting to manifest a greenish tinge. A mild stench hung in the air, making Jake wonder if the odor emanated from the injury or the lower half of the wet suit, which the man still wore.

Jake turned to Hector. "He speaks English, doesn't he?"

"All his threats were in English."

Jake faced the man again. "Knowing what I do of the kind of person you are and the people you represent, I find it strange that you would go out of your way to attempt boarding my vessel." Jake paused, looking for the man's reaction. "The question is, for what purpose?"

Jake's captive continued to ignore him.

"You followed us here…why?"

The man offered nothing, keeping his eyes focused on the ceiling.

"That arm of yours doesn't look too good. Guessing, I'd say the bone is shattered and gangrene is setting in. If we don't do anything about it, you'll probably die. And even if we're able to treat it, you could very well end up losing the arm, anyway."

"I will welcome death," the man suddenly blurted, addressing Jake for the first time. "Allah will embrace me in paradise."

"And I suppose you'll look forward to those seventy-two virgins the mullahs keep promising."

"Yes."

Jake sighed sadly. "Those religious misfits have been conning you all along. I'm told that nowhere in the Koran will you find any such reference. It's just a ploy concocted by radical Muslim clerics to coax guys like you into doing their bidding. I think you'll be greatly disappointed in the afterlife, my friend, but then again, I doubt heaven will be your final destination."

The man abruptly let out a string of gibberish, babbling in a language incomprehensible to Jake. Although he didn't understand the words, he knew it was Arabic, having heard it on numerous occasions during his tour in the Middle East. He could see the man was beginning to sweat heavily and that his eyes were beginning to glaze over.

Reaching out, Jake placed a hand on the man's forehead. Turning, he looked at Hector. "He's burning up." Pondering the situation, he made a decision. "Keep an eye on him while I see about making him healthy again."

Hector shrugged. "Maybe you should save yourself the trouble and just dump him over the side."

"Not on my watch," Jake said, striding from the compartment. Making his way to the main deck, he scanned the water off the starboard side. He was about to call for Achilles when the young dolphin suddenly reared his head above the surface.

"What do you wish of me, Jake Javolyn?" Achilles ululated.

How does he do that? Jake could not help but wonder. "Achilles, I need you to bring Destiny to me. It's very important. Can you do that for me?"

"I will do as you ask, Jake Javolyn," the dolphin replied.

Jake expected the juvenile to turn and head for the beach, but that didn't happen. The albino remained stationary instead, continuing to stare up at him.

After a few seconds, Jake arched a brow. "Achilles?"

"Destiny will be here shortly, Jake Javolyn," Achilles stated.

"Uh, do me a favor, Achilles," Jake said, doing his best to conceal the annoyance he felt.

"What is that favor, Jake Javolyn?"

"I prefer you call me Jay Jay, Achilles, and you don't have to use my name each time you address me."

"As you wish, Jay Jay."

Destiny showed up five minutes later, letting one of the other albinos tow her out to the Angel. As she climbed up onto the dive platform, Jake's breath came up short. He could see she was no longer wearing the white full-body wet suit that had fit her like a glove. Also missing were the strange goggles she had worn. Attired only in a skimpy white bikini, her skin had the smooth golden luster of sunlit honey, enhanced all the more by the sheen of water bejeweling her body. Though the girl was tiny, her limbs were long and lean, graced by a muscular suppleness often exhibited by swimmers. A silky mane of glistening black tresses partially hid her face, draping down past both her cheeks and reaching to her waist. Arching her back and grabbing her hair with both hands, she wrung the water from the thick mane, sweeping it back so that it fell to her buttocks. Her eyes lingered on Jake momentarily before speaking. "Achilles said you needed to see me."

"I need a favor of you," Jake answered, fighting back his arousal and nearly croaking out the words. "I need you to heal the man I captured last night. His arm is badly infected and I think it's broken."

"I'll do what I can," the girl said. Her voice was soft and euphonious, further meliorating her attributes.

Jake led her belowdeck to where the injured man lay. The man's delirium had now escalated and his incoherent jabbering had gotten louder. Hector's jaw drooped noticeably as Destiny stepped past him, his gaze befalling the girl as if in worship.

Destiny looked the stricken man over briefly before placing a hand on his brow. The man flinched suddenly, his eyes bulging wide like a person caught in the grip of some unseen force. Letting out a low startled gasp as if in pain, Destiny reeled slightly before regaining control of herself, then placed her free hand on the man's injury. After several seconds, she turned to Jake. "We must place him in the water where the others can help," she said, her tone hinting strain and weariness. "I cannot do this by myself."

Jake looked at Hector. "Give me a hand with this guy."

Moving the man topside proved awkward and cumbersome in the restricted quarters belowdeck, but after several minutes of struggle they had him on the Angel's rear platform. By then Zimbola joined in to assist. Before placing the man in the water, Jake took the time to strap a life vest securely around his torso. The captive seemed suddenly aware of his surroundings, and in his eyes Jake saw the look of a man being led to the executioner's block.

"I go to Allah willingly," the man uttered weakly, staring at Jake as Zimbola lowered him into the water.

"We're not going to drown you," Jake said.

Numerous wakes rippled the water as all the albinos converged toward the Angel's stern. One by one, they nosed up to the man on all sides, crowding in and forming a tight circle with Destiny positioned to the man's front. Even Achilles joined the group of adults. Surrounded by the sea mammals, the man looked clearly frightened. Jake could see it in his eyes.

As Jake watched, his captive stiffened noticeably when Destiny placed a hand on the wound. The conjoining of minds did its magic, however, and after a minute the girl lifted her eyes to Jake who continued to gaze down in wonder from the rear platform. "The infection is gone," she said, sighing deeply. "His arm is mending quickly."

Jake smiled and nodded his thanks as Zimbola hauled the man back up onto the platform and sat him down. The Jamaican then peeled off the remaining portion of the man's wet suit, allowing Jake to hose off his charge with fresh water. Once this was done, Jake gave the man a dry pair of coveralls to wear.

Prior to donning the coveralls, the man unwrapped the bloody strip of gauze from his arm and stared incredulously at Destiny's work. The swelling was now completely gone and only a tiny pink scar remained. "What form of…of madness is this?" he stammered, moving his fingers to test them. The full use of his arm was rapidly returning. He looked first at Jake, then eyed the girl with disbelief. His expression slowly hardened into a scowl. "Miracles such as this are not possible among non-believers. This can only be the work of a demon."

"No," Jake corrected. "This is the work of an angel. You should be grateful to her for saving your miserable, worthless life." Jake was suddenly besieged by a brainstorm, a possible way to breach the fanatical mindset of the man. "Could it be that this miracle is a sign from God for you to rethink what those deceitful Islamic mullahs have been preaching to you all along? Did it ever occur to you that this girl is one of God's servants, a messenger sent from heaven to show you the true path to enlightenment?" He let that sink in before continuing. "Look at her helpers. Are they not all white like angels?"

Jake's skewed logic seemed to have the desired impact, for the man seemed to mull his words as he turned back to face the girl in silence. Even as the man was led away, Jake could see he was in deep thought. With Zimbola's hulking presence discouraging any resistance, the man was taken back to the bunk in the Angel's forward section where he was shackled to the bulkhead as before and left under Hector's watchful eye once again.

When Jake went back up on deck he saw that Destiny had climbed back aboard. She sat at the end of the dive platform with her back to him, her feet dangling in the water and almost touching Achilles. With the exception of only one other dolphin floating next to the juvenile, all the albinos had dispersed to various parts of the cove. Jake identified the second dolphin as Natalie. Through the crystalline water, he could discern the long lateral scar running along her flank.

"It seems I owe all three of you a show of gratitude for saving my life," Jake said, sitting down beside Destiny. He pointed to the scar on his forearm. "This little souvenir could have been much worse, Natalie. You kept that big nasty mako from having me for lunch."

"Certain things are meant to happen, Jake Javolyn," Natalie trilled back. Her voice had a slightly different pitch than that of Achilles. *"There is no need to thank me. My actions on that day ultimately led you here where you were able to bond with Achilles."*

"Please call me Jay Jay. All my friends call me…tha-" Jake's words trailed off as he eyed the flustered expression on Destiny's face. She looked deeply troubled, staring down into the water as if seeing something repulsive beneath the surface.

"Why does that man hate you?"

Jake shrugged helplessly. "It's a long story, one you shouldn't concern yourself with."

"I have plenty of time to listen."

Jake studied the girl's face up close. She was a complete mystery to him, her and these extraordinary creatures floating at his feet. "I'll make a deal with you," he offered. "Tell me a few things about yourself and I'll tell you anything you want to know."

"There's not much to tell."

Jake restrained himself from laughing. "On the contrare, pretty damsel, but you're dead wrong on that count. It's not every day I come across a beautiful girl with a remarkable ability to heal life-threatening injuries, a girl who lives with talking white dolphins possessing hands. Either I'm having one incredible lucid dream or they've got me locked up in some psycho ward where I'm hallucinating all this."

Destiny smiled shyly at Jake's humor. "I can assure you I'm a real person."

"Then tell me how you came to live in this-," Jake looked around to take in his surroundings, "this most unusual place."

The girl swashed the water with her feet. "I was born here."

"You mean right here in this cove?"

"Yes."

"And these dolphins?" Jake looked down at Natalie and Achilles. Both creatures stared back at him intently, seemingly interested in every word he uttered. "How did they come to be here?"

"They were also born here. This is their home."

Jake nodded contemplatively, then glanced around. "A hidden paradise, I'd say. You're lucky to have grown up in so peaceful a setting. Do any others know about this place?"

Destiny seemed to withdraw into an abrupt silence over the question, dropping her eyes reticently to the water.

"I'm sorry," Jake apologized. "You don't have to answer the question if you don't want to."

The girl continued to gaze at the water. "Some of the locals have knowledge of this place, but they understand our need for solitude and leave us alone. With the exception of a few villagers, you and the other men with you are the first outsiders to ever set foot here ever since I can remember."

"What about Jacob?" Jake asked, spying the Haitian over by the fish pen at the far end of the cove. "How does he fit into all this?"

Destiny followed Jake's gaze. "Jacob raised me."

Jake lifted an eyebrow skeptically. "He's your father?"

The girl shook her head. "No. Jacob is my dear friend and teacher. He taught me everything I know about the world we live in. He saw to my education." She paused momentarily and indicated the albinos. "He educated all of us."

"Jacob seems to be a most extraordinary man. Not your run-of-the-mill fisherman, I'll grant you that. What did he teach you?"

"Lots of things."

"Like what?"

"History, philosophy, languages, geography, mathematics, genet-"

"Whoa! Slow down!" Jake interjected, impressed by the diversity of subject matter. "Did you say mathematics?"

"Yes. Jacob taught us such things as number theory, set theory, geometry, logic, algebra, trigonometry, calculus and statistics. He's gradually taken us to into higher mathematics like differential equations, linear algebra and topology."

Jake was dumbfounded. Having earned a college degree in mechanical engineering, he was quite familiar with higher mathematics and knew how convoluted the subject could be to the average person. He especially found it difficult to believe the albinos understood such abstract concepts. Nevertheless, he decided to put what the girl was telling him to the test. Turning to the juvenile, he asked, "Achilles, what is differential calculus?"

"It is a branch of mathematics concerned with studying the rates of change of functions with respect to their variables, Jay Jay," Achilles replied without hesitation.

The quick, unrehearsed response almost caused Jake to fall off the platform. To be sure he wasn't being misled, he tested Achilles again. "What about integral calculus, Achilles? Do you know what that is?"

"Yes, Jay Jay, it is a branch of mathematics that focuses primarily on advanced methods of finding lengths, areas and volumes of spatial objects."

Jake's head began to spin. "Tell me, Achilles, are you able to solve a differential equation?"

"Yes, Jay Jay. If the equation has a solution, I am able to solve it."

Jake was growing more perplexed by the moment. "But how? Don't you need something to write on in order to do this?" An image of Achilles scribbling out and then reducing an equation in the wet sand lining the cove's shore flashed briefly in his mind.

"No, Jay Jay."

Destiny suddenly chimed in to clear up Jake's bewilderment. "Unlike Jacob or most other humans, Achilles does not require the use of paper and pen to solve a mathematical problem. He's able to perform the calculation in his head."

Jake looked at Natalie. "What about the others? Do they also have this ability?"

"All of the albinos can do it."

Jake was awestruck yet again. "What about you? Can you also do this in your head?"

"In a way, yes."

"I don't understand."

"It's hard to explain. Usually I see the equations being reduced, but most of the effort is carried out by the others."

"You mean the other albinos?"

"Yes."

Jake shook his head. It was all starting to make sense. It certainly explained why he never witnessed any verbal exchanges between the girl and her companions or between the albinos themselves. "I find this most amazing. You actually see and feel what the others are seeing and feeling?"

"Yes, but it works best when I'm mentally conjoined with them at close quarters. The number of minds involved in the conjoining also makes a difference. I don't know why it works, it just does. Jacob thinks we somehow create a synergy that becomes greater than any one of us. The more of us that are conjoined, the more powerful the effect. But the bond weakens when great distances separate us."

Destiny suddenly grew quiet again, as if wondering how much she should reveal.

Jake sensed she was holding back on something. "So you use this conjoining to heal?" he prodded.

The girl seemed to overcome her reticence. "Yes. But when we're linked this way, we sometimes get insights or visions of things that aren't readily apparent. It's…it's as if we're looking beyond time."

"When did you learn to do this?"

"I've always been able to do this, ever since I can remember. I grew up thinking this was normal, to be able to see and feel what the others were thinking and feeling."

Jake mulled this over, intrigued by it all. "Where are your parents?"

"I never knew my biological father, only my mother. She lives here, too, but she's away."

"She must be a most unusual person to produce a girl like you. When-"

A dark shadow suddenly fell across the platform as a heavy load landed behind Jake and the girl, making Jake look over his shoulder. Zimbola loomed above him. "Excuse me, Jay Jay, but Doctor Grahm grows impatient for your company," the big man reminded him.

Jake realized he had forgotten. "Tell him I'll be with him in a minute." He shifted his gaze back to Destiny. "Can I have a rain check on this conversation?" he said apologetically.

"If you'd like."

"How about you and I have some lunch over by the falls at twelve noon?"

"Alright."

"I've been very selfish asking all the questions and not giving you a chance to ask anything about me," Jake apologized as he began to rise.

"I already have all I need to know about you, Jay Jay."

Jake was taken back. "How's that?"

Destiny looked out over the water, seeming to grope for the right words. "In healing you, I was given a glimpse of your inner being."

"Now that's a scary thought," Jake chuckled. "There's a lot of junk and loose baggage banging around in there. I'm almost embarrassed to ask what you found."

"You have nothing to be ashamed of."

Jake stood up, suddenly feeling uncomfortable. "See you by the falls at noon," was all he could think to say. With that he dove from the platform and began to swim for the beach. Achilles stayed with him, executing a series of quadruple somersaults on the way in.

- 31 -

Franklin Grahm greeted Jake with a warm smile. The scientist was with his two assistants and had various equipment set up close to the base of a steep bluff located at the northern end of the cove. In the deep confines of the gorge, it was here that Grahm would have the best chance of receiving an unobstructed telemetry signal relayed from an orbiting satellite.

"Quite a show you put on last night, my lad," Grahm praised. "I find it rather impressive the way you were able to stop those men from boarding and then destroying your vessel."

Jake's eyes drifted distractedly over the water, locking on the albinos closest to where he stood. He could see that Achilles was still shadowing him. "These dolphins played a large part in preventing a disaster."

"Yes they did," Grahm effused. "Magnificent creatures they are. This trip proved more fruitful than I'd ever imagined. How's the man you captured doing?"

"Healed," Jake said. "The girl and the dolphins did it. Kept the man from losing his arm, probably saved his life. A severe case of gangrene had already set in."

Grahm shook his head in wonder. "Most amazing."

Jake thought it best to get down to business. "Any feedback from those dolphins?"

The scientist pointed to a computer screen manned by Henderson. "See for yourself," he said ecstatically. "Your idea to fit Hermes with the Dee Bee Tee was a good one."

Looking over Henderson's shoulder, Jake caught a glimpse of a submarine's stern as viewed from behind underwater. Grahm had termed the small metallic device Jake had recovered off the seafloor following his encounter with Natalie as a DBT, a Delphine Biosonar Transmitter. As Jake watched, he realized he was observing the hear-see signals of the two albinos sent out to follow the sub that had attacked them. Remembering what Grahm had told him about the way the device operated, he knew he was not looking at a real-time transmission since the unit could only send a signal when the dolphins breached the ocean surface. "What's their current position?"

Henderson manipulated a few computer keys, then checked the lower part of the screen where several numbers where displayed. "Seventeen degrees, fifty-eight minutes, thirty seconds north latitude, seventy-five degrees, twenty-six minutes, four seconds west longitude," he said, enlarging the global coordinates on the digital monitor.

"Where's that with respect to Navassa Island?" Jake asked.

Henderson changed screens, pulling up a map of the Caribbean. A small dot flickered between Kingston, Jamaica and the tiny teardrop of Navassa. "About twenty nautical miles to the southwest," Henderson answered dryly.

This was not where Jake had expected the sub to be, way off the direct route between the cove and Navassa Island. Although this bit of information came as a surprise to him, he refused to let go of his conviction that the sub had tracked them here all the way from Navassa, shadowing them unseen on their tail during the trip. To him, it was simple deduction to conclude a connection between the people manning the sub and the San Carlo. *This was getting interesting,* he thought, *Islamic frogmen with hints of Seal-like training at Haiti's doorstep.* Mat had said the DHS had reason to believe Al Qaeda was currently operating in the Caribbean and that something big was coming down. A partnership between Colombians and Muslim terrorists was something he never would have anticipated, however. The colluding parties had sent the sub after him, of that he was certain. There was no other explanation as to why he would have been followed across the open sea. As far as he could see, his vessel offered no strategic value to these men, nor did Jacob's. And he refused to let himself believe the encounter was purely coincidental. So what was the objective of these men? Had immediate retribution been their goal for Jake's attack on the Colombians, they could have easily used the sub to ram the Angel long before they had reached the Haitian coast. It wasn't adding up. Some key piece of information was missing. It was only after he had repelled the boarding party that they had sought to ram him. That part of the incident made sense to him. He had pissed them off and they had sought revenge. But try as he might, he could not pin down their motive for tailing him to this place.

As Jake pondered all this, the thought that this hideaway was now compromised greatly troubled him. He could not dismiss the possibility that these people would return with vengeance in mind.

Jake became aware of Grahm staring at him. "Something on your mind, lad?"

"I'm trying to figure out why that sub followed us here."

Grahm's brow crinkled briefly. "What makes you think we were followed?"

"Just look at the evidence. We had an encounter with a hostile force in the aftermath of our conflict at Navassa. It's only reasonable to assume that sub was sent by the same people who attacked us. There's just too much coincidence. What I don't get is why they didn't try to even the score long before we got here? We were a sitting duck on the open sea, particularly since we weren't even aware we were being tailed."

Grahm nodded gravely. "I see what you mean. But in science, the explanation that ultimately turns out to be true doesn't always match the one that seems most obvious, no matter how much circumstantial evidence tends to support the initial assumption. Putting it more simply, what sometimes tastes like a rat and smells like a rat doesn't always turn out to be a rat."

"Alright then, give me another possibility."

Grahm suddenly appeared sullen, a look that did not suit his face. Turning in the direction of the waterfall at the far end of the gorge, he remained silent for several seconds before pivoting his head to glimpse the computer screen once again. "Could it be that last night's intruders have an interest in the dolphins as I do, that they came here with the intention of capturing a few of this incredible species? We cannot rule out such a possibility."

As Jake listened, he sensed something in Grahm's manner to suggest this was more than just mere speculation. "Who else would know about these dolphins other than those people who tried to blow us up from the air? According to the girl, we're the first outsiders to gain access to this place."

The scientist placed a hand on Jake's shoulder and steered him away from his assistants, walking him towards the water. "I think it's only fair I come clean with you," he said after they had taken half a dozen steps, his voice reduced to a low murmur. "When I gave you my reasons for releasing Natalie back into the wild, I left out something."

Grahm paused, a tinge of anguish in his expression. Jake could see that the doctor was having difficulty in divulging what he was attempting to tell him. "Go on," Jake urged.

"When Natalie was under my care back in Miami, I thought it prudent to keep her amazing attributes under wraps, knowing that if such information ever reached the wrong ears she could be taken from me and possibly end up under the care of people who would not have her best interests at heart."

Jake could not stop the cynical grin that crossed his face. "You mean like the government."

Jake's utterance caused Grahm to look at him in wonder. "Great guns, my lad, you continually amaze this old scientist. You have a keen perception of the way the world around us works."

"I've been around the block a few times."

Grahm went back to being serious. "Anyway, I felt it important to keep quiet about Natalie's unusual digital extremities and the fact that she could speak fluent English for fear that the government would enter the picture. After all, it was Uncle Sam who was subsidizing the major portion of my research."

"Weren't you concerned that Natalie's abnormal skin tone would draw attention?" Jake interrupted.

Grahm shook his head thoughtfully. "No. Although albino bottlenose dolphins are rare, they're occasionally sighted in the wild. So the fact that I had one in my laboratory would only have elicited mild curiosity at most. Anyway, in order to protect Natalie I had conveyed my concerns to her, making her understand that whenever anyone other than myself or my two assistants were near her that it was crucial she never spoke or exhibited her prehensile appendages."

"Did she follow your advice?" Jake asked.

"Yes she did. She was good at keeping a secret. But in spite of the precautions, I received a visitor one day, a man who claimed he knew all about Natalie's peculiarities and that he was willing to pay big money if I would relinquish her to his care."

"I assume this man was from the government."

"I suppose you could call it that since the military is considered to be a branch of the government. The man was a captain in the U.S. Navy."

This did not surprise Jake. He knew how interested the Navy would be in such a creature. "So what happened next?"

"I told him Natalie wasn't for sale, that she deserved to be free as soon as she was healthy again." Grahm unleashed a huge sigh, a far off look dominating his face. "In no uncertain terms, he told me I had better reconsider his offer or there'd be hell to pay, that he'd pull the right strings within the government and create all kinds of problems for me."

Jake could almost guess at what those problems would be, but he wanted to hear them anyway. "Like what?"

"Like dry up my funding and discredit my research in the eyes of the scientific community. He even threatened to get me fired from the university. And on top of that, he could have one of the covert branches of government just waltz in and have Natalie taken away on the grounds that she was a potential threat to national security if she ever fell into the wrong hands. He said it'd be a colossal mistake for me to underestimate the amount of clout he could exert."

"How do you suppose this man found out about Natalie?" Jake asked. "Surely you must have your suspicions."

Grahm looked dejected. "I just don't know. Graduate students and a host of other people often visited the lab. Some of them had clearance to use the Mac G4 where most of my files were contained. My staff and I were not the only users of the computer. Though the system was encrypted and secured with special access codes and passwords, a clever hacker might find a way to breach it. There's probably a myriad of possibilities."

Jake said nothing for the moment, mulling this over carefully. "So you think that submarine may have been sent by the government to apprehend Natalie and others like her?"

"I think it would be a mistake to dismiss such a possibility."

"What did you do after this man left?"

"I made hasty arrangements to get Natalie back into the environment where she was first discovered before he could follow up on any of his threats. In less than a day, I had her aboard the university research vessel I always used and sailed for Jamaica. I realized how selfish I'd been, keeping her holed up in the lab far too long in carrying out my research, way past the time she had needed to recuperate from her injuries. I was happy to free her, but I still harbored a strong desire to observe her in the wild, hoping to come across others of her kind." Grahm shook his head glumly. "Unfortunately my enthusiasm to fulfill this desire seems to have gotten in the way, and now it appears I may have inadvertently compromised the secret of this beautiful sanctuary forever."

Jake studied Grahm's downcast demeanor before commenting. "Would it ease your conscience, professor, if I told you the man I captured is in all likelihood a-"

A loud shout suddenly cut Jake off. "Professor!"

Jake noticed Parker beckoning wildly from a distance. It was only then that he realized just how much ground he and Grahm had covered walking along the water engrossed in heavy conversation.

"What is it?" Grahm yelled back.

"You better come see this. Hurry!"

Grahm and Jake plodded back through the sand at a near run, finally coming to a halt close behind Henderson again and staring at the picture Parker was pointing to on the laptop screen. The sub had surfaced and was now berthed against the side of a ship. As Jake continued to watch, two men were currently on the sub's deck steadying a rope ladder draped down the ship's side. Above their heads, a man could be seen clambering down the rungs.

"I don't get it," Jake blurted, unable to contain his confusion. He shot a quick glance at Grahm. "If the DBT is designed to catch and record bottlenose dolphin biosonar within a hydrous medium, how is it we're getting a visual of something out of the water?"

Grahm watched in astonishment, the look on his face seeming to mirror Jake's bewilderment. "I have to admit, I've never seen anything like this happen before." He let his eyes follow the imagery on the screen. "But while what we are witnessing is most unusual, I would have to venture it is not altogether impossible," he added after a moment of reflection.

"What are you saying?"

"Perhaps we're seeing a mental recreation of what Hermes' twin sister has observed above the water. By sending out a series of picture-speak signals aimed at her brother, the DBT will pick up the sounds as if they were speak-see signals on the rebound and relay them each time Hermes comes up for air."

"But these albinos don't communicate with each other the way normal bottlenose do," Jake shot back. "They have the ability to see and feel what the others are seeing and feeling."

The marine zoologist appeared dumbstruck, his mouth agape. "How do you know that?"

"Destiny told me."

Grahm hung onto Jake's words as if not believing what he was hearing. "Well, I'll be," he finally said. "If what the girl told you is true, it explains an anomaly I noticed yesterday."

"What's that?"

"On the way back from the island, I had Jeffry drop two hydrophones into the sea to record the acoustical interaction of these creatures," the scientist said, suddenly finding it difficult to contain his growing excitement. "When I failed to get the usual degree of delphine chatter, I thought the units were malfunctioning."

"So you weren't picking up any sounds from the pack."

"I wouldn't go so far as to say that, lad, no. Every so often a member of the pod would emit a speak-see pulse in order to scan the surrounding hydrosphere. Probably making sure no pelagic predators were in the immediate vicinity. But the level of noise was far below what I've come to expect over the years."

"Maybe it was the few grays accompanying the pod that emitted the sounds you picked up. From what Destiny tells me, the grays don't have the same abilities as the albinos. It stands to reason that without such unique capabilities, the grays would rely on echolocation and sound-based communication to a much greater degree than the albinos."

Grahm elicited his signature smile once again. "You're close to the mark on that one, lad. We were able to isolate the sounds and identify which member of the pod each emission originated from. While some chatter did come from the albinos, the grays had them beat by at least a factor of ten on that score."

Jake suppressed a smile of his own and let his eyes drift back to the computer screen. Somehow it gave him great comfort in knowing there was some evidence to support what Destiny had revealed to him, even though that evidence was marginal at best. "Know what I think?" he found himself saying, not waiting for an answer. "I think the two albinos trailing that sub are smart enough to comprehend the principle upon which your little contrivance works." He paused, attempting to get a read on how the scientist was taking this.

"Keep going," Grahm encouraged.

"I think they've figured out its shortcomings and found a way to help us back here by using your device in a manner for which it was not originally intended, performing what you described a few moments earlier to reflect conditions out of the water. In the case we are currently observing, Hermes remains quiet, letting his sister, Aphrodite, convey what she has seen in the form of picture-speak signals."

Grahm immediately sobered. "As I've stated before, my lad, you should have been a scientist."

"Maybe now we'll get a clue as to who these people are and what they're up to," Jake said hopefully, returning his eyes to the screen where he observed a second man climbing down the ladder to join the first. Almost immediately, the image began to break up, fading in and out before disappearing completely. "What just happened?" he asked, turning to look at Grahm.

"I suspect the satellite transmitting the signal just passed beyond our line of sight." The scientist lifted his gaze to scan the tiered walls of the chasm towering high above him. "In a place like this, our window of opportunity for receiving signals will be rather short in duration."

Jake directed his next question at Henderson whose fingers flew rapidly over the keyboard. "Has any of this been recorded?"

"It has," Henderson said tartly. "Give me a moment and I'll have it retrieved."

Within the span of a second, Jake found himself observing a replay of what he and Grahm had initially missed during their earlier conversation. Looking upon the aft section of the sub as if he was swimming behind it, he watched as the line of the hull suddenly tilted upward and broke the surface. In moments it plunged downward again in the midst of a billowing wash of whitewater as seen from below. The scene abruptly shifted. With its conning tower and upper deck now perched above the waves, the vessel came into alignment with the stern section of a huge seagoing freighter stacked high with boxlike cargo containers. Jake hoped to catch a glimpse of the letters painted high on the vessel's stern, but the sub's elevated superstructure blocked them from view. A hatch suddenly lifted atop the sub's conning tower and the head of a person abruptly protruded from the opening. Though the individual was too far away for Jake to discern much, it appeared that the person's attention was focused on the ship. The perspective of the ship changed as the sub swung its bow hard to port in a maneuver that drew it alongside the freighter. For one brief instant Jake was able to catch sight of more lettering adorning the ship's port side. Unfortunately, the lettering was presented for too short an interval and at too oblique an angle to be read. Subsequent imagery showed two individuals climbing down from the sub's conning tower onto the deck where they proceeded to grab hold of ropes flung down to them from the ship. Upon securing the ends of the rope to the sub's forward and aft sections, the men then steadied a rope ladder after it unfurled from above. Jake had already seen what came next before the picture broke up and then vanished again.

"Any chance of blowing some of these images up so we can get the name of that ship?" Jake asked, looking to Henderson once again.

The computer whiz turned his head and stared up at Jack as if annoyed by his presence. "Maybe," he spat gruffly. "It may be possible, but it'll take time, and right now I have other things to do."

Jake turned to assess how Grahm was taking this open display of testiness. The scientist gave a lackluster shrug as if to apologize for Henderson's abrading behavior, choosing to remain silent but moving his lips in a quiet gesture, one that conveyed to Jake that his request would be taken care of. Locking eyes once again with the freckled grad student, Jake flashed a congenial smile, fighting back the urge to wring his scrawny neck. "Well, do us all a favor and be sure to let me know if you make any progress in that direction once you get around to it," he said, keeping his tone pleasant. With that, Jake gave Grahm a wink and walked back towards the water.

- 32 -

Jake strolled along the water's edge, deep in thought yet vaguely aware of the proximity of the juvenile albino less than fifteen feet away. He could not get over the exotic lushness of the tiered walls overlooking the white sandy beach. The sand on which he walked had the consistency of fine sugar, and the gorge was like nothing he had ever set eyes on, a place that exerted a profound pull on his soul, its essence seeping into his inner being like twisting, vaporous tendrils drifting on the edges of time and space. He could not explain it. An indefinable, unseen force seemed to play all about him. Like an ethereal cloud of pure energy, it pulsed in measured cadence to the beat of the cosmos, sending out rhythmic vibrations that breathed life into everything within its grasp. There was magic here, a delicately balanced flux between air, water and earth that seemed to be just as alive as the very flora and fauna it sustained, keeping him in constant awe of this idyllic hideaway.

Inhaling deeply of the smorgasbord of sweet aromas permeating the air, he could not help but wonder if he had found Gaia or Gaia had found him. Either way, he could not shake off the guilt he felt. He had made an assumption, and by doing so, he had unintentionally endangered Destiny and the albinos. Based on Phillipe's run in with the Colombian fishermen along the waterfront back in Port-au-Prince, he knew these men were a bad lot, but then again they had been drunk at the time. In retrospect, he had no way of knowing the ultimate intentions of the San Carlo crew towards the girl and the three dolphins back near Navassa Island. As he continued to walk, the feeling of culpability nagged at him like a deeply embedded thorn. Had he not interfered, the outcome might have been quite different than what had actually ensued, with the girl and her companions still safe, but without the threat of requital that now hung over their heads like a cloud of poisonous gas. In mulling these thoughts, he had no way of determining whether his rashness had been the best course of action, and it was this that troubled him to no end.

The sound of metal grating against sand caused him to break from his reverie, and he lifted his eyes to observe Jacob coming ashore, pulling his small dory up onto the beach. "Good morning," Jake greeted him, managing a smile in spite of the guilt clinging to him.

Jacob regarded him with an intense, calculating air, then glanced at Achilles floating nearby. "You must be a very special person," he remarked. "Achilles is drawn to you like a hummingbird drawn to the scent of nectar."

Jake's smile turned rueful. "I'm not sure I deserve his friendship. I think I may have put your little realm here in great jeopardy. If the men operating that sub are who I think they are, they or their associates will most likely be back, and if that happens, this peaceful haven of yours may end up becoming a battle zone."

A trace of humor showed in Jacob's face. "Gaia is not my realm. Even though I live here, I do not own it." He glanced around for emphasis. "I, like all the creatures and plants you see about you, belong to her. In any event, Gaia will take care of herself."

Jake was momentarily speechless, unable to immediately respond. The Haitian seemed totally unconcerned with such dark speculation. "Then you are not afraid of what could happen, of what I may have brought upon you, of the possible danger I've put Destiny and these dolphins in?" he finally said, somewhat flabbergasted at Jacob's indifference.

Jacob grew serious. "Fear is like a toxin that can paralyze and poison if you let it. It is good to be aware of the danger it poses, but it cannot harm you if you do not react to it."

This bit of philosophy came as a surprise to Jake and he studied the Haitian with newfound admiration. He would have expected a man who lived in seclusion the way Jacob did to be especially fearful of the outside world. "Maybe you've never had to deal with the kind of men I'm talking about," he found it necessary to say. "Only through killing is their bloodlust satisfied."

Jacob merely smiled, seemingly unperturbed. "Perhaps that is why Gaia has embraced you. Maybe she has chosen you to defend her."

"Come again?" Jake puzzled, not understanding what he was hearing.

Jacob placed a hand on Jake's shoulder and pointed to Achilles. "Look around you. These unusual creatures are new to this planet, far more sentient in many ways than anything that ever came before them. They are extremely intelligent and very particular about with whom they develop attachments, yet they must sense something unique within you to have chosen you. They have connected with you through Achilles, bonding with you in much the same way they have bonded with Destiny. They are an extension of Gaia." The Haitian looked at Jake closely. "Tell me you have not already felt her pulse as all of us have who dwell in this place, the peace, serenity and joy of her blessing. Gaia is real. By denying her existence, you will not experience yourself, you will not discover your own pulse."

Jake felt strangely moved by Jacob's words. "What makes this place so different?"

"It is the very soul of this planet, the one refuge uncorrupted by the ravages of man."

Jake looked for outward signs of madness in the person standing before him, but could find nothing that would indicate lunacy. Jacob's eyes were bright and alive with intelligence. Here was a man at peace with himself. "How long have you lived here?" Jake found himself asking, wanting to learn more about this strange personage.

"Long enough to know that a change is coming," Jacob said, his manner suddenly light and cheerful.

"What do you mean?"

Jacob smiled cryptically. "Some things are best left unsaid until they actually occur."

Jake could see that Jacob was not the type of man to be pressed. "Destiny tells me you helped raise her," he said, steering the conversation in another direction. "Is your associate you mentioned her mother?"

A moment's hesitation ensued before Jacob answered. "Yes."

"This ability of Destiny to heal, was she born with it?"

"She acquired it from her mother, yes. I'm sure you have also noticed that all the albinos possess such a talent."

Jake shifted his gaze along the gorge above him. "You planted all those fruit trees?"

"Some of them. Most were already here before I came to know this place. Gaia existed long before I was born."

Jake pivoted his head, continuing to scan the layout of the orchards lining the tiered ledges. The intervals between trees seemed to be too uniform to be natural. Seeing this, he posed another question. "Then somebody else must have planted them?"

"Perhaps," Jacob said. "Long before Columbus set foot on these shores, a race of people called the Tainos inhabited this land."

Jake tested the word, rolling it off his tongue. "Tainos, huh! Sounds Spanish." He suddenly realized he had heard the word before, for Phillipe had claimed a portion of his bloodline as belonging to the Tainos based on what his grandmother had led him to believe. Whether this was actually true he had no way of knowing.

Jacob smiled at Jake's ignorance, deciding to give him a condensed history lesson. "The word Taino stems from the Arawak language spoken by the original natives who settled here. The word meant 'men of the good'. The

Tainos lived throughout the greater islands of Cuba, Haiti and Puerto Rico and had migrated from South America more than one thousand years before the arrival of Columbus. The culture that developed here in Haiti was said to be the most advanced of their race, and according to early Spanish historians, their population on this island numbered somewhere between three and four million people when Columbus first arrived in fourteen ninety-two."

"Why were they called men of the good?" Jake asked curiously.

"By all accounts, they were a gentle people. Generosity and kindness were dominant values within their culture, a culture that was geared toward a sustainable interaction with the natural surroundings. They had a great respect for nature and reflected this in their ceremonies. Their way of life prescribed a spirituality that cherished their primary food sources, as well as the natural forces of climate, season and weather. Edible food sources were in abundance back then. The land and nearby seas were rife with plants, fish and animals. Because the Tainos lived in harmony with a bountiful environment, their core nature was bountiful. Bounties from the earth were to be shared and they strived to feed all the people."

For no particular reason, Jake was greatly fascinated by what Jacob was relating to him. "The way you describe them, they sound like they were a very giving society. What else do you know about them?" he said, ambling leisurely beside Jacob as the Haitian began to move off in the direction of his tiny abode. He could see that Jacob did not mind giving him a history lesson, noting the smile he continued to wear.

"Actually very little is known about these people, and what I do know about them is based mostly on accounts compiled by historians from the records of early explorers venturing into the Caribbean. I remember reading about entries taken from the ship's log of Columbus during his first voyage into the Americas. Translated into its English equivalent, one quote in particular summed up quite succinctly the way Columbus perceived the Tainos: 'They are so ingenious and free with all they have that no one would believe it who has not seen it; of anything they possess, if it be asked of them, they never say no; on the contrary they invite you to share it and show as much love as if their hearts went with it.'"

"Too bad more people didn't follow their example," Jake said wishfully. "The world would be a much better place."

"To the Spanish, their world was like a tropical paradise," Jacob went on, "a veritable heaven on earth. The Tainos lived in the shadows of a diverse forest so biologically remarkable as to be almost unimaginable to the average person in this day and age. They enjoyed a peaceful way of life that modern anthropologists now call 'ecosystemic.'" Jacob stopped walking, stooping to pick up a shell that had washed up on the beach.

"I'm not familiar with the term," Jake said.

Jacob examined the shell momentarily before tossing it back in the water. "Envision a human population living in complete harmony with its environment, an environment where ecological degradation is non-existent, a habitat constantly nurtured and respected by its human counterpart. Now contrast that with the Haiti you see today, a place where extensive pollution, hunger and deforestation abound. In the wake of recent scientific revelations concerning high impact technologies upon the natural world, a culture that could feed several million people without permanently wearing down its surroundings is now viewed as much more practical and far less primitive than the way the first arriving Europeans perceived the Tainos civilization. Comparison of the lifestyle described by the early Spanish chroniclers and today's standard of living of the average Haitian indicates the Tainos were better fed, healthier and better governed using so-called primitive methods than the modern populations of today. The Tainos lived in small, clean villages of neatly appointed thatch dwellings along coastal regions and inland rivers. They were an ocean-going people who took pride in their courage and navigational skills on the open seas. They visited and traded with one another constantly and fished for countless varieties of fish, turtles and shellfish. Columbus was frequently astonished to find a lone Tainos fisherman sailing in the open ocean as he made his way among the islands. These people appear to have practiced a rotation method in their agriculture, harvesting nuts, corn, yucca beans, cassava, and other roots, and according to Columbus, they hunted fowl from flocks that darkened the sky. They were a handsome people who had no need of clothing for warmth. Their fondness for bathing was often frowned upon by the Spanish who invoked a royal decree forbidding the practice, thinking it did them much harm." Jacob paused to let Jake absorb all this.

"What ever happened to them?" Jake asked.

Jacob's demeanor suddenly saddened. "Most of them were wiped out. Columbus reduced the Tainos to slavery shortly after his arrival, exploiting them to work the limited number of gold mines that existed within the land. Within a single generation, their population was decimated. A large portion of the Tainos died off through the hardships imposed on them as slaves, while organized massacres and diseases contracted from the Spaniards took its toll on the rest. To the Spaniards, the life of a Taino had little value other than to perform grueling work in the mines. The wanton cruelty and disregard for human life by the fifteenth century Spanish in the conquest of the Indies is darkly legendary, and Taino miners often died of starvation, though food was easily obtainable. By 1515, just 23 years after Columbus first set foot on this land, only a few thousand Tainos were left. The genocide of the Tainos was one of the most brutal in history."

"So," Jake said shaking his head, "just as it happened with the Incas and the Aztecs, it was primarily greed which led to their annihilation."

Jacob nodded. "Virtually all expeditions conducted by the European powers of that age were motivated by greed, and Columbus' venture was no different. Columbus was quick to size up the local real estate and its inhabitants, doing it with a banker's eye. He was financed by powerful investors who wanted a return on their investment, and his ship's log betrayed the things he was most interested in finding: a trade route to the East, gold in great quantities, and valuable resources such as slaves, precious woods, and land. It is rather obvious that Haiti satisfied the last two."

Jake hated cruelty in any form, and he wanted to know more. "You mentioned massacres. Why would the Spaniards resort to this if such an act would kill off potential sources of labor for their mines?"

"Such cruelty stems from the type of people who came to the Americas during that era. Columbus brought fifteen hundred men to the Caribbean during his second trip, a mix of adventurers, ex-prisoners and former soldiers who came seeking their private fortunes. They were transmigrants looking to end their state of poverty, a situation that was widespread in Spain and plagued all social classes within the homeland. Many of this first wave who came here were poor Spanish noblemen with parasitic ways. These men had swords, steel armor, harquebuses, crossbows, trained attack dogs, and cavalry. Haiti rapidly became overrun with a lawless band who increasing demanded women, took captives by surprise, and announced their hunger for the yellow metal. As a result, the Tainos quickly lost their good will for the Spanish. The first actual clash broke out when a Spanish attack dog killed a Tainos chief. After the chief's subjects retaliated a short time later by killing a few conquistadors, the Spaniards perpetrated a massacre of the local village. The conquistadors enjoyed testing their swords on Tainos flesh, cutting off hands and heads at the slightest offense. Minor skirmishes often broke out and swiftly escalated into pitched battles. Sometimes the Tainos were able to rout Spanish soldiers, but unfortunately, these people ultimately proved to be no match for the cannon, steel swords, horses and dogs used against them. Retribution became first and foremost on the Spanish agenda, and one by one, the tribal leadership of the Tainos was crushed. The conquistadors were a treacherous lot, often suing for peace just before luring the Tainos into a trap. When the Tainos would put on a large feast following negotiations as a show of good faith, the Spaniards would attack."

Jake continued to walk beside Jacob, mulling the harsh history of this strange land. Something Jacob had said earlier came to mind and he asked another question. "This change you mentioned…the one you believe is coming. Do these dolphins have something to do with it?"

Jacob stopped abruptly, taking in a deep breath. "Mankind has mastered many things. Unfortunately our species has failed miserably in mastering its own human nature. In general, man has used his abilities incorrectly, causing terrible damage to our world and its inhabitants, destroying more than we are creating. Many want to gain at someone else's expense, often poisoning the planet's air and water just to satisfy their wanton greed. As a species it is obvious we are not fully developed. Some scientists believe man was created to supervise and protect this planet, to take care of this world in this dimension we perceive as reality. One has only to look at history and study the world around us to know that humans have fallen miserably short of this responsibility."

Jake's eyebrows went up at Jacob's reference to *this dimension*, but he held off asking what he meant. "So where do these dolphins come in?"

"On this planet, high intelligence has evolved in two contemporary life forms, one that lives on land and one that lives in the sea. One of the greatest neurophysiologists of the twentieth century, Dr. John Lilly, argued that dolphin behavior indicates a very intelligent, creative and self-aware mind at work. He maintained that, compared with humans, dolphins are at least equal or perhaps even greater in intelligence. With humans, tool production and other technological advancements are possible because humans have hands with opposable thumbs and fingers. Assuming that dolphins possess a comparable intelligence with that of man, without such an anatomical feature they cannot build machines even though they are capable of inventing with their minds."

"So with this new breed, you think man no longer has such an advantage?"

Jacob hesitated before answering, staring in the direction of the falls. "Only the test of time will be the judge of that."

Thinking back to some of the things Jacob had mentioned during the fireside discussions the night before, Jake looked behind him to note Achilles and some of the other albinos floating languidly on the water. "You were referring to these dolphins when you spoke of Gaia introducing something else to counter man's destructive tendencies, weren't you?"

Jacob merely smiled, choosing to remain noncommittal.

"Based on what Destiny told me, these albinos are incredibly intelligent, a major jump above your ordinary bottlenose dolphin on the evolutionary scale. From what I can gather, they're capable of communicating with one another without resorting to high-pitched clicks and whistles normally used by cetaceans. Preliminary findings by Dr. Grahm seem to support this. The girl sees and feels everything they see and feel through some kind of mind link. Most scientists refer to this kind of ability as telepathy. A creature that can solve a high order mathematical equation in their head has to be much smarter than even the most intelligent humans."

"I don't profess to know everything about these creatures," Jacob admitted. "How or why they have come into existence, I do not know. And although I have so far spent twenty-two years of close association with them, I can only speculate about their true purpose on this planet."

"You schooled them, educated them on a wide variety of subjects only a small percentage of human beings will ever get to learn. As far as I can see, there would be no need of such knowledge in a place like this. A man of your apparently exceptional intelligence doesn't strike me as a person who would do this without some purpose in mind. I believe you're holding back on something."

The sigh that escaped Jacob's lips seemed to suggest a great weight being lifted from his shoulders. "Over the years I have devoted a great deal of thought about man's shortcomings, his irresponsible behavior, and I keep coming back to one inescapable conclusion, one logical explanation as to why this occurs in so sentient and intelligent a species."

"What's that?"

"Most human beings are not yet fully developed." Jacob noted the way Jake's face clouded before adding more. "I am referring to the way humans use their brains. The brain of man is comprised of two hemispheres, but only one of these hemispheres typically dominates the thinking and actions of the average person. For most people it is the left side, and though they have developed their left brain hemisphere to an extraordinary degree, they have not yet learned how to use their right brain hemisphere effectively to think with and to obtain information that they can use to make better decisions and correct problems."

"I'm not following you."

"Following their biological birth, the average human has spent a lifetime developing the left side of their brain, the part that governs the five physical senses. Unfortunately, it is the right hemisphere that has remained underdeveloped, the part that some scientists believe to be responsible for subjective intuition, extra sensory perception and precognition. Among other things, there seems to be supporting evidence that the right hemisphere gives us a sense of spirituality. However, to categorize each hemisphere with certain abilities would be a gross oversimplification. But as a species, if we were to learn how to think with the less dominant hemisphere and then act with the more dominant one, we would function in the balanced manner nature intended, not in the unbalanced manner by which we are presently killing one another and destroying our planet. Learning to use the infinite capacity of the less dominant side of the brain to solve problems will help us to know one another better, allowing us to get all we need for ourselves without taking anything from anyone else, without hurting anybody. If used correctly, it will convert our entire planet into the paradise it was intended to be, ultimately ending the desire to fight and kill one another. Before the arrival of the Europeans to this land, I believe the Tainos were well on the road to this type of development."

"I still don't see how this ties in with these dolphins," Jake said.

Jacob noted Jake's perplexity and grinned again. "Unlike the human brain, the two hemispheres of the dolphin brain work independent of each other."

"Dr. Grahm mentioned something about that."

"While scientists like Dr. Grahm have not yet figured out what this means, we cannot rule out the possibility that dolphins are capable of complicated thought well beyond the way humans think, thought that is highly abstract in nature."

"Please go on," Jake encouraged.

"This may take some time," Jacob forewarned, "but if you are willing to listen, I will do my best to explain it."

Jake nodded. "You have my complete and undivided attention." There was something unique and intangible about Jacob's intellect that drew him to the man, something pure and noble.

Jacob stopped walking and sat down in the sand, prompting Jake to do the same. "Maybe our perception of the three-dimensional universe is the result of the way the human nervous system is structured. Perhaps it is merely an illusion, created by some limitation imposed on our consciousness. Maybe there are many more dimensions the human brain is unable to interpret because of this limitation."

Jake sat quietly, taking in the words.

Jacob continued his explanation. "This very limited three-dimensional interpretation by normal humans in this universe may actually be only a very small slice of a much greater reality that is simply beyond the detection of the neural hardware we possess. Recent advances in mathematics pertaining to string, fiber bundle and group theory seem to support the existence of higher dimensions, giving credence to the supposition that matter is really hyperdimensional in nature. In essence, there may be an infinite number of spatial dimensions, each one vibrating at a different frequency pattern that may be out of phase with this specific universe, or for that matter, any other universe. As such, the dimension we perceive is simply a subspace of a much greater realm. If such a theory is true, the space-time continuum of this universe may be only one of an infinite number of co-existing dimensions that are interconnected via a hyperspatial energy grid." Jacob paused, looking for signs of comprehension in Jake's face.

"I've read about some of these theories," Jake acknowledged. "In a roundabout way you're talking about the unified field theory. A physicist by the name of Servio Nakamauri presented a lot of what you're describing in a book he wrote called Boundless Dimensionality. Nakamauri discussed how mathematical use of higher dimensions provides a logical means for building a model that unifies all the known forces within our universe."

Jacob nodded with eyes widened slightly, apparently surprised at Jake's sagacity. "Yes, that is correct. I, too, have read his work. Assuming there is a cycling of energy between an infinite number of dimensions along this hyperspatial energy grid, different universes could be separated by the specific frequency at which this flowing energy vibrates in space, allowing separate dimensions to simultaneously co-exist within the same three-dimensional space our brains are wired to perceive. It is these specific frequency patterns that determine the parameters through which matter can form and the physics that govern it, and although these different forms of matter do not normally interact, maybe it is possible that strange or unusual circumstances may cause exceptions to this."

It was obvious to Jake that Jacob was laying the foundation for something even more esoteric than what he was presently describing. "Like the formation of interdimensional wormholes or vortexes that might connect with our own space-time subspace?"

"Well, yes, I suppose such anomalies in the fabric of our own space-time can cause such interaction. But what I am about to tell you goes far deeper than that. It is what mystics have affirmed throughout the ages, that human consciousness is not merely a passive perception or awareness of the universe. It is an active force that we can exert upon the universe to affect our individual or, if need be, our collective trajectory through four-dimensional space, assuming we use Einstein's premise that time is the fourth dimension."

"It sounds to me like you're talking about the power of prayer and wishful thinking to affect our destinies," Jake interrupted.

"In a way I am," Jacob asserted. "But as human beings, we tend to identify ourselves with our three-dimensional shadows, namely our bodies, and the matter we perceive around us are actually the projections of energy vibrating at a higher dimension. There is a connectedness. If we start with the assumption that hyperspace in its full context is an infinite-dimensional space, then there are an infinite number of energy projections and subprojections, each extending or stepping down from a higher to a successively lower dimension. With each step down, something gets left out and is unable to be perceived by the sentient beings within that dimension, and yet those unseen things are very real."

"So what you're saying is that this realm, this universe, depends on a higher dimension for its very existence."

"Yes." Jacob gave a slight shrug. "The concept is really nothing new. For thousands of years man has conceptualized the existence of a spiritual realm, indoctrinating it into various religious beliefs. But now mathematics and physics seems to be proving that a higher realm actually exists, a realm that theologians have instinctively pondered about throughout history. The mathematical proof of hyperspace corroborates such conviction, revealing to us that the ordinary world around us is only a partial view of reality, a reality that is encompassed by a much richer realm that we cannot normally see."

Jake felt a mild touch of disappointment at what Jacob alluded to, and the tone of his response reflected this. "As sophisticated and scientific as you make it out to be, isn't this simply another view of the supernatural?"

"Yes, but one where consciousness comes into play. You see, consciousness and hyperspace equate to one another in much the same way that matter and energy do. In this day and age, most people accept Einstein's matter-energy equivalence since it has already been proven. Unfortunately, no one has yet solved the unified field theory, and until that happens, there will be no way of showing how consciousness fits into the multi-dimensions of reality."

"You're getting way above this limited human intelligence of mine."

"Throughout the history of physics, scientists have pursued finding a relationship between the forces of nature, attempting to unify them into a singular, all-encompassing force. So far, only four known forces have been discovered - gravity, electromagnetism, and the strong and weak nuclear forces. Isaac Newton unified celestial gravity, the force that keeps the planets in their orbits and binds the galaxy, with the force that makes objects fall here on earth. Later on, James Maxwell unified the various forms of electromagnetism, including electricity, magnetism, and light, into a single, beautiful theory. And very recently, physicists have been able to link electromagnetism with the weak nuclear force responsible for radioactive decay. The strong nuclear force that holds the nucleus of an atom together against electrical repulsion is another force science is on the verge of integrating with these other forces. The biggest hurdle, however, is finding the relationship between gravity and the other known forces. In using fiber bundle theory to unify all these forces, mathematicians may ultimately find that there is another force lurking within the overall scheme of things, one that needs to be considered in order to make a working model of a unified field theory complete."

"And you believe consciousness is that missing force?"

"Yes," Jacob conceded. "But my viewpoint is only mirroring the same notion of a growing number of eminent physicists and mathematicians who now take the concept very seriously. In using the tools of modern physics, they have come to the conclusion that in attempting to fathom the structure of hyperspace and multiple dimensions they are actually looking at the very structure of the human mind itself. As they delve deeper into the mysteries of the physical universe, matter appears to be taking on mind-like qualities more and more."

Jake frowned heavily. "So in trying to develop a unified theory, these scientists see the human mind as one of the missing pieces of the puzzle, another component comprising the structure of creation?"

A sly, impish grin lit Jacob's face. "In a way, yes, but the human mind is only a small part of it. Sooner or later it might be mathematically proven that our own minds are actually projections from a much greater mind, a collective mind residing at a higher dimension. Working our way up through successive dimensions, each collective mind can be considered another projection of an even higher mind until the ultimate consciousness is reached. And that is the cosmic mind, the very essence of hyperspace and the basis of all reality. Most scientists who support this idea believe this collective cosmic mind is actually consciousness acting on itself. The proof of this will most likely happen when a theory is finally derived that simplifies and unites the laws of nature. When this happens it will lead to major changes in the way we as human beings think."

Jake spotted Achilles near the shoreline watching him, then swung his eyes back to Jacob. "The problem with conceptualizing higher dimensions is that they are impossible for us to visualize."

Jacob gazed idly in the direction of the Avenging Angel at anchor. "That is true. In many ways we humans are like blind men trying to conceive the grandeur of a sunset or a clear night sky littered with stars. Though a sentient being with sight may describe them to us, even the most eloquent words will fail to convey the utter beauty of such vistas. But there is a symmetry in using higher dimensions to simplify and merge the laws of nature. It is very much like looking down from the heavens to note that the earth is actually a spheroid rather than a flat surface. Only then does the planet become fully integrated into a coherent three-dimensional picture against the backdrop of space and the other celestial bodies rather than the two-dimensional landscape we normally perceive when standing upon it. By retreating into the abstract domain of mathematics, however, we are at least able to get a shadowy glimpse of higher dimensional space."

"Earlier you mentioned that our perception of the three-dimensional universe all around us may be an illusion concocted by the limitations of our brains. Are you implying that we live in a dream world?"

Jacob sighed even deeper than before. "From the standpoint that we are not seeing the entire fabric of everything that pervades our surroundings, yes. Things are being left out that our brains normally fail to perceive. All our experiences are based on our awareness of both the world in which we live and our inner thoughts and feelings, yet this personal awareness remains mysterious. Though we experience such things as imagination, emotion, creativity, reason, intuition and instinct on a daily basis, few of us can give a fully satisfying explanation as to what these things are. Within us is a cognizance that goes radically deeper than the thoughts and feelings we usually identify as ourself. The consciousness that comprises the root of our being is identical with the core of every other being, connecting us with each and all because it is also the root of their existence as well. As human beings we generally fail to grasp this given that we are ordinarily overwhelmed by the intensity of our own senses and our mental interpretation of them. Although modern cultures have instilled in us that mind and intellect are the arbiters of reality, these things have not always enjoyed such high prestige. Older cultures based on spiritual philosophies held different views. A basic tenet of Hindu philosophy, for example, holds that the mind, when unilluminated by the spirit, condemns us to inhabit a largely deceptive self-made world, a realm of illusion. Because most human beings are limited in roughly the same way, these misconceptions and self-imposed restrictions are collective and widespread. In most academic fields of today, the vast majority view consciousness from a materialistic perspective, believing it to be a byproduct of the biochemical and neurological complexity of the brain. In contrast to such narrow thinking, a growing contingent of scholars and scientists studying the subject are amassing a substantial body of evidence that points to a very different conclusion, that there is a grand purposeful design underlying all of creation and that all of existence is permeated by a superior intelligence."

"But it is our five physical senses that gives us a reference," Jake insisted adamantly. "It's hard to deny the validity of what we see."

"I think you will agree that a mirage is not real, yet we see it. And while a hologram appears three-dimensional, we cannot deny that it is actually flat. In a darkened room we may see a twig and mistake it for a snake, but when there is enough light we realize it was a twig after all. It is the way our brains interpret what we are seeing that determines reality. The world exists for us only when the mind and senses are directed towards it. Once we silence the senses and close our mind to it, we open ourselves to a fuller awareness."

"No offense, but I'm finding it difficult to buy into this argument of yours," Jake persisted.

Jacob gave the impression of a man with limitless patience. "Everything is in the mind. What we experience in dreams can sometimes be taken for reality. During deep sleep when your physical senses are not active, can you prove the reality of this world? After you wake up and another person tells you that the world existed while you slept, can you truly demonstrate that it was real while you dreamt? The life we live and the world we experience are actually based on the thoughts we project. No two lives are the same. Depending on what we see, hear and feel, a world is created. In order to experience a different reality, we must change our thoughts. In doing this, are we not really creating an illusion that appears real? It is only when we shut down all conscious thoughts that the world we know loses its reality, and that is when our awareness seems to shift to a new dimension."

Something weighed heavily at the back of Jake's mind and instinctually he threw another query at Jacob. "Where do you think the consciousness of these dolphins lay?"

From the look on the Haitian's face, he could tell the man had not expected such a question. Jacob sat quietly for a long moment before answering, and when he finally did, the words came slowly. "I believe they see the world much differently from the way humans do, that their sense of reality is much more profound than what we experience."

Jacob abruptly fell silent and Jake looked at him closely before pursuing the subject further. "Assuming everything you just described to be true, do you think they can see higher dimensional space?"

"Yes." The word came out of Jacob's mouth as if it was sacred and his face suddenly took on the expression of a man lost in deep thought. "The forerunners of these albinos held a marvelous advantage over the human species by not possessing prehensile extremities."

"How do you mean?"

"Without the ability to build machines, they were able to avoid becoming grounded in materialistic pursuits like most of mankind, allowing them to develop inwardly over the last fifty or sixty million years. It set the stage for the new breed to make the evolutionary transition that would transcend the dimensional gap we humans have trouble getting past. Dolphins were well on the way to learning how to control and repair their energy bodies, the true essence of all sentient beings that pervades the universe and hyperspace. But these new creatures appear to have taken it a step farther, somehow learning to master and draw upon this unseen power rather easily."

Bafflement lifted from Jake's face like fog burning off under a hot sun. "So that explains how these creatures are able to heal others so quickly." He mulled this briefly, then said, "But how do you account for this ability in Destiny? She seems even more adept than the others in this capacity."

"Destiny's mother is endowed with such a gift. Through genetics she has passed this trait onto her daughter."

"Are you telling me Destiny also sees beyond three-dimensional space?"

Once again, Jacob responded slowly. "Destiny is very unique. She may very likely represent a newly evolving class of human with senses that give her the means to interact with the fabric of hyperspace. But her thoughts and emotions are so intertwined with the pod, it would be too difficult to determine if she actually possesses such an ability alone and by herself."

Jake nodded at the logic. "So you're saying she may only see higher dimensions through the minds of the albinos."

"Not exactly. Separately, the consciousness of each of these albinos may not be able to see higher dimensions. But when linked with each other in a kind of synchronous mind meld, they can. It may very well be that only together are they able to achieve such an expanded state of awareness."

"You mean like forming a supermind."

"Very much so."

"But each of these creatures seems to possess their own distinct personality. What you're suggesting sounds as if each of them would lose their individual identities."

"Then you have a good grasp of what I am saying with the exception of one point that seems to be confusing you. True individual identity and the ultimate reality of hyperspace are not separate concepts. Each is something infinitely greater than what we may ordinarily conceptualize, and both are actually one and the same. Yes, on an individual basis each of the albinos is unique in their own right. In much the same way as humans and other sentient beings, each of them is characterized by common yet varying abilities and traits. It is their individual thoughts and skills that give each of them their identity. But in combination they seem to form a synergy that goes well beyond the sum total of their individual skills and abilities. Collectively they are able to forge a state of awareness much greater than any one of them by themselves, and in so doing every one of them has a loss of ego while this is happening. Although hyperspace is theorized to be outside the physical body, the only way of arriving there is to go inside oneself. By dissolving the boundary between inner and outer events in a collective manner are they able to view and act upon reality from a single, unified perception."

"And I assume that includes Destiny."

"Yes. Destiny's consciousness, as best I can determine, seems to be the pivotal point about which the delphine minds revolve."

"Which brings you and I back full circle to one of my earlier questions. But I'll rephrase it. What do you think is the purpose of these creatures?"

Jacob grabbed a handful of sand and let it spill from between his fingers as he pondered the question. "I believe the history of this planet is really an evolution of consciousness. If we chart this evolution, we see a tree with increasingly complex life forms coming into physical being and branching out in order to express more fully the consciousness behind existence itself. Perhaps the true definition of life is the physical linkage to its energy body residing in higher dimensions. As you look around this cove it is quite evident that a new species has emerged and, in the face of the dominant life form on this earth, is asserting its right to live. In the process of doing this, it is awakening to its cosmic calling and is mobilizing to resist the intelligence gone wild of the biggest threat to this planet, the irrationality of the Homo sapien. The disease called humankind, in all its combative, ego-oriented, divisive, exploitive, and technological madness, has brought such pressure to bear on nature that the life force behind creation has brought a higher life form onto the planet to save it. While mankind threatens all life and unconsciously is bent on self-destruction through its materialistic addictions and the unseen effects of these addictions on the biosphere, the emerging species is life-embracing and seeks to live in harmony with the dominant species, guiding it toward a collective change in its cultures, transforming its present temperament and showing it how to live in balance with the living world. In essence, the collective exertion of consciousness by these creatures will become an active force that can be used to alter what may appear to be our irrevocable destiny, bringing forth a new order founded on love and wisdom."

Jake found himself strangely touched by Jacob's words, sitting quietly and staring out over the water for a long moment. "Then you feel that these creatures are not here to replace man?" he finally asked.

"That may or may not be. As I said before, only the test of time will prove whether my assessment is right or wrong."

Jake kept looking for a contradiction to some of the things Jacob had mentioned and he suddenly thought he had found one. "What about the Gaia Hypothesis? How does it tie in with hyperspace?"

"Just think of it as another aspect of higher-dimensional consciousness, one that embodies this planet and all living things on it as being one single organism, a projection of a collective intelligence residing in hyperspace."

Jake struck again. "Why have you tutored these dolphins in so much knowledge? What use will mathematics be to them in a place like this?"

"In order for them to transform the conscious state of the human species they must be enlightened about the world humankind dominates. If they are to understand the underlying nature of man and the way he thinks, it is necessary for them to study the history of this planet and the foundations of all knowledge acquired by him, the very extensions of his mind. Are not such things as physics, philosophy and mathematics conscious interpretations by man of the world in which he dwells? Whether or not there is any fundamental truth in these subjects, they are still creations of his own awareness and are therefore his reality."

For some inexplicable reason Jake found himself growing impatient. "Is Destiny to be a key player in all of this?"

Jacob scooped up another handful of sand and let a stream of grains drop back onto the beach slowly. "She is the bridge between the two species, the salvation of both."

"I'm not following you."

Jacob brushed off his hands and stood up, staring back down at Jake with eyes that seemed to bear the weight of the world. "Without her, everything we know will cease to exist."

- 33 -

At precisely 12 noon, Jake stood near the base of the waterfall awaiting Destiny. Phillipe had recently taken him ashore in the skiff, dropping him off with a tiny charcoal hibachi, a pot full of fresh water, a few dinner plates, and a small ice chest packed with various provisions. Already he had the coals on the hibachi burning and the pot of water atop it close to a boil.

Forty minutes earlier, Achilles had towed him out beyond the outside reef and, using his cetacean biosonar, helped him locate and then retrieve the 9mm Colt 633HB submachine pistol he had removed from the man he had captured. During the short excursion, several other albinos had accompanied him, including Hercules. The weapon had lodged among some elkhorn coral at the base of a large coralhead, and it was there that Jake had spotted the antennae of three medium-size lobsters protruding from a crevice. Wearing only a bathing suit, his K-bar, mask, fins and snorkel, he had reached in and snared the prizes one at a time, stuffing them into the catch bag strapped to his waist. Now as he waited for the girl, he had the lobster tails laid out side by side on a plate in preparation for boiling them.

As Jake scanned his surroundings looking for the girl, something abruptly broke the water's surface close to the beach, quickly followed by more than a dozen sleek objects. All of the dolphins within the cove were there floating before him, including the previously injured grays. Rising within their midst,

Destiny's head suddenly poked above the ripples, her black mane shimmering in the sunlight. Jake stared in astonishment as the girl waded gracefully ashore, her slim figure glistening with beaded water clinging to golden silken skin. It was only a few minutes ago that he had observed the entire pod floating and frolicking at the cove's north end, a distance of perhaps sixteen hundred feet from where he now stood. Although he had no way of knowing for sure, he was almost certain the girl had traversed the entire stretch underwater, staying submerged with the group during the time it took them to reach the falls.

"I'm glad you could make it," Jake said happily, unable to pull his eyes from such a vision of innocence and beauty. He had to speak loudly for his voice to carry above the thundering water. "I hope you like boiled lobster tails."

Destiny smiled demurely, arching her back and wringing the water from her hair in the same manner Jake had seen her do before. "Lobster is my favorite seafood," she murmured, walking up the sandy incline.

Pleased with the girl's response, Jake dropped the tails in the pot, which was now at a full boil. Reaching behind a nearby rock, he pulled a small bouquet of wildflowers from where they lay hidden. "Please accept these as a small token of my appreciation for what you did this morning."

Destiny stared at the flowers briefly before lowering her eyes. "Doing what I did does not merit a reward," she demurred. With her naturally soft mellifluous voice, Jake barely heard her above the roar of the water.

"Helping others always merits a reward," Jake countered, placing the flowers in her hands.

Destiny turned and looked back at the dolphins watching them. She regarded the creatures for several moments before pivoting round to face Jake again. "I was only doing what I am meant to do, just as you are doing what you are meant to do. Each of us has a responsibility to fulfill."

The girl's response caused Jake to scrutinize her closely. There was something in her expression just below the surface. "And what am I meant to do?" he asked, completely mystified.

Destiny held his gaze, staring searchingly up at him before replying. "You are meant to protect. I would think that deep down you already know that."

Jake felt his jaw go slack and he quickly caught himself. Though well intentioned, the girl's words brought back a painful memory. "Your perception of me is all wrong," he said uneasily, looking away to conceal the guilt he felt. "I've already failed in that department."

The sound of the pounding water seemed to suddenly recede, and for an awkward moment Jake found himself with nothing else to say. He could feel the girl's eyes boring into him as if probing for something. "We all carry pain," she finally said, placing a hand on his shoulder. "Pain is joy turned upside down, inside out. Both are our companions, but we are truly in harmony with our purpose when we experience an inner state of joy. Certainly a man like you is no stranger to such a state."

Jake was amazed by the girl's depth of insight. He would never have expected something so profound coming from someone seemingly so sheltered from the harshness of the outside world. "I know the life I prefer to live, if that's what you mean," he replied, turning back to face her.

"Why don't we eat," she suggested, her face lighting up in a smile. She dropped down and sat cross-legged on the blanket Jake had spread out on the sand prior to her arrival, placing the flowers off to one side. "I have something I want you to see, but not until we've eaten."

"What's that?" Jake asked curiously.

Destiny became solemn. "Some things have to be seen and felt rather than told. You'll find out soon enough."

Jake nodded slowly, studying her closely to gather the meaning behind the words. Destiny's large brown eyes held the same inscrutable quality as the albinos, though he sensed something troubling her just below the surface. "Alright," he said. "I can wait."

It didn't take long for the outer chitinous layers covering the lobster tails to turn red and swell as the succulent underlying meat began to cook. Both Jake and Destiny dug in, dining on the tasty meal with gusto and washing it down with several cans of coke from the ice chest. Driven by hunger, conversation between the two was kept light. All the while the dolphins stayed close, watching the two of them with those frozen smiles.

Finally Destiny stood up and looked down at Jake, her expression solemn once again. "There is a hidden cavern behind this waterfall," she said. "Let me show you what I've discovered." With that, she turned and strode toward the nearby rocks.

Suddenly intrigued, Jake rose up quickly and followed. With surprising agility, Destiny worked her way up a craggy wall, climbing onto a stone ledge that wound behind the plunging water. The roar of the falls became deafening as Jake moved along the same path. Moss clung to the rock in many places, making the going slippery and treacherous, particularly where handholds and toeholds had to be negotiated. Jake was astonished at how easily the girl handled the difficult climb, displaying the nimbleness and balance of a mountain goat and showing no fear at all.

Pulling himself forward, Jake became aware that Destiny had vanished around an outcropping jutting close to the opaque curtain of dancing water. Turning the corner, a dark recess in the rock became visible, yawning wide and revealing only shadows in the subdued light penetrating the waterfall. As his eyes adjusted to the semi-darkness, he caught sight of the girl further back within the confines. She was hunkered down, removing something from a box stationed along one wall. A small burst of flame suddenly erupted and he realized Destiny had struck a match, which she then used to ignite the head of a torch protruding from a nearby crevice. Grabbing the handle of the torch, she dislodged it and advanced deeper into the cavern, casting an eerie flickering light on the cavern walls as she went.

An assortment of artifacts became visible to Jake as Destiny led him further back, all of them situated along the cavern floor on both sides. Walking behind the girl, he noticed dozens of pottery vessels and small wooden carvings adorning the base of each wall. Destiny stopped momentarily to point something out. The rock walls to each side rose higher here, and as Jake looked at what she was indicating, he recognized the narrow face of a Spanish conquistador peering out from beneath a metal helmet.

Destiny turned to gauge his expression. "It's one of several murals within this cave," she shouted, her words almost drowned out by the thunder of the falls as they echoed within the chamber. "It shows the first contacts between the Spaniards and the people that inhabited this land back in the fifteenth century."

Jake nodded, letting his eyes sweep the full limits of the painting, which stood nearly eighteen feet high. "Jacob gave me a history lesson about the locals from that era," he shouted back, continuing to study the layout of the mural. In the background behind the peering Spaniard, the painting showed a galleon at anchor and a scene of the Tainos giving offerings of bread to men with beards.

Moving deeper into the cavern, Destiny rounded a bend and brought Jake to another painting, this one larger than the first. It depicted a heavy wooden beam supported by timber columns on each end. Suspended from the beam were more than a dozen naked men and women hung by the neck, their arms tied behind their backs. Off to one side, two large mastiffs were shown tearing apart another naked man while several armored soldiers looked on. Destiny's torch revealed other inhumane horrors as she traversed the mural, and although Jake had been previously apprised of such horrors by Jacob, the skill of the unknown artist seemed to bring life to the images, making them far more revolting than anything the Haitian had described. It was as if Jake was observing scenes from hell. Bearded Spaniards armed with lances were portrayed chasing a band of Tainos through a forest. A succession of montages revealed how these men used swords to lop off various body parts of their captives. Decapitations and other grisly examples of human depravity were made all too real.

Destiny continued to lead Jake deeper into the cave, her torch now showing another mural, this one showing a cluster of Spanish galleons grouped tightly together in a pristine bay with boatloads of men coming ashore and forming a tightly packed river of humanity venturing inland. Further on, Jake perceived what were supposedly the roads to the mines, appearing like ant hills with an incessant march of new world arrivals prodding along captured natives burdened with heavy loads on their backs. A blow-up of several Taino slaves toiling under the whip of a nearby Spaniard in what seemed to be a mine came into view under the flickering light, their bodies severely emaciated from grueling work and starvation. Another picture showed several natives being burned to death as other Tainos were forced to witness the execution under the watchful eyes of armed conquistadors. Jake was observing human suffering at its peak, and it both sickened and enraged him.

As Jake moved still farther into the cavern, the sequence of horrors finally ended. Destiny slowed and turned toward Jake, her eyes reflecting a subdued mournfulness under the glow of the torch. "I grew up with these paintings," she said pensively. Where they now stood, the roar of the falls was much less severe and Jake could hear her more clearly. "I rarely come in here anymore, but when I do I usually avoid looking at what's shown on these walls. Both Jacob and my mother don't think its very healthy for me to see what atrocities men are capable of-" Her voice suddenly broke and it took her a moment to gather herself. "-of...of what men will sometimes do to their fellow man."

Destiny paused again, as if searching for the right words, and Jake could see that she was fighting back a tear. "But while these murals show a hopelessness, the person that painted them seems to have seen something in the future that gives hope."

Jake saw nothing in the paintings that suggested hope of any kind. All he saw was bloodlust and greed, the victimization of a gentle and giving nation. The brush strokes of the unknown artist depicted a segment of mankind at its absolute worst. He looked closely at the girl, trying to comprehend her meaning. "If hope is reflected somewhere in these paintings, please point it out to me," he said gently. "I just don't see it."

"Come," Destiny urged, her voice suddenly taking on a strange cryptic tone. "There's more for you to see."

Destiny lifted the torch and began walking again, taking Jake still farther into the dark recesses. The cave narrowed a short distance beyond, and under the torchlight he made out a jumble of fallen rock. The girl stepped carefully between some boulders and slipped sideways into a fissure, seeming to disappear and leaving Jake in near darkness. Jake realized her smaller frame worked to her advantage in the reduced confines and he had difficulty in following, struggling to squeeze his body through the tight opening. Once through, the cave widened to a width of about four feet, and Destiny stood awaiting him.

Jake discerned a narrow passageway with a series of steps that appeared to have been carved in the rock. The passageway rose sharply upward. With a barrier of rock now behind them, the din of the falls was now much quieter, reduced to a dull susurration that became subordinate to the sound of dripping water emanating from somewhere close by.

As Jake stepped up to the girl, she abruptly turned and led the way up the stone stairway. The climb was short, and moments later they emerged onto a landing. Destiny swung the torch around her to indicate the new surroundings. They were standing near the center of a fairly large room with smooth walls, ceiling and floor. The torch wasn't burning as brightly as it had before, leaving most of the room in shadow, but from what Jake could see the chamber appeared to be a perfect square. Like the corridor they had just ascended, it was much too smooth and uniform in configuration to have formed naturally. He assumed it to be man-made, chiseled out of solid rock.

"About five years ago, this extension of the cave became accessible after a section of rock at the bottom of the stairway collapsed," Destiny said, pointing to the top of the steps Jake had just negotiated. "What I'm about to show you came as a great surprise when I first discovered them."

Extending the torch off to one side, Destiny walked up to one of the rock walls, bringing light to bear on its surface. Jake judged the wall to be about twelve feet high and about twenty feet long. A mural covered its entire surface, and depicted on it was a woman in a storm-tossed sea, a cascade of whitewater rushing toward her as a towering wave crested nearby. The woman clung to the dorsal fin of a gray bottlenose dolphin to keep from going under, her face raised toward the heavens and clearly showing anguish as a jagged streak of lightning struck the water just behind her. A tangle of thin luminescent tentacles entwined both the woman and the creature supporting her, raising a series of heavy red welts on the woman's exposed skin. As if viewed through the glass of an aquarium, the scene gave perspective to the ocean below, revealing the source of the tentacles. A cluster of strange looking oblates floated just below the surface, and as Jake studied the painting, he noticed the distinct bulge of the woman's belly.

Destiny held the torch steady for several moments, giving Jake the time to take in all the details of the artistic work. Then without saying anything, she moved counterclockwise down the length of the mural to the adjacent wall where another scene had been painted. This one showed the same woman cradling a newborn infant in her arms as she stood waist-deep in water. Next to her floated a gray bottlenose with a newborn of its own, the calf completely white and focusing its gaze on the human child. In the background, a waterfall could be seen gushing a stream of whitewater emanating from the side of a steep chasm. From the perspective of the painting, the scene was one from the cove, the place Jacob referred to as Gaia.

Continuing on to the third wall, Destiny revealed yet another painting under the glow of her torch. A pod of six albino bottlenose dolphins charged through the sea. At the pod's center was another albino, considerably larger than the others, and riding on its back just forward of its dorsal fin was a girl. The girl was hunched forward and attired in an all-white body suit, her coal-black hair shimmering under a dazzling sun and billowing backward as if windswept. Jake immediately recognized the girl in the painting to be Destiny.

Stopping short of the fourth and last wall, Destiny seemed hesitant to move on, speaking for the first time in several minutes. "When I first saw the painting I'm about to show you, I didn't know what it meant until yesterday."

Jake raised an eyebrow, trying to assess what she was getting at, but as the girl swept the torch toward the final wall it all became clear. The mural displayed what could only be described as a modern day whirlybird hovering high above several albino dolphins, a dark-haired girl riding the largest one.

Destiny walked the torch off to one side of the mural, shining additional light on something there, and as Jake's eyes found what she wanted him to see, his blood suddenly ran cold. It was a man riding a waverunner. From all appearances, the watercraft looked suspiciously like the model he rode, a Kawasaki STX-12F, and mounted on its forward section was an over-under machine gun combination similar to what Jake had mounted on his own craft. The artist had shown both guns belching lightning directed up at the whirlybird, as if the rider of the waverunner was in pursuit of the helicopter. Although the man firing the machine guns was shown to be too far away to be clearly identified, the way the man was attired and his choice of personal weapons strapped to his body looked to be exactly the way Jake was normally outfitted when running the Kawasaki.

Jake stared transfixed, knowing it would have been impossible for someone to paint the mural in less than a day. The detail of the artistry was just too precise. As if to confirm this, he ran a finger over the wall's surface, checking to see if any paint came off. Rubbing his thumb and forefinger together and looking closely for any signs of wet paint residue under the torchlight, he determined that the wall was dry.

Destiny finally broke the silence. "When I first saw this painting, I didn't know what to make of it. It wasn't until our encounter with that ship yesterday that I knew the man in this mural was you." She turned to face Jake. "You are the protector, the reason why Achilles has chosen you for bonding."

Jake could only stare back, unable to voice any words.

- 34 -

Hennington was exhausted. After leaving Ternier's compound he had traveled the remainder of the night through the coastal and mountain roads that wound northward from Port-au-Prince. So far the journey had been arduous and painfully slow due to the poor condition of the roads they were forced to negotiate. Using a beat up jeep provided him by the Colonel, the ride had been uncomfortable and bumpy most of the way once they had left the main thoroughfares of Haiti's largest city. The roads were nearly impassable in numerous locations, covered with heaping amounts of debris from rockfalls and mudslides.

Accompanied by the same undercover police previously assigned to both protect and keep watch over him, he couldn't help but feel like a prisoner on a long leash. But he figured that was better than the alternative, and that was ending up in one of Ternier's congested and filthy jail cells harboring the numerous poor souls currently being incarcerated.

Although the early afternoon air was hot and humid, a chill ran through his body at the thought of the shadowy woman that lurked within one of the darkened chambers deep within the prison walls. He fully understood now the source of Ternier's deep-seated depravity, for here was a prime example of the apple never falling far from the tree. The woman was a sorceress and the Colonel's biological mother, a highly skilled practitioner of the black arts and the apotheosis of pure wickedness. He was nearly certain the woman was Erzulie, Baby Doc's former voodoo witch.

Sitting in the right front passenger seat of the vehicle, Hennington was jarred again as the driver tore over another pothole in the unpaved road, this one quite deep. The jeep bounced hard and veered momentarily out of control, coming precariously close to the edge of the high mountain road and seemingly about to plunge into a yawning abyss far below. Hennington felt his heart leap into his throat as he stared breathlessly at the dizzy drop lying in wait on his side of the open vehicle. The jeep careened wildly as it teetered for one split second on two wheels, and one of the men in the back seat let out a cry of alarm as the driver fought for steerage. The airborne side of the jeep slammed back down a moment later, and Hennington let out a shallow breath as all four tires found purchase once again.

"You trying to kill us all!" the other man in the back yelled in Creole. "Slow down."

Speechless, the driver could only nod, clearly shaken by the near mishap. He rounded a bend in the dirt road and seconds later the town of Saint-Marc came into view. The town sat on the sea at the base of a large hill where the ruins of an old fortress perched.

Hennington had never much cared for Haiti's fourth largest city, finding the place to be hot, dusty, shadeless and rather uninteresting, but he also knew the current calm could be deceptive. He found it hard to believe that more than four years earlier anti-government uprisings had stirred most of the city's population of 100,000 to revolt against President Jean-Bertrand Aristide's regime. As he remembered it, opponents of the now ousted Aristide had attacked the main police station, burned down the courthouse and thrown up a maze of blockades to thwart the police from taking back the town. Hundreds of frenzied looters had ransacked shipping containers along the harbor, stripping them of their cargos and setting the empty containers ablaze.

As Hennington thought about these things the driver descended the steep road, occasionally beeping his horn and screaming obscenities at those who blocked his path, mostly people leading horses, mules and donkeys laden with various goods and produce. He became aware of the heavy erosion marring the hills and knew that two years earlier, in the aftermath of torrential downpours brought on by a passing tropical storm, heavy mudslides sweeping down from the defoliated slopes had reeked havoc on some parts of the town, killing at least 1,200 people. Gonaives, an even larger city farther to the north, had fared far worse with about 200,000 of its 250,000 residents rendered homeless in the face of catastrophic flooding and mudslides that left more than 1,500 dead and 900 missing. Decaying corpses had been scattered everywhere. To avoid the spread of cholera and other deadly diseases caused by the human carnage, the surviving locals with the aid of the Red Cross had to gather up the bodies and bury them in mass graves. Hennington could see the changes the disaster had caused since the last time he had visited the area. Many of the structures were either completely destroyed or had become dilapidated shanties, rivaling some of the slums common to Port-au-Prince. As he studied the devastation he realized that the worst damage had been confined to the outskirts of the city. The closer they got to the main part of town, the less evident the destruction became.

Rolling along through the streets in the heart of the city, Hennington became aware of the charred remnants of the police station and courthouse, stark reminders of past political unrest. A short time later the driver pulled up to one of the cantinas along the waterfront and all four men climbed wearily from the jeep.

"This place has the best food and drink in the city," the driver said. "At least it used to be. I haven't been back here in years."

Hennington eyed the cantina's façade with skepticism before entering through the front door. The driver led the way with the other two men following in Hennington's wake. The broker was glad to get a respite from the sweltering heat. Unlike many of the watering holes found in Port-au-Prince, he was amazed to discover the air inside the establishment was cool and provided much relief. This was unusual, particularly since electricity was in short supply. With all of the Haitian cities cut off from the flow of electrical power anywhere from 16 to 22 hours each day, wasting such a scarce resource on air-conditioning was almost unheard of. In some of the more congested shantytowns, going without electricity for days at a time was quite common. In most places that served food and drink, the scant commodity generally went toward the refrigeration of perishables and beverages. He assumed the tavern was run on inverters that converted battery-stored DC power to AC current, and that required a sizeable bank of batteries. There was a major shortcoming to such a system, however, if it was to be used on a daily basis. The batteries needed a flow of electricity for recharging at the end of each day, something the nation's power company, Electricity of Haiti, could not provide to a reliable degree mainly because the power generators were always breaking down.

As he looked around, he saw at once that at least a dozen male patrons were clustered at one end of the bar, their faces alive in animated discussion. Curious as to what held everyone's attention, he stepped casually up to the counter off to one side of the crowd and eavesdropped on what was being said.

"-healed my son completely. His paralysis is now a thing of the past and he can walk again." The words were spoken in a maudlin tone by a man with ebony skin and brooding eyes.

"She has healed others suffering the same fate," another man said reverently. "She is a powerful mambo."

"I cannot deny the truth in what you say," a third man agreed, "but I have heard she keeps her face well hidden under a veil. They say she is hideously deformed, that her face would cause most people to run away in fear."

"There is nothing to fear from this woman," the first man stated. "She has brought only good fortune to Malique. All the fishermen who live there continue to fill their boats with fish. They sell their catch here and in Gonaives and are growing rich from it. They are blessed."

"She consorts with sea creatures," another voice piped in. "She uses them in her healing rituals."

"How do you mean?" one of the others asked.

"The people who are the sickest or the most gravely injured are placed in the sea and surrounded by several dolphins which she summons."

"She calls them?"

"No, they just seem to appear without any words being spoken by her."

"You have seen this?"

"Yes. The dolphins are not ordinary dolphins. Their skin is all white. They remind me of angels."

"Too bad this woman did not use her power to keep the mudslides from destroying parts of the city and killing people," someone else interposed.

"Why not just use her vaudun to keep the heavy rains away?" the bartender quipped. "It is the heavy rains that always cause the mudslides, are they not?"

A momentary lull in the discussion ensued as everyone stopped to consider the clever logic. It was the man with the brooding eyes who finally spoke first. "Maybe her vaudun is not strong enough to control the weather."

Several men nodded in agreement but remained silent, seeming content to sip their drinks. Hennington took the opportunity to get the bartender's attention, and it was then that the others became aware of the party of newcomers. Seeking to curry favor with the locals, Hennington ordered a round of drinks for everyone, including the man behind the bar. Alcohol tended to loosen tongues and he wanted to learn more about Malique and this woman.

He hadn't realized how thirsty he was until the barkeep slid a frosty mug of ale before him, and he quickly quaffed in down. It wasn't until his glass was refilled that he struck up a conversation with the man serving him. "How often does the power company provide you with electricity?" he asked nonchalantly, starting out with some small talk to break the ice.

The bartender smiled, presenting a wide gap between his front teeth. "I have no need of electricity from the power company."

"Oh?" Hennington was mildly surprised. "You do not need it to recharge your battery system?"

The proprietor pursed his lips and shook his head. "I have no need of a battery system."

"Then how do you run the air conditioner?"

"Gas powered generator. It gives me all the electricity I need to run everything in here, even the refrigerators."

One of the locals nearest Hennington leaned in close. "You should see the system he has out back. Hydrogen gas powers the generator to produce electricity."

Hennington looked quizzically back at the barkeep. "Really." He removed the white fedora he habitually wore and placed it on the countertop, letting the tavern's cool air wash over his cranium. "Where do you get the hydrogen?"

"That is a secret," the proprietor said evasively.

"Bull!" scoffed the man beside Hennington. "Everyone knows a fisherman from Malique brings you a dozen full cylinders every other day."

Hennington feigned disinterest, directing his eyes to several framed paintings hanging on the wall overlooking the bar. Perhaps this was going to be easier than he had originally anticipated. He did his best to introduce a tinge of boredom in his tone. "Where does this fisherman get the hydrogen?"

"No one knows," the bartender readily offered.

The opening was there and Hennington took it. "I could not help but hear mention of the mambo who lives in Malique. Could it be that she creates the hydrogen gas with her magic?"

The bartender shrugged. "I have considered such a possibility, but what does it matter. I am content to get refilled bottles of the gas as often a supply is available. As long as the generator works, I have no need of the power company's electricity."

Hennington continued to let his eyes wander over the paintings. There was something in the artistry that moved him, something exquisite, and as he stared upon the imagery, some suppressed facet of his inner being seemed to awaken. Oddly, he found himself beginning to reel. Startled by the strangeness of it, he pulled his eyes away nervously like a man looking down from a dizzying height, afraid he might fall if he did not avert his gaze.

Not wanting to appear overly eager for more information on the mambo, Hennington changed the subject. "Where did you get those paintings?" he asked. Guardedly, he let his eyes fall back on the art, unable to look away.

Turning to stare over his shoulder, the proprietor followed Hennington's gaze. "They are beautiful, are they not? I never tire of looking at them."

Hennington was about to ask another question, but his driver suddenly spat up the ale he had been chugging and staggered toward the front entrance. The man didn't look right, holding a hand to his mouth and appearing to choke back a mouthful of bile. An instant later Ternier's other two thugs bolted for the door, and moments later loud retching could be heard outside the establishment.

Someone further down the bar spoke up. "Looked to me like all three were going to upchuck right on the floor."

The bartender smiled in amusement, staring after the newly arrived patrons who had just fled the premises. "At least they kept it down long enough to leave. I hope they don't leave a puddle outside the door like the last one did. It hurts business."

The man standing next to Hennington stirred. "The paintings also come from Malique."

"Do you know the artist?"

"The artist prefers to remain nameless," the bartender stated. "I have tried to get the painter's identity, but even the fisherman who gave me these pictures claims he has no idea who created them."

"He did not offer them for sale?" Hennington queried incredulously.

"No, he said he wanted others to enjoy them. If I agreed to hang them on this wall, he offered them as a gift."

Steeling himself against any more strange stirrings, Hennington studied the artistic work with the critical eye of a connoisseur. He was, after all, a broker by profession and the work of a talented artist always had the potential of fattening his pockets with profits. There was a lucrative international market for Haitian art, and the possibility of having stumbled onto the creations of another Pablo Picasso in the making suddenly crossed his mind. Several of his wealthy clients were art collectors and had a strong fetish for unusual works. He was certain he could make a hefty return on such paintings, particularly if they could be gotten free of charge or next to nothing.

There were three paintings on the wall, all reflecting a theme hovering somewhere between abstractionism and surrealism. From where he stood, it appeared that the unknown artist had used an oil-based paint. Each of the creations depicted a strange mix of geometric shapes, textures and vivid colors intertwined with a grid of diverging and converging lines seemingly twisting back upon one another in a timeless dance. For some inexplicable reason, he let his eyes settle on the painting in the middle. It held his gaze, and the longer he stared into it, the deeper he was drawn. He could feel himself being transported to another time and place as fragmented imagery was pulled from the depths of his subconscious. A glimpse of his ancestry suddenly flashed before him, and with it a sense of infinity. The sensation of something long forgotten brushed his awareness like a faint puff of air wafting off jasmine blossoms, something obscure and buried deep within him. He tried hard to remember what it was, but it eluded him like a honeybee roving among a field of wildflowers. The feeling intensified, taking hold of him like the embrace of a loving mother.

Something clutched his arm and pulled him back. Hennington became aware of the bartender reaching over the counter and grasping his bicep, a knowing smile on his face. "You were a long way from here a second ago. I have seen others become lost in these paintings when they stare into them."

Hennington felt slightly embarrassed. "Would you consider selling me these paintings? I will pay you well for them."

The bartender's smile quickly faded and became solemn. "I am bound not to sell them. If ever I did, my business arrangement with the fisherman would come to an end. He requires that I keep these paintings on the wall for all to see who come in here, otherwise he will no longer sell me the hydrogen gas."

Hennington nodded at this, wondering why this unknown fisherman would require such an unusual stipulation. Normally he would have been more persistent in trying to acquire items representing a handsome profit, but he let the matter go. There was something purifying to the spirit at having looked upon the masterpieces hanging before him. For some unfathomable reason he felt like a man who had suddenly found himself after being lost for a very long time, but his thoughts were just too jumbled at the moment to give such a notion any credence. With regret, he pulled his eyes from the paintings, avoiding any further entrancement until he could clear his head. Try as he might, he just couldn't seem to grasp the full meaning of the mysterious symbolism exhibited within each picture, something almost...mathematical in context. The idea confounded him. Mathematics had never been a subject he particularly relished, that is, other than using it in calculating net profits and returns on investments.

He finally dismissed such weird musings and directed another question at the bartender. "How far to Malique?"

"Is that where you are headed?" the bartender asked.

"Yes."

"It is about sixteen kilometers up the coast, and only reachable by boat. The road that used to lead to the village was blocked by a mudslide long ago. It has been impassable ever since."

"Do you know where I can charter a boat to take me there?" Hennington inquired further.

The bartender swung his eyes to the man hovering next to him. "Franz here has a boat."

Franz took another sip from his drink before lowering the stein, his manner suddenly all business. "I am not a charter service," he declared.

Hennington peered back at him with the look of a man well accustomed to bargaining. "How much?"

Franz nudged his drained glass toward Hennington. "I do not conduct business over an empty glass."

Hennington pivoted his head back to the bartender. "Another round for everyone," he ordered.

- 35 -

The village of Malique finally sprang into view as the decrepit boat rounded a small headland. As he studied its layout, Hennington was momentarily taken back at how picturesque and peaceful the place was, noting that it did not fit the typical profile of other coastal villages. All of the structures were neat and tidy, with no piles of debris or garbage anywhere in sight. Coconut palms lined the rear of a white sandy beach, and as he looked beyond them he could make out other types of trees rife with fruit. Further upland he noticed hundreds, maybe even thousands of tiny saplings, each growing from a planter, with the planters arranged in uniform rows. His eyes darted to the shoreline. A long wooden pier, apparently in good condition, jutted out into the water with a fleet of fishing boats of varying sizes and shapes tethered to it.

Hennington glanced back at his entourage. He could see that all three men were now fully recovered from the inexplicable sickness that had come upon them earlier on, and as he watched their eyes rove over the village, he noticed they were just as surprised as he. Turning to Franz he said, "Malique appears to be doing exceptionally well for itself."

"It has for many years," Franz replied as he eased back on the throttle and scanned the pier for an empty place where he could disembark his passengers. "It is no doubt the mambo who lives here that brings such good fortune to the villagers."

Hennington decided the time was right to inquire about the man Ternier had instructed him to locate. "Do you know a man by the name of Ronaldo Trebek?"

"He is one of the fishermen who lives here."

"Can you show me where I might find him?"

Franz pointed out a tiny blue house at the north end of the village. "You should find him there. He should be home because his boat is tied alongside the pier." A minute later he dropped Hennington and his party off at the dock.

Various locals gave Hennington and his escort odd stares as they made their way to Trebek's house. As he passed them he nodded out of courtesy and wore a congenial smile, but refrained from stopping and striking up a conversation. The village was fairly small and it did not take him long to walk the short distance to Trebek's house.

The middle-age man who answered the door was a short blocky individual with a skin tone similar to Hennington's. His eyes widened appreciably when he noticed the three men standing behind the broker. "What do you want?" The man's wariness was readily apparent.

Hennington saw no need to be overly formal and decided to get down to business immediately. "Monsieur Trebek, my name is Chester Hennington and I am here at the request of Colonel Henri Ternier. May I come in?"

Trebek stood momentarily frozen, his face reflecting indecision over whether or not to slam the door shut. Several seconds passed before his expression abruptly drooped in resignation, and he stepped aside to let Hennington enter. "I will only speak with you," he grumbled. "The others must wait outside."

All three men hesitated, wondering over the wisdom in complying with Trebek's request. Hennington looked back at his escort, his eyes conveying diplomacy. "Perhaps you should abide by this man's wishes if we are to get even a small measure of his cooperation. The Colonel will be very displeased if we do not."

The leader of the group finally acquiesced, nodding with a begrudging scowl.

"There are some chairs out back and an apricot tree ripe for picking," Trebek offered the men. "You may help yourselves to some of the fruit if you wish." With that said, he closed the door.

Trebek gestured for Hennington to sit in one of the three wicker chairs adorning what could pass for a living room. "What is it Ternier wants of me after all these years?"

Hennington removed his hat and placed it on the small table adjoining his chair, then proceeded to mop his brow with the handkerchief he habitually carried. "Before we get to that, please understand that I am simply an emissary sent by Colonel Ternier to obtain certain information. I have nothing personal to gain in coming here."

"So Ternier is a colonel now. The last I remember he was a captain working for Baby Doc Duvalier. His ego and ambition went well together. Both were the size of a full grown mapou tree."

A shade covering the room's only window kept the home's interior fairly dim, but as Hennington's eyes adjusted to the faint light, he became cognizant of something on the wall facing him that caused him to sit up straighter in his chair. "That is a most unusual painting. I saw several more like it in Saint-Marc." The style was distinct, though the accompanying shapes and use of geometry by the unknown artist depicted something altogether new and different from the other creations. Once again he could feel himself being drawn irresistibly into the geometric pattern, and he quickly averted his gaze. "Can I trouble you for the name of the artist?"

Trebek appeared annoyed. "Is this what Ternier has sent you to find, the artist behind this painting?"

"No. The Colonel wants to know why you lost contact with him all these years."

Trebek fidgeted slightly and tapped his fingertips together, appearing uncomfortable with the question. "I am no longer the same man I was during Baby Doc's reign. I gave up being a spy long ago. Life has changed for the better here in Malique since those days, and I along with it. My allegiance has shifted to the welfare of the people who live here." Trebek uttered the words like a man ashamed of his past but satisfied with what he'd become.

Inexplicably, Hennington felt invidious of the man. "I have heard much about the good mambo who lives in this village. Perhaps she is the reason behind your change of allegiance."

Trebek stiffened noticeably, his face clouding with cynicism. "If Ternier has sent you to assassinate her, it will be a waste of time. The woman cannot be harmed."

"You have nothing to fear from me. I am not an assassin."

Trebek ignored Hennington's comment. "Amphitrite cured me of a serious illness many years ago. It was she who opened my eyes to what I had become back then. I have changed my deceitful ways ever since."

"That is the mambo's name? Amphitrite?" Hennington paused, mulling the word. "The Colonel claims she is a *cheval*."

Trebek cast cold eyes on Hennington. "She is no *cheval*."

"I have heard she keeps her head covered so as not to reveal her face. Could it be that she is cursed with the face of a wild beast?" Like most Haitians, Hennington was not immune to the tenets of voodoo, holding fast to certain beliefs predicated on the folklore that pervaded the land. Back in Port-au-Prince he had gotten a small taste of Erzulie's dark power and was terrified at what an adept of voudun could do. "Is it possible that she is strong enough to keep such a dark spirit from gaining control of her mind, though it may have gotten partial control of her body?"

"I have seen the mambo's face. She is a white woman with kind features."

"Then why does she keep her face hidden?"

"Because most Haitians would perceive a white woman having such powers with mistrust. It is only when she is in view of people not of this village that she covers her features."

Hennington nodded slowly. This confirmed what Ternier had already told him but he found it necessary to probe a little deeper. "I have been informed that the source of this woman's power is derived from a special charm she wears around her neck."

"What you speak of is an amulet that once belonged to Malique's former mambo. The white woman has taken possession of it and uses it during her curing rituals."

Hennington got right to the point. "The Colonel is very interested in acquiring that amulet. He claims it is an ancient family heirloom, one which the mambo has stolen from him. He has sent me here to get your cooperation in finding a way to take it from this woman."

Trebek stared icily at Hennington as if he were deranged. "What you ask of me is madness. I will not help Ternier."

Hennington had difficulty meeting Trebek's laserlike gaze and quickly turned his eyes away. The thought of having to go back to Erzulie's chamber of horrors sent shivers coursing through his body. Ternier hated failure and would be unforgiving. Trebek was forcing him to use harsh leverage to obtain the man's cooperation. "I think the townspeople would be very displeased to learn you were a spy for the Tonton Makout during Duvalier's rule."

Trebek did not react the way Hennington expected, though his eyes flashed with scalding menace for one fleeting second before subsiding into lugubrious resignation. "Do what you think you must, but I will no longer do Ternier's bidding."

"The Colonel has instructed me to offer you the sum of ten thousand dollars in United States currency for your services."

Trebek's face clouded with insult. "Do not try to entice me with the promise of material gain. That will only work on a selfish person motivated by greed. I no longer have a desire to be self-serving the way men like Ternier allow themselves to be. Over the years I have found that serving others in attaining a better life is much more satisfying and harmonious with who I truly am."

Hennington had trouble believing what he was hearing. In a place like Haiti the amount of incentive Ternier was willing to dole out would greatly improve the standard of living of someone like Trebek. "Are you sure this mambo has not dulled your sensibilities with her vaudun?"

The fisherman's face suddenly appeared ready to erupt with laughter, but then sobered just as quickly. "How can I expect a man like you to understand what this woman has done for the locals, myself included?" He paused wearily and rose from his chair. "She has provided a philosophy that unites all aspects of living. She has given new meaning to our existence."

As Trebek spoke, Hennington's eyes were drawn back to the painting on the wall like iron ingots to a magnet. *There it was again, something indecipherable yet not altogether alien. It was almost within his grasp. It...* Something loomed over him, blocking his vision, and he abruptly became aware of Trebek looking down at him oddly. "You can tell Ternier I will not help him."

Hennington stared back dazedly as if awakening from a deep sleep. "Where can I find this mambo?"

Trebek assayed him carefully, his expression reflecting indecision. "Attempting to harm her in any way will be foolish," he finally advised. "Go and see for yourself what others have discovered. You will find her with Lucette Baptiste, the wife of Emmanuel Baptiste."

Shards of some old memory surfaced at the mention of the name. Yes, now he remembered. Emmanuel Baptiste had been one of Baby Doc's staunchest enemies, a growing threat to the Duvalier regime of years past by virtue of the substantial public support he had garnered. There were some who believed that Baptiste should have assumed leadership of the floundering country following Duvalier's departure. Since the time of Baby Doc's exile, however, he hadn't heard anything of the man. That is, not until now.

"And where will I find Mademoiselle Baptiste?"

Trebek gave him directions, but before the two men parted company, the fisherman grabbed Hennington's arm. "Do not let yourself be manipulated by Ternier. He is truly an evil man without any chance of redemption. He would have destroyed this village long ago if not for the sudden arrival of the white mambo. She is the reason he will not come here himself. He fears her too much."

Hennington studied Trebek's face with newfound interest. This was something he hadn't known. "Why are you telling me this?"

"Ternier is ambitious. He is a man consumed with a need for power. Under the right circumstances he would seize control of Haiti. If that were to happen, past dictators like Papa Doc and his accursed offspring would appear like saints next to the cruelty Ternier would unleash on his people."

Hennington mulled this for a brief moment before replying. "History has shown that holding onto the reins of power in Haiti for very long is impossible."

"Call it a premonition, but Ternier may prove to be different." Trebek was suddenly radiating fear.

"How?" Hennington asked.

Trebek let go of Hennington's arm and turned away. "I am not proud of the man I used to be. As a member of the Tonton Makout I used to torture and kill to appease the bloodlust of Baby Doc. Back in those days I had worked with Ternier on several occasions in ridding the young Duvalier of his enemies. Under orders from Baby Doc we had captured two white men he suspected of being agents of the American Central Intelligence Agency."

Trebek paused and turned back to face Hennington, his expression detached as if seeing something from the distant past. "I never knew a man could take such pleasure in inflicting pain on another the way Ternier did.

Under excruciating torture one of these men revealed himself to be a former U.S. bomber pilot and not a CIA agent. With the help of the other man, he had spent the better part of twenty-eight years searching the waters of the Caribbean looking for something very valuable." Trebek expelled a heavy breath as if relieving himself of some oppressive burden. "He had knowledge of a lost H-bomb," he finally blurted, looking gravely at Hennington for his reaction.

Hennington stared back, his mind trying to grasp the full measure of this unexpected information. "Does Ternier have possession of such a weapon?"

"I would only be guessing if I told you he did, but Ternier did learn where it could be found. That is, if what the man told us to be true."

"Why was this man searching for an H-bomb?"

Trebek related everything he knew concerning the weapon, appearing not to hold back on anything he could remember. It all came pouring out like a hot, scalding liquid that had been pent up far too long, fragments of information that had been seared into his memory as though by a branding iron. Frank Jameison, a retired lieutenant colonel in the United States Air Force, had eventually died under Ternier's sadistic measures. But before he had expired, he had disclosed a most interesting story. Carrying out a simulated combat mission out of Homestead Air Force Base in Florida, a B-47 bomber under his command had become disabled over the Caribbean after colliding with an F-86 fighter jet in bad weather. The B-47 had quickly lost altitude, and with most of its instruments malfunctioning, the aircraft's crew was forced to fly blind within a cloud-strewn and darkened sky. Completely losing his bearings, Jameison was ultimately forced to ditch the plane into raging seas. The B-47 had flooded rapidly with water, and as it sank it took all those aboard with it, all except Jameison. The bomber had been carrying one of the most powerful nuclear devices of its time, a hydrogen bomb weighing close to four tons. With only an inflatable life vest keeping him afloat, Jameison floundered among tumultuous waves for several hours until a passing boat just happened by and rescued him. The boat's captain was an individual by the name of Mercades Myers, the other white man Ternier had captured and tortured.

As the sole survivor of a serious air crash, Jameison soon found himself under fire from the military. With an impeccable service record suddenly tarnished over losing such valuable military assets, Jameison was forced to resign his commission shortly after the accident. But he would not rest until he located the aircraft again and recovered the bomb. He spent the next 28 years of his life intermittently plying Caribbean waters in search of the downed bomber, often in the company of Myers with whom he had established a lasting friendship. His relentless efforts had eventually paid off, and he was certain he had found the plane's resting place. Misfortune would strike a second time for the man, however. Seeking to garner the resources he would need to retrieve the H-bomb, he had foolishly made a stopover in Haiti, a stopover that quickly led to his demise.

After listening to the tale, Hennington asked, "Where is this bomb to be found?"

"The exact coordinates I cannot remember, but a small island lies nearby. It bears the name Navassa. I have fished near there on several occasions." Trebek looked closely at Hennington. "If Ternier ever gets his hands on that bomb, the Caribbean will never be the same."

- 36 -

Amphitrite was well aware of the visitors long before word of mouth reached her. Though flashes of precognition would still hit her at the oddest times, they did not occur quite as often as they used to. Over the years she had found it difficult to accept such clairvoyance and some of the other unusual powers she possessed as part of the person she had come to be. The trauma of failing to remember her distant past had gradually ebbed away, leaving only a fulfilling contentment in its place. She was satisfied with her current identity, taking immense pleasure in being able to help others. The people needed her. Haiti was a land synonymous with human misery and dreadful poverty, where humanitarian crises consistently abounded, a place where a stable democratic government was about as alien as a blizzard to the beleaguered Caribbean nation.

The past twenty-two years had gone by swiftly in the face of strange happenings that no longer astounded her. It was near the beginning of that wonderous span of time that she had given birth to the only biological child she had knowledge of, a girl she had instinctively named *Destiny*.

She recalled the late night hour when Destiny had emerged from her swollen womb more than two decades ago. She had been floating waist-deep within the cove's warm and comforting water as her favorite but faint constellation, *Delphinus*, made its way across the heavens. Lucette had been there to assist during the miraculous event, acting as midwife, with Jacob pacing nervously along the shoreline. Amphitrite's ever present and faithful companion, Athena, had also been present, giving birth at almost the same moment, spawning a healthy female calf tail-first from her uterus. Amphitrite remembered Jacob's jaw-hanging reaction when he first set eyes on the exotic young albino, its two prehensile extensions not yet fully developed and jutting obtrusively from under its pectoral fins like the wings of a baby raptor. In time the appendages had grown into retractable jointed limbs that folded back covertly into recesses under the lateral fins. At the terminus of each limb was the semblance of something that approximated the hand of a primate, exhibiting four jointed fingers supplemented by an opposable, jointed thumb. As the white dolphin had grown, it had demonstrated the remarkable nimbleness, strength and dexterity of those amazing appendages.

It had been Jacob who had insisted on the name *Natalie* for the baby cetacean, this in honor of the actress Natalie Wood who had drowned off California's Santa Catalina Island five years earlier. Half jokingly, he had said the actress was now reincarnated in the form of a dolphin. Within six months, however, Jacob found it hard to jest when Natalie began to utter her first words, so great was his astonishment. He was again rendered speechless when Destiny began riding Natalie around the cove a short time later.

In the ensuing years, Natalie had matured at a faster rate than what was typical of a bottlenose dolphin, mating and then birthing other albino dolphins with the same attributes she, herself, possessed. The albino twins, *Coral* and *Reef,* were the first of her amazing offspring, followed two years later by another set of twins, *Hermes* and *Aphrodite*. It was the union of Reef and Aphrodite that produced *Hercules*, and the subsequent union of Hermes and Coral that sprang forth *Apollo* and *Artemis*, the youngest set of twins. Through her telepathic connection with Athena, Amphitrite knew that the birth of twins, particularly albino twins, was extremely rare among dolphins.

Amphitrite was aware of one thing in particular, that the genetic strain of mutated albinos Natalie had birthed only mated with others of their kind, and with the exception of Hercules, always generated mixed genders among the pair of paternal twins they in turn produced. Natalie, however, demonstrated an anomaly altogether different from her direct progeny in that she had the ability to mate with any common male bottlenose dolphin, bearing either one or two calves each time she delivered. In doing this, she was capable of breeding either grays similar to Thetis or albinos like herself, with the resulting offspring being either male or female, or mixed each time she bore twins. This proved to be substantiated after she had birthed her second set of albino twins, Hermes and Aphrodite.

Over the succeeding years, Athena had also stayed busy, producing a succession of calves. Following the birth of Natalie, however, her offspring were always gray and were unable to speak in human languages, although they were all born with the same prehensile appendages as the albinos. Incredibly though, every so often one of these grays would birth or sire an albino. That was one of the strange phenomena that had always puzzled her and Jacob, the fact that Athena seemed no longer capable of breeding any more albinos like Natalie while her succeeding offspring could, even if they mated with a common bottlenose dolphin lacking prehensile appendages. *Thetis* was one such progeny of Athena's, who in turn had given birth to *Achilles*. As Amphitrite reflected on these things, she knew that, not including the six white dolphins that helped her here in Malique, there were at least another two dozen albinos currently in existence possessing the same unusual and amazing attributes, all of them descendants of Athena. And greatly exceeding that number was a rapidly growing contingent of grays with those same amazing forelimbs.

Such thoughts paraded through Amphitrite's mind as she watched the small fishing vessel head up the coast toward Gonaives, its passengers glancing back in her direction as though in worship. This was the third such boatload this day. So far, she had cured half a dozen cases of cholera and an assortment of other physical afflictions, with most of her patients ending up teary-eyed and thanking her profusely for taking away their suffering. Word of Malique's benevolent mambo had slowly trickled out over the years, sparking an incessant stream of visitors seeking relief from their ailments. But there was a price for her services. All those cured were required to make an oath vowing to plant saplings given them and to help clean up their towns and cities of garbage and waste. Finally, the rolled-up canvas each was handed upon departure must be displayed in a public place where their neighbors and others could view it.

Amphitrite gazed at the departing vessel as it gained distance from the village. Two of its occupants she had not been able to help. She had long ago learned the mystical powers she and her dolphin retinue wielded were not infallible, that there would be people with corrupted natures that came before her from time to time. Such people, she knew from experience, had naturally dark souls with little hope of redemption. It was as if their own latent evil neutralized Amphitrite's ability to heal.

And for those she was unable to help, she had noticed something they all had in common: they could not gaze upon the dolphin art without becoming ill. But the degree of illness varied from person to person, with some becoming nauseous and suffering a splitting headache, while the most severe cases became debilitated with seething migraines that usually left them writhing and moaning on the ground in excruciating agony. The paintings, she knew, affected each person differently depending on their inner natures, with those she was able to cure experiencing a kind of euphoria whenever they viewed the art. But it seemed those truly harboring evil always became debilitated by some inexplicable malady when their eyes feel upon the enigmatic dolphin creations, and these were the ones that could not be cured.

The veracity of this supposition seemed suddenly in doubt as she recalled her daughter's encounter with the men manning the tuna trawler. Destiny had felt the appalling darkness coming off three of the four men Jake Javolyn had nearly destroyed with the torpedo. Only one had been an innocent, a young man held by the corrupt strands of circumstance ensnaring him. The others, however, had been content with the raw wickedness that lay ingrained within them, and Destiny had sensed those irreversible flames. Yet Destiny had been able to save them, making the decision to intervene and heal their otherwise mortal injuries before escaping the trawler's seine.

The thought caused Amphitrite to think back to the man who had tried to kill her back in the cove years earlier. She was certain the wound the Tonton Makout captain had suffered would have been fatal if not for her intervention. Perhaps the man would have lived anyway, but she could never be sure. She had held steadfast to the belief that her touch had stopped the man's bleeding. Maybe her psychic ability to heal had been stronger then, allowing her to penetrate to the very core of the man's iniquity in order to keep him alive.

It had been just before sunrise when she had slipped quietly from Jacob's cottage while everyone else slept, coming to stand over the trussed up Ternier. To this day she still couldn't explain to herself why she had freed the man from his bonds as he lay moaning incoherently in the sand. Somehow she had found the strength to drag him into the water, and even now the shear magnitude of the wickedness that had pulsated from him was strong in her memory. It had been the same kind of evil she had sensed during her encounter with Erzulie, something unforgettable like the hideous stench of decay from some dank, dismal dungeon that lingered on in one's nostrils long after the experience. She had known at once that Ternier was Erzulie's son. Puzzled by her own actions, she had held Ternier's head above the water as Athena towed them both through the cove's narrow inlet and then down the coast. Eventually they had reached the Devil's Horn, and it was there that she had pulled Ternier ashore and left him on the beach. But before leaving, she had scrawled numbers in the hard-packed sand close to where he lay. Strangely, she had known the numbers represented a specific latitude and longitude, the coordinates the Colonel had demanded of her, but for reasons she could not explain, she could not fathom why she was able to remember them so well when she could not recall any of her previous life. There was no need to give the man this information, especially when weighed against the atrocities he had openly confessed. He had killed her crew and left her to die, but even to this day, try as she might she still could not remember any of it. Nevertheless, something within her had compelled her to write those numbers in the sand.

Intuitively she had known Ternier would survive and that someday they would meet again under circumstances that would be potentially much more lethal. Something deep within her caused her to believe this with arrant certainty, its inevitability woven into the fabric of time and space long ago.

The type of people Ternier and Erzulie represented did not repulse Amphitrite. She harbored no enmity toward them. Judging the moral fiber of others was not in her makeup, and although many of the villagers regarded her as an absolute moral authority, she did not see herself this way at all. She sensed only a divine objective in her existence. She was a person whose previous identity had been erased by some unknown force in order to become someone sufficiently able to follow through on a grand and noble cause. If anything was absolute, it was her purpose. For her, compromise was not an option. The plan she was a part of was far reaching in scope, an enterprise that had seemingly and gradually taken shape of its own, and one that was still evolving. In its early stages, Emmanuel had perceived it as being impossible to carry out, an unwinnable scheme that was far too ambitious to succeed. But now even Emmanuel had embraced it, casting aside his own innate skepticism. And though Jacob had played a large role in its development by expanding upon the original rudiments first conceived by the albinos, it was her daughter who was the pivotal point in how it would ultimately play out. Destiny was the key and must be protected at all costs. Inasmuch as it hurt her deeply to know that many dolphin lives had been expended with the effort, primarily at the merciless hands of tuna fishermen, she could not condone her daughter placing herself at risk by coming to the aid of injured cetaceans. Even Athena had concurred with this. But Destiny had her own mind and, try as she might to convince her progeny otherwise, Amphitrite knew that it was a losing battle of wills.

Shifting her thoughts back to the present, Amphitrite watched the approach of the four men, their leader a short pudgy individual adorned in a suit of white linen coated with dust. She had been expecting them, having seen the same exact scene in a dream the night before. From the dream she had learned that the fat little man had been motivated by greed most of his life, a vice that often sprang out of a need to survive in a nation despairing from poverty. And while the man's deeds could be perceived as dark, she sensed the underlying nature of the man to be altogether different. Here was a person trapped by circumstances, a prisoner of himself and those he associated with. Mulling this, she suddenly felt a touch of empathy for the man as he walked to within arms length of Lucette and Louwanda, each standing resolutely blocking his path.

Amphitrite placed a hand on Lucette's shoulder. "It is all right to let this man pass," she said, letting her eyes drift over the man's clothing. "One of your ancestors was Tainos," Amphitrite found herself telling the man, speaking in French. "Did you know that?"

Hennington gawked back wide-eyed with disbelief. "How could you possibly know that? You are a stranger to me."

"We have met before, although you would not be expected to remember it," she replied loftily. "The existence you have so far lived has not been an easy one, for you have invariably made wrong choices. Not everything in life can be controlled the way we'd like them to be, but we can choose our response to the challenges we face. You are innately flexible, and that has been your strongest suit."

Hennington stared back hard, as if trying to see beyond the veil covering the woman's face. "I do not mean to be impolite, mademoiselle, but I have no idea of what you speak."

"You continue to travel the same path over and over, and in so doing you are constantly disappointed where you end up."

Amphitrite turned her head and studied the men standing behind Hennington, knowing each man carried a concealed handgun. The weaponry did little to mollify the fear registering on their faces. "Those who behave like earthworms should never be surprised when people walk over them." It was a common Haitian proverb. "Seek not destruction but rather seek change and positive ends. Those who have chosen to go against the will of the people, who chose profits over the betterment of human existence, shall soon enough discover their final wages to be oblivion. Do not abuse. Though God may often punish late, he punishes severely."

Amphitrite became conscious of the way Hennington eyed the amulet dangling obtrusively on the outside of her shawl. She had purposely let it be exposed for display before the arrival of these men. "Happiness cannot be bought or sold like goods or services. You cannot give or sell it to a person who lacks it. We often confuse happiness with pleasure, but pleasure is only a shadow of happiness, an illusion that tends to delude the inner being of a person. It is not happiness that belongs to the soul, for the soul itself is happiness, an extension of the Great Creator."

She hesitated briefly, reflecting on the words that automatically flowed from her lips with little thought. Over the years she had grown into the person she had become, and sometimes she found it strange how philosophical she must sound. Nevertheless she continued to sermonize. "The pursuit of physical gold is for those who as yet are only children, for physical gold is merely an imitation of the true gold. There is a great deal of difference between true and false gold. It is the longing for real gold that causes man to collect the imitation gold. Because gold represents the color of light and spiritual inspiration, man has unconsciously pursued this divine light by seeking an imitation of it much the way a small child satisfies itself by playing with toys. In this way man attempts to gratify this craving of the soul by seeking the false gold, ignorant that the true gold lies like a hidden spark deep within his heart, his innermost being."

Hennington stared as if mesmerized, unable to speak for the moment. His mind tumbled restlessly among a windstorm of human vices suddenly brought before him like molten silver, running and flashing without form, and he was all at once revisiting the painting hanging on the wall in Trebek's house, pulled into its imagery like a man caught in a powerful whirlpool. He tried to focus, but concentration was beyond him. He was spinning shamefully amongst a thousand dizzying liquid drops, each drop representing a virtue of some kind. They streamed by close to his fingertips, only to go racing off before he could grasp them. A perception of humility came and went, followed by sympathy, tolerance and unselfishness, rising and falling and taking him closer to something even more profound. His fingers abruptly located substance, and he was able to latch onto a single thought, that alchemy was possible here, that the silver might be transformed into something more desirable, something that might make him truly happy.

The intense blue light that burst forth from the amulet made the three men standing behind Hennington shrink back in fright a split second before they raced off in frenzied flight. Amphitrite was only doing what the dream had suggested, and that was helping Hennington find himself. There was something more to be done, however, something else she had seen herself carry out within the dream but did not fully understand, sensing only that the man standing before her would play a significant role in future events. She had long ago learned to trust her dreams implicitly.

She reached forward and lifted the white fedora from Hennington's head, then placed a gloved hand on the man's forehead. "Believe in the healing power of nature as your forefathers did, as your Tainos heritage cries out for you to do. The whole earth is a living organism. Our Mother Earth and all life upon it is a miraculous gift that must be treated with respect and loving care."

Removing the amulet from around her neck, she dangled it before Hennington, who looked uncomprehendingly at the offer. "I bestow this trinket onto you. Take it and do what you must with it." Amphitrite knew the charm held no real power. If anything, it was useful in focusing the strange powers she was able to invoke. In many ways it was nothing more than a placebo, acting only to reinforce the belief of the people in a woman they accepted as a priestess of the vaudun.

- 37 -

"I'm sorry, Jay Jay, but I believe your king has been checkmated once again," Achilles trilled, the dolphin's perpetually smiling face belying the apology.

Jake studied the board with a critical eye, trying to ascertain how his seemingly infallible defense had crumbled so quickly. He considered himself to be an excellent chess player, having taken either second or third place in several tournaments during his college days. But the albino juvenile had apparently found a weakness in his strategy and exploited it rather easily, sacrificing first a knight, then a pawn, and finally his black queen before driving Jake's king into a position of forced mate in six more moves. Throughout the game, each time Jake had moved one of the pieces Achilles had immediately responded with a countermove that appeared to take little effort in thought.

"Showoff!" Jake said, shaking his head in awe.

Achilles slid back into the water, retracting his left prehensile extremity as he did so. He had been using the appendage to move the chess pieces as he lay prone on the edge of the Angel's swim platform where he had engaged Jake in the ancient board game.

"Hey, come back here!" Jake protested halfheartedly. "I demand a rematch."

A stifled giggle next to Jake made him turn. "He's already beaten you three games in a row," Destiny reminded him.

"How does he do it?" Jake asked in mock frustration, looking to Destiny for sympathy. "Achilles plays speed chess, something this slow lumbering brain of mine is ill suited for. You should have given me fair warning."

"Achilles is still learning the game," Destiny said, trying hard not to laugh. "Some of the adults are even better players."

"If you're trying to make me feel any better, you're doing a poor job of it," Jake shot back, attempting to keep a straight face but failing. "Where did they learn such advanced play?"

"Jacob taught them the rudiments of the game, but then they just picked up everything else on their own. They're very quick learners."

Jake smiled sheepishly. "And here I thought I was going to show Achilles something new and interesting. Was I playing against Achilles only, or the whole conjoined pod mind?"

"Just Achilles," Destiny said sweetly. "He would never take such unfair advantage of you."

Upon leaving the cave behind the waterfall, Jake and the girl had somehow ended up back at the Angel as their conversations roamed over a number of enlivening topics. Though it became quite evident to him that Destiny was exceptionally intelligent and learned in a wide range of subjects, it also became obvious she was hopelessly naïve about the true nature of the modern world, having been sheltered from its boundless iniquities her entire life. To him, this was probably the most stimulating facet of her personage, a quality he could grasp, one that he found both refreshing and aglow with unblemished probity, untainted and pure like a drop of distilled honey. Yet she continued to baffle him, making him feel like a man stranded in a dream where nothing made sense and everything seemed unreal. And while the final painting she had revealed to him back behind the falls only added to his stupefaction, it also increased his sense of wonder over his surroundings, for if he was truly a man trapped in a dream, then nothing should make sense. *Expect the unexpected,* he had told himself. He did not want it to end.

He thought back to the skirmish at Navassa when he had raced back to the Angel to repel the attacking helicopter, fearful of the damage it could do to his crew and beloved boat. One of the albinos had leapt high into the air, snaring within its jaws a grenade dropped from the aircraft before hurling it back the way it had come. The aerial manueuver, he was sure, would have required something more than athletic prowess to pull off in the manner he had witnessed. No, it would have required anticipation at exactly the right moment, almost as if the creature had known in advance not only the destructive potential of the object it had intercepted, but also the precise moment it would be dropped in order for the dolphin to have sufficient preparation in gaining momentum and timing its leap precisely from beneath the water. He was positive something more than dumb luck would have been needed for the albino to do this, and that something was a glimpse of the immediate future, a flash of precognition. Just as the unknown creator of the cave painting had seen the future, so had the dolphin.

Certain of this, Jake had felt a nagging desire to further test the intellect of these unusual white creatures. In a subtle way he had brought out one of the two chess boards he carried aboard his vessel, asking Destiny if Achilles, who had been floating nearby, had ever been introduced to the game.

"I'll let you see for yourself," she had said, her face lighting up in a cryptic smile. Within minutes, the uncanny cleverness of the juvenile became apparent, clearly astounding Jake.

Jake dropped his reflections and brought his eyes to bear on Achilles again as the dolphin headed off to the north end of the cove where other albinos appeared to be gathering. "Where's Achilles going?"

"Art class," Destiny informed him, noting the frown that formed on Jake's features as he turned to face her. "Several times a week each member of the pod creates a work of art."

Jake looked back at the gathering with sudden interest. "Now this I've got to see with my own eyes."

"Come!" Destiny said, slipping gracefully into the water. The head of Hercules suddenly emerged above the surface next to her and she grabbed hold of the giant's dorsal fin, looking back up at Jake expectantly. "Well, are you just going to sit there or are you coming?"

Jake hopped off the platform and moved to the side of Hercules opposite Destiny before latching onto the creature's fin just above the area where Destiny clutched it. He immediately sensed the raw physical strength of the giant as the animal quickly gained speed, something several times more potent than what Achilles was capable of exerting. But this became secondary to the strange and alluring attraction exuded by the girl next to him. Already a strong friendship had grown between them, one that seemed to have existed for many years rather than a single day. Even so, she nevertheless remained a complete mystery to him. As he was pulled along he held the girl's gaze, her eyes less than a foot away and continually roving over his face, seemingly exploring the depths of his very soul as if she might uncover something altogether new and fascinating. This was a good day, he decided, one worth living. He let his hand slide down the fin until he made contact with Destiny's. Only then did he fully enjoy the ride.

- 38 -

The telemetry specialist sat at the terminal studying the console as he sipped from a steaming cup of freshly brewed coffee. It was currently several minutes past 7 p.m. in Toulouse, France, and he yawned tiredly as he monitored a map of the Caribbean displayed on the computer screen. Under the guise of working later on one of his company assignments, he had stayed at his workstation more than an hour beyond his normal shift, having been given ample incentive to do so. It wasn't every day an unknown benefactor was willing to pay him so handsomely for his services. Though the firm he worked for paid him an impressive salary as it was, he was willing to risk unauthorized use of company resources in furthering his financial objectives, particularly when the money was tax-free and had already been deposited in an offshore bank account he kept in the Cayman Islands. His job description allowed him unlimited access to the hardware and software comprising the computerized system he was presently using.

The Argos system was unique, utilizing both a ground and satellite-based network to collect, process and disseminate environmental data from fixed and mobile platforms worldwide. The system had been operational since 1978 and was established under a joint agreement between the Centre National d'Etudes Spatiales, better known as the French Space Agency, and two American agencies: the National Aeronautics and Space Administration (NASA) and the National Oceanic and Atmospheric Administration (NOAA). Operated and managed by Collecte, Localisation, Satellites (CLS), the specialist's employer for the past three years, the system had recently been upgraded with the addition of more advanced computer technology.

The hardware comprising the integrated system was unparalleled in its reach, incorporating well over ten thousand transmitters on a global scale that included a vast network of receiving stations. At the heart of the system were six NOAA series satellites following sun-synchronous, circular polar orbits at an altitude of 850 kilometers. At least two of these satellites were simultaneously in service most of the time, sending information to major processing facilities located in France and the United States. With such a configuration, any particular location on the planet could receive data from a satellite every six hours. No security clearances were necessary to gain access to the data, which was available commercially. Potential users of this data could readily purchase the necessary equipment from commercial companies for unlimited access to the satellite transmissions. In addition, there were no fees or licenses required by NOAA to receive this data. Archived data was also available from NOAA or various companies that stored it, either processed or in raw form, but acquiring such data usually incurred a reproduction fee.

This knowledge caused the specialist to smile ironically, for if such information were so easily obtainable to anyone who required it, why would some users need him? It was the intermittency of data streams received every six hours from orbiting satellites that created problems for many users, particularly when tracking ground-based signals. This was the area where he held an advantage. From where he sat he could acquire that same data at any time from linked ground stations all over the globe by using the recent upgrades. And it was this that put his moonlighting services in demand, this and a unique ability to customize software with programs that gave some users the same advantages he currently enjoyed.

Leaning back in his reclinable chair, he began propping his feet on an adjacent desk, but before he could get comfortable he became aware of the blip that suddenly began pulsing on the monitor. Abruptly, he sat back up. Shifting his eyes to a corner of the screen, he checked a readout that identified the modulated frequency of the signature signal he was scanning for. Satisfied that it was the correct one, he noted the coordinates that pinpointed the source of the transmission. The incoming signal, he knew, was almost real-time in nature and that the actual position of the source would be within 1000 meters of the coordinates shown on the screen. Such a discrepancy was typical when tracking signals emanating close to the equator where the Doppler effect would be more pronounced. Hitting a few keys, he homed in on the transmission's origination point by reducing the map scale, then changed perspectives, giving him a closeup view of that part of the earth as seen from one of the satellites at that moment. He knew that at least one of the satellites orbiting near the planet's north pole had to be in the right position to receive a signal.

An oblique panorama of the West Indies suddenly sprang into view. He immediately recognized the northern ends of Cuba and the Island of Dominica dominating the major portion of the picture screen. For the most part, the landmasses and seas were relatively unobstructed by any significant cloud cover. Increasing the magnification by a factor of ten, he zeroed in on the area southwest of the Windward Passage between the two large islands. The enlarged view showed a sector of ocean that dazzled him, displaying a rich variegation of indigo and turquoise hues that fell away to the southern horizon. A small oblong island loomed in the left foreground, and as he scrutinized it, he could make out what appeared to be a tall man-made structure overlooking its eastern side, probably the remains of an old lighthouse. Punching a few more keys, he pulled up the name of the tiny island.

Navassa.

Several nautical miles beyond the island, a flashing red dot indicated the location of the beacon sending the signal. Enlarging the magnification further, he was disappointed when only water filled the screen. Whatever was sending the signal, he concluded, was presently submerged below the waterline. He hadn't been informed about what the transmitting unit was mounted to, but from experience he assumed it would be a marine animal of some kind. Satellite telemetry was useful in solving many mysteries, including the migration routes of various animal species. Unfortunately, orbiting satellites were still unable to detect signals originating underwater mainly due to the limitations of the sending units used in studying marine animal behavior. To consume as little power as possible from the batteries that powered them, most units were designed to generate signals intermittently and just long enough to transmit vital data. During the course of his career he had often tracked leatherback sea turtles and knew that the transmitters mounted on their backs only switched on when the creatures were on the ocean surface. This caused him to deduce that the pulsing red dot shown on the screen was the last point of transmission and did not necessarily represent the current position of the sending unit.

He again sat back and pondered the task he had been hired to perform. He was only required to locate the transmitter's global position and track its movements subsequent to relaying this information to the anonymous party that had sought his services, nothing more. In order to gain access to this information, the unknown recipient needed a special receiver, a piece of hardware that was not available commercially. Fabricating such a unit was not for the layman, for specialized technical knowledge was required to produce one. That problem, however, had already been taken care of. The person responsible for setting up this gig had both built and supplied the hardware to the obscure recipient days earlier. All he had to do was download the data and send it off to its intended destination to fulfill his end of the bargain. His client, whoever he or she was, had retained him in good faith by paying his exorbitant fee in advance. He tried to visualize the type of individual willing enough to dole out such a hefty sum for so simple a piece of work. It had to be someone possessing considerable wealth. He had recently checked his Cayman account to confirm that the money had been deposited.

Maintaining a solid reputation for reliability in this covert line of work was important to the specialist, for it continued to set the stage for the amount of future moonlighting he could expect. Promoting himself through word of mouth had done wonders for his financial health during the last year. Precaution was paramount, for routinely exercising it protected both him and clients that didn't want their identities revealed. That was why he worked through intermediaries only, trusted individuals he had discreetly cultivated within scientific and military circles where his services were most frequently sought. One such intermediary was actually a close friend of his, a graduate student at the University of Miami and the person who had arranged this job. Unlike his friend, though, the specialist had completed his doctoral thesis in computer science three years earlier. He made a mental note to supplement his friend's Cayman account with the commission he had earned. He would make the electronic transfer of funds as soon as he concluded this business.

Swinging his eyes back to the screen he realized the current point of transmission had shifted by several hundred meters, but again nothing showed on the ocean surface. Damn, he should have been more observant, he chided himself. The carrier of the transmitter had to have breached the surface when he had looked away. It was driving him crazy to know what manner of beast carried the telemetry unit. He frowned in irritation, but an idea suddenly hit him and the frown abruptly faded. Perhaps it wasn't an animal at all, he surmised. Maybe it was a manmade object, maybe a submarine.

Curious, he decided to retrieve other data streams from the satellite's remote sensing instrumentation, starting with thermal imagery of the waters in the immediate vicinity of the submerged transmitter. If a submarine were there, it just might put out enough heat to give him a thermal footprint. Switching over to HIRS, the High Resolution Infrared Sounder, he became disappointed when a trail failed to appear. He gave this finding some thought. The lack of a thermal signature didn't necessarily mean that a sub was not present, particularly if it was an electrically powered sub. Usually it was only the large nuclear subs that put out thermal emissions sufficient to be detected by satellite, and that almost always occurred in cold polar waters where heat emissions from a sub contrasted more sharply with lower ambient temperatures.

In frustration he widened the scale, scanning a larger field. Although most of the screen exhibited blue, it contrasted sharply with a yellow-red zone occurring near the south side of Navassa Island, an indication of heavy phytoplankton concentration. This surprised him, for such concentrations were only possible if an upwelling of deeper water had taken place, and in the Caribbean upwellings were relatively rare. Upwelling brought nutrients to the surface, causing phytoplankton to erupt into frenzied growth. He had scanned the Caribbean Basin on numerous occasions during his first two years with CLS, but not since then. He did not remember having seen a concentration anywhere close to this magnitude. Seeking to confirm this he accessed the archives and pulled up a history of sea temperature imagery covering the same area dating back over the last year. Displaying a sequence of frames in reverse chronological order, each frame separated by one month, he could see the size and concentration of the algae bloom had remained fairly consistent during the past year. Pulling up additional frames, he went back in time another year. He only had to look at the first frame to confirm a smaller plankton bloom. Shifting back through several more frames told him what he was looking for. The plankton had begun to reproduce exponentially about thirteen months ago, exploding into riotous growth with a rich supply of nitrogen-laden nutrients brought to the surface from deeper, colder water.

His interest sparked, he mulled this. With the exception of the earth's polar regions where upwelling was common, surface waters in warmer climates remained relatively devoid of nutrients containing nitrogen. This was because phytoplankton absorbed such nutrients rather quickly while capturing sunlight and, through the process of photosynthesis, converted it into proteins, fats and carbohydrates. At sea, nutrients were not readily available and were not recycled in the same manner as on land. Marine organisms sank into the depths when they died, taking the nutrients bound up in their bodies with them. The specialist understood that nitrogen was the key nutrient for the proliferation of life, the basic building block of all amino acids, with food production dependent on it. The oceans of the world contained an almost limitless source of nitrogen from decomposed organisms, particularly in the form of nitrates, the concentration of which increased rapidly with depth before leveling off at around 3300 feet. Because fixed forms of nitrogen were vital to plant metabolism, he knew an upwelling from the depths would have a profound effect on the local ecology, for at sea phytoplankton formed the base of a living pyramid, providing sustenance for the myriad organisms comprising the pyramid above. A substantial increase in the supply of fixed forms of nitrogen would dramatically broaden the pyramid base, rapidly expanding the rest of the biomass supported by it by quickly working its way up the food chain. The numbers of tiny crustaceans and other grazers of planktonic sea grass would escalate swiftly with a large increase in available plankton, providing food for shrimp and other small organisms. These would then be consumed by sardines and other small fish, which in turn would serve to feed schools of tuna and other more complex life forms near the top of the pyramid. As he studied the various frames he was certain the area near Navassa had to be teeming with huge schools of fish at this very moment.

Upon learning this, he had to remind himself of his mission. Deleting the picture frames from the computer screen, he went back to real-time viewing. The monitor exhibited a new flashing dot, this one still closer to the island. Still seeing no sign of any creature on the ocean surface, he displayed the location of all three pulsing dots he had so far witnessed and projected a path of travel from them. Noticing that the spacing between transmission points was roughly equal, he focused on a spot ahead of the last point of transmission at a distance approximating the degree of separation between the preceeding points.

He only had to wait less than a minute before another point pulsed where he had anticipated. It was then that he saw a disturbance on the surface, and as he scrutinized the cause of it he realized he was observing the backs of two albino dolphins swimming side by side in perfect synchrony. Totally fascinated by the sight, he watched the creatures for one brief moment before they disappeared into the depths again. Only then did he relay the locations of the transmissions to his anonymous client.

- 39 -

Jake didn't remember seeing the large wooden raft at the far end of the cove, mainly because it had been tethered to the backside of the fish pen where it remained hidden from view. The raft was square in shape, accommodating one albino per side. Centered close to each edge of the raft was an easel fitted with a canvas that faced outward within easy reach of each dolphin. As Jake looked on, he could distinguish a palette containing an assortment of brushes, colored oils and other liquids situated on both sides of each easel. Already the creatures were busy, the upper third of their bodies jutting vertically above the water, their prehensile appendages fully extended and moving rapidly between canvas and palettes.

Awed by what he was seeing, Jake found it difficult to pull his eyes away from the scene before him. "They're all ambidextrous!" he uttered in disbelief, continuing to hold onto the dorsal fin of Hercules as the giant albino towed him and Destiny slowly around the small gathering.

Jacob smiled knowingly as he sat nearby in the small aluminum dory he used to maneuver around the cove. "Yes, they have the ability to compose with both hands simultaneously."

As if reading Jake's mind, Hercules ceased moving and hovered close behind Achilles, allowing Jake to observe the creation that was quickly unfolding on the young dolphin's canvas. "I don't claim to know much about art," Jake said, "but that looks to be some kind of abstract." He pivoted his head toward Destiny, then brought his eyes back to the painting. "What's it symbolize?"

"That all depends on the one doing the viewing," Destiny replied.

Jake studied the fast developing artwork. "The viewer will only perceive as much as they allow themselves based upon the capaciousness of representation," Jacob interposed. "For most people, the forms, images and composition will only touch what a person has absorbed throughout their existence. Works such as these will appeal to some, while invariably repulsing others. With some individuals, though, the context of what lies on a canvas may reach down to the very essence of the viewer, affecting that person in a unique and unexpected way."

Jake nodded, intrigued by what he was witnessing. "Yes, but what does Achilles want this painting to represent?" He turned back to Destiny. "Surely you must be feeling what he's trying to convey?"

The girl stared back, her eyes filled with infinite patience. "He doesn't know. Each of the artists before us is simply letting their brush strokes be guided by subconscious thoughts."

"What you are seeing is what some authorities within the art world would term '*unconscious autonomous creativity,*'" Jacob added, noting the blank look on Jake's face. "From the moment of birth, the brain is bombarded with stimuli which are arranged into coherent principles that will be accepted by other brains, but which may or may not represent the compositional elements of the psyche. On a basic level you are observing sticks with hairs carrying gobs of colored oils being haphazardly smeared on a surface, nothing more. But if you look deeper, taking this procedure and refining it to a degree that equates to painting without thinking, then you are viewing a form of creativity that portrays imagery that is symbolic of the infantile juxtaposition of thoughts." For emphasis, he glanced at Achilles' rapidly emerging creation. "Some might categorize this as surrealism, a representation of a superior reality associated with dreams and disinterested thought. Such a representation is unconnected with cerebral mechanisms, substituting itself in place of them as a solution to the principal problems of life."

Jake found himself groping for words. "You're getting way ahead of this limited intelligence of mine," he said, examining Achilles' painting with a critical eye. "But I see nothing haphazard. If anything, there appears to be order here." He pointed to the right half of the canvas. "Those lines...they seem to be converging, as if flowing towards a single point in space...as if going to infinity but not quite getting there. And near the top...the commingling of blue and yellow splotches in the midst of a white background...they somehow suggest both dolphins and humans in a purified state."

Though Achilles had not yet completed the work, the creation seemed to convey serenity to Jake, drawing him away from the penumbra of what he would have considered rational thought. All at once he felt cleansed, as if breaking free of the chains of consciousness where confusion and chaos seemed to predominate. He was falling, then rising, manipulating his free hand as if he himself were wielding one of the brushes stroking the canvas. All at once he was suddenly seeing the painting through the eyes of Achilles. The sensation startled him, jarring him back to the edge.

"You have a keen eye," Jacob praised, sensing that Jake was teetering on the brink of something newly discovered. He had seen that same look in others. "Paintings like these are usually unfathomable to the average person simply because such individuals are attuned only to the world they perceive with their eyes. The surrealist, however, strives to turn away from the illusions constructed by their five physical senses, looking inward toward an unfiltered and largely unexplored region of the subconscious. The surrealist seeks to depict a realm purified of all the social ills plaguing the world he or she lives in, escaping to a place where consciousness is only a small part. In doing this, the surrealist attempts to unveil a superior reality, one infinitely more complex and revealing than any metaphysics."

Hercules began moving again, slowly pulling Jake and the girl counterclockwise to the next side of the raft. The painting Jake observed was different from the one Achilles' was creating, alive with color and appearing to be nearing completion. "Coral is one of our more prolific artists," Destiny explained. "She and Reef have produced more paintings than any of the others."

"How many paintings has she completed?" Jake asked.

"This one makes three hundred and twenty four."

Jake's brow rose in astonishment. "What do you do with all of them?"

"We give them away."

"To whom?"

"To people. Mostly strangers who come to Malique wanting to be healed."

Jake digested this momentarily. "I take it there's some underlying purpose in these giveaways."

It was Jacob who gave a reply. "You might say that. Remember what I told you about mankind being insufficiently developed on the evolutionary scale to take responsibility for the planet, that the human species has not yet learned how to use the less predominant side of the brain for the benefit of the world?"

"I remember," Jake affirmed, noting that Jacob had drifted closer, his dory nudged forward by one of the other albinos not currently painting.

"And do you also remember my theory on why this new breed of dolphin has come into existence?" Jacob said, his tone oddly solemnizing.

Jake glanced over at Destiny, her gaze riveted on him as if in prelude to some new revelation. He lifted his eyes back to Jacob who was almost on top of him now. "You think they've been put here to show mankind the way to a better world."

Jacob nodded like a teacher satisfied with the answer given by one of his students. "Although I have no way of proving it, I believe these paintings can be used as one such mechanism in speeding up man's evolution toward becoming a more responsible species."

For one split second Jake thought Jacob must be mad. "How is that possible?"

"Tell me you do not feel anything when you look upon these creations," Jacob challenged. "Tell me you are not affected in some positive way."

As if to test what Jacob was saying, Jake let his eyes settle back on Coral's artwork. Almost immediately a burdensome weight seemed to lift from his inner being, making it possible for him to soar toward an infinite horizon where acts of love and kindness were in great abundance, a universe where greed and aggression did not exist. *What was he feeling? Bliss? Euphoria?* "It's hard to put into words, but something good seems to wash over me when I stare into these works," he found himself acknowledging. "But how can a painting induce such a reaction in a person?"

"Yes, how can it?" Jacob turned his eyes back to Coral who was focused on completing the painting. "I believe these creations somehow trigger a neurological mechanism in some people, stimulating the lesser used side of the brain, the part that is most creative, the area that is more inclined to follow a course of moral rectitude. While I can not tell you how or why it works, I can only tell you that it works."

"Maybe these dolphins know how it works," Jake suggested.

Jacob smiled, shaking his head. "Unfortunately they do not. It was only by chance that we learned of the strange effect these paintings have on some people. Over the years I have striven to educate these dolphins in many areas of man's accumulated knowledge, particularly the various types of art mankind has produced and treasured throughout the ages. Art, I felt, would be especially useful in giving them insight into the human psyche since nothing characterizes more fully the true nature of man than his artistic creations. Unlike most other formalized disciplines, art has remained virtually unconstrained in substance, representing a truly free expression of the beings doing the creating."

"Is surrealism their preferred mode of expression?" Jake asked.

"For the most part, yes," Jacob answered. "When I first introduced them to oil painting about seven years ago, they all began to produce works of the same general style even though each painting was unique in its own right. It was when we began giving these works away, however, that we discovered the profound effect they had on some people."

"When did you first notice this?"

"It was after several of the locals we know began to change their ways for the better. That was when they were exposed to several paintings put on permanent display in the village of Malique."

"And you think those changes were influenced by this dolphin art?" Jake said incredulously. "Isn't that stretching the envelop of speculation a bit?"

"Behavorial changes in people rarely occur on their own in an essentially unaltered environment," Jacob countered calmly, appearing amused at how Jake was handling this. "Usually it takes a rare event or the introduction of something new into their surroundings to elicit a modification in the way they act. Without elaborating on the full extent of my observations, I began to notice a relationship between these paintings and the way some people began to behave after viewing them. We now make it a priority to distribute these works among the Haitian masses living in some of the other cities in the hope of making the people more responsible in the manner they conduct themselves."

"Define what you mean when you say more responsible?"

"Contributing to the welfare of the nation, and for that matter, the world in general. Ceasing to overtax the planetary ecosystem. Cleaning up the garbage and refuse that pervades our environment, stopping the stripmining of our remaining timberlands and planting new trees. Helping our fellow man through hardship and difficult times. Essentially becoming environmentally and socially conscientious."

"Is that all, just demonstrating a concern for the environment and society?"

"For starters, yes."

Jake felt a need to test Jacob's convictions further. "Aren't such issues better left in the hands of government to follow through on?"

Jacob's expression abruptly hardened, hanging somewhere between a sneer and a grimace. "It is the people who must lead the way in taking responsibility for their actions, not government. History has shown that governments, all governments, sooner or later have a tendency to become corrupt and complacent, typically causing economic stagnation and social unrest. Here in Haiti that is especially true. It is the citizenry that must set an elevated moral standard, leading by example. Social cohesion must take root with respect to environmental and political issues if the planet is to survive. If we as a species are to evolve to a higher, more responsible level, the human vice of greed, the single most common disease afflicting mankind, must be diminished within the population. This vice is the remnant of the hunter-gatherer mentality that characterized the human race prior to the birth of agricultural-based civilizations, when the very survival of individuals depended on their ability to obtain sources of food. In those days, an excess food supply guaranteed a continuation of their existence and a propagation of their offspring. Unfortunately, this malignant trait is still inherent in most human beings, becoming a detriment in a modern world and contributing immensely to the problems hurting the planet."

Jake continued to hold onto Hercules' dorsal fin, his mind pouring over Jacob's philosophical viewpoint. "Your slant on greed is very enlightening," he admitted. "I never really thought of greed as being a disease. A moral failing, maybe, but not a disease." He decided to feel out Jacob a little more to get a better understanding of the man. "Some might argue that greed is a good thing, that it's the true driving force behind a free enterprise system, creating an economic climate that raises a society's standard of living and invoking technological breakthroughs that ultimately benefit everyone. Without a desire for monetary gain, a free enterprise system cannot flourish. In a broad sense, aren't greed and profit opposite sides of the same coin?"

Jacob took a deep breath, seeming to dissect Jake's argument. "What you say is true if exercised to a reasonable degree. But when taken to excess, greed can become a deadly mental illness that can cause severe social strife. History will attest that this often results in disastrous social upheavals and wars between nations. Did not the French and Russian Revolutions occur when the masses were driven by desperation to put an end to the extreme greed of the aristocracies oppressing and starving them? Did not the Spanish conquistadors in their fanatical search for riches and gold destroy the Tainos civilization? In an advanced stage, greed will lead to the enslavement of some human beings to do the work of others suffering from this sickness. Did not the trafficking of human slaves become one of the economic cornerstones of ancient Rome and the American Southern Confederation? This very nation emerged as a consequence of a rebellion against the greed of slavery."

Jacob suddenly smiled, replacing the gravity that was beginning to cloud his face. "Think of these paintings as a form of medicine, a potential cure for the madness brought on by excessive greed. In a way, they can be thought of as an alternate mode of healing used by these dolphins, a mode not requiring any physical contact and one that has the advantage of reaching far more people."

"Earlier you mentioned these paintings only work on some people afflicted by greed," Jake said. "Can I take it then there will be other people with this illness that cannot be cured?"

A hint of sadness manifested itself briefly in Jacob's expression. "Over the years these dolphins have healed many people suffering from a variety of illnesses, mostly physical ailments they were able to correct through direct physical contact in much the same way they healed the gunshot wound you sustained back at Navassa. Even though they know they have this ability, they have no explanation as to how it works. What they do know is that it does not work on everyone. Although I have no way of proving it, I believe most of the people they are unable to cure are truly evil individuals with dark natures. Perhaps such people are beyond help simply because deep down they are comfortable with who they are, choosing never to change their ways. It is my belief and the belief of Destiny and these dolphins that such people will remain unaffected by these paintings."

Jake swung his head back to Destiny to get a direct read on whether or not she agreed with this. The girl gave a slight nod of her head. Turning back to Jacob he said, "So through these paintings these dolphins think they can still reach significant portions of the Haitian population, suppressing greedy urges."

"Yes."

"That's a pretty tall order," Jake remarked blithely, "particularly in a country like this where people are trying to survive on a daily basis."

"Change will not come overnight. It will occur incrementally. But even that will be better than none at all."

A strange thought suddenly came to Jake. "Is greed the only human vice these paintings are capable of curtailing?"

"There is some evidence to suggest that some individuals with a propensity for violence will become less aggressive when exposed to them. In general, those affected seem to become more caring toward their fellow man, while those with dark natures appear to be immune. It might be that the type of person who is dissatisfied with their self image will become most susceptible to these paintings."

"You mean people who perceive themselves as morally deficient or degenerate?"

"Precisely."

"What about people harboring dangerous ideologies, the kind that threaten and kill people with differing viewpoints?" Jake pressed.

"It depends," Jacob said.

"I'm not getting your drift."

"Are these people rational? Are they attempting to achieve some kind of political objective through the artful combination of violence and the promise to cease hostilities if the objective is met?"

When Jake did not immediately answer, Jacob posed the question a different way. "Is the belief in the ideology real or fantacized?"

Jake appeared completely stymied. "What's the difference?"

"Very often a real belief has a logical or scientific basis. It usually has a degree of certainty restricted by mathematics and the hard sciences, whereas a fantacized belief is irrational as judged by the hard sciences."

"I'm still not following you."

"If the violence continues even after a supposed objective is met, then the ideology has been set up to act out a fantasy. In the eyes of the people holding onto the belief, achieving the objective merely holds symbolic value." Jacob paused, waiting for Jake's response.

"Can you explain this a little more fully?"

"It is a common human weakness to exaggerate our contribution to the world, more so than the world is usually willing to acknowledge. Only through our fantasies are we able to close this gap. If the fantasy involves taking part in a revolutionary struggle against perceived oppressors, the oppressed may imagine themselves marching to the right side of history. Quite often the oppressors are fabricated to fulfill a role, becoming nothing more than props in a theatrical play staged by the fantacizer. In a fantasy ideological movement the leader is not interested in altering the minds of the people he is fighting against. They are simply there as supernumeraries in his private psychodrama, symbolic figures set up for the sole purpose that he might act out his fantasy. The protest for him is not political in nature. It is not aimed at eliminating poverty or stopping economic imperialism. The protest is set up to make himself out to be a hero, constructed for his own edification. In such interactions the fantacist sees others as having no wills or minds of their own, caring nothing for them as individuals and casting them in roles he wishes them to play. In doing this, it never occurs to him that the other actors may be utterly failing to play the part expected of them. The fact that the fantacizer is normally surrounded by other individuals who are not fantacizing, or at least not fantacizing in the same manner, usually prevents his psychodrama from intruding into the domain of reality. But when an entire group or nation gets caught up in the fantasy, the repercussions can be disastrous to the human race. History is replete with such large-scale collective fantasies. For this to happen, however, there must first be a preexisting collective need to set the stage for such a widespread fantasy. This need arises from a conflict between a set of collective aspirations and desires and the austere injunctures of brutal reality.

Over time, this conflict is gradually transformed into a penchant for fantasy. Hitler's fantasy of reviving German paganism in the thousand-year Reich is a classic example of this. Mussolini's aim to resurrect the ancient glory of the Roman Empire is another. Such fantasy ideologies tend to take hold of those people history has bypassed or rejected, groups that feel they are under attack from forces they claim to be more powerful than themselves but nevertheless inferior in terms of true virtue."

Once again Jake was astounded by the depth of Jacob's intellect. The man was a walking library. "How would you classify religious fanaticism aimed at murdering innocents?" he found himself asking, unable to keep the bitterness he felt out of his tone.

A shrewd gleam came into Jacob's eyes. "Religion does possess a peculiar potential for intolerance and violence. Fanatacism and strife are natural byproducts of religion simply because it deals with ultimate truths. Many philosophers find this odd since most religions are based on love. But there is a fine line separating love from hate, and when crossed it can set the stage for some of the most brutal wars man has experienced. People are more apt to go to war over religious dogma than over other issues because for most individuals it deals with the very meaning of human existence and establishes a guideline of acceptable moral benchmarks on how to live their lives. While most of the wars that plagued mankind throughout history were fought under the guise of religion, I have no doubt that many of them were shining examples of collective fantasies on a widespread scale."

Jake mused Jacob's answer before pursuing his previous question from another angle. "So is it possible for these paintings to keep religious fanatics from killing others?" he needed to know.

"It depends how deeply they are imbedded in the fantasy," Jacob said. "If they see themselves as being morally chaste in carrying out their part in the fantasy, then I doubt these paintings will affect them in any way. As I explained to you during our stroll on the beach, there is some scientific evidence that suggests the less predominant side of the human brain to be the area that gives most people a sense of spirituality, the same area these paintings may be having some kind of an influence upon. If the spiritual belief is strong enough, then it is doubtful it can be altered from an outside source."

"But what if they suspected, even to a small degree, that they were being purposely misled by the person or people inciting the movement, the religious war?"

"It would be a serious mistake for an outside observer to view the leaders of such wars as power-hungry egotists using the religion as a cynical ploy to delude the gullible masses. Such leaders can only make others get caught up in the fantasy by believing in it so intensely themselves. For most of us, beliefs are generally a passive response, formed for the purpose of better understanding the world as it is. This differs radically from the fantacist who responds to the world in an intensely active way, developing a belief that is not used for describing the world but aimed at transforming it. As such, the fantasy ideology alters the character and conduct of those holding onto it."

Jacob took a momentary break from his discourse and sighed deeply. "In a sense, a deliberate form of make-believe is erected which becomes a means for making itself real. In such a fantasy, everyone and everything becomes a stage prop."

Jake felt all the more embittered over this analysis. "Being a prop in someone else's fantasy is not a pleasant experience, especially when that someone else is trying to murder you," he said, making sure to keep his ire from showing. "Those men who attacked us last night, I suspect them to be jihadists with a mission of terror in mind."

Jacob seemed to give Jake's comment careful thought before replying. "What you are saying could very well be the case although it does not fit in well with the modus operandi of the more radical elements of Islam," he said at last.

Jake had not expected such a reply. "How so?"

"We all want to make sense of the world around us, reducing it to something we know our way around, particularly when it is acting strangely."

Jake looked at him searchingly. "You think the attack was strange? The man I captured last night has all the earmarks of a Muslim extremist."

Jacob nodded. "Yes, it certainly does appear that way, but I nevertheless find it odd. For the modern day jihadist, there would be no glamour in attacking your vessel, especially in an out-of-the-way place like this where no media coverage would be available for broadcasting the incident. The Islamic extremists of today appear only focused on pulling off the spectacular, something specifically crafted to take root in the imagination of large populations of Muslims."

"You mean like bringing down the twin towers at the World Trade Center," Jake said.

"Exactly. Once the media got involved, bringing down the towers had an effect analogous to theater. It grabbed the audience within the Muslim world and made them feel part of the spectacle, revealing something they could easily and instantly identify."

"And what would that be?"

"Why that God was on the side of radical Islam, of course," Jacob stated breezily.

"Yes, I've heard all that before," Jake retorted, his face souring.

Jacob seemed not to notice. "In the Arab world, smaller acts of terror would have little meaning on the international stage," he rationalized. "An economic and political Goliath had to be brought down to prove beyond any doubt that God favored the extremists."

"So then what motive caused them to attack us?"

"Perhaps they wanted to hijack your vessel for some unknown purpose. After all, they did try to board it."

"True," Jake agreed, "but then they tried to ram it."

"But only after you repelled them," Jacob countered quickly. He fell into a silent interlude for several seconds before speaking again. "An attack on the heels of our earlier encounter is just too coincidental, leading me to believe a connection exists between the tuna trawler at Navassa Island and the men in the submarine."

"I did see a submarine near the island," Destiny interjected, speaking for the first time in several minutes. "The whole pod did."

Circumspection consumed Jacob's expression as he weighed this new disclosure. "Then to rule out that it was not the same one that followed us back here would be unwise," he postulated. "It only lends further support to a relationship between the tuna fishermen and the men operating the sub."

This was something Jake hadn't previously considered in spite of his conviction the sub had followed them all the way back from Navassa. "What you're suggesting is some kind of alliance between Colombians and Muslim radicals," Jake said dubiously, though not quite able to cast aside the absurdness of such a possibility. Although it seemed somewhat far-fetched, he found it difficult to dismiss such a link.

Jacob eyed Jake as if sensing his ambivalence over such a notion. "Have you ever heard of Akum's Razor?" he asked.

"You mean all things being equal, the simplest explanation usually proves to be the right one no matter how improbable it seems," Jake answered. "Yes, I-"

Jake stopped in mid-sentence as Destiny let out a small startled cry. Almost simultaneously, several of the albinos squealed loudly and Hercules shuddered convulsively beneath him. "What is it?"

The girl suddenly flinched as if in pain, closing her eyes momentarily before opening them again. "Hermes and Aphrodite are in trouble," she said, her voice conveying distress.

Jake looked at her closely, seeing the fear taking hold of her. "What's going on?"

Hercules flicked his powerful tail, abruptly swimming around the corner of the raft. Jake kept staring into Destiny's frightened eyes, searching for an answer. Turning his head, he followed her gaze. The albino on Coral's right was rapidly composing something, its prehensile appendages appearing like blurs as the paintbrushes held by them swept between the palettes and canvas. As if he was looking at a Polaroid photograph in the midst of development, a new image was quickly coming together, replacing the surrealistic work that had preceded it a short time earlier. As his brain interpreted the shapes swiftly taking form, he realized the new painting showed two white dolphins being netted and hauled from the water.

"We must go at once!" Destiny snapped, the urgency in her tone tugging at Jake like a hundred ton hawser being stretched to its limit.

"Where?" Jake asked.

The girl turned her eyes back to Jake as if suddenly aware of his presence again. "Navassa Island," she said anxiously.

- 40 -

Having been given advance notice where to look, the spotter plane had been close enough to cover the distance quickly and home in on the GPS coordinates relayed to it, converging on the heading. Holding to an altitude of one thousand feet above the water, the pilot suddenly discerned movement below him in spite of the sunglare reflecting off the surface. Locking his eyes on the disturbance, a smile lit his face as he glimpsed something resembling twin alabaster torpedoes cruising side by side. The sight rather surprised him for he had only expected to find one. He didn't want to get his hopes too high, he mused wistfully, but then again, one never knew when good fortune was in the works. For the moment though, he would keep this information to himself, knowing that his partner rarely saw things optimistically the way he did.

The objects remained visible for perhaps another second before submerging, but it was enough for him to confirm their direction of travel. Banking the aircraft sharply and swooping lower, he reduced the air speed and took on a new heading, angling the plane toward a spot ahead of the creatures.

Scanning the eastern horizon briefly, he spotted the vessel that comprised the other half of his team, a high-powered 60-foot Bertram that was rapidly converging on the same general area. The boat was fast and had been specifically retrofitted for the type of work they were about to carry out. He had done this many times before but had never used the equipment he was about to deploy.

The idea had first come to him about six months ago and he had wasted no time in hiring an acoustical engineer to put together the correct combination of electronic components and hardware to bring life to the concept. Though as yet untested under actual field conditions, he was confident that the unit would in theory have the desired effect on the marine mammals he was now tracking.

Depressing the transmit button on his radio, he hailed the Bertram on an encoded, secure channel using the prearranged call signs. "This is Bird of Prey. Can you hear me, Predator?"

"Predator on the approach. You're coming in very clear, Bird of Prey. I have you in sight."

"Be advised we have acquired the target, Predator. The package is about to be dumped."

"I hope that toy of yours works," a skeptical voice grumbled. "Otherwise this trip will have been all for nothing."

The pilot couldn't help but crack a smile, unable to share his partner's pessimism. "Well let's hope it's not," he muttered, turning his head and nodding to the two crewmen stationed further back in the cargo hold. In acknowledgement to the gesture, both crewmen disconnected the safety straps securing what he had called 'the package', a large bulky container weighing better than 1200 pounds.

Seeing that this was done, the pilot toggled a switch on the forward console. Several seconds passed before a noticeable vibration worked its way through the controls as the cargo bay doors opened outward and caught the wind. A moment later the vibration subsided as the doors locked into a fully opened position.

Bringing the twin turboprop lower, the pilot never tired of the feel of the Casa-212. She was a sturdy fixed-wing aircraft, the type of flying machine that was exceptionally versatile. He had picked it up cheap at a government auction, knowing the plane had been confiscated from the hands of drug runners. From all outward indications, the Casa has been well maintained. With the exception of the newly installed hydraulically powered cargo bay doors positioned amidships in the lower fuselage, he had done little to modify the airplane. The bay doors had been a necessary addition. The payload was just too large and heavy to be pushed out of the plane's side door, particularly when timing of the drop was critical to the operation. The success of the venture would depend on how close he could position the unit to the creatures.

The pilot had come up with the idea for the unit from recent studies that linked whale strandings with recent improvements in active sonar systems used by the U.S. Navy. Better known as SURTASS LFA in naval circles, the low-frequency sonar acted like a powerful floodlight in an undersea environment, generating sound levels equivalent to that put out by twin-engine fighter jets. Beached whales often exhibited the damage such a barrage of sound could do, showing internal bleeding around their brains and ears. Producing as much as 215 decibels of intense sonic wave energy, a substantial body of evidence was beginning to mount showing the harm LFA systems could do to marine life. Among other things, use of such technology in the open ocean was responsible for the formation of large emboli, or gas bubbles, in the organ tissue of marine mammals.

It was this type of technology he had deemed useful, a perfect complement to his line of work. But he had no desire to inflict bodily injury on the creatures below him. His deal with the man who had hired them required they be captured unharmed if he were to be paid what amounted to five times his normal fee for the delivery of just one live specimen. The fact that there were two of these unusual white dolphins within his grasp would double his windfall. And if the client refused to cough up the full amount for a second dolphin, he was certain he could put the additional creature up for sale in other markets. Foreign governments were clamoring for dolphins they could train as military assets and, in this case, would pay an exceedingly handsome sum for such a rare animal. According to the client, these marine mammals were exceptionally intelligent and possessed a most interesting anatomical feature atypical of the average bottlenose dolphin.

The unit he was about to launch was self-contained and designed to put out only sufficient sound energy to stun the animals, disorienting them just enough for his partner to get within range to sedate and net them. To accomplish that still necessitated a substantial output of sonic energy sent out in all directions from the device to ensure that the targeted dolphins would be temporarily incapacitated. Even so, a discharge of even that amount of power would be limited and short in duration. The energy source that powered the unit consisted of fifteen lithium-ion marine batteries, all of which accounted for most of the unit's weight. An array of loudspeakers protruding from a central hub ensured that the surrounding hydrosphere would be blanketed in sound.

Cutting back on the throttle a little more, the pilot reduced his air speed further as he descended to within fifty feet of the water before leveling off. Even though the unit was enveloped in what amounted to a belt of inflated bags to both cushion it from impact during the drop and keep it from sinking, he wanted to minimize the force with which it slammed into the sea as much as possible. He and his partner had expended a sizeable sum of money in developing the device, and protecting the investment was currently foremost in his mind. And if the unit performed up to his expectations, he was certain he could get at least a tenfold return on the cash he had laid out in producing it.

With his thumb planted lightly on the switch that would trigger the electronic release, he mentally counted backward as he eyed his drop zone. *Three…two…one…now.* "The package is away, Predator," he said loudly, his tone showing more emotion than he had intended.

"I saw it fall, Bird of Prey," the pilot's partner reported dully. "I'm heading straight for it now."

"Happy hunting, Predator. I'll stay on station to guide you to the prize. Bird of Prey signing off for now."

Reengaging more power, the pilot brought the nose of the Casa up and began to climb. As he did this, he turned anxiously in his seat to observe the expression on Hanson's face, the crewman assigned to monitor the operation of the unit. A look of intense concentration consumed the man's features as he listened intently to the sounds coming through the earphones clamped to his cranium. Several seconds passed before Hanson lifted his head to meet the pilot's eyes, his manner revealing nothing.

The pilot keyed the aircraft intercom. "Well?" he asked impatiently.

The stoicism displayed by Hanson suddenly transformed into a broad grin. "We have tone," he said jubilantly. Bringing his eyes to bear on the laptop before him, he added, "All the readings are pegged to max."

"Wonderful!" the pilot said happily, taking the plane into a moderate left bank and circling back the way they had come. "Now let's see if it does what it's supposed to do."

Looking out the side window, the pilot caught sight of the floatation bags bobbing in the distance. He visualized how the contrivance was currently working. Upon making contact with the sea, the primary component of the sonar unit was designed to fall away from the air bags, dropping fifteen feet below the ocean surface before a one inch umbilical cable connecting it with the floats stopped its descent. Almost immediately, the device would commence emitting the low frequency sounds at the required magnitudes, jarring the senses of creatures that depended on echolocation for their survival. A transmitter with antenna positioned in the cluster of floation bags would send out signals that indicated if the unit was functioning properly. Those were the signals both Hanson and his partner were currently monitoring. He also knew that the window of opportunity for capturing the dolphins was a small one. The amount of juice needed to generate the debilitating sound waves would quickly drain the lithium-ion battery system. Unless the second half of his team arrived in time to prevent the escape of the creatures, the animals would recover rapidly from their sound induced stupors and escape. From the few tests he had run on the device, he knew it would continue to put out sound pulses at the required level of impairment for approximately seven minutes.

Taking the plane out of its bank, he located the Bertram. Although it was still a significant distance away from the floats, it was closing the gap quickly. Nervously he studied the sea in the immediate vicinity of the sonar unit, knowing it was going to be close. A hint of something white just beneath the water suddenly caught his eye, and as he focused on the spot he realized the pair of albino dolphins had breached less than a hundred yards from where the floats bobbed. A smile worked its way onto his face as he studied them. Both creatures appeared to be floundering on the surface in confusion, their previous direction of travel now disrupted.

As he watched the pair, a new thought struck him. *Perhaps more of these white dolphins were in the area.* Squinting his eyes against the harsh sunglare reflecting off the water, he looked closely for other signs that might indicate the presence of more of this rare species. Sweeping his gaze left, a fleeting glimpse of something dark and huge appeared to race below the surface. He blinked in surprise, unsure of what he was seeing, but in doing so he lost sight of the object. Banking the aircraft slightly, he tried to pick it up again. He continued to scan the water in that spot for several more seconds before giving up the attempt, realizing what he had seen could very easily have been the shadow of a passing cloud. As if to confirm this, he cast his eyes above him, noting a succession of small clouds drifting overhead. On impulse, he turned his head to the north, becoming aware of the isolated chunk of land not too far away, the lush vegetation carpeting its surface contrasting distinctly with the blue horizon. It suddenly occurred to him that the white dolphins had been holding to a heading that would have taken them to the island, but so what.

Drawing his gaze away from the remote mound of greenery, he got back to the business at hand by veering the aircraft into another bank and taking stock of the scene below him again. The creatures were still on the surface, showing little movement. Gauging the present heading of the Bertram with respect to the animals, he thought it prudent to hail his partner once more. "Bird of Prey calling Predator."

"This is Predator."

"We have quarry, Predator," he said, speaking as if savoring the words. "Two of them to be exact, chased from the depths and eagerly awaiting your arrival. Let's see if you can nab both of them. If you alter your course by two degrees to port, you'll be almost in direct line with them."

A slight pause ensued as the context of the transmission was digested. "Two of them, you say," an astounded voice suddenly shot back. "Do you mean to tell me that unit of yours actually works?"

The pilot shook his head in exasperation as he watched the boat draw closer to the targeted creatures. "Haven't I always told you to have a little faith?" he said blandly, knowing the ball was now in his partner's hands.

In spite of the confidence he tried to convey in his tone, a growing sense of urgency began to take hold of him. Anxiously he checked his watch and ran a quick mental calculation. In another three minutes the Bertram would reach its prey. That would leave an overlap of approximately 30 seconds before the batteries powering the sonic device became depleted. Already he could distinguish a pair of gunners on the vessel's bow, each man armed with an air rifle that would launch a sedation dart. Over the years, both he and his partner had learned that having a second shooter at the ready was a necessary precaution in the event that the primary shooter missed the targeted marine mammal. Inasmuch as there were now two magnificent specimens ready for capture took away this measure of assurance if they intended on snaring both creatures simultaneously. And he definitely wanted both dolphins.

Before he realized what he was doing, he keyed the radio again. "Bird of Prey to Predator."

"What is it BP?"

The pilot put just enough inflection into his voice so there was no mistaking who was in charge of the operation. "Don't screw this up!"

- 41 -

The sudden eruption of sound pounded Hermes and his sister like a jackhammer, sending a cascade of debilitating pain to go coursing through their bodies. Totally disoriented and blinded by the paroxysm, they were forced to surface where they floundered helplessly. Only once in his lifetime had Hermes experienced anything close to the magnitude of sonic energy that was currently slamming into them, and he knew that a passing naval ship more than seven miles away had been the cause of the emission. But this was something even more enervating, making it impossible to navigate, let alone think.

Through the blinding pain he tried in vain to locate the source of the emanation, but was forced to keep his head clear of the water instead. With enormous difficulty he perceived Aphrodite doing the same. Peering about, he vaguely became aware of a flying machine high above. There was something else. A surface vessel was rapidly bearing down on them. Instinctively he knew both objects were somehow connected with the sound, and in that moment he became cognizant of the danger they represented. Though his remoteness from the main pod was substantial, he did not hesitate to send out a call of alarm through the impalpable mind link they all possessed, uncertain as to whether he would be heard. Fighting off the sonic blast as best he could, it took all his concentration to focus his thoughts on what was happening, and it was only when Aphrodite squealed out in panic that he realized the boat had come alongside them.

Looking back at his sister he could see something projecting near her blowhole, and as he reached out to remove it, a sharp sting in the vicinity of his dorsal fin made him flinch involuntarily. Within moments his pain began to subside even though the severe deluge of sound continued to pound away at him. Feeling suddenly weak and lethargic, he sensed himself beginning to sink below the surface. Forcing himself to fight back against the pull of gravity, he flicked his powerful tail, expecting to feel his body being launched high above the sea. Try as he might, his muscles failed to respond in the manner familiar to him. Torpidly, he rolled on his side, casting one eye on the vessel floating next to him. A grinning man hovered above him, wielding some kind of object. As he tried to grasp what it was, something sprang from it and abruptly expanded. Water kicked up around him, and the discomforting sensation of his body being entwined took momentary hold of his awareness. A mild weight began to tug at him, dragging him under. He tried to resist, unable to muster the energy.

With his mind strangely disconnected from his physical form, he mulled the consequences of this unanticipated circumstance objectively. Although his drowning would present certain setbacks to the project, it would by no means prevent the pod from achieving its ultimate goal. Regardless of his loss, they would go on, continuing to grow stronger in numbers. Comforted by this thought, he began to give himself to the sea. But before his head dipped below the water, another force seemed to pull at him, keeping him from sinking. Almost at the same time, the storm of sound assailing his senses seemed to taper off, quickly dwindling away to nothing. Movement caught his eye, and though restrained, he was able to turn his head just enough to distinguish the cause of it. Helplessly, he watched Aphrodite being pulled from the sea in the midst of a mesh-like netting restricting her movements. The sight seemed to galvanize him, and with a renewed effort he threw his full concentration into conveying the event to others of his kind.

- 42 -

Jake had the Kawasaki at full throttle, squeezing every ounce of power out of the small craft as he raced over the windswept ocean at close to 80 miles per hour. Destiny clung snugly to his back, her arms clamped tightly around his waist to keep from being thrown off balance as they careened crazily over the choppy sea. Every so often they would become airborne as a foaming whitecap launched them skyward, setting the stage for a jarring impact between hull and water that threatened to eject both riders.

Gusting winds made the open Caribbean a mite rougher on this day than what Jake had seen of late, but with a quartering sea at their rear, they would make Navassa in record time. Glancing at his watch, he estimated they had already covered 38 of the 45 miles in roughly 28 minutes. At any moment now, the island, and more importantly their quarry, should be coming into view. That is, if he didn't end up flipping the STX-12F under the less than ideal conditions that were at odds with their current velocity. Already they had had at least a dozen close calls upon being catapulted into the air, with the tiny bow of the Kawasaki coming dangerously close to plunging below the surface each time they landed. A high degree of risk was involved here, made all the more perilous by Hector's ingenious mechanical skills at maximizing the performance of reciprocating engines. The machine under him was even more powerful than its typical stock model due to Hector's tweaking. Jake could feel his forearms beginning to burn and cramp as he fought to keep from being dislodged from the steering bars, but he refused to let up on the gas.

When they had first left the cove, Jake had reservations about whether Destiny could take the brutal pounding she would be subjected to as the Kawasaki sped across the open sea with its throttle wide open. But now the safety of his passenger was no longer a concern. Destiny seemed to be holding up exceptionally well to the tumultuous ride. Though the girl was tiny, he was amazed at the pressure she was able to exert as she hugged his midriff during the bumpiest moments of the precarious voyage. This he attributed to the years she had spent in riding Hercules through seas that continually offered a heavy drag against her small frame.

As Jake continued to drive the Kawasaki with reckless abandon, he contemplated the circumstances beckoning him onward. Ever since meeting up with the girl and the unusual creatures she lived with, he had felt a strong compulsion to protect them. He just couldn't explain it. Perhaps this was a way to redeem himself for his previous failure, one that perpetually haunted him. Nevertheless, he would do whatever it took to foil the abductions he had seen in the dolphin painting. His immediate objective, however, was getting there in time.

"Turn a few degrees left!" Destiny yelled in his ear. "They're on the move."

Jake did as the girl instructed, aware that such a course adjustment would actually add to their rate of travel by giving them more of a following sea. That she was able to remain in mental contact with the captured creatures and provide input on the correct heading to take was extremely valuable if they were going to track down the albino abductors, yet this ability continued to astonish him.

Destiny leaned close to his ear again. "Oh, please hurry," she urged, her voice mired in trepidation. Despite the blast of wind rushing by, Jake could tell from her tone that she had no fear for her own safety. To him, the girl was without a doubt fearless, displaying only a concern for the creatures she was trying to save. "Can you go any faster?" she pleaded.

"Only if we sprout wings," Jake muttered, pivoting his head just enough for the girl to hear. He dared not take his eyes from the sea directly ahead lest he fail to anticipate which way to lean his weight. The last thing he wanted was to upend the small craft and spill both of them into the drink. At their present speed, he knew that serious injury would result to both of them if that were to happen. Destiny was proving to be a good passenger, though, seemingly anticipating Jake's every move as she shifted her weight in perfect unison with his as he fought to keep the Kawasaki on an even keel.

"I see them," Destiny suddenly blurted, keeping only her right arm hooked around Jake's waist and pointing with the other. "There!"

Bringing his full attention back to the horizon directly in front on him, a tiny speck above the ocean abruptly caught his eye. He quickly recognized it to be a plane, and as he kept the Kawasaki heading straight for it, he was able to discern a boat over which the aircraft circled.

Jake swung his head around again. "Are you sure that's them?"

This time Destiny's voice barely carried above the blast of wind. "Hermes and Aphrodite are aboard that boat. Their presence is very strong now."

Jake nodded, leaning the waverunner a little more to port as he aimed the Kawasaki on an intercept course with the vessel. From his perspective, it seemed the boat was on a heading that would take it toward the Haitian mainland, but it was as yet too far away to be certain. Ever since they had left the cove, his mind had been groping with how he would free the captured albinos if they were fortunate enough to catch up with their abductors. He had not had time to formulate a plan. Even worse, the type of people he would be dealing with and the resources they possessed were complete unknowns. Know your enemy. That's what they had always taught him in the Seals. And yet here he was, many miles from land at a complete disadvantage.

Resorting to the use of the Kawasaki had been the only option open to them if they were going to have any chance whatsoever of saving the dolphins. Unfortunately, making immediate chase had been the main priority and there hadn't been any time to arm the waverunner in the manner of a Code One. And even if there had, the automatic weapons would have done him little good. Firing live rounds in trying to free so valuable a cargo was something that would have put the creatures at risk. The only weapon Jake currently possessed was his K-bar, tucked firmly within the sheath strapped to his calf.

Lurking in the background of Jake's thoughts was the inexorable guilt grinding away at him. If not for him, Hermes and Aphrodite would be swimming with the rest of the pod within the safe confines of the cove. After all, it was he who had suggested to the girl the importance of tracking the sub using the DBT. He had never expected two of the albinos to volunteer so readily to the task.

Swiveling his head to the side, Jake asked, "Can you tell me how many people are aboard that boat?"

Several seconds passed before Destiny replied. "Hermes has seen five men."

Jake weighed this information carefully as he kept his eyes trained on the approaching vessel. The rudiments of an idea suddenly came to him and he explored it further. *Yes, it just might work.* Cutting back on the throttle, he leaned the Kawasaki hard to port, coming about by almost 180 degrees. Taking on the same heading as the boat carrying the albinos, he sped away from it. Although the distance separating them was still substantial, he increased it even more, hoping the waverunner's low profile had so far kept them from being spotted.

"What are you doing?" Destiny wailed. "Go back!"

"I have a plan," Jake shouted above the rush of wind. "Trust me on this." Opening up more distance from the oncoming vessel, he raced on for perhaps another mile before slowing and turning off the engine. Pivoting in his seat, he spun around to face the girl. "This is what I have in mind."

- 43 -

The man piloting the Casa-212 got back on the radio, unable to keep the delight he felt out of his tone. "Nice job, Predator. You certainly have a way with dolphins." Shooting a quick glance at his fuel gauge, he added, "Time for me to head back, though. I'm close to running on fumes. See you at the dock. Bird of Prey signing off."

Bringing the aircraft out of another steep bank, he brought the plane back on a straight and level flight, setting his course for home. As he looked up from the console, his eyes were immediately drawn to the bright red plume arcing high above the sea. A second later, his partner's voice came back. "Stick around one more minute, BP, and give me a heads up on that flare. I assume you see it."

"Only a blind man would miss it," the pilot keyed back, studying the source of the flare no more than half a mile off the Bertram's bow. Dipping the nose of the Casa, he swooped lower, getting a good look at two people waving their arms frantically as they sat aboard a small watercraft. "Looks like a man and woman on a waverunner. Probably run outta gas."

"Strange that they'd be so far from land," the pilot's partner said.

"Exactly what I'm thinking," the pilot agreed. "Give me a minute. I'm coming around for another pass." Banking hard and dropping one of the wingtips to within 50 feet of the water, he got a better look at both parties. Grinning, he keyed the radio again. "Appears to me the girl's quite a looker, Predator. Maybe you should just keep going. I'd rather you not be distracted in view of what you're carrying."

"No way, BP," the voice at the other end responded acidly. "That flare was red, signifying an emergency distress signal. Under maritime law, I have a moral and legal obligation to assist them."

"When was it you became such an upstanding mariner," the pilot quipped lightly, absolutely certain his associate had by now gotten a good look at the girl through the binoculars he kept near the helm. "Or is it more likely that ignoring a pretty face is just too much for you to handle."

A momentary silence ensued before the expected reply spilled from the radio like a swarm of angry bees pouring from a hive. "Up yours, BP. I'll drop the two of them off in Port-au-Prince."

"Suit yourself, Predator," the pilot said knowingly, well aware of the weakness his partner had for women. "See you back at the dock. Bird of Prey, flyin' away." Smiling at the cleverness of his rhyme, he gained altitude and left the stranded party of two far behind him.

- 44 -

Jake caught the line thrown to him as the Bertram drew alongside the Kawasaki. Letting the small craft drift back behind the larger vessel, he read the name *Sea Lion* on the Bertram's stern. Rising conspicuously above the back deck was a pair of heavy duty lifting davits designed for lowering and raising multi-ton loads to and from the water. Keeping his scrutiny casual, he could see the boat had been specially modified to take aboard sizeable cargos. Several crewmen milling about the deck cast curious glances at him and Destiny as they poured water over something below his line of sight. A handsome middle-aged Caucasian of medium build climbed down from the bridge and leaned over the rear transom, his eyes roaming hungrily over

Destiny before sizing Jake up in the manner of an animal trainer assessing a wild beast. "Quite a bit off the beaten path, aren't you?" the man stated. "Your waverunner break down?"

"Yeah," Jake said innocently. "Just conked out on us. Would you mind giving us a tow?"

The man rested a lingering gaze on Destiny again, seeming to ignore Jake for the moment. "Tell ya what," he finally said, "if you don't mind being dropped off in Port-au-Prince, I have no problem giving you a tow."

Jake produced a false smile. "Fine by us. Would it be okay if we come aboard?"

The man looked back at Jake, his expression seeming to convey a warning. "I guess that'd be all right so long as you keep out of the way. Pull your runner up against the swim platform and watch your step." He suddenly grinned from ear to ear, displaying a set of even white teeth. "I wouldn't want this young lady to slip and fall."

Jake pulled the Kawasaki up tight against the platform, and as he did so the man climbed down and extended a hand to Destiny, helping her aboard. The hefty six-shooter holstered firmly to the man's right thigh immediately caught Jake's attention, and he recognized it to be a 0.357 magnum with a six-inch barrel. The sight of it was imposing, giving the man an air of latent deadliness that implied a lack of hesitation in using it. Pretending to be oblivious of the weapon, Jake hopped onto the platform behind Destiny, making sure the tow rope was fastened securely to one of the Bertram's stern cleats.

"Loomins the name," the man said effervescently, addressing Destiny as he continued to hold onto her hand. "Ben Loomins. And you are?"

With doelike eyes, Destiny stared searchingly into Loomins' face longer than she should have, making Jake nervous that she would be unable to keep up the deception. From recent experience, he sensed the girl had an uncanny ability to probe down to the true nature of a person, any person. Physical contact appeared to be her primary means of doing this. And although he had seen her use this mode to heal, there seemed to be imponderable surges of energy that flowed from her touch, as if she were attuned to ferreting out the darkest and deepest secrets of a person. He wondered if she was doing this now.

It suddenly occurred to him that he'd heard of Loomins, though he had never met the man. Another name suddenly popped into his head as he searched his memory. Frank Jaffey was Loomins' associate, a pilot of colorful repute who operated mostly out of Haiti and some of the other Caribbean islands. A graduate of the U.S. Naval Academy, Jaffey had spent a good ten years as a fighter pilot, primarily flying sorties from aircraft carriers. Jake had met the man briefly in the midst of a lively poker game aboard the USS

Ticonderoga just prior to one of his Seal missions during the invasion of Iraq. Jaffey had been extremely lucky, winning most of the hands. And although Jake had no way of proving it at the time, he had the feeling Jaffey had found an undectable way of cheating.

"And you are?" Loomins repeated uncomfortably, his smile beginning to falter.

The word spilled demurely from the girl's mouth. "Destiny."

Jake thought it wise to intervene. "My friend warned me about taking this baby outta site of land," he said flippantly, looking back at the Kawasaki and shaking his head.

Seemingly awakening to Destiny's companion once again, Loomins let go of the girl's hand and swung his attention back to Jake. "So why'd you do it then?" There was an edge to his tone, as if annoyed by Jake's presence.

"Oh, I don't know," Jake replied, doing his best to inject cheer into his voice. "Always did have a reckless streak, I guess." As soon as he uttered the words, he realized they weren't far from the truth. Withdrawing his eyes from the Kawasaki, he turned around to face Loomins, making sure to keep his manner jocular. It was important he play the part of the buffoon, to keep Loomins lulled into complacency. The last thing he wanted was to arouse the man's suspicions. "I once tried to hitch a ride on a ten foot tiger shark and got bitten for my trouble," he added jestfully, raising his forearm to show Loomins the prominent scar. As Loomins surveyed the old wound, Jake took the opportunity to assess the man up close. It was in his nature never to underestimate an opponent.

"Never a wise thing to do," Loomins grumbled, lifting his eyes to Jake's face. "What's your name?"

"Nick Henderson." Jake had originally planned to use another name, but something that had been nagging at him made him use the identity of Grahm's testy assistant.

"So what was your starting point before ending up here?" Loomins asked, his gaze suddenly falling on the Kawasaki and studying it oddly.

"Southwest side of Tortuga Island," Jake stated. "Buddy of mine has an estate right there on the beach. Thought I'd do a little exploring, maybe see Navassa Island."

"You're lucky I found you," Loomins said icily, his tone chastising. "Venturing out into the open sea on a tiny craft like that is a dumb thing to do, especially when you're flirting with someone else's life besides your own. There's no telling what might have happened to this lovely young wife of yours if I hadn't come along when I did."

Jake got his first inkling of the man's subtlety. Loomins was both testing his relationship with Destiny and trying to curry favor with her by acting the part of the heroic savior. *Excellent,* Jake thought. *The man was lowering his guard already.*

Jake found it necessary to elicit a stupid lopsided grin. "Like I said, I've always had this reckless streak, but Destiny is not my wife."

Loomins' looked back at the girl with renewed interest. "My mistake," he apologized without sincerity, practically puffing up with delight. "I somehow got the impression you two were newlyweds on your honeymoon."

"No, just friends out for an afternoon spin," Jake clarified breezily.

Loomins looked back at the Kawasaki again, as if remembering something he had seen. "Why's the waverunner have those brackets up front?"

Jake had anticipated such a query. "My friend's an avid photographer. Those brackets are designed for mounting photographic equipment. You should see his house. It's alive with pictures showing tropical settings all along Tortuga and northern Haiti."

Loomins nodded as if satisfied with the explanation. "Uh huh!" Abruptly, he glanced at his watch. "I seem to be getting behind schedule. Come on back here and sit yourself down," he said, pointing to the short flight of stairs leading from the swim platform onto the Bertram's rear deck.

The girl was first up, and as Jake climbed onto the deck, he got his first glimpse of Hermes and Aphrodite. Both dolphins lay firmly strapped upon modified litters designed to restrict their movements. As Jake had hoped, Destiny said nothing.

"Interesting cargo you have there," Jake said, feigning ignorant curiosity over the creatures. "I never saw Beluga whales before."

Loomins let out a laugh filled with ridicule. "They're not Belugas, boy. Belugas are only found in cold Arctic waters. These are white bottlenose dolphins."

"I thought all dolphins were gray," Jake lied, hoping he wasn't overdoing the act.

Loomins appraised his trophies with a smug expression. "For the most part, that's true. But these babies are exceptionally rare, perhaps a brand new species never before seen."

Jake decided to test the man. "You mean because their skin is milky white?" He had to know just how much the man knew about these creatures.

Loomins stepped over to the nearest dolphin and inclined his head. "You ever see a dolphin with one of these?" he asked, reaching down and lifting the creature's left pectoral fin just enough to reveal a partially extended prehensile appendage protruding limply.

From the listlessness of both animals, Jake assumed they had been sedated with tranquilizers. Fighting the anger rising in him, he pretended astonishment. "Is that a hand?"

"Damned straight it's a hand," Loomins growled. "Each of these dolphins has two of them."

Jake shot a quick look at Destiny to see if she was staying calm. The girl's expression remained stoic as she gazed upon the captured creatures, although he detected a slight mistiness to her eyes. "I take it you're in the business of catching live dolphins," Jake said. "What do you do with them?"

Loomins released his hold on the dolphin and stared at Jake. "I sell them," he replied irritably. Turning in annoyance, he frowned angrily at two of the closest crewmen, both of whom Jake perceived to be Haitians. "I thought I told you to keep dousing these valuable specimens with seawater," he barked furiously. "You want this hot tropical sun to raise their core body temperatures. If they're not kept cool they'll die."

It became apparent to Jake that Loomins had a short fuse, but with the man's attention momentarily diverted, he took the opportunity to study the dolphins more closely. The eyelids of both cetaceans drooped noticeably. Hermes was the larger of the two creatures and the one Loomins had singled out to display the unusual appendage. The DBT unit that had been strapped to the albino's back was now gone, evidently removed by one of the boat's crew and stowed someplace.

Abruptly, Loomins turned back to Jake and looked at his watch again. "Try and amuse yourself for the time being," he grumbled, seemingly gaining control of his temper for the moment, "because that's about all the conversation you'll get outta me for now. Like I told you, I've got a schedule to maintain and, unfortunately, you're holding me up." Pointing to a large ice chest, he added, "Help yourselves to some cold beer if you're thirsty. Port-au-Prince is close to two hours away."

With that, Loomins spun around and began climbing a set of stairs leading to the bridge. As if forgetting something, he stopped and turned again. "Oh, and by the way," he said stiffly, locking eyes on Jake. "I would appreciate it if the two of you keep to the back deck and stay outta the way. Because of the potential liabilities involved, I don't usually let passengers have the run of my vessel." He paused, as if emphasizing the gravity of the request. "You never know if they'll do something dumb and get themselves hurt." Loomins let the veiled threat linger in the air a moment longer before turning and completing the climb. Ten seconds later, the boat's engine engaged noisily and the deck shifted underfoot as they got underway.

Feeling his thirst beginning to mount, Jake stepped over to the ice chest and lifted the cover, motioning Destiny to his side as he did so. Staring at a mixed batch of canned beverages interspersed among a mass of ice cubes, he assessed their current situation. "I think they drugged the dolphins," he said guardedly. Though the decibel level emanating from the vessel's engine was sufficiently loud to keep them from being overheard, he purposely avoided exposing his face to any of the nearby deckhands lest any of them be able to read lips. "Hermes and Aphrodite don't seem right. Are you able to talk with them?"

The girl gave a slight nod of her head, keeping her face turned away from the crew as well. "Both are barely able to communicate with me. These men shot some kind of sharp projectile into them and they became very weak."

"They were probably hit with tranquilizer darts. In their current state there's a good chance they'll drown even if we're able to free them and get them back in the water."

This bit of news did not sit well with Destiny. "Is there anything you can do?"

Jake looked over at the crewmen. There were three of them. "Hermes told you he had counted five men aboard this vessel, didn't he?"

"Yes."

"Well if his observation is correct, one man is still missing." Jake pondered this. Perhaps Loomins was not the type of man to leave anything to chance. With strangers aboard, it would be prudent to keep one man out of sight just in case the strangers had ill intentions. It was something Jake would have considered doing himself had he been in Loomins' shoes. "If we're going to do anything," he stressed, "it's crucial we find out where that fifth man is."

Destiny gazed up at him with soulful eyes. "How?"

Jake's mind moved into high gear, giving some thought to a standard military tactic used in the Seals. "We've got to create a diversion." Reaching down into the ice chest, he retrieved two Coca-colas and handed one to the girl. Popping the tab on the can he held, he took a swig. "Give me a moment to look around. There's got to be something aboard this vessel we can use."

Destiny grabbed Jake's arm. "The pod is on the way."

Jake gave this bit of news mild consideration, trying to figure what good it would do while the Bertram was underway. "You summoned them? When?"

"The moment we left the cove."

Jake gave her a bored nod, then stepped away. Making a show of stretching his arms and yawning deeply, he strolled past the deckhands, moving towards the Bertram's rear cabin. The three crewmen seemed not to notice, totally absorbed in carrying out Loomins orders. Wearing a bored expression on his face, he eyed his surroundings with a casual air. He quickly discovered that the windows to the rear cabin were tinted, obstructing his view of the cabin's interior and making him speculate whether he was currently being spied upon by the missing crewman from the other side of the glass.

A bulky object lay hidden under a heavy tarp situated to one side of the deck. Jake had noticed it earlier and had wondered what the tarp concealed. The glimmer of sunlight reflecting off something caught Jake's attention, prompting him to scrutinize the cause of it. Adjacent to the tarp, a tubular metallic barrel lay atop a pile of bunched up netting, its configuration closely resembling a handheld rocket launcher. Realizing there was something oddly familiar about what he was looking at, he studied it briefly before turning his head, mindful about drawing unwanted attention to himself. He suddenly understood how the albinos had been snared in the open ocean.

The object was a larger version of a webshot, a tool originally developed to capture wild animals without causing them injury. With a muzzle velocity of 100 feet per second, the device fired a net that expanded and enveloped the intended quarry, enfolding and restricting the movements of the creature unfortunate enough to be snared. Webshots had a short range, typically less than 40 feet, making it necessary that the shooter get close to the target he sought to bag. The device was sometimes used by law enforcement agencies when apprehending dangerous criminals, but Seal teams had also been known to employ the system, utilizing such technology to subdue an enemy combatant without wounding them. Some webshot systems had taglines that connected the launcher with the netting so that the captive animal could be retrieved.

Jake had fired a webshot during his stint with the Seals and was familiar with its effectiveness in neutralizing opponents who could then be interrogated. The system he remembered was a single-shot launcher with a 37-millimeter bore that discharged a 12-ounce projectile, giving the device a hefty kick when fired. Based on that experience, he was certain the larger webshot would have an even more powerful recoil than its smaller cousin, particularly since it would propel a missile carrying a net capable of entrapping a creature the size of Hermes. As if to confirm this, he stole another look at the pile of netting on which the webshot sat, judging the mesh to be strong enough to capture a creature nearly 12 feet in length and weighing close to 1000 pounds. Something else protruded from under the netting, and he scanned it fleetingly. The realization that he was looking at a webshot cartridge made his heart beat faster, and suddenly his mind scurried over the possibilities it represented.

How the men crewing the Sea Lion had been able to draw the albinos into the effective range of the webshot baffled Jake. On impulse, he again eyed the bulky object covered by the tarp, certain that these men had used something unique.

Turning, Jake looked back at Destiny. He was somewhat surprised to see her kneeling down between Hermes and Aphrodite, each of her hands touching the head of each creature. Even more surprising was the way the Haitian crewmen regarded her. They just stared, appearing unsure about the appropriateness of moving her out of the way. Destiny's eyes were closed in deep concentration, as if caught up in the midst of some unseen battle of the mind that required her entire focus.

With the crew's attention momentarily fixated on the girl, Jake decided it was now or never if he was going to make a move. Boldly, he stepped quickly to the door of the rear cabin and turned the knob, knowing what he would find on the other side. Closing the door behind him, he glanced to his right. Just as he had anticipated, a man wielding a carbine stood at the rear window. From the stunned expression on the man's face, Jake suspected he had been distracted in the same manner as the deckhands. Giving his opponent a fiendish grin, Jake pushed aside the rifle before it could be raised and landed a vicious kick that connected brutally with the man's stomach. With an almost imperceptible grunt, the man staggered backwards with the wind knocked from him. Following up on the attack, Jake snatched the weapon from the man's grasp and, in one smooth motion, clipped the man cleanly on the chin with the stock of the firearm. The man's body went slack almost immediately, but before his legs gave way, Jake caught him and gently lowered him to the floor. As the fallen foe lay comatose, something in the man's features made Jake do a doubletake. Though he was several years younger and sported a crooked nose, the man bore a striking resemblance to Ben Loomins.

Getting back to the business at hand, Jake turned and looked through the cabin's rear windows. The three deckhands were still preoccupied with the sight of Destiny kneeling between the albinos, seemingly unaware as to what had just taken place. With seasoned skill, Jake checked the carbine to see if it was loaded. Satisfied that a round was currently chambered in the weapon, he opened the cabin door and calmly sauntered back out onto the deck. One of the Haitians noticed him, abruptly going rigid when he saw the rifle pointed in his direction. Within moments, the other two men became cognizant of the threat Jake suddenly posed, and they too froze in fear. Wearing a devilish smile, Jake motioned the men over to the rear cabin where he made them lie facedown on the deck.

With the crew neutralized, Jake crouched down next to Destiny. "How're our friends doing?" he asked, looking cautiously above him for any sign of Loomins. The boat's engines continued to drone on monotonously in an unaltered tempo, giving him a partial assurance that the man at the helm was currently engrossed in piloting the vessel.

As if emerging from a deep sleep, Destiny opened her eyes and gazed wearily at Jake. "Their strength is returning," she replied, her tone carrying fatigue. "I think they'll be able to swim." Both dolphins stirred as she said this, and Jake sensed the creatures were now coming out of their drug-induced stupors.

Pulling the K-Bar from its sheath, Jake sliced the leather restraints holding each albino to its litter. Hermes was the first to fully revive, and Jake watched in amazement as the male extended its prehensile appendages to their fullest and began dragging himself along the deck in a series of waddling, flopping hops. A few seconds later, Aphrodite did the same, following Hermes to the rearmost section of the deck where access to the sea was easiest. One after the other, they reached up and grabbed hold of the starboard railing, heaving themselves over the boat's side and sending out a heavy spray as they hit the water.

Stunned by the impressive spectacle, Jake had difficulty finding his voice. "I think it's time we departed the company of these fine gentlemen." Guardedly, he glanced over at the deckhands as they continued to stare in wide-eyed astonishment at what they had just witnessed.

Destiny reached out and clutched Jake by the arm. She appeared physically drained. "Wait!" she said weakly. "There's something I must do first."

Jake was mystified. "What's that?"

"A man aboard this boat is dying. I have to help him."

A frown flooded Jake's face. "How do you know that?"

"I felt his pain."

"Where is he?"

Destiny pointed to the rear cabin. "In there."

Jake had difficulty accepting this news. "If it's the man I kayoed, I only gave him a love tap."

Destiny looked up at him, her expression devoid of judgement or accusation of any kind. "I cannot leave until I help him," she insisted.

Though her voice lacked potency, Jake could feel a powerful sense of purpose underlying her conviction. Momentarily caught in the grip of indecision, he glanced cautiously toward the bridge as he listened to the beat of the engines pushing the vessel steadily onward. Up until now, everything had played out in their favor, but their mission was not yet over. From experience, he knew how quickly that could change. "Alright," he agreed. "But try to hurry."

Gesturing with the rifle for the deckhands to get to their feet, Jake herded the men into the cabin with Destiny following slowly behind him. "Stand over there!" he ordered the Haitians. "If you behave, I promise no one will get hurt."

With diminished vigor, the girl moved to where the unconscious man lay and placed a hand on his forehead. Jake could see the man's breathing was labored and that his skin had paled considerably.

"What's wrong with him?" Jake needed to know, fending off the guilt he was suddenly feeling.

Destiny did not immediately answer, letting her fingers roam languorously over the man's cranium as if searching for something. "He...he has a ruptured blood vessel," she finally replied. Her normally mellifluous voice was languid and lacking vitality.

"I caused it?"

Destiny stopped momentarily to look back at Jake, her eyes full of sympathy. "This man had a preexisting condition, a...a brain aneurysm. Any blow to the head would have triggered it." Focusing her gaze back on the man, she placed both hands on his head and closed her eyes, once again seeming to draw on some hidden force from deep within.

Jake kept his eyes on the crewmen, careful not to let his vigilance relax, but at the same time attempting to get a read on what kind of a threat they might present. From the manner in which Loomins had spoken to them, there was a good chance they would not be eager participants in trying to interfere. As he studied their faces, however, it soon became apparent they were caught up in awed fascination as they watched the girl, almost as though in worship.

Anxiety began to take hold of Jake as Destiny continued to kneel over the man. He sensed she wasn't her usual self. Even with the Islamic militant he had captured, the girl had not taken this long to heal the injury. Then it hit him. Prior to this excursion, the albinos had always assisted the girl during healings. But now she was working alone. He could see it was visibly sapping her, sucking the very life force from her body.

With sudden concern, he moved to her side as she began to slump lethargically over her patient, but as he did so the man let out a prolonged gasp. The deathly paleness that had dominated the man's pallor moments earlier abruptly vanished, and slowly his eyes fluttered dazedly open, all signs of comprehension still absent from them. In that moment, Jake was certain the man would live, that whatever infirmity had plagued him before was now completely repaired.

Jake assisted the girl to her feet, wanting only to get her back aboard the Kawasaki and put distance between them and the Sea Lion. But when Destiny faltered on unsteady legs, he realized she would not be able to walk. "Time to leave," he uttered, slinging her over one shoulder while maintaining his hold on the carbine. Quickly, he carried her from the cabin and moved across the back deck. He had almost reached the short flight of stairs that descended to the swim platform when the engines suddenly changed pitch, falling off sharply to an idle. Underfoot, the deck shifted as the vessel lost momentum, and with it, an angry voice bellowed. "Hold it right there or, by god, I'll shoot you where you stand!"

Jake stopped in midstride and froze.

"Drop the rifle and turn around!" Ben Loomins ordered. "Try anything and I'll blow your fucking head off."

Jake did as he was told, knowing their luck had changed for the worse.

"What'd you do with my dolphins?" Loomins yelled, his eyes seething with rage as he climbed down from the bridge. The magnum pistol he carried was unholstered and aimed directly at Jake's head.

Jake knew he had to be careful how he replied. Loomins was beside himself with madness, and the wrong choice of words might put the man over the edge. With Destiny slumped over his shoulder in her current state, a remembrance of Afghanistan entered his mind, and he wondered if a similar outcome was drifting in on him with this sudden shift in the winds of fate. Overcome with these thoughts, he just stood there and said nothing as Loomins moved to within five feet of him with murder in his eyes.

- 45 -

The cove was not the same as Jacob looked out over the water. With the exception of two injured grays that were still recovering, the remainder of the pod was gone, including Destiny. This was not good, he thought. The pod had a pivotal role to play in bringing the plan to fruition, and Destiny was the catalyst that would make this possible. She was the key structural member upon which all the others balanced, the main pillar crucial to holding aloft their hopes and dreams, the very future of all life on the planet. Without her, everything would crumple and collapse under forces that were much too powerful to stop.

Jacob turned his thoughts to the man called Jake Javolyn. When he had first set eyes on him, he had been nearly certain he was looking at the man depicted in the cave painting. Never one to jump headlong to conclusions, however, he had found it necessary to test this assumption. On the ride back from Navassa he had formulated a scheme to assess Jake's moral rectitude, although Destiny had originally harbored scruples about carrying it out. Having healed Jake's arm, Destiny had already gotten a glimpse of the man's fundamental nature, and she was convinced Jake was the protector. Jacob, on the other hand, was not so quick to accept this. He had to remind the girl what a harsh mistress temptation could be, often corrupting otherwise good and noble men through the lure of incredible riches. After much urging he had finally had his way, persuading Destiny to bring the matter to the pod's attention. It had been decided that Achilles would show Jake the thurentra and gauge the man's reaction to the sight of precious metals littering the base of the hybrid organism. And though Achilles had told Jake that the production of gold and platinum held no benefit, from the young albino's perspective it was not altogether a lie. Gold and platinum were most commonly used as a medium of exchange. By themselves, such commodities provided no direct benefit to those possessing them since the metals constituted neither a viable source of nourishment nor consumable energy.

Jacob nodded inwardly without any regrets at having revealed the most alluring facet of the thurentra to a total stranger. It had been a risk, but one worth taking. Jake Javolyn had so far demonstrated a remarkable degree of moral integrity in refraining from making off with some of the riches he had seen. That made the man altogether rare, and one to be appreciated all the more. Javolyn had something they all needed if the plan was to succeed, and that was a willingness to attack evil head-on with no misgivings about using deadly force. It was a trait they all lacked.

As he pondered such thoughts, Jacob glanced around the cove. Both Dr. Grahm and Jeffrey Parker were still busy at one end of the beach fiddling with some of the electronic gadgetry they had brought ashore. Turning his head, he caught sight of Nick Henderson donning mask, fins and snorkel, apparently preparing for a swim away from the beach. He knew what the graduate student was up to. He had seen him fin out to where the thurentra lay submerged earlier in the day. And although Hercules had shooed him away, he had the feeling the contentious youth had already seen the glitter of gold beneath the water. Realizing his mistake in leaving such wealth unattended, he had asked the albinos to collect the glimmering grains and hide them in the usual place. Normally they did this only once every four weeks, but one could never be overly cautious, and now they they were scooping up the grains once each hour to make sure a noticeable pile did not accumulate. By his estimation, the thurentra was currently filtering out approximately eight pounds of highly concentrated precious metal from seawater each day. At most, Henderson would only see a few grains of the stuff settled in the sand, byproducts of the thurentra's strange metabolic process.

The thurentra's ability to collect such valuable elements had initially baffled Jacob when deposits of the metals first began accumulating about five years earlier. Through research, he had learned that seawater normally contained extremely small concentrations of gold in soluble form. Values ranged worldwide, with average concentrations reportedly running at approximately 13 parts per trillion. Through rough calculations, he had estimated the volume of seawater the hybrid organism was capable of drawing up from the deep each day, determining that the observed amounts of gold harvested would have been impossible to produce based on such negligible concentrations. The only other explanation Jacob could come up with was that the thurentra tentacles had worked their way into gold-enriched layers of sulfide compounds typically found at great ocean depths. He knew that the Caribbean Sea descended to a depth of four miles in the Cayman Trench whose eastern end was less than 300 kilometers from the cove's location. Continuing to delve into the subject, Jacob discovered that gold ores were often associated with sulfide deposits formed by hydrothermal vents commonly found in extremely deep regions of the sea where the earth's crustal plates were thinnest and moving apart. In such locations, superheated seawater emanating from cracks and fissures in the ocean floor dissolved minerals and metals in much higher concentrations than could occur in cold water. Upon reaching the frigid seafloor waters, dissolved precious metals and minerals precipitated out of solution, forming chimney-like vent structures, which eventually collapsed and formed again. Over long periods of time, immense mounds of these structures tended to build up, predominantly composed of iron and sulfide compounds. Sulfur-oxidizing bacteria found along these vents also had the potential of concentrating gold to even higher levels.

Although such facts lent ample support as to how the thurentra was able to produce such high-grade gold and platinum, Jacob failed to come up with a plausible explanation as to why the jellyfish-like creature was able to separate only these elements from the other metals and minerals, eventually bringing them to the surface waters in a purified state. Then again, finding an answer really didn't matter to him. The introduction of the precious metals into Gaia had opened new doors of possibility, both bad and good, depending on how you looked at them.

Jacob's mullings suddenly shifted to the mass genocide of the Tainos. Only a small portion of the once thriving population had survived, hidden away in the relative safety of this sanctuary long ago, of that he had no doubts. Concealed within the cave behind the falls at the far end of the cove, a mysterious linkage existed between the past and present. If word ever got out about what was produced at the bottom of the cove, he knew Gaia would be overrun with treasure hunters and soldiers of fortune, ultimately falling victim to the destructive nature of humanity's greed, something it had been spared from in earlier times, but that was mere speculation on his part. And inasmuch as he abhorred the potential harm the metal could bring to the pod, he had no choice in using it if the plan was ever to succeed. By his estimation they already had close to five tons of gold and two tons of platinum stored away within the cove and almost twice that amount at Navassa. On today's market, that equated to more than half a billion in U.S. dollars, enough to finance the future of the new species and a new beginning for Haiti. As time went on, he knew such staggering wealth would steadily increase as the thurentras continued to strain more and more metal from the ocean depths.

Jacob sighed with resignation as he watched Henderson flounder out into deeper water. He had warned everyone about touching the thurentra. To some people, the electric shock imparted by the organism could be fatal. In some ways, the thurentra acted like a huge capacitor, building an electrical charge much the same way certain types of eels were able to do. Aside from manufacturing hydrogen and gold, the creature had the capacity to produce electricity, and although he had been tempted to use such free energy to light his small cabin, he had refrained from doing so to avoid becoming dependent on the use of it. For the most part, he preferred to keep living standards within the cove simple, holding comforts to a minimum. To live ascetically was in harmony with his true nature. Aside from leaving his spirit uncorrupted by outside influences, it also avoided drawing unwanted attention that might otherwise complicate and disrupt the goals he, Amphitrite and Destiny had set for themselves.

Floating at anchor to the north side of the cove, Javolyn's vessel did little to console Jacob's misgivings about letting these strangers into his tiny kingdom. He suddenly berated himself for his possessiveness, reminding himself that Gaia was not his. Gaia was simply a concept he had rationalized through both observation and a wild stretch of the imagination. But the human mind, his mind, coupled with other unique intellects that were in some respects much more powerful than his, had fashioned possibilities that could be made real. There was a budding fantasy here, intensely envisioned and believed by those nurturing it, one that had the potential of becoming all too real in the not too distant future. Though beyond his understanding and control, certain things were meant to happen, the bringing together of circumstances that were rapidly providing the fuel for the fierce battle that was yet to come. Amphitrite had prophesized this. Both the stage and the props had been set, and they were about to act out their parts in the brewing storm of good versus evil that was swiftly building. But the script had not yet been set, something Amphitrite had also foretold. She had warned of the delicate balance and uncertainty woven into the cosmic structure. There would be choices to be made and actions to be carried out, with any wrong decision leading to disaster.

Jacob let his mind drift over what was at stake, instinctively knowing that taking the lead in a project of this magnitude would always be a risky endeavor, particularly when such leadership remained hidden from public scrutiny. But leaving both the dolphins and Haiti to fend for themselves was beyond consideration. He realized that he and his cousin still had another option open to them in spite of the distance they had so far traveled down the chosen path. Deep down, though, he understood that to retreat in pursuit of an easier life would have left him and Emmanuel devoid of all courage and ideals, something each of them would not and could not let happen no matter what the circumstances. Their course was now set, their conviction unshakable. They were going to act against tyranny, poverty and oppression. They would strive toward making significant positive changes to a world in desperate need of it.

As Jacob reflected on these things, he wondered how Emmanuel was making out. His cousin should have been back by now from a trip to Anguilla where he had completed setting up the corporate vehicle that would carry them to their objectives. Anguilla was the ideal place for registering an international corporation, mainly because the small Caribbean island required no corporate taxes. In essense, it was the ideal tax-free haven. All of them would be shareholders in *Tursiops Worldwide*: Destiny, Amphitrite, Emmanuel, Lucette, and he, himself. But it was the new species of albino dolphin that would hold the major interest in the budding venture. It was a concept that had originally taken root in the albino minds some years earlier when Jacob had thought it wise to teach them everything he knew about capitalism, big business and corporate structure. *Tursiops* would provide both the impetus and system required to attain their goals, and that was mainly achieving a much higher standard of living for the downtrodden masses.

Jacob smiled to himself as he thought about all the good a cash-rich corporation could do on the international level. He had to be realistic, using a practical approach to the way the modern world worked. Wielded properly, powerful corporations had clout, having the potential to manipulate heads of state and nations into serving their interests. The interests of Tursiops would remain altruistic, run by entities incapable of corruption. Tursiops would work in harmony with the ocean environment, developing and implementing alternative sources of clean renewable energy from the sea, and producing commodities that could be sold on the world market. If Tursiops worked out according to their envisioned plan, it would establish marine-based colonies all over the earth, predominantly in international waters. From an economic standpoint, it would provide vast amounts of energy and food at minimal cost to a consuming world by tapping into the oceanic reservoirs where almost limitless nutrients and previously untapped energy abounded.

Tursiops would unleash a flood tide of food, commodities and services revolving around sea mining and mariculture, initially bringing in an estimated $12 billion a year that would ultimately enrich Haiti and other poor countries. Conceptually, here was the island nation's best hope for escape from its plight of perpetual wretchedness, an opportunity that just might steer it clear from total economic collapse. Through the production of hydrogen, magnesium, and distilled water alone, sizeable revenues could be achieved that would finance the development of new technologies. Previous limits on food productivity resulting from land-based economies would be surpassed to an almost explosive degree through the use of maricultural and ocean farming, not only greatly improving the standard of living for Haiti, but for all nations of the world. Such an enterprise would provide a huge number of jobs for the poor, sprouting forth an economy of scale never before seen. In its wake, hunger would all but vanish, with a new social structure emerging and evolving in total harmony with the planetary ecosystem. A partnership would develop between man and dolphin that would open the doors to new horizons in scientific research. Spurred on by the albino super-intelligence, the advancement of science and technology would accelerate, with meaningful breakthroughs occurring at a faster rate. In the sea colonies, crime, brutality and social disorder would give way to intellectual, artistic, philosophical and spiritual pursuits, setting the individual free from the lone struggle for survival that had characterized old and contemporary societies. In short, a new beginning in human evolution would commence, unrivaled by anything that had come before it. Through the combined leadership of the company's board of directors, Tursiops would empower both Haitians and cetaceans to transform their lives in a single generation.

Such thoughts tended to heighten Jacob's expectations of the future. Sometimes you had to hit rock bottom before you could begin the arduous climb back up. Here was Haiti's way out of the hole it had become mired in. If everything went to plan, no longer would it be suppressed and tortured by successive waves of domestic and international politics that washed away all hope. Innovation would pave the way for change.

Yes, Jacob reasoned, *although such a grand undertaking would be immensely difficult to accomplish, it would not be unworkable. They just had to be resolute in holding onto their conviction, to keep believing the idea was possible. Over the years he had learned that anything was possible as long as you believed in it with every fiber of your being. And though it was Esmerelda who had first tried to make him understand this, it was Amphitrite who had actually made him feel the absolute power underlying it. There would be no try, no meager stab at hoping for the best, for such outlooks were too diluted in ambivalence to have any chance of success. No, the fantasy would be made altogether real by stripping away all negative leanings, all doubts. The power of their minds would work together, both human and delphine, to forge the path of their trajectories through time-space. Sentient intelligence would be used to mold the future. The mind was truly an integral part of the cosmos, and somewhere deep within this strange domain of seemingly endless chaos and swirling motes, an eerie symmetrical type of order existed that could be manipulated through conscious, and perhaps even unconscious, thought. Yes, perhaps there was a dimension where physical laws and mysticism eventually merged, intertwining and combining into a simple* structure, one that determined a reality of our choosing, a place immune to the winds of chance.

Movement aboard the Avenging Angel caught Jacob's eye, unhinging him of these thoughts. He watched as the hulking giant, Zimbola, led the man Jake Javolyn had captured to the vessel's rear platform, apparently giving the captive a breath of fresh air. Taking a moment to study the large man, he realized how fortunate Javolyn was to have such a devoted shipmate, judging that the man's outward appearance could be somewhat misleading to anyone who did not know him. Though physically imposing and obviously possessing great strength, there was also another side to the Jamaican that somehow reminded Jacob of Hercules. Zimbola, he was certain, was one of those exceptionally rare men that would follow a person to whom they held allegiance into the very bowels of hell itself. Here was an individual who would stand steadfast behind Javolyn against all odds no matter what the circumstances, with little or no concern for his own personal safety. Unwavering loyalty, Jacob knew, was an uncommonly noble quality in human beings, a trait to be admired and treasured whenever one was fortunate enough to find it. Strangely enough, it had a tendency to show up in the most unlikely places.

Shifting his eyes to the man being led by Zimbola, Jacob became aware of the painting in the captive's hands. To the Haitian, this was not surprising. He recalled what had taken place minutes before Jake Javolyn had bolted from the cove with Destiny seated behind him on the waverunner. Javolyn had hurriedly asked Jacob if he could borrow the painting produced by Achilles. "The painting is not mine to lend," Jacob had told him with measured solemnity, already sensing what Javolyn intended to do with it. "Only Achilles can give such permission." But before Javolyn could redirect the question to the youngest member of the pod, Achilles had quickly swam over to him, holding the painting above the water. *"I would be honored if you would keep this, Jay Jay,"* the dolphin had said, his speech coming out in a high-pitched squeal.

So Jake Javolyn hopes to turn the Islamist by means of the albino art, Jacob thought to himself as he observed the bearded captive holding the painting in both hands. Even from where he stood, he could discern the look of deep contemplation etched on the man's face. As Jacob witnessed the scene taking place at the stern end of Javolyn's vessel, two conflicting questions struck him. *If the man was truly a follower of Islam, was his faith strong enough to sustain itself in the face of the strange effect such art had on some people? Or was it that the man was simply unhappy with who he was, what he had become?* Here was a test, one that might lend support to Jake Javolyn's previous assertion, though to Jacob it did not make any sense. This made him reexamine it all over again. *Was the man a blind follower of distorted Islamic tenets, false doctrines concocted* by militant zealots for the purpose of satisfying hate through the mass murder of innocents? Had the man actually been part of a team set on carrying out some vile deed of destruction?

Sitting down in the sand, Jacob studied Zimbola's charge at a distance with the impartial eyes of the true scientist, looking for any overt signs in the way the man was being affected by what lay on the canvas. Not having anything better to do at the moment, he continued to stare out of curiosity, trying to ignore the restless anxiety churning in the back of his mind over the fate of Hermes and Aphrodite.

- 46 -

The leader of the three mujahideens continued to stare at Raduyev with those same sad eyes the Chechen well remembered. Raduyev fought back the scowl that surged up from the pit of his stomach, meeting the Pashtun's striking blue eyes with a fierce, defiant glare of his own. He would not be fooled by Sherkhan's seemingly downcast manner, knowing what lay just below the surface.

"You were late," Sherkhan stated, finally breaking the brooding silence he had manifested ever since being met at sea. Though his voice came out in a bland monotone, Raduyev sensed a subtle reprimand in the tone. "The captain of the freighter was very displeased. He did not like having to wait as long as he did for you to show up. Had you forgotten our planned rendezvous was to take place under the cover of night and not in broad daylight?"

Raduyev was not about to tolerate any criticism. "A small problem arose that delayed us," he retorted testily. "What does it matter, anyway?"

Sherkhan's eyes narrowed. "The captain risked drawing attention to his vessel," he pointed out.

"But that did not happen," Raduyev scoffed.

"A ship flying the Yemeni flag and drifting out in the middle of the Caribbean without the engines engaged is very conspicuous," Sherkhan went on blandly. "It could easily cause passing vessels or aircraft to come and see if there is a problem. We have a schedule to maintain and you put this mission in jeopardy by exposing this submarine." Pausing, his normally morose features abruptly hardened in preparation for the words that followed. "I would like to think the right man is leading us." Letting out a seemingly bored sigh, he added, "Kalid tells me you had taken this vessel to the Haitian coast where you lost Bashir. Is this true, and if it is, for what purpose did you make this unscheduled trip?"

Raduyev shot a look of contempt at his second in command before turning his gaze back to the Pashtun. "I warn you not to insult or berate me. His Supreme Holiness, Osama Bin Laden, himself, may he live forever, has personally placed me in charge of this mission. By insulting me, you insult him."

Sherkhan touched his forehead and gave a slight bow. "Forgive me, my Muslim brother. For all eternity may you reside at the right hand of Allah in the next life that awaits you. God is great, and he will surely reward you for bearing on your shoulders this most sacred duty. As you have already proven, you are a great and noble holy warrior, one of the very strongest among us. Your skill as a fighter is fast becoming legendary, making some among us believe a man like yourself could only have been forged by the Almighty Allah to carry out his work. Guided by your hand, we will bring the Great Satan to his knees, and if God wills it, perhaps even inflict a mortal blow to Islam's greatest enemy. I, along with these two other servants of Allah, have come to aid you as was planned. We are fully prepared to follow you in fulfilling this most holy task, and if need be, to shed our blood in the sanctity of martyrdom. I only ask that you do not let personal vendettas cloud your judgement."

Raduyev glanced maliciously at Kalid once more. It was apparent Kalid had told Sherkhan everything. But the Pashtun had shown respect with his words of appeasement, and slowly, Raduyev allowed his heated glare to cool. "There is much work still needing to be done," he finally said, "considerably more than our small band can complete in so short a period of time. We will require many more strong backs if we are to meet our timetable. That is why I have arranged to have some more people brought here."

Sherkhan showed surprise. "Why was I not told of this before?"

"You had no need to know of this," Raduyev replied coldly.

"These people...they are Muslims?"

Raduyev was in no mood for any more insurrection, unable to keep the sarcasm from his voice. "I do not think you will find many people of the Islamic faith among these islanders. No, a sizeable contingent of heathen infidels will be brought to us. We will use them as slaves to speed up the backbreaking labor needed to clear away large amounts of rock within these caverns."

From the Pashtun's expression, Raduyev could tell his old comrade in arms was not very comfortable with this idea. "And how will these people be brought here?" Sherkhan asked.

"They will arrive on the southern shore of this island, ferried in by boat two days from now."

"Under the cover of darkness?"

Raduyev scowled deeply, his eyes flashing with anger once again. He was growing tired of Sherkhan's questions. "We will meet them at midnight and escort them down here through the passage that extends to the island's surface." He cast his eyes to one end of the underground chamber where a string of electric lights disappeared into a narrow crevice set back in the rock. "Some of these passageways will have to be widened if we are to assemble and then install the second delivery system clear of these caves."

Sherkhan nodded with mild satisfaction, appearing quite at home in his present surroundings. With the exception of the deep pool of water dominating the center of the chamber, the place was not unlike the rocky underground fortresses he had spent so much time living in back along the Pakistani border. He let his eyes roam approvingly over the length and breadth of the cavern that housed *Allah's Sword*. "Osama would be pleased to see what you have already accomplished. You have chosen well in establishing such a base. From here, you will be able to carry out any number of missions undetected."

A satanic grin replaced the scowl that had been preponderating Raduyev's face, ameliorated all the more by the strange glow cast by the electric bulbs lighting the subterranean grotto. "It will be the first strike conducted from this sanctuary that will be the most important. God willing, we should be able to launch our attack on schedule."

"Then you have already located the weapon?" Sherkhan speculated, his normally insipid voice feeling strangely tense within his own throat.

"Yes, the coordinates were very accurate."

Sherkhan glanced around again. "How will you bring it up? I see nothing at your disposal that can lift a weapon of that size."

Raduyev indicated the crates that were currently being removed from the sub by the other men. "That is the means by which we will lift the weapon."

Sherkhan stared blankly, not understanding Raduyev's meaning.

"I have struck an accord with others who have no love for the Great Satan," the Chechen explained. "They will provide the machinery for bringing the weapon up from the depths. The heroin you have brought will be a down payment on the use of their ship and winches. Once the bomb is recovered, the bomb will be exchanged for the remainder of the heroin aboard the Spirit of Aden."

Once again, Sherkhan's manner became uneasy. "Can these people be trusted?"

"Their very cupidity will keep their affiliation with us safe. Like most infidels, they are blinded by greed. They salivate for a continuing supply of the white heroin, which is in great demand on the black markets of America and Europe. It is these people who will give us money and other necessities in exchange for this much sought after narcotic. For the time being they will serve as an important ally, one that will increase our chances of success. These same people will provide us with the slave labor we so desperately need."

The expression on Sherkhan's face reverted back to one of melancholy. "What about the Haitian colonel? Can he be trusted to guard our secret?"

A malicious little laugh sprang from Raduyev's lips, echoing eerily within the confines of the cavern. "The man's hunger for power will keep him silent. He seeks to seize control of Haiti once the Americans are preoccupied with the death and destruction we will unleash upon them."

The Chechen smirked inwardly as he remembered the havoc created by Hurricane Katrina after it had laid waste New Orleans in 2005. Bloated by complacency and the bungling of inept bureaucrats, the United States government had been ill prepared to take on such a crisis, failing miserably in the way it had handled the devastation and chaos in the wake of the monster storm. The blow they now planned to inflict would be far worse, ultimately precipitating anarchy of apocalyptic dimensions. After that, Iran would step in, using its newly acquired nuclear capability to finish the job.

Gaining control of the glee taking hold of him, Raduyev grew serious again as he gave Sherkhan's question more thought. "You were not informed that it was the Haitian colonel who had offered us the weapon?"

Sherkhan shook his head slowly. "During the last year I have had little contact with our exalted leaders, spending most of my time eluding capture by the Americans." The Pashtun abruptly fell pensive, seeming to mull something weighing heavily on him. "So it would appear this colonel is using us as a tool to satisfy his own ambitions, much the way we are using these infidels you speak of to bring up the weapon."

"The man's feeble grab for power is of little concern to us," Raduyev replied, punctuating it with another small laugh. His mind rested briefly on the staggering stipulations Bin Laden had agreed to in order to procure the bomb. The extent of the Colonel's greed stunned the imagination. For one, there was the down payment of $50 million in euros deposited in a discreet Cayman bank account controlled by the Colonel. Then there was the Yemeni arms dealer they had set up in Port-au-Prince to stockpile the weapons the Colonel would require. Both of these things Bin Laden had readily arranged in order to learn the bomb's location. But then there was the delicate multi-party deal Bin Laden had been able to broker with North Korea and Hezbollah in order to ensure the success of their plan, a multifaceted transaction in which the Colonel would also be a beneficiary. But Bin Laden had been getting short of funds as it was, and he had thought it economically prudent to resell the bomb to Hezbollah at an exorbitant profit, figuring Iran's scientists could get it in working order far quicker than than his own people. And finally there had been the other two items the Colonel was to receive once they had the bomb in their possession.

Raduyev dismissed these thoughts, knowing Bin Laden would be highly displeased if these last two items failed to be delivered, for they would still need the Colonel's cooperation in the aftermath of the first strike. Ever since Afghanistan had fallen, his people had needed a new country from which to operate with impunity, and Haiti was the perfect country from which to plan and execute renewed attacks against the United States.

"Let him set himself up as a king," Raduyev grunted. "Eventually we will take control of every island nation within the Caribbean, converting all those who do not oppose us to the rapture of Islam." He paused, and his face broke out in a vicious scowl. "And the ones that choose to oppose us we will crush."

For the first time since meeting up with Raduyev, Sherkhan elicited a smile. It was a smile that told Raduyev how much common ground both men shared, an expression of resolute purpose. But lurking beneath it, Raduyev sensed there was something else, something cold and calculating. He sighed inwardly, resigned to the burden of leadership. So be it, he would be careful around Sherkhan. This mission rested solely on his shoulders, and rightfully so. Sherkhan had been correct when he had fawningly stated that he, Yeslam Raduyev, had been forged by the Almighty Allah to carry out such a holy undertaking. He was by far the strongest warrior among them. And though he lacked the depth of religious conviction held by the Pashtun, it was he that would be the one to make all the decisions, the one that would alter mankind's history by paving the way for the Islamic theocracy yet to come in this part of the world. Once the Great Satan fell, all the other western nations would topple like dominos. One by one, they would come under Muslim control, falling to the dictates of Islamic law.

All at once, the thought of Javolyn squeezed in on him like an oppressive black cloud, reminding him he still had some unfinished business to take care of. The trip back from the Haitian coast had been difficult on him, and he had been forced to swallow yet another humiliating defeat at the hands of his nemesis. But it was then that he was able to piece together the circumstances that had led Javolyn to this region of the world. He had overheard tidbits of conversation between Javolyn, Daniels and Myers during the Seal mission led by Captain Sheridan. It all made sense. Having disposed of the irksome little Jew did little to console his dissatisfaction. No matter what it took, he made himself a vow that he would not rest until he killed Javolyn. But right now he had more pressing duties that required his attention.

Reminding himself about the deal he had made with Ortega, he suddenly found solace in the edge it gave him. He thought about it some more. Maybe it was possible Javolyn could be brought to him, one way or the other. Raduyev had carried out his end of the bargain by carefully recording the location where he had last seen the strange white dolphins, the place where Bashir had disappeared. For such information, Ortega had agreed to get him one hundred drums of badly needed diesel fuel, some of which would be necessary to replace what he had expended in taking the sub across the Windward Passage. Ortega was a man much like himself, a man not to be denied the pleasure of revenge. But if Ortega could not get Javolyn, he just might succeed in capturing the girl that had ridden the dolphin, whoever she was. Ortega, he had guessed, had more than a simple desire for retribution regarding the girl. No, he had sensed something more. The Colombian had seemed especially interested in both the girl and the creatures she had been seen with. Yes, it just might work, he told himself. With the girl as bait, perhaps Javolyn could be lured right into his hands.

As Raduyev entertained these thoughts, he was unaware of the depraved grin that had worked itself onto his face and the strange manner in which Sherkhan was studying him. Vaguely, he became cognizant of an oddly familiar sound reverberating within the grotto, and all at once he realized it was the sound of his own laughter. This did not disturb him, for sooner or later he knew he would have his vengeance.

- 47 -

Ortega climbed up to the helipad amid the San Carlo's superstructure, weary from the oppressive heat and humidity. It was late afternoon in the harbor of Port-au-Prince and the sun was nearing the final stages of its descent beyond the western horizon. Upon seeing Fernando still at work repairing the damaged turbine, Ortega's fatigue abruptly evaporated, replaced by a savage burst of rage. "How much longer?" he roared impatiently, the extended delay becoming unbearable.

Fernando jumped up with a start. This was the third time in the last two hours his boss had come up to take inventory of his progress. The pilot hated being in Ortega's line of fire, knowing what could happen when the man's temper flared. The fact that he was a far better pilot than Pedro did little to make him feel safe as Cardoza's lieutentant glared at him with malice in his eyes.

"Another fifteen minutes and she'll be flyable, boss," he said nervously, barely finding his voice.

"Then I'll be back up fifteen minutes from now," Ortega growled. "Have the blades spinning and be ready to go!" Turning on his heels, he started to climb back down but suddenly stopped. "Tell me, Fernando, how difficult would it be to rig this bird with an electronic gattling gun?"

The weapon to which Ortega was referring was something Fernando had spoken of in past conversations with a few members of the San Carlo crew, usually over a mug of ale in some sleazy backwater cantina infesting one port of call or another. Having worked as a helicopter mechanic in the U.S. Army for more than twenty years, Fernando had considerable knowledge about mounting sophisticated weaponry to military aircraft. At the age of 17, he had served in Vietnam and had retrofitted Hueys and LOHs with M134 miniguns, which could spew 7.62mm rounds at a rate of up to 4000 per minute.

"It can be done, but it'll stick out like udders on a cow on a helicopter this small. That type of gun is normally mounted on a chopper's port side and has a tendency to impart a heavy counterclockwise yaw to the aircraft when fired."

"I'll be the one to worry about that," Ortega admonished harshly. "I am making the arrangements to procure such a weapon. After what happened yesterday, I think it would be wise if we had such a capability."

"But what if we were to get boarded by the U.S. Coast Guard?" Fernando objected meekly. He knew full well the risk Ortega's suggestion posed. Once mounted to the aircraft, disconnecting such a system and effectively hiding it before it came under the scrutiny of a boarding party would be highly difficult.

Ortega stared back, smiling coldly. "I'm sure you'll figure out how to get around that."

Fernando felt like a trapped animal as he watched Ortega's head disappear below the platform. Almost three years had gone by since he had found employment with these people, and as he had come to learn, a group comprised of the most sadistic homicidal maniacs he had ever known. In Vietnam he had seen how the stress of battle and escalating body counts could harden most men, reducing some to what amounted to cold-blooded killers devoid of all emotion or compassion. But members of the Cardoza clan were far worse. They were a mean-spirited bunch, sharing a common passion for killing and deriving some kind of perverted joy out of the sight of suffering and death.

At the time of his recruitment by the Colombians, Fernando had been completely ignorant about the true nature of the organization, only knowing the pay was greater than anything he could ever hope to garner back in the States and that within five years he would be able to retire, living the good life on the beachfront property he would eventually purchase back in Florida. He well remembered the excitement he had felt over his good fortune when he had first found his current job, but as he recalled it now, he knew that early retirement would never be an option open to him. Ortega would see to that. It was too late for him to get out, his flying and and mechanical skills much too valuable for the drug ring to let him go.

Fernando dropped his introspections and went back to work on the aircraft, realizing he had been dwelling on his current predicament way too long. But as he turned a bolt, he could not help but examine the various ways he might be able to escape the Cardoza ring for good. There was a moral decay all about him, far more encompassing and offensive to the senses than the overpowering stench of rotting fish that pervaded every corner of the vessel he was forced to live on. With one exception, he hated the miscreants who crewed the San Carlo. But he had managed to keep such hatred under wraps and well guarded, not wanting to end up as shark bait or a meal for Cardoza's pet tiger back in Colombia. There was only one person aboard the ship he associated with on a regular basis, and that was Antonio, the youngest among them. Though there was a marked age difference between them, Antonio could be considered a friend. For some reason, the lad looked up to him, probably because, like him, Antonio did not share the same penchant for killing as the others had shown. Sooner or later, though, the crew's bloodlust was going to get the lad killed. The day before remained clearly etched in his mind. A stranger had nearly ended Antonio's life, a man riding a waverunner retrofitted with some unusual weaponry. And now he knew that Ortega would not rest until he found that man. With Ortega, it would become an obsession. In Southeast Asia, he had gotten a firsthand look at what an obsession could lead to if left unchecked. Usually a lot of people died.

After turning the final bolt to the required torque, Fernando installed the safety wire that would keep the bolt from working its way loose under the high frequency vibration every component of the helicopter would be subjected to once the turbine engine was fully engaged and the aircraft was in flight. He enjoyed working with his hands, repairing damaged machinery or building things from scratch. To his way of thinking, constructing was so much more satisfying than destroying, and he had seen enough destruction to last a lifetime.

As he completed the task, Fernando's thoughts returned to the man on the waverunner. He held no animosity toward the man, feeling only a strange kinship with him instead. It was obvious the stranger had only sought to protect the girl and dolphins, using a weird combination of weaponry to do this. Maybe this individual had been the one to configure the weaponry to the waverunner. In that thought alone, there was a common bond. And the man, no doubt, had a love of dolphins, risking his life to save the creatures. This in itself made him diametrically different from Ortega, who he knew hated dolphins, killing them with grenades at every opportunity, or letting them get caught up in the seine net and pulled through the San Carlo's powerblock where their bodies were shredded to pulp.

Securing the engine cowling, Fernando turned his head and looked toward Haiti's capital city. Rarely did he leave the ship whenever the San Carlo was moored within the harbor of Port-au-Prince, knowing how unsafe the streets could be, especially after dark. From where he stood high up on the tuna trawler, he could just make out the gang-controlled slums of Cite Soleil. Much to Ortega's displeasure, they had been forced to come back here two days ahead of schedule in order to replace the destroyed runabouts. Already Pedro and several crewmembers had gone ashore, rowing their way into the waterfront on one of the trawler's skiffs. The Colombian crew always seemed upbeat prior to taking a shore leave here, holding a particular fondness for the place. They would be in their element. From experience, he knew they would come back to the San Carlo drunk and obnoxious, bragging about what they had done to some poor bastard, usually a street urchin unfortunate enough to cross paths with them.

Looking at his watch, Fernando realized the fifteen minutes given him by Ortega was almost up. Climbing into the pilot's seat of the Bell Ranger, he flicked several switches before firing up the engine. As the power train hummed to life and gradually built to a deafening roar, he ignored the gauges lining the instrument panel, listening instead with a critical ear to the changing pitch of the overhead blades as they gained momentum. The sound of the aircraft and the vibrations coursing through it would tell him if anything was wrong. Satisfied that everything was functioning the way it should be, he scanned the various gauges as a final check, knowing precisely the readings he would see. He was not disappointed.

- 48 -

There was something odd about the powerboat below them that made Ortega take a second look. "Take us closer to that vessel down there, but not too close," he instructed, pointing to where he was looking.

Fernando did as he was told, banking the helicopter to starboard and taking it lower. He could see the boat was headed for Port-au-Prince, and as he got closer, his eyes were immediately drawn to the small watercraft being towed behind it.

"Notice anything?" Ortega asked.

Fernando glanced sideways to read the sickening smile on the Colombian's face. Knowing it would do no good to play dumb, he told his boss what he wanted to hear. "Yeah…minus the weaponry, the watercraft being towed looks like the same one used against us yesterday."

Ortega grinned the way a man might at having just discovered a cache of diamonds. "But the boat doing the towing is very different from the one we encountered near Navassa Island," he pointed out. "Bring us lower, but keep your distance. I have no wish to be fired upon like yesterday."

Dropping to within 500 feet of the water, Fernando took the Bell Ranger in a wide circle over the vessel's wake. Two objects suddenly broke the surface, catching the eyes of both men. "Well now, this is proving to be very interesting," Ortega said. "Funny how these white dolphins keep showing up with that waverunner." Almost as soon as the Colombian uttered the words, the albinos sounded, disappearing from sight.

Ortega fell into a protracted silence as the towing vessel picked its way through a scattered fleet of old and decrepit fishing boats. "What do you want me to do?" Fernando asked impulsively, wondering what his boss was thinking.

Several more seconds transpired as Ortega alternately shifted his gaze between the powerboat and the water to its rear. "Resume your original course," he ordered at last. "I want to be in Saint-Marc before sunset."

Relieved by Ortega's decision, Fernando brought the helicopter back on their original heading, ascending higher once again. As they climbed to altitude, Ortega periodically craned his head around to glance back at the vessel as it plied its way toward the harbor entrance. "I have seen that boat before," he muttered gruffly, almost as if talking to himself. "Finding it again should be easy."

Inwardly, Fernando shuddered at the way the words were spoken.

- 49 -

Sitting within the darkened cramped space of the storage locker, Jake continued to cradle Destiny's head in his lap. The girl was still out. Checking the luminous dial on his watch, he could tell they had been penned up this way for well over an hour. Not wanting to risk any more funny business from the two of them, Ben Loomins and his brother, Charlie, had marched Jake at gunpoint into the Bertram's forward section, locking him and Destiny in a tiny closet located in the galley. The quarters were so tight that Jake had been forced to crouch down with the girl awkwardly cradled in his arms in order for the two of them to effectively fit inside. With only a sliver of dim light finding its way through a crack in the locker door, Jake had groped around clumsily in the limited space, hoping to find something useful to extricate them from their holding cell. Handicapped by the unconscious girl pressed up snugly against him, though, he had decided to give up the attempt for the time being, seeing the futility of trying to escape with Destiny in her present condition.

Although passivity was not in Jake's nature, he had purposely avoided gambling with Destiny's life, submitting instead to the role of prisoner. Somehow he would find a way out of this mess, but not until the girl regained consciousness. Having been forced to sit hunched forward in such a constricted manner, he could feel the muscles in his back and neck beginning to tighten up painfully. With both knees already numb from being scrunched up against the door, he exerted as much pressure against it as he could muster, hoping the wood comprising it would crack under the strain. He visualized the door in his mind's eye again, having assessed it just before being crammed into the small compartment. The door was a good two inches thick, probably consisting of solid oak, with a heavy steel bolt situated on the outside keeping it firmly secured. From the way he was restrained, he had no room to apply even feeble leverage to force it open.

As he listened to the steady, almost hypnotic thrum of the boat's engines, something banged lightly against the Bertram's hull close to where he sat. The sound, he guessed, was the dolphins' way of letting him know they had not deserted them. Hermes and Aphrodite had been doing this periodically ever since he and the girl had been caged up.

Stroking Destiny's head with the fingertips of one hand, Jake felt her suddenly stir. "Where are we?" she asked, her voice calm and not showing any signs of the listless coma she had been in a moment earlier.

"They've got us locked away in a storage compartment. Loomins got the drop on me before I could get you off this vessel. You were out cold."

Destiny found his hand in the darkness and squeezed it. "At least we were able to free Aphrodite and Hermes," she commented, trying to rise as she said it.

"Don't try to get up," Jake warned. "It's tighter than a jammed suitcase in here."

Destiny stopped moving and remained silent for a long moment, as if letting the full magnitude of their predicament settle over her. Finally, she spoke. "The rest of the pod is here. They'll help us."

Jake stifled a laugh. "What are they going to do, come down here and open this door?"

Destiny ignored the humor. "Coral wants you to picture the mechanism that keeps this door locked."

"Why?"

"I'll explain later. Do you remember what it looks like?"

Jake was puzzled over such an odd request. "It's a sliding dead bolt that latches the door."

"Good. Now just keep thinking about it."

Having nothing better to do at the moment, Jake did as the girl asked, if only to soothe her. He visualized the bolt again, keeping it lodged firmly in his mind. The sliding mechanism was in a closed position, just the way he remembered it before it had been thrown back with a loud clank to allow them entrance to their current prison. A sudden flickering seemed to intrude its way into his thoughts. No, it was more than a flickering. He was being prodded and nudged by ethereal wisps without form or substance as he concentrated on the latch. A vision of the bolt sliding open abruptly flashed into his brain, and even before he became aware of it, the numbing pressure against his knees was swept away like a puff of air. The sudden eruption of light flooding the closet made him blink in surprise as the door suddenly swung open. Letting his eyes settle on the outer compartment, he could see that no one lurked in the dimly lit galley beyond.

Immediately stunned by what had just taken place, he looked at the girl in confusion. "How did you do that?" he gasped, mouth agape.

Rising from his lap, Destiny turned and stared down at him. "We all did it together…you and the rest of us."

Still confused, Jake could only gawk back, too tongue-tied for any more words. He tried to rise, but with all his joints now stiff from lack of movement, he had difficulty standing. He realized his legs had fallen asleep, tingling with a dull numbness. Continuing to sit, he extended his feet out in front of him, wincing with the effort. Legs, he knew, needed occasional movement if they were to remain flexible. For the blood to keep flowing, it was important the muscles were periodically stretched out. But now that circulation had been restored, the tingling in his limbs escalated rapidly to an excruciating ache. "Give me a minute to loosen up." *Funny,* he thought, *she's been cooped up as long as I have and she's limber as a cat.*

Above the steady drone of the engines, the sound of footsteps could be heard. Someone was making his way down the stairwell toward the galley. With renewed effort, Jake hobbled to his feet and pushed the door to the storage closet closed, sliding the deadbolt into place. Reaching out, he grabbed Destiny by the arm and pulled her along with him as he limped spastically through an open doorway leading to the next compartment forward of the one they were in. They had just enough time to find a place of hiding on the opposite side of the bulkhead separating the two compartments.

Jake went rigid as a voice rang out above the din of the engines. "I hope you're comfortable in there." For one fleeting moment he thought they had been discovered, but then he heard a loud banging which told him otherwise. Risking a peek around the edge of the doorway, he saw Charlie rapping a closed fist against the bolted locker door, the same carbine he had wielded earlier clutched at his side. "You were lucky to catch me off guard," Charlie went on, "but that won't happen again. I guarantee it." Turning away from the closet, Charlie opened a refrigerator and retrieved a chicken leg. Gnawing on the leg, he left the galley and went back topside.

Jake released the breath he had been holding back. "That was close."

"What now?" Destiny asked.

From the way the girl was looking up at him, Jake could tell she was expecting him to come up with another plan. Scanning their present quarters, Jake spied his K-Bar lying on a bunk behind him. Just before being jammed into the storage closet, Charlie had removed the knife from the scabbard strapped to Jake's leg and tossed it into the compartment where they now stood.

"There's got to be something down here we can use," he said, reinserting the blade back in its sheath. His legs were almost back to normal.

Destiny moved forward toward the boat's bow and opened a door. Staring over her shoulder, Jake noticed an assortment of supplies inside the compartment. A hodgepodge of coiled rope, extra anchors, rolls of netting, and small wooden crates took up most of the space. Squeezing himself into the congested room, he spied various tools attached to fixtures along each side.

He suddenly smiled as his eyes came to rest on one item in particular. Another webshot was mounted conspicuously on the wall, this one a smaller version of the one he had seen up on deck, and as he rummaged further, he quickly discovered a box of cartridges for the device.

- 50 -

Charlie Loomins was sprawled comfortably on a couch in the Sea Lion's rear cabin, chewing contentedly on the last morsels of meat from the chicken leg. Absentmindedly, he tossed the bone aside and let out a loud burp.

"I hope you enjoyed that."

Charlie practically leapt up from the couch at the spoken words, his brain addling in bewilderment. His brother, Ben, was currently piloting the vessel and the Haitian deckhands were not allowed in here. He scooped up the carbine lying next to him and swung the barrel toward the source, but before he could aim the weapon, Jake fired the webshot from the top of the stairwell.

Twelve feet from where Charlie stood, the gas-powered gun kicked hard, discharging a compressed wad of netting at a velocity of almost 100 feet per second. Six feet from the launch point, the net mushroomed open, expanding to engulf its target. Finding himself suddenly entangled in the mesh, Charlie only managed a surprised grunt as he toppled to the floor with the netting contracted about him like a closed fist.

Jake was on his jailer in an instant, leaning a knee into the small of the man's back to discourage further movement. "Now I don't want to hurt you and you don't want to be hurt," he said mildly as he wrestled the carbine free of Charlie's grasp and pulled it from between the mesh. He could see the reason the gun had not discharged in the short scuffle even though Charlie's finger had been squeezing hard against the trigger. The safety was still on.

Jake handed the weapon to Destiny. "Hold onto this!" he instructed as Charlie began to squirm like a landed marlin. The man was putting up more of a fight than he had expected. "Don't make me konk you like before," Jake threatened.

"How?" Charlie whined, ignoring the threat. "How'd you get out?"

Jake pondered the question momentarily. *Yeah, how?* "I'll never tell," he found himself saying, forcing a hammerlock on his captive and grabbing him by the back of the belt with his free hand. "Now just behave yourself and I promise I'll try to be as gentle as possible."

Still wrapped in the net, Charlie was dragged forcefully along the floor and down the stairs. A minute later, Jake had him stowed safely away inside the same storage locker that had imprisoned him and the girl.

As Jake bolted the door, Destiny looked at him with a hint of amusement in her eyes. "What next?"

"Now we simply walk out onto the main deck and you jump overboard."

"What about you?"

"I've got to retrieve the Kawasaki. I'll catch up with you." Jake could see she didn't like this part of the plan.

Not wanting any further discussion on the matter, Jake hefted the carbine and peered through the window facing the rear deck. Having nothing else to do, the three deckhands had their backs to him as they leaned up against the stern railing. From the way they were gesticulating, they appeared to be debating something.

Seeing the opportunity before him, Jake turned to Destiny. "Stay behind me and get ready to jump!" Opening the door leading out onto the rear deck, he moved up behind the Haitians as their discussion continued. Keeping his eyes trained on the men, he pushed Destiny toward the vessel's port side. "Now go!"

Destiny climbed the railing and leapt just as the three crewmen turned. With seemingly raptured interest, they watched as the girl disappeared headlong into the sea, her arms outstretched gracefully before her in a perfect dive. Strangely, they ignored Jake, pivoting around instead to search the boat's wake for where the girl might surface. But the girl was nowhere to be seen.

Jake could not help but notice the large amount of fishing vessels dotting the sea all around him. From experience, he knew the Sea Lion was nearing the harbor entrance outside of Port-au-Prince. Several familiar landmarks located to the east confirmed this.

"Excuse me, gentlemen," Jake said, keeping his air casual as he walked past the deckhands and unhooked the gate leading to the swim platform. "I'll be taking my leave now."

Something in their mannerisms told Jake they would not be a threat. He moved quickly to the cleat tethering the Kawasaki and untied the line, glancing up one final time toward the bridge as he did so. Leaving the carbine on the platform, he dropped himself over the side and held onto the line. When he poked his head above the surface, the three Haitians could be seen in heated conversation again, gesturing wildly as the Sea Lion drew rapidly away.

Something brushed lightly against Jake's body, and an instant later the head of Achilles bobbed next to him. *"Once again, you do us great honor, Jay Jay,"* the young albino ululated.

"Where's Destiny?" Jake asked nervously, scanning the sea all around him.

"Over here," a voice beckoned. Riding Hercules, Destiny suddenly emerged from the opposite side of the waverunner, her face lit up in a happy smile. Within moments, the remainder of the pod converged all around them, nuzzling in close to Jake and the girl.

"I think it's time we headed back," Jake suggested, staring hard at Destiny. "Would you like to ride with me?"

"Only if you promise not to go any faster then the pod can swim."

Jake threw her a happy grin. "You got yourself a deal."

- 51 -

Dr. Franklin Grahm knelt beside his fallen young assistant, wondering why the lad hadn't heeded the warning. As of late, Nick Henderson had become increasingly contentious and moody. The marine zoologist breathed a sigh of relief, however, when the computer whiz finally responded to the CPR administered to him by Parker. Letting out several large gasps just prior to regaining consciousness, Henderson awoke with a start and immediately expelled the water he had taken into his lungs, coughing so harshly that he vomited up his last meal in the process.

Finally catching his breath, Henderson stared up at the others hovering above him, his face a mask of confusion. "What happened?" he stammered dazedly.

Grahm took a moment to glance up at Jacob. The grizzled Haitian wore an expression that implied he had been expecting such an event. "We heard you scream and Jacob pulled you ashore," Grahm said. "You apparently made contact with the thurentra and received a severe electrical shock. Can you stand?"

"I think so." With Parker assisting, Henderson staggered shakily to his feet, and as Grahm studied him, his eyes were once again drawn to the jellylike substance adhering to the grad student's forearm.

"Hold still!" Grahm ordered as he unsnapped one of the pockets on his utility belt. "I believe you have some of the thurentra on you."

Anger welled up in Henderson's eyes. "That thing shocked me?" The question was phrased more like an accusation, as if Grahm's explanation of what had just happened had finally sunk in.

Parker helped to immobilize Henderson's arm as Grahm scraped some of the translucent orange goo onto a small glass slide. "Jacob warned you against touching it," Grahm reminded him. "You should have listened."

"I thought it was just a ploy to keep us from seeing the-" Henderson abruptly shut up, falling silent as he suddenly became aware of Jacob standing nearby.

Parker stared sharply at him, still holding his arm. "Seeing what?"

"Nothing."

"Tell us what you saw?" Parker pressed, unwilling to let the matter go.

Henderson pulled free, almost savagely, but Grahm had already gotten enough of a sample. "There's nothing to tell."

"Go sit in the shade, Nicolas!" Grahm muttered in a soothing tone, trying to quell the brewing argument. "You need to clear your head."

"I'll do that," Henderson grumbled irritably. Turning, he strode away, seeming eager to get away from all three men.

The scientist turned to Jacob. "Once again, I must extend my apologies for the lad's impetuosity. I hope you will not consider this unfortunate event as an overstay of the hospitality you have already given us."

Jacob shrugged with indifference. "Sometimes it is best that reckless stubbornness run headlong into the very thing it had been advised against. That way we are more likely to heed future warnings."

Grahm nodded in agreement. "Perhaps it will improve his judgement as well." He indicated the glass slide he was holding. "I hope you don't mind if I analyze this?"

Jacob assessed Grahm curiously, as if seeing something he needed to examine more closely. "And if I did?"

Grahm's disappointment was evident. He had not expected this. "Why… I, uh, would respect your wishes, of course," he stuttered.

Jacob stared at the scientist a moment longer as if trying to gauge the full extent of his earnestness. "You are obviously a man driven by scientific curiosity, a man that has an insatiable need for answers." He suddenly smiled. "Please…go ahead and do what you must. I have no desire to obstruct you."

Both Grahm and Parker watched as Jacob headed off in the direction of the thatched dwellings set back from the beach. "A most interesting individual," Grahm commented. "Somehow I get the feeling a man like that could accomplish anything he put his mind to."

"I was kind of thinking the same thing," agreed Parker.

Remembering what he was holding, Grahm extended an arm to Parker. "Run this sample through the blot scanner, then send it back to Miami as soon as you're able to establish a satellite uplink. Access the DNA microarray imaging program on the Big Mac. I'd like to know how closely this matches known varieties of sea cucumbers and coelenterates."

The program to which Grahm referred was the latest version of one that had undergone modification over the last two years. It both simplified and expanded the usefulness of the older protocol of DNA microarray technology. Normally it was Henderson who handled such duties, but Parker had sufficient knowledge of the system to carry out Grahm's directive without any problems.

Parker started to walk away, but Grahm stopped him as a strange thought came to mind. "Include Natalie's genome for comparison."

A look of genuine surprise was evident on Parker's face. "You think there's a genetic relationship?"

Grahm sighed, then shrugged. "There's a mystery here, one that seems altogether impossible and yet…" He groped for the right words but couldn't find anything adequate enough to express what he was feeling. "God only knows what we'll find."

Parker studied Grahm for several seconds without speaking, then finally turned and trudged away.

Grahm watched his protégé head off to where most of their equipment had been set up to one side of the cove. He had a special fondness for Parker. The lad was bright and easy to work with. Henderson, on the other hand, had his quirks, but without him Grahm was convinced he would never have been able to develop the unique programming needed to translate delphine sounds. Unfortunately, Henderson was a rude and unruly sort, and as of late had become even more so. Perhaps he shouldn't have brought him along.

There was something else about the youth that had begun to peck away at the back of his mind. *Was it betrayal?* Too many recent coincidences made it difficult to shed his suspicions. And he noticed that Henderson had never really developed a close attachment to Natalie the way he and Parker had. Intentionally, he let his thoughts shy off in another direction, ashamed of himself for considering the possibility that Henderson couldn't be trusted.

Almost by reflex, he glanced over at the cove's entrance. Still no sign of the pod. He was worried about the fate of the two captured dolphins, knowing what could happen to these incredibly intelligent beings if they fell into the wrong hands. They were not meant to be isolated from their own kind, to be penned up in some laboratory far from the sea. Here among these people, the creatures were treated with love and a deep abiding respect.

In the midst of these mullings, the girl came to mind. Already he had developed a strong affection for her. If he had had a daughter, he would have wanted her to be just like Destiny. The thought sent an unexpected surge of yearning through him. The same haunting image that had plagued him all these years suddenly popped into his head. His wife, Harriet, had been pregnant at the time she disappeared. Had she given birth, the child would have been the girl's age.

Longing for the woman he loved, Grahm wandered aimlessly along the beach, unable to enjoy the magical spell of the place Jacob called Gaia. The nostalgia he felt was a gruff reminder of what had happened so many years ago, and as he wallowed helplessly in its grip he realized how cowardly he was. *Yes,* he finally admitted to himself, *failing to face the truth was a form of cowardice, wasn't it?* By coming here first instead of diving down to explore what remained of the vessel his wife had used to sail the Caribbean had only tended to reveal his utter gutlessness. *Was he truly afraid of what he might discover?* After all these years, he still couldn't bring himself to accept her loss, knowing that some small part of him actually believed she had not really perished.

With great difficulty, he stopped berating himself. He knew he was torn between two conflicting choices. There was still a mystery he had to unravel about this place, so much more he needed to learn about these magnificent white creatures and their interaction with the girl who rode and communicated with them through some unknown mind link. Destiny was altogether special, someone he felt inexplicably drawn to. Without knowing why, he felt a deep sense of loss with the girl now gone, and he would not leave until she returned safely. But he also had another need, one that required he go back to Navassa Island to locate the sunken sloop. Burdened by this impasse, he knew he had to satisfy both needs very soon. Like a man trapped in a stupor, he continued to roam the beach without purpose, every so often gazing haplessly toward where the dolphins would re-enter the cove.

- 52 -

An evening twilight was rapidly falling upon Saint-Marc, bathing the old fortress that sat above the town in an eerie reddish backwash of glowing incandescence. Somewhere in the distance, the sound of an approaching whirlybird grew gradually in volume, slowly drowning out the low rhythmic beat of reggae emanating from one of the taverns farther back along the waterfront. Like a gnat emerging out of the southwestern horizon, the aircraft took on size and form as it rushed toward the small group of men tracking it. Circling once, it descended swiftly, taking on a heading that would bring it to a lesser used area of the docks. The Bell Ranger flared sharply, throwing up a cloud of dust that partially obscured the setting sun. Hovering briefly, it settled down gingerly on one of the run-down wharves, almost as if testing the aging timbers that would support it.

Dabbing the sweat from his brow, Hennington stood back far enough from the savage blades to avoid the storm of grit that was cast in all directions. Wearily, he watched as Ortega climbed out of the cockpit and came toward him, the man's head lowered forward like the oncoming prow of a ship as he moved under the whirling rotor. Unlike all his previous meetings with the Colombian, the sight did not elicit the same level of fear in the broker. Ever since leaving the mambo he had felt cleansed, purged of the guilt he had unknowingly carried up to then. His own reckless greed, he had come to realize, had been the cause of this guilt. But because a great burden had been lifted, he was no longer afraid.

Stepping forward to meet Ortega, Hennington left his bodyguards standing farther back, not wanting them to hear what would be said. As always, he could see the threat of violence in Ortega's eyes as the man first looked at him before shifting his gaze to Ternier's thugs.

"This had better be important," Ortega grunted with impatience, speaking in Spanish as he always did when the two men spoke. "Did you forget about our little arrangement? Never call me on my satellite phone unless absolutely necessary. This is the second time you contacted me in the last day."

"It is imperative I get back to Port-au-Prince tonight."

Ortega appeared shocked at Hennington's audacity. He suddenly gave the impression of a volcano ready to erupt. "Do you think I am a taxi service?" he snarled.

Hennington spoke fast, trying to pacify the Colombian's soaring anger. "The Colonel will not provide you with the people you requested unless you fly me back at once," he lied. "He has some important business to discuss with me and suggested I contact you to help me out."

For one fleeting moment, Hennington expected Ortega to strike him. Slowly, the pent up rage emblazoned on his face began to ease. "There is only room enough for two more aboard this bird," he growled, looking beyond the broker at the three Haitians.

"Then only one of these men will accompany me," Hennington replied.

Ortega reached out and grabbed Hennington by the forearm, making the broker flinch in pain at the strength of grip. The message was clear, reaffirming just who was in charge here. "You have not forgotten about the weapon I asked for?"

Hennington had not forgotten. He had made the appropriate arrangements earlier the day before, several hours before being sent by Ternier to go to Malique. "You will have it by tomorrow."

"You are certain of this?" The Colombian applied more pressure, but Hennington sucked up the pain, refusing to give Ortega the satisfaction of seeing him squirm. "I would hate to be disappointed."

"My contact is very reliable."

A cruel smile affixed itself to Ortega's face. *"Bueno. Muy Bueno."* He kept the grip of steel locked firmly in place a moment longer before letting go.

Hennington managed to keep his face expressionless as the blood returned to his fingers. "Walter McPherson has arrived in Port-au-Prince. He is eager to take delivery of the frozen dolphin carcasses."

"He understands this will be strictly a cash transaction?"

"He understands perfectly."

Cardoza's lieutenant appeared pleased. "Life is good." As an afterthought, he looked down at Hennington's legs. "I noticed you are no longer limping, my fat friend. You are healing much more quickly than I would have thought possible. Perhaps I went too easy on you." He stared for another moment before placing a hand on Hennington's shoulder and moving him toward the helicopter. "Come! The Colonel awaits you."

Looking over his shoulder, Hennington motioned the leader of Ternier's thugs to follow. He smiled inwardly at his own deception. Before Ortega had arrived here, he had stressed to the leader how upset Ternier would be if the Colonel were denied the immediate delivery of the medallion by the fastest means possible. The other two men would therefore have to make the cumbersome journey back to Port-au-Prince without them.

Instinctively, Hennington ducked down as the chopper blades began to crank faster overhead. Walking was definitely easier now. He could even walk stooped over like he was currently doing without his knee bothering him. Much to his amazement, his painful limp had all but vanished soon after leaving the mambo, and he no longer moved like a cripple.

Climbing aboard the aircraft, he now understood beyond a shadow of a doubt that the mambo had seen something in him that he had been blind to all these years. Oddly, he remembered most of the things she had said. It was true, he had continued to travel the same path over and over again, and in the process, had been constantly disappointed where he had ended up. Somehow the woman had made him see something he had failed to see all his life. Happiness could only come from deep within, that it could not be bought or sold like much of the merchandise and services he provided. For some people, they had to be comfortable with their self-image before they could develop a true joy for life. He was now curious to discover who he actually was, hopeful that deep down he was not really a coward, that there existed at least a shred of courage within him. And though there was misery all about him, self-fulfillment might be possible if he no longer strived for the false gold. Perhaps there was a chance for him after all.

As he buckled himself in, Hennington shifted his thoughts back to the strange images that had flashed through his mind when the mambo had placed her hand upon his head. Even as the helicopter began to rise and gain speed, those same images continued to stay with him, blocking out all sensation of the darkening ocean flitting swiftly by below.

- 53 -

With Destiny sitting behind him on the waverunner and the rest of the pod leading the way, Jake finally entered the cove late into the evening under another gibbous moon. Rather than have Zimbola lower the docking chute on the Angel's stern, he decided to leave the Kawasaki tied up alongside the trawler for the time being. Having not had anything to eat since noon, he was now ravenous, wanting only to get something in his stomach. Unfortunately, Zimbola, Phillipe and Hector had other ideas, eager to get an account of the day's events. Not wanting to disappoint them, Jake gave them a brief recount of what had happened, deciding to leave out how the lock to the storage closet had been opened.

Destiny had soon disappeared, wanting to attend to the two recovering gray bottlenose dolphins. Jake's plan to have a quick meal in the Angel's galley was quickly aborted when Achilles suddenly chittered noisily off the vessel's larboard side. *"Jacob invites everyone to dinner, Jay Jay,"* the albino trilled. *"Will you be coming ashore?"*

"Will Destiny be there?"

"Yes, Jay Jay."

"Then tell Jacob I accept his invitation."

Jake watched as the juvenile turned and swam toward the shore. The brazier Jacob had grilled fish on the night before was already burning brightly, occasionally outlining several figures moving about close to its flickering glow. Breathing deeply, he took in the rich fragrance hanging in the air, wondering what it would be like to spend his remaining years in such a place. There was life here, pulsing and vibrant, ceaselessly rapturous to the spirit.

Turning, Jake noticed Zimbola hovering nearby. "How's our captive doing?"

The giant cocked his head, scratching his huge cranium and smiling oddly. "I do not know what to make of it, but he has been staring at that painting like a starry-eyed puppy all day. He will not put it down."

"Has he given you any more trouble?"

"No...there must be strange magic in that painting to make him behave like that. I think the white witch-"

Zimby abruptly caught himself, seeing the frown that immediately clouded Jake's face. "Perhaps the girl did something to him during her healing ritual."

News of the man's docility was not altogether unexpected by Jake. He, himself, had experienced the strange power of the dolphin art. On impulse, a wild thought came to him. "Bring him ashore, Zimby. I'd like him to eat with the rest of us."

Zimbola nodded impassively, showing no surprise. Having spent most of the day keeping an eye on the prisoner, Jake knew his friend would have voiced an objection if he thought the man was still potentially dangerous or could not be controlled. "That may not be so bad an idea," the Jamaican concurred.

Going belowdeck to his stateroom, Jake retrieved his satellite phone and put in a call to Mat Daniels. He would have placed a call to him earlier, but recent mitigating circumstances had forestalled him from doing so. Mat picked up on the fourth ring.

"Daniels at your service."

"What's cooking, buddy? It's Jake."

"What happened to you? I've been waiting for your call all day."

"Don't ask, it's a long story."

"Will I be getting the present you spoke of anytime soon?"

Jake remained silent for several seconds as he contemplated a decision. "Sorry to disappoint you, pal, but I seem to have lost the package. I do have one piece of intel that may interest you, though."

"Speak to me."

"If I were you, I'd keep my eyes on the lookout for a hundred foot sub. There's one roaming the waters between Haiti and Navassa Island."

"You saw it."

"With my own two eyes."

Mat waited for Jake to say more, then grew impatient. "Come on, fella, you're holding back on me. I know you have more to tell."

"Sorry, old buddy. That's all I can give you right now. I'll be in touch as soon as I find out more. Gotta run."

"Jake!" Mat shouted, catching Jake before he could end the call.

"Yeah."

"Take good care of yourself."

Jake could not help but smile. "You know what your problem is, Mat?"

"What?"

"You worry too much."

Five minutes later, Jake waded ashore, having taken a much needed invigorating swim from the Angel to the beach. Turning to look back at the Angel, he could discern movement on the water as the other members of his crew were currently taking the skiff to join him. Facing the fire again, he saw Grahm coming over to greet him.

Grahm extended a hand. "Let me congratulate you for what you did today, lad."

Relunctantly, Jake clasped the proffered hand. Praise such as this made him feel uneasy. "I only gave Destiny assistance. She was really the one who made the rescue possible."

"You're much too modest. From what Jacob tells me, you did a lot more than just assist." Grahm turned his head toward the water. "The youngest member of the pod seems to be very fond of you."

Jake followed his stare, seeing Achilles watching him. "Sorry I wasn't able to recover the DBT," he said, eager to change the subject. "Those dolphin hunters probably still have it."

"That's quite all right, my lad. I brought a few more along on this trip."

Jake thought it appropriate to pursue another topic. "Did your assistant have any luck in identifying that freighter the sub met?"

"As a matter of fact, he did. *Spirit of Aden* was the name on that ship."

"What about its registry? Were you able to get a view of the flag it flew?"

"Yes. I didn't recognize it, so I consulted Jacob. The man is a walking encyclopedia. He identified it as a Yemeni flag." Grahm scrutinized Jake's expression in the glow of the brazier. "You look troubled."

Jake looked on as the skiff from the Angel neared the beach. He could see it was being nudged along by two albinos, although he couldn't tell which two. "Nothing to concern yourself about," he said, showing Grahm a smile and turning him in the direction of the fire. "What say we eat? I'm starving."

As they walked toward the fire, Jake sensed Grahm had something else to talk about. "Would you mind if we delayed that trip to Navassa Island until the day after tomorrow?" the scientist asked, his tone bordering on embarrassment. "I know our original business arrangement hinged on only chartering your boat for a period of three days at most, but unfortunately the funds I have available will be inadequate to cover anything more than that." Grahm paused, his discomfiture growing heavy. "If there's-"

Jake cut him off. "Don't give it another thought. I'll take you to Navassa day after tomorrow and hopefully we'll find your boat. We'll work out the tab later. After what's happened the last two days, I'm going to need a full day of rest anyway." He glanced around for Destiny as he spoke, locating the silhouette of her petite form sitting on a rock next to Jacob as the Haitian grilled fish steaks on the brazier. From the aroma wafting off the fire he could tell they were having grouper again, and his stomach began to churn hungrily in anticipation.

Breaking away from the scientist, Jake stepped over to Jacob and exchanged a few pleasantries before squatting down beside the girl. "How is Thetis and the other gray doing?" he said softly. With the exception of the waterfall's dull roar in the background, all was quiet and he did not want to disturb the ambiance of the evening.

A gentle wash of light from the grill spilled briefly off Destiny's brown eyes as she turned her head. She watched as Zimbola led the man she had healed the day before to the edge of the gathering. "Both should make a full recovery by tomorrow," she said in a lackluster tone.

Perplexed by the girl's unexpected sullenness, Jake groped for words. "That's good," he managed, trying his best to brighten her mood. "I'm sure that will make Achilles feel a whole lot better."

Destiny did not respond, keeping her gaze focused elsewhere.

Up close, Jake could see she was preoccupied with something weighing heavily upon her. "What's wrong?"

"I discussed with Jacob what Hermes and Aphrodite told me. He thinks a special type of sonar was used to stun them."

Destiny's statement brought to mind something Jake had been taught during BUD/S training. Working underwater when military sonar was activated was dangerous. A ship's sonar could be lethal to a diver at close range. It only stood to reason that sonar emissions of a lesser potency would temporarily disable a living organism rather than kill it.

Jake thought back to the vessel they had escaped. There had been something aboard it covered by a tarp. "Remember the plane we saw circling the Sea Lion?" he said.

Destiny nodded.

"I think that plane was acting as a spotter to direct Loomins to the dolphins. If the plane dropped such a sonar device near the dolphins, it would explain why they were captured so easily."

It seemed more logical to Jake that the plane would carry such technology rather than the boat, owing to its greater speed and spotting ability. Ben Loomins wanted the dolphins essentially unharmed if the creatures were to have any salable value. One possible way to accomplish this might very well involve the use of sonar of sufficient magnitude to temporarily incapacitate but not cause injury. The device that sent out the emissions would have to be dropped almost on top of the creatures before they could race away beyond its limited effective range. Had the Bertram been the carrier of such a contrivance, he doubted it would have been able to get close enough to debilitate them. The crew of the Sea Lion would simply complete the capture by first sedating and then netting the stunned albinos. Hauling aboard the sonar emitter would be the crew's final task before getting underway.

"Has this ever happened to any of the albinos before?" Jake asked curiously.

The question caused Destiny's eyes to well up. "Never."

"Then I have to assume Ben Loomins and his brother may have come up with a new way of capturing dolphins in the wild."

Jake expelled a long breath laced with frustration. The girl was hopelessly naïve. Glancing toward the water, he could just make out several albinos staring in his direction. "I think it would be wise to have the pod stay clear of Navassa Island for the time being. Loomins will most likely revisit the place where the albinos were last spotted."

The suggestion seemed to startle the girl and she looked away. Her reply was barely audible. "That's not possible!"

Jake was momentarily speechless. He could see no reason why members of the pod would have a need to venture out into the open sea. Everything they required was close at hand right here in the cove. An abundant food supply was readily available. The large holding pen Jacob had built at the cove's northern end was kept well stocked with fish. He started to open his mouth, but before any words could be uttered, a shadow fell across him that was followed by a light touch on his shoulder.

"Let us take a stroll together, Mr. Javolyn," a voice interceded. The tone was low, affable.

Jake was surprised to see Jacob standing over him. From the way Destiny's mentor hovered, he had the impression the man had overheard the last part of the conversation.

"If you please," the Haitian persisted. "I have a few things to discuss with you."

Rising to his feet, Jake glanced back down at the girl, unable to grasp what she had meant. *Why was it not possible?* Vaguely aware that Grahm was now manning the brazier, he let Jacob guide him away from the others milling about the fire. He assumed the man needed to converse in private.

Jacob led Jake leisurely along the water's edge, seeming to mull what he was going to say. Jake waited patiently for him to speak as they continued to walk slowly in the direction of the waterfall.

"A lot has happened in the past several days," Jacob finally began. "Two days ago, you were a complete stranger to Destiny, a person with untested qualities." He sighed deeply, as if culling out the appropriate words. "But now you seem to have been accepted by the pod, a man who they are able to trust. This comes as a great surprise to me, because they are creatures that do not readily surrender trust."

Jake abruptly stopped and stared at Jacob. "What about you? Am I someone you think you can trust?" He took it for granted that Jacob had seen the painting on the wall of the cave, but still he felt compelled to ask.

Jacob smiled elusively. "You saw the gold! You were not tempted by it?"

The directness of the question caused Jake to flounder like a man having his legs swept out from under him in a sudden rush of whitewater. It took him several moments to regain his footing. "You set me up?" he sputtered incredulously.

Jacob shrugged without pleasure. "Yes...admittedly it was a test of sorts, a way of determining the kind of person you are."

The stirrings of indignation welled up from the pit of Jake's stomach. "Did I pass?"

"That depends on how you answer the question." Jacob studied him as though Jake were under a microscope. "Does the fact that so much wealth lies within these waters tempt you in any way?"

The pique Jake was feeling slowly abated, giving way to tolerance. Try as he might, he couldn't fault Jacob for testing him in light of what the lure of gold had done to both men and entire nations throughout history. The desire to satisfy greed spawned temptation. Greed was an inborn part of human nature, one of humanity's ugly imperfections firmly rooted in most people. It was a stubborn trait, often acting like a persistent virus that would not go away, sometimes lying dormant just below the surface for long periods before recurring to manifest its wicked symptoms. It was a vice that many human beings had to deal with in their own way. Those who failed to conquer it usually ended up being enslaved by it, sentenced to a life of chronic wickedness.

Without knowing why, Jake's pending business arrangement recently negotiated with Hennington took hold of his thoughts, and he found it necessary to gaze deep within himself, searching an array of feelings. Hennington had given him an opening, and the temptation to capitalize on it had quickly consumed him. An exorbitant pile of potential cash had been intentionally dangled before him, and like a drooling hyena hungering for a meal he had automatically reached for it, but then demanded more. Undeniably, he had been enticed by the promise of easy money for the delivery of something entirely unknown, tossing good judgement to the four winds. *Did putting the squeeze on a greedy man also constitute a form of greed, or was it simply another form of survival?*

In asking himself these questions, Jake felt the first tendrils of guilt wending their way into his conscience. He tried rationalizing it, attempting to resolve the conflict, but soon realized he was at a moral crossroad without direction. Rarely did he indulge in self-analysis, but then again, Jacob was asking him to look for flaws in his own moral convictions. *Was it possible for a person to actually evaluate their own probity with any degree of honesty?* Strangely, Jacob's query caused him to reflect on why he had come to Haiti in the first place.

Instinctively, Jake voiced the only answer that was within him. "You don't have to worry about me. Your gold will remain safe." With heartfelt sincerity, he knew he was being truthful.

Jacob held his gaze a brief moment longer before turning his head to look back at the fire. "We, who reside in Gaia, live a simple existence. In a place such as this, we have no need of gold." He let out an audible breath. "The precious metals will serve a useful purpose, however."

Jake was suddenly inquisitive. Though he had only known Jacob a short time, everything the man did seemed to have an objective. "What kind of purpose?"

Jacob wheeled slowly about to face him again. "As I explained to you earlier today, nature has a way of recruiting the very sentience she has created to fulfill certain goals that will benefit her. There is much more going on about you that you could not possibly know, things that will eventually become clear to you if you should ever decide to keep more lasting company with these wonderful creatures." For emphasis, Jacob glanced over at the small pack of albinos shadowing them just off the beach.

With his thoughts racing on ahead, Jake tried to find meaning in Jacob's carefully contrived wording. *Lasting company? Where's he going with this?*

Unexpectedly, the abstruse things Destiny had said the night before flashed in his mind's eye like a burst of lightning, intensely bright and blinding. *"Thetis begs you to reconsider. Failing to bond with Achlles will place the pod in immediate danger, setting it on an irreversible course of imminent doom. She believes there is still hope, but only if you remain linked to Achilles. Without this link the pod will cease to exist."* Oddly, he had not forgotten the words, although he was still unable to fathom their full implication.

Jake suddenly latched onto the very thing that had puzzled him a little while ago. "Why is it necessary for these dolphins to go near Navassa Island?"

In the moonlight, Jacob's expression became somber, and Jake could see he was having difficulty answering. Jake had to wait only a moment longer before the Haitian's response came tumbling out. "The thurentra you saw is not the only one. There are others."

The revelation hit Jake with the abruptness of a spotlight suddenly turned on to illuminate the contents of a dark basement. At least he could now begin to connect a few of the dots. "And those others are at Navassa?"

Jacob gave an affirmative nod.

Reading the Haitian's demeanor, Jake now sensed a subtle change in the man. The wall of hermetic guardedness that always seemed to reside just below the surface was now being lowered, albeit very slowly. Perhaps Jacob would trust him afterall. "I assume they're able to produce precious metals like the one in this cove."

"Some of them, yes, but not all."

"You mean they're not all alike?"

"Some of them would surprise you." Jacob smiled as if the memory of how the unusual organisms had come into existence was a constant source of wonder to him.

"I take it, then, that members of the pod make periodic visits to Navassa to harvest the gold and platinum."

A strange gleam came into Jacob's eyes, one that Jake perceived as amusement. "Among other things," the Haitian volunteered. "Some of the thurentras also produce magnesium in great quantities."

"Magnesium, huh!" The mention of the metal caused Jake to think about the diversified uses the element had around the world. A huge demand currently existed for its lightweight, high-strength properties, making the metal a prime ingredient in all types of structural components. "Do you do anything with it?"

Jacob's cryptic smile broadened. "Oh, yes." He started to amble down the beach again, now seemingly very comfortable with Jake's presence. "Dr. Grahm has informed me that you will be taking him back to Navassa Island two days from now. Achilles can show you some of the other thurentras if you would like to see them."

The onset of frustration suddenly enfolded Jake, tightening around him like a boa constrictor. The perils that obviously existed around Navassa were all too real. The possibility of danger still lurked there in the form of Colombian tuna fishermen, militant Islamics, and dolphin hunters. "I don't think it would be wise for any of the pod to venture anywhere near that island for a while," he grumbled, aware of the tenseness his own voice held.

A deep weariness suddenly replaced the smile Jacob had been wearing. "Sometimes you have to keep going, no matter what the risks. A crucial mission is at stake here."

Once again, Jake was bewildered. "What do you mean, mission?"

Jacob stopped walking and sat down in the sand, lapsing into an annoying silence.

To Jake, the Haitian's laconic manner was becoming tiresome. Unlike the expansive individual he had conversed with earlier on, the man sitting before him now seemed to have fallen into a state of taciturn withdrawal. He wished Jacob would stop beating around the bush and get to the point. With growing frustration, he sat down beside him, expecting him to at least offer more.

A passing cloud abruptly eclipsed the moon, turning the water darker as Jacob swiveled his head to scrutinize Jake up close. In the darkness, his face became unreadable. "A plan has been devised that may ultimately save the planet," he finally said.

Jake stared dumbly. "A plan? What kind of plan?"

Slowly, Jacob began to explain, and as he did, Jake's eyes widened in astonishment. As Jacob talked, the words continued to pour out faster and faster, leaving Jake nearly spellbound. He quickly gathered that Jacob had finally decided to trust him completely, not holding back on anything. Over the next hour he listened with rapt attention, no longer noticing his famishing hunger clamoring to be satisfied.

- 54 -

When Jake came back to the fire, Destiny was immediately at his side, giving him a heaping plate of grouper fillets and a stein of fresh water. The girl watched as he wolfed down the food like a ravenous animal.

"Far and away, this has to be the tastiest grouper I've ever eaten," Jake said, washing down the last morsel and smacking his lips.

Destiny looked at him intently. "You understand now why members of the pod must go to Navassa Island?"

"They must be very noble creatures to risk their lives this way." Jake glanced around at the shadowy figures still lingering nearby, his eyes searching the duskiness before settling on the person he perceived to be Nick Henderson. Jacob had told him about the grad student's mishap. "Do they really think the human race is worth saving?"

"The ability to change lies deep within all of us," Destiny replied.

"If that's true, why isn't everyone making a conscious effort to change for the better?"

The girl turned her head, her gaze singling out one of the men in the limited light. Jake saw she was looking at his captive. The man sat quietly next to Zimbola, staring passively out over the water. "People sometimes need help," Destiny clarified.

"I suppose you're referring to the albino art?"

"The art has its uses, yes. But acts of kindness and compassion can also go a long way in making a difference."

Jake let a small amused laugh fly from his lips. "I hope you're not going to suggest we turn the other cheek and kiss the people trying to kill us." Indicating the creatures still partly visible out on the water, he quickly added, "These dolphins have got to learn to fight back when they're attacked."

Destiny had no response.

Jake's thoughts raced back to Navassa, remembering the incredible leap one of the albinos had executed in intercepting a grenade intended for the Angel. Though the creature had flipped the small bomb back toward the helicopter with near miss results, he could not help but wonder if the dolphin had had the option of destroying the aircraft had it wanted to. "Have any of these creatures ever actually fought back?" As soon as he uttered the words, he knew they had flown from his mouth a little too vehemently. He realized the warrior in him was talking.

The girl dropped her eyes to the ground, idly digging her toes in the sand. "Striking back in anger is not in their nature. They are incapable of aggression."

Jake fought back his rising frustration. "Then their passivity against assault will become a major liability, making their task all the more difficult. Perhaps none of them will even survive in attempting to carry out this plan."

"They are aware of the risks," Destiny replied, the words spilling out swiftly.

Jake pointed to the Islamic that had tried to kill him. "You see the man you healed. There are many people in the world just like him who are intent on killing people just like us. In order to survive, we have no choice but to fight back."

"But you chose not to kill him," Destiny countered softly.

In Jake's mind, a replay of the underwater fight with the man flashed before him as if he were viewing a movie. He had gone for a killing strike with the bang stick and the man's elbow had unexpectedly gotten in the way. "Only pure luck saved him," Jake shot back.

Destiny searched his face with gentle eyes and her riposte was mellifluous. "You could have let him drown or die from his wound, but you didn't. Instead, you chose to let me heal his injury. Even now you let him come ashore to eat with the rest of us."

Jake found himself unable to find any words as he stared back at the girl.

The girl held his gaze for an extended moment before looking toward the captive again. "I have spoken to him and he has asked for our forgiveness."

"He what?" Jake blurted, completely dumbfounded.

Destiny smiled disarmingly. "His name is Bashir!"

- 55 -

Bashir continued to stare out over the water, marveling at its muted shimmering surface. There was something sublime about the wavering light, a harmonic balance between beauty, serenity and… something else. It mystified him, oddly reminding him of the painting with its…its…he couldn't seem to put his finger on it. It lay just beyond the fringes of his comprehension. Casting off the frustration, he exhaled slowly, depleting his lungs before refilling them with the scented air. With his mind now relaxed, he refocused his eyes once more on the water. The feeling assaulted him again, the potency of both starlight and moonglow merging smoothly to produce a symphonic interplay of fascinating oscillations, both past and present. Yes, it was all there before him, a magical cosmic dance that enlivened the spirit. And hidden within it, a universal truth that could not be denied. It existed on its own, far from the bounds of religious doctrine.

In the midst of his spell, discrepant movement amid the glimmerings made him break from his reverie. He looked closely, perceiving it was well beyond where a gentle rise of wavelets lapped soothingly against the sandy shore. *They were watching him again.* For the moment, the mysterious white creatures had made him a subject of interest, seeming to probe his inner being from where they floated. He sat transfixed, feeling an abnormal calmness suddenly wash over him. With the hulking giant sitting close at hand, he should have felt threatened, but strangely he did not. Unaccustomed to such peace and tranquility, his thoughts began to drift over distant memories, recollections he now viewed as abhorrently unpleasant. For perhaps the first time in his life, he was seeing things clearly, unobstructed by circumstance and dogmatic teachings. *Yes, the hate had blinded him, taking away his ability to think.*

He tried putting it all into perspective. *Hadn't he changed in the last eight hours? No, that wasn't quite right. More likely he had found his true self, a unique part of him buried deep that was incapable of change.*

Orphaned at an early age, Bashir had grown up in the midst of wretched poverty in the slums of Beit Lahiya on the Gaza Strip, the youngest of six brothers. Though he barely remembered the woman who had birthed him, he knew she was the reason five of her oldest sons had blown themselves up on suicide missions. This desire for martyrdom had been incessantly encouraged within his family, so strong was his mother's hatred of the Jews, and it was this intense loathing that had caused her to finally take her own life as a way of killing Israelis.

By the time he was twelve, he had been recruited into the ranks of Hamas, enjoying a certain amount of prestige through the ultimate sacrifices of his mother and brothers. The Hamas leadership had become both surrogate mother and father to him, brimming with the word of God and the certainty of their cause. *Yes,* he had to admit to himself, *the Palestinians were most likely the first terrorist people on earth.* Over time, Hamas had spread its deadly preachings, steadily gaining support until it had finally taken over the reins of power in a country besieged with struggle. Winning a stunning landslide victory in a democratic election held in Palestine a little more than a year ago, the militant ruling party had provided additional glue for unifying the various Islamic radical groups into a loose coalition. Hezbollah, Al Qaeda, Islamic Jihad and a host of others were now further emboldened to pursue their objectives within the region. Militant Islam had grown stronger, taking another step forward in its hate-filled agenda aimed at destroying Israel and establishing a Muslim caliphate all over the world.

Caught up in the fervor of jihad, Bashir had nearly let himself follow in the footsteps of his mother and brothers. He had come close to submitting to the will of Muslim mentors much older and wiser than he. Gleefully, they had smuggled him into Tel Aviv laden with a belt of high explosives strapped hidden on his body, expecting him to spackle the walls of a certain restaurant with infidel flesh. At the time, he had perceived himself as being well prepared for martyrdom, ready to claim his place in Paradise by carrying out the task assigned him. On the last minute, however, he had removed the bomb and fled, somehow finding his way beyond the Israeli border into Jordan.

Journeying to the port city of Al Aquabah, he had managed to get work aboard a tramp steamer bound for Bandar-e Abbas, Iran. From there he eventually wound up in Pakistan. Ashamed of his cowardice, he had avowed before Allah to atone for his failure. As if in divine answer, he had chanced into the man called Kalid and confessed his sin. It was Kalid who had recruited him into the brotherhood of Al Qaeda.

In joining Al Qaeda, he had been a fool. Only now did he grasp the fact he had been sightless, for he knew the leadership of Hamas had considered Bin Laden's agenda to be far too destructive even for their own slaughterhouse sensibilities.

As he pondered his past, he could not refute the constant indoctrination of outrage they had instilled in him. But now all he could see were a faction of Muslim supremacists forcing their dictates upon others. The painting had gently compelled him to look deep inside himself, making him realize that he did not want to kill innocents after all. With this discovery, one overriding question kept plaguing him: *Was it truly the will of God that all non-Muslims be killed for their blasphemous existence?*

The answer rang loud and clear within him. *No!*

Such an idea now seemed completely and irrevocably inane, totally repulsive to his sensibilities. His newfound insight pointed to one conclusion, and one conclusion only, that the purity of Islam had been infected with an ugly malignancy, a moral corruption. The Muslim religion had been contaminated by the aspirations of men like Bin Laden and Raduyev, men who preyed on the blood of innocents. This was not and could not be God's way by any rational stretch of the imagination. The Islamic militant's justification for jihad had been grossly distorted. Using violence as a vehicle of expression was simply not God's way. He did not need the Koran to tell him this, for the Koran was merely based on a collection of words open to interpretation and often misused by biased minds. Rather it was an absolute sense emanating from somewhere deep within him that imparted such a conviction, something that simply was and could not be soiled by anything pernicious.

On impulse, Bashir turned and looked back at the girl. It was she and the creatures that had provided him with this insight, the instruments by which he could see himself for what he truly was. The painting had only been a means of conveyance, a tool, but the essence of both the girl and the dolphins had been been firmly embedded within the depicted forms and texture. *These divine angelic beings have shown me the way.*

With his thoughts meandering over these things, he was suddenly caught in the grip of a sudden realization, giving him a premonition of horrific destruction yet to come. Undeniably, he had been part of the plan, but now he had to make amends, certain he would be unfit for Paradise if he did not. *I must do what I can to stop this insanity,* he swore to himself.

Wondering what he could possibly do, several voices seemed to vibrate all at once in the depths of his soul. *We will help you!* they chimed in unison.

The inner voices spoke to him again, and Bashir suddenly knew the angels of Allah would take him to the place he had to go.

- 56 -

Without any words being said for the moment, Jake and Destiny ambled toward the falls, leaving the company of those still gathered around the fire. Sensing something was wrong, Jake studied the girl out of the corner of one eye, not wanting to be overly intrusive. For the second time this evening she appeared lost in thought, as if deeply preoccupied with something. He started to open his mouth to say something, but the sound of loping footsteps approaching from the rear made him turn. Out of the darkness, Phillipe raced forward to meet him.

"Bashir is gone!" the boy shouted breathlessly.

Jake's face immediately clouded. "Gone?"

"Yes, he is missing. Zimby looks for him."

- 57 -

Late into the evening, Amphitrite walked out on the deserted pier. Jimenez, one of the local fishermen who often assisted her, was at her side, while Athena and several albinos were nearby in the water below. With little breeze to disturb the array of berthed fishing boats tied up against the timber structure, the dock was eerily quiet. Coming slowly toward her, she could discern a trail of luminescence on the ocean surface as something neared the platform on which she stood. Within moments, the imposing bulk of Hercules came alongside the pier, a man clinging to the dolphin's dorsal fin. Appollo and Artemis arrived a few seconds later, silently poking their heads above the water and staring wordlessly up at the woman.

Amphitrite turned to Jimenez. "Please help this man up the ladder," she said, making the request in English and talking loud enough for the clinging man to hear.

The Haitian fisherman climbed down and offered a hand to the stranger, helping him onto the wooden rungs.

Slowly, the man climbed up onto the platform, his silhouette appearing to scrutinize Amphitrite with uncertainty. "Who are you?" he asked, water dripping from his body. With the subdued glow of moonlight at the stranger's back, it did little to show his face.

"My identity is of no importance at this moment," Amphitrite replied calmly. She studied the man closely as though she might learn something new. She had heard the voiceless call and knew that the man before her had slipped unseen from the cove, aided by the others. "I am told you have journeyed up a poorly chosen path and that you wish to retrace your footsteps in order to stop something terrible from happening. Is this correct?"

The man looked back down at the creature that had carried him here, but Hercules was gone. In the darkness, his shroud of perplexity seemed to thicken as he turned again to face Amphitrite. "Will you take offense if I ask you to lower the veil covering your face?" There was apology in his tone.

The question amused Amphitrite. From the others, she had already learned a few things about the man. "In the culture from which you come, I thought it was unacceptable for a woman to reveal her face?"

Even in the dim light, the stranger's mannerism suggested surprise. "I am a long way from such a place."

Amphitrite lowered the shawl slowly to her shoulders, keeping her face to the moon.

A startled intake of breath was heard as the man stared. "I see another angel…an angel who looks very much like the one that healed me."

Amphitrite smiled. "The person you speak of is my daughter, Destiny."

"Destiny has shown me much kindness," the man responded, his voice containing awe.

"Yes, I know," Amphitrite said, keeping the smile in place. "She tells me your name is Bashir." She hesitated briefly. "Before I can help you, Bashir, it is important that I place my hand on your head."

"There is no need of that," Bashir answered. "I am fully recovered from my injury."

"You may have other injuries that you are not yet aware of." Amphitrite was not referring to any impairments of the flesh.

"Very well," Bashir conceded, the words coming out in a sigh. "I suppose an angel can see many things."

Amphitrite raised her left hand and planted it softly on Bashir's forehead, closing her eyes as she did so. Probing by this method did not always work, and for the moment she saw nothing. Through her daughter and the others, she had learned about the man's capture by the one who had helped Destiny rescue the dolphins. In healing Bashir's wound, the pod had gained only partial insight into the man's fundamental nature, knowing he had been part of some unknown objective in the Caribbean. And though an indistinct wickedness seemed to surround that objective, the man himself seemed to be more of a victim rather than an evildoer. Yes, she had known of these things beforehand through the ethereal flickers that often flitted in and out of her consciousness like the delicate songbirds fluttering weightless about the cove.

The vision that suddenly came to her, however, pierced her mind like a cold dagger, making her cringe. For what seemed like an eternity, she bore up to it, assaying the full context of what she was seeing. Finally, with knees quaking, she withdrew her hand.

Turning, Amphitrite locked eyes with Jimenez. "This man must be delivered to Navassa Island tonight. Will you take him there?"

Jimenez nodded, more than happy to oblige.

Amphitrite turned back to Bashir. "I bade you a safe and successful voyage, Bashir," she offered, still reeling from what she had seen. "God go with you!"

"Two of his angels have already helped me," Bashir said earnestly. "I am sure he will continue to guide me."

Amphitrite stood still, watching the two men climb down into Jimenez's boat. She continued to stand there long after the boat had disappeared into the night. Over and over, one thought kept echoing in her brain. *So it begins!*

- 58 -

The Colonel's eyes bulged in disbelief, wondering if the trinket's authenticity was for real. He had never expected Hennington to actually bring him back the medallion, only that the broker return with news of the cheval and the valuable talisman it possessed. "Am I to understand she simply handed this over to you?"

No emotion of any kind showed on Hennington's face. "She did."

The old scar on Ternier's jaw tingled at the memory of the accursed thing that had taken the form of a white woman. It didn't make sense to him. *Why? Why would she give it up so readily?* The thought tormented him, thundering through his mind as he paced around his office like a caged lion waiting to be fed.

Ternier halted abruptly. *Unless?*

He recalled the amulet's searing heat the last time he had clutched it. The pain had been agonizing. His mother, Erzulie, had suffered a similar fate when her hands had bled painfully upon holding the ancient talisman so long ago.

Suspiciously, Ternier eyed the trinket in Hennington's hand as if it were a vial of poison. "You may place the object on my desk," he instructed curtly. He would not repeat his past mistake. With hands clasped stiffly behind him, he resumed his pacing, once more projecting the regal bearing that was so much a part of him. "And what did you learn about Ronaldo Trebek?" he said, changing the subject.

"Other than the fact that he still lives in Malique, there is not much to tell."

"I assume you spoke to him?"

"Yes. The man prefers to spend his days as a simple fisherman."

Ternier mulled this, finding it difficult to believe. He hadn't yet decided what to do about his former accomplice. The fact that Trebek had knowledge of the hydrogen bomb might possibly compromise the grand plan he had devised, and that was not good.

The Colonel turned his eyes back to Hennington. The broker's mannerism struck him as odd. There was something different about the way he spoke and carried himself. "You have nothing else to tell me?" he asked, regarding the man closely.

The broker met Ternier's stare with uncharacteristic calmness. "Malique is only reachable by boat, seaplane or helicopter these days. The road that used to lead there has remained blocked by a mudslide that occurred many years ago."

The reference made Ternier grimance inwardly, yet another reminder of the cheval's strange power. In response, his eyes were again drawn to the amulet, now lying innocently on his desk. *Surely she will be powerless without it!*

An overwhelming desire to be alone suddenly came over Ternier as he thought about the cheval. He needed time to think without any distractions. Stepping back to his desk, he sat down heavily, casting his eyes back on Hennington. "Leave me!" he ordered.

Hennington rose from the chair he had been sitting in, but stopped short of moving any further. "The San Carlo is back in the harbor."

Ternier's eyes were drawn to the amulet once again, and for the moment he ignored Hennington.

Not getting a response, Hennington rephrased the declaration. "Sebastion Ortega has arrived back in Port-au-Prince with his flagship."

The Colonel stared blankly at the amulet. "I am well aware of that," he said, the words uttered dully. The sight of the trinket continued to hold his attention. "She comes back earlier than expected."

"Ortega would like to take delivery of the merchandise a day earlier than planned."

Ternier looked up sharply in annoyance, his eyes suddenly coming alive with a flaming, hypnotic vehemence. "Leave me!" he hissed, waving the broker away as if he were some form of loathsome vermin. "I will contact you when I am ready and not until then."

For one brief moment before turning to leave, Hennington met Ternier's withering gaze, and in that moment Ternier could not detect the slightest trace of timidity in the man. *Could it be that the cheval has done something to him?* The thought disturbed him to no end. People without fear could not be controlled. *Perhaps it will be necessary to take him before my mother again.*

After Hennington had left, Ternier focused all his attention back on the amulet. Cautiously, he extended a hand to touch it, but held back, startled that his hand was shaking. For several minutes, he sat and stared, trying to overcome the fear gripping him. *I will not let her do this to me!* he scolded himself. Maddened with rage, he poked the trinket gingerly with a finger, withdrawing his hand even more quickly. He felt no heat. Emboldened, he touched the charm again, holding his finger against it a little longer this time. There was no pain. With wary temerity he covered the amulet with his palm, noticing how cool it felt. With unrestrained glee, he snatched it from the desk, caressing it lovingly as one thought raced through his mind. *My future is now assured.*

- 59 -

Walter McPherson was in no mood to accept failure, especially after following Grahm and his two assistants to this godforsaken place. Everything he had ever heard about Haiti's economic plight had been confirmed by his own eyes. He found it difficult to believe this land had once been the richest country in the western hemisphere. But after getting a taste of the island nation's people and infrastructure, he now understood why it was by far the poorest. Port-au-Prince was a virtual slum, a hopeless haven of unimaginable poverty and squalor. *Port-a-Potty would have been a name more befitting,* he thought as he recalled the taxi ride from the airport that had taken him here to the La Casa Grande where he was currently staying.

With the hotel located in Petitionville, supposedly the city's richest suburb, he had endured an unpleasant and bumpy ride over a barely passable road that looked like a semi-dry riverbed shrewn with deep ruts and potholes. Burning tires interspersed among a seemingly endless succession of dilapidated shacks off to both sides of the road had further downgraded the dismal journey. The cab he had ridden in had not been much better and had only tended to intensify his discomforture with the gloom all about him. A dented, rusting hulk with blown springs, it jarred him to the teeth each time it met another discontinuity in the surface upon which it rode. On top of that, the vehicle was missing a functioning horn, taillights, windshield wipers, spare tire, mirrors, and a host of other essential safety features. On the way in, swarms of emaciated, sunken-eyed beggars had surrounded the car yelling, *"Blanc! Blanc!"*, either hustling prostitutes or demanding money.

Reputed to be one of the few prestigious hotels adorning the outskirts of the city, he found the La Casa Grande to be a major anticlimax. Adding to his woes, his room was currently without running water. After being subjected to several discreet knocks on his door since arriving, he had finally learned to ignore the solicitations of sleazy prostitutes looking for an easy mark. And once again, the leaky air conditioner was not working.

It was late at night, and with the exception of a lit taper casting eerie shadows on the walls, the room was bathed in an ominous gloaming. The electricity had cut out again, making him glance longingly out the room's window overlooking the hotel's center court. Glowing softly in the darkness, a line of burning candles outlined the sunken bar situated in the swimming pool, their minuscule flames reflecting off the water which beckoned invitingly. When he had first arrived here, an artificial waterfall spilling profusely into the pool had given him a false impression of the place. But without power, the plummeting stream had ceased flowing, driving home the condition of his oppressive surroundings. Every so often, a rising crescendo of shouting from the hotel's casino intruded rudely into his quarters, a stark reminder that the establishment's clientele would not be discouraged from laying down bets.

With his clothes rapidly becoming damp with sweat, he was in no mood to be confronted with yet another disappointment. He had expected more from Frank Jaffey, a man who had distinguished himself in the U.S. Navy as an exceptional fighter pilot. "You're telling me you bagged two specimens, then lost them," he blurted angrily, his tone on the verge of a shriek. He shook his head in disbelief. "You actually had them aboard your vessel and somehow you lost them."

Jaffey looked over at Ben Loomins, impaling his partner with a vicious glare. "Unfortunately, yes. We had 'em, but then they escaped."

McPherson affixed both men with a glare of his own. "You mind elaborating?"

Jaffey shot another venomous look at Loomins. "Yeah, explain to the Captain how you managed to blow such an incredible catch."

Loomins shrugged helplessly, clearing his throat as he did so. "Everything went perfect until we picked up two people adrift on a waverunner."

"We?" Jaffey grumbled, his eyebrows rising in protest. "Don't make me a party to your screwup, asshole. You took it upon yourself to take aboard two strangers."

"They appeared innocent enough," Loomins sputtered. "They were stranded on a waverunner dead in the water. What was I supposed to do, just leave 'em and keep going on my merry way? Maritime law requires I lend assistance."

"Bullshit!" Jaffey shot back. "You picked them up because you saw a pretty face."

McPherson was bewildered. "One of the people was a girl?"

"Yeah," Jaffey confirmed. "Ben, here, is a real sucker when it comes to women. He can't help himself."

Loomins' face reddened with both anger and embarrassment. "I had the situation under control. I locked up the two of them in a storage locker. Somehow they found a way to get out."

"What good did that do?" Jaffey snarled. "The damage had already been done."

McPherson looked from one to the other in confusion, his fuse rapidly shortening. "Two people sabotaged the operation?" *Is that what they were telling him?*

Jaffey nodded contemptuously. "They freed the creatures…right under the nose of my vigilant partner, here."

"Screw you!" Loomins snapped.

McPherson was at the end of his rope. "Stop this blame game and tell me what happened," he spat heatedly. "In good faith I advanced the two of you $80,000 to bag me a specimen, so I'd like to know precisely how these dolphins managed to slip from your grasp."

Loomins shook his head in frustration. "The girl's boyfriend cut the restraining straps holding down the dolphins. They were able to walk themselves across the deck on those hands of theirs and pull themselves over the railing."

McPherson's jaw dropped. "You saw this?"

"No, but the deckhands did. I was up on the bridge piloting the boat."

"I thought your plan was to tranquilize them before hauling them aboard," McPherson reminded him.

"They were tranquilized!" Loomins argued.

"Apparently not enough."

"There was enough sedative in those darts to take down a rhino," Loomins persisted. "I checked the dosages myself."

McPherson paused, looking doubtful. For several seconds he pondered what Loomins was telling him before riveting the man with an accusing stare.

"Wasn't that rather stupid to leave these people with the run of the boat?" he admonished. "Nobody tried to stop them from freeing the dolphins?"

Loomins fidgeted nervously. "My brother was keeping an eye on them," he muttered.

McPherson let out a reproachful laugh. "A lot of good that did."

"The girl's boyfriend sucker-punched Charlie while he was watching the girl. She was doing something to the dolphins."

"Like what?"

"I don't know. I wasn't present to see for myself."

"What about your deckhands? They just stood there?"

"The guy had taken Charlie's rifle and kept them away. That's when he cut the dolphins loose."

McPherson scoffed derisively. "And I suppose that's when these creatures just got up and left."

"Yes." Loomins uttered the word as if he found this hard to believe himself.

"So what happened next?"

"The girl revived my brother who was still out cold." Loomins was speaking rapidly now. "According to the deckhands, she seemed to do the same thing to him that she did to the dolphins. Charlie used to be a professional fighter, but came away from the sport with a glass jaw. The doctors said he had a non-operable brain aneurysm. Any blow to the head could prove fatal to him."

"What did this girl actually do?"

"Not much of anything other than place her hands on his head."

"But you didn't see her do this."

"No. I was told that when Charlie started to come to, the girl collapsed. Her boyfriend was in the process of moving her back aboard their waverunner when I caught them. That's when I decided to lock them up in the storage locker."

McPherson stood motionless for a long moment, trying to make sense of this strange sequence of events. "If he was attempting to get back on the waverunner, I have to assume it was still operable. I take it you never checked to see if it would run." The look he gave Loomins was devoid of all respect. "You were set up. This whole story about a waverunner on the fritz was simply a ploy to get aboard your vessel. Those people had to have known in advance what you were carrying."

Ben Loomins appeared crestfallen, holding his tongue.

"Did you notice any other vessels in the vicinity while capturing the dolphins?"

"None."

McPherson turned to Jaffey. "What about aircraft?"

"The sky was clear," Jaffey stated.

"And that waverunner was nowhere in sight at the time?"

Both men shook their head.

McPherson eyed each man coldly. "Just look at the facts, gentlemen. Those people had one objective, and one objective only. And that was to free the dolphins. Somehow they had advance knowledge of the capture and came up with a plan to get aboard your vessel." He paused, throwing a sideways glance at both men. "That is, unless this whole story you're giving me is all horseshit. Perhaps you want to keep these dolphins for yourselves. Maybe you think you can get a better price elsewhere."

Both Jaffey and Loomins bridled at the suggestion. "Once we make a deal, we stick by it," Jaffey growled, suddenly looking like he would have no misgivings about striking McPherson. "I'm no longer in the military, Captain. You're not speaking to some low-ranking midshipman trying to pull the wool over the eyes of the big brass. You better think twice before you throw any more wild accusations around like that."

McPherson gazed back, unruffled. "So then how did these people manage to free themselves from their confinement?" he finally asked, his tone mocking.

Jaffey glanced at his partner. "I don't know!" Loomins said peevishly. "It's been driving me crazy how they managed to escape from that locker. It should have been impossible. A heavy dead bolt locked them in there. They somehow found a way to slide it open from the inside."

"And when they got out?"

"They found one of the netting devices we keep aboard and caught Charlie by surprise in the boat's salon. They snared him with the webshot and locked him away in the same storage locker. After that, the girl jumped overboard and her boyfriend retrieved his waverunner. I wasn't aware of the escape until I got back in the harbor."

"I assume your deckhands saw both of them leave but failed to alert you at the time?"

Loomins reddened with embarrassment again. "Yeah... they witnessed the whole thing but didn't try to stop them. These Haitians who work for me are a superstitious lot. A belief in voodoo runs deep in these islanders. They referred to the girl as a *white witch*. They were fearful of bringing misfortune on themselves had they alerted me right away."

"Why would they call this girl a white witch?"

Loomins shrugged. "Who knows? I can't even begin to imagine how their minds work. But from what they told me, there's more of these white dolphins than just the two we captured."

McPherson perked up suddenly. "What do you mean?"

Loomins smiled thinly. "My crewmen counted at least nine of those creatures trailing behind the boat while we were underway. After the girl jumped overboard, they spotted her riding the largest among them."

McPherson turned and looked back at the swimming pool, a heavy trickle of sweat pouring from his brow. He wondered how much longer he he would be able to endure a hellhole like this. He should have been rewarded for his troubles in coming here by now, flying back to the states in Frank Jaffey's Casa-212 with the prizes he had come to retrieve. This sudden revelation, however, had sparked a new set of possibilities into the scheme of things. Perhaps he would walk away with so much more than he had originally anticipated.

Spinning around, he gaffed Jaffey with a penetrating stare. "If there's that many of this unknown species, then you and your partner should have no trouble getting a chance to redeem yourselves."

"Where do we look?" Jaffey said testily. "Do you think all these dolphins have emitters strapped to their bodies? Ben removed the one we found on the male during the capture. Without a signal to home in on, it'd be like looking for a needle in a haystack."

McPherson smiled bitterly. "Gentlemen…one thing I've learned is that when in doubt, go back to the point of origination."

"What are you getting at?" Ben asked.

"The plan is simple," McPherson said. "Go back to where you bagged the dolphins and see if you spot any more."

Jaffey nodded. "I suppose what you're suggesting is as good as any other plan." He hesitated, appearing to give the idea some thought. "All right… we'll give it a shot."

An angry scowl abruptly crossed Loomins' face. "If I ever get my hands on Nick Henderson, he'll wish he never poked his nose into our business."

McPherson gaped at Loomins as if the man had backhanded him squarely across the mouth. "Who?"

- 60 -

Jake Javolyn kicked his way deeper through the murk, carried along by a strong current. The poor visibility surprised him, and he wondered if a storm had passed this way in the last several hours. Indistinct shapes suddenly materialized below him, and as his eyes penetrated the gloom, he started to make out ridges of jutting coral parading by in the midst of a white sandy plain. Although he was fairly deep, perhaps 60 feet below the surface, he felt no escalating pressure, nor a desire to breathe. The thought that this was rather strange ran briefly through his mind. He had been down for some time now without a tank of air to sustain him.

Letting the current take him, he glided effortlessly above a forest of calcareous growths, noticing how bleached and lifeless the formations were. Instinctively, he knew the coral had been dead for many years now, killed off by runaway pollution. The sight failed to disturb him as the flow of water swept him on. He had long since grown used to seeing such sterile habitats while conducting many similar explorations up and down the Haitian coastline, all of them with the same objective. There was a plus side to such barren desolation that would make his search easier, however, and that lay in the unchanging nature of the rocky structures. Without living polyps to generate new growth, the shape of dead coral would remain relatively constant for many years to come, wearing away only gradually through the grinding turbulence of storm-tossed seas.

Something abruptly caught his eye as he looked on, and as he stared, the silhouette of a lone human hovered in the distance ahead, unaffected by the strength of the current. The figure motioned to him, pointing below at something for him to see. Swept closer, he glimpsed the thing being indicated. It was a gargantuan sea turtle, etiolated and unmoving, its broad concave shell stretched out before him.

No! That wasn't what he was seeing at all. Rather, it was a formation of bleached brain coral that had the configuration of a sea turtle. Dumbstruck, he gazed in wonder as a sense of elation quickly engulfed him. The very thing he had been searching for all these months finally lay before him. With a little luck, his quest would soon end.

Looking up, he started to wave his thanks to the lone figure, but the figure was gone. Turning, he glanced about in confusion, wondering what had become of the stranger. But deep down he knew it had not been a stranger. With a start, he gazed in all directions again. It had been Myers. But that was impossible. Myers was dead.

An overwhelming need for air took hold of him, and with sudden alarm he realized he had been down far too long. Fighting back the temptation to breathe, he placed his fins on the formation beneath him, preparing to push off hard and launch himself toward atmosphere high above. But something had hold of his ankles and he could not move. A wave of horror ran through him as he looked down. The diver that had almost got him the night before was back, holding fast to his legs. He tried to kick away, but he was now physically spent and his legs failed to respond. With choking awareness, a wash of water flooded his lungs, and with strangling brutality, a cold blackness rushed in on him.

Jay Jay! A voice cried out from across the galaxy. *Jay Jay!* The cry was closer this time, accompanied by a heavy thud. *I know the location of the turtle coral. I will show you where it is if you wish to go there.* In moments, the nightmare receded into nothingness as Jake found himself back in his quarters, the last tendrils of sleep ebbing away quickly. Another thud landed on the Angel's hull, and he lifted the curtain from the window to investigate. Achilles was there, the dolphin's dark orbs scrutinizing him through the plexiglass.

Rubbing the sleep from his eyes, Jake climbed out of bed. The thought that Bashir had disappeared the night before rushed in on him, and he tried to postulate where the man might have gone. Maybe he... *I can help you find the turtle, Jay Jay.* Jake stopped short, glancing about him. The cabin was empty.

Scratching his head, he wondered if he was still dreaming. Though it had come to him as a barely perceptible whisper, he had distinctly heard a voice. *Am I losing my sanity?*

No, you are perfectly sane, the voice answered. *And you are no longer dreaming.*

What's going on?

Another thump sounded against the hull. *Look out the window, Jay Jay!*

Jake glanced out the window, only to see Achilles again.

The young albino stared back with that permanent smile of his. *I am not currently phonating, Jay Jay. You have become attuned to projected thoughts emanating from me. I was able to see your dream, Jay Jay. You have been searching for that particular formation for some time now without any success. I can bring you to the turtle. I know where it is!*

Jake could only stare back in amazement, wondering if this, too, was another part of the dream as well. Maybe he would find himself waking up at any moment.

- 61 -

The skulls stacked against the wall behind Erzulie grinned hideously in the dimly lit chamber as Colonel Ternier laid the amulet down before her. "I believe this is bona fide, mother," he said, reading the wary look on her face.

Erzulie examined the trinket carefully, not yet willing to make contact with it. As if to neutralize any lurking spells, she reached into one of the many glass jars on the table before her and sprinkled some powder upon the object, chanting a repetitive phrase incomprehensible to Ternier. The chanting went on for nearly a minute before a startled gasp escaped her. The talisman began to give off an eerie red aura, the scant light reflecting dully off Erzulie's face and imparting an expression not much different from the skulls.

"What do you think, mother?" Ternier asked, unable to contain himself any longer. He had never grown used to these mystic rituals.

As if in answer, an inhuman bloodcurdling scream pierced the air within the chamber, emanating from one of the torture cells further back in the prison. Ternier listened, enraptured, glad that the chamber's steel door was still ajar so as not to impede the cries of a tormented soul. The sound of agony always pleased him. For several seconds he wallowed glaze-eyed in the shriek before it finally trailed away into a hopeless wail.

Erzulie's eyes and mouth appeared to retract into broadening, blackened hollows under the feeble emission radiating from the amulet. "You have done well, my son. Nothing can oppose us now!"

An upwelling of immense satisfaction rose up from Ternier's loins and worked its way onto his countenance. "I have another surprise for you, mother."

Erzulie looked up to scrutinize her son more fully, the pits within her face widening even more. "Yes, my son?"

"I have apprehended Emmanuel Baptiste."

Erzulie glanced back down, the glow from the amulet now appearing stronger and changing over to a deep blood-red. "This charm has the power of the rada contained within it," she said, her voice gravelly and filled with emotion. "The cheval gave it up because she and all those she protects have fallen out of favor with the rada. The amulet would have been useless in her hands, maybe even a danger to her." Placing her gaze back on her son, she asked, "When and where did you catch Baptiste?"

"Less than two hours ago at the airport. Baptiste was disembarking from a flight originating out of Anguilla. One of my people working in customs recognized him even though the man was traveling under an assumed name."

Erzulie seemed to smile, though her features continued to be obscured in shadow. "Already the power held within the charm manifests itself. It tells me the rada now favor us." Lifting the amulet, she placed the chain attached to it around her neck, letting the ancient piece of jewelry dangle between her shriveled breasts where it glowed even brighter. "With this behind you, you will be unstoppable, my son. The power you now enjoy will be but nothing compared to that which awaits you." She paused, seeming to savor the feel of the object against her chest. "Where is Baptiste being held?"

"He is in this very prison. Would you like me to bring him to you?"

"Not just yet, my son. I will need time to meditate. There are other considerations more pressing at the moment."

"I assume you are referring to Malique, mother?"

Erzulie turned her face up to Ternier again, her expression appearing even more skull-like than before. "The fulfillment of revenge is not much different than harvesting fruit. The taste grows sweeter as the fruit ripens."

The Colonel was used to his mother speaking in metaphors. She had always talked this way, and Malique was the fruit to which she referred. Their intended raid on the village many years ago had left a bitter taste in both their mouths because the fruit had not sufficiently ripened. But Malique was now ripe for the plucking, and the analogy made him anticipate the potential sweetness all the more.

Yes, he would honor Ortega's request, and the tiny fishing village would provide the needed bodies. It would be easier this way, allowing him to avoid accounting for too many missing prison inmates. A few prisoners disappearing every so often was one thing, but to have nearly two dozen vanish all at once left him exposed to possible repercussions by an assortment of human rights groups, and even worse, incarceration by The Hague. With United Nations troops still in Haiti, it was important he evade bringing such attention to himself. But then again, the day when such accountability would not matter any more was fast approaching.

"I will make the necessary arrangements, mother," Ternier said.

Erzulie rested her gaze on the amulet once more. The talisman continued to glow with a strange ominous intensity.

- 62 -

Jake held on tight as Hermes towed him along, his mind feasting on several concerns. One of those concerns was Bashir's sudden disappearance the night before. Deep down he had the feeling the pod had something to do with it, but decided to keep the matter to himself. It was a beautiful Caribbean morning with near-flat seas, and he had no desire to break the spell. Several others had accompanied him on the outing, including Destiny, Hercules and Aphrodite, Hermes twin sister. With Achilles out in front of the small contingent and leading the way, they had left the cove and were currently traveling south toward a place called the Devil's Horn, a distance of roughly four miles down the coast.

Originally, Achilles had wanted to be Jake's mode of transport, but because Hermes was bigger and more powerful than the juvenile albino, the pod had thought it best to have one of the adults do the pulling rather than have the smallest member of the group run the risk of fatiguing himself. From what Jake was seeing, however, the adult consensus was off the mark, for the young dolphin appeared to be bursting with energy. Every so often along the way, Achilles would execute a series of acrobatic flips, soaring high into the air each time. On several of the aerial maneuvers, Jake could have sworn the juvenile had reached a height of close to 60 feet above the water, turning five and sometimes six complete somersaults during each leap.

In watching these antics, Jake wondered whether the young albino was just happy or simply showing off. Either way, he was justifiably impressed with the athletic prowess displayed by Achilles. But he still remained no less than astounded by what had happened earlier. Even now, his brain continued to reel over the mind link he had attained with with the juvenile. How the cetacean had been able to read his mind, he could not even begin to fathom? And though the mental union had not lasted long, he was beginning to have a clue as to what *bonding* meant. Try as he might, though, he had not been able to reestablish a mental link with the juvenile since the mind-boggling event.

As they continued to make their way south, Jake turned his head to espy Destiny and her mount. To Jake, the girl was a sight to behold as she rode Hercules, her long dark mane trailing behind her and glistening like burnished coal under the morning sun. Once again, she was outfitted in that all-white wet suit which fit her body like a second skin. Destiny was truly in her element as she hunched forward atop the huge albino bull, the same dive mask he had seen before strapped snugly against her face. Periodically, the girl would glance in his direction and throw him a warm smile, seemingly glad about his presence.

As it was, Jake was eager to discover the location of the turtle-like formation, something that had eluded him for a long time now. Without words having been spoken, Achilles had claimed to know where it was. For this jaunt, he had opted to keep his choice of equipment simple, wearing only a shorty wet suit, mask, fins, snorkel, and his trusty K-bar, preferring to leave the waverunner behind and ride Hermes instead. The supposedly short trip was to be nothing more than a brief reconnaissance to confirm if the calcareous structure was the one he had been searching for.

Several times during the excursion, Jake had tried to ride Hermes in the same manner exhibited by Destiny astride her own mount, but finally gave up the attempt. Destiny, it seemed, had a riding technique all her own, naturally conjoining with Hercules as if both beings were actually one. In watching her, Jake could not help dispel the impression that Hercules had been created for this very purpose. Whereas the girl sat just forward of the giant's dorsal fin and held onto straps specifically designed for looping around the creature's pectoral flippers, Jake was forced to grip his own mount's dorsal fin, letting his body trail back as the bottlenose switchbacked through the sea.

Hermes was a powerful animal, and as Jake was towed onward, he was struck by the idea that here was a newly evolved sentience whose mind was likely even more powerful than its body. Some of the things Grahm had told him during the initial voyage to Navassa Island jumped to the forefront of his thoughts. Cetaceans had developed intelligences at least equal if not greater to that of the Homo sapien, having inhabited the planet far longer than man. Grahm had explained to him that without hands for building machinery, the forerunners of this creature could only develop inwardly, possessing thoughts and cultures far different from that of its human counterpart. But something had now changed, something both extraordinary and wonderful. Equipped with digital extremities in combination with an intellect that showed every indication of being superior to man's, the emergence of this newcomer on the planetary scene opened a whole new frontier to all types of possibilities, possibilities that were confided to him by Jacob last night. And from what he'd already seen, it was very probable that the creature to which he clung also possessed both *telepathic* and *telekinetic* abilities. *Yes,* he concluded, *it was quite possible this species was one up on man in every way.* Convinced of this, he felt honored that he had been accepted by these amazing beings.

With such thoughts dominating his awareness, Jake did not realize Hermes had stopped moving. Looking around, he now saw that the jutting headland known as the Devil's Horn lay directly to the east. Almost immediately, Hercules swam alongside Jake so that Destiny could speak to him.

Hiking the dive mask to her forehead, she indicated the area over which they floated. "The formation is directly below us."

"How deep?" Jake asked.

Destiny paused, apparently consulting with the others in the silent mode of communication she used. "About twelve meters," she finally replied.

Jake adjusted his dive mask in preparation for descending, but Hermes did not move.

"Achilles will take you down, Jay Jay," Destiny said.

Jake nodded, noticing the juvenile was suddenly beside him. Hyperventilating for several seconds, he filled his lungs to capacity and grabbed hold of Achilles' dorsal fin. Abruptly Achilles dove.

Just as Jake had experienced in the dream, he felt the strength of the current as he descended. Visibility was not particularly good in this locale, perhaps a step down from what was typical in most undersea habitats along the Haitian coast. The water carried a lot of suspended sediment, and he could see no more than 40 feet through the murk. This was understandable, considering the proximity of a small river discharging on the southern side of the Horn. He had taken the time to look at a map of the area just before coming here, noting the river winding its way down from the higher elevations to the east.

The pressure built rapidly as Achilles arrowed for the bottom, and Jake's ears popped as he swallowed to relieve the escalating discomfiture on his eardrums. Within moments, ridges of coral suddenly sprang into view as the juvenile maintained a purposeful heading. All at once the young dolphin stopped flicking its tail, taking on a lazy glide that brought it over a lower portion of the reef, giving Jake the opportunity to let his eyes adjust to the size and shape of the rocky formation below him. Achilles made three full circuits around the structure, allowing Jake ample time to take in the sight.

A gigantic sea turtle lay sprawled out on a bed of white sand, its broad heart-shaped carapace bleached a pale brown and extending a full 10 meters in length. From above, Jake was amazed at the anatomical correctness of the formation. It appeared to match perfectly the physical characteristics of a real sea turtle, exhibiting four flipper-like legs, a tail, and a bulbous head that jutted ostensibly from beneath the shell in all the right places.

As if knowing Jake had seen enough, Achilles dipped lower, dropping below the edge of the turtle's convex shell. Beneath this level the coral was substantially recessed, and as Jake's eyes adapted to the reduced light, he could see that the carapace of the formation overhung a pedestal of rock that formed the base of the structure. From this perspective, the coral outcropping gave the appearance of a giant mushroom. Two lone spider crabs, their shells encrusted in brown algae, scuttled out of his way as he let go of Achilles and slipped under the umbrella of coral. Swimming beneath the overhang and making one full lap around the center column, Jake gauged the distance between the sandy bottom and the underside of the shell to be remain fairly uniform, about four feet in height all the way around. One area back toward the turtle's tail contained a significant buildup of calcareous rubble. It was here that he focused his efforts, moving aside small chunks of rock.

The available light dimmed further as Jake began to work, making him glance briefly behind him to investigate the cause. Congregated together, Destiny and all four albinos hovered suspended just below the edge of the overhang. Overcome by curiosity, they peered in at him. Turning back to the task at hand, Jake resumed his labors and dug deeper, displacing several larger coral fragments before his hands encountered something incongruous with the rubble. Running his fingers along it, he felt a flat surface. Encouraged, he cleared away more rock. Some kind of a metallic box, possibly aluminum, sat embedded among the loose stone.

Working more quickly now, Jake uncovered the front face of two more boxes, each face about two feet wide by eighteen inches high. Extending an arm, he managed to get a hand behind a corner of one of the boxes. Although the confined space afforded him little in the way of leverage, he positioned his body as best he could to exert as much force as possible. The box barely budged, its contents apparently quite weighty.

With lungs now burning, Jake made a decision, and that was to bury the boxes once again. Quickly, he pushed rubble back in front of the containers and withdrew from the rocky enclosure. Achilles was standing by to take him to the surface, and upon gripping the juvenile's dorsal fin, Jake was whisked swiftly to the air above.

Inhaling ponderously upon gaining atmosphere, Jake eased his aching lungs. He looked at his dive watch, realizing he had been down nearly five and a half minutes. Turning his eyes toward the land, he took a moment to study the shoreline, gauging his current position with respect to several conspicuous landmarks along the headland. From where he floated, he guessed he was approximately a quarter mile directly off the rocky promontory.

"There is no need for you to memorize where you are, Jay Jay," Achilles ululated, as if reading Jake's mind. *"When you wish to return here, I will take you."*

Jake took in the words, growing used to the way Achilles always seemed to be one step ahead of him. "I'll remember that, Achilles." Pivoting his head, he noticed Destiny sitting atop Hercules close behind him. Though he half expected her to ask about the boxes, the girl sat quietly, leisurely stroking the giant albino's head.

"You're probably wondering what those boxes contain," Jake huffed, continuing to breath heavily from the lengthy dive.

Destiny smiled lazily. Though she had been submerged as long as Jake, she showed not the slightest sign of strain. "I have been brought up to respect the privacy of others," she said softly. "Hopefully your search is now at an end and you will find peace within yourself."

Jake had not expected such a reply. "But you were down there watching me," he panted, still hungrily gulping air. "You're not curious about why I came here?"

"I was only concerned for your safety. It is normal for every member of the pod to look out for one another. These waters off the Horn can be dangerous."

As his oxygen debt diminished, Jake's breathing began to slow perceptibly. "I need to confirm what's in those boxes, but not now," he offered. "When the time is right, I'll come back here with the Angel and bring up what's down there."

"When that time comes, we'll be ready to help if you need us."

Jake nodded in appreciation. "I just might take you up on that offer." He looked north. "What say we head back? I've seen all I need for now."

Achilles gave Jake just enough time to lower his face mask and insert the snorkel in his mouth before flicking his tail hard and taking off in the direction of the cove. It soon became evident that the young albino would not be denied towing him on the return trip.

- 63 -

Though things like this no longer surprised him, Grahm nevertheless continued to stare in wonder at the data displayed on the laptop screen. Everything Jacob had claimed about the thurentra was proving to be true. The Big Mac in Miami had done its job, identifying a genetic marker common to both the hybrid organism residing on the cove floor and a species of sea cucumber found in Caribbean waters. What was even more interesting was the discovery of a second DNA sequence within the thurentra that inferred a match with a fragment of Natalie's genome.

Grahm turned to Parker. "You're certain Big Mac scanned the genome of every known variety of coelenterate."

Parker gave a lackluster nod. "Yep. Probably came close to burning out her circuits with the survey she made. It was quite extensive."

Frustration showed on Grahm's features. The face of his long departed wife suddenly loomed in his mind's eye. Had she still been alive, she might have provided valuable insight in the search. "Then its got to be a species of coelenterate never before catalogued."

"Assuming it actually belongs to the coelenterate phylum," Parker was quick to point out. "I only instructed Big Mac to focus on the coelenterates."

Grahm shifted his eyes to the inverted funnel positioned above the water where the thurentra lay. "It stands to reason a life form capable of transforming or mutating other organisms into newly evolved creatures has never before been catalogued. Jacob's description of the organism fits that of a jellyfish, and right now, that's what I'm sticking with."

Parker whistled. "So you think this unknown variety of jellyfish is a genetic cousin of Natalie's and the other pod members."

Grahm scratched his beard. "It certainly seems to look that way."

"This trip isn't over yet," Parker said. "Who knows…maybe we'll get lucky and find this jellyfish before we're done."

"Perhaps," Grahm agreed tiredly. He sank down on a nearby flat-topped rock and rubbed his eyes. He was a scientist and men of his profession needed proof to collaborate observations simply because things weren't always what they appeared to be. Here was at least an inkling of evidence backing up how the thurentra came into being. Dispelling the skepticism he had felt over the merging of a sea cucumber and an unknown form of jellyfish was not easy for him. A discovery like this was unprecedented in the history of biological research. Newly evolved organisms were just not produced in the manner Jacob had described. And yet he could not reject the supporting evidence, though of and by itself it was not conclusive. Such thoughts caused his mind to explore another possibility.

Was Jacob's application of the Gaia Theory so absurd after all? Had Mother Nature actually come up with a remedy for neutralizing man's destructive nature, of putting mankind back on the right track? Grahm's eyes locked on several white fins cleaving the water in the vicinity of the waterfall. *And if such a divine purpose were truly in the works, maybe these dolphins had been specifically created to fulfill a certain role.*

Caught up in this idea, Grahm explored it further. If allowed to propagate and multiply, who knew what achievements this new breed might accomplish. With prehensile digits they could build machines, but in so doing mankind might perceive them as a threat. In the laboratory he had seen with his own eyes how quickly Natalie could take a complex pipe puzzle, disassemble it, and then put it back together in no time flat. Then there was the Rubik's Cube. Natalie had solved it easily, no matter how randomly it was reset each time. If an albino could do that, then designing and fabricating new types of machinery and electronic gadgetry was more than likely only a step away in their technological advancement.

Back in Miami, Grahm had been astounded to discover that Natalie had already known how to play chess. Even Nick Henderson, an exceptional player in his own right, had been no match for the female dolphin. This recollection brought a humorous smile to Grahm's face, for he knew that Henderson had considered each of Natalie's three victories to be nothing more than flukes. Following the third loss, Henderson had refused to play anymore.

Grahm mulled this over. Only now did he fully comprehend the extent of Henderson's bias. His young assistant exemplified humanity's narcissistic need to believe man to be the preeminent thinker, doer, and feeler on the planet. Henderson was a perfect example of man's self-perceived superiority over all other living species, even in light of the fact that the brain size of some cetaceans had grown equal to and then surpassed the size of modern man's some thirty million years ago. The current Tursiops truncatus alone, Grahm knew, had been around on the order of fifteen million years with a brain size on a par with the present day Homo sapien. Without prehensile extremities with which to develop a written language, it only stood to reason that delphine history would be stored away in such large brains, passed down from generation to generation. If that were true, the knowledge locked away in those minds would be vast.

As one of the foremost delphinologists on the planet, Grahm understood that past increases in brain sizes of both humans and cetaceans indicated a rising curve of further evolution in the cranial capacity of the two species. But it was the cetacea that still held a sizeable lead. With a mass of 9,000 grams, the brain of a forty-ton sperm whale was six times heavier than that of a human's. Even so, the consensus among most scientists was to place these brains in a category below man's, rationalizing that large bodies required large brains to control their behavior. They also argued that since larger-brained cetaceans had no hands, they had no need to develop intelligence. But Grahm's opinion went counter to such reasoning, holding to the belief that cut off from the need for building, for food preservation and preparation, and for external forms of transportation, cetaceans in all probability had highly advanced ethics and laws, developed over eons and passed on to succeeding generations. In spite of having no direct experience of living in the sea, man still insisted upon imposing the criteria for intelligence relating to cetaceans, refusing to see that some of those large brains were actually superior to human brains in unique and different ways.

In working with dolphins over the years, Grahm had become more than convinced they harbored a complex inner reality quite different from that of man. With dolphins, group survival took precedence over individual members. Necessities for survival took in the group as a whole, with sick or grieving pod members cared for by the healthier animals. However, when such care put the survival of the group in jeopardy, the injured member would voluntarily commit suicide by simply ceasing to breathe.

Perhaps the most notable cetacean ethic was their special regard for man. Generally speaking and with few exceptions, dolphins and whales appeared to avoid injuring a human, even under extreme degrees of provocation. And although Grahm had no way of actually proving it, he suspected that cetaceans viewed man as an incredibly dangerous species in concert. Even with incomplete knowledge about man, contacts at sea with members of the human race often revealed to cetacea how harmful mankind could be, not only to the environment but to all life in the hydrosphere. Experiences with whaling and tuna fleets alone were good enough examples of the detriment man posed. Factor in massive oil spills, the effects of ship's sonar, undersea explosions, widespread pollution of the oceans, and naval warfare, and cetaceans had enough fragmentary knowledge about the nature of the human race to know that man could easily wipe them out if he so chose.

Grahm turned his eyes in another direction. Henderson was at it again, snorkeling around the thurentra like a bloodhound on the scent of elusive quarry. There was something unusual going on out there to arouse the lad's curiosity, of that he was certain. His young assistant had grown increasingly withdrawn over the past 48 hours, appearing to be preoccupied with the hybrid organism. But whatever was sparking his interest he was keeping to himself.

In the last several days, Grahm had seen a different side to Henderson, and he didn't like what he was seeing. Although the grad student had always been a bit cantankerous and surly, those traits had become far more pronounced as of late. Among other things, Henderson was proving himself to be a racist, showing an open hostility and disrespect towards Jacob. It was now apparent Henderson had preconceived notions about how these islanders should act and behave, and Jacob was not conforming to the image Henderson had expected of him. Henderson was being stubborn. He had put reason aside, wanting to delude himself into believing all Haitians were illiterate and ignorant. As smart as the lad was with computers, Henderson refused to accept the premise that no race, culture or ethnic group held a monopoly on intelligence and that exceptional intellect could spring up from any quarter in the human species.

Unconscious of his own action, Grahm shook his head as he continued to watch his stubborn assistant fin around the thurentra, wondering if Henderson would be foolish enough to get himself zapped a second time. *Serves him right if he does.*

Movement at the cove entrance abruptly caught Grahm's eye, and he realized Javolyn and the girl had returned with four of the albinos. The sight brought a smile to his face, particularly that of the girl. And while he had no idea why, a feeling of joy seemed to take hold of him every time he set eyes on her. Strangely, it warmed him to see Destiny in Jake's company. The two seemed right together. Even stranger was how natural it appeared for both of them to be whisked along by the albino dolphins.

Grahm felt a tinge of envy as the group turned toward the beach, wishing he, too, could share such a bond with these noble creatures. The way they had taken to Javolyn in so short a time still continued to puzzle him, but then again, maybe they could sense certain qualities in the makeup of an individual that determined the full measure of their interaction with that person. He couldn't even begin to imagine what kind of thoughts pulsed through those marvelous brains. With fifteen million years of advanced evolutionary development already behind the Tursiop's neurological hardware, he had to assume their view of the universe and existence itself had to be worlds apart from that of human perception. But then enhance those brains further through a mysterious event that had all the earmarks of an evolutionary jump, an elevated sentience had emerged with immeasurable mental capabilities, giving it a potential that now dwarfed man's.

As Grahm watched the group work its way toward the beach, he realized it would take more than his remaining years to fully grasp the underlying philosophies of these newcomers to the planet.

- 64 -

Bashir worked his way down through the fissures in the rock, slowly making his way toward the subterranean grotto. The fisherman called Jimenez had dropped him off on the southern side of the island just before dawn, leaving him with a small sack of cornmeal, a flask of freshwater, and half a dozen mangos for sustenance. Finding the concealed entrance that would lead him to the hidden submarine pen had not been easy, and he had wasted many hours groping his way through the objectionable thickets that overgrew the karst before stumbling upon the opening. His knowledge of its exact location relative to other topographic features had been rather obscure. Unlike Yeslam and some of the others in the team, he had had far less opportunity to venture out onto the island's upper plateau.

His body ached in various places, the result of having to travel on foot over jagged bedrock that riddled the island's interior. The sun had not yet arisen by the time he had first gained the island's upper terrace, and in the dim twilight he had misjudged a small but craggy pocket overgrown with cacti. The ensuing spill he had taken had left him bruised and bleeding in several places, and irksome quills of cactus had broken off in his hip. And coming into contact with the poisonwood trees that abounded over the rough terrain had only added to his discomfort, for his skin now itched wildly where rashes had broken out. He didn't care. He would do what he could to put a stop to this madness.

A strange detachment from what he was doing seemed to urge him onward, all the while his mind vaguely aware he had no actual plan to follow. Still, he continued to follow the passageway, descending deeper through the honeycombed rock that comprised the island's substrata. A series of electric bulbs strung out along the power cable that wound its way toward the underground stronghold provided ample light as he labored his way lower.

Already he could hear the generator to which the cable was attached, the sound of it reaching his ears in a barely audible hum.

As Bashir descended lower, he thought about the man in charge of this operation. From his association with Yeslam Raduyev, he had learned the Chechen was actually the nephew of the infamous Limash Sabayev, a fanatical Muslim fundamentalist who had been killed more than a year earlier. Sabayev had been a rebel warlord and the most wanted man in Russia. Through sheer audacity, Sabayev was responsible for more high-profile acts of terrorism than any other Chechen. In a bid to rid Chechnya of Russian domination, Sabayev had been reputed to have allied himself to Al Qaeda, purchasing nuclear weapons for Bin Laden in three former Soviet states – Turkmenistan, Ukraine, and Kazakhstan. Rumor had it that those weapons were a mix of suitcase and tactical warhead bombs.

Regarded as little more than a foot soldier by his superiors, Bashir had not been privy to many of the details of his group's mission, although he had learned enough to fill in some of the missing tidbits of information concerning the operation. Raduyev was actually the youngest of seven nuclear experts that worked for Bin Laden, all of them Central Asian Muslims. In an attempt to secure a lasting alliance with Al Qaeda, Sabayev had offered up his nephew as part of a long-term scheme that had the potential of bringing down the country Bin Laden deemed the Great Satan. Blond-haired Chechens were much sought after by Bin Laden, owing to the reduced scrutiny such individuals would draw upon themselves. Initially, Yeslam had been planted as a one-man cell, thereby minimizing contacts until certain objectives could be achieved. Through carefully forged documents, Raduyev had gained entrance into the United States where he had first earned a degree in nuclear engineering before seeking admission to Navy Seal training. Knowledge of military techniques used by the Seals would be invaluable to the plan, which would involve clandestine undertakings at sea.

Bashir occupied himself with such thoughts as he inched his way down to the final turn in the winding passageway where it gave way to the subterranean grotto. Above the soft drone of the generator, voices could be heard. With great caution, he poked his head around the last barrier of rock, his eyes falling on two nearby figures with their backs to him.

"-very soon." It was Raduyev talking.

"I am still uneasy about bringing these infidels here," the other man said. "Down one man already, it will be difficult to control so many people in these constricted caverns."

The voice of the second speaker caught Bashir by surprise. Although he had known three other militants would be joining up with Raduyev, he hadn't been informed that one of them would be Gullu Sherkhan.

"You are beginning to sound like a woman more and more each day," Raduyev chided. "We will need a large labor force to widen the tunnels if our plan is to succeed."

Bashir found it difficult to believe Sherkhan's apparent calmness in the face of such open admonishment. Back in Afghanistan, an underlying friction had always existed between the two men, but now something had changed.

"Where will these people sleep?" Sherkhan said evenly, choosing to ignore the insult. "There is little room down here for so many."

"We will keep them working around the clock in the tunnels above," Raduyev snapped. "They will have little time for rest. We will push them hard, dividing ourselves up in shifts to oversee and ensure their efforts."

Sherkhan shrugged resignedly. "What about tools? Even among us, we don't have enough to go around."

Raduyev shifted around to glare at the Pashtun, and Bashir barely managed to pull his head back in time to keep from being seen. "More tools will be brought to us when the labor force arrives. I have already arranged for that."

"What about food?" Sherkhan pressed. "These people will require nourishment if we expect them to keep working. I have examined our stockpile of food and fresh water. Our supply is too limited to give any of it away."

Raduyev's response came back as a snarl. "Feeding these islanders does not concern me. We will use them until they can no longer serve us."

Bashir remained hidden, daring not to sneak another peek as he eavesdropped, but no further conversation ensued. He waited another minute before sidling his head around the bend in the rock, only to discover both men were now gone. He was still unsure of his next move, mulling over what he had just learned. This was something else he had been in the dark about.

Apparently Raduyev had made a deal to have people abducted and brought to this place for the sole purpose of performing slave labor. The most startling aspect of the plan was the manner in which those people would be treated. The idea caused Bashir to take a hard look at himself, making him realize what kind of a monster he might have become if not for the way fate had interceded to take him into the hands of those angelic beings. They had rescued him from defiling his soul forever, opening him up to reveal the person he truly was. Men like Raduyev were brutal and evil to the core. Raduyev was incapable of showing someone the mercy and compassion the captain of the Avenging Angel had given him. He found it hard to believe he had actually looked up to the Chechen before his capture. The one they called Jay Jay had treated him kindly. Even though his captor had had every right to let him die, the man had instead chosen to have his wound tended. On top of that, he had fed him and brought him ashore to eat with the others.

It was these thoughts that further galvanized Bashir, causing him to see the utter contradiction an individual like Raduyev represented. Here was a man whose fundamental faith was at irreconcilable odds with sober logic. More than ever now, he knew that Raduyev had to be stopped, and with renewed conviction he suddenly became cognizant of what he must do next.

- 65 -

Jake sat next to Destiny at the north end of the cove near the fish pen, their location farthest from the waterfall. At this distance, the sound of the plummeting water was only a dull susurration, allowing him to speak in a quiet tone. "Pardon me for bringing up the subject, but I'd like you to explain to me why these dolphins refuse to fight back against people trying to hurt them. I would think their extraordinary intelligence could be used as a weapon." He paused uncomfortably, waiting for her to say something.

Destiny gave a minute shrug. "It's not in their nature to fight back. They're incapable of aggression."

Something registered in the back of Jake's head, realizing she had said the same thing the night before. The idea puzzled him. For a creature to avoid striking back in self-defense was a concept altogether unique from his point of view. "You've led a sheltered existence, living in this cove all your life. The world beyond this place can be mean and nasty much of the time. If these dolphins are going to survive, they've got to learn to defend themselves in a proactive way."

Jake stared at Destiny's face closely, trying to see if he was getting through to her. Her expression seemed filled with empathic understanding, like that of a teacher patiently listening to the complaints of a stubborn child. "Causing harm to others is not in their nature," she reiterated softly.

The girl's reply prompted a montage of past battle skirmishes to go flashing through Jake's mind. Defending himself and others was an inborn trait that came naturally, never requiring much in the way of thought on his part. By nature, he was a man of action, seldom given to deep reflection. "Sooner or later we all have to do things we don't like…that is, if we choose to go on living. Keeping your skin intact from an aggressor doesn't necessarily mean you have to injure or kill that person." For emphasis, he eyed Achilles floating leisurely nearby. "Back at Navassa I saw a member of your pod make an incredible aerial leap to intercept and toss aside a grenade thrown from that helicopter attacking us. That action prevented anyone from getting hurt, including the bad guys."

Destiny's face remained soulful, her eyes holding his gaze and infused with seemingly limitless compassion. Delaying a response, she reached out and stroked Jake's cheek with a gentle tenderness. "It was Hermes who did that," she finally said. "He was protecting your vessel and crew."

The girl's touch was soothing, and Jake felt his inner frustration quickly defusing.

He sat quietly for the moment, enjoying the light caress of her fingertips, vaguely mindful that those same appendages were capable of miraculous healing. A familiar stirring suddenly took hold of him, and it took all his will to fight off the urge rapidly consuming him. To conceal his embarrassment, he wrestled for words, practically choking them out. "Are you telling me these dolphins are only capable of protecting others, but not themselves?"

Destiny withdrew her hand slowly, looking at Jake strangely. "We must always be aware of the consequences of our actions. Even when we think we are justified in what we are doing, the act can sometimes cause unintended suffering."

Jake caught the inference. "You mean like when I kayoed Frank Loomins?"

Destiny stared back blankly, innocently. "I'm not familiar with that word."

Jake's surprise lasted less than a second, giving way to a wry smile. He should have automatically assumed the girl's sheltered life among the gentle creatures she lived with would have left her ignorant of terms descriptive of violence, and 'kayo' was one such term used to describe it. "Kayo means to knock out, to render someone unconscious with a blow to the head."

The girl nodded uneasily, and out of the corner of his eye, Jake saw the water splash as Achilles flinched.

Jake thought it necessary to explain himself further, remembering something he had gained from perusing books on existentialism. Destiny had mentioned that, among the diverse subjects Jacob had educated her and the pod on, philosophy had been one such field of study. "Isn't the morally right thing to do in any situation governed by the consequences of the actions under consideration? Had I not done what I did, we might never have been able to save Hermes and Aphrodite. Sometimes there are no alternatives available to achieve the desired result."

Destiny's reply was non-judgemental. "You acted in a manner consistent with who you are. You were only doing what you were meant to do. Your nature is to protect."

Jake found himself growing weary of such sinuous logic, not knowing what else to offer on the subject. The girl was obviously hopelessly naïve. He suddenly felt inclined to nudge the conversation in another direction. "Are you and your friends happy living away from the rest of the world in this secluded place?"

Destiny sniffed the air. "I have always sensed an inner peace within Gaia. Knowing that it pulses with the purity of life gives me and the others great joy."

Jake steered the conversation even further, planting his eyes on Achilles again. "Have you ever considered how much your life and the lives of these dolphins will change once Jacob's plan is set in motion? A plan like that is quite grand and far-reaching in scope."

Destiny elicited a weak smile, noting Jake's concern. "The plan is already in motion. It has been for some time now."

"Yes, I understand all that. But what happens when it begins to take on a fruitation that becomes visible to the rest of the world? From what I gather, I'm the only one outside your tight-knit little group who has knowledge of this plan, and I'm honored by the trust Jacob has shown me in revealing it. But I also know this project will be perceived as a threat by some people once they get wind of it."

Destiny appeared unperturbed, and Jake wondered if it was her naivety that was showing again. Some elements of the human race could be quite ruthless and downright vicious when it came to protecting their own interests, particularly when some new innovative enterprise threatened the piece of the pie they had established for themselves. For one, oil companies and oil-producing nations would not be receptive to the idea of cheap, environmentally friendly forms of alternative energy, seeing it as disruptive to the monopolies they had so painstakingly set in place over the last hundred years. He had no doubt they would take whatever measures necessary to stop *Tursiops Worldwide* from achieving its goals. Then again, there was the potential terrorist aspect to consider. Sea-based energy-harvesting and mining operations that benefited the world would be viewed as economic targets by Islamic extremists and other militant groups seeking to make a political statement. Such sites would become fair game for sabotage and attack. And once the thurentra's ability to siphon valuable precious metals from the sea became known, it would draw the attention of all types of unsavory characters, causing them to descend upon Gaia and other thurentra habitats like a school of barracuda. A foreboding coldness settled over him as he thought about how the lure of easy riches and gold had led to the destruction of the Tainos by greedy men.

"Both my mother and Jacob have foreseen such a possibility," Destiny acknowledged. "But they believe most of the world will embrace the goals we're trying to achieve."

"It's the people who don't share your views you have to be concerned about," Jake said bitterly, finding it difficult to disengage himself from the cynicism he felt.

"If there's any possibility of saving the planet, of making the lives of everyone that much better, then we would be derelict in not even trying to make such a thing possible simply because the risks were too high."

"Is that you talking, or is it Jacob?" Jake looked away. "I just don't want you and your friends getting hurt."

Destiny studied Jake's face, once again seeming to probe his inner being. "A moment ago you asked me if I was happy existing in a place you perceive as being unaffected by the outside world." Her words flowed softly, mellifluously. "There is a connectedness that you don't see…that I wouldn't expect you to see-"

Jake cut her off, unable to suppress his growing frustration any longer. "You'd be surprised by some of the things I've seen. It would horrify you." He suddenly caught himself, ashamed at how harsh his words must have sounded. In a gentler tone, he added, "Take my word for it, you'll be exposing yourself to dangers you never even imagined."

Destiny's calm air remained unchanged. "What we see can often be deceptive. An object floating on the ocean surface can sometimes have a submerged portion that lays hidden and extends very deep. Eventually you will find that many of the things most visible to you are nothing more than illusions."

"The danger I'm talking about is no illusion. It's very real."

"There is also much good in the world," Destiny countered patiently.

"Yeah," Jake agreed halfheartedly. "But, unfortunately, I don't see enough of it going around."

Destiny glanced over at Hermes and Hercules as they swam over to join Achilles, then turned back to regard Jake with balmy, enchanting eyes and the trace of a knowing smile. "Just because you're not able to see or feel something doesn't mean its not there."

Jake wanted to tell her he only believed what he could see or experience with his other senses, but he pulled up short of saying so, aware that Destiny had lifted a hand to his temple. He lost sight of his thoughts, feeling oddly relaxed by the solace of her touch. The scent of wildflowers wafting down from the upper ledges seemed suddenly stronger, making him light-headed. He had slept somewhat fitfully the night before, and a bout of drowsiness seemed to be creeping up on him, leaving him momentarily speechless. With heavy eyelids, he was vaguely conscious of a soothing, melodious warbling coming from the nearby dolphins. The trilling commingled with the chirping of the songbirds filling the air. Lulled by the sound, he gazed dazedly, letting himself drift into the deepening pools of Destiny's eyes. Like a cloud of mist, they engulfed him. A feeling suggestive of the healing he had undergone two days earlier accosted him, accompanied by something even more profound than before.

A voice reminiscent of Destiny's and the ululations of Achilles, Hermes and Hercules seemed to echo across the cosmos in a soft, comforting whisper. "Conjoined with the minds of my friends, here, I am able see and feel something far bigger than any one of us, something beautiful that has given us special purpose. We have a duty, an obligation to fulfill…there are things we were meant to do. Turning away from this responsibility would be tantamount to a grave injustice, one that would leave only misery in its wake."

Jake had difficulty responding, overcome by the somnolence rapidly consuming him. "Misery already exists everywhere," he murmured, the words spilling lethargically from his mouth like thick maple syrup. "Here in Haiti…it…is…especially….baaad."

"Then we must look to change it," the foursome chorused soothingly.

Jake stared mesmerized. Lying behind the words was a rainbow. Intrigued, he reached out to grab it, but came away with nothing. Confused, he tried to reorientate his ethereal being and latch onto it again, only to find his hands come up empty a second time.

Do not try to grab the rainbow, Jay Jay! It was Achilles speaking to him. *You will never be able to hold onto it.*

It's right there! Jake insisted. *I see it!* Stubbornly he reached for it again, disregarding what Achilles was telling him.

If you think about it, Jay Jay, you will realize rainbows have no distinct location, nor distance. Paradoxically, they do have a direction. A rainbow is actually a phenomenon, a good example of the duality all phenomena exhibit. In one sense, a rainbow certainly seems real, appearing as an arc of brightly colored concentric stripes, but in another sense it does not really exist because it is a by-product of light and the prismatic properties of mist.

But light is a form of energy, Jake pointed out, *comprised of electromagnetic waves. Isn't electromagnetic energy real?*

Relative to the perceptions of the sentience perceiving it, yes, Achilles agreed. *Condensed energy forms matter, and a particular pattern of matter lays the foundation for the building blocks of life. It is this wellspring of energy that gives the universe structure, an infinite realm of superimposed dimensionality in which all living organisms are part of the whole, including humans. In their current state of evolutionary development, most humans are able to perceive only an infinitesimal portion of the energy grid that comprises creation in its entirety. Because of this, it is difficult for your species to embrace the full spectrum of beauty that embodies nature. All living things are an integral part of this spectrum, interdependent on the other energy bodies.*

Jake realized the rainbow had vanished, replaced by the painting he had seen Achilles create. As he studied it, a heightened awareness took hold of his senses. *These paintings are very much like portals, aren't they?* he found himself asking, although he was certain he already knew the answer. *They give some of us a fleeting glimpse of the universal energy grid, a subtle sense of the big picture.*

You are very perceptive, Jay Jay, Achilles said. *Though we did not consciously intend for it to happen, it turns out our art can be used as a tool. For those it affects, it allows them to look deep within in order to see beyond themselves. We surmise we subconsciously embed a higher mathematics in the overall composition formed by the various colored paints that are given form and texture by the brush strokes.*

Albert Einstein tried to give mankind a simplistic picture of the universe through mathematics, Jake replied.

This time it was the voice of Hermes who answered. *Yes, Einstein was one of your great thinkers. He understood man's limitations in his perception of the world around him, believing reality to be an illusion, albeit a very persistent one. According to him, man experiences himself, his thoughts and feelings, as something separate and disconnected from other things and phenomena...a kind of optical delusion of his consciousness. This delusion imprisons him, restricting him to a personal affectation for only a few people near him. But Einstein also saw that man could free himself from this prison by widening his sphere of compassion.*

What led him to that conclusion?

Einstein believed interdependence to be a fundamental law of nature. Without compassion for all living organisms, the human species cannot possibly grasp the interconnectedness of all things. Feeling genuine compassion means wanting others to be free of suffering. Without compassion, humans are prone to focus on the distinct differences and individuality of other life forms and objects instead of seeing the integrated whole. All things on this planet are interrelated. The oceans, clouds, forests, mountains and flowers are part of a system that is really one. Everything survives through an interaction of subtle patterns of energy, causing phenomena to arise that are also connected with this dependence. Nothing exists separate from the whole, for if it did, it would quickly decay and dissolve. To believe ourselves as existing independent and autonomous from everything else is out of accord with true reality. Einstein saw through the illusion, knowing that such thinking lay outside the bounds of ultimate wisdom.

But modern science has already discovered this interdependence, Jake argued. *Fields of study like oceanography, ecology, and eco-biology have made considerable advances in recent years.*

Your claim is valid, Hermes capitulated. *But unfortunately the vast majority of humankind still remains detached and aloof of these facts in spite of acquiring such knowledge. The callous disregard for the environment shown by the most pernicious elements of your species is frightening. You only have to look at the damage your civilization has wrought on the earth by making the petroleum-based fuels your primary energy source. Even though humans are aware that burning such fuel can cause global warming and acid rain, most turn a blind eye to the harm done. Only by instilling compassion will they fully realize the consequences of their actions, the wrong they have committed. Bad deeds and, in some cases, even bad intentions have a way of coming back full circle on the entity responsible for them.*

So this is your mission, to broaden mankind's compassion?

Among other things.

Einstein tried to unify all the forces of nature in one simple equation and failed, Jake felt it necessary to say. *Have your kind also made such an attempt?*

Hermes did not immediately respond.

Jake grew impatient and tried to coax an answer from the albino. *With those superior brains, I have to assume all of you have tried.*

Hermes hesitated a moment longer before answering. *Just as Einstein had failed, so have we.*

But you must have gotten closer than Einstein to solving this mystery?

The puff of a collective sigh seemed to brush up against Jake's mind. *Mathematics is a nexus to the eternal beyond,* Hermes explained. *In its purest form, it is a bridge between visible and hidden worlds, a means of turning the mind away from transitory physical perceptions of matter which is really illusionary and leading it to the contemplation of truly existing constants that never change. Another of your great thinkers, Pythagoras, understood this. From our perspective, mathematical thought is the language of the divinity that resides deep within the consciousness of all sentient beings, a form of inner communion. This language makes use of abstractions that correspond to nothing in one's experience. It is a vehicle for transcending the world of illusion into a realm of universals, drawing the soul towards a domain of higher being. In using it to its fullest, the thinker must learn to feel this thought in a reverent way if he or she is to become one with the eternal. The thinker must be able to cast off all beliefs and biases, striving for an emptiness that lies beyond duality.*

Jake tried to grasp the wisdom being imparted to him. *What do you mean by emptiness?*

Emptiness is a melting away of the ego, the self. It was now the group talking in a collective voice. *It is a purified state of mind that rids itself of the qualities we normally assign to reality. In such a state, what we usually identify as normal perception is contradicted, replaced with no attachment to any preconception of what truth may ultimately prove to be. It is a frame of arcane ignorance, a final state of perfection in which the thinker is possessed by the ultimate truth, rather than the ultimate truth being possessed by the thinker.*

A clarity of mind the likes of which Jake had never before experienced suddenly gripped him, awakening him to a feeling of inner calm and happiness he had never known. He let the sensation wash over him, wallowing in its glow before continuing with the discussion. *So by failing to achieve complete emptiness, you're not able to mathematically unify the known forces of the universe?*

That is correct! Achieving absolute emptiness might be analogous to exceeding the speed of light in the four-dimensional universe your human brain normally perceives.

I'm not sure I follow you.

If your mind is already restrained with Einstein's premise that such a speed cannot be surpassed, then going beyond light speed in a realm consisting of only four dimensions, three of space and one of time, is impossible.

But Einstein mathematically proved its validity, that the speed of light was a universal constant.

Yes he did. Referenced to a four-dimensional time-space universe, his logic was sound. But tied to a system consisting of higher dimensionality, such logic is flawed.

One of Jake's conversations with Jacob came flooding back. *Jacob is convinced higher dimensions actually exist, that what we believe to be reality is really a subspace of a much greater realm. He believes all of you are capable of seeing beyond this subspace when you're linked together collectively. Is this true?*

We are able to attain instances of exceptional insight into the true reality that pulses all about us, yes. Sometimes we are able to arrive at conclusions that are not just probable, but undeniable. On such occasions we soar to a place that is eternal, unified and never varies. In such a place our sense of certainty is unlimited.

Yet in unison you're unable to achieve a state of absolute emptiness.

Yes. While it is possible to approach it asymptotically, we never quite get there.

Why is that?

Our motivations are not sufficiently pure. Our compassion for your species falls short of being utterly self-disregarding, and our seeking of ultimate truth is tainted with bias.

What kind of bias? In asking the question, Jake sensed a subtle change in the minds surrounding him.

We still believe in the good that lies within mankind.

Jake pondered what was being revealed to him, but quickly gave up, realizing he was trying to ponder the imponderable. These intelligences were endowed with a wisdom far more advanced than he.

We would like to show you something, the group said, interrupting Jake's perplexity.

What's that?

Achilles' painting floated before Jake's eyes again. *Do not try to make sense of what you see before you for the moment.*

For one fleeting instant, Jake perceived he was seeing beyond infinity. An upwelling of something suddenly came flowing from a singular point that he sensed to be the back side of a black hole, growing in luminosity and oscillating harmonically as it wended its way toward him. Tendrils of it shot out to loop around his being, imparting an overwhelming, yet vaguely familiar warmth that took his breath away.

The emission you perceive is composed of the true essence of hyperspace. It is what gives matter pattern and form.

Caught in its grip, Jake felt rarified, barely able to gasp out his next question. *Is it pure energy I'm seeing?*

Look closer, Jay Jay! Feel it for what it is!

Baffled, Jake continued to stare. *If it's not energy, then what am I sensing?*

It is the very thing that binds the totality of nature, the unifying force that connects everything in existence.

The lucidity that suddenly struck Jake slapped up against him like a wave crashing against a levee. Dumbstruck, he realized he was sensing pure love. Aware that he was now linked to the minds surrounding him, he felt his base consciousness rekindled, the part of him that was intrinsically pure and unpolluted with blinding presumption. There was harmony here, a synchronous joining of spirits in which one consciousness hovered at the center of the globular cluster, the focal point about which the others spiraled. Drawn to the gravity well, he fell into orbit, feeling the tug of the glowing astral body that was Destiny.

A rapid dawning began to impinge on Jake's awareness, and he instinctively grasped the nature of the things he was seeing. The laws of physics were different here. Gravity assaulted him from multiple directions simultaneously, pulling and pushing in such a way as to cancel out the combined effect. He wasn't really moving at all. Time had no meaning where he presently floated, that is, if he could call it floating. As best he could tell, he found himself entwined in a vast dodecahedron, a volume of space bounded by twelve planes extending to infinity where they intersected.

Enraptured, Jake felt his being reasserting itself much like the sun reemerging from the clouds to overlook the landscape that had previously remained obscured. He now understood the power of healing, the awesome nature of the energy coursing through him. Properly evoked and channeled, it could mend the mind as well as the body. This was the stuff that caused what most humans deemed as miracles, phenomena that contravened normal occurrences in the subspace his lower mind had come to know. But miracles were actually shadows of phenomena from dimensions above that intruded into everyday experience. In this current realm, miracles were not impossible. In this place miracles didn't transgress any physical laws. Unconditional love was the luminous side of the cosmos, the positive energy that made all things possible, its purity able to strip away the physical deceptions that trick the unenlightened senses. Like sweet harmonious music, it filled the heavens, resonating between the stars with an astounding number of keys. It was so clear to him. Here was an ally, offering its limitless vibratory tones to the enlightened composer. How the composer chose to play those keys would influence the world, setting off chain reactions of cause and effect.

Jake was suddenly jolted by one particular bit of insight. *You can see the future from here, can't you?*

The answer that came back was encouraging, though not absolute. *Sometimes, but most future outcomes are too shrouded in mist to be predetermined.*

With utter joy, Jake turned back to ask another question, but as he did so the dodecahedron shrunk into a galaxy that spiraled away beyond his reach. Caught off guard by this unexpected event, he groped at nothingless, feeling stranded and helpless in the midst of the great void. Cut off from the light, he plunged headlong into the darkness that formed the negative half of creation, vaguely aware of the voice echoing back at him in recession. Overcome with despair, he listened as it faded toward the far side of existence.

Do not let the darkness deceive your senses, for it can easily lay the foundation for foolish presumption, the voice warned. *There is a danger in such presumption. It has a self-fulfilling power.*

Something nudged him gently from behind, and as he twisted around to investigate the cause of it, he found himself staring up into Destiny's face.

The girl seemed amused. "You fell asleep."

"How long was I out?" Jake said groggily.

"Not long. Just a few minutes. I thought it best to let you get some rest, but you started thrashing around and I decided to wake you."

"Sorry for konking out on you. That was pretty rude of me." Sitting back up, Jake realized the entire pod had assembled just off the shore, their permanent smiles turned in his direction. As he stared back, fragments of the dream tingled his thoughts like the ghosts of a distant memory. In that moment, he wondered if it had been a dream at all.

- 66 -

Through his informant in the U.S. Coast Guard, Sebastion Ortega had learned there would be no overflights of the island on this day. From past experience, he knew such information was highly reliable. Nonetheless, he kept a vigilant eye for the approach of any cutters or aircraft as the Bell Ranger set down at the prearranged landing site for the second time in the past 56 hours.

Hastily, Ortega jumped from the aircraft and scrambled over to the spot Omar had designated for exchanging messages. As the main rotors continued to beat the air behind him, he glanced in all directions. Satisfied that nobody was currently lurking about, he lifted the stone situated against the base of a nearby tree. Lifting the lid on the metal container that lay beneath, a scrap of paper awaited him. Snatching the paper, he stuffed it into a pocket before inserting his own note, then closed the lid and replaced the stone. Scanning his surroundings one more time, he got back aboard the helicopter and buckled himself in as the pilot pulled the collective. Within minutes, the island was well behind them as Fernando guided the aircraft directly for Port-au-Prince where the San Carlo still lay at anchor in the harbor.

Pulling the paper from his pocket, Ortega unfolded the note, his eyes roving hungrily over the contents. Several seconds went by before his face broke out in a malicious grin. Omar had come through for him. Carefully, he read the note again before resting his gaze on the numbers at the bottom of the message. Scrawled in red ink were the latitude and longitude of the place where his attacker had gone following the firefight.

Unable to contain his growing excitement, he reached for a chart of the Haitian coastline and unfolded it, tracing with a finger where the lines of reference met. Without him being aware of it, his jaw hung open at what he saw. To make sure he hadn't made a mistake, he rechecked the location, making sure his eyes weren't deceiving him. *No. It was right there.* The coordinates fell just a short distance below the small circle he had penciled in on the chart earlier. Though this was actually good news, he found it eerily strange that the rendezvous point given him by one of Ternier's men was so close to where he might find his quarry.

Ortega was almost tempted to have Fernando change course, swinging more to the north where a quick recon of the area could be made. But as he thought about it, he realized such a move might prove too shortsighted by taking away all element of surprise, and surprise was something he needed if he was going to capture the girl and those strange white dolphins he had seen. Performing an overflight might tip his hand, alerting those people that another attack would be forthcoming. In addition, it was important he get back to the

San Carlo right away. The electronic gattling gun had now been delivered, and Fernando would need the remainder of the day and a portion of the night to get the weapon system fully retrofitted to the Bell Ranger.

As they continued to head east, Ortega could not keep the smile off his face. The revenge he had been hoping for was now becoming a certainty.

- 67 -

For most of the afternoon, Jake prepared the Avenging Angel for an early morning departure, checking and rechecking diving gear as well as weaponry. With what he had so far experienced near Navassa Island, taking the necessary defensive measures was his top priority. If they were attacked again, he would be ready. Earlier on, Destiny had left him to attend to personal matters, but already he missed her company.

Using the trawler's skiff, he had Zimbola, Hector and Phillipe make several trips to the falls where they filled five 20-gallon canisters with fresh water each time, eventually topping off the potable water tanks aboard the Angel. Upon completing the task, they then assisted Grahm and his assistants in bringing back aboard the equipment the scientist had brought ashore.

Satisfied that everything was in full readiness, Jake cooled off by taking a swim, eventually angling toward the beach. On the way in, Achilles joined him, staying by his side until he was hip deep in water. As he waded onto the beach, Jacob came over to greet him.

"I would like to show you something," the Haitian said.

"You've shown me quite a bit already," Jake replied.

Jacob nodded, his expression serious. "It may seem to you that we are isolated from the rest of the world here in Gaia, that keeping current with world affairs is not possible."

Jake stared, wondering what Jacob was getting at. "Now that you mention it, the thought has occurred to me."

Jacob looked in the direction of his tiny dwelling. "I have at my disposal something that allows me access to all types of information."

"Like what?"

"If you will come with me, I will show you."

Abruptly, Jacob turned and began walking. Overcome with curiosity, Jake followed. Stacks of books, magazines and periodicals cluttered Jacob's cottage. The Haitian moved some of these things aside to reveal a laptop computer. "While this might appear to be a typical computer, I can assure you it is not."

Jake studied the contrivance, looking for oddities. A mass of wires and electronic components seemed to spill from the rear of the device, appearing to terminate in two dissimilar cables that extended to the ceiling of the abode where they disappeared through the thatched roof. "What makes it so special?"

Jacob allowed himself a wry little smile. "These dolphins have an exceptional grasp of modern electronics and computer technology. They have modified the hardware and circuitry comprising this computer. They have also taken the internal programming and made it more efficient. With this device, I am able to access the worldwide Internet where I can peruse the information of my choosing."

Jake studied the assemblage of parts. "Are you telling me they rewired this thing?"

"Yes."

"How do you power it?"

The smile on Jacob's face broadened. "Sunlight provides the necessary power."

Jake felt his jaw dropping. "You have a solar collector on the roof?"

"Not on the roof," Jacob said, staring up at the ceiling as if seeing beyond it. "At the top of these cliffs." He touched the thinner cable with a finger. "This cable attaches to the solar array and provides the electrical energy that powers the computer. The other cable connects with a transceiver that allows wireless Internet access."

"Very impressive," Jake uttered.

"Would you like to see how quickly the system is able to boot?" Without waiting for an answer, Jacob pressed one of the buttons on the keyboard. In less than three seconds, the screen showed the computer was fully engaged and ready for processing.

Jake was stunned. "I've never seen a laptop boot so quickly."

"From here, I can research any subject, keying the topic of my choice into the available search engines. At this point, the device functions like any other wireless laptop, only it processes at a much higher speed."

Jake lifted his eyes to scrutinize Jacob's face. "Why are you showing me this?"

The Haitian paused, drawing in breath. "I wanted you to see the exceptional genius of these creatures."

"They've pretty much demonstrated that to me already," Jake conceded.

"Yes, but their minds are like sponges. They are able to absorb the fundamentals behind any type of technology and then refine it further. Imagine what they can do for mankind."

Jake let out a dubious laugh. "I can imagine a lot. It's what some segments of mankind can and probably will do for them that troubles me." He shook his head sadly. "Governments all over the world would love to get their hands on these protégés of yours once they learn what they're capable of. First and foremost, they would regard these creatures as potential military assets, to be used as they saw fit. Dr. Grahm has already told me about a man who tried to take possession of Natalie back in the states. He thinks that man was affiliated with the U.S. Navy. What happened yesterday is only the tip of the iceberg. I would think that should be enough to convince you that there are people out there who will stop at nothing in order to capture these dolphins."

"These creatures are well aware of the risks that face them," Jacob said dryly.

The statement had a familiar ring, and Jake suddenly remembered Destiny telling him the same thing. "Are they? I don't think they've seen enough of man's dark side to make such an assessment."

The shadow of a smile rippled across Jacob's features. "That is why they have chosen you."

Jake gaped in disbelief. "Chosen me for what? There's nothing I can do for them that would amount to much. I'm just an average Joe trying to make his way in the world like everyone else."

"On the contrary, Mr. Javolyn. You have already shown yourself to be anything but average. Perhaps they see you as their champion, their protector."

"If that's the case, then their expectations of me are way too high. I'm just one man, a little guy without much in the way of resources to combat the forces that will ultimately come after them."

Jacob gave a commiserating nod. "Sometimes circumstances arise that are seemingly beyond our control, making us feel insignificant when we see what we are up against. Nevertheless, these same circumstances often dictate our true calling whether we like it or not."

"They've got me pegged all wrong. I'm not the guy they think I am."

"Then you would abandon them in their time of need?"

Though said softly, Jake perceived the question to be more of an appeal, almost as if Jacob knew it would hit a sensitive nerve within him. "I...," he began to say, but quickly realized he had no answer within him worth giving at the moment. Flustered, he groped for a way out of the corner Jacob had trapped him in. "These creatures are far smarter than me. I would think they're clever enough to come up with defensive measures much more sophisticated than my meager Stone Age methods."

Jacob stared back quietly, a deep abiding intelligence residing behind his weathered exterior. "Do you remember the place they let you see?"

"The place south of here?"

Jacob sighed deeply. "No. I'm talking about a place where the laws of physics as we know them do not apply."

Abruptly, the dream Jake had experienced came flooding back. Stunned by the implication, he had trouble finding his tongue. "It wasn't a dream, was it?"

Jacob's reply came slowly. "No."

"Then you've also experienced it?"

Though Jacob's outward demeanor manifested graveness, an underlying kindness seemed to be lurking just below the surface. "Yes, I have also been there," he acknowledged reverently. His eyes glinted with the memory of wonder. "It is a place that only a few of us have been fortunate enough to see." He studied Jake closely, letting the revelation take root before continuing. "Do you know why these dolphins have taken to you?"

Having no answer, Jake could only shrug.

"They see a kindred soul, a being not unlike themselves."

All at once, the spell Jacob had cast was suddenly broken, replaced by a cloud of guilt. "Then they're wrong," Jake retorted. "I was a soldier. People have died because of me. I've killed more than a few. Unlike me, these creatures are incapable of hurting anyone."

Jacob smiled warmly. "Yet you are a man who has no reservations about coming to the aid of someone in danger, a person who will place the lives of others above his own."

Such praise made Jake feel uncomfortable. "You give me far too much credit. If anything, the things I did were nothing more than knee jerk reactions to the situations at hand. Unfortunately, I gave little thought to the consequences of those actions. As I told you before, my actions have probably compromised the safety of this place, doing far more harm than good."

"Then Destiny and these dolphins will need you all the more," Jacob persisted.

With Jacob's imploring eyes resting on him, Jake felt oddly defenseless. "I have several commitments which cannot be ignored," he said, looking to escape the way the Haitian was pressing him. "Dr. Grahm is one of those commitments. As you know, tomorrow I sail back to Navassa to search out a sunken vessel he believes is his. Both you and Destiny are welcome to come with us. I have additional space aboard the Angel that can accommodate the two of you."

Jacob's expression turned somber. "Thank you for the invitation, but I have business of my own which also cannot be ignored. Perhaps Destiny will accompany you, though I cannot speak for her."

Jake felt a need for further appeasement. "If that offer you made earlier is still open, I would like to see these other thurentra you mentioned."

"Achilles will show them to you."

To Jake, the connotation was clear. Achilles would be going with him in any event. Strangely, he liked the idea. He was growing used to the albino's company. "Tell me," he said, looking back down at the modified laptop, "have these dolphins provided you with any other innovations?"

A subtle brightening in Jacob's manner seemed to take place. "Let me show you," he beckoned, moving toward the door and leading Jake to the rear of the dwelling. Pulling back a large tarp, he exposed a dozen identical steel cylinders, each nearly five feet in height. Connected to the cylinders was a jumble of tubing of varying diameters that joined with other components, some of them pressure gauges. The Haitian said nothing as Jake studied the array of equipment.

Jake raised an eyebrow and looked over at Jacob. "Compressed air?"

Jacob shook his head. "Hydrogen gas! A second pipe tees off the one that feeds the cooking grill. It runs under the sand before connecting with the system you see before you. As the gas trickles in, it is compressed and stored in these cylinders."

Jake stared perplexed. "Where's the compressor?"

An amused smile was evident on Jacob's face. "The heavy machinery normally required for pressurizing gas is not needed here."

Jake eyed the system skeptically. "But how is that possible?"

"To be honest with you, I do not completely understand how it works myself. The dolphins have developed a process that utilizes nanotechnology at its core." Jacob pointed to one particular fixture. "It is here that the hydrogen gas is first subjected to a magnetic field where it is polarized, inducing Van der Waal forces within the molecules."

"I've heard the term before," Jake interrupted, "but I'd appreciate it if you'd refresh my memory as to exactly what a Van der Waal force is?"

"It is the weakest type of intermolecular force, caused by a skewed symmetry in the electron configuration of atoms. Once polarized, the molecules of a gas attract each other like magnets, though the effect lasts only a fraction of a second."

"I assume this makes the gas temporarily denser."

"Yes. By polarizing the gas, it is being prepared for what comes next." Drawing his finger further along the tubing, he indicated another component, this one appearing like a cone-shaped frustum. "This is the heart of the system. It is here the polarized gas passes through a specially fabricated filter. The filter has a nanostructure that further alters the configuration of the molecules, greatly magnifying the Van der Waals forces within them. This force draws the molecules much closer together so that they come out the other side of the filter in a liquefied state. The filter channels the hydrogen in only one direction and is able to withstand the huge pressure differential that gradually builds on opposite sides of it, because once the gas is on the downstream side, the binding forces immediately weaken and the hydrogen changes back over to a gas."

The filtering device held Jake's attention. "The dolphins fabricated the filter?"

"*Grown* would actually be a better description of how the filter is made," Jacob clarified. "The material that comprises the filter was grown in the sea."

Jake could only nod as he continued to marvel over the relative simplicity of the setup. Though he understood little about nanotechnology, he had read enough on the subject to know that the essential properties of matter were determined at the nanoscale where the atomic structure of substances could be customized to behave a certain way.

"What about the power needed to operate the system?"

"Same as before. Energy from the photovoltaic solar collectors on the cliff above provides the necessary power. Surprisingly, the system does not require much in the way of energy to work."

"Where did you get the solar collectors?" Jake asked.

Jacob smiled again. "The solar collectors are also unique in that, they too, were grown in the sea. Most photovoltaic cells on the market today are highly inefficient, typically converting only about five percent of the sunlight impinging on them into electrical energy. The material the dolphins have grown is able to convert better than forty percent of the sunlight hitting it into electricity."

Jake shifted his gaze to the cylinders. "What do you do with the bottled hydrogen?"

"Believe it or not, I give most of it away," Jacob replied.

"To be used how?"

Jacob let out a deep sigh. "For most Haitians, getting electricity on a routine basis is problematic in this country. In Saint-Marc and Gonaives, there are several cantinas that receive the bottled hydrogen every few days. The gas powers generators that have been specifically modified to burn hydrogen."

"I see," Jake said. "So these establishments don't have to rely on electricity coming from Haiti's power grid for their electrical needs?"

"That is correct." Jacob grinned. "Examples of the dolphin art you observed earlier are showcased in those cantinas. A deal has been made with the proprietors to keep those paintings on permanent display if they are to keep receiving the hydrogen."

Jake's admiration for the Haitian escalated a few more degrees as he thought about what the man was trying to accomplish. "Have you ever considered setting up a web site on the Internet for displaying the dolphin art?" he suggested. "I would think you could reach a much broader audience if you did that."

"It has already been done," Jacob declared, his expression reverting back to solemnity once again. Lifting the tarp, he placed it back over the gas cylinders and the system that filled them.

A sense of guilt continued to grip Jake as he watched Jacob secure the tarp. "I'll be sailing at first light tomorrow. If you should change your mind about coming, the offer still stands."

Jacob looked away, directing his gaze elsewhere. "As I said, Mr. Javolyn, I have duties that will require my attention."

Jake turned to leave, but stopped short. "Would you do me a favor?"

"That will depend on what you ask of me."

"Please call me Jay Jay. Those whom I consider friends call me that."

Jacob abruptly turned and scrutinized him for several seconds. "Obligations often accompany friendships. Are you certain you want me to be your friend?"

As Jake stared back, he realized the Haitian did not take such a relationship lightly. "Yeah," he finally said. "I'm sure."

- 68 -

It wasn't until much later in the day that Jake decided to visit the outer reef beyond the cove. Towed along by Achilles, he was able to locate enough lobsters to feed everyone at dinner, stuffing nine of the crustaceans into the catch bag he had brought with him. While holding onto Achilles during the return trip, Jake removed the snorkel from his mouth, taking the opportunity to converse with the albino.

"Jacob showed me some of the inventions developed by your pod," Jake said. "They were quite impressive."

Achilles reduced his speed, coming almost to a halt. *"We have other concepts that will eventually gain embodiment in fully functioning prototypes,"* the juvenile trilled back.

"Like what?"

"All will be revealed in good time."

"Jacob tells me you'll be going to Navassa Island with me."

"Yes, Jay Jay, I will follow your vessel.

"I don't suppose it will do any good to talk you out of it. As you've already discovered, Navassa is a dangerous place." Carrying on a conversation with the dolphin no longer seemed strange to Jake, though he perceived the albino's trilling speech to be somewhat childlike and incompatible with the extraordinary intelligence behind it. To him, Achilles' profound wisdom made the juvenile seem far older than his years would suggest.

"There is a path to be taken no matter what perils exist along the way."

Achilles' response was just as Jake had expected. Readjusting his grip on the dolphin's dorsal fin, he said, "Will the rest of the pod be coming?"

"Yes, Jay Jay."

"What about Destiny?"

"She will also be with us."

The news brought a sense of relief to Jake. He would much rather have her with him than leave her behind. As it was, the cove's sanctity had been compromised and, with him gone, would be vulnerable to intrusion by unwelcome parties. This particular thought made him think of the gold that lay hidden within the tiny realm, and he suddenly found it necessary to ask the dolphin another question. "There is something I must know, Achilles."

"You want to know why Jacob rejects the very things most of your species covets."

"You're reading my mind again," Jake said. He wasn't sure if he liked this. It made him feel violated.

"Your thoughts tend to be very powerful at times, Jay Jay. I seem to be naturally attuned to receiving them."

Jake wasn't sure if this was a statement of fact or an apology.

"Jacob sees such things as money and power as corruptive influences to one's moral rectitude," Achilles went on. *"While they are a means to an end, they have no true value. To Jacob, only knowledge that is used unselfishly holds true value. Some of your greatest thinkers maintained this view. Albert Einstein was one such person who held no desire for material riches. For him, finding the answers to universal mysteries was his form of self-enrichment. And like Einstein, Jacob also believes that reality can only be grasped through pure thought."*

"But Einstein's matter-energy equivalence led to the development of the atomic bomb," Jake found it necessary to point out. "By sharing this knowledge with the rest of the world, the consequences of the act proved to be a detriment to the entire planet."

"Einstein was not responsible for how the knowledge was used. He was averse to unleashing nuclear energy for destructive purposes. It is not nuclear weapons that kill, but the sentience using it."

"I can't argue that point," Jake concurred. He thought about Jacob's philanthropic goals. "Do you really believe the pod's plan for a sea colony will work?"

"From a financial perspective, yes. Already we have amassed enough of the metals humankind deems as precious to make it possible. Such a resource will provide us with more than enough options with which to carry out the objectives we have established for ourselves."

"I assume you'll also grow much of what you'll need in the sea."

"Your assumption is a good one, Jay Jay. Once we get beyond the initial startup costs, the ocean will provide the sea colony with everything it will require in order for it to be fully self-sufficient and autonomous."

"I only have one suggestion to-".

Achilles cut him off before he could complete the sentence. *"You think we should put our minds to developing defensive systems for protection."*

"I wish you'd stop doing that," Jake objected. "I find it rather discomforting having my thoughts thrown back at me before I'm able to utter them."

"I am truly sorry if I have offended you, Jay Jay," Achilles apologized, *"but your thoughts sometimes come to me as though you have already spoken them. From this moment unward I will try to be more mindful of your wishes."*

Jake sighed. "Forget it, okay." Hefting the catch bag above the water, he gestured toward the lobsters it held and grinned. "I'm starting to get hungry, my friend, and these little critters have an overdue appointment with a pot of boiling water.

Achilles let out a sound Jake could have sworn was a laugh. *"That is the one thing about your species to which I have never grown accustomed."*

"And what would that be?"

"Your need to cook the food you consume."

"Hey," Jake said in mock protest, "if you haven't tried it, don't knock it."

The juvenile emitted the analog of a snicker. *"What makes you think I have not?"*

Rendered speechless by Achilles' unexpected response, Jake had to hold on tight as the albino suddenly forged ahead and shot for the cove.

- 69 -

The trip back to Navassa Island had gone without incident, with the most difficult part of the journey occurring at the outset. With the tide in his favor and the dolphins marking the way through the narrow passage in the reef, Jake had managed to keep the Avenging Angel's hull clear of the coral that lay in wait on both sides of the channel. Sea conditions had been especially cooperative, with virtually no wind to stir the ocean and a diluted azure sky welcoming onward both the vessel and its escort of white dolphins. At Jake's urging, Destiny had chosen to come aboard rather than ride Hercules, dividing her time between him and Grahm as Zimby took over at the helm.

Ten miles out to sea, the Angel had overtaken a 35-foot open boat making its way slowly to the north, its gunwales forced dangerously low in the water from the ponderous cargo it held. The sight was nothing new to Jake. Since coming to Haiti he had seen many such vessels overflowing with Haitian migrants looking to escape the wretched poverty of their homeland. In looking upon the grave faces staring up at him, he knew their chances of reaching Florida's mainland were slim. As it was, their boat was unstable and would be prone to swamping or capsizing in the face of rising winds. And if the sea didn't take them, interception by the U.S. Coast Guard was another obstacle in their path. Feeling empathy toward the boat's passengers, Jake had watched it recede far behind as the white cliffs of Navassa gradually drew closer.

Upon nearing the island, no other vessels were in sight as Natalie scooted out in front of the Angel's bow, showing where the boat should be positioned if Grahm was to find the remnants of his old sloop. The fact that Natalie still remembered the exact location of the sunken sailboat astounded Jake, and as the Angel's anchor was being set, he couldn't help but wonder if such an expectation might be just a little overly optimistic. But then again, their present position was matching the coordinates Grahm had given him. With that in mind, he quickly suited up and, donning a scuba bottle, dropped over the side of the swim platform, eager to see what awaited him on the bottom. Aside from the dolphins, he would be the only one to make the initial dive on the wreck. Basically, he wanted to keep his stay near the island as limited as possible. Though Navassa and its surrounding waters were closed to visitors, Grahm had in his possession a valid permit issued by the U.S. Fish and Wildlife Service for performing scientific studies on the local ecosystem.

For Jake, diving under conditions of dead calm was extremely rare, and as Achilles swooped in to tow him to the sea floor, he took note of his surroundings. The ocean appeared to be composed of glazed glass, giving off a glossy sheen of variegated colors predominantly comprised of indigo and turquoise. A mid-morning sun hung in a cloudless blue sky, adding to the tranquility as it reflected off the mirror-like surface that was unmarred by wind or tide.

With Achilles pulling him downward, he glanced up, marveling at what he saw. At a depth of 60 feet, the air-water interface above appeared like a sheet of thin ice with a boat trapped motionless in its grip. As he descended deeper, he discerned Natalie and two other members of the pod hovering just above a bottom profuse with life. Colonies of healthy coral abounded everywhere, providing a craggy backdrop upon which multitudes of reef fishes darted and thrived. Drawn closer to the other dolphins, he suddenly became aware of a sunken vessel lying on its side, its hull and deck almost unrecognizable beneath a heavy blanket of encrusting coral and sponges.

Releasing his hold on Achilles, Jake swam alongside the vessel, trying to estimate its overall size. Dense groupings of damselfish and wrasses scattered at his approach, with several large parrotfish appearing unperturbed by his presence as they continued to feed on live coral. After a minute's worth of inspection, he was convinced he was looking at the remains of a sloop, though it was evident the boat's mast had been torn away. Floating adjacent to a section of railing encrusted with fire coral, he checked his depth gauge, noting that it read 95 feet. Adjusting his facemask, he gazed up toward the surface. A massive school of barracuda drifted lazily above him, the shear magnitude of numbers giving the appearance of a passing storm cloud. Barely discernable above, the silhouette of the Angel's hull could be seen, draped by streaming shafts of sunlight that penetrated the depths like fat laser beams. As Jake stared, the cloud of barracuda abruptly parted, giving way to a creature of considerable size. Hercules had come to join him with Destiny clinging to his back. At his current depth, Jake was amazed that the girl was not wearing a scuba rig.

Turning back to the task at hand, Jake unclipped from his harness the chipping hammer he had brought with him. Subjected to almost four atmospheres of ambient pressure at his present depth, he had little time to waste. The maximum bottom time he would be afforded without having to undergo decompression would be limited to 25 minutes.

With practiced efficiency, he glided to the vessel's fantail and went to work, hacking away at the horny material stubbornly adhering to the hull. Within minutes he was able to expose the bronze nameplate Grahm had described. He had brought several other tools with him, one of them being a small crowbar with a wire brush taped to it. With this, he brushed away the softer growth, running a gloved hand over the plate's raised lettering. Satisfied with what he read, he inserted the tip of the crowbar behind the plate and applied leverage. He had barely begun to pull hard when one of the fastening bolts gave way. Jimmying the bar behind the plate in other locations, he was able to snap several more bolts until it hung loosely. Giving the bar one final yank, the plate came free, upon which Achilles rushed in, snatching it with one of his prehensile appendages before it could sink to the bottom. Abruptly, the juvenile turned and shot for the surface.

Jake watched with mild amusement as Achilles raced upward through the curtain of barracuda, entertained by the way the school scattered like a blizzard. His smile quickly faded when he realized Destiny was still nearby, sitting calmly astride Hercules. The girl's ability to go without breathing for such a lengthy period was a point of continual amazement for him, and he scrutinized her for several more seconds before turning and focusing his attention back on the wreck.

Sunken vessels had always fascinated Jake, and he was itching to gain entry inside the hulk. The sloop lay on its port side, and as he studied it, he discovered an area near the starboard bow where the hull appeared to have been breached. He would have considered squeezing through the hole if not for the heavy concentration of sea anemones congregating around it, knowing how painful their stings could be. As he scanned the wreck, he realized sea anemones were in abundance, their polyp-like arms waving to and fro as they filtered nutrients from the water.

In studying the vessel, Jake was impressed at the transformation that had taken place during the past 22 years. Various species of coral and soft sponges crowded the hull, with the ever-present population of anemones clinging anywhere they could gain a foothold. The reef had become an adoptive mother, claiming the vessel as its own.

Moving to the side of the wreck where he could view the deck and superstructure, Jake noted a mound of broken calciferous branches lying below an open hatchway. As he examined the mound, he realized it had been part of a dense stand of black coral that had established itself along the sloop's topside deck. It soon became apparent to him that the sloop's hatchway had been cleared of the obstructing black coral that had overgrown it. Picking up several of the broken fragments, he scrutinized them closely, noting that no algae or other forms of marine growth had taken root where the branches had been fractured. In his estimation, the breaks were recent, hinting that someone had already worked the wreck within the past several weeks. Supporting this assessment was a heap of thick hemp rope and rusted chain lying adjacent to the mound, their surfaces lined with a slick coating of algae. Nudging the heap, he could see two small Dansforth anchors attached to the chain. To him, it seemed as if the rope and chain had been recently removed from the sloop's hold.

Jake dropped the fragments and swam for the cleared hatchway, its blackened interior appearing like a dark window. In preparing to enter, he stopped short, noticing that Achilles had returned. Clutched in the dolphin's hand was the end of a rope that trailed toward the surface. This had been prearranged prior to the dive. Grinning at the juvenile's helpfulness, Jake took hold of the rope and tied it off to the sloop's rear starboard railing, then dove down to the hatch opening. Poking his head in, he flicked on the underwater flashlight he carried, aiming the beam in front of him.

With the exception of a few small reef fish and a couple of lone crabs, he so far found the cabin to be unoccupied by any potentially dangerous denizens of the deep, particularly morays. Morays loved confined spaces. With their habitat suddenly invaded, such eels would see the intruder as a threat and possibly attack. Cautiously, he made his way forward. All unsecured objects within the cabin lay haphazardly strewn against the vessel's port side, the side on which it rested. Squirming his way toward the forward compartments, he found more of the same disarray.

Jake knew that Grahm's primary reason for coming here was to find out what had happened to his wife. With that in mind, he searched diligently among the wreckage for human remains, something that might indicate the fate of the passengers. Gradually he worked his way through the galley, reaching the crew's quarters. For the next 15 minutes he poked around, moving as far forward within the boat as the obstructing debris would allow. Although he found numerous signs of past human habitation, the place was devoid of anything remotely conforming to the skeletal anatomy of a human. Unless the salvaging party that had preceded him had removed any dead, as best he could tell, no one had gone down with the sloop.

Backing up, he turned himself around and made a quick exit from the wreck. Achilles was there to greet him. He looked around for Destiny, but the girl nor her mount were nowhere to be seen. Only one other albino was nearby, and from the lateral scar marring its flank, he recognized Natalie. From his perspective, this was a good thing. He needed the remainder of the pod to maintain vigilance. With the possibility of that rogue sub on the loose, he had no desire to have the Angel's crew caught napping. He had discussed this with both Zimbola and Destiny before the dive, and the girl had agreed that the dolphins would keep a sharp lookout, fanning out in all directions around the Angel. If any of them detected the sub, the girl would alert Zimbola of its approach.

Glancing up at the sloop's railing, Jake reached for the nylon rope and checked his watch. Having been down almost 24 minutes, he thought it wise to begin his ascent. As he rose higher, he noticed the immense school of barracuda had moved downstream, leaving the water between him and the Angel clear of any other life forms. With Achilles at his side, he continued upward slowly, careful not to exceed the speed of his vented air bubbles rising toward atmosphere.

Grahm stood anxiously on the swim platform when Jake poked his head above the surface. "Did…did you find anyone?" he stammered nervously, the question uttered as if the man were afraid of what he might hear.

Jake shook his head before lifting his facemask to his forehead and spitting out the mouthpiece. "I found nothing that would suggest human remains," he clarified softly, keeping his tone sensitive.

The news seemed to elicit both relief and disappointment in the scientist's face. Clearing his throat, Grahm said, "The brass plate Achilles brought up proves it's the *Tursiops*."

Jake removed his fins and climbed from the water, noticing that everyone else had assembled on the Angel's stern, that is, all except one. He looked around sharply. "Where's Destiny?"

Phillipe pointed at the nearby island. "I saw her go in that direction, Jay Jay."

Shedding his tank and weight belt, Jake squinted his eyes and scanned the water in front of the distant cliffs. There was no sign of either the girl or Hercules. Inexplicably, he felt uneasy. Turning, he looked at the juvenile albino floating adjacent to the platform. "Is Destiny okay, Achilles?"

"You should not worry, Jay Jay," Achilles trilled. *"Destiny is not in any danger."*

Jake nodded, mollified by the answer for the moment, but kept his gaze fixed on the dolphin. "Any sign of that sub?"

"No, Jay Jay."

Zimbola caught Jake's eye. "There be anything for Zimby to pull up?" he asked, indicating the cleated off rope.

"Sorry, big guy, but I didn't see anything worth salvaging."

Jake went on to explain to Grahm what he'd seen, cognizant of Grahm's lingering anguish. "We're tied off to your boat," he said gently. "You want to throw on a tank and have a look at her?"

Grahm nodded, looking glum. "Paying my last respects is only appropriate."

Jake pointed to some scuba equipment on the rear deck. "Phillipe has gear laid out for you and your assistants."

"That's very kind of you," the scientist murmured. He turned to Parker and Henderson. "Are you lads up for a dive?"

Jeffrey Parker smiled exuberantly, giving Grahm a thumbs up. He appeared eager to hit the water. Nick Henderson, who had been uncharacteristically quiet as of late, did not share the same enthusiasm. "If it's alright with you, I'll be staying topside, professor. I'm still not feeling up to speed."

"That's quite all right, Nicolas," Grahm said resignedly, almost as if he had expected this. "Jeffrey and I will go without you."

While both men suited up, Jake scanned the surrounding water with the binoculars. There was still no sign of Destiny or other members of the pod. It wasn't until Grahm and Parker descended on the wreck, however, that he decided to take action. "Hold the fort," he told Zimbola as he began slipping on his mask, fins and snorkel again.

Zimbola did not look too pleased. "Where you be going?"

Jake stood perched by the rail. "Nowhere in particular." With that said, he launched himself over the side, letting his mind focus on only one thought: *Take me to Destiny, Achilles.*

As he plunged below the surface, Achilles was right there waiting for him, and within seconds he was being whisked rapidly across the water.

- 70 -

About 100 meters from a place called South Point, Achilles stopped flippering. South Point was the name shown on Jake's chart representing the southeast side of Navassa Island. Holding onto the juvenile's dorsal fin, Jake studied the abandoned lighthouse poking above the crown of green vegetation topping the karst.

"Please take this moment to hyperventilate, Jay Jay," Achilles advised. *"From here we must go below the surface."*

"How deep?" Jake wanted to know.

"We will descend to a maximum depth of 16 meters below the surface for a brief period."

Jake nodded, then began purging his lungs of excess carbon dioxide. Seeming to know when his passenger was ready, Achilles dipped below the surface, arrowing at a steep angle toward a submerged outcropping overgrown with plangent, lush corals. As the dolphin powered deeper, a narrow recess in the reef suddenly came into view, and an instant later Jake was pulled into the dark opening. All traces of sunlight quickly vanished, and he felt like a man being swallowed by a black pit as the albino raced swiftly along. And although the feeling was strange, he had no fear. He trusted Achilles implicitly, intuitively knowing the albino would not endanger his life.

The ride went on for perhaps another half minute through pitch-blackness before a faint luminosity accosted his eyes, and within seconds the light grew stronger. Moments later, he was back in atmosphere, looking up at an immense subterranean cavern bathed in the soft glow of an eerie green light that seemed to emanate from multiple sources located both above and below the water.

Jake took in several deep breaths before dipping his face below the surface again, staring around in amazement. A strange subaqueous architecture abounded below him, its swirling geometric patterns suggestive of those commonly exhibited by seashells. The structure was vast in size and organic-looking, its smoothly curving free-flowing lines appearing to extend toward the far sides of the cavern. Underwater visibility was very clear, allowing him to see at least thirty dolphins in the immediate vicinity, all of them engaged at various tasks as they used their prehensile appendages to move and manipulate material. But the creatures were not albinos.

Jake lifted his head above the surface again and removed the snorkel from his mouth. "What is this place, Achilles?" he gasped in wonder.

"This is what Jacob likes to call Gaia Two," the juvenile trilled back. *"It is both a manufacturing facility and a place of learning. As you can see, it is still under construction."*

Jake continued to stare in awe, a multitude of questions dancing through his head. "What do you teach here?"

"We educate others of our kind on the great plan."

"Plan? Are you referring to your pod's idea for a sea mining corporation?"

"I am referring to the world yet to come, Jay Jay."

It was then that Jake became aware of Destiny as she floated toward him astride Hercule's broad back. She was aglow with excitement, and Jake could not dispel the idea that perhaps he had something to do with her current state of mind. "As you'll soon discover, this place holds many wonders," she announced happily.

Jake gestured at the water as the girl joined him. "What are they doing down there?"

"They're erecting a skeletal framework," Destiny effused.

Repositioning his facemask, Jake placed his head back in the water. Studying the dolphins at work, he now realized they were emplacing wire mesh that connected with strands protruding from the bulkier material that formed the organic-looking structure below him. Suddenly remembering what Jacob had told him about the other thurentras, he raised his head above the surface once more. "Is that wire made from magnesium?"

"Mostly," Destiny answered. "But magnesium in its pure form is soluble in sea water and will easily corrode. But alloyed with small amounts of manganese and aluminum, it has a tensile strength comparable with that of structural steel and will not dissolve."

"Manganese, huh. Where do you get it?"

"In this cavern, there are twenty-two thurentra. Several of them produce polymetallic nodules primarily comprised of manganese."

"What about the others?" Jake asked. "What do they produce?"

"Mostly magnesium oxide, better known as the mineral periclase, comes from fifteen of the thurentra, while four of them produce gold and platinum."

Jake was impressed. "Okay, but how is the wire produced? You're not going to tell me the magnesium wire comes in the extruded form I see below us, are you?"

Destiny appeared amused. "Yes."

Jake felt his jaw dropping again. "You're yanking my chain?"

The girl seemed confused. "I don't know what that phrase means."

"You're kidding, right?"

Destiny looked back at Jake with endless patience showing in her eyes. "Why would I mislead you about a thing like that, Jay Jay?" she said softly, angelically. "There are three other organisms that feed on the polymetallic nodules. The alloyed magnesium that comes from them is in the form of long strands of wire."

Jake nodded in understanding. "Now I get it. So the wire mesh defines the shape of the finished structure, becoming the framework for the heavier material that makes up the shell. I assume these dolphins also install that material, too."

"The shell is grown through electrolytic action. Seawater is saturated with calcium carbonate in the form of positively charged ions. Once precipitated out of solution, it is able to solidify into a kind of sea cement, the same material from which these caverns are made. By applying an electrical current through the wire, the wire becomes a cathode upon which calcium carbonate agglomerates. Because magnesium is a good conductor of electricity, voltage will readily flow through it, allowing the accretion of sea cement to adhere around it. Anodized this way, the magnesium is virtually corrosion-proof."

"What produces the electric current?"

"The thurentras!"

Jake thought back to his first glimpse of the thurentra back in the cove. Achilles had warned him against touching the hybrid organism. And from what Grahm had told him, Nick Henderson had learned this lesson the hard way. "As far as I know, electric eels are the only creatures capable of building an electric charge of any significance."

"A thurentra can produce an electrical potential many times greater," Destiny offered. "Making contact with them can be quite dangerous."

"Can I see them?" Jake asked.

"They all lie at the bottom of this cavern. In order to view them, we must swim through the interior of the structure you see being built."

Jake felt himself growing excited. "I'm game."

Without waiting for a reply, he began hyperventilating again, preparing himself for an extended dive. When he was ready, both Achilles and Hercules jackknifed downward in unison. Growing accustomed to the juvenile's switchback motion, he was learning to hold on with less and less effort. Turning his head, he was able to get an up close look at the other dolphins as they labored away. These were the gray strain of the new breed, the ones that did not converse in human languages.

Pulled through a series of rounded, smoothly winding corridors that more or less descended around a central hub within the structure, Jake scrutinized the source of illumination within the meandrous passageways. A substance appearing like a glowing green moss periodically lined the interior walls. Towed deeper, he felt his eardrums pop as he swallowed hard to neutralize the growing weight of water pressing in upon them. Rounding a final bend, the bulbous outline of a thurentra came into view. But unlike the one in the cove, this one was much larger. Accumulated at its base he could see mounds of chalky white sediment, the substance seeming to ooze from the bottom of the organism. As he looked on, a gray bottlenose swam in to scoop up some of the material, filling a bowl-shaped object clutched in its fully extended hands. The dolphin twisted around briefly to regard Jake just before moving away, and for an instant, Jake had the feeling the dolphin was Thetis, Achilles' mother.

Achilles hovered for the moment, giving Jake the opportunity to study the bloated organism lying before him. Hundreds of tentacles joined with the main body of the thing, all of them pulsing like veins leading to a heart. A steady stream of bubbles flowed from the crown of the creature, rising up into a suspended flared pipe that captured the escaping gas. The pipe appeared to consist of the same agglomerated sea cement as the rest of the dolphin-made edifice, rising vertically to join with an overhang situated above it.

For the next two minutes, Achilles guided Jake past fourteen more thurentra, all of them nearly identical to the first and strung out along a huge arc that followed the foundation of the edifice. The sixteenth hybrid was different, however. Scattered around its base was a lush mounded carpet that sparkled under the pale green light cast upon it.

As if to gauge the reaction of his rider, Achilles held still as Jake pondered the sight. Here were two of the rarest metals on the planet, elements in scarce supply that mankind deemed as exceptionally valuable. And yet a plentiful stockpile lay before Jake's eyes. It was an abundance of wealth that could elevate humanity's poorest into a life of leisure and endless pleasures, something many people would kill for to acquire. It was the stuff investors flocked to in times of political instability and economic crisis, mediums of exchange that provided the backbone to international monetary systems and gave most governments their underlying puissance. From humanity's perspective, this was what made the world go round, true power distilled into its most abstract material form. Gold was potential energy transmogrified into whatever the possessor desired, whether it be land, ships, planes or food.

Jake eyed the gleaming mounds, vaguely aware just how much the metals had escalated in value in the face of inflating global economies primarily tied to soaring energy costs. Plain and simple, the world seemed to have an unquenchable thirst for oil. Demand for the black liquid continued to climb, with emerging markets like China and India adding considerable pressure on OPEC to produce ever greater quantities of the fossil fuel in recent times. Historically, the price of gold tended to follow what the world market was willing to pay for a barrel of oil. And though he had not stayed current with its latest value, he remembered that it was about one month ago that gold had hovered around $920 an ounze when the price of oil had hit $130 per barrel. By his estimate, the wealth that lay piled before him was staggering.

Flippering forward, Achilles showed Jake three more thurentra surrounded by similar glittering masses, altogether tons of it. Here was additional concrete proof of the things Jacob had spoken of, the underlying and necessary financial muscle that would allow the plan to proceed further and gain momentum.

Stunned by the sight of such immense riches, Jake found himself analyzing the implications of it all. Destiny and the albinos had at their disposal the means to take down any possible barriers that stood in their way, legal or otherwise. An intermediary like Jacob, having lived apart from the world's mainstream most of his life, might not be the best choice to negotiate those issues in an effective way, or so he assumed. Such a task would require the skills of someone more hardnosed and ruthless, a person used to operating on the edge of legitimacy. He was surprised at the name of one individual that suddenly came to mind. But although Chester Hennington was well suited to fulfill such a role, Jake knew the man could not be trusted. While Hennington was used to dealing with unsavory sorts, the broker's uncontrollable greed would ultimately prove to be a liability.

Jake quickly dismissed these thoughts, scooping up a handful of the precious grains and letting them spill back into the gleaming mounds shrewn below him. Gold and platinum could buy widespread cooperation from governments that might otherwise seek to disrupt new and innovative ventures taking place in international waters, even though those ventures might fall outside their jurisdictions. A fertile environment of laissez-faire was essential if the pod's vision of a multinational corporation on the open seas was going to succeed. Precious metal was more potent than actual money in that it didn't really require a banking transaction for it to exchange hands. Used in the modus operandi conforming to the real world, it could be employed as an incentive, greasing the palms of already tarnished officials and bureaucrats wherever they might present a problem. Most likely, international laws would be amended to deal with an autonomous sea colony operating beyond the boundaries of any nation. As such, Jake could easily imagine the United Nations, the most corrupt quasi-legal authority on the planet, getting into the picture. With its image already sullied by a growing resume of egregious behavior and corruption, most notably the infamous oil for food scandle tied to the former Hussein regime in Iraq, the world body might actually be used to the advantage of *Tursiops Worldwide*.

Jake's awe was quickly superseded by pragmatism as he pondered these things, and he suddenly grew uneasy. Though the gold would provide the needed leverage, such wealth would also leave the plan vulnerable, for he realized a good portion of the yellow metal would have to be sold or exchanged in order to purchase the equipment and machinery required to get the initial colony started. Eventually the metals would leave behind a trail that might inevitably lead back to the cove or even this cavern. The very thing men had fought, plundered and died for throughout the ages was here for the taking, easily accessible once it was known what lay hidden under the island. As far as he could see, the albinos would not try to defend the precious cache. To them, the metal held no actual intrinsic value, being viewed as nothing more than a tool to be applied in a manner consistent with how the world operated.

Pivoting his head, Jake espied Destiny looking over at him as she sat astride Hercules. Though optimistic over the plan, the girl had only experienced a small sample of what lay in store for the pod. And while her sense of duty was steadfast and to be admired, her naivety and givingness were sure to become stumbling blocks that got in the way. He had already gotten a firsthand look at an underlying fragility in her makeup. He had seen her tears over the prospect of Thetis dying, and he could not help but wonder if she would be able bear up to losing any of the pod should the plan go awry.

Jake put these thoughts aside, feeling a need to breath again. As if knowing this, Achilles abruptly altered his motion and shot for another passageway, following the tubular corridor as it wound its way upward in a steep spiral. More than a few gray dolphins broke from their labors and moved out of the way, allowing the two albinos with their riders an unobstructed path to the surface. Reaching atmosphere, Jake sucked in air, curiously monitoring his dive watch as he did so. He had been down nearly six minutes and yet he had felt little strain.

"I would like to see more," Jake said, addressing Destiny as she floated beside him on her mount, "but I think it would be wise to check up on the Angel first."

"There is no sign of the submarine, if that's what you mean," the girl assured him. She spread her arms expressively, describing a semicircle. "Most of the pod is still stationed all around your vessel, patrolling the sea several kilometers from where it sits at anchor. If they see anything considered to be a threat, you'll be immediately notified."

"Even so, I better let Zimby know what's going on. He might get it in his head something's wrong and pull anchor."

Destiny nodded in agreement, then abruptly cocked an ear as if focusing on a sound only she could hear.

"What's going on?" Jake demanded.

"Artemis has detected the approach of a surface vessel heading toward the island from the east."

That was all Jake needed to hear. Pumping up his lungs with several enormous inhalations, he gulped down a final breath before Achilles dove. Leaving the pale green light in his wake, he let himself get hauled back through the blackened cavity that would take him to the world above.

- 71 -

Walter McPherson felt bored as he sat aboard the Sea Lion, though he was glad to leave Port-au-Prince far behind him. The very idea that Frank Jaffey and Ben Loomins had made such a place their base of operations repulsed him. Never before had he seen such squalor, and from what he'd heard, gang violence within the beleaguered city had gotten so out of hand that many businesses and factories were closing shop. Haiti's problems were inveterate and seemingly irreversible, with nothing in sight in the way of viable solutions to raise it out of the muck in which it was mired.

Staring out over the ocean, McPherson hoped his luck would change for the better on this day. One way or the other, he was determined to bring back at least one healthy specimen of this mysterious breed. Already he had taken delivery of the dead gray dolphins with those strange hand-like appendages. Chester Hennington had not been helpful about how the creatures had been captured, keeping the identity of the seller anonymous. Surprisingly, the chubby little broker had appeared distant and preoccupied during their discrete meeting, even after receiving a hefty bundle of cash to complete the transaction. Though the carcasses were currently packed in ice aboard the Casa, it gave him little comfort in knowing these unusual trophies might be all he came away with on this grueling trip.

As if in answer to this thought, Jaffey's voice suddenly blurted over the radio. "Bird of Prey to Predator!"

Standing at the helm, Ben Loomins keyed the mike's transmit button. "Go ahead BP."

"I hadn't expected this, but it seems I'm receiving a signal on that little doodad his majesty gave us."

Though McPherson was fed up with Jaffey's subtle innuendoes, he cast aside his annoyance in light of the other tidbit of information the radio message held.

The inkling of a smirk was evident in Loomins face as he glanced over at the naval captain. "That sounds very interesting BP. What's our next move?"

A short pause ensued before Jaffey responded, his speech erratically garbled by static but understandable. "Bird of Prey advises you to home in on acquired target. Stand by for numbers."

Trying to leash his growing excitement, McPherson watched as Loomins scribbled down a set of coordinates. It had been he, McPherson, who had provided Jaffey with the doodad to which the pilot referred, a piece of hardware that had actually been designed by Nick Henderson. It was a tool used for tracking the movements of dolphins outfitted with something Henderson had called a DBT device. Based on what he was hearing, it sounded as if there were more creatures out there with such a sending unit strapped to their bodies.

McPherson smiled inwardly at the exorbitant price he had paid in order to recruit Henderson's cooperation. He wondered how Dr. Grahm would react if the scientist ever found out how one of his young assistants had been so easily bought off. Turncoats like Henderson, it seemed, were everywhere these days, opportunists who had no scruples about taking a bribe whenever it crossed their path. Manipulating people through bribery and monetary incentive had become a way of life for McPherson. Coming from an exceedingly wealthy family had taught him at a very early age how money could be used to one's advantage, and he had taken the lesson to heart, employing it to invoke a successful military career. It was a game he fully enjoyed playing.

But in this case, it had not been he who had approached the grad student to make him turn traitor. No, it had been the other way around. Henderson had somehow ferreted him out from among an elaborate maze of military channels, making him privy to a new breed of dolphin with extraordinary attributes. It had been Henderson who had offered to give away the secret for money, and McPherson had readily accepted. But Grahm had refused to cave under the captain's threats to turn over the dolphin, unexpectedly fleeing Miami with the creature in tow a short time later. Just before leaving, however, Henderson had managed to get word to him of Grahm's plans. Mailing him the device Jaffey called a doodad and the manner in which it could be used, the computer whiz had explained how they could stay in contact using the device. When the time was right, Henderson would alert him where to find these magnificent creatures, that is, provided he wired another sizeable deposit into a certain offshore bank account.

Letting his thoughts coast along while Loomins repeated back the coordinants over the radio, McPherson was absolutely certain the man who had stolen the two albinos right out from under Loomins' nose was not Nick Henderson. The man Ben Loomins had described was much too muscular and conditioned to match Henderson's scrawny physique. By assuming Henderson's identity, though, the thief must have had some knowledge of what Henderson had been up to. But this time around, things would be different. He would make sure of that.

Loomins keyed the transmit button again. "Have you established the target heading, BP?"

Jaffey's voice came back buzzing with static. "You're gonna love this, P, but it ain't moving at all."

Loomins swiveled his head and looked over at McPherson again, seemingly entertained by what he saw in the captain's face. "What's your ETA, BP?"

"I'm just gaining altitude, P. You should be seeing me in approximately seventeen minutes. I strongly recommend you stay well clear of the target until I'm able to get there and drop the package. Is that understood, P?"

A formidable scowl overcame Loomins' features. "There's no need to remind me, BP," he stammered, his face suddenly reddened with bottled up rage. "I know the procedure."

"Just refreshing your memory, P. I wouldn't want to see you blow this a second time. Bird of Prey out."

McPherson said nothing as Loomins put down the mike in agitation. Still steamed over the remark, Loomins matched the coordinants given him with a spot on a chart laid out before him, circling the location so hard with the point of a pen that he cut through the paper where a small island in the shape of a tear-drop was shown.

Studying the location, McPherson found it interesting that this had been their original destination all along. Perhaps the area was where many more of these creatures congregated. The possibility that he might actually be onto the mother lode of this new species brought on a renewed feeling of elation. With such creatures in his custody, he would have a powerful bargaining chip in furthering his career, something that would set the stage for new innovations in naval military tactics, something that would undoubtedly bring him back into the good graces of his superiors and advance him very rapidly to the rank of rear admiral. Having made the decision to stay aboard the Sea Lion rather than Jaffey's plane was so far proving to be a wise choice. This way, he would make sure nothing went wrong should they get another chance at snaring one of these amazing animals.

Focusing eager eyes on the balmy horizon off the vessel's bow, he could just make out the hazy white band that was supposed to be Navassa Island, the vicinity where the first two dolphins had been bagged. In order to limit the Casa's time in the air and save fuel, Loomins had sailed for Navassa well in advance of Jaffey. Once the plane caught up with them, it would scoot out ahead and unload the system that would ultimately incapacitate the unique creatures, making them easy to net.

Checking his watch, he estimated when he might gain sight of the plane. By nature, he was not a patient man. For some strange reason though, he wanted to prolong the joy of anticipation he was currently experiencing, savoring the thought that the prizes he sought were almost within his grasp. This was the most excitement he had had in a long time.

- 72 -

Jake left Achilles at the dive platform, climbing up onto the Angel's stern where Zimbola, Phillipe and Hector awaited him.

"We be receiving company," the Jamaican said, pulling the binoculars he held from his eyes and handing them over to Jake.

Jake spotted the vessel Zimby had been studying, then lifted the optical device and peered through the lenses. Though the boat was more than a half-mile distant, he recognized its lines immediately. "How long they been sitting there?" he asked.

"Not long. She's a fast lady. Come outta the south like a mako on the hunt, then cut her engines just as quickly."

Scrutinizing the vessel further, Jake had a clear view of the boat's larboard side as it floated without power. No breeze had sprung up yet and the sea lay flat. "That's the Sea Lion," Jake offered, raising the glasses to the sky overhanging the horizon to the east. "If my guess is right, we'll be seeing a spotter plane joining her very shortly." Handing the binoculars back to the big man, he glanced over at Hector. "We've got a Code One on our hands."

Hector nodded gravely, then scrambled away with Phillipe following.

Jake turned and stared up at the Jamaican. "I take it Grahm and Parker are still on the wreck."

Zimby checked his watch. "They still have fifteen minutes."

Craning his torso over the side, Jake looked down at Achilles and started to open his mouth.

"*There is no need to speak, Jay Jay,*" the young albino twittered. "*Destiny and the others have already been informed of the danger. We will take the necessary precautions.*"

Though Achilles was reading his mind again, Jake was no longer surprised. The juvenile began to submerge when the tendrils of an idea worked its way into Jake's thoughts. "Achilles, wait!"

The albino stopped and looked back up. "*I will do as you say, Jay Jay. The probability of success is actually quite high.*"

Jake felt himself smiling. Achilles was thinking right along with him on this one.

- 73 -

Logging off the laptop computer as he sat in his thatched dwelling, Jacob could not remember feeling so lonely. With the entire pod gone, the place he called Gaia seemed inordinately serene today, as if all the other life forms, both fauna and flora, residing within its midst were aware that Destiny and the dolphins were missing. Even the roar of the falls seemed to have waned, evidenced by a flow of water that lacked the usual potency. The feeling was exacerbated all the more by Emmanuel's prolonged absence. Taking into consideration unforeseen delays so common to incoming flights bound for Port-au-Prince, he knew his cousin should have returned by now. Something was definitely wrong.

The familiar sound of another watercraft suddenly reached his ears, and within moments he was standing on the shore awaiting Jimenez as the fisherman nudged the sand with the bow of his boat.

"Have you gotten any word on Emmanuel?" Jacob asked in Creole, as if expecting the man to alleviate his fears.

Jimenez shook his head gravely as he hopped onto the shore. "Lucette is beside herself with worry. She has not slept in days." He looked past Jacob, setting his eyes on the two dwellings set back from the water. "Do you have bottles for me?"

Jacob nodded, grabbing one end of the first empty cylinder slid over the boat's gunwale. Further conversation between the two men was not necessary. There wasn't much more to say anyway. They were following a set schedule. Jimenez had visited the cove on many previous occasions, each time for the dual purpose of picking up cylinders topped off with hydrogen gas and collecting more of the dolphin paintings. A brooding silence took hold of both men as they began unloading the spent bottles filling the boat, a routine they had carried out twice each week now for almost the last two years. Once the load was replaced with recharged cylinders, Jimenez would deliver the gas to the owners of four cantinas, two in Saint-Marc and two in Gonaives. But first the dolphin art would be dropped off with Amphitrite.

Word of Malique's benevolent mambo had spread far and wide in the last year, sending people in droves to the tiny seaside fishing village in the last several months. What had started out as a trickle was slowly turning into a flood. With a growing influx of sick and injured seeking to be cured, more and more of Amphitrite's time had been taken up, necessitating that she remain as close as possible to where she could do the most good. Both her and Jacob had agreed long ago that Gaia would be off limits to the masses, particularly since a human intrusion of significant number could easily offset the delicate ecosystem that existed within it.

It didn't take Jacob and Jimenez long to complete the task of loading recharged cylinders into the boat, and minutes later Jacob found himself waving a final farewell as Jimenez rounded the bend leading to the rocky inlet. As always, Jacob's mind began to fill with a variety of matters, both large and small, and as he strolled idly along the shore, his thoughts fell back on ways of reversing global warming.

By his estimates, global warming was accelerating, spurred on by increasing demands for oil. In the last two years, Asia had surpassed North America in the consumption of petroleum. Already, China had become the second-largest importer of the liquid fossil fuel next to the United States even though the typical person in China used only 10 percent on average what the typical American consumed. Jacob had done enough research on the subject to know that every day, 200 million automobiles in America guzzled roughly 11 percent of the world's daily output of oil. Not surprisingly, the United States was actually the only industrialized country that was less energy-efficient than it had been two decades earlier. Since 1980, when gasoline was still relatively cheap, Americans had made the switch from smaller cars to gas-guzzling SUVs and minivans, all of which currently accounted for about half of all cars in the United States as opposed to just 7 percent in 1990.

Americans, it seemed, lived in a car-driven culture, establishing themselves as the most energy-inefficient consumers on the planet. This inefficiency was exacerbated all the more when many U.S. citizens moved from the cities to the suburbs and exurbs, with 75 percent of the population choosing to commute longer distances each day. Only 5 percent of Americans relied on public transportation to get to work, a far cry from the 20 percent of Europeans who used bus or rail to reach places of employment. At present, two-thirds of America's petroleum consumption went toward transportation. At the present rate of consumption worldwide, about 1.1 billion tons of carbon dioxide was currently being produced annually by road vehicles.

Both Jacob and the pod had done calculations, making logical assumptions based on research about the spiraling tempo of oil consumption worldwide. Starting with the current year, if China and India paralleled the same growth rate South Korea had undergone since 1980, those two countries alone would end up consuming three times as much energy as the U.S. does today 25 years from now. Developing and then solving third, fourth, and fifth order differential equations, they had discovered that the amount of carbon dioxide dumped into the atmosphere would reach a critical level long before that took place. Mathematics had given them an advance look at the disasters that would befall the world if such irresponsible actions continued to go on uncurbed much longer. It could not be refuted. Sea levels would rise dramatically. Jacob glanced dismally all about him. Portions of Gaia would become submerged, destroying the dwellings he, Destiny and Amphitrite lived in, though he well knew it would take many more years for that to happen. Malique would also drown in the ensuing floodwaters, as would the entire Haitian coast. The frequency of hurricanes would escalate, with the destructive force and accompanying size of such monster storms becoming greater than anything mankind had previously seen. But even before mankind felt the full brunt of those disasters, Jacob was convinced of another potential calamity that was even more disturbing, and that was the threat of horrific war. Amphitrite had prophesied this many years earlier, foretelling of a conflict that would be triggered by diametrically opposed ideologies fostered by segments of humanity, compounded further as oil-hungry nations fought to control the major petroleum supply lines flowing out of the Middle East. It was a war that had the potential of decimating the human race long before global warming could take its toll.

With the collective pod mind assisting him, Jacob had constructed one mathematical model after another, each leading him to the same conclusion. Change was desperately needed if catastrophe was to be averted. This was not a political issue to be hashed over and endlessly discussed by feckless politicians and inveterate societies. Decisive actions had to be taken, and very soon if the impending cataclysm was to be averted. Based on recent satellite measurements published in one of the scientific journals he had recently read, the second-largest ice cap on the planet, the ice sheet covering Greenland, was melting into the surrounding oceans at a rate three times faster than it did four years earlier. The Greenland sheet accounted for about 10 percent of all the ice on earth.

He thought about the last item he had been researching. That item was *salps*. Salps were low member organisms in the ocean food chain, transparent jellyfish-like creatures about the size of a human thumb. Swarming by the billions in hot spots that have been known to cover immense areas of the seas, salps had the ability to transport tons of carbon each day from surface waters to the ocean depths where it could be kept from re-entering the atmosphere. The oceans absorbed a small percentage of all atmospheric gases, including greenhouse gases like carbon dioxide. Increases in this gas from burning fossil fuels continued to exacerbate global warming, with the planetary hydrosphere absorbing significant amounts of it and becoming more acidic in the process. This increasing acidity was beginning to contribute significantly to the destruction of many coral reefs around the world.

With barrel-shaped bodies, salps propelled themselves through the water by drawing water in the front end and forcing it out the rear in a jetting action. Passing over a mucus membrane within the organism, the water was vacuumed clean of all organic material. Salps consumed all types of microscopic carbonaceous plants from surface waters, including phytoplankton, which used the carbon dioxide to grow. They swam, fed, and produced waste continuously, taking in small packages of carbon and transforming them into bigger packages that sank rapidly in the form of fecal pellets. When salps died, their bodies also had a tendency to sink relatively fast, becoming a dead-end in the food web provided they remained uneaten on the way down.

Jacob had learned that one particular species of salp, Salpa aspera, multiplied quickly in dense swarms that flourished for months, covering as much as 100,000 square kilometers of ocean surface and transporting up to 4,000 tons of carbon to deeper water each day. During daylight hours, they were known to swim deeper to avoid predators and the effects of damaging ultraviolet rays. Ascending back up at night in a vertical migration, they aggregated and reproduced when food was abundant. Because of this behavior, they released fecal pellets in deep water where few animals were able to ingest them. In this way, they allowed the oceans to absorb excess carbon dioxide in a manner that prevented it from re-entering the atmosphere. Jacob well knew that in order to permanently remove excess buildups of this greenhouse gas from the atmosphere, the carbon had to be removed from the planet's active bio-cycle.

As of late, Jacob had been exploring more and more possible ways of reversing global warming caused by escalating build-ups of carbon dioxide in the atmosphere, and he had quickly discovered that salps had shown much promise toward this end.

Fertilizing the oceans with iron was another method that also showed great potential, and one that might prove valuable in proliferating phytoplankton blooms in areas where upwelling was absent. A strong biological response occurred when dissolved iron was added to the topmost region of the hydrosphere, causing algae to quickly multiply and absorb excess carbon dioxide in the upper water column. But from the research Jacob had uncovered, algae blooms alone were not enough to be an effective solution to removing greenhouse carbon dioxide from surface waters since the carbon would return to the biosphere in the exhalations or metabolic processes of the animals that fed upon the algae. Applied in combination with phytoplankton-consuming salps, however, he saw that a rapid carbon export to deeper water was quite possible.

Jacob already knew of the existence of one huge phytoplankton bloom, and it was very close to Navassa Island. Years earlier, he and Amphitrite had seeded the water there with three other thurentra. Those organisms had been created by splicing the mysterious oblate jellyfish with the largest variety of sea cucumber they could find. And while he had never actually seen them, based on what the dolphins had told him, the resulting hybrids had grown to immense proportions, drawing huge volumes of cold, nutrient-rich water from the oceanic depths where dissolved nitrates and nitrites were plentiful. With their taproot network of tentacles reaching down thousands of feet along the sea bed, the water they brought up was 40 degrees lower than the 80 degree water at the surface. This he had discovered by using a Fahrenheit thermometer to measure the temperature of the water rising directly above the thurentras pumping it. It was this hybrid-induced upwelling that had caused the immediate surface waters adjacent to Navassa to become rife with life, with vast schools of tuna drawing the attention of huge fishing trawlers he had seen near the island as of late.

When mixed with the warm surface water near Navassa, the colder upwelling also provided another benefit to the local environment. It cooled the surrounding water. With average ocean temperatures at the surface rising with global warming, water vapor was being released in linearly increasing amounts, slowly working its way toward a critical runaway greenhouse effect where the release of water in gaseous form into the atmosphere would jump dramatically. Jacob well knew that water vapor was far and away the most powerful of all the known greenhouse gases, able to absorb infrared energy over a much broader spectrum than carbon dioxide.

Jacob thought back to the hydrogen gas he had just helped Jimenez load into his boat. The use of hydrogen as an alternative fuel had no environmental downside provided the resulting water vapor produced from burning it was kept from entering the atmosphere. If the vapor was contained, hydrogen was a clean, renewable source of energy, and one that could be used to lead the way in achieving a scientific revolution that would transform the world.

In the last several weeks, Jacob's mind had been churning with possible projects Tursiops Worldwide would pursue once the first sea colony was established, and he tried to busy himself with such thoughts. But nagging inexorably within the midst of such noble musings was Emmanuel's prolonged absence. It was imperative that Emmanuel return with the necessary paperwork that would launch the corporation the albinos had envisioned. They needed to get started right away in order to avoid a looming catastrophe. The fate of the world depended on it.

Making a decision, he rowed himself out to the pinnace and cranked up the motor. He would go to Malique and see Amphitrite. Perhaps she had had another one of her extraordinary visions. Maybe by now she would know what had become of his cousin.

- 74 -

Frank Jaffey took the Casa in low, swooping over his partner's craft at close to 200 knots. Although the signal had stopped, he still had a fix on its point of origin. The vessel that lay at anchor further ahead caught him by surprise, however, and he toggled the transmit key. "Bird of Prey to Predator, you ever see that boat before?"

"Come on back, BP, you're breaking up."

Jaffey keyed the mike again, altogether forgetting about radio protocol. "The boat off your port side. You recognize it?"

A momentary pause ensued before Loomins answered. "Negative, BP. Why do you ask?"

"Never mind, Predator. What say we bag us some dolphins?"

"Just drop the package, BP, and we'll do the rest."

Jaffey took a good look at the unknown vessel as he overshot it, seeing two divers removing scuba gear on the boat's rear platform. One other person was assisting the divers, and all three looked up sharply to observe the plane as it passed less than 300 feet above them. "No can do until an actual target is spotted, P. Give me a moment to circle."

Coming around hard, Jaffey let his eyes roam over the water, trying to take in every square meter of the ocean surface. He could not recall having ever seen a sea so flat. Conditions were perfect for spotting quarry from the air. Banking hard left, his gaze came to bear on something white amid the surrounding indigo. "Well, well, look what we have here," he said aloud to himself, letting a wide grin spread over his face. Abruptly, he again keyed the transmit button. "I've got a target, Predator. I'm coming around for a drop run," he blurted excitedly. "Stand by to come on in on my command!"

"I read you, BP. Standing by."

Jaffey kept his eyes locked on the target, keeping it off his port wing as he guided the aircraft on a course parallel with the island. He needed to open up some distance with it before swinging back around and setting up his drop vector. Timing was everything if the operation was going to be successful. So far, the prize appeared to be fully cooperative, seemingly unaware of the plane buzzing noisily overhead.

Satisfied with the distance he had opened up, Jaffey dipped his port wing again, taking the Casa into a lazy bank before preparing the aircraft for a final approach. Gradually, the target swung into the center of his windshield, and several hundred meters directly behind it was the boat carrying the divers, its bow facing him.

Cutting back on the throttle, he continued to maintain perfect alignment with the creature floating languidly on the sea below. His preoccupation with the quarry was intruded upon as the vessel behind it suddenly rocked back on its stern, its bow rising ostensibly above the water. Disregarding the distraction, he steered the plane lower, engaging the hydraulics that would open the bay doors situated at the Casa's belly.

Thumbing the intercom button, Jaffey gave an order to the others stationed in the rear. "Stand by for a drop!"

Over his headphones, a voice came back curtly. "Ready when you are."

Jaffey started a backward count in his head as he checked his altimeter and air speed, content that everything was proceeding exactly as it should. *Five...four...three...what the devil?*

In that instant, a watercraft shot out from behind the anchored vessel, racing rapidly along the boat's starboard side and heading directly at him. Much too seasoned a pilot to let his concentration waver, Jaffey resumed his interrupted mental countdown. *Two...one...*He triggered the electronic release.

"Package away!" he cried.

Nearly two seconds elapsed before a response blared back loudly. "Package delivered!" the same voice confirmed.

Throwing more power into the engines, Jaffey pulled back on the yoke, lifting the Casa's nose skyward and banking sharply left.

"Predator to BP!" Jaffey was nearly deafened as Loomins voice suddenly cracked from the earphones like gunshot. "You've got a visitor! There's a guy on a waverunner under you!"

Jaffey banked the plane harder, coming around as fast as possible to have a look, but before he could complete the turn, Loomins voice sounded again. "It's him!"

It took Jaffey only a fraction of a second to make the connection. "Calm down, Predator. You're getting yourself all worked up for nothing. There's nothing he can do to stop us now."

By this time, he had opened up enough of an angle to glimpse the waverunner, and with a start, he realized the man driving it was bearing directly at the sounder he had dropped. Nervously, he shifted his gaze further back to locate the white dolphin he had targeted, but the creature was nowhere to be seen. The package had just splashed down and was bobbing violently as it settled into its watery cradle. It required a fairly stable orientation for the sonar emitter to disengage from the floatation bags and sink below the surface, and that would take roughly three more seconds.

With rising panic, Jaffey turned his eyes back to the man racing along below and was immediately dumbstruck. He could only stare helplessly at the trail of whitewater that streaked away from the waverunner, a trail that was reaching for his piece of electronic gadgetry with disconcerting swiftness.

- 75 -

Jake had concealed both himself and the Kawasaki upon which he sat under a tarp, awaiting the right moment to launch the waverunner after the plane had buzzed them. Seeing the aircraft swing wide before taking on a glide path that would bring it straight for Achilles, he gave the order for Hector to deploy the water chute. Sliding down backwards to meet the sea, he noticed the familiar shift in the boat's superstructure as the Angel settled back on its haunches.

Turning the ignition switch, Jake felt the Kawasaki purr to life, its engine seemingly ready to take on any challenge. Twisting the throttle to full, he held on tight as the waverunner leapt forward like a greyhound eager for an all out run. Leaning his weight, he exploded past the Angel's starboard side, reaching maximum speed within seconds. With the sea like a sheet of glass, he knew the watercraft under him would have the striking capability of a cobra.

The plane, he could see, had its cargo bay doors fully ajar as it homed in on the juvenile's position, and an instant later something fell from between them. The very scenario Jake had predicted was now taking place before him. In that moment, Achilles' dorsal fin disappeared from view, leaving only a few ripples marring the sea's glossy surface.

Continuing to plow straight ahead, Jake moved aside the swivel guard that blocked the arming switch to the right side torpedo. A flick of the toggle was all he needed to prepare the 40mm missile for launch. Aligning the waverunner with the plummeting object's projected point of impact, he let his thumb find the launch button that would send the torpedo on its way. With his gaze now focused on the thing accelerating toward the sea, he knew his timing had to be precise.

The geyser that erupted when the object met the water was truly spectacular, but Jake had no time to admire the resulting plume. With a deft thumb, he depressed the launch button and watched the torpedo leap away.

A white spumy rope appeared to spring forth across the water, growing rapidly in length as it raced forward on a vector that was straight and true. Unlike his encounter with Mat's boat, Jake had not tampered with the projectile to reduce its potency. This was a standard 40mm torpedo, packed to the brim with hellacious explosive. Even a glancing strike against the thing currently settling on the water would send out a shock wave of sufficient magnitude to severely damage it, or so he hoped.

Cutting back a quarter turn on the throttle, Jake sheared away from the target, getting clear of the impending explosion and taking on a heading that was ninety degrees to port. Even so, the booming blast of compressed air that caught up with him was more than he had expected as the torpedo detonated. Looking back at the damage, he could see various components of the object still aloft, flung high in all directions from the force of the strike. Within moments, they fell back into the sea, with only the remains of several floatation bags hanging in tattered disarray on the ocean surface.

The possibility that Achilles had failed to escape the ensuing shock wave in time to avoid injury weighed heavily on Jake's mind, and he glanced about anxiously in an attempt to locate him. As if to calm his worry, Achilles suddenly rocketed from the water close to the Angel, performing one of his signature quintuple somersaults.

Letting go with a relieved sigh, Jake altered the Kawasaki's heading by several more degrees to face the oncoming vessel, his expression suddenly turning grim. Though he held no particular animosity toward Loomins and his partner, he would do whatever it took to keep them from capturing any more dolphins. With cold deliberation, he armed the sixty, prepared to discourage any retaliatory responses made by the crew of the Sea Lion as it bore closer.

- 76 -

McPherson had trouble believing what he had just witnessed. From a distance, he had watched as Jaffey made the airdrop. No sooner had the sounder splashed down, it had been destroyed, blown to pieces by a person skimming across the sea on a waverunner. Nearly speechless, he turned to stare at Ben Loomins. "You're sure it's the same guy?"

Driving the Sea Lion forward with the engines wide open, Loomins was beside himself with rage. "Fuckin' A right it's him." For emphasis, he put the spyglasses to his eyes again, taking another look at the man riding the waverunner. "But this time he's gonna pay," he added, his face contorted in ugliness. He put down the glasses and pulled the magnum pistol from the holster strapped to his thigh, clicking open the barrel to make sure the firearm was fully loaded.

"What are you going to do?" McPherson asked in annoyance, looking at Loomins as if he were insane. The sight of handguns had always made him feel uneasy. This whole situation was rapidly disintegrating, turning into something way beyond his control. Becoming a party to any egregious incidents had not been part of his plan, and he surely had no desire to be implicated in one that might possibly mar his naval career.

"I'm gonna kill that bastard!" Loomins screamed. "I'm gonna blow his god damn brains out!"

Jaffey's voice suddenly blared over the radio. "Stand down, Predator! Do not approach the waverunner!"

Loomins ignored the command, continuing to drive the vessel onward as fast as it would go.

The radio blared again. "What the fuck you doing, Predator?" Jaffey's voice boomed in panic. "I told you to stand down, the guy on the runner has torpedoes! Stay clear of him!"

The words caused the blood in McPherson's veins to freeze. *Torpedoes?* A vague remembrance of something to do with waverunners and torpedoes unhinged itself from the back of his mind, but he had no time to dwell on it now. Instead, he grabbed Loomins' by the arm, yanking hard to pull him out of his focused rage. "Did you hear him?" he yelled tremulously. "Stand down! You want to get us killed?"

Loomins lifted the pistol, pointing it directly in McPherson's face and cocking the hammer. "Get the hell off my bridge!"

In Loomins' eyes, McPherson could not mistake the cauldrons of murderous hate. Abruptly, he released the man's arm and backed away, certain Loomins would shoot him if he did not comply.

Loomins waved the gun. "Off my bridge!" he bellowed.

McPherson scampered down the ladder, not having any desire to provoke Loomins any further. Reaching the rear deck, he saw Charlie leaning against the port railing with the Haitian crewmen. The whole group was staring around the side of the vessel, following the movements of the distant waverunner. In Charlie's hand was the carbine rifle he had seen before.

"You've got to stop your brother!" McPherson shouted. "He's gonna get us all killed."

Charlie glanced his way momentarily. "Ben knows what he's doing."

"Jaffey said the sounder was destroyed by a torpedo," McPherson explained hurriedly, aware of his own rising panic. "The guy out there might have another one. He can sink us."

The full impact of McPherson's words seemed to awaken Charlie, for Charlie's mouth suddenly came ajar. "Holy shit!" he cried. Bolting for the ladder leading to the bridge, he started to climb the rungs, but the vessel abruptly lurched and he lost his grip on the hand-railings.

McPherson's eyes went wide as a cloud of wavering darkness seemed to loom up from the sea, portions of it swarming all around and then engulfing the Sea Lion in frenzied, bludgeoning violence. Like a cresting wave, it heaved up and hammered down upon him. Something slapped wetly against his chest and before he could fully grasp what was happening, his entire body became entrenched in a rush of flapping, slippery chaos. Shielding his face with out-flung arms, he tried to ward off the silvery-gray throng before being knocked from his feet.

Amid the turmoil, he felt the vessel lurch under him again, this time more violently. Horrified, he sensed the Sea Lion teeter precariously to one side before righting itself in a sustained list. As if in protest to the way the vessel was being violated, the clamor of the engines rose in a distressed shriek, only to die away a moment later by whatever was smothering the props.

A dead quiet descended as the confusion ended almost as quickly as it had started. Getting hold of his senses, McPherson tried to rise. With great effort, he forced aside the mass of wriggling, slithering bodies bogging him down, barely managing to stand erect. *What in god's name?*

"Help me!" The voice belonged to Charlie. Mired deep in the squirming throng, he tried to get to his feet, failing miserably in the attempt.

McPherson stared dumbly at the mass of fish overwhelming the deck. Wading through the bodies, he realized he was bleeding as a red trickle worked its way down his arm. Bringing a hand to his cheek, he located the source, flinching when his finger found where the flesh had been lacerated. Heaped high all about him were barracuda, perhaps thousands of them, their cylindrical bodies continuing to shudder convulsively under the hot sun, their teeth appearing like tiny daggers jutting from protruding lower jaws.

Afraid he might get bitten again, McPherson ceased moving, aware that the Haitians were now busy pushing fish over the side.

"Jesus Christ," Charlie hollered, "will somebody get these god damn fish offa me."

The drone of the Casa slowly grew in pitch, and like a man in a stupor, McPherson looked up to watch the aircraft shoot above him with less than 50 feet to spare. With the Sea Lion now dead in the water, he continued to follow the plane as it took on a course that would take it back at the man on the waverunner.

- 77 -

She had never been able to understand why she was the hub of the pod, the sentience through which all the others focused their mental energies whenever the synergy inherent of a collective mind needed to be achieved. Such comprehension was irrelevant anyway. To Destiny, knowing when to form a mind meld with the others was instinctual, as natural as satisfying one's hunger for food. Like the moon exerting its pull on the oceans to produce the tides, it was a phenomenum that simply was.

She had seen Jay Jay destroy the mechanism dropped from the aircraft, the thing that had enervated Hermes and Aphrodite. And she had seen the watercraft that had previously captured them bearing straight for him, sensing intense anger emanating from the vessel. And yet there was fear, too. Based on what she knew of its crew, there were also innocents aboard the boat, Haitians that worked for Ben Loomins.

A potentially deadly confrontation had quickly arisen, one that had necessitated defusing, for if left unchecked only misery would follow. And misery was something she and the others felt obligated to dispel whenever they came across it.

Inciting the nearby shoal of barracuda into a frenzy aimed at swarming the Sea Lion had been far easier than expected. The mental suggestion she and the others had imparted to the horde was something they had never before tried. And though the act had caused the death of numerous fish, she felt no remorse. Unlike a human, the mind of a barracuda was very limited, entirely governed by instinct and incapable of conscious thought. Whatever members of the pack had perished would ultimately become food for other predators in the food chain, their essence continuing to live on.

As Destiny looked across the water at the vessel drifting aimlessly without power, she sensed the outrage lessen, replaced by confusion and frustration. Still linked to the others, she could clearly feel it. The negative emotions pulsing from Ben Loomins had ebbed sufficiently for a shred of rational thought to take hold of the man. But there was something else hanging in the air, something far more puissant than Loomins' ire.

Startled by the strength of it, she stared back at the island. An overpowering iniquity seemed to lurk somewhere to the northwest of her position. It was the same feeling she had experienced during her first sighting of the submarine, but much more pronounced this time. Her mother had taught her long ago never to ignore perceptions that lay beyond the boundaries of her physical senses, for when they occurred, they often portended undesirable events yet to come, events that might be averted. And while such extrasensory attunement was infrequent, tending to come at the oddest moments, Amphitrite had stressed it could be taken as a forewarning from God to be on one's guard.

Bashir, Destiny knew, was currently somewhere on the island, taken there by Jimenez to right a wrong he had abetted. What exactly that wrong was, she had no knowledge, though she did perceive it had something to do with the sub.

Do not try to understand everything going on about you, her mother had emphasized. *You have a special purpose to fulfill in this world. All will eventually become clear, but first you must take heed of the inner voice that resides deep within you.*

Turning her gaze in another direction, Destiny spotted Jay Jay as he steered the waverunner back up the retractable launching chute extending from his boat's stern. From her vantage point, she could see the Sea Lion was far enough away from the Avenging Angel to pose no threat. For the time being, the Loomins brothers would be busy trying to repair their vessel.

Satisfied with the outcome, she let her eyes linger on Jay Jay as he climbed off the Kawasaki, now snug within its berth atop the Angel's rear superstructure. Here was the man prophesied by the painting on the cave wall, the man she had come to think of as 'The Protector' long before fate had brought them together. She had known only a few men in her life, all of whom she loved dearly. And although Jacob, and to a lesser extent Emmanuel, had become father-figures to her, the feelings she held for them in no way came close to what she felt for Jay Jay, for whenever she was near him her heart beat faster. This was a different kind of love, one that utterly confused her, and yet one she could not deny.

She had gotten insights into such love from the novels Jacob had given her to read, a love that could only exist between a man and a woman. And now she was actually feeling it for what it truly was. Though eternal like the limitless wellspring of pure love flowing forth from infinite dimensionality, there was a physical side to the emotion she was experiencing. It was a deep yearning, an inexplicable hunger akin to the albino matings that occasionally intruded their way into her awareness.

With great difficulty, she tried distancing herself from such thoughts, knowing she should investigate the source of evil originating from somewhere further back on the island. Strangely, she was besieged by a sudden impulse, recognizing that Bashir needed her help.

Just before Hercules submerged, she cast her eyes upon the Avenging Angel one more time. Those aboard the vessel still required Jay Jay's protection. The unknown danger she sensed was all too real for him not to remain where he was. One threat had just passed, only to to replaced by the possibility of another, one that might prove to be far worse.

And she realized, too, that the safety of Dr. Grahm was especially important to her. Without knowing why, she felt an unaccountable closeness to him. Oddly, this last thought stayed with her as Hercules dove beneath the surface.

- 78 -

From the bridge, Ben Loomins watched the Casa shrink to an indistinct dot before disappearing over the horizon. The last thing his partner had told him was that he would return with a boat to tow the Sea Lion back to Port-au-Prince if the vessel remained inoperable.

He knew Jaffey must be ready to kill somebody by now. A short time earlier, Jaffey had made one mad water-skimming pass at the man on the waverunner, trying to ram him with extended landing gear. Their assailant had easily dodged the maneuver, veering off to one side at the last moment and adding insult to injury by firing on the aircraft with an automatic weapon. After that, Jaffey had immediately backed off, circling at a distance and remaining clear of both the waverunner and the vessel that had launched it.

Loomins could not recall his partner ever sounding so enraged over the radio. Normally, Jaffey tended to be the most levelheaded between them. "That bastard shot a hole in my wing!" Jaffey had screamed. "I'm losing fuel!" Just before flying away, Jaffey had had the presence of mind to inform him about one little oddity he could clearly see from the air. "There's a really big dolphin down there, a white one with someone riding it."

Disgustedly, Loomins mulled these things as he dropped his gaze to the mass of fish strewn over the rear deck. The Haitians were still busy clearing away hundreds of barracuda swamping the boat, most of them inundating the vessel's port side. Slowly, the Sea Lion was coming back on an even keel.

He could tell Charlie was still shaken by what had happened. In all his years at sea, both he and his brother had never experienced anything that had come close to this.

"What now?" McPherson said, staring up at him.

"We try and get this boat up and running again," Loomins said heatedly. "The props won't turn."

"How could something like this happen?" McPherson persisted.

"I don't know!"

McPherson turned his gaze in the direction of the other boat anchored a quarter mile away. Every so often, a white dolphin made an impressive leap close to the vessel. "Maybe these white dolphin are tamer than we think." As he spoke, the creature made another spectacular leap. "That one there seems to be with the people aboard that boat."

Loomins felt his frustration growing. "Nothing I can do about it unless I get the props turning again. They're froze up solid." As an afterthought, he said, "Stay on the lookout for more of those creatures. Frank told me he saw a big one with somebody riding it."

"Maybe it's that girl you let get away the other day," McPherson criticized smugly. "You know, the one your crew calls the *white witch.*"

The sound of barracuda being tossed into the water abruptly ceased, halting the biting retort about to fly from Loomins' tongue. He glanced sharply at the Haitians to see why they had stopped. All three of them stared speechless at McPherson.

"Get back to work!" Loomins snarled.

For the moment, all three men ignored the command, pulling their eyes from McPherson and looking nervously at the surrounding water.

"If you want to keep working for me, you'll do as I say," Loomins threatened.

With great reluctance, the men went back to work, their efforts now considerably slower.

Loomins looked over at his brother. "Charlie! Grab a mask and hop over the side. I need to know what's fouling the shafts."

Charlie pointed to the other vessel. "What if that guy decides to take a run at us while I'm in the water?"

"Are you blind?" Ben decried. He addressed his brother as if speaking to a child. "Can't you see his waverunner's back on that boat? Get your ass in the water!"

Charlie stared up at him defiantly. "No way I'm gonna let myself become chum. Look what these fish did to me." He indicated his wounds. "Their teeth are like razors. If I go in the water I might get torn to pieces."

Ben turned heated eyes back to McPherson. "What about you? You got any balls?"

The naval captain bridled in annoyance. "You forget who's in charge here. You work for me. Already you seem to have forgotten about the $80,000 I advanced you to deliver me a dolphin, and so far you've screwed up twice."

Ben gawked fixedly down at McPherson for a long moment, his mouth hanging agape. "God damn!" he finally bellowed, moving to the ladder and climbing down from the bridge. "Get me the dive gear, Charlie! I'll do this myself!"

It took Ben less than three minutes to shed most of his clothing and don the scuba gear. The magnum pistol was turned over to Charlie's keeping. One by one, he stared contemptuously at the others. "I guess I'm the only one around here with any moxie. The rest of you are nothing but spineless wimps!" With that said, he lowered his dive mask and jumped into the sea.

- 79 -

Destiny had never fully explored all the underwater terrain surrounding Navassa Island. Neither had the other members of the pod. What she was looking for did not require exploration, however. Homing in on Bashir's location was more like following a scent, though the use of her olfactory senses to accomplish this was not needed.

The island was like a huge mesa of honeycombed limestone jutting above the sea, the top of a submerged mountain rising from the oceanic depths abutting the Cayman Trench. Hidden within the upper portions of this geologic structure were a vast maze of interconnected tunnels and vaults, all of them created over the eons by the incessant action of carbonic acid eating away at the remnants of the ancient coral reef comprising the rock. The huge subterranean grotto housing the thurentras was only one of numerous caverns that lay concealed beneath the island's surface.

As Hercules skirted the lush coral, Destiny studied the life-encrusted topography intently, knowing they were getting close to Bashir's position. Passing a collapsed section of reef, a sense of deep foreboding suddenly grabbed hold of her, its malevolence springing forth from an inky maw that yawned wide. Here it was again, the raw strength of it nearly disorienting her. The feeling passed quickly as Hercules ignored the opening and continued on for perhaps another hundred meters, eventually finding a darkened crevice amid a thriving forest of elkhorn coral. Intuitively, Destiny knew they had reached the right place as Hercules sent a pulse of biosonar into the cavity to gauge its configuration.

Rising 60 feet to the ocean surface, both Hercules and Destiny recharged their lungs before descending once again, this time entering the opening. With her mount periodically emitting bursts of sonar, Destiny was able to catch vivid mental pictures of what lay before them. Like the tunnel that led to the structure the dolphins were constructing, this one gradually wound its way upward, although it was more constricted in several places. At one particular bend, Hercules was barely able to squeeze through, and Destiny had to hug the dolphin tightly in order to avoid portions of jagged rock protruding down. A short distance beyond this point, they emerged into a small dome-shaped cavern partially filled with water, the chamber inundated with ebony blackness.

With his built-in sonar, Hercules continued to share the images he was receiving, and in spite of the total darkness Destiny was able to perceive a shelf of rock off to one side. Wide enough to accommodate her small frame, the shelf was only slightly submerged. Climbing from the albino's broad back, she stepped onto the ledge, her feet covered by several inches of water. A sense of Bashir's presence suddenly came to her again, now much stronger than before.

Somewhere ahead, a light flickered, and with it the sound of someone talking. Wading through the water, she groped her way through the darkness, guided by the cavern's arched wall where it met the shelf. Following the sound, she was able to hear the voice more clearly. Stealthily, she poked her head around a bend where the light still glimmered.

Standing several meters away were two men in heated discussion, the muted light from a handheld lantern dancing eerily off the face of one of them. Destiny recognized the man immediately. It was Bashir.

- 80 -

The damage Ben Loomins found was startling. A mass of hemp rope and rusting steel chain had somehow managed to become entangled around both drive shafts, taking them out of alignment. Attached to the chain were small anchors that had gouged the props, severely bending the blades. His vessel was not going anywhere.

How this could have happened seemed impossible. Dubiously, he eyed the void of deep indigo falling away beneath him. Off to one side more than a hundred feet from where he floated, he could see a huge congestion of barracuda filling the sea, but now they were moving away. In open water like this, the calamities that had wreaked havoc on his vessel were not supposed to happen.

Irately, he finned forward under the hull, checking for more damage. As yet, he had refrained from dropping anchor, letting the boat continue to drift slowly along. In any event, the water was probably too deep where he now floated to attempt dropping anchor anyway. Whatever current existed was slowly taking the Sea Lion further away from the unknown vessel that had launched the waverunner. The farther away he got from the man who had destroyed the sounder, the better, he finally conceded. As best he could tell, his assailant had weaponry far superior to the meager firepower he currently possessed.

The bodies of dead barracuda, some of them shredded and torn beyond recognition, continued to splash down into the sea on both sides of his vessel, attesting to the labors of the Haitians still clearing the deck above him. Torpidly, they drifted along with the boat, littering the water all around him. Sudden movement caught Loomins' eye as something large and torpedo-like darted in, snatching one of the fish in a mouth lined with serrated teeth. Caught off guard by the sight, he felt his heart buck in his chest like a stallion unexpectedly coming upon a rattler. Other large shapes quickly shot in to feast on the carnage, and he realized he was in the midst of a rapidly developing feeding frenzy. Sharks were flitting all about him, some of them three times his size.

With legs pumping, Loomins turned and sped for the boat's rear platform, wanting only to get out of the water. He had been stupid to let the crew keep on dumping fish while he made the dive. One thing after another was going wrong, and he berated himself for not having thought this out better. Reaching for one of the struts supporting the platform, he pulled himself along under the cantilevered overhang. Something rough and abrasive brushed rudely against him from behind, and with a strength born by terror he got a hand on the ladder hanging down into the water.

Just before pulling himself clear of the thrashing mayhem beating the sea all about him, Loomins became aware of one more anomaly, one that he found to be every bit as strange as the chain that had mysteriously fouled his props. With his breath catching in his throat, he suddenly shivered uncontrollably. Inexplicably, he realized the sea had become very cold.

- 81 -

"You do not understand," Bashir pleaded. "Bringing misery to others will contaminate your soul forever. There will not be seventy-two virgins waiting to give you pleasure in Paradise. If you continue with this insanity, only the fires of hell await you."

"You have betrayed us!" Kalid spat angrily. "You have betrayed Islam."

"No, my brother, it is you who has betrayed Islam. The killing of innocents is not Allah's way. If you continue on this course of madness, you taint the true Muslim faith, you defile your soul forever."

"Infidels are not innocent. They seek to desecrate Muslim cultures and Muslim lands, polluting them with unholy and obscene decadence. The Great Satan's bombs have killed many of our people. It is our obligation as Muslims to destroy those who are an abomination in the eyes of Allah. The Prophet prescribed this to be the duty of all those who follow the true Word."

"Your mind is twisted by hate."

"Have you forgotten your sworn allegiance to Allah? Under the banner of jihad you made an oath to vanquish all those who are unclean, vile and evil."

"I beseech you to rethink what you are doing, Kalid."

"I should kill you," Kalid threatened, "but I am sure Yeslam would be very displeased if I did not leave this task to him. You are no longer one of us."

"Yeslam is not a fit leader. He uses Islam as a pretext to do as he pleases." Bashir studied Kalid's face carefully. "Do you truly wish to follow this man?"

Kalid seemed hesitant to respond, and Bashir could see he had struck a chord of dissent. When Kalid finally answered, the words came out dull, devoid of all emotion. "Osama, himself, entrusted this mission to Yeslam. Our great leader, may he live forever, has ordained it. Do you presume to question his judgement?"

"Bin Laden deludes himself into believing he is fighting some kind of holy war, that he is doing God's work. He has often said that he looks forward to martyrdom in a showdown with the American troops hunting him. Yet he remains hidden among the Pashtun like a coward, imposing himself on their unique hospitality while others carry out his murderous decrees. I have given him much thought as of late and find him to be a man without a fiber of moral decency or honor. He is nothing more than a deceiver, a vicious killer who is obsessed with spilling the blood of others. When the war with the Soviets ended in Afghanistan, he looked for other excuses to justify his passion for killing. That was when he decided to prey on the Americans and other Western cultures to satisfy his thirst for blood, hiding behind the veil of Islam and inflaming Muslims to hate anything outside the boundary of our religion." He stopped his diatribe momentarily to gauge the look of horror that was steadily growing on Kalid's face. "Yes, I do presume to question the judgement of such a man, for he places missions like this in the hands of people with the same moral temperment as he, himself, possesses. Godless murderers without any sense of honor or faith."

"You are mad!" Kalid croaked in disbelief. "You have completely lost your sensibilities."

Bashir was truly saddened. Kalid was beyond reason. "No, my Muslim brother," he uttered softly. "It is you who has lost yours. I will pray for you."

"But who will pray for you?"

It was not Kalid who had voiced the question. Bashir spun around to see Raduyev loom up out of the darkness. In the light cast by the lantern, the Chechen's expression was perfidious and cruel, but Bashir was not afraid. He had come back here to do what he could to stop a colossal tragedy from occurring, knowing he might die in the process. Raduyev was a brutal and unforgiving sort, a man who would kill as easily as drawing in a breath of air.

For over a day now, Bashir had poked around in these caverns deciding on a course of action, doing his best to remain hidden from the others. Driven by thirst, he had raided the food stores, making off with some of the limited fresh water and rations, including the lantern. He had thought he had been surreptitious in doing this while most of the Al Qaeda team slept, but now he knew otherwise. Kalid had obviously awoken and spotted him skulking about, eventually following him into the unused passage he had taken to remain out of sight.

As he stared at Bin Laden's lieutenant, Bashir had to assume Raduyev must have tailed Kalid and overheard most of the ensuing confrontation that had just taken place. Opening his mouth, Bashir blurted the only words he could think to utter in that instant. "You deserted me. You left me to die."

Raduyev ignored the accusation. "How did you get back here?" he hissed warily, looking beyond both men to scan the unlit portions of the chamber. "Someone must have helped you."

"Yes," Bashir affirmed proudly. "But it was not just someone. It was the angels of God who saved me. They rescued me from the madness that was slowly consuming me."

The Chechen studied him oddly before projecting a pernicious sneer. "Angels would not waste their time on a pitiful blasphemer like you," he rasped cuttingly. "You have offended Allah and all those who serve him. You are lower than a Jew. You are the filth that comes from the bowels of a Zionist pig."

Bashir let out a disdainful little laugh. Caught up in mind-clouding hate, men like Raduyev never seemed to grow tired of using anti-Semitic slurs as a form of insult. Ever since having been saved by the strange angelic beings, Bashir's thinking was the sharpest it had ever been, and it suddenly dawned on him that in the Muslim world most political legitimacy was acquired through the bashing of Israelis. With this in mind, he responded with the only logical reply within him. "Then perhaps I will learn how to create rather than destroy."

Raduyev's expression abruptly stiffened, his eyes ablaze with the threat of mayhem as his hand came to rest on the hilt of the Bowie knife strapped to his side. "You think Jews do not destroy?" he said scornfully.

"They only destroy in self-defense. Look at what they have done with just a tiny sliver of desert. Perhaps we can learn from them."

Ashamedly, Bashir could not help but measure the accomplishments of his own Palestinian people against those of the Israelis. In the Arab world, illiteracy, poverty and disease still reigned supreme while Israel boasted a $100 billion economy with less than one-thousandth of the world's population. During a brief but enlightening discussion he had had on the beach the other night, the man called Jacob had gently pointed out several unavoidable truths that, though disturbing, had opened his eyes. Israel had the highest ratio of university degrees per capita on the planet, possessing some of the world's finest medical, scientific and technically sophisticated research facilties. By comparison, the record of his own people was sorrowful, with the predominantly Sunni Palestinians achieving next to nothing that could be considered beneficial. Even the network of high-tech greenhouses the Palestinians had inherited from the Jewish settlers upon Israel's withdrawal from Gaza ended up falling into ruin and vandalization. After more than 60 years, the Palestinians of Gaza continued to live off foreign aid, putting their efforts into building rockets and bombs instead of a future, and teaching their children to intensely loathe everything associated with Zionism. The hate of his people was poisoning their minds, preventing them from pursuing anything even remotely constructive. Unfortunately, there seemed to be a bottomless pool of young Palestinians who sought to satisfy the rage instilled in them by radical Muslim clerics incessantly preaching anti-Semitic hatred.

Bashir knew that the recruitment of Muslim men to the call of jihad was escalating. Both Hezbollah and Hamas were steadily growing in numbers these days, gaining more and more political support among the Muslim moderates to wipe Israel off the face of the planet. They never seemed to tire of provoking the Jews through suicide bombings, kidnappings, hijackings, murders or other forms of mayhem, periodically prodding the Zionist bull into retaliating, then running to the United Nations for protection. Every time this happened, it seemed, the UN tended to openly condemn Israel for its use of disproportionate force, interceding itself into the conflict before the retaliation could escalate to a point that would obliterate the paramilitary infrastructures of either Hezbollah and Hamas.

Based on what he had heard over the last several years, Bashir was convinced that Hezbollah had gained dramatically in strength. Firmly rooted among

Lebanon's general population, Hezbollah had no scruples about using civilians as human shields to discourage Israeli bombing strikes. Using Lebanese residential homes as launching sites, they fired Katyusha rockets designed to kill Israeli citizens. Tactics like this worked well in their favor, serving them on the public relations front that molded world opinion. Collateral damage caused by Israeli bombs in taking out a launch site often killed women and children, drawing widespread condemnation from other nations.

Now that his thinking was clear, Bashir could plainly see the escalating fatalities and misery such strategy brought to the people of Lebanon. These things, however, were of little concern to Hezbollah. Lives were unimportant, only results. A state within a state, Hezbollah was a Shia Islamist political party within the Lebanese government. Fortified by members of the Iranian Revolutionary Guard, it received substantial financial backing from the Iranian government, essentially making it Iran's attack dog. And the government of Iran, led by a group of rabid Islamo-fascists, had vowed to exterminate Israel. Iran, he was certain, would never relent on this primary goal, constantly testing the will of the international coalition.

To its credit, Hezbollah had often demonstrated innovative skills in carrying out its objectives, and Bashir wondered about all the good that could be accomplished if this same creativity were ever used toward constructive rather than destructive ends. As had been proven many times, Hezbollah seemed to have an uncanny ability at raising vast sums of money to fund its operations, most of it funneled into terrorism, guerrilla warfare and media coverage that both justified and glorified their efforts.

The recent alliance between Bin Laden and Hezbollah struck Bashir as odd, however. In the past, Hezbollah and Al Qaeda had pursued different agendas, with Hezbollah focusing primarily on Israel and fomenting sectarian violence in Iraq, while the Sunnis of Bin Laden had previously confined themselves mainly to Afghanistan, Pakistan, Yugoslavia, Bosnia and Chechnya, but were now stepping up their presence in Iraq, as well. Hezbollah wanted to eradicate the Zionist state while Al Qaeda wanted to destroy the United States. Al Qaeda's Sunni Wahhabist ideology was largely incompatible with Hezbollah's relatively liberal brand of Shia Islam. Surprisingly, Bin Laden had initially demonstrated a distaste for the Shia suicide bombings and attacks on civilian targets in Iraq, and he had openly condemned Hezbollah for preventing Palestinians from using Lebanon as a staging area for incursions against Israel. Hezbollah, on the other hand, had denounced Al Qaeda for killing innocents, claiming its own resistance toward the Jewish state by whatever means to be justified and legitimate. In spite of these differences, something had changed in recent times, though Hezbollah continued to publically deny any links to Bin Laden's organization.

And Bashir now understood what had united the divergent militant groups. In order to wipe out Israel, Iran needed Israel's closest ally neutralized, and that meant collaborating with Al Qaeda to take down Bin Laden's greatest enemy.

All these things coursed in the back of Bashir's mind as he stared back at Raduyev. He could see his brash retort had the equivalency of a stinging slap. In the feeble light cast by the lantern, the Chechen's face darkened, glowering with malignant hatred.

In a flash, Raduyev drew his blade, positioning the point of it under Bashir's chin. "The words of a Jew-lover are nothing but gibberish to me," he ranted. "Tell me who brought you here or I will send you off to the fires of hell this instant."

"I already told you," Bashir said calmly. "I was helped by angels."

"Liar!" Raduyev screeched. Grabbing Bashir by the throat with his free hand, he pulled the knife back in preparation for a lethal underhand strike that would plunge the shaft deep into the Palestinian's abdomen.

Bashir offered no resistance. He was prepared to die now that he was completely free of the dogma and ignorance that had blinded him from the truth his entire life.

"Stop!" a voice suddenly cried out, the sound ringing through the chamber.

Spoken in English, the outcry had come from somewhere behind Bashir. As Raduyev continued to clutch his throat, Bashir noted the look of shock this sudden intrusion had evoked in the Chechen's expression. With eyes opened wide, Raduyev stared over Bashir's shoulder, trying to discern the presence lurking in the darkness.

Pivoting his head around as far as the Chechen's restraining grip would allow, Bashir tried following Raduyev's gaze.

"Stop!" the voice repeated firmly. "Don't hurt him!"

It was then that Bashir saw Destiny's slender form materialize out of the blackness.

- 82 -

It had never been Destinys intention to become involved in the disputes between men. Conflict, she knew, was the result of fear, and fear only intensified the perception of separateness that kept people at odds with one another. But then conflict always seemed to leave misery in its wake, and as she watched the scene that was taking place before her, she knew she could not let Bashir die.

"I have seen you before," said the man holding Bashir by the throat. "You were riding an accursed white dolphin."

Destiny moved closer, fully exposing herself in the light spilling from the lantern. She had heard enough of the confrontation to know these were the Islamic extremists Jay Jay had talked about with Jacob. "Please let this man go," she implored. "He means you no harm."

For one seemingly unending moment the man stared back at her as if she was crazy. All at once, he threw his head back and let out a harsh, rabid laugh. "Allah is truly a wondrous and accommodating god. He delivers into my hands the very thing I have been thinking about these last several days." Abruptly, his expression changed into a sneer. "I do not know how you got in here, but you will soon pay a most painful price for meddling in our business."

Up close, Destiny sensed something emanating from the man that was altogether different from the first individual Bashir had been arguing with, and it made her blood run cold. An aura of negative energy seemed to surround him. It was the same iniquity that had invaded her awareness a short time earlier. Here was a man whose soul belonged to the dark side of creation, a sentience she intuitively understood would be immune to the benign effects of the dolphin art.

Bashir struggled against the hand gripping his throat. "There is nothing you can do against an angel," he gasped. "She has the power to heal severe injuries in seconds."

"Silence!" Raduyev snapped. "I forbid you to speak any more." He looked over at the other man. "Grab her, Kalid!"

Destiny remained still as Kalid stepped toward her, keeping her gaze fixed on Raduyev. "Release Bashir at once." She could see a tinge of confusion manifest itself fleetingly in his eyes, knowing immediately that such a man fed off the fear he was able to instill in others. By showing no fear, she was diminishing his command of the situation.

"Did you hear what I said, Kalid?" Raduyev yelled. "I told you to grab her!"

Ignoring Kalid, Destiny stood her ground, continuing to lock eyes with Raduyev. She was not going to leave without Bashir.

Overcoming his hesitation, Kalid reached for her arm. Blue sparks suddenly flared, accompanied by the sound of a sizzling pop as his fingers made contact. Kalid screamed as he was flung back violently, his body slamming against the cavern wall and crumbling to the floor. The acrid smell of ozone hung heavily in the air.

In slack-jawed disbelief, Raduyev stared at Kalid's unconscious form. Shifting his eyes back to Destiny, he said, "What manner of satanic trickery is this?"

Bashir managed to pry Raduyev's fingers from his throat. "Your twisted brain refuses to accept what your eyes have just seen," he admonished disdainfully. "Trying to capture one of Allah's angels has sentenced you to eternal suffering in the next life." Taking advantage of the Chechen's bewilderment, he moved quickly to Destiny's side, bringing the lantern with him.

Destiny looked back at Raduyev. "Do not try to follow us," she said, the hint of a warning firmly implied in the words.

Raduyev did not reply, totally aghast at what he had just witnessed.

Turning, Destiny led Bashir back to the pool of water flooding the adjacent cavern. "You'll have to hold your breath for at least two minutes if I'm going to get you out of here," she told him.

Bashir gave her a venerating nod, his eyes filled with pious awe. "For you, my sweet angel, I will hold my breath for all eternity. Forever will I be your humble servant, to do anything you wish of me."

"Be sure to keep your head low," Destiny instructed as Bashir straddled Hercules' wide back. With that, the albino bull dove.

- 83 -

The sight of Destiny with Bashir sitting behind her as they rode Hercules surprised Jake. He had been keeping to the Angel's pilothouse where he had been maintaining an uninterrupted vigilance of the Sea Lion as it continued to drift without power nearly a half mile away. Descending to the main deck, he moved quickly to the boat's dive platform where he helped the girl come aboard. Meeting Jake's cold stare, Bashir smiled meekly up at him as he continued to hold fast to the large albino, seemingly unsure if he should follow.

"You have nothing to fear from this man," Destiny assured him after he had taken the girl aside. "Bashir is not the same person that attacked you back at Gaia. He has changed."

Jake studied Destiny's earnest expression. "How did you find him?"

Destiny looked away. "All will be revealed soon enough, but now is not the time."

The girl's comment jarred something loose from Jake's memory. Achilles had made a similar statement the day before, though it was in response to a different question. Such evasiveness puzzled him. "I need answers," he insisted hotly, wondering if Destiny's naivety was impeding her judgement. "Bashir is an Islamic militant. I've had experience with men like him and deception is part of their ideology. How do I know he can be trusted?"

Destiny turned her face up to Jake again, her eyes searching his. "His mind is no longer fettered with irrational fear. Of this he has purged himself. Fear is the underlying cause of all human conflict, the wedge that separates people and brings on hate. In shedding his fear, Bashir has become fully aware of our commonality, the unifying force that connects us all."

Jake turned his head to observe Bashir standing beside Phillipe and Zimby. All three were laughing at something said, possibly a shared joke. Perhaps what the girl was telling him was true, but then again, one could never be completely certain. "All right," he finally conceded. "I'll rely on your judgement for the time being, but if he causes me any problems I'm holding you responsible."

A mischievous glint suddenly showed in Destiny's eyes, adorned by a mirthful smile. "Oh…and what do you propose to do if it turns out I'm wrong about him?"

Jake took immediate pause. This was the first sign of outright flirtation he had seen in the girl, a quality he had assumed was not in her character. "I, uh…I'll think of something," he stuttered. "Perhaps a good spanking will be in order."

"What's a spanking?"

Staring down at her, Jake realized her innocence was showing again. Now it was his turn to be evasive. He made an effort to give her his best enigmatic grin. "You'll find out if such punishment is ever warranted."

Destiny responded with a mock pout. "Then I guess I'll never get to learn the meaning of the word."

Jake became reflective. "You're quite sure about Bashir, aren't you?"

The smile on Destiny's face turned serious. "Very sure. A change in one person is like a ripple on the water, radiating out to affect everything it touches. If enough people underwent the same positive change that has transformed Bashir, the whole world would become a better place. Strife and war would become a thing of the past."

Jake fell silent, musing over the girl's logic. Obviously she was seeing things that were alien to him, things he had difficulty understanding. The dream with the rainbow had given him only partial insight to the mysteries Destiny and the dolphins shared, but now his memory of it had all but evaporated, leaving him devoid of most of the things he had previously grasped. Still, some shreds of it continued to stay with him.

Looking in the direction of the Sea Lion, Jake said, "I don't think Ben Loomins is very happy right now. I assume you had something to do with what happened."

Destiny nodded demurely. "I only wanted to keep him away from you. Someone might have gotten killed."

Jake frowned, knowing what she really meant. Destiny didn't want anyone aboard the Sea Lion dying as a result of his actions. "But you must have known about the chains Achilles tied off to his propellor shafts. Loomins was just sitting there waiting for his partner to show up. The chains would have been enough to stop his vessel."

"I had to be sure," Destiny said softly. "Those chains were old and corroded having sat on the bottom all those years. Achilles wasn't convinced they wouldn't break."

Jake let out a long weary sigh. "And you thought I would've fired upon Loomins if he kept coming?"

"You might not have had any other option. I wanted to prevent such a possibility from happening."

Jake narrowed his eyes, looking for clues in the girl's face that would reveal more. *Had she seen something?* Using their collective mental capability, had she and the pod made some kind of statistical analysis of all the information available to them and come up with a probable future event? Trying to second-guess what was going on was starting to wear him out.

Deciding to steer clear of the subject, Jake said, "I'm getting ready to pull anchor. Dr. Grahm has seen enough of his boat and would like to be leaving. As for myself, I've got to be in Port-au-Prince tomorrow."

Destiny stared up at him, her demeanor serene. "Will I ever see you again?"

"Only if I'm still welcome back at the place you call Gaia."

"You'll always be welcome there, Jay Jay. The pod has accepted you as one of their own."

"I have one problem, though."

"Yes?"

"What do I do about Bashir?"

Destiny turned around to observe the Palestinian. "Bashir is now my responsibility. I'm sure Jacob can use his help…at least for the time being."

"I just hope you're not being overly optimistic about this change in him. I'd hate to see him revert back to what he was."

"Bashir sees the world through different eyes now. Free from the confusion that had plagued him all his life, he has finally found himself. He no longer has a desire to harm anyone. I sense within him a need to build rather than destroy."

Jake thought about the dolphin art again. Having been exposed to its strange power, he believed what Destiny was telling him to be true. But as he began making preparations to get underway, he suddenly realized there might actually be a potentially bigger threat aboard his vessel than the one Bashir posed. With bells and whistles going off in his head, he became aware of the way Nick Henderson kept staring at the Sea Lion floating in the distance.

- 84 -

A jumble of thoughts wended their way through Raduyev's neurotic brain, most of them perverse and ugly. This was the second time he had been thwarted by the dolphin girl. What angered him even more was Bashir's insistence that she was an angel sent by God. But now that he had time to analyze the strange occurrence he had witnessed, he was convinced such a claim was absurd. Bashir was stupid to think Allah would pit one of his angels against followers of the one true religion. Physically, Bashir had been the weakest among his team. It only followed that his mind would exhibit the same shortcomings as his body, easily fooled by another's duplicity. Obviously the girl had purposely misled the Palestinian into accepting this false belief. Most likely she had been armed with some kind of defensive weapon hidden under the wet suit she wore, perhaps some kind of a taser that produced a powerful but non-lethal electrical shock. It was the only plausible explanation he could come up with to rationalize what he had seen her do to Kalid.

Initially, the event had left Raduyev stunned, and by the time he had regained his wits, both Bashir and the girl had vanished, disappearing beyond a heavy grouping of stalagmites. Using the flashlight he carried, he had followed, ignoring Kalid's inert form sprawled on the cavern floor. He had not traveled far before discerning a faint glow. Drawing the 9mm Browning from his shoulder holster, he had advanced rapidly toward it. The lantern Bashir had taken with him had sat deserted on a rocky ledge, its light reflecting off a pool of darkened water. Movement had caught his eye, and he had turned his light to follow it. A huge white dolphin had dipped below the surface, the girl and Bashir sitting in tandem astride its back. The unexpectedness of the sight had caused him to react too slowly. Nevertheless he had aimed his pistol and emptied the clip, nearly deafened by the shots echoing hollowly about the low-slung chamber. When nothing had floated to the surface, he could only surmise the bullets had missed their targets. After that, he had scrambled hurriedly to the island's surface to investigate where they had gone. Obviously they had escaped through one of the many underwater tunnels that riddled the island and were on their way back to the boat that had taken them here.

He had been right. From a concealed position that overlooked the sea, he had watched Bashir and the girl ride the huge white dolphin out to the vessel he had failed to destroy two days earlier, and as he studied the boat through the spyglasses, his rage continued to mount. Once again, his chance at retribution had been foiled.

Silently he cursed the girl, vowing to get revenge. If not for the repairs that were currently taking place on Allah's Sword, he might have been able to take the sub out to where the boat lay at anchor and ram it into a mass of splintered wood. But now all he could do was observe the people aboard it, powerless to do anything. Magnified through the optics of the spyglasses, he had a clear view of the man he had failed to kill, and his hatred abruptly climbed to a new height.

Seething with rage, he swung the binoculars by seventy degrees to the west to observe the other vessel he had noticed a short time earlier, this one further out to sea. Through the lens, he could make out several members of its crew working hard to clear the rear deck of fish. Another crewmember was shedding scuba gear, and by the manner in which the man was gesticulating, Raduyev could see he was clearly angry.

Disregarding the sight for the moment, he brought the glasses to bear on the first vessel once again, realizing its anchor was being hoisted. With intensified frustration, he continued to watch as the boat swung around to take on an eastern heading, the lettering on its stern taunting him all the more.

Watching the vessel depart, a sudden realization closed in on him with the power of a hydraulic vise. His hidden base had now been compromised. Bashir knew enough about the mission to bring it to a screeching halt should that information fall into the wrong hands. And with the Palestinian traitor currently aboard Javolyn's vessel, he could only assume such a possibility to be inevitable. That left the Chechen with only two options. Either he would have to eliminate Javolyn and those of his crew very quickly, or he would have to accelerate his original timetable. He already had one Rodong rocket in readiness, and that he could fire any time he chose.

As the departing vessel gradually grew smaller in size, only one thing provided Raduyev with a modicum of appeasement, and that was the information he had supplied to Ortega. *We shall soon see who is the true avenger*, he consoled himself.

It was just after sunset when the San Carlo crept close to the tiny seaside village. Setting its anchor, it floated no more than 500 meters offshore, awaiting its intended cargo. Standing on the walkway outside the unlit bridge, Sebastion Ortega aimed a powerful spotlight shoreward, blinking it on and off three times. Several seconds elapsed before he was answered in kind, though the signal coming from the village consisted of only two short flashes followed by two more after a brief interval.

Satisfied, Ortega glanced at the luminous dial on his watch before turning to Pedro. "We have fallen behind schedule," he announced acidly. The odor of something in the air made him look at the man a little more closely. In spite of the stench of rotting fish hanging over the ship, the smell of liquor on Pedro's breath was almost as pungent. Cardoza's nephew, it seemed, continued to offend him on a daily basis. "I want these villagers brought aboard as quickly as possible. Any more delays and I will hold you personally responsible."

Pedro shrugged as if such a threat were inconsequential. "I have no control over how fast these Haitians can climb a ladder."

"Just do it!" Ortega growled.

Pedro shrugged again, saying nothing as he moved to the stairs that would take him to the lower deck.

Watching him go, Ortega could not help but think how easy it would be to put a bullet in the back of the man's head. But doing that, he knew, would bring the wrath of Cardoza down on him, the only thing that had always kept his desire to do away with Pedro in check. He had seen firsthand what Cardoza's pet tiger had done to others, and he had no wish to suffer the same fate.

Ortega was in a particularly bad mood, having taken the trawler to the coordinates given him by Omar before coming here. Lowering one of the newly acquired motorboats over the side, he had sent five of his men ahead while he and Fernando had taken the helicopter in a coordinated raid designed to catch by surprise all those residing in the hidden cove. Unfortunately, the place had been deserted. Both the man who had attacked him back at Navassa and his boat were missing. Being denied the baleful things he envisioned doing to the man continued to grate on him as though he were being dragged over jagged coral, and now more than ever he needed some form of satisfaction.

Even more disappointing was the absence of the girl and those incredible white dolphins seen with her. The thought of this only served to increase his irritable mood, and as he watched the loading of human cargo, he entertained himself with the various ways he might go about finding them. Remembering the other vessel he had spotted from the air during his flight to Saint-Marc, he made himself a promise to seek the boat out at the first opportunity. But right now he had a delivery to make.

And following the delivery, the San Carlo was committed to assisting Omar with something else. Even after the trawler got underway, Ortega continued to muse over what that something else entailed.

- 86 -

It was late evening by the time the Avenging Angel pulled abreast of the cliffs concealing the cove entrance. Out of the darkness, another boat arrived at the same time, its size much smaller than the North Sea trawler.

"It's Jimenez," Destiny informed Jake. "Let him come alongside." The dolphins had detected the watercraft's approach long before it materialized out of the gloom, and now the girl sensed something to be very wrong.

As the boat came alongside, Destiny recognized another man in the boat with Jimenez. It was Ronaldo Trebek.

"Everyone in Malique is missing," Jimenez told Destiny, his voice crackling like dry twigs caught in a flame. "I came here looking for Jacob, but he is not in the cove. I found it strange that his boat was tied to the main pier in the village, but he was no where to be found."

Destiny listened with Jake and Grahm at her sides. Something nudged her consciousness and she became aware of the other creatures that had always stayed close to her mother. Hearing their whispers, she immediately went rigid.

Though foretold several years earlier by Amphitrite, Destiny had never thought it would come to pass. Erzulie had once again come to Malique leading a band of men.

Acknowledging Jimenez's searching eyes, she found it difficult to utter the words aloud. "They have all been taken away."

In the glare of the Angel's deck lights, Jimenez appeared to shrink back in horror. And while Trebek seemed downcast, Destiny could see her words had not impacted him in the same manner.

"Who took them away?" Jake demanded.

Destiny was momentarily confused. Fighting through the disorientation, she was able to perceive occasional glimpses of what had taken place. Glancing about her, she looked in the direction where urgency was most needed. "Both mother and Jacob are prisoners of Erzulie. They have been taken south."

"Who is Erzulie?" Jake asked.

Destiny turned to stare up at him. "A witch of the voudun. Her son is a ranking member of the Tonton Makout."

Jake shifted his gaze to Zimbola who hovered close. "Zimby, that name mean anything to you?"

Zimby stiffened with graveness. "They are the worst type of scum. It is rumored that a man by the name of Ternier is their leader. He runs the prison in Port-au-Prince."

The mention of the name elicited something residing deep inside Jake, causing him to stare sharply at the Jamaican giant. "Henri Ternier?"

Zimby nodded grimly.

"How long have you known this?" Jake asked in surprise. The name had remained lodged in his memory ever since Myers had told him a man called Henri Ternier had murdered his grandfather.

Not a trace of guilt showed in Zimbola's face. "Long enough to know that revenge will not bring back Mercades."

The first twinges of anger boiled up from the pit of Jake's stomach, but he quickly gained control of himself. "You should've told me this before."

"Would it have made a difference?" the Jamaican replied.

"It might have," Jake retorted, becoming aware of the perplexity this sudden turn in the conversation had invoked in the faces of Grahm and his assistants.

Jake brought his attention back to Destiny, his manner pressing. "What about the others? What happened to them?"

"West," Destiny answered dully. "Most have been put aboard a ship that is heading west. It's the same ship you fought against."

"You mean the fishing trawler?"

"Yes."

Jake watched Destiny's face anxiously. "Jacob and your mother...do you sense them?"

Destiny nodded. Her mother's presence was very strong now though she knew she was many miles away.

"Can you take me to them?"

"I think so."

Grahm spoke up for the first time, looking completely bewildered as he stared at Jake. "What do you intend on doing?"

Jake thrust out his jaw, his face a mask of determination. "I'm going to rescue a friend."

"You want me to do what?" The speaker's tone indicated incredulous disbelief.

Jake faced the man he had come to see with a calm air. On his way back to Port-au-Prince he had made a brief satellite call, arranging this impromptu rendezvous on the fly. The face-to-face meeting just beyond the harbor limits was necessary. He could not afford the risk of having this discussion overheard in a monitored phone conversation.

"I'm asking for your help, Mat," Jake said. "This job will require a true professional."

"But breaking into Haiti's National Penitentiary. You're joking, right?"

"No, Mat, this is no joke. You ever hear of the Tonton Makout?"

Mat fell silent for several seconds. "Yeah. They were a paramilitary group here in Haiti. The Duvalier's used them to keep the population in check when they ruled the country. The Makout were disbanded years ago."

"Wrong," Jake shot back, looking to see how Mat reacted to what he said next. "They're still around and they work for a guy named Henri Ternier who runs the prison. You remember the name, don't you? He was the one who tortured and killed Myers' grandfather, Mercades Myers."

"How do you know this is the same man?"

"I don't, but whether or not he is, I still have to spring some people from the prison he runs."

"And you think we'll just be able to saunter in there and break them out."

"Damn it, Mat, don't make me call in my marker."

"I know I owe you, buddy, but what you're asking is nothing short of nuts, something that could easily mushroom into an international incident. If word ever got out that a member of the DHS abetted a prison break in a sovereign nation, the media would never let it go, not to mention the mess it would put Uncle Sam in."

Jake hesitated before letting out a remorseful sigh. "You're right, Mat. Only an asshole would make such a stupid request. Forget I ever asked you, I've got to go."

"Wait a second, Jake, tell me you're not going to be so dumb as to go this alone."

"There are some things in life that cannot be ignored, and this is one of them."

"But why?"

"Because some friends need help and the people holding them will torture them if I don't get them out of there. I'm talking about people whose only crime is trying to make the world a better place."

Mat did not immediately reply, lapsing into a deep and prolonged silence. Finally, in a changed voice that was soft and conciliatory, he said, "All right, Jake, count me in. Tell me how you'd like to do this."

- 88 -

With brooding eyes, Chester Hennington stared pensively at the man looking back at him. Though the reflection remained the same as it always had, he knew that inwardly he had changed. Why then, he continued to ask himself, had he arranged for Ortega to rendezvous with Ternier at Malique. Hadn't he betrayed the woman?

But deep down he knew the answer. The white mambo had intended for it to happen. With unrestrained willingness she had given him the amulet, knowing it would be handed over to Ternier. But she had done something to him. Using some strange miraculous power she had opened him up, giving him the means to transcend both his mind and body to connect with his soul. And in so doing she had rid him of an immense burden, cleansing him of all the rot that had built up inside. But in the process, he had become a party to something that would normally defy reason under normal circumstances. He had continued to do what he had always done, following the same path for which his talents were best suited. This confused him all the more. Now free of the guilt that had always nagged away at him, he had nevertheless provided aid to three of the vilest men he had ever known.

It was the only explanation he could come up with. The white mambo had wanted this to happen even though it would place the entire village in jeopardy, including herself. None of this made any sense.

Nonetheless, he felt no compulsion to interfere with the web that was rapidly forming, though those ensnared in its strands would surely meet their doom. Falling into Erzulie's clutches would be a fate worse than death, of that he was certain. And yet all he could do was look on like a man awed by the sight of a huge spider about to sink its deadly fangs into a helpless victim, too horrified to do anything to stop it. Without understanding why, he felt no remorse over his own feckless behavior, realizing he was willing to let events unfold regardless of how hopeless they appeared.

The Girl Who Rode Dolphins

With deep resignation, Hennington dropped this thought, focusing on another matter. Another of his clients had finally contacted him and a package needed to be delivered. It was important he notify Javolyn right away.

As he reached for his wireless phone, the device unexpectedly rang. "Who is calling?" he asked in French. But from the number displayed on the phone's small screen, he already knew.

The voice that answered was cold and impatient. "Come to my office at once!"

Wearily, Hennington got up and reached for his white jacket, mildly surprised that Ternier had arrived back so soon from Malique.

- 89 -

With Mat providing suggestions, Jake began putting together a plan. Ronaldo Trebek proved to be an invaluable asset as they hashed out the obstacles they were sure to encounter. Trebek had insisted on accompanying Jake back to Port-au-Prince once he had learned where Amphitrite and Jacob had been taken. Standing over a chart table aboard the Angel, all three men studied the layout of the prison compound Trebek had sketched out.

Trebek tapped a finger on the drawing, emphasizing one particular area. "It is here where you will find them," he proclaimed emphatically.

Jake raised an eyebrow. "How can you be sure?"

Trebek lowered his eyes and fidgeted slightly, suddenly appearing self-conscious. "Long ago, I was a member of the Tonton Makout. Having to admit this is a source of personal shame for me. I used to work with Ternier and know the way his mind works." He placed a finger on the sketch again. "There are holding cells in this area that were used for interrogation and the torture of political dissidents. Ternier has always had a penchant for torturing his enemies. It gives him pleasure. I can assure you he still uses those cells for this purpose."

Jake's expression hardened, and Trebek found it necessary to look away. Placing a finger on the paper again, he added, "At the end of this hallway is a steel door that leads to Erzulie's chamber. To gain entrance to this area, you must first get past the guards posted at the door blocking the opposite end of the hallway."

Mat shook his head. "That's the least of our problems. Just getting into the compound is what concerns me. I've seen that penitentiary. It's like a fortress."

"There is a way in," Trebek intoned enigmatically. "One where you will not meet any resistance."

"Where?"

"Here!" Trebek indicated a place further back from the north side of the prison. "This is your way in, an entrance to an underground tunnel." He drew a line that terminated inside the prison close to the interrogation area. "This tunnel dates back to the days when Haiti was a French colony."

Mat still looked skeptical. "And you think it'll be unguarded, or at the very least unsecured."

"Yes."

"Explain!"

"Only Erzulie and her spawn use this tunnel. Ternier is Erzulie's spawn. The locals who know of this tunnel keep clear of it, believing a terrible curse will befall them should they ever wander into it."

"You can take us to this tunnel?"

Trebek hesitated, his expression turning grim. "I will lead you into the prison."

"I assume you know the danger you'll be putting yourself in if you do that," Jake offered.

A small wistful smile came to Trebek's face. "It is but a small price to pay. Think of it as a form of atonement for past sins. I can never truly repay the white mambo for saving me from a former life ill spent."

"I will also go with you," Zimbola said, crowding in close to stand beside Jake.

Jake opened his mouth to object, but before he could voice his disapproval, Destiny stepped forward to join the discussion. "I'll be coming as well." Up to this point the girl had been standing off to one side, her manner subdued and distant.

"That's not a good idea," Jake said, bristling at the suggestion. "Way too risky. I'd rather you stay aboard the Angel until this business is finished."

Upon learning what had happened back near Malique, he had insisted Destiny remain with him in order to keep her safe. Putting her back in the path of danger was something he would not allow.

Destiny locked eyes with him, and within them Jake could see a massive unwillingness to go along with what he wanted. "There is more to this than you can see," she said in that soft mellifluous voice of hers. "People I dearly love are being held captive in that prison. I must go."

"No way." Jake was adamant.

"This is not a matter of choice. I must go to clear the way for the future."

Zimbola placed a gentle hand on Jake's shoulder, stilling the protest about to be launched from his lips. "Going without the girl is not a good idea."

Jake spun, turning a sulky glare on the Jamaican towering over him. "Are you out of your mind, Zimby? You want to get her killed?"

Frustration showed in the giant's expression. "The girl will bring balance to the plan. She will provide the light against the darkness that will block our way."

"Say it in terms that have meaning to me," Jake snapped irritably, his tone scalding.

"Without Destiny's help, Erzulie will defeat us. A witch of the voudun is very powerful and can only be countered by one strong in white magic."

Jake's face soured even more. "You're wasting your time if you expect me to buy into that voodoo crap. I've told you before, black magic doesn't exist. This Erzulie is just a woman who can be stopped with a bullet like anyone else."

Zimbola looked ridiculously helpless under Jake's cold stare. Here was the subject that had caused them to butt heads whenever it arose, an irritating source of disagreement that had often come between them in the past.

Destiny came to Zimbola's defense. "You have to trust what your friend is telling you, Jay Jay." Her tone continued to remain dulcet and disarming, but Jake could not mistake the underlying conviction her words conveyed. "A gun barrel will not be enough to stop Erzulie," she stressed.

Jake was momentarily taken back. He had not even considered the girl to be capable of believing in such nonsense. To accept voodoo was to believe in the supernatural, an acceptance of phenomena at variance with the world he was able to grasp.

Abruptly, Jake shrank back within himself. *Hadn't the girl already demonstrated her ability to invoke events that were discordant with the physical universe he had come to know?* Having to confront such a quandary flustered him, and he suddenly found himself at a crossroad. And then it hit home. With unsettling clarity, he knew he had to let Destiny have her way. All his instincts were now clamoring for him to withdraw an obstinacy he could no longer justify.

Discharging a reluctant sigh, Jake found himself caving. "You'll stay behind me! You won't leave my side!"

"I will not hinder you," Destiny agreed.

Mat, whose head had been swiveling back and forth in confusion over the interplay, looked alarmed. "Jake, are you nuts?" Though Mat was a close friend, he had never liked calling him Jay Jay. Dismayed, he turned to stare at Destiny uneasily, then swung back to face Jake. "You'll be putting this whole mission in jeopardy if you let her come."

"There's no time to explain, Mat. You wouldn't believe it if I told you anyway." Jake kept his eyes on Destiny as he said this. "All I can tell you is that we'll be worse off if we don't take her. You'll have to trust me on this one."

Mat shook his head, glancing sideways at Destiny in perplexity. "Voodoo and witches. Now I've heard it all."

- 90 -

Suspended upside down by a rusty chain looped severely about his ankles, the man whimpered weakly. The chain had cut deeply into the flesh, causing a dark brown mass of congealing fluid to form about the links. Scattered all over the man's naked body, red and purple clusters of burns and welts puckered grotesquely. As if in supplication to the harsh discolorings, the contents of the man's bowels had dribbled shamelessly down his back.

Sniffing the rank air, Ternier licked the drool collecting on his lips as he took in the sight. The combined smell of blood, urine and feces had always excited him. By keeping the man alive a little longer, he had prolonged his own pleasure.

Apprehending Emmanuel Baptiste had provided Ternier with far more than he would ever have expected. The legal papers found in Baptiste's possession had initially surprised him, but then after careful scrutiny, the documents had raised some compelling questions. First and foremost, a business venture of the magnitude described by *Tursiops Worldwide* would require considerable financing. And it was the source of this financing that had interested the Colonel the most.

Ternier stepped closer to Baptiste's inverted form and turned to one of the men beside him. "Remove the hood!" he ordered.

The man nodded gravely, then stooped low to untie the hood covering Baptiste's head.

The Colonel immediately assumed the mien of a maestro pleased with the results of his work. Baptiste's face was swollen and pasty almost beyond recognition. It was the look of a man close to death.

Prodding Baptiste's head with the tip of his boot, Ternier watched the man swing back and forth several times before speaking. "I ask you again, how were you going to finance this operation?"

Though Emmanuel's eyes were reduced to mere slits by the distended flesh surrounding them, his gaze seemed to focus on the man standing above him. Somehow finding the strength, he spit forth a wad of bloody saliva that fell short of Ternier's boots.

"Go ahead and kill me already!" he moaned between labored gasps. "I will never tell you!"

The Colonel shook his head ever so slightly, eliciting a small sadistic laugh. "Such stubbornness will do more harm than you ever imagined." Pivoting his head, he looked over at the other man in the room. "Bring in the woman!"

Through eyes horribly swollen, Emmanuel had trouble recognizing the female being supported between two burly guards, her legs dragging limply behind her. Slowly the fuzzy image coalesced, and Emmanuel's straining heart pounded so hard it seemed his chest might burst. A dizzying moment passed before he became cognizant of the deafening animal wail that filled the room. It was the sound of incredible despair, a cry that had surged up from the depths of his being to echo hopelessly off the cell walls.

The woman that had been brought into the room was his wife, Lucette.

- 91 -

Amphitrite lay without complaint in the darkened chamber, her ankles and wrists shackled in such a way as to leave her spread-eagled horizontally on a raised slab of concrete. Adjacent to her on an identical slab, Jacob was similarly pinioned.

From a nearby table, Erzulie cackled raucously as she played with the amulet dangling between her gnarled fingers. "You were wise to relinquish this little trinket," she rasped, the words sounding as if rising through a throat filled with gravel. "The whisperings of the rada cannot be ignored. It was only a matter of time before they realized one such as you would be unworthy to possess it. You had no choice but to give it up. The amulet would have become a danger to you had you insisted on keeping it." Once again she cackled triumphantly. "Is this not so?"

Amphitrite did not reply, twisting her head around just enough to see the amulet glow with the ominous redness of a burning coal within Erzulie's claw-like hands.

"Is this not so?" Erzulie repeated, this time screeching out the question in a shrill, hideous shout.

"The wisdom of the rada is not for me to question," Amphitrite offered appeasingly. "Their motives are often hidden and rarely understood. The fact that you are now the amulet's possessor reveals their intentions."

The answer seemed to satisfy the crone. "Yes, yes," she readily agreed. "It was their wish that I should have it."

Erzulie suddenly rose and drifted closer. With her hood lowered, the room's gloomy interior did little to conceal the woman's frightful ugliness. "But now it is my wish that you pay for the humiliation you had put me through so many years ago."

Amphitrite could only watch as the witch of the voudun leaned over Jacob.

- 92 -

Upon being escorted to the prison by the four policemen Ternier had assigned to Hennington, the broker was immediately taken to the interrogation area he had been shown before. Led to one of the cells abutting the corridor, he was appalled by the sight of the man and woman within the room.

"Do you know this man?" Ternier asked, his hypnotic eyes studying Hennington closely.

Overcoming his initial shock, Hennington shook his head slowly. "He is unfamiliar to me." He managed to keep his face neutral despite seeing the results of Ternier's depravity.

The Colonel continued to scrutinize him carefully, his gaze bearing down on him like sharpened spikes. "You do not remember him from your trip to Malique?" With his hands clasped stiffly behind him and his gaze never leaving Hennington's face, he began pacing off a leisure circuit of the two dangling forms. "I find that rather strange since Malique is but a tiny hamlet. Surely you must have seen this man."

Hennington could only shrug. "My stay there was very brief. Perhaps this man was out fishing. All the men there are fishermen."

Ternier nodded. Seemingly satisfied with the explanation, the intensity of his gaze abated a notch. Saying nothing for the moment, he turned his back to the broker, stepping slowly back around the two people hanging inverted. "The condition of these people does not upset you?" he said at last.

Hennington fought down the impulse rapidly taking hold of him, and it was not fear. Something flashed in the back of his brain as he looked upon the two parties ravaged by torture, and he was suddenly reminded of the inhuman abuses inflicted upon his Tainos progenitors.

Ternier's manner took on an added measure of sternness when Hennington failed to answer. "You seem to have lost your tongue?"

Hennington could feel the rage building within him, and he had great difficulty masking his emotions. Ternier's cruelty was without limit, on a par with the conquistadors that had decimated his ancestors. With a boldness he hadn't known was possible, he looked deep into the mesmeric orbs that had terrified him not so long ago, and within them he sensed a growing trace of confusion. He now understood why he had been summoned here. Ternier had deemed it necessary to perpetuate the fear that kept him under his thumb.

Encouraged by the comprehension quickly enfolding him, Hennington probed deeper. Instilling fear in others was the only thing that gave Ternier his power. Like the insatiable demon he was, the Colonel fed ravenously from it, but without such sustenance he would rapidly weaken and become nothing.

In that instant Hennington saw the Colonel's regal bearing begin to unravel. In that instant he saw the Colonel not as a man but as a vile thing to be eradicated the way one might crush a disgusting cockroach beneath one's heel. And in that fleeting interval of time he came to realize his transformation was now complete. The nexus his entire existence had been inexorably aimed at had finally been reached. The greed and cowardice had now been erased forever, replaced by something he could never be ashamed of, something absolute and good.

Drawing strength from it, he sprang with a swiftness he never thought possible, and as he rose up to clutch Ternier's throat, the sound of gunfire did little to deter him from the thing he sought.

- 93 -

With Trebek leading the way, the group of five moved along a maze of seedy alleyways bordering on the waterfront. Exhibiting the cunning silence of jackals on the hunt, they traveled swiftly under the cover of darkness. The hour was late, with the streets of Port-au-Prince mostly deserted. Terror always lurked in the shadows following sunset, and because of it the city belonged to the ever-present gangs prowling the night.

As if to confirm this, a large band of *zenglendoes* brandishing machetes and knives suddenly skulked out of the gloom to surround the group. But at the metallic sound of rounds being chambered with obvious intent, the thugs scattered like gazelles, and within seconds the alleyway was once again left deserted.

Clutching the MK-23 Stoner at high-guard, Jake carried the most firepower among the group. The MP-5 submachine gun wielded by Mat provided ample backup to the Stoner, as did the infantry-version M-60 held by Zimbola. Earlier, Jake had taken the time to instruct Trebek in the use of the 9mm Colt submachine pistol he had acquired from Bashir, and from the way the Haitian handled the weapon he could see the handling of firearms was nothing new to the man.

And although he knew it would have been absurd, Jake had offered his USP-9 semi-automatic pistol to Destiny as an added measure of protection. As he had anticipated, the girl had readily declined the invitation, appearing repulsed by what the gun represented.

Jake kept his senses on full alert as he followed Trebek, wanting only to reach the prison compound as quickly as possible. With the prospect of torture awaiting those taken by Erzulie, he knew every second counted.

It was another five minutes following the encounter with the *zenglendoes* that Jake was able to perceive an abrupt rise in a narrow alleyway strewn with garbage and debris. Straining his eyes against the darkness, he could just make out a place where the trash was heaped high. It was here that Trebek brought the group to a halt.

Trebek motioned Jake to his side and pointed above the mound of garbage. "The prison is located up there along higher ground," he said, keeping his tone low. Directing his gaze at the trash heap, Trebek pointed again before moving behind the mound.

Jake followed on his heels and flicked on the combat light he had taped to his Stoker. Pointing the weapon, he probed the darkness. Completely hidden behind the piled up garbage was the mouth of a small culvert set back in an earthen slope, its entrance yawning darker than the surrounding night.

"This is the way in," Trebek whispered. "We must be very careful from here on."

Jake noted the nervousness in Trebek's voice. "You don't have to take us any further if you're having second thoughts about doing this," he proposed, offering the Haitian a way out. "We can take it from here."

Trebek expelled breath like a slowly deflating balloon, as if tempted to take the offer. Seeming to make a decision, he looked back at Destiny. "No!" he affirmed with finality. "I have a debt to pay."

"It's your call."

Trebek took a deep breath, then turned quickly and entered the dark opening. The rest of the team formed up in single file, advancing on his heels. Jake was second, with Destiny and then Mat following closely behind. Zimbola carried up the rear toting the sixty and more than a thousand rounds of belted-ammunition draped loosely around his massive shoulders.

Once inside, Jake had Trebek and Destiny flick on the flashlights he had given them. Almost at once the dual beams caught the skeletal remains of a decomposed corpse. It hung limply by the neck from a hook embedded in the tunnel's brick-lined ceiling, tatters of withered flesh continuing to adhere to the bones in various places. An amused grin adorned the skull, its empty eye sockets staring back at the group as if daring them to venture into the black void that lay beyond. The smell of rot and decay hung heavily in the air like an oppressive invisible vapor.

Trebek halted at the sight, standing frozen for several seconds before retching convulsively. Gaining control of himself, he swung around to address Jake, his voice racked with the strain of gagging. "There will be more of this, but you will soon get used to it."

Jake fought down the bile rising in his throat. He had seen the aftermath of similar death and had never gotten used to it. He turned abruptly to see how Destiny was responding, but the girl gave no visible signs of gagging though her eyes were moist with emotion. "Are you all right?" he asked.

"I'll be okay."

Jake looked back at Trebek. "Let's keep moving."

Sidestepping the suspended cadaver, Trebek pushed on with everyone falling into step behind him. As they penetrated further into the tunnel, a potpourri of human and animal bones littered the passageway, either dangling obtrusively from the arched ceiling or scattered about the mud-encrusted floor.

Along the way a wooden bench blocked their path, its surface supporting a row of human skulls smiling ominously up at them. Glistening with wetness, the skulls sat snugly rooted in a base of hardened wax that kept them affixed to the wood. Directly above, water dripped oppressively from a fissure in the ancient brick that formed the culvert's flattened oval construction. The droplets plunked down heavily upon the skulls in a steady cadence, the sound imparting a chilling resonance to the unnerving sight.

A cacophony of hushed squeals startled everyone as several things went skittering underfoot, and Jake could have sworn he saw several rats the size of a fully-grown alley cat brushing past his legs.

A succession of other benches blocked their path as they made their way deeper into the culvert, each bench lined with human skulls in the same manner as the first, and as the team pressed on, they eventually came upon a sheet of cloth draped across the passageway, the fabric smeared with grime. Trebek halted in his tracks, playing the beam from his flashlight over the material. Drawn crudely in blood in the center of the cloth was a skull and crossbones. Cautiously, he prodded the barrier with the barrel of his Colt. Satisfied it was not rigged with any surprises, he went to push past it.

"Stop!" Destiny cried. A cold chill had begun accosting her seconds earlier, and in her mind it had now taken definitive form. Her mother and Jacob had been taken into the prison via this route, and she was hearing the warning one of their captors had voiced when they had passed this way.

Trebek immediately froze, pivoting his head around slowly to see what the girl meant.

"A trap awaits you just beyond the cloth," Destiny clarified gravely. "Do not go another step!"

"How do you know that?" asked Jake.

Before Destiny could answer, Zimbola sidled his looming bulk past Mat and interceded. "A white witch can see things others cannot."

Jake let his eyes linger on the big man momentarily, the giant's face inscrutable in the dim light reflected off the cloth barrier. Swinging back around, he scrutinized the girl once again. "What kind of trap are you seeing?"

"A pit with sharpened wooden stakes lies just behind the sheet."

Jake stepped past Trebek and pushed the cloth aside, shining his light on the earthen ground on the opposite side.

"The pit lies hidden under a false floor," Destiny advised grimly.

Jake swung back around to face the girl. "Is this the only thing we have to be concerned with right now?"

"For right now, yes."

Jake tugged hard on the sheet, tearing it loose from its overhead fasteners, then looked back at Mat. "Help me with one of those benches back there!"

With each of them hefting a side, the two men moved a skull-laden bench into position and heaved it into the area Destiny had indicated. Abruptly, the ground gave way and the bench disappeared into the concealed sunken pit with a dull thud. Directing his beam down into the hole, Jake could see the fate Trebek had narrowly escaped. The bench lay at an odd angle ten feet below him, hung up on a dense cluster of pointed spikes. One of the skulls had torn loose from its waxen base, its left eye socket penetrated fiendishly by one of the pointed shafts.

"Please be careful," Destiny warned. "Those stakes are tipped with a lethal poison."

Jake studied the width of the pit. Only a narrow ledge remained along the tunnel's right side with sufficient breadth to allow passage. "Everyone watch your step," he cautioned. "There may be more booby traps."

Further on the team was welcomed by several more suspended cadavers in various stages of sickening putrefaction, each one seeming to beckon the group onward. One after the other, the gruesome sights left no doubt as to what the group would be facing. All the while Jake kept his senses on full alert, prepared for the unexpected but also trusting in Destiny's uncanny ability to forecast the presence of danger.

It wasn't long before the team came upon a fork in the tunnel, and Trebek came to a halt, suddenly appearing unsure of himself.

"Which way?" Jake asked.

Trebek scratched his head, looking truly confounded. "I do not remember this."

Jake turned to Destiny. "Any suggestions?"

The girl studied the twin passageways for several moments, her expression mired in concentration. "The tunnel to the right will take us where we need to go."

"And the left?"

"Only danger lies in that direction."

"Right it is then," Jake concurred, confident that Destiny had chosen correctly.

Guardedly, Trebek ventured right with the rest of the group following. He had not gone more than ten paces before the passage began to slope downward. Gradually it took on a moderate grade, and it wasn't long before the illumination from the light he held showed the decline before him plunging beneath a pool of stagnant water, the surface slick with a coating of organic slime and giving off the foul stink of raw sewage.

Trebek looked back at Jake. "They have flooded the tunnel!" His tone was dismal and he appeared spooked. "It was never like this in the old days."

Stopping at the water's edge, the Haitian seemed to stare at something lurking further out in the pool. Within seconds he backed away and spun around. "Do...do you see it?" he stammered in horror. He had the manner of a man suddenly besieged with terror, glancing back over his shoulder as if afraid the thing he had seen would emerge from the pool to pounce on him from behind.

Jake moved Trebek out of the way and played his light searchingly over the water. "I don't see anything. What did you see?"

Trebek had difficulty speaking, continuing to remain wide-eyed. "It...it-" He had only gotten a fleeting glimpse of it, a hideous thing with jagged teeth. And now it was lurking somewhere below the slime, waiting to rise up and sink those puncturing fangs into anyone foolish enough to get close.

"Do not let your eyes deceive you," Destiny interposed, her voice placid and calming. "What you saw is an illusion created by Erzulie. There is nothing there to harm you." Reaching up, she placed a hand on Trebek's temple. "If you look hard, you will see through the illusion."

The Haitian's panic slowly abated, his wild-eyed stare changing over to one of embarrassment. He pulled his gaze from the fetid water, turning to Destiny's calming influence. "You are right," he acknowledged. "The monster I saw was one of the mind. I-" The sudden alteration in the girl's expression made him stiffen again.

Destiny was rigid, shuddering. Something icy cold and terrible was closing in. Sensing the approach, she spun around and gasped, staring back the way they had come.

Jake turned quickly to follow her gaze, his eyes stabbing into the darkness. He was able to discern something resembling coal tar, a growing splotch within the tunnel's black void. It flowed down the slope of the passageway, oozing slowly forward like heavy crude dumped from a barrel.

The warning sprang from Jake's mouth before he realized he had yelled it. "Zimby, behind you!"

Zimbola whirled, piercing the darkness with his light, and his breath hitched tight in his throat. The lead forms drew back, throwing up skeletal arms to block off the light, and Zimbola saw eyes that burned red with the raging embers of hell. Stacked behind them in the darkness were similar forms, a compressed horde of emaciated inhuman things composed of hideous rotting flesh and fungus-encrusted bone. The mass of things hung back momentarily under the sudden illumination, seeming to coalesce even more as they crammed the passageway. And then in unison the horde surged forward as though intent on destroying the very light clinging to them.

Trebek's eyes enlarged to the size of engorged dotted grapes and he wailed aloud, his previous fright regenerated by the mob of vile things closing in. "It is Erzulie's walking dead!" he screamed. "We are all doomed!"

The lead forms pressed forward, letting loose with a horrifying mix of hissing and screeching. Hobbling and limping on decayed limbs, they moved like old decrepit men suffering from some disabling malady, and Zimbola could not pull his eyes away from the claw-like hands that reached toward him.

"We are doomed!" Trebek repeated shrilly, shrinking back toward the pool of slime at his back.

With both Mat and Zimbola in his way, Jake could not use his Stoker. He sprang forward, brushing past a dumbstruck Mat and reaching Zimbola's side. Zimby stood frozen, his belief in witchcraft crippling him with terror and nearly seizing up his convulsing heart as it jumped in his chest.

The lead forms were almost upon them, their putrid breath leaking from between broken and splintered teeth blackened by rot, and Jake felt the sickening oiliness of it climbing up into his nostrils and coating his throat. Almost retching, he lifted the Stoker's barrel, pulling back on the trigger just as claws caked with offal raked out.

The front rank disintegrated. Bits of grizzle and decayed bone flew backward as though spat from a meat grinder, spattering other bodies coming up from behind. The carnage suddenly worsened as Mat opened up from Zimbola's opposite side, and within the tight quarters the din of both weapons was shockingly loud. All at once the giant Jamaican stirred, the thunder of the guns jarring him from his bout of paralysis. He blinked just once before the sixty in his enormous hands came alive, and in moments the horrible things clogging the tunnel were quickly torn apart as all three men hosed the corridor.

Jake ceased firing, grabbing Zimbola by the arm and yanking him hard as the sixty continued to bark. "Save your ammo, big guy!" He had to shout to be heard.

Relunctantly, Zimbola let up on the trigger, staring wide-eyed and shaken.

Though incomprehension filled Mat's face, he was able to overcome his initial shock. "Tell me that didn't happen!" he suddenly vented, breathing heavily.

Something tumbled dully down the slope of the tunnel as he said this, and his eyes came to rest on the maimed skull as it rolled to a stop at his feet. One of the sockets was empty where a bullet had gouged it, but the remaining eye was bloodshot and scalding, fastened on him and continuing to burn fiercely as though aware of his presence.

With his stomach beginning to churn, Mat kicked the vile thing away. "Man, that's disgusting."

Jake had no time to mull over what had just happened. He was growing impatient, knowing any more delays could result in a failed mission. Based on what he'd seen so far, it was a foregone conclusion that the longer Destiny's mother and Jacob remained imprisoned, the more likely they would suffer a cruel ending. Consulting his wristwatch, he noted the time. "We've got to keep moving, even if it means wading up to our necks through this filth."

Trebek nodded penitently, the shadow of fear still heavy in his eyes. He needed to get away from this part of the tunnel. "I will not fail you again."

Jake tossed him the light. "Go then and take point!"

"Keep to the exact center of the tunnel," Destiny instructed. "You will find a narrow walkway concealed less than a centimeter below the water's surface. The water is much deeper to either side."

To Jake it made sense. If what the girl said were true, it would be the means by which Erzulie could get through the tunnel. It was also one more reason why the culvert had been left unguarded. Even if the locals were bold enough to overcome their fear of Erzulie's grisly artwork and get past the hidden death trap and those vile things to make it this far, a seemingly impassable pool of raw sewage would provide a final psychological barrier of revulsion to discourage them from venturing any further.

As the team treaded tentatively out onto the water, no one commented on the girl's incredible foresight until it became evident her prediction was correct.

Treading his way carefully atop the disgusting liquid waste, Mat leaned close to Destiny. Keeping his voice low, he asked, "Are you sure you were never in this place before?"

"Never."

"If you ever want a job with the DHS, please let me know. You'd save us a lot of trouble."

With the tunnel continuing to decend deeper, the waterline rose higher, causing the male members of the team to duck their heads lower and lower to avoid the sloped ceiling. It wasn't until the team had covered another 30 meters before the gradient finally leveled off and began to rise again. This was a relief to Zimbola who had been forced to negotiate the lowest level of freeboard in a near squat. When at last the giant stepped clear of the offending pool, his immense exhalation did not go unnoticed by the rest of the group. It was evident that the potential for falling into the decaying offal had repulsed him far more than anyone else on the team.

Continuing to lead the way, Trebek soon located the tunnel's terminus where a set of concrete steps rose before him. "This I remember," he said, shining his light up at the rusted underside of a recessed trapdoor at the top of the stairway.

Jake stared up at the entrance that would provide them access into the prison. Trebek had briefed him thoroughly on the layout of the area immediately above the trapdoor, at least what the Haitian could remember. Although there was no way of knowing how security protocol had changed within the prison in the past 22 years, Trebek had said that even the guards refrained from going near the passageways Erzulie regularly used.

Destiny moved to Jake's side, glancing up at the corroded metal hatch above them. "You will find the door unlocked," she said, seeming to read his mind. "The room above is empty."

Jake elicited a grim-faced nod. "I hope so, otherwise this little ordeal will have been a complete waste of time." He turned to acknowledge the rest of the team, finding it necessary to reiterate only a few items of the battle plan he had previously laid out. "Everyone check your weapon and keep to the plan. I'll go first. No one is to follow me until I do a recon. I don't want anyone poking their head above that trapdoor until I give the all clear. Let's all avoid getting our heads blown off, shall we." His eyes roamed from face to face. "Are we all on the same page?"

The Girl Who Rode Dolphins

Mat smiled back at him, a knowing gleam in his eyes. "You just look after your own hide. And for once in your life try not to do anything stupid like putting yourself in the line of fire."

Jake ignored the words, turning to Destiny one more time and studying her face. In her eyes he could see fear, but the fear he read was entirely selfless, set aside only for the people around her and those they had come to rescue.

"Stay behind Mat and Zimby!" Jake told her. "You can count on them to protect you."

Wearing the same face that had taken him through many a horrendous battle in the past, Jake bounded up the stairs with the agility of a cat, moving into position just below the trapdoor. Bracing himself, he applied upward pressure on the corroded metal plate until it pivoted on its hinges. Surprisingly it offered little resistance. Cautiously, he raised it higher, cringing at the squeal of rust impeding the pivots. Bringing his eyes level with the upper floor, he quickly swung his head to both sides to insure no one was lurking nearby. A small concrete room surrounded him, its stark interior dimly lit by light streaming in through a grimy glass window reinforced with wire mesh. Noting that the trapdoor was positioned close to the back wall, he could see the room was unoccupied. This was one of the holding cells Trebek said was used for interrogation, and the light making its way in came from the adjacent corridor.

Jake lifted the lid higher, keeping a firm grip on it as he clambered up through the opening with the Stoker at the ready. Careful not to let it come clanging down, he lowered the lid to the opposite side until it came to rest against the concrete wall behind him. Strangely, he began to reassess Zimbola's notion that Destiny was a white witch. Everything the girl had so far predicted had proved to be true.

Striding silently to the glass window, he surveyed the abutting corridor from his darkened position. Off to his left he saw the heavy metal door that, according to Trebek, was Erzulie's quarters. When he had first been told this, he found it rather odd that a woman would choose to live within one of the most deplorable prison strongholds in the Western Hemisphere, a place that reeked of human suffering and decay. But now having seen examples of the woman's fascination with death, he was beginning to understand why.

As if to epitomize this newfound thought, a muffled cry of agony suddenly breached his ears. Following the sound, he perceived the scream to originate from somewhere off to his right in the adjacent corridor, possibly in the holding cell next to the one he was in. Shrill enough to penetrate the concrete wall separating the two rooms, the cry hung in the air for several more seconds before dying away.

Stepping back along the glass, Jake increased his field of vision, now looking in the opposite direction. The grating screech of a door opening on rusted hinges followed by ringing footsteps caught his ear. Several people were coming down the hallway. Listening intently, he heard the door let out another protest before clanging shut with abrupt finality. It was then that he caught a glimpse of four men striding into view before they entered the adjacent cell.

Recognition hit him like a sledgehammer, and with a start he realized one of the men was Hennington. *What the hell is he doing here?*

Moving quickly, Jake sidled up to the holding cell's door and tried the handle. The door was locked. This was a point Trebek had failed to mention, and one in which Jake should have paid more attention. It was only reasonable to assume the door of a holding cell would only open from the outside. Silently, he let out a curse in spite of knowing it would only present a minor inconvenience.

The alarm that had been sounding in Jake's head was ringing more shrilly now, fueling his need to act. In two bounding strides he shot across the room, suddenly aware of the darker blotches staining the cell's walls and floor and the chains hanging idly from the ceiling. A history of depraved violence entrapped him, reaching out from all quarters like the sinister hands of a demon. But Jake was not to be deterred from his goal, completely immune to the residues of terror.

Mat was perched just below the trapdoor opening, waiting eagerly for Jake to give the all clear. Handing Jake his weapon, he pulled himself through the entrance in a flash. In less than fifteen seconds, the rest of the team followed, with Trebek the last to emerge.

Using a combination of whispers and hand gestures, Jake let the others know of his improvised plan. Zimbola nodded, then aimed the M-60 at the cell door as the others in the group huddled farther back. The weapon thundered within the confined space as a short burst disintegrated the door lock.

Leaping forward, Jake threw all his body weight behind a kick that sent the door crashing open. Dashing into the corridor, he bolted immediately to his right in anticipation of the resistance that would surely come from the far end of the hallway. Already the massive steel door that separated the interrogation area from the rest of the prison was beginning to swing open. It was obvious the guards stationed on the other side were eager to investigate the cause of the disturbance.

The Stoker bucked harshly as Jake let go with a burst of discouragement. A shower of sparks exploded against the heavy metal barrier, and abruptly the door slammed shut. And although the hallway before him was now empty, the adjacent interrogation cell was not.

- 94 -

At a glance, Jake took in the scene of horror, noting the man and woman hanging upside down by the ankles and bleeding profusely. Five Haitian men stared back at him, shocked by the threat of the smoking weapon in his hands.

Jake was even more shocked. The sight of Chester Hennington struggling with a seventh man was something Jake would never have expected. Little more than an insignificant flea to his much bigger adversary, Hennington was shoved violently away, his small pudgy frame sent slamming into a nearby wall.

With Mat backing him up, Jake poked the barrel of the Stoker into the room. Hennington's opponent brought smoldering eyes to bear on the sudden intrusion, his orbs burning into Jake with sizzling hatred.

"Colonel Ternier I presume?" Jake growled coldly. "I've heard a lot about you, and none of it at all flattering."

Ternier straightened to his full height, throwing all the dignity and authority he could muster into his bearing. "Who are you and what do you want?"

"I'm your worst nightmare," Jake rasped, "a man who will have no qualms about sending you and your cohorts to the farthest reaches of hell if you don't disengage these two people from those chains this instant."

Ternier fidgeted slightly, still laboring to present the regal posture that defined him. "You are insane," he hissed brazenly, his eyes rebellious and boring into Jake with hypnotic intensity. "Only a madman would attempt to come in here by force. I do not think you have the slightest idea what you are up against."

Jake felt the heat of his own ire growing rapidly in temperature. "You see this weapon I'm holding. It can fire 750 rounds a minute. Try my patience any more and I'm turning your miserable hide into dog chow." For emphasis, he aimed the Stoker directly at Ternier's head, caressing the trigger with an eager finger. "Don't make me ask you again to get those people down."

Ternier wrung his hands, his attempt at haughtiness beginning to unravel like strands of a rope under too much strain. Turning his head slightly, he barked an order to several of the men standing behind him. "Do as he says!"

Within moments, both the man and woman were lowered to the floor, their ankles free of the chains.

"I know these people." The words came from Trebek who was stationed to Jake's rear. "It is Emmanuel and Lucette Baptiste."

A look of genuine surprise shot across Ternier's face as his eyes fell on Trebek for the first time. "You!" he hissed contemptuously. A string of guttural invectives abruptly left his lips as he lapsed into Creole.

"Speak English!" Jake snapped, giving the Colonel a deadly stare. "Otherwise I might be tempted to pull this trigger." Though he understood some of the local dialect, he wasn't quite sure what had just been said.

"He calls me a traitor," Trebek translated scornfully. "He says I have betrayed the trust of the Tonton Makout."

Trebek returned the Colonel's skewering glare with a scowl of his own. "But I never had the same appetite for torture and murder as this man," he uttered gruffly.

A vicious sneer suddenly descended on Ternier's face. "Such words are unbefitting of you, Ronaldo," he said, keeping the conversation in the language Jake could comprehend. "As I remember it, you used to take great pleasure in punishing others."

"I am no longer the same person you once knew."

Ternier let out a condescending laugh, but before he could reply Jake silenced him by pointing the Stoker menacingly. "Does the name Mercades Myers stir anything in that memory of yours, Colonel?"

The question seemed to throw Ternier off balance for one microsecond before he managed a look of supreme innocence. "I am unfamiliar with that name."

"You killed him, you murdering bastard!" The screaming accusation did not come from Trebek.

The Colonel's expression turned baleful again as he swiveled his head to locate the new speaker.

"You killed him the same way you killed so many others," the speaker went on. The voice belonged to Hennington. "Only a monster would do the things you do to other people."

Out of the corner of his eye, Jake noticed the broker rising from the floor. "I don't know what you're doing here, Chester, but I think it would be wise if you moved behind me," he advised, speaking out the side of his mouth.

Hennington complied, moving to stand behind Jake.

"Now I want everyone's hands raised real high where I can see them," Jake ordered, addressing Ternier and the others. He leveraged the command by waving the Stoker threateningly again. "All of you! Up against the wall!"

From further down the hall, Zimbola called out to Jake in a booming voice. "All secure, Jay Jay. The other holding cells are empty."

Satisfied for the moment, Jake focused his attention back on Ternier again. "Where are the others?"

A smug little smile flashed briefly on Ternier's face. "Whatever do you mean?"

"A man called Jacob and a woman called Amphitrite," Jake shot back angrily. "Where are they?"

"Forcing your way into the prison of a sovereign nation is a violation of international law."

"So is the inhumane treatment and torture of innocent people."

Ternier appeared to regain some of his former arrogance. "The man and woman you seek are dissidents of Haiti. They threaten the political stability of this island nation."

Mat moved forward to stand at Jake's side. "This guy's stalling. A friendly little chat with him is a waste of time."

Emmanuel suddenly stirred, letting out a prolonged moan.

"Get Destiny in here!" Jake barked at no one in particular, wondering why the girl had not entered the room to attend the victims of Ternier's sadism.

"Destiny is not here," Trebek blurted out in dismay.

"Where is she?"

"She was standing in the hallway a minute ago, but now she is gone."

Jake could not believe what he was hearing. Facing Mat, he said, "If any one of these assholes so much as twitches, blow his head off."

Mat's expression turned fiendish. "It'll be my pleasure."

Shoving past Hennington and Trebek, Jake glanced anxiously up and down the hallway.

As Trebek had stated, Destiny had vanished.

- 95 -

Erzulie had been too busy to notice the heavy steel door barring the way into her chamber swing silently open, nor did she see the petite silhouette framed in the entrance a split second later. Then, just as noiselessly, the door swung closed, with the bolt sliding back into place with little more than a whisper.

The nature of the psychic link Destiny felt was on a level she had never before experienced, a guiding power that inexorably drew her forth like a moth drawn to the flame. As if she were a wisp of air, she slipped into the gloomy lair with wraith-like stealth, now fully aware of what she must do. A minute earlier she had been able to distort the curvature of space-time just enough to cushion the din of gunfire so that the sound of it did not alert the witch of the voudun. Evoking this had been a simple mental exercise, one she was able to bring about with the combined help of her mother and the albino dolphins currently awaiting her in the harbor. Opening the door to the chamber should have been impossible to a normal human being, but this had also been accomplished without the girl ever having to make physical contact with the seemingly impenetrable barrier.

In a far corner of the chamber, Erzulie leaned over a small black cauldron. "You are going to love my little potion, my darlings," the witch sibilated gleefully. "Filling this pot with rainwater that fell on the sixth day of the sixth month and heating it to a boil works best."

Erzulie stepped back, holding out the amulet. A red light suddenly pulsed from it, brought to bear on the water in the cauldron and bringing it to a sizzling boil almost instantly. Reaching behind her, she began dumping one after the other the contents of several small bowls into the pot. "Six hairs from a pig…six feathers from an owl…six scales from a snake…extract from the bark of a 66 year old mapou tree."

Happily the hag stirred the mixture before pulling a jar from a shelf and dropping whatever it contained into the pot. "And six teeth from a six day old cadaver."

Without emotion, Destiny watched Erzulie go through the strange ritual, cognizant of her mother and Jacob pinioned to the concrete slabs. And although Amphitrite appeared to be physically restrained, she knew the appearance was a false one. For it was really the mind that mattered, and the thoughts and mental images pulsing from her mother's mind were enormously powerful, merging in harmonic resonance with her own.

"And last but not least," chortled Erzulie, "six hairs from each of you." Having said the words, she sprinkled something held between fingers resembling talons into the steaming brew.

A sense of agonizing pain suddenly invaded Destiny's being as she continued to stand unobserved by Erzulie. It was Emmanuel's and Lucette's torment she was feeling. And while their suffering had been a necessary placation in the midst of the immense evil engulfing her, their pain would soon culminate, replaced by the healing that would soon come. With arrant certainty, she knew they would survive, with both of them living in a state of discovery rather than recovery. She understood the role pain would play in their lives. They would remember their trauma not as an enemy without purpose, but as something transforming to the spirit. They would absorb and process it before making it a part of a more vigorous and adaptive consciousness. And in the end they would become stronger and wiser for it.

Years earlier, Destiny's mother had described the vision that had come to her in a dream. The iniquity gripping Haiti had festered far too long, and like all wickedness, would ultimately come around full circle to feed on and then destroy itself. Erzulie and her spawn were the embodiment of absolute evil, doing the only thing evil was capable of doing, and that was doling out more misery. By nature they were predatory creatures, desiring only the means to bring about human suffering. Possession of Esmerelda's amulet provided them with such means, or so they believed. And according to the dream, their obsession with destruction and death might one day come to an end, but only at great risk to those bold enough to oppose them.

Destiny knew not hatred, for within her the concept held no meaning. It was an emotion she had never experienced, and therefore one that could not sully the purpose she had been born to fulfill. As Jacob had explained to her many times in the past, the world was much too full of destructive emotions and actions that defied reason, all of which posed a detriment to the planet. Sometimes people could make things so difficult that plain old logic escaped them. National swoons, just as national hysterias, had a way of obliterating rational thought. Anger and hatred, it seemed, were rapidly approaching a critical level that was taking humanity to the very brink of extermination. If his refined view of the Gaia theory was correct, perhaps there was some super intelligence at work that had engendered beings such as herself and the albinos in order to remediate the harm that was being done.

"I have heard of that marvelous mind of yours, Jacob," Erzulie said aloud, looking over at her male captive as he lay restrained atop the stone. "You are a man of great intellect I am told, a pundit who thinks it is possible to pull Haiti from the squalor that has plagued it for centuries." The witch let out a shrill laugh. "You think this corporate venture you have designed will make your vision a reality."

From where Destiny stood she could see Jacob move his head to heed the witch's rantings, though he said nothing.

"Such an enterprise would require vast sums of money, would it not?" Erzulie went on. "Now where do you suppose a lowly fisherman like yourself would be able to find so much wealth?"

When Jacob failed to respond, the witch grew angry. "There are many ways to loosen a man's tongue, most of them very painful and usually fatal." Erzulie cocked her head, her manner suddenly calm again. "But to destroy such extraordinary intelligence would be foolish when it can be put to better use."

Dipping a ladle into the cauldron, Erzulie removed a small portion of the heated liquid. "Yes," she said as she walked toward Jacob. "While killing you would give me great pleasure, I have decided to let you live to serve my son, Henri."

Moving to within inches of Jacob, the witch cackled harshly. "With your help, Henri will become the undisputed king of the Caribbean, a man other leaders will bow to. Cuba's Castro, Venezuela's Chavez, they will be nothing compared to Henri once he is able to pluck the fruits of your vision."

"I will never help your son!" Jacob spat. "You and your offspring are a pox on Haiti. Kill me already and be done with it!"

"Oh, but you will help him," Erzulie disagreed, seemingly amused by Jacob's vitriolic outburst. "No one has ever been able to resist the effects of this potion. It will shackle your mind. It will make an obedient slave of you. Pleasing your king and his mother will be your only desire. You will be unable to recall your former self, who you once were. Only your magnificent intellect will remain intact, subservient to Henri's will."

"I reject this black mysticism of yours. You will never take possession of my mind."

In the dim light, Destiny saw the hideous grin that took hold of Erzulie's ugly features. "Your Haitian heritage is your vulnerability. It resides at the center of your being and will prove to be your enemy. Scientific beliefs and logical leanings are merely superficial layers of who you think you are. Ingrained deep down inside you is the very thing that will cause you to surrender to my magic. You cannot escape it. Has not our little encounter many years ago already demonstrated this to be true?"

"I am not the same man you fought against back then."

"You are Esmerelda's grandson. That is enough."

Jacob suddenly gagged, his jaw clenching in an effort to keep his lips sealed. He appeared to struggle briefly before his mouth jerked wide as if being pried by invisible hands.

Erzulie cackled shrilly. "See how easily I am able to manipulate you. You are like a puppet, powerless to fight the strings that control you."

Extending the ladle above Jacob's open mouth, the witch began to pour the liquid, but before it could reach its target Destiny intervened. Diverted by some unseen power, the hot fluid reversed its flow and splashed up into Erzulie's face with explosive force. The witch immediately stiffened, appearing frozen solid by the unexpected assault, and time seemed to hang still for one brief moment before a high-pitched squeal strong enough to shatter glass left the old hag's lips. As if in protest, various jars within the chamber burst into fragments simultaneously, and the stack of human skulls lining one of the walls abruptly collapsed.

Now free of the restraints that had bound her to the concrete slab, Amphitrite suddenly arose to face the maddened witch of the voudun. A second later, the shackles holding Jacob fell away, and he immediately sprang to his feet.

Amphitrite spoke for the first time, her voice calm and without emotion. "We are leaving this place, Erzulie. If you still have the courage to come after us, Navassa Island is where we will be."

It was then that the witch noticed Destiny for the first time. Her mouth hung open as she transferred a shocked gaze from mother to daughter, alternating her eyes between the two. "I should have known a cheval would have spawned another," she hissed. "But now I will kill both of you."

"Your powers have been weakened," Amphitrite said. "That cocktail you brewed has sapped your strength. You of all people should know the negative consequence of getting mapou extract on you instead of its intended victim. It will take hours for you to regain your strength."

Erzulie raised the amulet to test Amphitrite's supposition, but when the charm barely produced a few feeble sparks, the witch let out a frustrated scream. "I will follow the three of you to the ends of the earth. You will never escape me."

Amphitrite stared back without fear. "As I have already said, you have only to go to Navassa Island to find us. But I warn you, you will place yourself in great peril should you be foolish enough to go there."

Amphitrite turned and raised an arm. Forty feet from where she stood the latch securing the doorway slid sideways and the heavy steel barrier swung open. Ignoring the string of profanity railed by Erzulie, she walked calmly toward the exit with Destiny and Jacob beside her.

- 96 -

Jake remained immobile, ready to meet any opposition coming forth from behind the door as it opened. A deep sigh of relief escaped his lips when Jacob appeared, and the tightness in his gut relaxed a notch when Destiny and another woman stepped from the gloom a second later. The door slammed shut behind them with booming finality, and Jake felt the floor beneath him shudder as the sound echoed down the hallway like cannonade.

Jacob gave him a grim nod that seemed to conflict with the small smile Destiny displayed. "Jay Jay, this is my mother, Amphitrite."

Jake stared in disbelief, finding it difficult to accept this, for the woman with Destiny appeared to be not much older than her daughter.

Sitting in the Avenging Angel's salon, Nick Henderson turned his head to glimpse the painting propped against a wall. Almost immediately his face soured. Try as he might, he saw nothing to indicate anything exceptional within the pattern of lines and colors.

"Do you see it, Jeffrey?" Bashir effused excitedly.

"I think so, but for me it's more of a feeling than a visual perception. What about you, Professor?" Parker asked Grahm. "Does it spark anything within you?"

"Yes indeed," Grahm said, nodding absently. "I must admit, I have never been moved by art, but there is a certain mesmeric quality to the work that automatically draws me in. If I could sum up with one word what I'm feeling, I'd say that one word is *hope*."

Henderson stifled his growing irritability. The dolphin painting was no different from any of the abstract art he had seen in museums. It instilled nothing within him when he looked at it. As a matter of fact, it gave him a splitting headache if he stared at it too long as he was doing now.

Averting his eyes, Henderson massaged his temples. He was bored out of his mind. Those around him were just killing time awaiting the return of Javolyn and the people that had accompanied him. Their unending obsession with Bashir's painting was beginning to grate on him. On top of that he didn't like the camaraderie that had developed between Grahm and Javolyn. The professor had been much too accommodating in agreeing to stay aboard the Angel while Javolyn and the others had gone off to rescue Jacob and the girl's mother.

Served the Haitian right for being abducted, Henderson thought. Though Jacob seemed inordinately intelligent and learned, there was some arcane quality about the man that rubbed him the wrong way. Most likely it was Jacob's doomsday forecasts concerning the fate of the planet and those absurd theories of his that were the cause of this. In any event, he disliked the man intensely.

He hated Javolyn even more. He had run into a few others like him at one time or another in his life. Strong athletic types had always offended him, mainly because they always seemed willing to stick their necks out under the banner of some noble cause, prepared to risk life and limb in order to perform what they deemed to be a good deed. Yes, he truly loathed the way they tended to attract the prettiest girls, usually luring the damsels with their superior muscles rather than their inferior minds. A deluge of resentment and jealousy suddenly swept over him as he pictured the way Destiny had taken to the Angel's skipper. While he had hungered for the girl from the first moment he had set eyes on her, the girl had hardly given him a second glance. And from what he had noticed lately, it was obvious she was in love with Javolyn.

The man Javolyn had met up with just outside the harbor seemed to be cut out of the same mold. Obviously an old friend, he thought it odd that Javolyn had purposely kept Bashir out of the man's sight until the rescue team had left the vessel.

A sense of impending helplessness gripped Henderson as he contemplated the constantly shifting events that had recently occurred. Surprises were at every bend, keeping him off balance. The final payoff he had sought had so far eluded him. To assuage his disappointment, he let his mind revert back to the possibility of gold, certain he had spotted gleaming mounds of it at the base of the thurentra when they had first entered the dolphin hideaway. But then strangely it had all disappeared. Refusing to believe his eyes had been playing tricks on him, he had snorkeled around the thurentra at every opportunity, feigning scientific curiosity as an excuse for his actions. In short order he had managed to pick what amounted to a handful of shiny grains from the cove's sandy floor, confirming that his eyes hadn't deceived him after all. As far as he could tell, the little he had found gave the appearance of gold. Maybe even platinum. And if that were true, it meant there was a sizeable cache of precious metals hidden somewhere within the verdant hideaway Jacob called Gaia. Yes, the more he replayed it over in his mind, the more he was convinced that Jacob had instructed the dolphins to hide the gold before those aboard the Angel became aware of it.

Henderson felt imprisoned being stuck aboard the Angel, and something akin to claustrophobia suddenly closed in on him as he continued to dwell on all the things that had happened over the last several days. McPherson must be steaming by now, and rightly so. Capturing the albino specimens should have been a relatively simple operation. He had done his part, providing the naval captain with the hardware that would show the location of a dolphin wearing a DBT. The plan had worked just as he had envisioned it, at least initially, but then Javolyn had stuck his nose in and screwed everything up. The man had a proclivity for danger, always spoiling for a fight. If not for Javolyn's interference, McPherson would have the dolphins by now, and in the process would have dished out the remainder of the money he had agreed to pay. That was the deal. Secretly activating the spare DBT aboard the Angel during their second visit to Navassa had given McPherson and his associates another signal to home in on. But once again Javolyn had butted in, keeping the captain from paying up.

"Are you feeling all right, Nicolas?"

Henderson realized Grahm was scrutinizing him. "Huh?"

"Are you ill, lad?"

"I just need some air. It's stuffy in here."

Rising, Henderson went out on deck and leaned over the railing. In the moonlight he could make out the dorsal fins of several albinos as they floated near the stern. Idly, he watched them for several minutes, the thought of the gold continuing to nag away at him like the promising aroma of ambrosia. As far as he knew, he was the only person outside Jacob's small circle that had any knowledge of the other thing the thurentra was able to produce. Maybe if he took in McPherson as a partner, the two of them could come up with a way to take control of the little hideaway the girl and Jacob called home. And even if they never found the hidden cache of gold, they'd still be able to collect all future outputs of the yellow metal discharged by the strange organism. Better yet, perhaps one of the dolphins could be captured and ransomed in exchange for all the gold that had previously been produced.

Damn! He was having trouble thinking. Looking at the dolphin art had made him dizzy and his head felt like it was going to burst. Bringing both hands to his forehead, he began to rub his temples vigorously.

Another thought suddenly loomed up. *What if Javolyn's little foray failed and everyone in his party were either captured or killed?* With both the girl and Jacob out of the way, he'd be able take over the dolphin hideaway and harvest the thurentra's produce. It would take some resources to carry this through, most likely hiring a boat and some people to help him, but once all the albinos went back to the cove he would be able to block off the entrance with a net. Then he'd be able to enrich himself further by selling each specimen to the highest bidder.

Plagued by these musings Henderson began to grow feverishly energized. Here was the chance for him to become rich beyond his wildest dreams. Deviously, he began to plot other possibilities. As he sifted through various options, one idea stood out from the rest. Perhaps sabotaging the Angel's engine would give him the assurance he needed. Even if Javolyn's rescue mission were successful, he could not possibly escape the harbor with an inoperable vessel. Then maybe Haitian authorities would be able catch up with him. In any event, such a delay might at least prevent Javolyn from escorting the girl back to the cove just long enough for McPherson and his associates to regroup and kidnap the girl right here in the harbor. Jacob would surely reveal where the gold could be found in order to get Destiny back. Of course, he'd need to send a message to McPherson in order to initiate such a plan. But once McPherson learned of the gold, he'd be a fool not to go along with such a scheme.

Convincing himself that it could work, Henderson moved to the hatchway that led to the engine compartment and began to lift the cover. In his excitement he failed to hear the footsteps that plodded the deck behind him.

"Is there something I can help you with?"

Henderson spun, startled by the intrusion. Hector stood before him, his expression grim in the moonlight.

Groping for words, Henderson barely managed to stutter them out. "Oh, uh...North Sea trawlers have always fascinated me. I...uh...wanted to see your engine."

Hector shifted his stance, bringing his face to within inches of Henderson's. "The engine room is off limits to anyone other than ship's crew."

"Is that the captain's policy?"

Hector pivoted his head sideways and spat, then turned back to stare coldly at Henderson. "Nope, it's my policy."

Henderson felt rattled, his cheeks beginning to burn under Hector's steady gaze. "My apologies," he blurted, finding it necessary to back away from the shorter man's fireplug frame. Quickly, he changed the subject. "Do you think it's wise to let Bashir have the run of this vessel? I mean, isn't he some kind of terrorist?"

Hector's manner remained unchanged. "Destiny feels the man is no longer dangerous and Jay Jay believes her."

"What if the girl is wrong and Bashir waits for the right moment to strike?" Henderson countered, putting a full measure of sarcasm into his tone. "He could sabotage this boat very easily with everyone's guard let down. He could kill us all in our sleep. Must I remind you that his people tried to destroy this vessel?"

"He no longer thinks as he once did."

Henderson's irritability returned with a vengeance. "How do you know that? No one changes so quickly. Tell me you don't actually believe that stupid painting in there caused him to change his behavior?"

Hector studied Henderson for a long moment, raising his eyebrows before responding. "The painting does not affect you?"

"Oh, I'm affected by it, all right," Henderson railed, unable to keep the anger he was feeling from showing in his voice. "Looking at it for too long makes me ill."

"I am sorry to hear that," Hector said evenly. "The painting seems to give the rest of us great pleasure when we stare at it."

Henderson felt like he was talking to an idiot. With growing impatience, he tried another tact. "You realize your boss is risking all our skins by attempting this little raid of his. If he's caught by Haitian authorities, we could all go to jail. I understand the jails in this country are among the worst in the world."

"Jay Jay will not fail."

"What makes you so certain?"

"Jay Jay used to be a Navy Seal."

"And you think an ex-Navy Seal is invincible?"

"Jay Jay is not like other men."

Seeing the look on Hector's face, Henderson was convinced his words were falling on deaf ears. Having worked with computers most of his life, he had grown used to the orderliness such hardware had given him. But here in Haiti, there was no order to anything, and as of late, nothing seemed to make sense anymore.

Staring over Hector's shoulder without meaning to, Henderson once again glimpsed the painting through one of the salon windows. Abruptly the pounding in his head resumed. Turning to avoid the sight, he set his eyes shoreward and shuddered involuntarily, wondering why a man like Javolyn would choose to stay in a place like this, operating out of a land that offered only squalor. When he had first arrived in Port-au-Prince, he had been horrified at the fetid trash lining the streets and the untreated human waste flowing freely in the drainage canals. On the way from the airport, he had seen the head of a man lying in the road, the decapitated body sprawled obscenely a few feet away. The man that had driven them from the airport had said ransoms were now commonplace in Haiti and that an old woman walking her dog earlier that morning had been swept up for ransom. When her unarmed husband had come to her defense, the man had been literally beheaded by the kidnappers abducting her. The slum-ridden city was a dangerous place. Everyday hundreds of extremely violent thugs held it hostage. Law and order were practically nonexistent here, almost completely overshadowed by anarchy.

The thought of Javolyn and the others trying to play hero annoyed Henderson to no end. Javolyn was nuts to venture into the city at night, an urban wasteland where most of the 7,000 UN peacekeeping force spent the bulk of its time simply protecting foreign service staff against the roaming gangs.

As he continued to stare shoreward, Henderson's knees nearly buckled as his eyes suddenly focused on something hovering high over the city, a thing pulsing with a strange assortment of lights. *No, that's not possible,* he told himself. Convincing himself he was merely hallucinating, he tore his gaze from the glowing object. Strangely, the thing's essence made him envision the hand of an avenging deity.

"I think I'll get some sleep," Henderson said tiredly, noticing the way Hector kept staring at him. Obviously the man had not seen the thing floating in the sky.

Henderson abruptly winced in reaction to the stabbing pain that shot through his brain. The throbbing in his skull was almost unbearable now. If he didn't lie down in the next minute, he just might collapse.

"Yes, you look like you could use some rest," Hector agreed, though his voice held no sympathy. "You do not appear very well."

Henderson went belowdeck to the small bunk Javolyn had assigned him, the nausea he was feeling bringing him to the brink of retching. Just before reclining, however, he had the presence of mind to reactivate the spare DBT he had kept in the case stowed under the bunk. Maybe he could still attract McPherson's attention yet again, just as he had previously done during their last trip to Navassa Island, thus bring him and his cohorts here to this place in the harbor. Maybe by now the Sea Lion was up and running again. Then he could present his plan to the Navy captain. And if McPherson failed to show, he could always send him a coded electronic message describing that there was considerably more to be gained than just the new breed of dolphin. In any event, he had to rest, for at this moment he felt as if he was going to die.

- 98 -

Cruelty and injustice were two of the things Javolyn hated most, so when Amphitrite insisted all prisoners be freed within the adjacent holding block, he had no objections against doing this.

"Tell your goons to drop their weapons and open the door!" Jake ordered.

The Colonel hesitated, his eyes flicking in expectation toward his mother's quarters at the far end of the corridor.

"Do it!" Jake barked. "Do it or so help me, I'll kill you where you stand."

Ternier brought hateful eyes back to Jake, briefly studying the anger emblazoned on his face before turning and sliding open the portal on the steel door that separated him from the next cell block over. Cautiously, he kept his face off to one side as he spoke through the opening. "This is Colonel Ternier," he said, speaking in Creole. "This prison has come under attack by insurgents who are currently holding me hostage. I want all of you to place your weapons on the floor and open this door."

A moment passed before the door swung slowly open, squeaking gratingly as it did so. Standing behind Ternier's large frame, Jake prodded him through the doorway with the Stoker's muzzle. Eight guards stood in frozen puzzlement on the other side, all of them glancing nervously at the weapon Jake wielded.

The sight of human misery overcrowding the nearest cell caused Jake to stare back in utter disgust at Ternier. "Tell your men to open all these cells!" he growled, finding it difficult to control his trigger-finger.

"You realize you will be creating an international incident if I do this," the Colonel warned.

"No I won't," Jake snapped. "A piece of scum like you will keep this whole thing real quiet, knowing that once the World Court got wind of what's been going on in here, you'd be brought up on charges for crimes against humanity."

Ternier's eyes flashed as if a flare had been ignited behind them. "The men in these cells are dangerous. Releasing them will only bring more crime to the streets of Port-au-Prince. You cannot-"

Something ethereal began to take form in the air, causing the Colonel to stop in mid-sentence and stare.

Dumbstruck, Jake studied the thing that hung before him, recognizing it immediately. A three-dimensional image of the dolphin painting that had been brought aboard the Angel suddenly came into sharp focus. But unlike the static painting depicted on the canvas, the replication that shimmered before him was dynamic, surges of energy rolling along the oddly snaking geometric lines that gave the art its unique definition. A sense of utter happiness splashed over him as he drank in the thing's intoxication, unable to tear his eyes away.

Ternier jerked spasmodically, suddenly falling to both knees. Grimacing, he let out a thunderous roar, clasping his cranium between quivering hands. A split second later, several of the guards emitted piercing screams and collapsed, writhing uncontrollably on the floor and holding their temples as if striken by some unseen enemy battering the inside of their skulls.

Riding the wave of euphoria washing over him, Jake became vaguely aware of Destiny and her mother stepping past him and throwing their arms wide. Instantly, the pulsing hologram slid down the hallway. Incredibly, the door to each jail cell swung wide open as the glowing thing swept past. A mixed chorus of joyful cries and agonizing shrieks echoed incoherently within the corridor, the rapturous outbursts at odds with the screams of physical distress. Slowly, many of the inmates began to rise and stream past the bars that had imprisoned them, appearing to be caught up in something blissful and incongruous with their befouled and oppressive surroundings.

Jake felt a hand close on his wrist and, dumbly, he turned.

"We must go, Jay Jay!" Destiny urged softly. Her face was angelic and filled with joy. "We have done all that was meant for us to do here."

Jake had to rouse himself as if awakening from a deep sleep. Pivoting around, he faced the others in his party, noticing the jubilance etched on each face. "Let's move, everyone!" her managed to croak. Stepping back the way he had come, he felt Destiny grab his wrist again.

Destiny pointed in the opposite direction, looking down the length of the hallway that was rapidly flooding with the prisoners that had crammed the cells. "This way!"

Jake started to protest, but Trebek gave voice to the same thing he was thinking. "Going that way is too dangerous. It will take us through the main gates of the prison."

"It's alright," Destiny said. "No harm will come to us if we move quickly."

Jake shifted his eyes to Amphitrite, seeing the same elation reflected in her manner as that of her daughter, a look that conveyed assurance. Behind those eyes, destructive thoughts were not possible.

Spinning around, Jake saw that Ternier and his acolytes currently posed no threat, all but two of them still clutching their heads as if being pelted by stones. Only a few of the inmates still remaining in the closest cell displayed the same throes of agony, squirming wildly on the cell's grungy floor. Of those inmates able to walk, however, he could see the afterglow of rapture lighting their faces. With the exception of Emmanuel and Lucette, all those in his party exhibited similar fugues. Even Hennington appeared spellbound. Still incapacitated from his recent ordeal, Emmanuel Baptiste hung listlessly over one of Zimbola's enormous shoulders while his wife was being borne along by Mat in a comparable carry.

"We'll do as Destiny says!" Jake barked. "Let's move, people!"

Working their way through the gathering throng, Jake led the others as fast as the mob would allow, moving along with the flood of inmates flowing down the hallway.

- 99 -

It was nearly sunup by the time Jake and the others met up with Phillipe. The lad had been awaiting their return just offshore at one the dilapidated docks situated along the waterfront. Jake's party had now doubled in size by those he had rescued, and it had taken two trips in the skiff to get everyone safely aboard the Angel. Everyone, that is, except the girl and her mother. Because several of the albinos had also been there to meet them, Destiny and Amphitrite had chosen to ride the dolphins out to the vessel. Upon Jake's insistence, even Hennington had been urged to go along in order to avoid Ternier's wrath once the Colonel recovered from the strange debilitation that had struck him and his henchmen.

Getting out of the prison had been surprisingly easy, though Jake had found it strange that every door that should have barred their way had been left wide open. With no guards to obstruct them, they had trudged unthreatened through the dingy corridors of the detention center, pushed along by the exodus of shabby detainees seeking freedom. Eventually they had found their way out into the streets. Amazingly, no one had tried to stop them, not even the gangs that normally roamed the back alleyways within the capital city. But as the group raced on, the sight of people writhing on the ground or stooped over in sickness continued to stay with them, their shrieks of pain filling the air like the cries of demons rising up from hell. In stark contrast to this, many more of the locals stood outside their hovels with faces glazed and blissful, their rapturous gazes riveted skyward as though caught in the grip of an evangelistic revival.

It was only when Jake looked up that he understood the reason for what he was witnessing. Struck by the surge of euphoria that descended to engulf him, he nearly stopped in his tracks to take in the beautiful sight. There, high above the city, something glowed with the vibrant luminosity of a multicolored neon sign hanging against the stars. Here it was again, the same phenomenum he had witnessed back in the prison. Like the benevolent hand of some omnipotent god, an enormous hologram of the dolphin painting floated majestically in the heavens, its three-dimensional imagery of pulsing lights intertwining soothingly before shooting to infinity.

- 100 -

Once aboard the Angel, Mat took Jake aside. "Where can we speak privately?"

Jake immediately led him up to the boat's pilothouse. "What's on your mind, buddy?"

"What do you plan on doing now?" Mat asked.

Jake felt the adrenalin that had carried him through the night beginning to ebb away. "I've got other business to take care of," he said.

"Yeah...like what?"

Jake was at an impasse. He had already committed himself to the gig Hennington had arranged for him, but then again, he hadn't forgotten about the villagers that had been abducted from Malique and taken away aboard the San Carlo. For what purpose they had been kidnapped, he could only guess.

Although his first impulse was to head west in the hopes of intercepting the tuna trawler, he was now desperately low on cash, and without it he would not be able to buy the fuel that would replenish his badly depleted tanks. The price of fuel had skyrocketed in recent months and the cost of it had nearly depleted his funds. Without sufficient fuel, he could not even consider trying to hunt down the trawler.

Letting out a big sigh, Jake gave voice to the only thing that made sense to him right now. "For starters, I'm going to bring the people we saved back to their homes."

Mat did not appear very pleased. "And then I suppose you'll be picking up where you left off, engaging in those illegal smuggling runs you've grown so fond of lately."

Jake looked away. "A man's got to eat."

Mat's displeasure soured further. "I just don't get you anymore. Making a piss hole like this your base of operations doesn't fit the Jake I know."

"Some people change."

"Yeah…," Mat nodded in agreement, "some people. But you're not one of 'em. I watched you closely tonight. You're still the same guy I used to sweat and bleed with. You haven't changed one little bit. What gives that you're not telling your old Uncle Mat?"

Jake stood mute for a long moment, cognizant of the way Mat was scrutinizing him. Perhaps it was time for him to come clean with his old friend. "You remember our little stint in Tora Bora?"

"I'd have to suffer amnesia to ever forget it."

"Well, I made a promise to Myers back then, one I aim to keep."

Mat kept staring. "Go on."

"He made me promise I'd find his kid, the one he told us about."

"Uh, huh!"

"Phillipe is Myers' kid."

Mat's jaw dropped. "You mean the boy that works for you?"

"Yep."

"Now that you mention it, I thought I saw something in him that reminded me of Myers. How'd you ever find him?"

Jake shrugged. "Just lucky, I guess."

"Well, it seems to me you fulfilled your promise. Yet you continue to stay in these waters. Why?"

"I still have another promise to keep," Jake confided.

A look of genuine intrigue suddenly transcended Mat's countenance, but he said nothing, waiting for Jake to offer more.

"You remember the treasure Myers told us about?"

"Yeah. All of it was seized by Haitian authorities."

Jake felt it difficult to extinguish the smile wanting to creep onto his face. "Wrong!" he corrected. "They only got half of it."

Mat absorbed this tidbit of information for several seconds. "Are you telling me Mercades managed to hide half the booty?"

"Yes."

"So where is it?"

"It's hidden in the waters north of here…at least that's where I think it is."

"But you're not sure?"

"To tell you the truth, I've been so busy lately, I haven't been able to confirm if I've actually located it."

"So what happens if you find it?"

"Phillipe will get most of it."

Mat's eyebrows rose. "Really."

"Yeah. That was the other half of the promise I made, that I'd recover what was left of the treasure and make sure Phillipe was the primary recipient."

Mat stared at Jake, unable to conceal the admiration he was feeling for his friend. "I see," he said. "Does the boy know this?"

"Not yet."

Mat looked around him, studying the layout of the pilothouse before shifting his eyes to the deck below. "This was Mercades boat, wasn't it?"

Jake nodded.

"And Zimbola was Mercades' loyal friend that Myers had told us about?"

"Right again."

"So I take it this vessel also belongs to Phillipe."

Jake shook his head. "The Angel has two owners, each with an equal share…Zimbola and myself."

Mat let all of this sink in, seeming to analyze what Jake had revealed. Finally he said, "So what happens if you recover the treasure?"

Jake expelled a long hearty sigh. "I really haven't given it much thought."

"You'll at least stop running illicit contraband, won't you?"

Jake could not help but produce an enigmatic grin. "Well I just don't know. There's something about those running gun battles at sea that gets a fella's blood going. It's a habit that's gonna be hard to break."

Mat grinned back. "Always the wise ass."

"I've learned from the best."

Mat's expression suddenly mellowed into one of deep reflection. "Now tell me, buddy, what the hell's going on with the girl and her mother? Am I going crazy, or are those women actually psychic?"

Jake sighed again. "I wish I knew the answer, and no, you're not going crazy."

"So how did you get mixed up with them?"

For the next ten minutes, Jake gave Mat a rundown of the events that had led him to the girl near Navassa Island and the ensuing trip to the cove, including his fight with the crew of the Colombian tuna trawler. When Jake told him all about the strange white dolphins Destiny communed with and the other unusual powers she possessed, his friend stared back as if Jake had lost his mind.

"I wish you'd stop putting me on, old buddy," Mat said, his tone holding no humor. "You must think I was hatched out of an Easter egg to buy into a whopper like that."

Jake noted the look of disbelief in his friend's eyes. "I know it's a hard story to swallow. Even though I've seen what I'm telling you with my own eyes, I have trouble believing it myself. But tonight you had a front row seat in witnessing what Destiny is capable of, things that would normally seem impossible to most people."

Pointing to the barely distinguishable scar on the back of his upper arm, Jake said, "See this. About four days ago I took a bullet through the triceps, compliments of the Colombians I fought against. Destiny was able to heal the wound completely in a matter of seconds just by touching it. From what I've been told, she inherited this ability from her mother who has the same power."

Mat shook his head skeptically. "I don't know…this whole story seems far too weird. I mean, come on, voodoo and white witches of the vau…what do you call it?"

"Vaudun."

"Whatever!" Mat was beginning to look annoyed. "It's all just too much to accept, especially the part about dolphins with hands and how they're able to carry on a conversation in human languages."

"These dolphins are fairly new to the planet," Jake explained. "My guess is they're the result of some kind of evolutionary jump. From what I've seen, they seem to have an intellect way above human intelligence. Somehow Destiny is able to establish a communal mind link with them that, at least in part, is responsible for the unique powers she displays."

Jake assessed the doubt still clouding Mat's face and sighed. "I can see I'm still beating a dead horse here." Turning, he grabbed a flashlight hanging from the bulkhead and began to exit the pilothouse. "Follow me! I've got something to show you that might change your mind."

Leading Mat down to the vessel's rear deck, Jake leaned over the port side. He was about to call to Achilles when the albino poked his head above the water.

Shining the flashlight down into the dolphin's face, Jake said, "Mat, I'd like you to meet Achilles."

"*Hello, Mat,*" Achilles trilled. "*You must trust the things Jay Jay tells you.*"

Mat appeared stunned. "Are my ears deceiving me, or did that dolphin just speak to me?"

"Achilles, please show Mat your hands!" Jake requested.

Using his tail for leverage, Achilles rose higher out of the water to display the abnormal appendages he possessed.

"Catch!" Jake blurted, tossing the flashlight down to the young dolphin.

Exhibiting precise dexterity, Achilles caught the flashlight in his left hand, then tossed it back up to Jake.

"Now do you believe me?" Jake asked, turning to look at Mat.

Utter astonishment manifested itself on Mat's face. "Holy shit!"

"Here's something else for you to chew on," Jake intoned. "Achilles, tell Mat what the *pi* ratio of a circle represents and give him the actual number out to the eighth decimal place."

"*Pi is the circumference of a circle divided by its diameter. It is both a universal mathematical constant and an irrational number, having an infinite string of digits with no discernable pattern emerging from its numbers. The first time the sequence one through nine is encountered, it is over five hundred million digits into the ratio. The pi ratio calculated out to eight decimal places approximately equals three point one, four, one, five, nine, two, six, five.*"

Mat continued to look flabbergasted. "Jesus Christ, how does he know that?"

"Let me show you something else," Jake said, ignoring the question. As he led Mat into the Angel's salon, only Grahm, Parker, Trebek, Hennington and Jacob currently occupied the cabin.

"Does that painting look familiar?" Jake queried Mat, pointing to the dolphin art leaning up against the wall.

As Mat cast his eyes upon the canvas, Jake could see the effect it had on his friend, a profound nurturing of the spirit.

Mat stared, silently transfixed as if in a stupor, seeming to forget about Jake's presence for the moment. "I...I saw something very much like this during our escape from the prison. I thought I was hallucinating at the time."

"Looking at it makes you feel good inside, doesn't it?"

Mat nodded distractedly, unwilling to pull his gaze away from the masterpiece. "Where...where did you get this?"

"Achilles produced this painting," Jake stated. "Members of his pod have produced a lot of paintings like this. Even though each work of art is different, they all seem to have one thing in common, and that's the remarkable effect they have on people."

The painting continued to dominate Mat's attention. "How can a painting do this?" he asked, his tone indicating awe. His eyes seemed to rove over every facet within the artistic expression.

"I have no explanation," Jake said, "though Jacob, here, believes it triggers some kind of neurological mechanism in the lesser used side of the human brain."

Finally managing to withdraw his gaze, Mat looked at his watch. "Well, good buddy, I'd like to stick around and continue chatting, but I have other business to take care of. If my boys are as punctual as they've shown me in the past, they should be pulling alongside at any moment."

No sooner had Mat uttered the words, something bumped lightly against the Angel. Moving back out on deck, Jake saw the hulking silhouette of *Relentless* abutting the North Sea trawler's starboard side. Two members of Mat's team stood near the boat's stern, lending a hand as Mat climbed aboard.

Just before the DHS vessel pulled away, Mat smiled back at Jake. "If it's not too much of an imposition, I'd sure like to have one of those paintings."

"I'll see what I can do about getting you one," Jake said.

"Don't be a stranger, buddy. Stay in touch." And then Mat was gone, his boat purring off into the twilight of dawn like a phantom drifting across the water.

As Jake watched his friend depart, he suddenly realized he hadn't seen Destiny or her mother in some time now. As if responding to his concern, Achilles suddenly surfaced close by, and before the question lurking at the back of Jake's mind could be vocalized, the adolescent albino gave him an answer totally unexpected.

"Destiny and Amphitrite have gone, Jay Jay," Achilles warbled.

"Gone?" Jake blurted. "Gone where?"

"I cannot tell you at this time."

The comment left Jake almost speechless. "Why can't you tell me?"

"Do not be mad, Jay Jay. Destiny has made me promise not to reveal her whereabouts until three hours from now."

"What's wrong with telling me right now?" Jake fumed.

"I am bound by a promise."

Jake scanned the water all around the Angel. There was no sign of any other dolphin. "Excluding yourself, Achilles, are any other members of the pod still here?" he asked.

"*Two others still remain,*" Achilles said.

"Who?"

"*You and Jacob remain.*"

Jake began to grow frustrated. "Achilles, please…I must-"

The hand placed on Jake's shoulder made him spin around. Hennington stood before him.

Jake studied the blend of humbleness and anxiety written on the broker's face. "What were you doing in the prison, Chester?"

"For many years now I have been Ternier's pawn, a man possessed by both selfishness and fear," Hennington confessed. "But it was the white mambo who turned me away from my own insatiable greed and the coward I had become."

It took Jake several seconds to deduce what was being said. Apparently Colonel Ternier had used the broker as his personal agent, capitalizing on Hennington's unique talents for shady dealings in order to enrich himself. Like Bashir, however, Hennington had undergone some inner transformation for the better, a cleansing of the spirit brought about at the hands of Destiny's mother. Perhaps Hennington was going to walk the straight and narrow from here on out.

Jake nodded in understanding. "You realize Ternier will kill you if he ever finds you."

"I can no longer allow myself to live in fear."

"What about our little business arrangement?" Jake found it necessary to ask. Though the idea of running illegal contraband did not sit well with him, he desperately needed cash to refuel the Angel. Deep down he knew this would be his last smuggling run.

Shame flashed briefly across Hennington's face. "Do you know what *supernotes* are?"

Jake stared blankly.

"Supernotes are extremely high-quality copies of foreign currency."

"You mean counterfeits?"

"Yes."

"You're telling me that was to be the shipment?"

"Yes."

"Which currency and how much?"

"United States greenbacks in one hundred dollar bill denominations. About $140 million in all."

Jake was dumbstruck by the amount. "Where was it coming from?"

"Pyongyang, North Korea via Kingston."

Something stirred in the back of Jake's mind. While in the Seals he had learned of North Korea's state-supervised currency printing plants that churned out high-grade counterfeit currency, primarily in the form of American greenbacks but also in Japanese yen, Thai bath, and in recent years, euros. These were high-speed banknote presses similar to those used by the U.S. Bureau of Engraving and Printing.

"And who was to be the recipient?"

Hennington leaned against the railing and looked down at Achilles, staring briefly at the dolphin before turning back to Jake. "The man you recently made an enemy of was to be the recipient."

"Henri Ternier?"

Hennington produced an affirmative nod. "The Colonel is an ambitious man and is waiting for the right moment to take control of Haiti."

"Coups are nothing new to this country," Jake said, unperturbed by the news. "Keeping a secure grip on the reins of power is generally short-lived. I don't think Ternier would have any more success than his predecessors, especially with U.N. troops stationed here to counter a government takeover. Even if he initially succeeded, the U.S. wouldn't stand for it. Uncle Sam would march right in and kick him out."

The broker frowned gravely. "Ternier knows this. That is why he has aligned himself with some powerful allies. He has been planning his move for a long time now, and when conditions are in his favor he will strike."

"He's told you this plan?"

"No, but I have acted enough on his behalf to figure out the things he has set in motion."

Something shifted heavily along the fringes of Jake's consciousness, and his mind was suddenly forging ahead like a tugboat abruptly cut loose from the tow-line it had been straining against. "So North Korea is one of his allies."

"I think so."

"What makes you believe that?"

"Counterfeit bills are normally purchased with bonafide money at anywhere from thirty to seventy percent of their face value, but the Colonel was to receive the counterfeits without having to pay anything in exchange."

"Sounds like Pyongyang's intent on funding something free of charge. What was Ternier gonna use the phony money for?"

"To buy weapons and the cooperation of U.N. troops and other factions within Haiti. He has already bribed several U.N. commanders not to interfere in his activities. And because of it, he has managed to stockpile an impressive arsenal of weapons for a military coup. A continuance of this type of corruption would be child's play for him."

Jake tightened his eyes sullenly. "Yeah, but how would he prevent the U.S. from coming in here and ousting him?"

Hennington played a brooding gaze over Jake's face, drawing a deep breath before replying. "By introducing turmoil in your own government through some catastrophic event. An incident even greater than what you Americans refer to as nine-eleven would strain Washington's resources enough to divert its attention completely away from Haiti, possibly forestalling indefinitely, maybe even permanenantly, any military response aimed at restoring order to this insignificant country."

The hazy picture lingering at the back of Jake's mind suddenly became a little clearer, and an image of the rogue sub sprang to the forefront of his thoughts. "You mentioned other allies of the Colonel. Did he make any deals with Islamic extremists?"

"I was his go-between in arranging a meeting between a Colombian and a man representing an Asian heroin cartel. The cartel man went by the name Omar. Whether or not he was a Muslim I cannot say. What I can tell you is Ternier has strong ties with a powerful Colombian drug lord called Cardoza. One of Cardoza's lieutenants, a man called Sebastion Ortega, met with Omar for the meeting."

"What was the purpose of this meeting?"

"I do not know because I was not present when it took place. I simply arranged for it to happen. But some kind of a deal had been struck involving the delivery of at least twenty able-bodied Haitians to Omar."

"What were these people needed for?"

"Again, I do not know, but it was Ternier who actually provided Ortega with the people Omar requested. They were abducted from the village of Malique early last night."

To Jake, the picture was now beginning to come into sharp focus. "Where and when was this meeting held?"

"At Navassa Island almost five days ago. That is where the people were taken."

This bit of information put Jake's thoughts in a tizzy. The Colombian-Jihadist connection he had theorized was now being confirmed, and instinctively he knew where Destiny and her mother had gone.

"I have a problem, Chester," Jake found himself saying, "one I'm hoping you'll help me with.

Hennington held Jake's gaze, the expression on his face open and unguarded, and Jake saw a new quality to the man he hadn't seen before. "I'll help you any way I can, Jake," the broker offered.

Jake had never liked asking anybody for anything unless a problem involved people other than himself. "The Angel needs fuel, and at this moment I lack the cash to pay for it."

Hennington did not bat an eye, reaching into his pocket and stuffing a thick wad of bills into Jake's hands.

Jake nearly choked with gratitude, but before he could offer any thanks, Trebek came out on deck to join the conversation.

"Did you tell him?" Trebek asked Hennington.

Jake alternated his gaze anxiously between the two men. "Tell me what?"

The broker met Jake's questioning eyes and sighed tiredly. "We have reason to believe Ternier knows the location of a hydrogen bomb lost by the United States military many years ago."

Even though the early morning air was warm, something akin to frostbite raced wildly through Jake's bones, and he berated himself unmercifully for having neglected the thing bubbling like fermenting ale in the recesses of his brain, a thing he had failed to follow up on ever since capturing Bashir. Why he hadn't pressed the man for more information he could not explain to himself, though he suspected it had something to do with his trust in Destiny. The fact that Ternier was somehow linked up with Islamic terrorists was proof enough that something cataclysmic was about to happen.

With growing apprehension, Jake listened carefully to the story related to him by both Hennington and Trebek. When they had finished, Jake knew he needed additional facts, and he rushed to locate Bashir who he assumed was still aboard the Angel.

"We cannot find him anywhere," Zimbola eventually informed Jake following a thorough search of the vessel.

Staring back over the side, Jake was about to question Achilles on the matter, but the juvenile spoke up before Jake could utter a word.

"Bashir has left with Destiny, Jay Jay," Achilles twittered. "But I still must keep my promise."

Jake looked back in frustration, knowing how binding a promise could be. Abruptly, he called out to his first mate. When Zimbola appeared, he said, "Pull anchor!"

"Where we going?" the big man asked.

Jake fingered the wad of money in his hand. "First we top off our tanks, then we head back up the coast."

Racing into the Angel's salon, Jake found Grahm and Parker talking quietly with Jacob. "Leaving you here to catch an outgoing flight would put you and your assistants in too much danger, Professor," Jake stated gruffly. "For the time being I'm going to leave the three of you with Jacob back at the cove. Later on I'll come pick you up and drop you off in Kingston where it's a lot safer."

Grahm's expression turned to one of deep concern. "Where are you going, my lad?"

Jake hesitated, unsure if he should disclose his plans, but not seeing any need for secrecy, he came right to the point. "I'm going back to Navassa."

- 101 -

Carried along by Hercules, Destiny glanced over at her mother, strangely moved by the sight. The technique used by Amphitrite to ride a dolphin was entirely different from her own, mainly because the creature that most often bore her was considerably smaller and anatomically different than Hercules. Nevertheless, Athena still had the ability to plow through the sea with a remarkable degree of efficiency in spite of the load she carried. And if Athena somehow tired, there was always one of her progeny to take over the task of towing Amphitrite.

Surrounded by an entourage of other pod members, Destiny tried to grasp the full magnitude of what lay before them. But contrary to the occurrences she had been able to foresee at the prison, any gleanings into future events now seemed to be blocked by a blanket of mist. The familiar harmonious resonance that had always preceded precognition was completely absent, leaving a disconcerting uncertainty hanging in its place. The communal conjoining of minds did little to penetrate the fog, and the notion that she might actually be the cause of the problem clung to her perceptions like annoying cobwebs in a dusty room. As she contemplated this, the sensation transformed into something more potent, intruding its way into her thinking like some clumsy beast entering a chamber filled with fragile glass, and begrudgingly, she suddenly knew it could not be denied nor ignored. She had compromised herself. She had fallen in love, and in so doing she had contaminated the purity of the vinculum she held with the others. Bias now took away her selflessness, putting the pod at risk. Try as she might, she could not rid herself of the thing she felt. In loving Jay Jay, she had sought to protect him rather than allow him to provide the support she and the others would require in their quest to meet head-on the danger that was fast approaching. They were nearing a critical nexus in the time-space continuum, and the battle that had to be fought could not be avoided. To a large degree, she was failing the purpose she had been created to fulfill by keeping Jay Jay out of the fight. And yet she was powerless to do otherwise.

Tormented by these thoughts, Destiny pressed on, vaguely aware of how her mother and the others regarded her. As always, there was not a shred of condemnation or accusation directed at her. By nature, they were all inherently gentle creatures, and it was not within them to judge. They were simply following a course of action guided by something on a subliminal level.

Destiny noticed Bashir weakening as he sat directly behind her. Once again they were sharing the same mount. With his arms clasped securely about her waist, she had felt the man's strength gradually ebbing over the last few kilometers. But Bashir would be needed, of that much she was sure, and the respite he required would be forthcoming very shortly. Having been summoned earlier on, Jimenez was not far off and would soon meet up with them. Then Bashir as well as she and her mother would climb aboard the fisherman's pinnace and sail the remaining distance to Navassa Island with the dolphins leading the way.

A sense of impending disaster suddenly seized Destiny in a crushing grip, causing Hercules to flinch spasmodically as he continued to push north. The feeling spread quickly to the other dolphins ringing her, and all at once they let out a high-pitched squeal of distress.

- 102 -

The winch screeched in protest under the strain, then abruptly quieted as the unknown load finally came to rest on the San Carlo's stern deck.

Holding back the grin he felt, Raduyev kept his emotions in check, looking instead to the questioning frown coming to bear on Sebastion Ortega's face. The Cardoza lieutenant was staring fixedly at the canvas tarp wrapped tightly about the thing pulled from the depths. And from what Raduyev could see, it was obvious Ortega was more than just a little curious about the object salvaged from the sea floor.

"When will this ship of yours arrive?" Ortega asked indifferently.

The Chechen studied Ortega's mien carefully before answering. The man's eyes betrayed the boredom he was trying so hard to exude. The Colombian desperately wanted to see the thing hidden under the tarp. But the deal between them had already been struck, and Ortega had no need to know the tarp's secret.

"We will make the transfer just after nightfall," Raduyev said, shifting his attention to the two divers climbing from the sea. He was quite pleased with the way they had conducted themselves during the recovery operation that had just taken place in 140 feet of water. The mujahideen fighters Gullu Sherkhan had brought with him were showing skills he had not expected. Even though the task required nothing more than locating the load and attaching a shackle to it, he was still impressed with how quickly they had carried it out.

Raduyev stared back at the thing brought up from the ocean floor. In the sunlight, the canvas tarp shrouding it glistened green with a budding growth of algae. This was to be expected given that the tarp had been left submerged during the last three weeks. After all, it was he who had done most of the work in preparing the thing for recovery, risking the bends during more than a dozen separate dives executed from the sub over a span of nearly two weeks in order to complete the task. The coordinates provided by Henri Ternier had proved surprisingly accurate, making it fairly easy for him to locate the military aircraft that had carried the object. Much of the plane had been buried in sand that had accumulated around the airframe, pushed up against and almost covering it as a result of passing storms over the last several decades. Getting to the object had not been easy, requiring him to use a cutting torch in removing part of the fuselage so that the thing could be lifted out. Airlifting the sand smothering it had proved less difficult, and in the end he had managed to expose its bulk. Girthing the thing with chains had proved much more problematic, however, and he replayed in his mind the arduous task of having had to dig out more sand covering the frame supporting the 12-foot long bomb in order to get the links around it in two places. Then it had required eight large air bags, each with a lifting capacity of roughly 460 kilograms to nudge the 3,500 kilogram bomb off its cradle just enough to allow him to wrap the weapon in the tarp that now kept it hidden from prying eyes. Entwining the tarp with additional chain had not been as time consuming, and after that he had deflated the lift bags and let the load fall gently back into its cradle, certain that the chance of accidental detonation was extremely remote.

Based on what he knew of the bomb, it was a Mark-15 with an explosive yield somewhere between 1.9 and 3.6 megatons. Beneath its metal shell was 80 kilograms of conventional high explosives, a removable capsule housing the plutonium trigger, a mass of highly enriched uranium, and the lithium-6 deuteride compound, the actual fusion material which comprised most of the bomb's volume. Constituents of Bin Laden had researched military records on the lost bomb, discovering that it was one of 11 nuclear bombs lost by the Americans during air and sea accidents, what the Pentagon referred to as "Broken Arrows." And although the U.S. Air Force had long insisted the plutonium capsule needed to trigger the weapon had been removed from it before the ill-fated flight, his examination of the bomb showed it to be entirely intact. Supporting this was a pentagon memo from 1966, which seemed to indicate that the bomb was a complete weapon.

As Raduyev mulled this, Ortega drew in a deep breath, his nostrils flaring to analyze the muggy air wafting over the sea. Staring off into the distance, the Colombian set his eyes on the dark mass of clouds building off to the east.

"We may be getting some weather, my friend," Ortega stated. "Nightfall may come earlier than expected with those clouds headed this way."

Raduyev had noticed the darkening sky earlier, though he didn't think it would amount to much.

Ortega shifted his gaze in another direction. About a quarter-mile away a large school of whales had congregated, various behemoths within the group spouting as they breached. "Those are humpbacks, my friend. You do not normally see many whales in these waters, but the feeding must be good to attract so many."

Raduyev barely nodded, not really caring.

Ortega swung around to face him, his manner turning icy. "I checked out the location you gave me. The place was empty."

Though there was only the slightest hint of challenge in Ortega's tone, the Chechen was rather glad the man's attention had shifted away from the bomb. Producing a lazy shrug, Raduyev shifted his gaze to the island not too far from their present position. "I fulfilled my end of the bargain. The coordinates I gave you were accurate. That is where those people had gone."

Ortega nodded stoically, his eyes flitting over the Chechen's face like those of a poker player deciding if he should raise the bet. "There was a cove a short distance back from the cliffs, just as your message had indicated. It was very well hidden, a natural sanctuary."

"Did you find any signs of occupation?"

"*Si*...I discovered living quarters, two small cottages. One of them contained a laptop computer and was filled with books."

Raduyev fought down the bile suddenly rising in his throat. Having to discuss the place where he had failed to crush Javolyn was just one more ugly reminder of how he had been bested by the former Seal. In spite of his annoyance, he felt it was time to bring to light the thing chaffing away at the back of his mind. "Did you learn what those men were doing in these waters?" He made a show of letting his eyes fall on the boat tied up alongside the trawler to indicate what he meant. Apparently the San Carlo had come across the vessel while heading out to meet him.

"What makes you think anyone was aboard her?"

"I saw this boat drifting without power near the island yesterday. Six men could be seen on her deck."

A nefarious smirk came to Ortega's face. "Several of my crew are interrogating them as we speak. They claim to be dolphin hunters. I saw this boat a few days ago heading toward the harbor in Port-au-Prince. It was towing the same waverunner used to attack us."

Several seconds passed as Raduyev studied the Colombian's expression. "You will not find the man you are looking for among those you have captured."

Ortega's smugness vanished immediately. "How do you know that?"

Raduyev felt his something clench deep down in his gut. "The person you seek was a Navy Seal at one time, a man called Jake Javolyn."

A dark frown sprang onto Ortega's face. "You know this man?"

"I have a vendetta to settle with him. He and that accursed girl we saw with him were out here yesterday, but they sailed away."

Ortega reined in his anger. "What were they doing?"

"I do not know." Raduyev brought his eyes back on the tethered vessel. "But I think they may be the reason why this boat became inoperable."

Ortega's face darkened further. "Maybe these dolphin hunters know something about him?" Contemplating his own question a moment longer, his expression changed into a sneer. "Follow me belowdeck, my friend. Perhaps they can provide us with some answers."

- 103 -

Destiny was amazed at the size of the creature rising up from the depths to trail behind them. It was immense, the largest shark she had ever seen, and from the mental feedback she was getting from the others, it appeared to be a tiger. And as she well knew, the teeth of a tiger were the most dangerous of all sharks. Even without biting down on prey, they were capable of causing extensive damage to flesh with as little as a raking strike during a slack-jawed attack.

But as she sensed the animal's approach, she felt a familiar presence driving the creature on. Erzulie was following them.

Through some arcane ritual of the black arts, the sorceress of the voudun had found a way of pouring her essence into the predator pursuing them. And while the witch was seeing them through the shark's eyes, it was Erzulie's will that was controlling the monster, compelling it to attack.

Normally the albinos should have been able to easily outpace it. Compared to the new breed, tigers were relatively slow swimmers, only capable of reaching a maximum speed of 32 kilometers per hour, with short bursts of higher speeds lasting no more than a few seconds. But Erzulie was forcing the 30-foot monster forward at an incredible rate, making it drive its 6-ton bulk through the sea at a speed that at least equaled their own.

With the threat rapidly closing in on them, the group went into a defensive posture. Every member of the pod suddenly altered their formation, flaring out to both sides in flanking maneuvers to surround the beast. It only took Destiny a moment to realize where the shark's attention was directed. The monster had targeted her mother, or at least the dolphin she was riding. Being the slowest member of the pack, Athena was the most vulnerable.

Discovering the shark's intent, the pod quickly adjusted its movements. Hermes and Aphrodite darted in to intercept it as it closed the gap on Amphitrite. At the same instant, Apollo and Artemis circled around, rushing up on the shark's rear as Coral and Reef raced to Destiny's side. With Destiny having no time to give Bashir a full explanation as to what was happening, she simply asked him to release his hold on her. No sooner did he comply, Coral extended her powerful forelimbs to pluck him from Hercules' back. A look of surprise came over the Palestinian's face as he was carried off to one side out of harm's way.

The tiger's jaws parted wide, displaying flattened triangular teeth with notched and serrated edges. Waving its wedge-shaped head from side to side, it lashed out with frenzied vigor, eager to have its razor-sharp weaponry come in contact with dolphin flesh. And while the albinos nearest the jaws were successful in remaining clear of the slashing strikes, they were ineffective in discouraging the beast from its targeted prey, that being Amphitrite and her mount.

Destiny held on tight as Hercules dove deep, responding to the imminent threat. She felt his heart pound thunderously within his powerful body as he rapidly gained speed. Flattening herself against the dolphin's back, she reduced the drag on the albino as much as possible, knowing what Hercules had in mind. The giant leveled off and began to rise, increasing his momentum further, and as Destiny looked up, the tiger's bulk blotted out the sun hanging above the ocean. It was then that she realized how close those snapping jaws were to Athena.

Hercules flicked his tail with a final explosive snap, slamming beak-first into the beast's belly with such force that Destiny was nearly flung free. Stunned from the impact, the albino bull fell away slowly, dropping languidly into the abyss beneath him.

Destiny focused, channeling most of her life energy into her mount, desperately trying to revive him. Apollo and Artemis swooped down to help, keeping Hercules from falling any deeper by supporting his body with their own. Reef, Hermes and Aphrodite quickly joined in the rescue, and conjoining their minds with Destiny's, concentrated on bringing Hercules back to full consciousness. Within moments, the giant albino responded, and with renewed purpose, prepared for another assault against the colossal shark.

But another assault was unnecessary. Already the enormous tiger was plummeting into the depths as if in slow motion, its heart completely ruptured by a combination of overstress from the impossible demands Erzulie had forced upon it and the crushing impact of Hercules' charge.

A flood of relief washed over Destiny as she glanced up toward the surface, noting that her mother and Athena remained unscathed. Riding Hercules back to the surface, she waited for Coral to restore Bashir to his former perch behind her. With the others forming up around her and Amphitrite, they once again resumed her northerly heading.

Another half hour passed without further incident, after which time Jimenez finally chugged his pinnace into their midst. Few words were exchanged as Bashir and the women climbed aboard, and a moment later the entire group set out for the place where an unavoidable but necessary showdown had been prophesized long ago.

- 104 -

Erzulie let out an agonized scream. She had felt the trauma inflicted on the tiger shark as if the pain were her own, and she clutched her chest protectively as if the heart beating within were on the verge of bursting. The paroxysm passed quickly, however, and she exhaled sharply as though a knife had pulled from her lungs.

Henri placed a hand on her shoulder. "What is wrong, mother?"

Erzulie gasped, drawing breath hungrily. "They…they have beaten me again." She stared in bewilderment at the quartz crystal at the center of the amulet, no longer able to view the pod they were pursuing. Once again, the chevals had escaped her.

Ternier's face contorted into a mask of blistering rage. These chevals were causing him nothing but problems. "It does not matter," he consoled her. "Once we reach Navassa Island we will join forces with our allies. Our combined strength will be more than adequate to defeat these chevals once and for all." All at once his anger changed over into a malicious grin. "Sebastion Ortega will be especially pleased to know the girl and dolphins will practically fall right into his waiting hands."

Erzulie nodded absently, continuing to eye the ancient charm as if doubting its potency for the first time ever. "Perhaps that is the reason the rada are urging them to Navassa."

The Colonel took a moment to espy the sea sliding past one of the boat's starboard windows. The rumble of the engines was somehow reassuring to him as they pushed the craft toward the island. The sound only tended to reassert his sense of power. He had grown rich over the past several years in spite of the vast fortune the hurricane had taken from him many years ago, affording him the luxury of the modern yacht he now possessed. It was a sleek vessel, far too good for the men he had chosen to crew her. He had commissioned its construction in Miami two years earlier, and it was only three weeks ago he had finally taken delivery of it.

"We will destroy them completely this time," Ternier reiterated. "And once Omar launches his missle, Haiti will finally be ours for the taking."

Erzulie released the amulet, letting it fall back into place between her withered breasts. "When will that be, my son?"

"Very soon, mother. Very soon."

- 105 -

Sitting at his computer console in Toulouse, France, the telemetry specialist noted the location of the pulsing signal. Enlarging the magnification further, he was was momentarily surprised to find that it did not originate from one of those strange white dolphins he had seen several days earlier. This time the signal was coming from a boat, and from the look of the watercraft, he sensed her to be exceptionally seaworthy. Yawning, and without giving it much thought, he relayed the information to the anonymous client. But on this occasion the transmission would be broadcast automatically every three minutes. For all practical purposes, he was finished doing what he had been paid to do.

The hour was late and boredom was creeping up on him. Sipping some of the steaming coffee from the mug he held, he decided to take another look at the thing that had grabbed his attention once before. With his free hand, he punched several computer keys, and almost immediately the color-coded imagery of sea temperatures surrounding Navassa Island filled the screen.

Surprised by what he saw, he almost spilled his coffee. Thinking his eyes might be playing tricks on him, he accessed the history file, retrieving the latest stored frame and comparing it against the current image. There was no mistaking it. The algae bloom had grown, its size broadening significantly without any reduction in concentration. That meant the amount of upwelling near the island had increased.

Acknowledging the irregularity as something of passing interest, he changed screens, pulling up real-time satellite visual imagery of the waters where the upwelling was occurring. With the exception of a ship sitting stationary several hundred meters from the pocket of cold water that delineated the sector of upwelling, nothing else was visible. Lowering the magnification, he broadened the picture. Off to the east, a heavy patch of cloud cover blocked a view of the ocean. More than likely a storm was brewing, and from the looks of it, the water just south of the island was going to be subjected to a heavy blow.

Finding nothing else of interest to arouse his curiosity, the specialist saved the latest images, storing them away in the system's data banks. Propping his feet up on the desk, he leaned back in his chair, and within seconds fell off into a light sleep.

- 106 -

Jake stared first at Jacob, then at the others. Firmly rooted in all four faces was a look of conviction. Nevertheless, he felt it necessary to convince them otherwise. "There is no telling what we'll be facing at Navassa," he advised. "All I can say is each of you will be putting yourself in danger if you insist on coming along. You might even get yourselves killed."

Jacob appeared unruffled. "I am not afraid of dying."

"The same goes for me," Hennington insisted.

"You will have to physically eject me from this vessel to keep me from going," Trebek growled.

Jake turned to Grahm. "What about you, Professor?"

The scientist sighed wearily. "Count me in!"

"What about your assistants?"

"Nicolas is still ill. We can drop him off in the cove. Jeffrey will tend to him."

Jake nodded in agreement. "Makes sense." He shifted his eyes to Jacob. "Provided Jacob doesn't mind."

"I do not mind."

"Phillipe will accompany them," Jake said. "We'll drop them off with provisions to tide them over." He had considered leaving Emmanuel and Lucette with them as well, but it was Jacob who had insisted they would be better off aboard the Angel where he could tend to them. Though Amphitrite and Destiny had healed their injuries, they still had not fully recovered from their ordeal.

The boat's intercom suddenly buzzed, and Jake answered the bridge. "What's up, Zimby?"

The Jamaican's deep voice boomed from the speaker. "Kingston has issued a weather advisory, Jay Jay. There may be a storm headed for Navassa. Do we hole up at the cove, or do we keep going?"

"We'll be dropping Phillipe off with Jeff Parker and Nick Henderson. After that, we sail for Navassa, storm or no storm."

- 107 -

Ortega felt only contempt for the man tied to the chair before him. The one admitting to the name of Walter McPherson had so far shown a total lack of courage, practically blubbering like a baby. While the Loomins brothers had proved much tougher, it had taken very little persuasion to get McPherson to open up. Pedro had barely begun to administer the type of beating he was so fond of doling out, and McPherson had spilled information like a media newscaster, spewing much more than expected.

Fingering the device recently retrieved from the Sea Lion, Ortega motioned Pedro away from McPherson. Pedro scowled savagely, backing away begrudgingly. He did not like being denied his pleasure. He was just getting started.

"So what exactly does this little thing do?" Ortega asked, ignoring the look Cardoza's nephew was giving him.

McPherson grimaced, his right cheekbone now swollen and taking on a bright purple sheen. "It's a telemetry device. It transmits the location of whatever it's tied to."

"And this was taken from one of the two white dolphins captured a few days ago?"

McPherson answered with a frenzied nod, his eyes filled with fear.

Out of curiosity, Ortega turned to observe the scornful expression etched on Omar's face, judging the Islamist to be equally revolted by McPherson's shameful display of gutlessness. "If this device transmits a signal, where do you keep the receiver?"

"We don't have one aboard the boat," McPherson whined.

"Then how are you able to determine the signal's location?"

"The tracking unit is kept aboard a spotter plane which guides the Sea Lion into position."

"And then what do you do?"

"The boat's crew stands by while the plane drops a sounder to incapacitate the dolphins." McPherson was speaking very quickly now. "After that the crew moves in to drug them with sedation darts just before netting them."

"By what means does this sounder you speak of incapacitate them?"

"It sends out a blast of sonar just strong enough to stun them."

"You said two white dolphins were captured. Did they by any chance show any unusual appendages?"

The panic that had been showing in McPherson's face instantly changed over to astonishment before subsiding into perplexity. "I...I'm not sure I understand what you mean?"

Ortega studied his expression a moment longer, then looked over at Pedro and gave him a subtle nod.

Pedro's mouth displayed a sadistic grin, and he pounced on McPherson with renewed eagerness, balling a fist and throwing a punch.

By moving his head at the last moment, McPherson was able to avoid the brunt of the strike, his jaw taking only a glancing blow. "Okay...okay," he yelled, tucking his chin down against his chest to protect it from further harm and straining wildly against his bonds. "They had these strange foldout forelimbs with hands."

With a stern look, Ortega warned Pedro off again. "So how did they manage to get away?"

McPherson glanced timidly over at Pedro to make sure he was not about to launch another blow. "Two people sabotaged the capture. They pretended to be stranded on a waverunner. Loomins picked them up, a man and a woman...they freed the creatures."

"Describe these people."

"I wasn't there when it happened," McPherson groaned. "You'll have to ask Ben Loomins."

Tied to another chair, Ben Loomins was out cold, his face showing Pedro's nasty work. Slumped in a chair next to him, his brother, Charlie, was in similar condition.

Ortega looked to another of the San Carlo's crewmen standing close to the unconscious man. "Wake him up!" he ordered.

The crewman lifted a bucket of water and splashed its contents over Loomins' drooped head. Coming awake and sputtering weakly, Loomins stared groggily about him.

Squatting down to look into his eyes, Ortega said, "Describe the people who freed the dolphins you caught."

Loomins blinked dumbly for several seconds, the question seeming to be beyond his understanding.

"The people who freed the dolphins you captured," Ortega repeated in an ugly snarl. "Describe them!"

Intense rage suddenly took hold of Loomins. "A man and a woman freed them," he bellowed, as if the memory of the incident angered him far more than what Ortega was doing to him. "The woman was about five feet tall and very pretty…she had long black hair and looked to be about eighteen years old at most." Loomins face glowered still hotter. "The guy was about six feet and looked like a weight-lifter…I think he had green eyes and a trident tattooed on his left forearm."

Ortega lifted his eyes to glimpse the hatred emblazoned on Omar's countenance. "Does that sound like Javolyn?"

Before Omar could reply, another crewman entered the room. "A vessel is approaching from the east, Sebastion."

Ortega mulled this. According to his sources, the nearby island was not scheduled for any military surveillance or scientific expeditions in the immediate future. Skewering Pedro with a vicious glare, he said, "I am going topside for the moment. You will refrain from hurting these men any more until I come back. Is that understood?" He needed to know more about these strange white creatures, and the men tied to the chairs might have a lot more to tell him. The last thing he wanted was Pedro beating the life out of them before they could provide him with additional information.

Pedro barely acknowledged the order, exhibiting the manner of a carnivore denied a chunk of bloodied meat laid before it.

With that said, Ortega left the room, somewhat mystified that Omar was still accompanying him. By the time he made his way back up on deck, the unknown vessel was within hailing distance under a sky that had darkened considerably, its bow working hard against a restless sea. He could see the weather was rapidly deteriorating.

"They request permission to come alongside," the same crewman informed Ortega. Using a handheld radio, the crewman continued to stay in contact with the San Carlo's bridge.

Ortega studied the vessel as it drew closer. She was a rusting hulk with the lines of an ocean tug that had spent too many years at sea without ever seeing drydock. "Ask them what they want?"

The crewman did as he was told, bringing the radio to his mouth again and carrying on a short discourse with the bridge. "They say they are here to tow the other boat back to Port-au-Prince."

Ortega sneered wickedly. Things were getting better and better. "Tell them to pull up to our port side and throw us some lines."

With the Avenging Angel finally holding to a steady course, Jake wondered if he had made the right decision. As expected, Phillipe had not liked being left behind. Even Parker had objected to being put ashore, much rather preferring to accompany Grahm. But once Jake had explained the perils they were sure to encounter, Parker had eventually given in, seeing the wisdom in keeping out of harm's way. Not surprisingly, however, was Henderson's desire to get his feet back on dry land. As a matter of fact, the electronics whiz had seemed all too eager to revisit the cove.

Hector had told Jake how Henderson had fallen ill after looking at Achilles' painting, and it was this that made him continue to dwell on the decision he had made. While in the prison he had seen the way the painting had adversely affected Ternier and most of the men that served him. People with inherently vile natures, it seemed, were apt to become sick, at least temporarily, when exposed to the dolphin art, forever removed from the boundaries of redemption. And it was this observation that had served to further both his dislike and distrust of Henderson.

As the coast receded farther behind him, a feeling of deep-seated uneasiness began to take hold of Jake, gradually mounting with each passing minute as if to match the growing sea. Already the Angel was beginning to pound its way through quartering swells as the storm approached from the east. The sky had darkened considerably, exacerbated all the more by the approach of nightfall.

Ever since Hennington had informed him about the nuclear warhead, Jake had tried to contact Daniels, putting in a satellite call to his friend every few minutes to warn him about the bomb. But each time he had done this, the call had gone unanswered.

Checking his current GPS coordinates, Jake could see they were now less than ten minutes from Navassa, even taking into account the reduced headway they were making under the deteriorating conditions. Already the island's southern shore was showing up on his radar screen, and some distance back from it was a sizeable blip that told him all he needed to know.

Jake turned to note Zimbola eyeing the screen from his position at the helm. "If that's the San Carlo, she's not moving."

"She be sitting at anchor, I suppose," the Jamaican offered. His gaze came to bear on another blip just beginning to impinge on the screen as he said this. "And she be having company."

Jake scrutinized the screen again, studying the object making its way slowly toward the first vessel. "If we can see them, I have to assume they can see us."

"What shall we do?"

Several ideas flashed quickly in Jake's mind, but only one held any merit, though even that seemed pretty foolhardy. Nevertheless, he had to give it a try. "I want you to bring us to within a half-mile of those ships and then hold your position. Don't go any closer! If any vessels come in this direction, I want you to back away."

Zimby looked confused. "So we just be sittin' here?"

"For the time being, yes, but I want everyone at the ready, all weapons locked and loaded like before."

Suspicion crept onto the big man's face as he stared at Jake. "What you be doing?" he asked, emphasizing the *you*.

"I'm going over the side for a closer look."

Zimby gazed back as if Jake were nuts. "The sea, she be gettin' angrier by the minute. How will you make it back?"

"Let me worry about that, okay. Navy Seals trained in weather like this all the time. Mercades' grandson would have considered it nothing more than a stroll on the beach."

Zimbola looked doubtful as the Angel suddenly rolled, then pitched hard under him.

"Besides, Achilles will be with me."

"Are you sure that dolphin still be with us?"

"Oh, he's still with us alright." Jake could feel the juvenile on the fringes of his awareness, an all too familiar presence that had continued to grow stronger during the last several hours. It was a sensation that would not go away.

- 109 -

With a utility belt holding six spare ammo clips wrapped snugly about his waist, his USP-9 submachine pistol riding his right thigh, and his K-bar strapped firmly to his right calf, a feeling of invincibility began to consume Jake as he held on tight to Achilles' compact form. Even so, he knew such a state of mind could be counterproductive, perhaps reckless, and Mat's chastening stare loomed briefly in his thoughts, a sober reminder that many lives were depending on him. At least try to be a little cautious, he chastised himself.

Jake suddenly shivered involuntarily, aware that the water temperature had dropped markedly. Achilles was only breaching the surface whenever Jake needed air, otherwise avoiding the heavy surge where avalanching whitecaps made the going more difficult. Somehow the dolphin could sense whenever

Jake's lungs were in need of recharging, and it was only at these times the young albino would also take the opportunity to breathe. For some inexplicable reason, though, Jake's ability to remain submerged had improved significantly in the last several days, and he wondered if it had something to do with the bond he shared with the juvenile.

Keeping his dive gear to a minimum, Jake had foregone the use of his swim fins, only strapping on his dive mask with snorkel and wearing the same shorty wetsuit he normally utilized in these waters. With Achilles doing all the work, he didn't require swim fins anyway. But now he was freezing, and he could feel the first signs of hypothermia creeping up on him. Why was the sea so damned cold he couldn't help but ask himself?

We will pass beyond the boundary of the upwelling shortly, Jay Jay, Achilles informed him, apparently reading Jake's thoughts again. *You are experiencing the water pulled from the oceanic abyss by the largest of the thurentra that are below us.*

Jake now understood why the area immediately adjacent to the island abounded with huge schools of fish, and no sooner had the thought crossed his mind he sensed an abrupt upward shift in the ambient water temperature just as Achilles had said. Already he was beginning to warm up again.

Another minute passed before the juvenile broke the surface, and it was then that Jake glimpsed the two ships, taking in the scene with a critical eye before focusing his thoughts. *Bring me to where those boats are tied alongside the smaller of the two ships, Achilles.* It had become quite clear to him that speech vocalizations were no longer necessary for him to communicate with the albino.

Earlier in the day the juvenile had finally owned up to where Destiny and Amphitrite had gone, confirming what Jake had assumed all along. Regardless of this, their safety continued to weigh heavily on his mind.

Your concern is my concern, Jay Jay.

Then they are still okay?

At this moment, no danger befalls them. They are currently on Navassa Island.

Achilles sounded again, eventually surfacing within 20 meters of the tethered boats. Though it was now very dark, light cast from the few deck lights turned on aboard the tending ship provided just enough illumination for Jake to identify the watercraft used by Ben Loomins. The Sea Lion was straining hard against her mooring lines as she rode the heaving sea alongside the San Carlo.

Take me to the stern of the Sea Lion, Achilles!

Doing as Jake requested, the albino dove, following a parabolic course that brought Jake just beneath the Sea Lion's swim platform. Grabbing hold of one of the struts supporting the swim platform, Jake held on as the vessel above him pitched heavily with the surge.

See if you can detect anyone aboard her, Achilles!

The juvenile immediately shot deep in a bid to gather momentum that would take him into atmosphere, and a moment later Jake caught a glimpse of the dolphin's sleek form as Achilles leapt from the sea. Less than two seconds elapsed before the answer Jake sought rang clearly in his thoughts. *The watercraft appears to be abandoned, Jay Jay.*

Stay close, Achilles! I'll call you if I need you.

Pulling himself along the platform's undercarriage, Jake found the edge, gripping it firmly as the Sea Lion plunged into the trough of a passing wave. Timing his move, he used the boat's ensuing upswing to pull his body completely from the water. A wash of foaming turbulence surged over the platform as he landed on hands and knees, and he was nearly swept back into the sea as the vessel began to drop again.

Scrambling quickly, he fought for balance, making his way up onto the vessel's rear deck as it reeled violently underfoot. With a free hand, he pulled his dive mask down around his neck to improve his field of vision. Holding onto the railing, he looked upward, checking to see if anyone was currently stationed along the side of the ship above him. Satisfied that he had gone unobserved, he slipped into the Sea Lion's main cabin, prepared to take down anybody that might be lurking there. But upon conducting a rapid surveillance of all the compartments belowdeck, he soon discovered Achilles' assessment to be accurate.

The Seal rule of never leaving a room or place of concealment unsecured behind you before proceeding on ahead was too thoroughly engrained in him not to have carried out a complete search of all the spaces belowdecks, and as he turned to move away from the most forward compartment, he spied something familiar. The webshot he had used on Charlie Loomins had been placed back in storage, a cartridge taped snugly to its stock.

Reaching for the device, Jake tore the cartridge loose and chambered it into the barrel. Checking to see that it was still in working order, he made sure the safety was on before slinging it over his shoulder and making his way back up on deck.

A driving downpour had begun sometime while he had been inside the vessel, and the sting of raindrops against his face pelted him unmercifully as he squinted through eyes reduced to mere slits. A caving ladder had been left hanging down the San Carlo's side, the end of it reachable only when the Sea Lion was above mid-rise as it rose and fell along the ship's hull.

Waiting for the right moment, Jake was able to grasp the third rung from the bottom before the deck of the Sea Lion fell away beneath him. With arms straining, he quickly pulled himself higher, his feet finding the first rung, and in a matter of seconds he climbed the remaining distance to the deck above.

Luck was still with him, for the inclement weather seemed to be discouraging any members of the ship's crew from venturing outside. Stealthily, he hastened along the deck before finding a companionway leading to the superstructure above. Another stairway took him yet higher, and from what he remembered of the ship's layout, he knew the helipad was located just aft of the bridge. From such a vantage point he might be able to see much more.

Jake froze, the sound of voices suddenly drifting back at him above the rush of wind and rain for one fleeting instant. Remaining still, he perked his ears and listened. Several seconds passed before another burst of conversation reached him, but the words were too garbled to garner their meaning.

Leaning over the railing, Jake latched unto one of the tubular joists supporting the helipad, swinging his body outward and working his way hand over hand along the framework. The driving rain had made the support slippery, and at one point he nearly lost his grip. Moving more cautiously, he pulled himself along, grabbing a succession of other structural members until he reached the opposite end of the platform's underside.

A bolt of jagged lightning suddenly flashed close to the island, briefly connecting the maddened sky with the roiling sea, and seconds later a thunderous boom came rolling over the water. In that instant, Jake caught a glimpse of the other ship, its dark mass momentarily illuminated within the cloak of tumultuous darkness surrounding it. And though the sight was fleeting at most, he knew he was looking at a freighter. The vessel was holding to a position about 300 meters from the San Carlo's port side, and as best as he could tell, she had not dropped her anchor, apparently standing by as she rode out the gale. But for what purpose, he wondered? Usually when ships rendezvoused in such a clandestine manner, a transfer of cargo was almost inevitable. And if something was going to be transferred, he had to assume the storm was delaying the operation.

As the lightning faded, Jake managed to get a hand over the edge of the platform, pulling himself up until his eyes were just above the level of the helipad. The Bell Ranger that had attacked him almost a week earlier sat perched, its main rotor fastened down to its tail boom and quivering under the assault of wind. Two men were at work with their backs to him, one of them holding a flashlight steady while the other turned a wrench. Unprotected from the elements, both men appeared to be soaked to the bone.

Jake lingered in his current position a moment longer, trying to ascertain what the men were doing. And all at once recognition hit home with brutal clarity. He was very familiar with the type of armaments typically retrofitted to rotary-wing aircraft, and there was no mistaking the electronic gattling gun jutting obtrusively from the helicopter's port side. With such a weapon, the Bell Ranger would have a firepower capability greatly superior and far more lethal than anything Jake could throw back at it. Once airborne, the aircraft could be used to destroy the Angel with a single strafing run.

As Jake studied the scene before him, the man with the wrench looked up at his partner and said something, but his words were incoherent, drowned out by a blaring clap of thunder. Another burst of lightning erupted, and Jake ducked down below the blinding glare suddenly flaring over the helipad. Thunder crackled again, and then the sea was plunged into darkness once more.

No longer intent on caution, Jake removed the webshot and placed it on the deck, then heaved his body over the edge of the platform. One of the crewmen had disappeared, and a flicker of light at the far end of the helipad told him where the man had gone. The beam of the flashlight continued to bob as the man descended the steps leading to the next level down.

With the stealth of a jungle cat on the verge of a kill, Jake sprung to his feet, gliding like a ghost as he slipped up behind the other crewman. The cry of dismay that left the man's mouth was immediately cut off as Jake clamped a forearm snugly against his throat in a rear-naked choke. Applying pressure, he held on tenaciously until the man began to slump. It was only then that he released the hold.

Laying the man on his back, Jake knelt down on one knee and pulled the K-bar from its sheath, keeping the point positioned near the man's Adam's apple. He could see the man was barely conscious, gasping to suck in air.

"If you cry out or struggle, I'll kill you!" Jake snarled, keeping his face just close enough to be heard above the storm's din. "Nod if you understand me!"

The man lay rigid under the knife as another bolt of lightning flashed, his eyes focusing on the wet steel as light from the electrical discharge glinted off the blade. Abruptly, the man nodded.

Jake glanced behind him to make sure his six was still clear before resuming the conversation. "I have some questions and you will cooperate by answering them! Are we on the same page?"

The man nodded again.

"People from the village of Malique were kidnapped and put aboard this ship yesterday. Where are they?"

"They're not here," the man croaked. "They were taken to the nearby island."

"Where on the island?"

"I don't know."

"How were they transferred?"

"By boat. They were moved there this morning before dawn."

"For what purpose?"

"If I knew I would tell you. I'm just a pilot, not privy to the deals Ortega makes."

Jake thought back to the information Hennington had provided him. "Sebastion Ortega?"

"Yeah."

An assortment of thoughts began to race through Jake's mind. "The person Ortega has been consorting with out here, a man called Omar…where is he?"

"As far as I know, he's still aboard this ship."

Jake let that sink in before pumping the man further. "What about the boats tied up alongside this vessel? Why are they here?"

"The one boat was picked up earlier today. It was floating without power. From what I've been told, the other boat was sent to tow the first boat back to Port-au-Prince. Ortega has taken the crews from both boats down into the hold of this ship for questioning."

Shifting his gaze to the darkened sea, Jake indicated the unknown freighter, its dark bulk barely visible as it maintained position. "What's that ship doing here? I have to assume she's waiting for something to be transferred over to her?"

"Something was pulled from the sea floor and brought up on deck several hours ago. I don't know what it is, but as soon as this storm lets up, Ortega's gonna have it moved to the Aden."

The name evoked something Grahm had told Jake, and he looked back toward the freighter. "What else can you tell me about that ship?"

"She's called the Spirit of Aden. She flies a Yemeni flag." The man stared up earnestly. "That's all I know."

It was becoming increasingly evident that the man lying before Jake was being more cooperative than he had anticipated. "What branch of the U.S. military did you serve in?" Jake continued to grill.

"U.S. Army. How'd you know?"

Jake placed his free hand on one of the gattling gun barrels. "Only a person with extensive military training in aircraft maintenance would possess the know-how to mount one of these to a helicopter."

"It's not something I wanted to do," the man said ashamedly. "I'm not proud of being a party to the things Ortega does. He and most of his crew are nasty sonofabitches. He'd feed me to the sharks if I didn't follow his orders."

"Then why do you work for him?"

"Because I was too stupid to know what I was getting myself into when he hired me to fly this bird. But now it's too late for me to get out. Ortega would have me killed if I ever tried to quit the organization."

The sky lit up with still another eruption of lightning, leaving the pilot's face fully exposed in the dazzling, evanescent glare. He was not a young man, perhaps in his late fifties or early sixties, possibly of Latino descent. Before the light faded completely, Jake was able to discern something in the man's eyes that suggested he was telling the truth.

Another bout of intense electrical activity lit up the night, the crash of thunder so severe that it drowned out all possibility of further dialogue for the moment. Pelted harshly by the driving downpour, Jake felt the helipad actually quiver under the onslaught. A rapid succession of earth-shattering thunderclaps seemed to explode directly overhead, hammering down on the San Carlo as he waited anxiously for the disturbance to subside. The possibility that he risked getting fried out here in the midst of all this metal weighed only briefly on his mind, knowing it was a risk that had to be taken. More than two minutes passed as he hovered over the man, but finally the din abated.

Before Jake opened his mouth to resume the interrogation, the pilot spoke. "You've come to free the people Ortega kidnapped, haven't you?" Not waiting for an answer, he added, "I'll help you any way I can."

"How do I know you can be trusted?" Jake rasped.

The pilot hesitated as thunder rolled overhead again with deafening pandemonium. A procession of receding strobe-like flashes ignited within the curtain of cloud scudding low over the water. "I guess I'd ask the same question if our roles were reversed," he managed to say above the sound. Though he shouted to be heard, the words were barely perceptible. "But you're gonna need help and I'm the only option you have right now. So you can either trust me or not. Take your pick."

Before Jake had time to mull this over, the pilot spoke again, more quickly this time. "Somebody's coming back up here. You better hide before you're seen."

Jake shot a quick look toward the stairs. Someone was shining a light, the beam stabbing the darkness from below. Swiveling his head back, he talked rapidly. "I'll be watching you closely. If you give me away, I won't have any problem shooting both you and whoever is climbing those stairs."

"Hurry!" the pilot urged.

Having no choice but to heed the warning, Jake sheathed the K-bar and scurried back to where the webshot lay, sliding his body back over the edge of the platform until only his head poked above it. The worst part of the storm seemed to have passed now, with the rain starting to taper off and the roar of thunder beginning to fade off toward the west like the dull thumping of a distant battery sending artillery rounds off into the night.

Jake watched as the glow of a flashlight reached the top of the stairs, his right hand reaching out onto the helipad deck and resting on the stock of the webshot should he need it. The light danced along jerkily as its holder moved to join the pilot. Jake's heart pounded heavily, all his senses on full alert for any signs of betrayal by the man offering to help him.

"*Con quien estas, Fernando?*" the interloper said, the beam from the flashlight playing briefly over the pilot's face. "*Yo escuche voces!*" Jake couldn't tell if it was the same man as before, but he understood the words. *Who were you talking to, Fernando? I heard voices.*

Fernando was back on his feet, appearing to be working on the gattling gun once again. "I'm surprised you were able to hear me at all above the thunder," Fernando said loud enough for Jake to hear. "I was reminding you not to come back up here unless you had the coffee I asked for."

The other man handed something over to Fernando. "Why are you talking in English?"

"Old habits die hard, Antonio. Don't forget, I spent more than twenty years working for the U.S. Army."

Fernando paused, and Jake saw him bring something to his lips.

"That's good!" Fernando said, continuing to keep the conversation in English, his voice sounding light and jubilant. "Colombian coffee is the best in the world."

Jake remained at the ready, keeping his finger poised on the webshot trigger should he have to use it. For the most part, the snaring device was his current weapon of choice. Though it would not be nearly as effective as the USP-9, it would be non-lethal and far less noisy, and the last thing he wanted was to alert the others aboard the San Carlo that their vessel had been infiltrated by an unfriendly.

"Do you think this weapon will fire?" Antonio asked.

"If it doesn't, Ortega will have my hide."

The wind had now died down considerably, and Jake did not have to strain his ears to discern everything being said. From his place of concealment downwind of the two men, the sound of the conversation drifted directly at him. And although the helipad was still shrouded in darkness, he was able to perceive Antonio run a hand along one of the gattling gun barrels.

"Ortega will become even more dangerous with such a weapon," Antonio stated. "He will probably use it along with those grenades he likes to toss down on dolphins whenever he sees them."

"Killing dolphins is an obsession with him," Fernando agreed, his voice reflecting disgust. "But I don't think he would attempt to destroy any of those white dolphins we saw when this ship came under attack by the man on the waverunner. Ortega wants to capture them alive."

Jake felt his blood begin to boil. As long as he had breath in his body, he would make sure no one nabbed or harmed any member of the pod ever again. Nevertheless, he kept still, listening intently as he watched Antonio's dark form squat down next to the newly installed weaponry system.

"He is even more interested in getting his hands on the girl we saw riding one of them," Antonio said. His tone held sadness, almost as if he knew that sooner or later Ortega would succeed in doing this.

"You don't want to see the girl get harmed, do you?"

"Of course not." Antonio sounded indignant. "Is your memory beginning to slip, old man? Have…have you forgotten the story already?" he stammered in annoyance.

"Tell me what happened again," Fernando said calmly, almost fatherly. "The story fascinates me."

As Jake listened, he had the impression Fernando was purposely guiding the conversation along solely for his benefit.

"She owed me nothing. I was dying and she saved me." Antonio's voice took on a slight quaver. "Something ruptured inside me when the torpedo struck our boat and flung me into the sea. I could feel my life slipping away. The girl could have left me to die, but she chose to come back, even with her own life still in danger. I know it sounds impossible, but her touch stopped the bleeding and I felt whole again." He paused at the memory. "There are no words to describe what I felt when she did that to me."

"Yes…she did the same thing to everyone in your boat," Fernando said. "But unlike you, the others continue to hate her. I believe they would try to hurt her at the first opportunity."

"They are all ungrateful scum!" Antonio spat bitterly. "It is unfortunate we are forced to work alongside these animals."

"What about the man who fired the torpedo? If you had a chance to kill him, would you do it?"

"I cannot blame him for protecting the girl. Pedro wanted to keep her from escaping the net and we were trying to stop her from doing that. His courage is something to be admired."

"What if Ortega ordered you to kill him?"

Antonio did not immediately answer. Rising to his feet, he moved over to the top of the steps, directing the beam from his flashlight below as if checking to see if anyone was lurking there. Coming back to where Fernando stood, he said, "If Ortega ordered me, I would not do it."

Fernando posed another scenario. "What if the man needed help? Would you help him?"

"Why do you ask such questions?"

"Curiosity, I suppose. I have always been a student of human nature. There is nothing more noble than putting one's own life at risk to aid another in need. Life-threatening situations have a way of molding most men, making some much nobler than others. In Vietnam I saw how danger brought out the best and worst in people."

"What about you? If Ortega told you to use this weapon on the same man, would you do it?"

Even from his position, Jake could not mistake the heavy sigh that escaped the pilot.

"I hope I'm never faced with such a situation," Fernando said.

"But if you were?" Antonio pressed.

"I could never pull the trigger on such an honorable man," Fernando admitted. "If I did, I wouldn't be able to live with myself."

"But then you would be a dead man for not following Ortega's order," Antonio pointed out.

"Yes," Fernando agreed. "And so would you."

Both men remained quiet for a protracted moment, each seeming to ponder that possibility. In the midst of this, Jake's uneasiness escalated further, and he glanced quickly in the direction of the island. Somewhere on that desolate hunk of craggy rock was Omar's base of operations. Everything he had so far learned in the past several days pointed to that one conclusion. If large enough submerged tunnels and hidden subterranean caverns existed beneath the island that could be entered from the sea, it was possible the Islamists had discovered a place to hide a submarine. And because Bashir had been an integral part of that operation, the former terrorist would know exactly where the base was located, including its precise layout. That, and that alone, had to be the reason why mother and daughter had taken Bashir with them. Bashir would lead them to where the villagers had been taken. Omar needed those people for something, otherwise why bring them there? Keeping them alive and under control would become burdensome, a task that would require constant supervision by his small force of men and place an enormous strain on the limited supplies he had on hand.

Jacob's description of the way the conquistadors had enslaved the Tainos for the purpose of working the mines abruptly entered Jake's thoughts. The Spaniards of old had been brutal, slowly starving their captives into a state of emaciation as they worked them to death. A vision of such carnage began to fill his mind with stunning clarity, and now he understood what Omar had in mind. The Islamic radical would use the Haitians to enlarge the chambers and passageways comprising his submarine base until they could no longer serve him. Feeding them would not even be a consideration. They would be used like subhuman chattel the way the conquistadors had used the Tainos.

As Jake thought this out, he couldn't understand why Destiny hadn't asked for his help. Ever since meeting the girl, helping her had become a routine undertaking, something she had readily accepted. It didn't make sense that she would suddenly avoid using his skills in attempting to free the abducted villagers. Certainly that was her main objective in going back to the island in the first place, to free them.

The sound of Fernando's voice pulled Jake from these musings. "What's to become of the men Ortega questions?"

"Knowing Ortega, he will probably kill them. He has already sent the three Haitians found aboard the first boat off to the island along with the people taken from Malique. I'm told they had been successful in catching two of the white dolphins."

"What did they do with them?"

"They lost them."

"How?"

"Two people tricked their way onto their boat and cut the dolphins free. Omar thinks one of them was the same man who attacked us. The dolphin girl was with him when it happened."

As Jake clung to the edge of the helipad, he felt it begin to vibrate, and almost at once the sound of heavy machinery being activated cut the air. Turning his head, he blinked as several floodlights abruptly came alive further back along the ships's stern. A cable was being attached to the lifting rig used for deploying the ship's small tug. It was the same boat he had seen towing the San Carlo's seine, and on its deck was a large object, its bulk wrapped in a tarp. And although the sea had not moderated enough for the crew to pick the tug from its cradle and sling it over the side, Jake had the impression those responsible for launching it were anxious to send it on its way at the first opportunity. As the boat was being readied, Jake saw several deckhands lock their gazes on the freighter as it continued to hold station off their port side. He held no doubts as to where the tug was going.

Spying half a dozen crewmembers moving under the lights, Jake thought it best he leave his present position. If any one of them happened to look up in his direction, there was the possibility he might be spotted.

Re-shouldering the webshot, he pulled himself back along the supports in an effort to reach the stairs, but held up immediately as another light flickered below him. Quickly, he scrambled back amongst the framework, managing to stay hidden in the shadows as another crewmember ascended to the platform above. With the ship continuing to sway in the face of buffeting waves and gusting winds, the crewman staggered awkwardly up the steps as he fought for balance, his arms holding two wooden boxes. After the man had passed, Jake scrambled back to the stairway and moved lower.

Part of the conversation he had just overheard bothered him, and in spite of the danger Ben Loomins and his brother were in, he knew he could not let them die. He had not forgotten Destiny's perspective on the ripples of causation, and inwardly he saw her beautiful face staring up at him, a face full of kindness and compassion. If the brothers were murdered, their deaths would be on his head because he had been directly responsible for their boat breaking down.

Stacked one atop the other at the base of the steps, Jake noticed two more boxes similar to the ones the crewman had been carrying. Lifting the hinged lid on the top box, he discovered a dozen concussion grenades. He was intimately familiar with the type. These were MK3s, tarred cardboard canisters filled with TNT. Such grenades did not throw out shrapnel, relying instead on their shear explosive power for killing.

Plucking two grenades from the container, he hooked the spoons over his utility belt of spare ammunition clips, then closed the lid and moved forward. Seeking entrance inside the ship, he had to jump back into shadow once again as two men suddenly emerged out on deck.

"-cannot wait much longer," one of the men complained. "The cargo must be sent over now."

"Too dangerous," the second man said. "We risk losing the tug if we try to launch her now. Your precious cargo is way too heavy. Without calmer conditions, the tug will swamp or capsize."

"The Aden's captain grows impatient. He has a schedule to maintain."

"So do I," the second man growled. "But I cannot ignore the weather."

Jake was only able to discern their dark forms as they filed past, but something in the voice of the first man held a ring of familiarity, though he had trouble placing it. By contrast, the accent of the second speaker was far different, heavy with a distinct Spanish inflection.

"Where is the rest of that shipment?" the Spaniard demanded. "So far you have only given me half of what you had promised. Have you forgotten our deal?"

"You will get it," the first man hissed back. "I already told you, it is aboard the other ship. But first the bomb-" The speaker abruptly went silent.

The Spaniard immediately halted, seemingly very interested in what had just been said. "A bomb you say. Is that what sits on my ship? A bomb?"

When the first speaker failed to answer, Jake realized a slip of the tongue had just occurred.

"What kind of bomb?" the Spaniard pressed.

"You have no need to know."

"Oh, but I do," the Spaniard blurted heatedly. "Judging from the size of it, it is a very large bomb. An accidental detonation could sink this ship. Lowering it into the sea under these conditions might set it off. Perhaps I should take a look at this bomb."

"We made a deal!" the other man snarled.

The Spaniard began walking again, and the other man followed. Jake listened as their bickering continued, the sound of the argument gradually ebbing away as the men distanced themselves from his place of concealment.

Something seemed to flutter in the back of Jake's mind, and he realized Achilles was speaking to him.

Another vessel approaches, Jay Jay!

What kind of vessel?

It is what those of your kind refer to as a cruiser. It has an overall length of nearly 25 meters.

Jake did a quick mental calculation. An 80-foot yacht was nearing the San Carlo. *Keep me posted on what that vessel is up to, Achilles!*

Slipping into the passageway the arguing men had exited, Jake became aware of the overpowering stench within the ship. Outside the vessel, the smell had not been nearly as offensive, most of it carried off by the gusting winds. But without the movement of air, the odor of rot clung to everything like a thick blanket, making him think back to the prison in Port-au-Prince.

Finding no one to challenge him, he found a companionway as the ship lurched lazily under him. A clamor came faintly to his ears, and as he began to follow the sound it quickly died.

Several doors lined the short hallway Jake found himself in, and just as he was coming abreast of the last door, it suddenly opened. In that instant he came face to face with a swarthy Colombian. Like a deer suddenly caught in the headlights of an oncoming vehicle, the Colombian just stared, a surge of confusion consuming his features as he looked Jake straight in the eyes. Nearly a half-second elapsed before bewilderment turned to shock, but by then it was too late as the point of Jake's right elbow shot up and caught the man directly in the throat. A choking gasp barely left the man's lips as Jake followed the blow up with a crushing uppercut that landed cleanly under the man's chin. The Colombian's head snapped back, and before he could slump, Jake pushed him back through the doorway, stepping into the room the man had been vacating and closing the door behind him.

A tiny bunk adorned one end of the enclosure, and as Jake looked around he could see it was a tiny stateroom, not much bigger than a large closet. Scanning the compartment for items he could use, he spotted a roll of duct-tape lying in one corner, and just above it a filthy rag was draped over a hook protruding from the wall. Grabbing both items, he stuffed the rag into the man's mouth, making sure it stayed in place by placing several wraps of the heavy adhesive around the man's face. The Colombian was out cold and offered no resistance, so it was relatively easy for Jake to finish the job by binding his ankles and wrists and trussing them together behind his back.

Leaving the man on the floor, Jake cracked the door to the room slightly ajar and peeked out, making sure the hallway was empty before venturing out again. Finding another companionway at the end of the hallway, he descended deeper into the ship's hold. No sooner did he reach the bottom of the stairs, the sound of yelling resumed. An intermittent chorus of shouts and screams grew louder as he made his way down another hallway. The corridor turned by ninety degrees, and he found himself facing a steel door with a small glass window smudged with oil and grime.

On the other side of the door, someone hollered angrily. Sidling up to the door, Jake risked a peek through the glass. Six men were strapped to chairs, with one of them currently taking a beating from a pugnacious individual standing over him. Three others of the San Carlo's crew hovered nearby, each of them wearing a cruel grin as they watched what was being done.

Jake recognized the man doling out the beating almost immediately. It was Pedro, the Colombian Zimbola had hammered unconconscious back in Port-au-Prince. With his face and neck still discolored by splotches of heavy bruising, Pedro's expression was hideous, a mask of insane rage as he struck the man tied to the chair before him.

Pedro drew a bunched fist back again, and his victim yelled before the blow landed. "Up yours!"

A dull smack could be heard as Pedro's fist struck, and even with the welts swelling the victim's face, Jake thought he recognized Frank Jaffey.

"Tell him already!" one of the other men screamed. "Give him what he wants!"

Jake swung his eyes along the glass and was momentarily shocked to discover an old acquaintance. Walter McPherson was the last person he would have ever expected to see.

"For god's sake, tell him!" McPherson screamed again.

From what Jake could ascertain, the Colombians were much too engrossed in the punishment being meted out to notice him peering from the other side of the glass, and he did not let the opportunity go unheeded. Deciding that the grenades he had appropriated might get in the way, he removed them from his belt and placed them on the floor. He then unslung the webshot from his shoulder and took a deep breath. Grabbing the doorknob, he flung the door open, and in one smooth motion he leveled the webshot at Pedro and fired.

Even as the net mushroomed open, Jake was across the room in a flash, catching the closest crewman on the temple with the butt of the snaring device before his foe even realized what was happening. Jake slid past as the man fell, and in a single stride he was on a second man with blinding quickness. The crewman was slow to react, and Jake was able to snap a crunching front-kick between the man's legs. Lifted off the floor from the force of the kick, the man was immediately rendered unconscious by a jarring right that had all of Jake's weight behind it.

The last man was more alert, and before Jake could move in on him, the glint of a blade lashing out made him pull up short. Parrying the slash with the barrel of the webshot, he executed a lightning riposte by lunging, jamming the muzzle of the device up into the man's nose. He then pulled back as blood spurted. His adversary bellowed out in pain, lifting an empty hand to a face now appearing like a blood-gutted mask. Startled by the amount of gore smearing his fingers, the man turned flaming eyes on Jake, impaling him with the uncontrolled fury burning deep within them.

Jake recognized the all-consuming insanity, clearly aware of how dangerous the man had become. His opponent reversed his grip on the knife, preparing to rush at him in a foolhardy lunge, all sense of self-preservation completely evaporated by an animalistic need to destroy. The man had a squat, powerful build, making Jake feel like a matador awaiting the charge of an enraged bull.

Calmly, Jake stood his ground as the Colombian lowered his head and let out a horrendous roar before charging. Waiting for the right moment, Jake timed his move perfectly as the man came straight at him. With a natural fluidity, he simultaneously sidestepped and leaned back to avoid the point of the blade as it arced down at his head in an overhand strike. As his foe thundered past, he swung the webshot by its barrel, slamming the stock into the Colombian's head with all the force he could muster. The man dropped like a boulder, all 250-plus pounds of him, falling to the floor facedown and staying there.

It was only then that Jake took stock of how his first victim was faring. Pedro was struggling madly, effectively entangled in the webshot's tenacious netting.

"We've got to stop meeting like this," Jake said, his tone holding a trace of humor as he stepped unhurriedly towards the entrapped man.

Pedro squirmed even harder, answering Jake with a torrent of profane vitriol issued in Spanish. The invective was abruptly silenced as Jake spun the webshot around and casually drove the stock against the back of Pedro's head.

With all four opponents laid out cold, Jake brought his gaze to McPherson. "Now why would a captain in the U.S. navy be out here hunting dolphins?"

For several seconds, McPherson could only stare, his face swollen and bleeding in various places from the beating Pedro had given him. "You...look familiar," he finally stammered.

"I should," Jake remarked bitterly. "Think real hard and maybe you'll remember my name. But right now my main concern is getting all of you off this ship. After that, you're on your own."

"It's him!" someone else said. "He's the sonofabitch I told you about."

Jake gazed over at Ben Loomins, ignoring the comment. The man looked none too pleased to see him in spite of what he had just done.

Drawing his K-bar, Jake moved first to Jaffey, cutting him loose from his bonds. Groggily, Jaffey looked up at him, one eye swollen shut. "Try getting your wits about you and help me free the others." He pointed to the bull-like Colombian he had felled. "Use his knife to cut them loose!"

With all of the battered men still hurting, little was said as everyone was finally set free. Looking through the glass window to the corridor beyond, Jake could see it was still empty. "Sit tight a moment!" he said to Jaffey. With a push on the door, he moved out into the hallway and retrieved the two grenades he had left there, hooking them back onto his belt.

Opening the door again, Jake looked back at the others. "Follow me!"

Moving back the way he had come, Jake kept his pace slow enough for the others to keep up. Upon reaching the main deck, he poked his head out into the night air. Feeling the wind on his face, he could tell it had died down even further, now no more than a moderate breeze.

An analog of Achilles' voice suddenly reverberated in the back of Jake's mind. *Jay Jay, the cruiser is headed for Navassa Island.*

I hear you, Achilles. Thanks for telling me.

Turning to face Frank Jaffey, Jake said. "I'm going to create a diversion. As soon as you hear a ruckus, you and your men get back aboard the tug and get the hell away from here as quick as you can."

Jaffey nodded gravely. "If I ever come out of this with my hide intact, I'll consider the slate wiped clean between you and me. You've cost me a lot of money, fella, but I'm willing to let that slide under the present circumstances."

"Maybe you are, but I'm not," Ben Loomins chastised, glowering at Jake contemptuously. "When this is over, you and me have some unfinished business to settle. I wouldn't be in this mess if it weren't for you."

Jake spoke calmly. "Maybe I'll take you up on it, pal, but right now I'd get ready to move if I were you." With that said, he scurried toward the ship's stern, knowing what had to be done.

With Bashir leading the way, Destiny and her mother moved furtively among the maze of subterranean caverns, illuminating the way before them with the hand-held underwater lights Jimenez had given them. It had been late afternoon by the time Jimenez had finally taken them to within 10 kilometers of Navassa, dropping them off unseen while the sea was beginning to take on a hefty chop. From there they had covered the remaining distance to the island, leaving Jimenez to sail off alone beyond the reach of the approaching storm. Prior to using the hidden subaqueous passageway that led to the thurentra grotto, they had spied the tuna trawler from a distance, and it was then that Hermes and Aphrodite had broken away from the pod to investigate.

Awaiting a report from the albino siblings, the two women had made a cursory inspection of the latest progress carried out on the submerged habitat still under construction, scrutinizing only the upper portion of the structure. At seeing the strange edifice being built by the team of gray dolphins, Bashir's eyes had widened with wonder as he stared through the dive mask Jimenez had lent him.

They had not stayed long, however. Upon receiving observations made by Hermes and his sister, they had moved on again, riding their mounts back out to sea through a noticeable surge that had worked its way into the hidden tunnel. Bashir had trouble holding his breath for even relatively short stretches beneath the surface, and with the full brunt of the storm now upon them, they were forced to keep close to atmosphere where the turbulence was the most brutal. Nevertheless, their mounts easily fought their way through the sweeping waves, eventually locating the same submerged tunnel Destiny had used when she had rescued the Palestinian.

"I must be careful where I step, my beautiful angels," Bashir warned in a low voice. He directed his light at the cavern floor before him, searching the immediate vicinity meticulously before taking a few more steps. "It is possible Yeslam has prepared a few surprises now that he knows his base can be reached from another underwater route."

"What kind of surprises?" Amphitrite asked.

"Yeslam may have placed explosives with a trip-wire. Being angels, you cannot be harmed by such a device. But if I am killed, I will not be able to help you unless I also become an angel."

"We are not angels, Bashir," Destiny corrected softly. "We're as mortal as you are."

Bashir stopped short and turned to face the girl. "Surely you jest with me," he said, refusing to accept what had just been uttered.

"I'm sorry if I have misled you. I would never think to jest over such a matter."

"But...you have the power to heal...the mind as well as the body. I saw you render Kalid unconscious without lifting a hand. Only an angel has such power." In the semi-darkness, Bashir sounded dismally disappointed.

"Yes, you did." Destiny concurred. "But this ability is not entirely mine. I had help."

Bashir's disappointment quickly turned effusive again. "If you had help, then it is only the Almighty Allah who bestows you with such miraculous power. Either way, he both favors and blesses you. Even if you are not an angel as you claim, he treats you as though you truly are one."

Destiny produced a helpless smile. Trying to convince Bashir otherwise was going to be a losing battle. She thought of an appropriate reply, but before she could utter a word, the sound of voices reverberated among the cavern walls.

Bashir turned off his light, and Destiny and Amphitrite did the same. "We must be very cautious from this point on," he said quietly. Just as he finished saying this, a soft glow could be seen emanating from somewhere up ahead. "The main chamber is very close."

The threesome crept silently forward, with Bashir periodically lighting the way to check for booby traps. Another half-minute passed before Amphitrite let out a curt warning. "Do not take another step, Bashir!" She paused. The sudden intuitive flash allowed her to sense the danger that blocked their way. "Shine your light on the ground before you!" She could see it clearly in her mind, directly in front of Bashir.

Bashir stooped low, flicking his light on again. Less than a meter from where he stood, a thin wire was stretched tautly less than 12 centimeters above the floor. Moving forward, he traced the wire and located an object lodged tightly into a crevice off to one side. With great care, he worked it free, then moved it carefully away from the rock wall to put slack in the wire attached to it. Holding the thing, he regarded Amphitrite with increased awe. "Allah allows you to see through divine eyes," he whispered reverently. "Yeslam has seen fit to place a Claymore mine in this tunnel. He has six such devices. Hopefully this will be the only one barring our way."

Amphitrite said nothing as Bashir gave the trip-wire a soft tug, removing the detonation cap from the mine. Gently, he placed the Claymore off to one side where it would no longer pose a threat. Turning off his light, he crept forward once more. The glow from up ahead had grown stronger, and seeing the way before them was becoming easier.

Destiny felt concern. Unlike her mother, she had failed to sense the threat, though she suspected the reason why. Her mind had become too clouded with other matters. Achilles had relayed recent events to the others, and through them she knew that Jay Jay had come back to Navassa to find her. The very thing she had wanted to avoid was now rearing its ugly head, a thing that put the man she loved in great danger. *No, it was more than just danger. Jay Jay would die.*

The future had been clearly shown, memorialized on the chamber ceiling behind the waterfall, painted long ago by an unknown but clairvoyant Tainos artist. Clutched within the jaws of a fierce Bengal tiger, a man was depicted being torn apart. When she had first discovered it at a much younger age, the sight had depressed her, and later on she had found it necessary to fabricate a makeshift ladder so that she could climb up to the overhead mural and cover it with mud. But at the time, little did she know she would fall in love with the stranger shown there.

Deep in her heart, however, she knew that such an act would do little to change what had been prophesied long ago. Whether or not that future could be altered as Jacob and her mother had often contended, she did not know, but now more than ever she would use every fiber of her being to forestall the event she feared most.

- 111 -

Jake used the cover of darkness to his advantage, keeping to the shadows and slipping unseen to the ship's larboard side. Moving swiftly, he came across a cluster of 55-gallon drums strapped securely to the deck. Intermingled with the rank odor of rotting fish was the unmistakable smell of diesel. Using his K-bar, he pried the cap from one of the drums, then cut the straps holding it in place. Tipping the drum on its side, he let the fuel splash out onto the deck.

Under the spotlights further back toward the stern, he could see the tug still sitting in its cradle, a small group of men standing next to it. With the possibility of a hydrogen bomb resting within the small vessel, Jake felt the full burden of what he was up against, and it pressed down upon him like a thousand tons of earth. One way or another, he had to keep the tug from being launched.

With overwhelming purpose, he pulled one of the grenades from his belt and pulled the pin. Letting the grenade slip from his fingers, he turned and raced forward toward the ship's prow, making a mental count in his head as he did so. Just before reaching four, he ducked down behind a crate of heavy hawser.

The ensuing blast sent a shock wave through the air, and a split second later several oil drums erupted in a titanic explosion of heat and light. A wall of flames abruptly engulfed the side of the San Carlo, further enhanced by a succession of secondary blasts as other drums flared. Amid the expanding inferno, shouts could be heard as men rushed to see what was happening.

Satisfied, Jake hied to the other side of the ship to observe the men he had freed taking advantage of the confusion. One by one, they climbed down the caving ladder leading to Jaffey's towing vessel. All too slowly another minute passed before the boat got underway, and with a lumbering motion far too subdued for Jake's taste, it began to veer off to the south.

Remaining hidden in shadow, Jake turned to study the havoc he had caused. Crewmen were scurrying like ants to get the inferno under control. The flames had spread and were licking high, engulfing a sizeable portion of the ship's superstructure and effectively blocking access to the flight deck. And even though a margin of safety separated him from the firestorm, the heat from it was rapidly becoming unbearable.

With several options open to him, Jake chose the one that seemed most sensible under the present situation. Doing something to sabotage the transfer of the bomb could wait. The fire was delaying that transfer, and if the Colombians failed to bring it under control, it was probable such a transfer would not take place at all. Helping Destiny was now his main priority, and if he could help her free the people abducted, he would refocus his efforts on making sure the bomb did not fall into the wrong hands. Right now it was crucial that he join up with her as quickly as possible. She was much too naïve to understand the type of men she would be facing. And if he did not get to her at once, she and her mother would surely get themselves killed.

Slipping from his place of concealment with the stealth of an eidolon, he strode rapidly to the starboard railing, nearly colliding headlong into two crewmen looking to get clear of the flames. Both men came to an immediate halt, staring in stunned silence at Jake's presence. Fully exposed under the harsh glare of the inferno, their expressions turned to alarm.

Jake was the first to react, automatically resorting to the physical assets that had made him a standout athlete, those being speed and quickness. Snapping a front kick to the genitals of the man on his left, he shifted his body weight a millisecond later to flatten the man on his right with a left hook that struck like lightning. Not taking the time to appraise his work, he pulled the dive mask that had been hanging around his neck up onto his forehead.

Someone shouted. Almost immediately, something pinged off a metal support adjacent to Jake's head, making him duck back into shadow. A hail of bullets followed, caroming off a cluster of steel members directly in front of him and sending a shower of sparks flying. Snatching the USP-9 from the holster riding his thigh, he tore the watertight plastic wrap from the submachine pistol. Normally, the weapon would have fired even during immersion, but using a protective seal gave him an added degree of assurance it would still operate in spite of its previous submergence.

From the direction of the ship's bow, two more members of the crew were moving toward him. Illuminated by the flames, their faces glowered with rancor, one of them wielding an axe, the other an AK-47.

Cocking his weapon, Jake opened up with a short burst. One of the rounds caught the man holding the axe, spinning him around and knocking him to the deck. Abruptly, the man's partner dove for cover.

More shouts reached Jake's ears, and he turned to see two more assailants making their way along the gangway behind him. Letting loose with another burst, he stopped them in their tracks, scoring a hit on one of them.

With deft quickness, he removed the spent clip and inserted another from his utility belt. Pivoting back around, he spotted the man with the AK poking his head out from behind a bulkhead. Jake brought his weapon to bear and squeezed the trigger, spewing half a dozen rounds. The man managed to retract his head just in time to avoid being hit. For good measure, Jake spun around and sent a spray behind him again. Jamming the weapon back into its holster and pushing down the Velcro flap that secured it, he pulled his dive mask into place. Calmly, he pulled the remaining MK3 from his belt and pulled the pin. Almost delicately, he placed the grenade at his feet just before vaulting over the railing.

Keeping the dive mask pressed firmly against his face, he dropped twenty feet into the sea's cooling embrace, happy to escape the inferno's searing heat. Ten feet below the surface, Achilles was right there waiting for him.

A cascade of bullets ripped the water above. Jake felt a mild sting on one of his buttocks, but didn't think the skin had been penetrated. Slowed by the denser medium of water, several rounds zipped dangerously close before losing velocity. Languidly, they fell away.

The machine gun fire abruptly stopped as a weak shock wave whipped past, and Jake knew the grenade had detonated, the force of the blast carrying down from the ship's deck and rippling out into the surrounding water.

Take me to Destiny, Achilles!

The young dolphin did not move, appearing not to have read the request hanging in Jake's thoughts.

Still submerged, Jake petitioned Achilles again, surprised that the juvenile had not heeded him. Keeping the appeal at the center of his mind, he focused on a parallel thought. *Achilles, I-*

I am very sorry, Jay Jay... but I...I cannot do that.

Jake was astounded at the intensity of sorrow resounding in the dolphin's response. If dolphins were capable of crying, he could have sworn he was sensing a monumental amount of emotional pain emanating from the albino.

What's the matter, Achilles?

Achilles did not immediately answer, and Jake suddenly became aware of the mental barrier being erected, something analogous to a wall of solid steel through which nothing could penetrate. The depth of emotion Jake had been touched with was now gone, and an aura of sterility seemed to surround the newly evolved cetacean. The bond that had connected them was beginning to break.

I have been instructed to take you back to your vessel, Jay Jay. The thought was delivered like a blast of polar air, cold and devoid of all warmth.

Tell me what's troubling you, Jake pressed, grabbing hold of Achilles' dorsal.

Achilles turned and gathered speed. He did not respond to the question.

Can you hear me, Achilles? What's wrong?

Achilles would not answer, and Jake could only hold on as he was pulled through the sea with disconcerting swiftness.

- 112 -

The inexplicable illness had eventually passed, and Nick Henderson felt restless. Unable to sleep, he arose from the sleeping bag he had laid out on the sand and walked to the water's edge. Almost an hour had elapsed since nightfall had descended, and with an intermittent cloud cover obstructing most of the starlight, the cove was very dark.

Wading out into the water until the wavelets washed up around his knees, he looked to where he thought the thurentra lay submerged, his mind continually churning over the treasure the organism produced. He had purposely kept to himself ever since Javolyn had put him and the others ashore, and with Parker and Phillipe currently holed up in Destiny's tiny thatched cottage, Henderson could now conduct the search he had yearned to undertake, this time unobserved and without interference. With all of those annoying white dolphins gone, he was free to investigate the places where the gold would most likely be hidden.

Glancing behind him, he eyed the soft glow emanating from the doorway of the small abode. More than likely, Jeffrey and Phillipe were engaged in a game of chess, something Phillipe seemed to enjoy playing. Regardless, with more of that migraine-inducing dolphin art hanging obtrusively along the cottage's interior walls, there was no way he was going inside to see what they were up to in any event.

Leaving the water, Henderson walked back to where his sleeping bag lay, pulling his mask, fins and snorkel from the duffel bag situated next to it. Rummaging further, he groped for the dive light amid other personal items, finally locating it near the bottom of the bag. The dive light was fully charged and would last him a little over an hour.

With the dive gear in hand, he made his way down the beach, following the sound of the waterfall. The roar of plunging water gradually grew louder, eventually drowning out the softer sounds of nocturnal animals foraging among the lush foliage that dominated the cove walls.

He had given it a lot of thought, and through a process of elimination, he had come up with the best place to hide a cache of gold within the cove's confines. For one, it would be the dolphins that did the hiding, not Jacob. The gold had been hidden fairly quickly, and with Jacob occupied with his guests, the Haitian could not possibly have moved it. That meant the cache had to be submerged. And if that were actually the case, what better place than the base of the falls where eddies of aerated turbulence would obscure underwater visibility.

With his dive booties already on, Henderson made his way close to the base of the falls and attempted to slip his swim fins on in the manner he had seen Javolyn use. Hopping on one leg, he stumbled off balance and fell down, skinning his knee on a rock as he did so. Cursing in anger, he struggled some more, finally succeeding in donning the rest of the gear. Tentatively, he stepped clumsily into the water. He had always hated having to walk erect with ungainly fins strapped to his feet, and with the rocky shore before him, the task was made all the more difficult. Unable to see the curtain of falling water within the backdrop of night, he was suddenly unnerved by the sound. It thundered ominously like the rumble of some enormous lurking beast.

The dive light did not immediately come on when he flicked the switch, and he had to smack it with his palm several times before it came to life. Lowering his face into the water, he directed the beam against the rocky bottom and pushed himself further out, his excitement over what he might find overcoming his fear of the ebony blackness that lay beyond.

Henderson had been disappointed when McPherson had failed to show back at Port-au-Prince. Surely the signal emitted by the DBT had been strong enough to follow. But Henderson had a more direct way of contacting the naval captain, and hopefully the message he had sent had been received by now. Unbekownst to Javolyn and the others, he had managed to send off an electronic communiqué just before the Avenging Angel had sailed from Port-au-Prince. The unit he had provided McPherson had an additional feature he had thought prudent to install, and that was an electronic text receiver, one that automatically translated the communique's encryption.

He had still been nauseous when he had transmitted a second message via the wireless laptop he always kept close at hand. That was right after Javolyn had dumped him off. And while Parker had glanced his way at the time, Parker had no way of knowing what he had been up to. The special program he had developed did the encoding. He knew he had been taking a risk in sending it, but then again it was a risk he had felt worth taking. Surely the naval captain would not try anything underhanded and grab the entire booty for himself, especially since there would be plenty to go around. Now all McPherson had to do was home in on the DBT signal. Out of sight within his duffel bag, the DBT was still transmitting.

Cautiously, Henderson swam toward the thundering falls, now keeping his head above the surface. Shining his light out in front of him, he spotted the curtain of aerated water, making sure to stay well clear of it. Finning to his left, he skirted the gravity-driven deluge. Eddies tugged at him with surprising force, and he had to work hard to avoid being sucked under. The far end of the waterfall was suddenly before him, and he kicked with all his strength to gain the backside. There was still a good amount of turbulence here, and he hugged the rock wall to escape being pulled toward where the flow was heaviest.

The rock behind the waterfall was relatively smooth, and he had trouble locating a finger hold where he could rest. A small projection was suddenly before him, and gratefully he grasped it. For the next two minutes he breathed heavily, regaining his strength. Fully rested, he began to make exploratory dives along the face of the rock, periodically dropping to the bottom and looking for anything unusual. The water was not very deep, and the base of the rock was strewn with sand and pebbles. Hampered by poor underwater visibility, however, he had no success at finding anything that remotely resembled grains of gold.

At one point during his search, he stumbled across an opening in the cliff face, a rift wide enough to easily accommodate him. Ebony blackness surrounded him as he made his way between the rock, and even the beam of his light failed to penetrate the turbidity below him by more than a few feet. Fighting back his fear, he continued on into the confined space, discovering there to be no flow at his present location.

The fissure began to narrow as he penetrated deeper, and as he finned on, it changed direction. Rounding a bend, he distanced himself further from the base of the falls. As he studied the layout before him, he suddenly became excited, for he knew this would make a perfect place to hide treasure.

Aiming the light above him, he gauged the overhead clearance, daunted by the tight space. A succession of rocky crags overhung the water, providing air pockets that afforded little room for maneuvering. Willing himself forward, perhaps another thirty feet, he saw where the crevice appeared to end. A short distance out in front of him, the rock met the water.

Filling his lungs, he jackknifed his body awkwardly, his legs flailing spastically above him. The attempt caused him to bash one of his legs against the rock, and skinning a shin, he cried out in pain. Abruptly, he pulled up and massaged the stricken area. Being in such cramped quarters made him nervous. He was suddenly not so eager to do this, and he almost decided then and there to abort the dive. But with the promise of riches beckoning him on, he overcame his fear, but just barely.

He jackknifed again, this time succeeding in getting his fins below the water. Kicking himself downward, he maintained contact with the rock wall using his free hand. He had only descended a few feet when something glinted below him. With his heart pounding, he stabbed his dive light deeper. He could not believe what he was seeing. A glittering mass inundated the bottom. At this location, the water was not very deep, maybe just over his head.

Overcome with joy, he plunged his fingers into the material, pulling up a heaping handful and bringing it close to his face. Shiny grains spilled loosely from his palm. Jamming his hand back into the mass, he had trouble digging down. The granular substance was very heavy and resisted him.

Needing air, he rose back to the surface and lifted the dive mask from his face. Holding the light to the grains held in his hand, he stared in wonder. He was utterly amazed at his good fortune. It was gold all right. And if he were not mistaken, there were lesser quantities of platinum mixed in.

Unable to contain himself, he took another deep breath and dropped down again. For the next ten minutes he busied himself with gauging the total size of the treasure. It filled the bottom of the cavity for almost 25 feet. In his estimation there had to be tons of it below him. He was going to be rich beyond his wildest dreams.

Filled with an elation he had never before experienced, Henderson spat out his snorkel and let out a triumphant cry. *He was going to be rich! Far richer than anything he had ever imagined!*

Swept away with emotion, he barely heard himself above the rumble of the falls. In his excitement, he accidentally slammed the dive light against one of the outcroppings. Euphoria quickly turned to panic when the light flickered briefly before going out altogether.

Frantically, he struck the light with his palm. When it failed to come on, he tried the switch, jiggling it on and off like a frenzied madman. The dive light would not cooperate. Screaming out in frustration, he thrashed around, abruptly smacking the top of his skull into an overhead projection. Clutching his head with both hands, he applied pressure against the injury, groaning in agony and nearly blacking out. The pain gradually ebbed into a dull throb, and it was only then that he realized he had let go of the light.

Groping around with renewed violence, he tried to find it. Being slightly buoyant, the light had to be floating close to him, but try as he might, he failed to locate it. Completely disoriented, he didn't know which way to go to get out of the fissure. With a strength born of shear panic, he clawed his way along one of the walls, and in moments he banged his head again. *Shit!* He was going in the wrong direction. With his mind in a tizzy, he reversed direction, losing contact with the wall. In desperation, he kicked hard with his fins, only to slam up against the rock again. Abruptly, he stopped, panting hard and frozen with fear.

Cut off from all light, the bass rumble of the falls dominated his senses, and his mind began to careen in disarray. Something seemed to brush up against his body, making him flinch. The realization that he was not alone struck home with frightening force, and he kicked his legs insanely to fend it off. Within seconds he grabbed hold of himself, wondering if his imagination was playing tricks on him. *No!* He had definitely felt something touch him. The thought sent an immense shiver coursing through his body, and the illness he had experienced hours earlier suddenly returned with a vengeance.

He tensed again. Whatever had touched him was back. Treading water, he moved quickly to get away from it. There was a presence close at hand.

Unable to elude it, he was suddenly besieged by a strange image that sprang to the forefront of his thoughts. Instinctively he took refuge in it, instantly understanding there was another means of escape. The thing he had seen shimmering in the night sky high above Port-au-Prince was there before him again. All at once he was moving, flowing along one of those lines that seemed to connect with infinity. Yes, he would travel at the speed of light to get away.

But something was hindering him. It had caught up and latched on, squeezing with a pressure that was incomprehensible. Dizzily, he grabbed his temples and fought for breath. His head was going to explode.

Bearded men wearing steel armor and crude metal hats were storming past. Armed with lances, swords, and blunderbusses, they charged through a pristine tropical forest, some of them with large canines on leashes. They were after something, their faces rancorous with brutality.

Bowled over by their passage, he could see what they were chasing. Scantily clad men and women, small in stature, were scrambling for their lives. Body parts were scattered across the forest floor, and those unfortunate enough to be run down were being hacked to pieces, their screams filling the air. A massacre quickly unfolded before him, and as he looked on, he found himself oddly stirring to the gruesome slaughter, much too fascinated to avert his gaze.

A young girl lay sprawled on the ground next to him. She was gasping for breath, unable to go another step. Something in one her hands caught his attention, and he saw at once that it was a small idol made of solid gold. Transfixed by the sight, he rose to his feet and stared down, drawing the sword he carried. Confronted with two choices, he chose the one most satisfying. A single tear trickled down one of the girl's cheeks as her eyes met his, but he felt only pleasure as his arm swung the blade in a killing stroke. He would have his gold. The girl's life was of no importance.

The scene faded, and once again he became aware of the pressure inside his skull. It had intensified. The presence was causing it, something unseen yet nevertheless there. Looming all around him, it swarmed in upon his senses, a sentience immeasurably vast. In the blink of an eye, he was able to grasp its fundamental nature, and with startling clarity he suddenly came to accept the things Jacob had hypothesized. Strangely, the presence was not vengeful. He was not even certain it was aware of itself. Nevertheless, it had a purpose, and that purpose was to survive. In fulfilling that purpose it would bring into balance those entities threatening its existence. And if the imbalance could not be corrected, then the offending entities would simply be destroyed.

It began to dawn on him that the presence was speaking. It had always spoken to him, though he had never noticed. It had a voice. The rumble of the falls was its voice. No, that was only partly right. There was so much more to it than that, something all encompassing in its profundity. He was beginning to see it clearly now, and he could not discount the rustling of the trees nor the whisper of the wind. Though soft and lilting, was the serenade of a songbird any less important than the roar of the surf? And yet these were only some of the things that gave it voice.

With his mind now reeling in the midst of such comprehension, Henderson began to tremble with renewed intensity. Only then did the possibility that he might never again see the light of day enter his thoughts.

- 113 -

Jake was totally caught off guard. Upon climbing back aboard the Avenging Angel he found his vessel to be completely abandoned. A feeling of total dismay gripped him as he conducted a frantic search of every compartment, only to discover there was no one aboard. The North Sea trawler had been left adrift, completely deserted.

Crestfallen, he sat down, his mind trying to piece together what might have happened. Adding to the mystery was Achilles' recent behavior. The young albino had broken off all communication with him, remaining silent in the face of all Jake's queries.

The return trip to the Angel had taken much longer than expected, mainly because the vessel had drifted a significant distance from where Jake had left it. With the clarity of hindsight, he realized Achilles had been searching for the Angel, apparently trying to locate it by reaching out with his biosonar in all directions. Upon finding it, the dolphin had simply dropped him off at the stern end and then swum away.

Jake climbed up to the pilothouse and got a fix on the boat's current position. He could see that the wind and waves had driven it nearly 11 kilometers from where he had left it. Making a few educated assumptions about the vessel's rate of drift during and after the storm, he calculated that the helm had to have been deserted for at least 90 minutes for the Angel to drift that distance. A glance at his watch told him the boat had been abandoned somewhere between 10 and 15 minutes after he had left it. Without anyone to steer the vessel into the oncoming sea, it was a wonder the Angel had not swamped or capsized during the gale.

With this in mind, he could only surmise that hostile forces had managed to storm the Angel and take captive all those on board. *But how?* Zimbola and Hector had been armed to the teeth, prepared to defend the boat at the slightest sign of trouble. At the very least, Zimby would have spotted the approach of another vessel on radar and taken evasive action.

Jake was dismal. None of it made any sense.

Combing the vessel, he could find nothing that would indicate a skirmish had taken place. Everything was pretty much in order, everything except for the missing crew. No bullet holes, no overt damage, and no signs of blood. And Zimbola would never leave his beloved boat under any circumstances. No matter what, he would have held position, standing by for Jake to return.

With these things overwhelming his thoughts, he stared off into the distance. The flicker of a lazy glow emanated from the direction of Navassa. The fire he had started on the San Carlo was still ablaze, though from the intensity of the light, he judged that it would soon burn itself out.

Bringing his eyes to the instrument panel, he noticed that the engine was still idling. Dully, he stared at the gauge, contemplating his next move.

The radio suddenly hissed, interrupting his thoughts. A garble of static blared from the speaker. "…you listening…Avenging..gel."

Jake reached for the microphone, prepared to answer if someone was actually hailing him. A good ten seconds of unbearable silence followed before the radio hissed again. "…advise you respond…ing Angel if you ever want …your comrades alive."

Eagerly, Jake depressed the transmit button. "This is the Avenging Angel. Please identify yourself, whoever you are?"

Another burst of words flowed from the speaker, this time coming in crisp and clear. "Intruding into the affairs of a sovereign nation is not a wise thing to do, Avenging Angel." The voice sounded content, self-assured, and Jake realized he had heard that same voice before.

Jake waited for more, but the person behind the voice fell silent.

"What do you want?"

The reply came back quickly. "The same thing we all want. Satisfaction."

Another pause ensued, and Jake fought down his growing irritability. "Just state your business."

"You will come ashore at the nearby island. You will come to the base of the old lighthouse on the eastern side. And most importantly, you will come alone."

"And if I don't?"

A heavy pause hung in the air. "Then your friends will pay the price of your obstinancy," the voice said smugly. "All ten of them."

Jake's mind was sent spinning. *What was going on here?* There had only been eight people aboard the Angel when he had left it. Zimby, Hector, Grahm, Jacob, Hennington, Trebek, Emmanuel, and Lucette. But the voice on the radio had said there were ten. *Was it possible Destiny and her mother had been captured as well?*

He brought his gaze back to the glow many miles away. It was now very faint. Lifting the microphone back to his mouth, he said. "I'll do as you say. But harm a hair on their heads, and you'll wish you'd never been born."

Not waiting for a reply, Jake turned off the radio. He couldn't help berate himself for having left Zimby and the others to fend for themselves while he had gone off to play hero. And now they were going to pay with their lives for his stupidity.

Filled with self-loathing, he engaged the prop and turned the Angel around, bringing it on a new heading.

- 114 -

The sound of suffering reached Destiny's ears long before the misery could be seen. The men in the adjacent cavern were as cruel as those depicted in the cave murals back at Gaia. The cry of pain had come from Samuel. He had only sought to protect Louwanda and had been struck down.

Bashir was the first to intervene, leaping on ahead of Destiny and her mother. "Stop this insanity at once," Bashir yelled. Striding boldly from the darkened passageway, he stared reproachfully at Kalid. "You will invoke Allah's wrath if you do not release these people immediately."

Kalid turned, his mouth hanging agape at seeing Bashir again. His eyes widened further at the sight of the two women entering the chamber behind him.

Destiny took in her surroundings at a glance. The subterranean grotto was very large and well lit in those areas where human occupation existed. A series of electric bulbs were strung out at intervals along a portion of the perimeter. Closest to her, other lights were positioned along the lowest stalactites hanging from the cavern roof. Further back along one of the walls, rows of wooden crates were stacked high, and adjacent to the crates was a makeshift eating area outfitted with cooking grill, two tables and foldout chairs. Beyond that, an array of sleeping cots took up more space. Droning dully in the background, the low hum of a generator could be heard. The light revealed a nearby pool of water, its surface perfectly flat and giving off a silvery sheen under the electric glow. The pool appeared to be substantial in width, extending off into a void of inky blackness where the light could not reach.

Three other bearded men also turned to witness this sudden intrusion, each of them holding a rifle. Samuel lay at the feet of one of them, moaning in pain.

Herded amid a grouping of stalactites were twelve Haitians. Several of them were struggling under the weight of a wooden crate each had been forced to carry. At seeing Destiny and Amphitrite, their anguish abruptly turned hopeful. Destiny could see that most of them were from Malique, but not all. Standing among the villagers were the three crewmen she had seen aboard Ben Loomins' boat.

Overcoming his initial shock, one of Kalid's constituents stepped forward, his eyes flitting pensively between Bashir and the two women. Destiny studied his face, profoundly moved by the man's drooping, lugubrious eyes that resembled those of a bloodhound.

The man brought his gaze back to Kalid, who continued to stare speechless at Destiny. "Do my eyes deceive me or has Bashir arisen from the dead?"

The question had been spoken in Arabic, and though Destiny did not speak such a language, she was able to translate the question through her mental link with the albinos. The albinos were currently keyed into her senses and those of her mother, observing and listening to what was taking place.

With the capacity to converse in numerous human languages, they continued to interpret what was being said.

The man with the bloodhound eyes spoke again when Kalid did not reply. "Has Satin grabbed your tongue that you cannot speak, Kalid?"

Kalid finally found voice, and his words were sodden with fear. "Keep your distance from the girl, Gullu. I do not advise touching her. To do so is very dangerous." He pivoted his head slightly, staring at Amphitrite with wary eyes. "The other woman may be equally dangerous."

"They are only dangerous to those who oppose them," Bashir said, his tone simmering with haughtiness. "What you see standing before you are two of Allah's messengers." He riveted Kalid with reproachful eyes. "Do you still refuse to accept the power Allah imparts to his angels?"

Gullu looked back at Destiny, studying her intently before transferring his gaze to Amphitrite. "Do you profess these women to be angels, Bashir, servants of the Almighty?"

Destiny detected mockery in his tone, though confusion filled his face.

"Yes," Bashir said, his manner softening. "They will show you the way as they did me."

Gullu turned back to Kalid. "Tell me what he speaks of?"

"Bashir has deluded himself into believing these women are angels. He claims they have the power to heal mortal wounds in seconds."

"Only Allah has such power," Gullu said scornfully.

Gullu stepped closer to Kalid, peering into his eyes. "Why do these women frighten you, Kalid?" He posed the question as if amused.

A flood of shame washed over Kalid's face. "Over a day ago the younger one knocked me unconscious when Yeslam ordered me to grab her. She was with Bashir in these caverns. Yeslam believes she is armed with a concealed taser capable of delivering a severe electrical shock."

Gullu's expression immediately clouded. "Yeslam told me none of this. Up to now, he led me to believe Bashir was killed during your little escapade along the Haitian coast."

Bashir laughed heartily. "Yeslam has shown himself to be the liar he truly is. He seeks to hide the truth from those willing to follow him. Angels of Allah have no need of concealed weapons. In their hands lies the power behind all of Paradise."

Bashir spun around to regard both women. "Perhaps it is time to demonstrate Allah's power to these non-believers."

Destiny had no desire to deny Bashir his delusion. Both she and her mother were perfectly content to let him act as their spokesman. Some inner, yet inexplicable sense told them Bashir had to perpetuate such a falsehood if they were going to free the villagers.

Destiny felt the full synergy of all the albino minds come together in something akin to a controlled explosion, the force of it reaching out to her and Amphitrite. Without understanding the actual mechanism that caused it, a hologram of the dolphin art materialized out over the subterranean pool, pulsations of multicolored light dancing swiftly along the twisting and intertwined curvature of the 3-dimensional geometry.

Bashir pointed, drawing all eyes to the breathtaking image. "Search your feelings as you look upon the power of God."

Gullu and Kalid stared, suddenly mesmerized.

A howl of pain broke the air, and Destiny saw two of the bearded men closest to the villagers drop their weapons and sink to their knees, each clutching his head as if struck by an invisible demon.

"Search your feelings!" Bashir repeated imploringly, his voice rising further and quavering with emotion. "Ask yourself if it is truly Allah's way to destroy and kill."

The hologram continued to hang in the air, holding the attention of everyone except the two fallen men. Amphitrite stepped forward, coming to stand before the one called Gullu. Gullu seemed not to notice, spellbound by the thing floating over the water. Placing a hand on his forehead, she said, "Let go of your hate. Hate is an illness that prevents you from being whole." She was about to say, *"Holding onto it will impair your ability to think clearly and will destroy your soul forever,"* but she sensed something within the man before she could convert the thought into words.

The essence Amphitrite was feeling was laid bare, easily read much like an open book. And in reading the man, she was suddenly reminded of Chester Hennington, for here was another victim caught up in the web of circumstance. The threat of violence against Gullu's family back in Afghanistan was a tangible thing, and it was this threat that had forced him into abetting the people he served. But the shadow of tragedy was also evident, for Gullu's son had been murdered by these same people.

Removing her hand, Amphitrite stepped over to Kalid and performed the same ritual, quickly sensing the man would no longer present a danger.

Destiny remained immobile, watching her mother move to the last standing man. The two fallen men were beyond help. Tormented by something unseen, they continued to writhe convulsively on the cavern floor.

Bashir grabbed Kalid by the arm. "Where are the others?" he demanded.

Kalid stared enraptured, his gaze still clinging to the hologram of lights, and Bashir had to shake him hard to get a mumbled response. "Azzum and several others have taken the submarine. The rest of the team is in the passageway that leads to the surface."

Bashir turned quickly to Destiny. "Our work is not yet complete."

Yes, Destiny thought, *our work is far from over.* Even from down here she could feel Erzulie's iniquity pressing still closer. Erzulie and her son were now on the island, and there were others nearby who pulsed with the same intensity of evil. In unison they presented an incredibly powerful force, an alliance that might actually defeat the pod's combined strength. And if that were to happen, millions of people were going to be killed. Forged from the dark side of creation, the entities they were pitted against could never be turned.

And with the pod's latest member purposely kept from the impending fight, she wondered if they had any chance of winning at all. She knew she was being selfish, knowing her actions were jeopardizing everything they had worked so hard to achieve. But she could not bear the thought of Jay Jay dying.

Expelling a long breath, Destiny let the albinos channel another surge of energy through her. It was then that the hologram floated past everyone, disappearing into the tunnel that would take them to the surface above.

Bashir ran over to where Samuel lay and helped him to his feet. He started to move in the direction the hologram had taken, but suddenly stopped. Stooping, he picked up the two firearms dropped by the fallen men. Although both men had stopped writhing, they were breathing hard, their hands still pressed tightly against their skulls as though attempting to subdue the demons trapped within them. Bashir stared down contemptuously at one of them. "It does not surprise me that you feel only pain, Mahmood. Those who are truly evil cannot be saved." Walking over to the edge of the pool, he flung the weapons into the water.

An odd feeling descended on Destiny as she watched the guns sink from view. Almost at once she realized Jay Jay was still in danger. *Yes,* she clearly felt it now. Jay Jay was being lured to the island, and that was the last place she wanted him to be. The thought caused her to break her focus, and she suddenly realized she was failing the others, failing the purpose she had been destined to fulfill.

The entire planet may be lost if you try to help him. It was her mother speaking. *What has already been implanted in the fabric of true reality may very well be unchangeable, my daughter.* The thought Amphitrite was conveying was not meant to chasten, though it did hold immense emotional distress.

Destiny could not help herself. Strangely she was filled with feelings she was unable to suppress. *Forgive me, mother, but I must go to him.*

Sprinting to the water's edge, Destiny dove just as Hercules broke the surface. Molding herself to the albino's back, she held on as the dolphin powered into the depths.

- 115 -

Jake brought the Avenging Angel around to the east on the darkened ocean, holding to a wide arc that kept the vessel well clear of the San Carlo. It was important he stay beyond the range of the tuna trawler's radar, especially since Ortega had at his disposal a helicopter armed with an electronic gattling gun. He thought it prudent to assume the fire he had started had not engulfed the ship's helipad. And he could never be sure the pilot would actually defy Ortega's order to use the weapon against him.

Even if he were spotted on radar, Jake reasoned, the Colombians had no way of knowing the identity of his vessel or who was aboard it. The Angel would be seen as a blip on the screen, just another boat making its way through the Windward Passage in the middle of the night.

It was understandable that the San Carlo's captain would be enraged over the fact his vessel had been infiltrated and sabotaged. But while some of his crew had come into direct contact with the man responsible for damaging his ship and freeing the dolphin hunters, they had also seen that same man leap over the side. With no other boats close to the San Carlo, they might assume the man had either drowned or been forced to swim to the nearby island.

Steering the Angel to the eastern side of Navassa, he turned the bow towards the west. With a portion of the island now between him and the tuna trawler, he would remain hidden from the San Carlo's radar.

As he brought the Angel still closer to the shoreline, his own radar picked up another vessel in close proximity to the island's southeast side near Lulu Bay. Continuing on in, he closed to within 100 meters of the shore before dropping anchor.

His vessel rocked stiffly in the swells as the Dansforth bit, and he heard the surf hissing against the nearby bluffs, every so often drowned out by the boom of a crashing breaker. The sea had calmed down considerably since the storm, but it was still fairly rough.

Jake stared in the direction of the sound. With no moonlight available, a veil of complete blackness hid the shore. And whoever was baiting him ashore remained hidden in that blackness. He was at a complete disadvantage. No matter what, he would have to venture into the trap that awaited him if he was to have any chance at all of freeing those taken hostage. Used as bait, ten lives lay in the balance.

Faced with such an internecine dilemma, Jake set about preparing himself for what lay ahead.

With the surf hissing at his back, Jake made his way up the escarpment with the aide of the NV goggles. He had tried giving Mat one more call on his satellite phone before leaving the Angel, but he could not even get a signal. After that he had swum ashore, towing the things he would need on a small inflatable float trailing well behind him on 200 feet of nylon rope. The surf had been quite nasty, and he had been tumbled around in the breakers. But he had purposely moored the Angel near this particular spot because it was the only place this side of the island where there was a narrow break in the low-slung limestone cliffs, a fissure just wide enough to provide a way up. He remembered it well, having climbed it once before when he had made a brief exploratory stopover at the island a year earlier.

Already he was limping, having been slammed up against some rocks in the turbulence. Still, he had managed to pull the float up on the rocks with him, and climbing higher to get clear of the billowing spray, he had removed those items he had sealed in plastic wraps. Toweling himself off, he had slipped on coveralls and a pair of sneakers. With great care, he had sewn one particular item into the inside collar of his coveralls, mindful of the threat it posed. After that, he had strapped on other equipment, including the night vision lenses, before beginning the sharp ascent.

Climbing as fast as he dared, he doubted a trap awaited him at this particular area. In the veil of darkness, the escarpment was exceptionally dangerous here, unstable in many places, and it would have presented as much of a hindrance to an enemy as it did him. The karst could be treacherous, concealing a multitude of small but deep crevices where cacti and razor-sharp thorn brush often grew. The recent rains had left the ground slippery, and he had to be careful where he stepped to keep from destabilizing the loose rocks and rubble that lay before him. Regardless of this, he was unable to prevent a small avalanche of stones from skittering down the escarpment every so often, but the hiss of the surf at his back was loud enough to mask the sound.

During the climb, he made it a habit to periodically scan the lay of the land above him through the NV lenses, when at last he was able to glimpse the pinnacle of the old lighthouse. The island's lower terrace was now behind him and the escarpment had become less steep, ascending to the plateau upon which the lighthouse stood. Even so, the route he found himself taking meandered its way erratically in the rising karst, mainly to avoid the worst areas of dogtooth coral, and he realized he still had a distance to go to reach the lighthouse. The wind had subsided even more since he had come ashore, and with the limestone cliffs now far below him and hushing the occasional boom of a breaker, a grim stillness descended over the island.

Readjusting one of the straps on his rucksack, he was automatically reminded of the thing it held, and once again he lifted his gaze to the lighthouse. The feel of the Stoker in his hands did little to lighten his mood as he studied the structure that used to keep shipping at a distance. Hampered by a rugged landscape studded with jagged limestone and dense thickets of underbrush, the going would still be slow. The vegetation had thickened, and as he climbed higher his muscles tensed like coiled springs in readiness for an unexpected attack. In the terrain that now lay before him, he knew that an ambush or booby trap would be easy for someone to set up. In spite of this, he took a deep breath and forged on, foregoing any measures of Seal-like stealth, for they were expecting him.

Drawing closer to the lighthouse, something rustled nearby, making him go rigid. Through the night scope, he was able to catch sight of a bird launching itself toward the tower, but the startled creature quickly disappeared from sight.

With the walk-around observation deck of the lighthouse beginning to loom high overhead like the brim of a jaunty derby, Jake knew he would be meeting opposition at any moment. He was glad he had brought the night vision glasses. In the darkness it would have been near impossible to wend his way through such treacherous terrain without stumbling into something injurious. Taking inventory of the tall structure, movement suddenly caught his eyes. There were people up there on the lower turret.

Before he had a chance to assess the situation, a sibilating whoosh cut the night air. A moment later, a flare lit up the landscape, and Jake was nearly blinded by the intense glare. Immediately, he lifted the NV lenses from his eyes, blinking back the spots dancing before them.

Something blared loudly, and he realized someone was speaking through a megaphone. "Do not be shy, Mr. Javolyn. Your presence is required if we are to begin this little party." The speaker paused, eliciting a little chuckle of delight. "After all, you are the guest of honor."

Jake ducked down, glancing all about him as the flare wafted slowly down on its tiny parachute. Carried by the wind, it drifted off to the west.

The megaphone blared again. "If you please, Mr. Javolyn. There is no need for caution. Otherwise you will force me to resort to harsher measures." The speaker was practically laughing now.

Another whoosh reached Jake's ears as a second flare streaked skyward. Someone yelled, the sound coming from above. With the flare igniting, he could see a person being dangled from the lower turret. The person was being hung upside down by a rope tied to his ankles.

Jake realized it was Trebek.

"I advise you to show yourself, Mr. Javolyn. Ronaldo never did like heights. We can drop him right now if that is your wish."

Jake held back a moment longer, caught in the throes of indecision.

"From the things I have learned about you, I am sure you will not want his death on your hands." The speaker's tone had taken on an edge.

Jake lowered the Stoker to the ground, pushing it off to one side near the base of a small tree rising from a depression. Quickly, he removed the holster carrying the USP-9 from his thigh and placed it next to the Stoker. He did the same thing with his K-bar, NV glasses, and utility belt with its spare 150-round magazine for the Stoker, making sure the items were effectively shielded by the side of the depression. Scooting forward to where the foliage thinned, he glimpsed a group of armed men. They stood in a small clearing abutting the base of the lighthouse, their gazes searching the underbrush in which Jake lay hidden. With a critical eye, he gauged his current position with respect to the base of the lighthouse, knowing that anything beyond 20 meters would doom him to failure. He realized it was going to be close as he slipped his arms from the rucksack. *Too damn close!*

Careful not to snap any twigs, Jake looped one of the rucksack's shoulder straps over a tree branch at the height of his head, mindful of how he oriented it. He then took a deep breath, and before the descending flare had a chance to fade completely, he strode boldly out into the small clearing with his hands raised high.

Another flare rose skyward and ignited. "A most wise decision, Mr. Javolyn," the speaker lauded imperiously. "I am sure your friends will be very grateful for what you are doing for them."

Several men converged from opposite sides as Jake separated himself from the underbrush. Unceremoniously, they prodded him forward with Kalashnikovs until he was within twenty feet of the tower.

A sickening scream suddenly erupted, followed by a heavy thud a moment later as Trebek's body impacted harshly with the ground.

A deep sigh arose from the loudspeaker. "Such a pity Ronaldo had to die. But then again, it is a fate all traitors deserve."

Like phantoms in the flare's fading light, the dark forms of more men emerged from behind the lighthouse. One figure glided silently forward and something analogous to a blazing gush of crimson flame shot out, leaping from the figure to a pile of tree branches stacked high. In spite of the recent rains that had drenched everything on the island, the flame quickly overcame the resistance of the wet wood, taking root and sprouting rapidly into a sizeable bonfire. In moments, dense clouds of billowing black smoke and steam belched upward as the pyre sizzled and blazed.

"As I told you, Mr. Javolyn, meddling in the affairs of a sovereign nation was not a very wise thing to do." This time the words were spoken without the aid of the megaphone.

Jake turned in the direction of the speaker. Light cast from the bonfire revealed the man's face as he walked close to where Jake stood. The man was Henri Ternier.

"I've come here just as you asked," Jake said, keeping his temper at bay. "Now let the others go."

The Colonel let out a small laugh. "I see you have come unarmed, Mr. Javolyn. No knife, no guns." As the Colonel said this, the silent figure that had lit the fire skulked forward to join him. The figure wore a cowl and cloak, seeming to float rather than walk as it approached.

Jake's eyes were immediately drawn to the pendant hanging from the figure's neck. It burned with an ominous intensity, giving off the color of molten steel.

"Let the others go!" Jake repeated, aware that his words had come out in a snarl. He could not help himself. Diplomacy was not an option here. Men like Ternier offended him to the very core.

One of the men surrounding Jake jabbed the stock of his Kalasnikov hard into the small of his back, sending a wave of pain rippling through his body. Jake regained control of his buckling legs and spun around. In that instant he was willing to die if given a moment's gratification at killing his attacker with his bare hands.

The man's sneer abruptly wavered at seeing the look on Jake's face, and he backed up a few paces in spite of the weapon he held.

Jake turned back around to face Ternier. The Colonel grinned loftily, the light from the flames exposing teeth that made Jake think of a nocturnal predator toying with cornered prey. In the end, though, the predator would indulge in tearing the prey apart. "Are you a gambling man, Mr. Javolyn?"

Jake did not answer, choosing instead to glare back defiantly at the predator that was preparing to sink deadly fangs into him. Ternier was the type of individual he would love to have a go at one on one.

Ternier answered for him. "Of course you are. But you are obviously a fool as well, for only a fool would be stupid enough to break into Haiti's National Penitentiary and come away thinking there would be no price to pay."

"Do what you will with me, but let the others go," Jake snapped irritably. He looked past Ternier, hoping to see one of the others the Colonel had kidnapped, but all he saw was Trebek's crumpled body.

"I might consider letting the others go if you provide me with some information," said Ternier, unruffled. "It is but a simple request."

"And what might that be?"

"The whereabouts of gold, Mr. Javolyn."

Jake stared back, keeping the glare in place. "I would think a two-bit counterfeiter like yourself would have no need of gold."

A trace of somberness worked its way into the Colonel's grin. "You have a sharp tongue, Mr. Javolyn. I have a special way of dealing with people who show impertinence, one you will find to be very unpleasant."

Jake needled Ternier more by producing a sneer. "You forget, I've already gotten a firsthand look at this special way of yours. Sooner or later, a whole gang of human rights groups will be screaming for your hide once word reaches enough ears about what you've been doing to people. Once the Hague investigates you, you'll be toast."

The gibes had the desired effect, and Jake saw some of the Colonel's smugness fall away. He readily understood that the man before him was unused to people not showing fear with the threat of torture and death imminent. Instilling fear was Ternier's source of strength.

Ternier stared for a long moment, his eyes stabbing into Jake like crazed, hypnotic daggers. "We seem to be getting away from the main point of discussion, Mr. Javolyn. Jacob's cousin informs me they have amassed a substantial cache of gold and platinum. They had planned on using it to launch a global enterprise, one that might prove to be highly profitable when one considers these intelligent dolphins that will play a large part in the operation."

"If such a cache exists, what makes you think I would know about it?"

Ternier searched Jake's face with a penetrating gaze for a long moment. When he finally spoke, his tone was filled with culture and refinement. "I was hoping I would be talking to a reasonable man, but your stubbornness leaves me no choice. You have no idea what you are dealing with, Mr. Javolyn." He turned and looked down at the cloaked figure standing next to him. "This woman is a voudun priestess. She has powers that many people outside of Haiti would find to be, shall we say, unimaginable, what some might even call impossible. It was her magic that allowed us to board your boat unopposed."

The Colonel turned to address one of his men. "Bring out the large one."

The man disappeared into the shadows. Moments later, a hulking form surrounded by several men was escorted from the darkness, and Jake realized it was Zimbola.

Jake brought his eyes back to Ternier, attempting to get a read on what the Colonel had in mind.

Ternier addressed Jake again, his cultured voice seemingly at odds with the crazed look dominating his expression. "Your friend, here, informs me you are a highly skilled fighter, Mr. Javolyn. A warrior of sorts." Glancing sideways, the Colonel let his eyes linger on Zimbola for several seconds. Though Ternier was a big man, the Jamaican was even bigger.

Ternier continued, his tone turning sardonic. "I have often wondered which is the better combination of assets, physical size and strength, as opposed to skill and quickness."

Jake studied his friend, noticing that Zimby didn't look right. It seemed to him as though the Jamaican's eyes were staring right through him.

"Therefore, I propose a contest, Mr. Javolyn," Ternier said. "Yes…a contest between you and your friend, one in which there can be only one survivor." With his face warped into a nauseating grin, the Colonel turned to the giant and pointed a finger at Jake. "Heed the words of your master, Zimbola. At the third beat of the drums you will kill the man standing before you."

The Colonel swung around and nodded to a man sitting on the ground behind him, and Jake could see the man's legs were wrapped around a set of bongo drums. The man tapped the left drum, then the right a second later. On the third beat, the cowled figure at Ternier's side suddenly whirled, casting a handful of powder into the fire. A burst of red light immediately flared and the flames leapt up wildly, nearly blinding Jake.

And in that moment Zimbola lunged. The attack came with such swiftness that Jake barely had time to react. Quickly sidestepping, he moved just beyond Zimbola's outstretched arms.

"Zimby…what are you doing?" Jake yelled in disbelief over the rising tempo of the drumbeats. "It's me, buddy. It's Jay Jay."

The giant came at him again, this time swinging a fist the size of a cannonball that would have taken Jake's head off had he not ducked under the massive paw.

"What have you done to him?" Jake gasped incredulously, espying Ternier out of the corner of one eye.

The Colonel let out a fiendish laugh that modulated eerily with the rhythmic drumming. "Your friend has been turned against you, Mr. Javolyn. He is now your enemy."

The group of soldiers encompassing Jake and his attacker moved in closer to tighten the circle, and Jake found himself with less room to maneuver.

"If you wish it, I can stop this little contest," Ternier offered magnanimously, raising his voice to be heard above the sound of the drums. "Just tell me where the gold is."

"Screw you!" Jake bellowed, dodging Zimby for the second time. He was well familiar with the Jamaican's immense strength and had no desire to be caught in the grip of those pulverizing hands. He had once seen Zimby lift the front end of a Ford pickup completely off the ground. Zimby was undoubtedly the strongest man he had ever known.

Zimbola lunged again, and Jake barely eluded those massive arms. The circle of men closed in further as the drums pounded faster, heavier.

"Zimby!" Jake yelled again. "What's wrong with you, buddy? It's me, Jay Jay!"

Doggedly, the black giant stalked him, cutting him off in the shrinking ring. Light from the bonfire glinted briefly off Zimby's eyes, and Jake was startled to see they were as glazed as black ceramic. There was no emotion in his friend's face. None at all!

Jake winced, his legs nearly failing him as something poked him hard in the back. Glancing behind him, he saw one of the soldiers withdraw the muzzle of his assault rifle. Spinning around, Jake managed to move just in time to avoid another swiping blow.

Jake yelled at the top of his lungs. "Wake up, Zimby! You've been drugged." In the background he heard Ternier's malicious laugh. It blended ominously with the flurry of the drums, now a wild frenzy of irritating noise that reached into Jake's head.

"He cannot hear you, Mr. Javolyn," the Colonel chortled mockingly, shouting to be heard. "He will only do what I tell him. It is only a matter of time before he catches you."

Bobbing and weaving, Jake used what little space he had left to keep away from his oversized friend. Zimbola was relentless, continuing to pursue him with tenacious intent.

Jake abruptly stopped and held his ground, the drums pounding furiously, the cadence growing steadily louder. Stubbornly, Zimbola lumbered in at him, a huge unstoppable juggernaut bearing an expression as vacant as wind-carved stone. Timing his move, Jake leaned away from another windmill punch capable of crushing most men. Countering, he landed a hard right to the giant's jaw.

Jake's knuckles abruptly throbbed, his brain racked by the clamor of the drums. He had hoped the blow would jar his friend from the strange trance consuming him, but he realized it had about as much effect as a fly slamming up against a concrete wall.

"Snap out of it, Zimby!" Jake roared. "They've got you drugged."

Zimbola pivoted his body and swung with the other arm, forcing Jake to duck yet again. Vaguely, he became aware of the men jeering him as he scrambled back to the center of the circle.

One voice rose up above the jeers, above the drums. "The gold, Mr. Javolyn…tell me where the gold is hidden and I will put a stop to this."

Jake ignored Ternier, noting the impatience gripping his tone. He waited as Zimby lurched toward him, sliding under an outstretched arm and coming up behind the giant's bulk. Leaping onto Zimby's back, Jake placed his left forearm across the giant's windpipe in one smooth motion. Locking his left hand in the crotch of his right arm, he placed his other hand at the back of the Jamaican's head and squeezed. The use of a rear-naked choke was his only option.

Zimbola whirled, and Jake hung on. The drums were at a fever pitch now, and Jake caught sight of the drummer as the giant spun, the drummer's hands blurs of motion as they pounded out the tormenting, insane din. Tightening the hold further, he wrapped both legs around Zimby's massive body. Zimbola struggled fiercely as Jake applied pressure. The giant staggered one way, then another as the encircling men continued to taunt.

Reaching up with both hands, Zimbola attempted to break the hold by prying his banana-sized fingers under Jake's forearm. Obstinately, Jake held on, squeezing with all his might. He now had the hold firmly in place.

Zimby reeled wildly to one side, colliding with several of Ternier's men and knocking them to the ground. The drums were screaming now, almost as though crying out in sympathy with the Jamaican's pain, and Jake barely heard him above the dizzy crescendo. Zimbola was wheezing, fighting to draw breath. The wheezing grew in both pitch and desperation, at odds with the overriding thunder of the bongos, and it turned into a gasping whistle as the giant's throat was gradually compressed. Starved for air, the Jamaican sank to one knee.

Jake's head throbbed, the insanity of the drums undermining his will, a staccato of crazy enervating sound hammering within his brain, and it was all he could do to keep his focus from being disrupted. His only intent was to take the fight out of his friend, and with a sudden spurt of awareness, he realized his concentration was in danger of slipping away if he did not clear his mind of this overpowering distraction. Continuing to maintain the pressure, he kept himself plastered up against Zimby's back like a leech, afraid to let go too soon.

Zimby tried to rise back up, then abruptly fell to both knees. Gradually, he lowered his head, and Jake felt the man's powerful body begin to sag. The next ten seconds seemed like an eternity as the Jamaican slowly slumped forward, his face finally coming to rest on the hard ground.

Jake immediately released the hold, and as he did, the fever pitch of the drums suddenly cut out, leaving a marauding silence in their wake. The stranglehold that had been slowly tightening on his brain immediately eased and he found himself clearheaded once again. Looking down, he was regretful at what he had just done, but there had been no other option. A rear-naked choke could kill if applied too long, and the last thing he wanted was to put his friend's life in jeopardy. Forcing Zimby onto his back, he pushed hard on the giant's chest to get him breathing again.

Jake felt himself winded and sweating profusely. It had taken everything he had to bring down Zimbola, and now he felt himself paying the price. As he sucked in breath, he became aware of the hushed atmosphere within the clearing. Ternier's men stood quiet, staring as though they had just witnessed the impossible.

Ternier's voice broke the silence. "Very well done, Mr. Javolyn. I have to admit I am rather impressed. It would appear that physical size and brute strength was no match for skill and quickness in this particular case."

The Colonel paused, then sighed, and Jake saw another malicious grin break out on the man's face. "Perhaps I have not challenged you enough. Perhaps I should pit you against a man with abilities more on a par with your own." Turning, Ternier looked at one of his cronies and barked an order. "Bring out the other one."

As the soldier left, Ternier stared back at Jake. The Colonel seemed to be enjoying himself. "One way or another, Mr. Javolyn, I will eventually learn where the gold can be found."

Jake scowled scornfully. Ternier was obviously toying with him. He wondered how the Colonel had been able to sense his presence before he had reached the lighthouse. His eyes settled briefly on the cowled figure standing beside Ternier. The pendant continued to glow eerily red, appearing like an angry bloodshot eye.

Led by several men, another figure emerged from the darkness. The bonfire crackled harshly, sending out a cascade of flickering light that quickly revealed the man's face.

Jake was momentarily shocked, and he had difficulty believing what he was seeing.

Ternier's tone was gloating. "No, Mr. Javolyn, your eyes are not deceiving you. I can tell from the look on your face that you had not anticipated this."

Jake continued to stare dumbfounded, wondering how Ternier had ever managed to capture Mat Daniels.

- 117 -

Jake stared speechless at his friend. Mat wore the same blank expression as did Zimbola.

"I will let you in on a little secret," Ternier said, enjoying Jake's bewilderment. "It was Mr. Daniels who allowed us to get aboard your boat."

Jake said nothing as he studied Mat, numbed by what he was seeing.

"Voudun can be a powerful weapon, Mr. Javolyn. It is an ancient art few people outside the Caribbean truly understand. Applied in the right manner, it can be used to subjugate people and influence the course of human history."

Jake found his voice, strangely recalling one of Jacob's little lectures. "You're a dreamer, Ternier. You see yourself as some emerging dictator who will gain control of Haiti. History books are replete with brutal madmen like you, deranged lunatics who used people to suit their own demented fantasies. Fact is, the misery they created was generally short-lived because the world always has a way of ridding itself of deluded Hitler-types."

Ternier stiffened, his eyes bulging savagely, utterly taken back by Jake's tirade. "My plan is infallible," he said angrily, his comportment momentarily unraveling. "I am not like other men. I have things at my disposal that will ensure complete success."

"You mean like a hydrogen bomb?!"

The Colonel showed surprise. "So you know about that." Nodding, he said, "I have to assume Trebek told you."

"You're truly a stupid man, Ternier," Jake continued to antagonize. "Only an idiot would provide Islamic radicals with such a catastrophic weapon."

Ternier's mien seemed to implode at the insult, and his rebuke came out in a deep guttural hiss. "They will prove to be a powerful ally."

"Temporarily, maybe. But if they ever manage to use this bomb on American soil, then what? They have ambitions just like you, one of them being to take over the world."

"Once I am in power, any attempts to usurp me will fail."

"Oh, really. What makes you so sure?"

Ternier's growing anger suddenly tapered off and a smirk took hold of his face. "Because like you, they will have no idea what they are up against. Think about it, Mr. Javolyn. If I am able to turn your friends against you through the power of voudun, I will surely be able to disrupt any plans to overthrow me in the future, no matter how well thought out."

"You assume too much."

Ternier's smugness dissolved. "Enough of your meaningless prattle. You are about to learn what happens to people who meddle in my affairs." The Colonel turned to several of his men. "Bring out the one called Polanski."

Another man was soon led from the darkness, and Jake recognized him to be one the three agents he had seen assisting Mat Daniels.

"Let us see how well you fare against two combatants, Mr. Javolyn." Upon saying this, Ternier lifted his eyes to the turreted observation deck near the top of the lighthouse, nodding and motioning with a hand.

Jake followed Ternier's gaze. A terrified scream broke the air as something was being dangled in the same manner as before. It was the cry of a woman.

Ternier looked back at Jake, a surly smirk plastering his face. "Your efforts to save this woman will have all been for nothing if you should lose this little contest, Mr. Javolyn."

Jake's dismal failure at keeping another female alive suddenly came back to haunt him as he stared up at the woman. Even though she hung partially hidden in shadow at a height of 130 feet above him, he somehow had the feeling the woman was Lucette.

Struggling for words in the midst of his helplessness, Jake said, "Before you have your fun, Ternier, I'm curious about something?"

Ternier continued to smirk expansively. "Yes?"

Jake looked over at Mat and the other DHS agent. Both men continued to stare dumbly off into space. "I'd like to know how you managed to capture these men."

"As I told you, Mr. Javolyn." The Colonel glanced briefly at the cloaked woman standing at his side. His manner seemed to reach a new level of pomposity as he spoke. "Voudun exercised by a powerful priestess can be highly effective." He paused again, as if to give his explanation more meaning. "But initially, it was not voudun that led to the capture of your friend."

"If not your black witchcraft, what then?" Jake needed to know.

"The very thing that tends to corrupt most men," Ternier said smugly. "A thing called greed."

Jake stared over at Mat in disbelief. "I'm not-"

Ternier's curt laugh cut off Jake's confused reply. "No, Mr. Javolyn. It was not your friend who became greedy, but the man standing next to him. Men in key places can be very valuable, particularly a representative of your country's Department of Homeland Security. I thought it prudent to keep this man on my payroll. I find it rather gratifying that so many people within your government are so easily bought off by those who have the means to purchase their cooperation."

Jake glared contemptuously at the DHS agent. "This man is an informant?"

The Colonel nodded slowly, smiling viciously as he did so. "This surprises you?" Letting out another laugh, he said, "Unfortunately, Mr. Daniels happened to be in the wrong place at the worst possible time. He and his crew were in the process of boarding a vessel on the open sea when I came upon him. The vessel he boarded was carrying some very special contraband meant for me."

Jake thought back to the smuggling run he had failed to undertake for Hennington. "Let me guess," he said sarcastically. "Over a hundred million dollars in United States greenbacks shipped from North Korea, all of them counterfeit."

Ternier's hauteur turned frosty. "Your knowledge of my business arrangements is becoming irksome, Mr. Javolyn. No doubt it was the fat little broker who provided you with this information."

"Yeah, I was the stooge originally designated to make the pick-up for you."

Ternier cocked an eyebrow. "Most interesting. I take it you were the same smuggler Mr. Hennington had used to make other deliveries on my behalf."

Jake's retort was flippant. "Guilty as charged. But I've wised up since then. I'm no longer in the business of smuggling, especially for people having delusions of grandeur. But I'm still curious about how you managed to capture Mat Daniels."

Ternier presented Jake with another sick grin, seeming to take great pleasure in telling more. "Ah, yes…it seems Mr. Polanski, here, killed the other two agents working for Mr. Daniels. He apparently had no problem shooting them in the back during the boarding process. Mr. Daniels was more fortunate, only receiving a slight concussion for his unsuspecting ignorance. Money has a most peculiar way of changing a person's loyalties."

"So once you were able to take him prisoner, you drugged him," retorted Jake bitterly. "After that you used him and his vessel to come within hailing distance of the Angel, getting Zimbola to lower his guard. By making him think he was being approached by friendlies, you were able to capture everyone aboard her."

"You are most perceptive, Mr. Javolyn. But it was so much more than a drug that was used to control these men. Drugs generally have a limited effect on influencing the behavior of a person. Ancient voudun potions are much better. They strip away a person's will, leaving a puppet in place to do a master's bidding."

A deep groan sounded at Jake's feet, letting him know that Zimbola was regaining consciousness. Judiciously, he took it upon himself to step beyond the giant's reach.

Ternier's demeanor suddenly hardened. He no longer seemed amused. "I have wasted enough time on you with idle chatter. Now it is time to pay the price of your meddling."

Jake thought quickly. "What if I gave you the location of the gold?"

Smugness returned to Ternier's face. "So you do know where it is hidden, after all."

"Yes. But first you must order your men to pull the woman back into the lighthouse if you want me to tell you."

Ternier hesitated, mulling the offer. "As you wish, Mr. Javolyn. It costs me nothing to spare the woman's life a little longer." The Colonel looked above him and shouted an order, and Jake watched as Lucette was pulled back into the tower.

Ternier brought his gaze back to Jake, staring expectantly. "No more games, Mr. Javolyn. Now tell me."

"You're standing over it."

Ternier eyed the ground under his feet. "Am I to believe it is buried right here?"

"This island has a subterranean cavern close to where we're standing. In it you'll find the gold, tons of it."

The Colonel's eyes bulged greedily. "Tons of it, you say?"

"Yes, tons of it. Maybe more than three hundred million dollars, I'd say."

The Colonel's face abruptly clouded with skepticism. "You better be telling the truth, Mr. Javolyn. I can make your inevitable death an eternity of agony should you be lying to me."

"I'm telling you it's right here under us," Jake said flatly.

"Show me the way to this cavern!"

"It's only reachable by water. There's a submerged tunnel on the southeast side of this island that connects with the cavern."

"That does me little good," Ternier snapped. "I am not a diver, nor are any of my men. Is there no other way into this cavern?"

"Possibly. Based on what I've seen, the bedrock comprising this island is riddled with a labyrinth of caves. But trying to find another way in might take months."

Ternier began to rub his jaw idly, seemingly frozen with indecision.

"Maybe you should consult with your Islamic buddies," Jake recommended snidely. "Most of them are trained frogmen. They even have a submarine at their disposal."

The Colonel stopped rubbing his jaw, gaping back at Jake with a strange look in his eyes. "A submarine?"

"You didn't know that?" Jake shook his head disdainfully. "You supply men like that with abducted Haitian citizens to be used as human slaves and you're in the dark on what they've been doing out here? I'm rather surprised that you don't know more about the people you're dealing with, Ternier."

The Colonel produced a caustic frown. "I shall not warn you again to curb that sharp tongue of yours, Mr. Javolyn."

As Ternier said this, two of his thugs moved in close to Jake, prepared to bash him with their Kalashnikovs. Both looked to the Colonel, awaiting his acquiescence, but Ternier stopped them by holding up a hand. "Not knowing everything about the activities of my affiliates does not concern me, only the end results. It is simply their primary objective that holds any importance." The broad grin that suddenly supplanted his expression appeared all the more perfidious by the crazed look in his eyes. "And that objective is nearly upon us."

Jake answered with a gruff chiding smile. "It'll take months for them to get that bomb in working order. It's been submerged far too long to have any chance of working. Before they're able to make use of the nuclear material it contains, this island will be swarming with U.S. troops."

Ternier appeared unperturbed. "Before this day ends, that bomb will be well on its way to Iran. Their scientists will have the know-how to prepare it for a nuclear strike in short order. But long before its ready, a nuclear missile of lesser yield will be launched from this very island. The missle will be capable of reaching the nearest American city."

Stunned by what he was hearing, Jake felt the smile drop from his face like a lead ingot. The ease with which Ternier had uttered the statement left him little room for doubt. "Miami is the closest American city!" he gasped. "You're telling me they're gonna nuke Miami?"

Jake's appall seemed to energize Ternier. "Your government will be crippled by even a small nuclear strike." The Colonel's words were saturated with a bluster meant to sting. "The devastation it will cause will wreak havoc. Your government showed the world how inept it was at handling the damage caused by a hurricane hitting New Orleans. Think how much more impotent it will be in the face of anarchy resulting from a nuclear catastrophe."

Jake felt like he was being crushed by the onus coming to bear down on him. The burden of saving nine lives had just escalated, for it was now the fate of millions that suddenly came to rest squarely upon his shoulders.

- 118 -

From the sea, Destiny had seen the flares lighting up the night sky and exposing the pinnacle of the old lighthouse overlooking the Windward Passage. It was an area of the island that lay directly above the subterranean grotto containing the dolphin refuge.

Climbing aboard the Avenging Angel as it rose and fell in the swells, she had found the vessel to be abandoned. As she watched the last of the flares fade, she instinctively knew that Jay Jay had gone to the lighthouse.

She was somewhat familiar with the terrain governing the island's surface, and she knew that even in broad daylight it would be difficult to wend one's way through the jagged bedrock and dense thickets hugging the landscape. But with these same obstacles hidden in darkness, traversing the land would be outright treacherous.

With this in mind, she dove back into the sea and mounted Hercules. There was another way of reaching the lighthouse. A passageway existed that ran from the dolphin refuge to the surface. And it exited roughly 80 meters to the north side of the tower's base, a naturally concealed cleft in the rock situated in a cluster of trees. On several occasions in the past, she had used the passageway to reach the surface. Clinging to the rock walls was the same living matter that provided bioluminescence to the dolphin refuge under construction. Moving through the passage had not been difficult. Each time she had emerged from its entrance, she had made her way over to the lighthouse and climbed the stairs leading to the top of the structure. And although the scene that always awaited her was breathtaking, the awe she felt seemed to be offset by some inexplicable force that lay just beyond her senses.

As Hercules swam for the south side of the island, Destiny knew she was failing the others. And with that failure, something had changed. A new sensation seemed to emanate from the other minds, its epicenter originating from one consciousness in particular. Yes, she felt it more fully now, suddenly cognizant of what was taking place.

Almost immediately her sense of purpose deserted her, causing her to flounder in the midst of uncertainty. Whatever clairvoyance she possessed was now gone. The collective pod mind had been compromised. Having bonded with Jay Jay, the youngest of the albinos had taken on some of the traits that made Jay Jay what he was. And now it had spread to the others.

- 119 -

At Yeslam's orders, Azzum had assumed command of Allah's Sword, keeping the sub at a depth of 3 meters below the surface as it cruised close to the island. Originally, he had been instructed to hold the sub in a standby position between the two ships, keeping to a depth well below the ocean turbulence brought on by the passing storm. With a communications buoy fully deployed, he had left a radio channel open, awaiting a message from his team leader. Over an hour earlier, a message had finally come, and Yeslam had been livid with rage. The San Carlo had been attacked. Someone had managed to get aboard, setting off a raging fire that had further delayed the transfer of cargo. The man who had caused the fire had killed several of the ship's crew and jumped overboard. Azzum was to conduct an immediate search of the water bordering on Navassa's south side. He was to be on the lookout for anything unusual.

Azzum frowned as he studied the sonar blip on the sub's monitor. The object he was viewing might actually be a small whale, but he could not be sure. Earlier in the day, a school of humpback whales had been sighted near the island. But then again, maybe it was one of those accursed white dolphins his entire commando team had come to hate. He knew that Yeslam was very interested in capturing the girl seen with those dolphins.

Azzum's mind drifted as he considered this. If he could capture the girl himself, he might regain favor with Yeslam. His leader had been extremely displeased with him ever since he had been knocked unconscious during their foray along the Haitian coast. The man who had bashed him in the head was obviously a warrior like himself.

"Shall I continue on this heading?"

The question caused the other two crewmembers to look pensively at Azzum when he failed to answer. They were spread thin by current circumstances, and the sub's normal contingent of crew had been honed down by necessity for this particular operation.

"Azzum!"

Azzum looked sharply at the man piloting the sub. "Do not yell!"

Nabu lowered his voice. "The object has disappeared. Do you want me to continue on this heading?"

Azzum stared at the monitor, his reverie now broken. The blip had vanished. "All stop!" he barked. With eyes locked expectantly on the screen, he waited for the blip to reappear. When it did not, he said, "Give me bearing and range on the last known position of that object, Nabu."

Nabu did as instructed. "Compass bearing is fifteen degrees. Range is three hundred and twelve meters."

Azzum mulled this information for several seconds before making a decision. "Nabu, you will bring us to within fifty meters of where the object vanished and hold that position."

Nabu followed the order. His expression soured when he realized Azzum was stripping off his jumpsuit. "Azzum, what are you doing?"

"What does it look like, you fool?" Azzum said gruffly. Nabu was beginning to get on his nerves. "I am suiting up. Prepare the airlock. I will make an exploratory dive to see where the object might have gone."

Alarm showed on Nabu's face. "What if Yeslam needs us?"

"I will not be gone long," Azzum persisted. "Something strange is going on out there. I can feel it."

Azzum moved quickly to where the dive equipment was stored further back toward the stern. Eying the three DPVs resting in their holding racks, he decided to take the one Yeslam always used. The headlight on that one provided more illumination than the others, plus it had a built-in sonar device, which the other two lacked. It was perfectly suited for an exploratory dive. Exploratory dives excited him. They sometimes led to unusual finds. It was only a month ago that he and Yeslam had come across a sunken sloop close to where the sub now hovered. Apparently Allah had decided to reward them, for the treasure they had retrieved from the sloop's hold had been immense, and the feel of gold doubloons had been intoxicating. There had been thousands of them. And within the cache of ancient treasure, they had also discovered sealed containers containing 23-year old bearer bonds issued by a bank in Zurich worth millions. The find had been brought back to their submarine base and stored there.

As Azzum struggled clumsily into his gear, the possibility that Allah might reward him yet again tickled his thoughts. He paid particular attention to the weapons he would carry, making sure to secure them firmly to his anatomy. He was one of Allah's true warriors and he would act as one. The thought that he had already lost one weapon weighed briefly on his mind, but he shrugged it off, certain that he would soon atone for his previous failure.

- 120 -

Ortega locked heated eyes with Omar. He did not trust the man, but then again he trusted no one. The two men had been bickering almost incessantly ever since Omar's slip of the tongue about the bomb. "You disappoint me, my Muslim friend," he said irritably. "You should have been more open with me. Our arrangement appears to be one-sided." He flung his hands wide to indicate the heavy damage inflicted on his ship. "Your indiscretion is going to cost me plenty. Three of my men are dead. Three others are either so badly burned or wounded that they are of no use to me."

Raduyev parried with a fierce scowl of his own, his hand hovering near the haft of his Bowie knife. He had also incurred a loss. One of his mujahideen fighters had been killed by a bullet to the head. "Do not try to hold me accountable for your lack of security," he fumed. "The fuel oil you promised me is completely destroyed because you failed to have lookouts posted. I needed that fuel."

Ortega was tempted to pull his handgun at that moment, but the thought of all that white heroin stopped him. There was a lot of money at stake, money that could easily be skimmed from Cardoza. Perhaps his relationship with Omar could still be salvaged. In a calmer voice, he said, "You are certain the man responsible for this is Javolyn?"

The scowl on Raduyev's face darkened further. "Few men would have been capable of getting aboard this ship in that storm. Javolyn is one such man. He fits the description your men gave of the attacker." He spat out the words as though they left a foul taste in his mouth, and his eyes darted in the direction of the island. "He is somewhere out there."

"If he is, we will find him," Ortega vowed, fighting to keep his tone under control. He had seen the flares over the island. "Perhaps the Haitian colonel will capture him."

Raduyev snarled savagely. "If he is captured, he is mine."

At the moment, Ortega had no desire to argue this point. He could not risk any more delays. In a tone meant to pacify, he said, "If I find him, I will give him to you as a gesture of good will, my friend."

Raduyev did not reply, and Ortega could see the intense hatred continuing to burn fervently in his eyes.

Ortega shifted his gaze, barely able to discern the San Carlo's tug making its way slowly toward the freighter. Once the fire had been brought under control, they had finally been able to launch it.

The Spirit of Aden was still holding position off their port. If not for a tiny sliver of moon suddenly poking through an opening in the clouds, he doubted the vessel would have been visible at all. He was glad to be rid of the bomb. He was eager to have it hoisted aboard the Yemeni ship so that it could be exchanged for the remainder of heroin they had agreed upon.

And once he had the heroin, he would go after the dolphin hunters Javolyn had helped escape. The one called Jaffey had offered a cache of gold as a bargaining chip in exchange for their lives. But unfortunately, Javolyn had interrupted Pedro's persuasive measures before Cardoza's nephew could extract its exact location from the man.

Ortega wrestled anxiously with this one particular thought, and all at once a flash of insight entered his thinking. Could it be that his prosperity was about to take another new turn for the better?

On impulse, he left Raduyev standing where he was and made his way down to his private stateroom within the ship. The item he sought still lay on the bed where he had left it. Hefting the object, Ortega studied it more closely this time, pressing a few buttons on the device before the same digital readout was displayed.

Ortega was unaware of the indulgent smile that transcended his face as he read the numbers. Yes, he was now certain what those numbers represented. After the device had been discovered, he hadn't had time to fully scan through the limited menu exhibited on its tiny screen, but now he realized it also had a text messaging capability.

He was now convinced what the unit was used for, noting that it was about twice the size of the sender they had found aboard the broken down Sea Lion. This was the receiver McPherson had claimed to be aboard the spotter plane used for tracking the dolphins. But then again, perhaps the Naval captain had not lied at all. Perhaps McPherson hadn't known the receiver had been brought aboard the salvage tug Jaffey had come in.

A sense of elation took hold of Ortega as he pondered this, knowing he had been right all along to follow his gut instincts. This was indeed a stroke of good fortune. Having one of his men perform a final search of the salvage tug one more time had proved worthwhile, because it had been shortly after the receiver was found that Javolyn had allowed the dolphin hunters to escape in that same vessel.

Pulling up the latest text message, his eyes widened in awe at what he read. Just to be certain he wasn't misinterpreting it, he reread it several more times before placing the device back on the bed. Just before leaving the room, however, he drew up sharply. Pedro was a sneaky bastard, and the last thing he wanted was Cardoza's irksome nephew snooping around his quarters and finding the unit. He had always suspected Pedro of being an informant to his uncle, and he certainly did not want this newfound information leaking out to the powerful drug lord. But then again, the brutish Pedro was rather stupid and wouldn't give the unit a second glance anyway. Nevertheless, he felt it prudent to at least hide the thing from plain sight by placing it under his pillow.

Somewhat satisfied, Ortega locked the door to his quarters before making his way up to the main deck.

- 121 -

Emerging from the cave north of the lighthouse, Destiny groped her way through the heavy underbrush before locating the narrow path she remembered so well. The path would take her to the ruins of two small houses adjacent to the base of the lighthouse. These, she knew, were the old keeper's quarters, at least what remained of them. Bathed in a soft glow of light emanating from some unknown source on the opposite side of the lighthouse, the towering structure presented an imposing silhouette overlooking the landscape. With a waning moon now peeking intermittently from behind an umbrella of low-slung clouds, she had just enough illumination to follow the tiny trail without stumbling into any unseen obstacles. Something stirred briefly in the overhead branches of the thicket she was in, and she attributed it to be the sound of a startled bird fluttering its wings. The sound quickly died, and all was still again.

Upon reaching the dilapidated keeper's quarters, she stopped. Something moved, appearing inky against the pervading darkness. More movement caught her eyes, and she ducked down to keep from being seen.

A voice suddenly rang out, ominous and sibilating. "Do not try to hide from me, cheval. It is a waste of time."

Destiny stared frozen as a shadowy figure emerged, a tiny orb giving off a blood-red emission as though it were the eye of an angry cyclops slowly coming for her. Almost at once, she knew what she was seeing.

"I have been waiting for you," Erzulie hissed, the words pouring from her mouth like grains of salt sliding along a coal chute.

Destiny rose to her feet, looking beyond the witch for anyone accompanying her. For the first time in her life, a sense of complete helplessness accosted her. The omnipotence of the group mind was now gone, leaving only the spectre of something vague and uncertain in its place.

"As it turns out," Erzulie went on, "your pathetic rescue ultimately proved fruitless. The only thing you have accomplished is to increase the power you have relinquished to me."

The cackle that suddenly escaped the crone's lips was the harshest sound Destiny had ever heard.

- 122 -

With the DPV's powerful headlight illuminating the way before him, Azzum had followed the azimuth given him by Nabu. The azimuth had taken him to the place where the unknown object had disappeared. It was there he had discovered a dark opening in the reef.

Hovering only briefly outside the opening, he had decided to investigate what lay inside. Steering the DPV along the tunnel that awaited him, he soon came upon a subterranean grotto. Its immensity awed him. The cavern was far greater in size than the chamber that housed Allah's Sword, and as he glanced about, he became aware of the pale light that seemed to bath everything in a soft greenish glow.

His eyes were quickly drawn to the swirling geometric patterns that lay just below the water's surface. Amazed by the sight, he re-engaged the DPV's propellor, tipping the unit so that it would take him deeper. Overcome by curiosity, he followed one of the curving surfaces. Whatever he was seeing had an oddly familiar texture, and the geometric whorls of a conch shell suddenly came to mind. Nevertheless, the structure did not look natural. Extruded wire mesh protruded along one area where the surface appeared to terminate. Frowning, he glided to a halt, running a gloved hand over the wire. His fingers tingled strangely with the touch.

What is this place? he asked himself, suddenly glancing around in all directions. He had the feeling he was being watched, but as his eyes penetrated the limpid water, he saw nothing that might indicate danger.

Re-powering the propulsion unit, he aimed it deeper. He would learn what was going on here. Following a corridor that appeared to spiral its way down, he eventually located an area where the walls flared outward.

His gaze immediately fell on lengths of rope, intertwined about one another and pulsing rhythmically. Under the DPV headlight, the rope-like strands appeared multicolored and segmented, and as he followed the strands, he saw that they joined a huge bloated organism. He could see similar organisms strung out at intervals behind the first one, each one seeming to roost upon a bed consisting of a thick, milky slurry.

Azzum followed the line of organisms, puzzled by the sight of gas bubbles discharging from the crown of each creature. The bubbles disappeared into inverted funnel-like tubes situated directly above the rising gas. Something glittered further ahead, and as the DPV pulled him closer, his eyes bulged under his dive mask. Almost immediately, he knew he was looking at gold. Mounds and mounds of gold with the consistency of coarse granular sand. His recent participation in the recovery of sunken treaure from the sunken sloop had left a lasting impression of what real gold looked like, and he was certain he could not be mistaken.

Just to be sure, he began scooping up handfuls of the stuff. The grains were metallic, all right, and weighty, too. Feeling it filled him with joy and he knew in that instant he would not share this find with the others. Though he was a holy warrior, he had never acquired the same level of zealousness held by his peers. He had always refrained from believing himself to hold the same religious conviction as his comrades. He would have been lying to himself had he done that. Born into dismal poverty, he had pursued a life of robbery and murder before joining Al Qaeda. He liked killing; it gave him pleasure. Nevertheless, Allah, in his infinite wisdom, had sought to reward him, probably because he was now devoted to only killing infidels.

Azzum eyed the bloated creature squatting in the midst of the gold, aware that the organism might actually be responsible for producing the valuable metal. If that were true, then the amount of metal would continue to accrue at a steady rate. Stricken with wonder, he turned the DPV so that its beam shone on the unsightly thing. More fully illuminated, he could see its pulsing surface was awash in bright colors. *What are you that you are able to produce such riches?*

The same weird feeling as before suddenly accosted him, seeming to clutch at his heart this time. Cautiously, he looked all about him again. He could not help it. He had the distinct sensation he was being observed.

Convincing himself he was letting his mind play tricks on him, he brought his eyes back to the organism in front of him. Reaching out, he placed a hand on the thing.

The jolt he felt lasted only a millisecond. Then there was only an all-consuming blackness from which there was no return.

- 123 -

The radio squawked harshly on Raduyev's belt, making him step away from the others so as not to be overheard. As he lifted the radio to his ear, his eyes continued to follow the unloading of the shipment sent over from the freighter. The exchange of cargos was nearly complete. Only two more loads remained to be transferred before Ortega would have the quantity of white heroin originally promised him. And with the hydrogen bomb now safely aboard the other ship, a critical phase of the mission he had been assigned had finally come to an end.

"Have you spotted anything?" Raduyev grunted, speaking in English. He had instructed his crew that call signs were not to be used and that radio protocol was to be avoided. Though the broadcasting range of the radios they were using was very limited, one never knew if the transmissions might be intercepted, and the last thing he needed was for the wrong people to overhear someone speaking Arabic in these waters. They would speak in generalities that offered little to an eavesdropper.

Nabu's voice shot back in urgency. "Azzum left us to investigate something picked up on sonar. He has been gone more than an hour and has not returned."

The statement caused Raduyev's temper to flare. He could not afford the loss of another man. "Come home!" he growled. The prearranged command meant for Nabu to bring Allah's Sword back to base.

"What about Azzum?" Nabu persisted.

"Forget about him!" Raduyev snapped, livid with rage. "You will wait for me at home!"

A reply came back after a short pause. "We will wait for you there."

Raduyev's mood continued to deteriorate. He now realized his mistake in letting Azzum assume command of the sub during his absence. Perhaps it would have been far wiser to have left Kalid in charge. Kalid was not a diver and would have been unable to venture outside the sub.

As Raduyev put the radio back on his belt, he noticed Ortega striding toward him. "It seems we are both busy with radio calls, my Muslim friend," the Colombian boss said coldly. "I have just received a call from the Haitian colonel. He claims to have captured Javolyn."

The Chechen gaped in disbelief, unsure if he was hearing correctly. "I hope you are not joking with me."

"I am not in a joking mood," Ortega said gruffly. "Ternier requests you go ashore immediately. He will meet you at the lighthouse."

Raduyev glanced up at the ship's helipad. During the fire, he had seen the flames lick their way up close to the flight deck. "Is your helicopter still operable?"

Ortega nodded, his eyes still icy. The explosion Javolyn had caused had left a lasting strain on their relationship. "Yes. I will fly you there. I want to look into the eyes of the man who has caused me so much trouble."

Raduyev stared closely at Ortega's face. From the Colombian's tone, it sounded as if Ortega was having second thoughts about his earlier offer of appeasement. "Javolyn is still mine. You will not interfere with what I have in mind for him."

Ortega shrugged, still appearing annoyed. "Perhaps the Colonel has ideas of his own. From what I hear, he is a man very creative in the way of revenge."

The Chechen stiffened, not liking what Ortega was insinuating.

- 124 -

Jake heard the blades of the Bell Ranger beating the air as it approached. With its searchlight probing the terrain beneath it, the helicopter quickly found the small rectangle of open space near the base of the tower before setting down. Some of Ternier's men had recently fed the bonfire, and the light from it flickered with renewed vitality, providing a sinister aura to the two men who emerged from the copter's cabin.

As the men drew closer, recognition of the one on the right caused Jake to go rigid. Something leapt from the depths of his soul with such savagery that several of the Colonel's men had to prod him back with their Kalashnikovs. The vehemence he felt toward Raduyev was overpowering and he had great difficulty restraining it. Like a reawakening beast that had been locked away in a cage far too long, it surged up with ferocious hunger. And now the beast had to be fed.

Raduyev walked to within ten feet of Javolyn, his face twisted in hatred. "I knew that someday we would meet again," he rasped, ominously fingering the hilt of his sheathed Bowie knife.

Ortega moved to Raduyev's side, sizing Jake up with a grim appraisal. "So this is the man who attacked us."

Colonel Ternier stepped close to the two men. "It appears we all have a score to settle with Mr. Javolyn, here."

Jake stared back in silence as he regained control of his emotions. It was crucial the beast be held at bay for the time being, otherwise it would perish within its cage without any chance at retribution.

Raduyev turned, skewering Ternier with the same scalding gaze. "Whatever you have planned for this man must be put aside. I have plans of my own for him."

The Colonel met Raduyev's gaze with a calculating grin. "For the time being I suggest that no injury be inflicted on Mr. Javolyn. He is currently much too valuable to be harmed."

Ortega scowled murderously. "The only thing of value will be this man's death."

"Do not rush to judgement so quickly, gentlemen," the Colonel said. "It seems Mr. Javolyn knows something I am sure will slake your need for vengeance." Ternier paused, continuing to grin as he studied both men. "At least temporarily."

Raduyev stared back at Jake, his eyes savage and filled with extreme menace. "I have no time for riddles, Ternier."

Jake noticed a slight waver in the Colonel's smile at the Chechen's lack of respect, but Ternier remained diplomatic. "Then perhaps I was mistaken in assuming you would be interested in a worthwhile venture, Omar, one that might very well help finance your objectives." Ternier paused again, waiting for a response, but Raduyev showed no interest as he continued to glare belligerently at his old nemesis.

Annoyance flared briefly in the Colonel's eyes. "I am offering you a share of something that can make you exceedingly wealthy should you choose to take it."

Ortega turned sharply to face Ternier, his cruel demeanor suddenly easing with the prospect of further enrichment. "A share of what?" he demanded.

"I have learned of a substantial hoard of gold that exists somewhere on this island. According to Mr. Javolyn, it is in a subterranean vault directly below us. Unfortunately, the only way into that vault is through a submerged tunnel located off the island's southern shore. Divers will be needed to access that tunnel."

Ternier eyed the Islamist. "You possess the necessary equipment and training to reach this gold."

Raduyev said nothing for several seconds, continuing to glare at Jake as though he might spring upon him at any moment. Finally, he said, "And if I help you recover it, you will turn Javolyn over to me?"

The Colonel gave him a chilling smile. "You have my word."

"I assume we will all get an equal share of this prize," Ortega grunted.

The Colonel's voice was placating. "Are the three of us not partners? Sharing the gold equally goes without saying."

The Chechen threw hate-filled eyes back at Javolyn. "What makes you think this man will show us the way to the gold?"

Ternier appeared to swell with smugness. "It seems Mr. Javolyn is a man who is foolishly ruled by loyalty. He will do anything to keep his friends alive."

Ortega nodded in agreement. "I have seen one of them... a girl who rides a dolphin. Not too long ago Javolyn risked his life to save her."

"Yes," Ternier said, his smile broadening. "The girl's life is a powerful motivator."

Ortega's interest escalated. "You have this girl?"

The Colonel gave Jake a cryptic grin before gesturing to one of his thugs. "Show these men the girl!"

The statement rocked Jake to his heels. He had not even considered that Destiny might be among those held by Ternier. Ten minutes earlier he had accounted for all ten of the captives Ternier had claimed during their radio conversation, having seen the remaining six led from the lighthouse. Jacob, Grahm, Hennington, Hector, Emmanuel and Lucette had all been taken away before the arrival of Raduyev and Ortega. Mat, the traitorous Polanski, and Zimbola had also disappeared, with the black giant taking Trebek's broken body with him. Apparently the Colonel enjoyed doling out psychological torture as much as he did physical. Ternier was like a crafty poker player, showing his cards only when necessary.

Apprehension filled Jake as Destiny was led around the side of the lighthouse by two soldiers. Floating behind her was the cowled priestess he had seen earlier, the strange ornament around her neck still glowing a choleric red.

At seeing Jake, Destiny squirmed free of the hands constraining her. "Jay Jay!" she squealed.

The soldiers moved quickly to regain control of their charge, but Ternier raised a hand. "Let the cheval go!" The order was barked in a bored monotone, almost as if he had expected such a scene.

No one interceded as Destiny bolted for Jake's protective embrace, hugging him fiercely. "They didn't hurt you?" she cried.

"I'm okay," Jake said.

Destiny looked up into his face, her eyes misty. "They have Jacob and the others."

"I know," Jake replied bleakly.

"Enough of this pitiful prattle!" Ternier scolded impatiently. The Colonel looked sharply at several of his men. "Separate them!" he bellowed.

The soldiers moved in to pry the girl from Jake's arms. As she was pulled violently away, he lashed out with the swiftness of a viper, slamming a fist into an exposed jaw. The man he hit was sent sprawling to the ground, knocked cold.

Jake fell to his knees as something blunt slammed into a kidney, but Ternier stopped his henchmen before they could retaliate further.

The Colonel's eyes bulged grotesquely, his composure now worn thin. "Any more attacks on my men will result in severe punishment to the cheval, Mr. Javolyn," he warned mordantly. "The same thing will happen to her each time you fail to cooperate."

"We are wasting time!" Raduyev snarled.

Ternier studied Jake closely as if to assess his compliance with the warning. "I do not think Mr. Javolyn will give us any further problems," he chortled.

- 125 -

Destiny felt terribly vulnerable and alone as she was led to a place away from the others. And although she knew what must be done, she no longer comprehended how to do it. Something empty resided in her chest, a void around which the fire of her living body existed. She sensed the futility of the paradox, for the fire held no flame. She was floating over unknown ground, and held within her cupped ethereal hands was the tender organ of her own beating heart. Confronting insidious forces was something far more difficult than she had ever imagined.

And those same forces were responsible for all the obstacles standing in her way, crude malicious barriers that took all happiness away from life.

Something Jacob had once told her came flooding back. Happiness was a concept within the mind, nothing more. There was no road that led to such a place, for happiness was merely the voyage, not the destination.

Her mother's face suddenly flashed before her. *You will become stronger and wiser for your pain.* The thought made her feel lost, for she wasn't sure if Amphitrite was speaking to her at this moment. Fearful of what would happen to Jay Jay, her sense of the others had gradually faded. It was she who was responsible for what was happening, for if Jay Jay were to die, his death would be on her hands.

She suddenly became aware of a new emotion surfacing within her, and it rose with such potency that it blocked out all sense of the hurt and guilt she had been feeling. It was something new to her, something that up until now she had never before experienced.

Consumed by this surging state of mind, she realized Jay Jay had been right all along. Gentle persuasion and passive restraint would not be enough to counter the vile natures of the people seeking to do them harm. It was now time to fight back!

- 126 -

With a guard on each side of her, Destiny stared back in defiance at the old crone. She had been taken back to the old keeper's quarters on the far side of the lighthouse.

"A powerful mambo once tried to defy me, cheval," Erzulie gloated in a reptilian voice that was somewhere between a hiss and a cackle. "But your fate will be the same as hers."

"What have you done with the others?" Destiny asked, her revulsion of the hag continuing to build within her.

The crone ignored the question as though she had not heard it. "You are probably wondering how I was able to sense your presence when you arrived here." The witch held the amulet in front of the girl's face, dangling it smugly. "I have always had the power to possess a creature's mind, seeing through its eyes and controlling its movements. But this little trinket amplifies this power even more. There are many birds on this island-"

Erzulie suddenly tensed. The amulet's steady glow abruptly wavered, beginning to blink eratically, its emission of crimson light now turning a deep green. Without warning, the earth heaved beneath her feet, followed by an ear-shattering boom a split second later. In that instant, she knew that something had gone terribly wrong.

Jake had had enough. He had stalled for time as much as he dared, but now he knew it was time to act. Ternier, Ortega and Raduyev had gotten aboard the Bell Ranger and flown off, leaving him guarded by a contingent of fifteen men, including one stationed on the lighthouse's turreted observation deck above him. With Destiny and the others having been taken away, he was now free to put his plan into motion.

The light from the bonfire had gradually dimmed into a feeble glow and the men closest to him were keeping a respectful distance, though they made him kneel on the ground with his hands clasped stiffly behind his head. Jake had anticipated something like this, and he casually probed with his fingers for the tiny device he had sewn in the lining of his collar. The device was a remote entry key, the kind used to unlock the door or trunk of an automobile from a distance. It was part of an accessory kit he had purchased for remotely deploying the Angel's waverunner launching ramp when berthing the Kawasaki. Luckily he had not gotten a chance to install it, for now it would serve a far better purpose. The radio signal it would send was designed to activate its counterpart, a torsion spring that normally acted as a car trunk release, but he had rigged the electronic release to something else. He had been especially lucky he hadn't triggered it during his struggle with Zimbola, for a jury-rigged remote detonator could be quite unpredictable. From where he knelt, he estimated he was right on the edge of its transmitting range. And that was 20 meters.

Taking a deep breath to steady his nerves, he prayed he was within range as he located the triggering button through the cloth. Twisting around so that the remote aligned with the target, he suddenly flopped forward and pushed down on the button, pressing his face flat against the ground and shielding the back of his head with both hands.

One of Ternier's men began to shout, but the protest of anger never left his tongue as an invisible battering ram seemed to catch the man from behind and send him flying like a leaf caught in a gale. The shock wave rending the air was thunderous, the force of it scattering Ternier's thugs like piffling windblown debris. The rucksack Jake had left concealed at the edge of the clearing had held a homemade bomb. He had been able to construct it using the explosives contained in two of the waverunner torpedos he kept aboard the Angel.

With ears ringing, Jake wobbled dazedly to his feet. Grabbing a Kalashnikov dropped by one of the fallen men, he sprang into action. As soldiers staggered to their feet, he hosed them, cutting them down before they even knew what was happening. In seconds, he emptied the weapon. Flinging it aside, he picked up another, spraying several more men as they tried to get to their feet.

Reflexively, he ducked down at the hammering clatter of return gunfire. Dirt was kicking up all around him. He glanced up to espy muzzle flashes coming from the observation deck above. Pulling the AK to his shoulder and taking careful aim, he stood rock-steady and squeezed down on the trigger, intent on emptying the clip. The firearm bucked, cooperating just long enough to send out a short volley before jamming, and Jake knew his marksmanship had not failed him as a bloodcurdling scream filled the air. The moment was dramatized all the more as one of the logs within the bonfire shifted and flared, suddenly illuminating the object accelerating down from the heights with a spiking burst of light, and Jake followed the flight of the falling man, unable to look away. The man continued to shriek in terror, twisting and twitching and clawing at the air until he met the ground with a heavy thump, and then all was quiet again.

Jake threw down the Kalashnikov and bolted like a jackrabbit for the thicket off to his right, expecting another storm of return fire to follow him. When none came, he risked a glimpse over his shoulder, seeing more of Ternier's thugs struggling to their feet like drunken sailors.

Grimly, he found his way into the underbrush, and in moments he was able to locate the weapons he had left behind. With resolute purpose, he strapped on his K-bar and USP-9, finally snapping his ammo belt into place before snatching up the Stoker.

Gripped by the same coldness he had felt back in Tora Bora, he moved back to the edge of the clearing. The Stoker shuddered like a jackhammer as he fired from the hip, cutting down four more men clustered together. With a total disregard for his own safety, he ambled calmly out into the clearing, looking to kill anything that moved with the awesome firepower held in his hands. The body count quickly escalated, and it did not take him long to account for fifteen dead men, all of them strewn about the clearing like torn and twisted rag dolls.

No matter what it took, he would get Raduyev for what he had done to Myers. But right now he had Destiny and the others to think about.

- 128 -

Destiny saw the fear etched on the faces of the men guarding her. The stillness hanging in the air seemed to have unnerved them even more than the sporadic bursts of gunfire that had erupted moments earlier.

Shifting her attention back to the hag, the girl watched as Erzulie gazed intently into the amulet's crystal. The light ensuing from the trinket had now changed back to a deep blood red.

The hag turned to the soldiers. "Stay here and keep guarding the cheval," Erzulie ordered in that halting reptilian tone. "If she gives you any problems, kill her."

Within seconds, the witch was gone, seeming to float off into the night.

A disconcerting silence ensued, and Destiny sensed the growing uneasiness of the two guards. Both men fidgeted nervously as they awaited Erzulie's return.

Something clunked dully, making the men whirl around in fright. The sound had come from behind them. From the other side of the lighthouse, the bonfire continued to burn, though it had dimmed considerably. Eclipsed by the tower's dark looming bulk, the fire cast a soft glow to each side of it.

The silence was broken again, this time by multiple clacks coming from one of the back walls comprising the keeper's quarters. Both men turned and fired at the sound, taking their attention away from the girl.

Destiny caught sight of a dark shadow rising up, and in that instant an eruption of gunfire exploded at close to point blank range. *Brrrup, brrrup.* A lance of stabbing flames shot out, the sound of it drowning out the staccato fire of the guards.

The shadow reached out and grabbed her arm, and she knew at once the shadow was Jay Jay.

Jake stared down at the two fallen men, making sure their crumpled bodies did not move. "Where are the others?" he asked.

Destiny eyed the dead men. Though she felt a detached empathy, their deaths did not revolt her. She suddenly realized that some people would have to die if the pod was going to survive and continue fostering their objective.

Getting her wits about her, Destiny stared up into Jake's face. "I don't know. I saw them earlier, but they were led away."

Jake opened his mouth to say something, but stopped short, and Destiny noticed his eyes impinging on something over her shoulder. With his free arm, he moved her slowly aside and leveled his weapon.

Destiny spun as Erzulie's voice rasped out from the gloom. "Your weapon will be useless against me."

Jake was not about to take any more chances. He had seen what this seemingly innocuous old crone had done to Zimbola and Mat, and so he fired, the muzzle of his Stoker flaring a bright orange as it spat a lethal hail designed to destroy. A shower of sparks erupted in front of the witch, the storm of bullets unable to penetrate whatever was shielding her from the deadly barrage.

Jake stopped firing and lowered the Stoker, stunned that Erzulie was still standing. The pendant she wore pulsed savagely, radiating ebbing doses of flaming crimson as though shedding an excess of stored energy. The pulsing quickly died and steadied.

"You cannot hurt me," Erzulie rasped hoarsely. "Protected by the charm of my ancestors, I am invincible."

"Perhaps you assume too much!"

Erzulie froze. The words had come from behind her. Whirling, the crone faced the intruder.

Both Jake and Destiny watched as another dark form materialized out of the gloom. With stolid calmness, Amphitrite stood before the witch.

"So...the mother cheval dares to come here," Erzulie hissed. "You make this easier than I had thought."

"The amulet's empowerment is an illusion, witch," Amphitrite said. "The power contained within it will ultimately destroy all those who seek to use it wrongly. Your obsession in using it for evil and self gain offends the forces behind it."

Erzulie floated off to one side so that she could observe all three people. "No," the crone countered angrily. "The rada have bestowed this power to me because I am the rightful owner. They saw you as unworthy and forced you to give it up. Deep down you knew it would have been too dangerous to keep it for yourself."

"Giving the amulet up was only a ploy," Amphitrite said without emotion. "Without it, you would have been too cowardly to come here."

Erzulie cackled in amusement, but Destiny detected a waver of confidence in her tone. "You delude yourself, cheval. I have come here to carry out the wishes of the rada. This amulet gives me the power to destroy all those who oppose my son. The rada wish to see Henri rule, for he is the only one capable of restoring Haiti to its former glory. With Henri as king, Haiti will become one of the world's great powers. It is only befitting that the people you are aligned with will contribute immeasurably in making this possible. Henri is fully aware of the business venture Jacob and Emmanuel have concocted and will take control of their plan, using them as pawns to increase his wealth and power."

Destiny sensed the smile that formed on her mother's face, though in was partially obscured in shadow. "If you truly believe this, then destroy me now," Amphitrite challenged. "As I recall, you tried to do this many years ago. You failed then, just as you are about to fail now."

Erzulie hesitated, suddenly seeming unsure of herself. "I have had enough of your interference," she sibilated bitterly, her words coming out in a hateful rush. "You will not only die, you will die in unbearable agony."

As if in response to the witch's declaration, a swirling mist rose up around her cloak-shrouded form. The amulet began to glow more fervently, the pent up energy within it building rapidly.

"You will feel the fires of hell burning within you," Erzulie hissed brusquely. "You will bear the torments of a thousand suffering souls. You will-"

The amulet's choleric red abruptly changed over to a greenish emission, pulsing with such blinding speed that it dazzled the eyes. The fabric of Erzulie's cloak began to smolder where the amulet hung against the cloth, and the pungent smell of scorched flesh began to fill the air. The witch screamed, flapping her hands wildly against her chest as though trying to squash an unseen insect alighting there. The scream grew in pitch, escalating into a horrible screech as the hag's cowl burst into flame.

Amphitrite stood immobile as the fire spread rapidly to consume the hag, her features impassive and sedate under the light cast by the flames. Driven into an agonizing frenzy, Erzulie lunged, intent on engulfing Amphitrite in those same flames, but Amphitrite stepped aside and the witch flew past. The crone managed five more steps before falling to the ground, the fire sizzling flesh as it burned savagely.

Erzulie continued to scream for another ten seconds before her cries began to wane, eventually stopping altogether. When the flames finally died, only a charred corpse remained.

"Come," Amphitrite said, turning to look at both Jake and Destiny. "We must hurry. There is still danger."

- 129 -

Colonel Ternier's eyes blazed in anger as he examined the contents of the final metal chest. "You disappoint me, Omar. There appears to be a discrepancy here."

Raduyev's face clouded as he scanned the stack of cases under the beam of his own flashlight. Ternier was right. By his own count, he was five cases short. "If there is a shortfall, it is because all the cases have not been delivered as yet," he replied, suppressing his bewilderment. Silently he cursed Kalid for not completing the task. The man had more than enough laborers at his disposal to have gotten the job done by now.

Ortega paced impatiently off to one side, appearing like a shadow in the pall of night. Farther back from him, the Bell Ranger's dark silhouette sat quietly. "I am not a shuttle service, Colonel," he said testily. "My time is very valuable and I have business of my own that cannot wait."

The three men had landed in the middle of the small clearing adjacent to the topside entrance leading to Raduyev's hidden submarine base. Debts had to be settled and additional business discussed before they could pursue seeking out the gold with Javolyn's forced cooperation.

Ternier turned to the Colombian and huffed in annoyance. "Has no one ever told you patience is a virtue, Mr. Ortega. You will be amply remunerated for the use of your aircraft…unless, of course, you feel the girl is not a fair exchange."

Ortega stopped his pacing but said nothing.

The Colonel swiveled his head back to the man he knew as Omar. "When can I expect the rest of the merchandise?"

"Give me a minute to converse with my people," Raduyev said stiffly. "I am sure a reasonable explanation exists for the delay."

"Of course," Ternier agreed coldly. "But if it turns out you are unable to make good on the remainder, I will expect payment in full in United States greenbacks equal in value to that portion missing. By my estimation, you are still short by twenty-five million dollars."

Raduyev was puzzled by what was happening here. Even before they had left the lighthouse, he had radioed his base, but Kalid had not answered. They had first flown out to the San Carlo to make sure the remainder of white heroin had been sent over from the freighter. Once aboard Ortega's ship, he had tried contacting Kalid again, but to no avail. To make matters worse, something had gotten caught up in the tug's props while the small vessel was on its way back to the Aden to receive the final load, further delaying the operation. Rather than wait for the final shipment, they had gotten back aboard the copter and flown to where he now stood.

To Raduyev it seemed all these infidels had their hands out. The extent of their greed seemed to have no bounds. The Chechen felt the anxiety building within him as he stepped out of earshot of both men. His business with Ternier needed to be concluded very shortly. Once he got the Colonel out of his hair, he would launch the rocket the North Koreans had provided. His base antenna was situated only ten meters from his current position, well hidden in a cluster of trees. Certainly he would be able to reach Kalid from here.

Raduyev lifted the small radio to his mouth, his finger resting on the transmit button, but before he could utter a word, the radio squawked gratingly. Someone was jabbering excitedly. From the sound of the speaker, he knew Nabu was hailing him.

Raduyev had difficulty keeping his voice calm and it came out in an angry whisper. "What is going on? Why has Kalid not brought up all the cases? We are five short!"

"There is a problem!" Nabu cried. His tone was hysterical. "Our base has been breached. The Haitians have taken control-" The transmission suddenly cut out.

Raduyev felt an icy hand reach out to close on his innards, but before the Chechen could find his tongue, the radio came alive again, this time with the voice of a new speaker. The voice was Bashir's. "Your mission is finished, Yeslam! I will not let you kill innocent people."

The radio abruptly cut out again, leaving Raduyev staring at the device in stunned silence.

"You seem perturbed, Omar."

Raduyev looked up. Ternier hovered close, gazing at him expectantly.

"I assume there will be nothing to mar our relationship," the Colonel said. There was an ominous edge in his manner. "I would hate to think you will not honor your end of our bargain when I have already honored mine."

Ternier was reminding him of their arrangement. The Colonel had given him the precise coordinates of the lost hydrogen bomb in exchange for items recovered from the hold of a sunken sloop. Ternier also had provided him with the coordinates of the sloop's location, and Raduyev had done the rest.

It had always puzzled the Colonel why the cheval had scrawled those numbers in the sand where she had left him unconscious so many years ago, a place known to the locals as the Devil's Horn. Upon regaining consciousness, he had given those numbers to memory, having a boding sense of their meaning. After much rumination, he had eventually consulted a navigational chart, and sure enough those numbers had conformed to the latitiude and longitude of a location very close to Navassa Island. He had remembered seeing the island in the distance shortly before they had ditched the seaplane in the ocean. With the wind blowing hard in that direction, it was only logical that the sloop would have been pushed close to the island before sinking. But what had amazed him even more was the proximity of the sloop to the lost hydrogen bomb. Both had been less than 500 meters from one another. This he had taken as a positive omen, one that foretold of the glorious destiny that awaited him. And he had been further rewarded when Omar had gotten word to him that the sloop had been found and its contents recovered. With the exception of the bearer bonds that were still missing, the ancient Spanish treasure he had taken from Mercades Myers so long ago was now back in his possession once again. So be it if it had lied in wait for him at the bottom of the sea all these years rather than the Cayman bank vaults where he had originally planned to store it. Twenty-two years earlier, Baby Doc had entrusted him with the delivery of several cases of bearer bonds worth millions to a discreet bank account in the Caymans. At the time, Duvalier had known his reign was almost at an end and had decided to loot the Haitian national treasury. In carrying out Duvalier's orders, Ternier had simply added his own booty to the stolen bonds, arranging transport of the goods via a seaplane taking off from Saint-Marc. Baby Doc had been furious with rage when he had learned the assets he had absconded with had gone down in the sea, but Duvalier's fear of Erzulie had kept him from seeking retribution on her one and only son, and Ternier had escaped with his life.

The Colonel mulled the current situation. The stockpile of weapons Omar had promised were in secured locations in Port-au-Prince, ready to be distributed on his command. He also had in his possession the counterfeit dollars coming from North Korea. His plan had now ripened sufficiently to initiate. But now the bonds were still missing, and he was not going to be satisfied until Omar delivered them into his hands.

"You will get everything agreed upon," Raduyev rasped, throwing venom into his words. He was growing weary of these greedy infidels. "But a problem currently exists and I will require the use of your soldiers to rectify it."

Ternier grimaced, drawing back in horror as if Raduyev had just doused him with a bucket of scalding water. "What kind of problem?"

Raduyev felt a rush of heat rise to his cheeks, taking momentary comfort that it was still nighttime, otherwise the Colonel would have noted the red flush spreading across his face. "It seems the Haitians you provided me have overwhelmed my people and taken over my base."

Ternier stood frozen, remaining speechless for several seconds. "You had assured me the missile would launch before daybreak," he sputtered in outrage, all his former aloofness seeming to dissolve into a heated meltdown. The Colonel looked at his watch. "Dawn will be upon us in less than ninety minutes."

"The Rodong will go off as planned!" Raduyev assured him. "But I will need your assistance."

Ortega moved closer, looking from one man to the other. "What is this I am hearing about a missile?"

- 130 -

Standing on the bridge, the Spirit of Aden's captain stared nervously at his wristwatch. It was crucial he set sail before first light. "What is the holdup now?" he asked his first mate in exasperation.

"The tug from the San Carlo has broken down again," the first mate stated.

"I thought they had removed the netting fouling its props."

The first mate shrugged. "They did, but it seems they have picked up more."

The captain gazed across the water at the tuna trawler's dark outline. "Hail the San Carlo and inform them they have exactly 50 minutes to pick up the remainder of the cargo," he ordered. "After that we will depart these waters with whatever they have failed to off-load."

The first mate nodded before carrying out the order.

The captain looked at his watch again, his uneasiness continuing to mount. As a devote Shiite Muslim and operative of Iran's Revolutionary Guard, he knew he should be smiling but somehow he could not bring himself to do so just yet. Aboard his ship was the very thing he had come for, a weapon capable of unspeakable destruction once Iranian scientists loyal to the mullahs restored the device to its full potential. With such a weapon in their possession, Iran's nuclear ambitions would be greatly accelerated. With such a weapon, they would bring America's dominance in world affairs to an abrupt end.

Yes, he assured himself, he would allow himself a smile only when his ship was safely underway.

- 131 -

Mat Daniels broke from his stupor with a start, bewildered by his surroundings. He was currently sitting in semi-darkness among a small group of people on the back deck of a large modern yacht. Three men bearing Kalashnikov assault rifles stood nearby, none of them paying him any attention. The men were leaning over the vessel's gunwale, looking intently at something in the water. The sound of distant surf told him a shoreline was not too far away.

Taking inventory of the faces nearest him, he recognized most of the people he had last seen aboard the Avenging Angel - Chester Hennington, Zimbola, Franklin Grahm, Hector, Jacob, Lucette and Emmanuel Baptiste. One other person sat to the right of Emmanuel, and as he leaned over to get a glimpse of the person's face, his pulse quickened.

All at once, a flood of lost memory washed over him. He thought it had all been a dream, but now he knew for sure that one of his men had betrayed him. Joe Polanski was a murderous traitor.

A terrified shout caused Mat to stare back at his captors. One of the men appeared horrified. The man gesticulated wildly at the larboard water and cried out in panic. The deck abruptly lurched as something crashed into the hull with jolting force.

Knocked to his side, Mat noticed a dark form loom up from the sea. Huge and monstrous against the backdrop of night, it rose still higher until it towered above him. Reaching an apex, it hung suspended for one brief instant before pitching forward, ever so slowly at first as it gained momentum. Too late to escape the descending mass, the gun-toting men screamed out in terror as a 100 tons of whale flesh crashed down upon them.

Mat felt the vessel's deck disintegrate underfoot as fiberglass and wood splintered. Another huge body rose up and fell, followed by two more as the vessel's stern end was quickly transformed into wreckage by successive hammer blows.

Staggering to his feet, Mat stared in amazement as the deck leaned back, the boat's aft section now tilted below the waterline. The vessel was sinking rapidly.

With water rising up around his legs, Mat saw the others around him responding to the situation. Zimbola was already reaching for several life rings hanging nearby. Without hesitation, the black giant handed one off to Lucette before tossing another to Emmanuel. Spotting two more life rings, Mat followed suit, doling one out to Grahm and another to Jacob.

Vaguely, Mat perceived Hennington share a float with Hector as the deck began to disappear beneath them. Somehow his eyes found Joe Polanski in the midst of the turmoil, noticing that the DHS agent had climbed a nearby stairway to get clear of the rising water.

Mat's breath caught in his throat. In Polanski's hands was a Kalashnikov, the barrel leveled directly at Mat's head. Even in the dim light, Mat was able to discern the sneer where the stock of the weapon abutted Polanski's face. The vessel suddenly lurched just as Polanski pulled the trigger, and water kicked up five feet away from where Mat floated.

Polanski regained his balance and aimed again, but before he could get off a second shot, another gargantuan shadow surged up from the sea. Throwing up his arms in a futile bid to shield his face, Polanski let out a horrific scream. His cry was immediately cut off as the whale's bulk mashed down with the destructive force of a massive wrecking ball. In moments, the vessel disappeared from sight, leaving a bubbling froth behind.

Mat stared all about him as he treaded water. He could discern seven bobbing heads floating nearby. Using a breaststroke, he swam over to the nearest one, finding Grahm. "Are you okay?" he asked.

"I believe so," Grahm sputtered, spitting out water.

Another person floated over, and Mat could see it was the Haitian he had helped Jake rescue.

"Do you hear the sound of waves?" Jacob said. His tone held encouragement. "I think we should swim toward the sound."

"What happened?" It was Hennington asking the question as he shared his float with Hector.

"I think we just witnessed an attack by humpback whales," Grahm replied. "I would never have believed such gentle creatures were capable of such destruction unless I saw it with my own eyes."

Zimbola's large head moved into their midst, each of his hands grasping a life ring as he towed Emmanuel and Lucette. Moving to within arms reach of Mat, he stared closely at Mat's face. "Erzulie no longer controls us with her black magic, my friend. We are free of her power."

"It is because Erzulie is dead," Lucette blurted.

"How do you know this to be true?" Zimbola asked.

"Only the death of a voudun mambo can erase the spells she has invoked," Lucette assured him. "Erzulie must be dead."

Mat spun in the water as something splashed behind him. Upon the dark sea he could make out the profile of a fin knifing along the surface.

As if to alleviate Mat's sudden apprehension, Jacob spoke up. "The pod is here to help us."

Upon saying this, the heads of several dolphins poked above the water two feet away from where Mat floated.

- 132 -

A sense of fear gripped Ternier as the Bell Ranger set down next to the lighthouse for the second time. It was an emotion he had rarely experienced over the course of his life, one that made him feel utterly weak and not in control.

"What is going on here, Colonel?" Raduyev snarled belligerently, eyeing the dead soldiers scattered about the clearing. Twenty meters behind him, the Bell Ranger's rotors continued to swish the air at low RPM.

Ternier stared dully at the fallen men, their bodies revealed by what remained of the bonfire he had started earlier. This was too much for him to bear. His boat destroyed and now this. In flying back to the lighthouse, they had flown over the area where his vessel had been anchored. Under the helicopter's spotlight, only debris had littered the water. The sight had sent a chill racing through his bones. And now the chill had deepened.

"Your stupidity has allowed Javolyn and the girl to escape," Raduyev accused in a feral growl.

Ternier had difficulty speaking. His eyes continued to rove dully over the dead men, afraid of what else he might find if he searched further. His mother was a powerful voudun priestess. Armed with the ancient amulet bestowed upon her by the rada, she should have been invincible. All his life he had relied on Erzulie. She was the underlying source of his power. Without her he would be little more than a low-ranking official within the Haitian hierarchy. With his mind churning in confusion, he wondered how something like this could have happened.

The escalating pitch of the helicopter cranking its blades made Ternier spin around in alarm. Ortega had been right behind them a moment ago, but now he was back aboard the aircraft.

Raduyev shouted at the top of his lungs, waving his arms frantically. "What are you doing? Stop!"

The Bell Ranger lifted off before the Chechen thought to bolt forward, and both men could only stare as it headed out to sea.

- 133 -

The thought that he might actually be dealing with idiots had come to Ortega only after he had learned about the missile. He had fallen victim to a scheme far bigger than he had ever imagined. Both Ternier and Omar had made him a party to something he would have avoided had he known their primary objective. Social and economic stability in the United States was important to the drug trade. Stability insured open borders and a continuation of the profits his organization enjoyed. Stability meant reduced vigilance by the U.S. Coast Guard. There was an inherent predictability in stability. But a catastrophic upheaval of any kind had the potential of disrupting that trade, and he liked things just the way they were.

But now he was being cheated. Just before landing at the lighthouse he had received a radio call from the San Carlo that had infuriated him. He had controlled his temper, however, giving his passengers no indication of what had been said. He was not in the habit of supplying headphones to those who sat in the rear seats, and without them his passengers had no way of knowing the contents of the communiqué.

As Fernando piloted the helicopter beyond the San Carlo, Ortega spotted the tug. The vessel was still adrift without power. The cloud cover had all but dissipated, allowing the moon to cast a rich golden glow upon the water below.

"Bring us to a hover above them and shine the searchlight at their stern," Ortega instructed.

Three Colombians looked up as Fernando brought the aircraft lower. Under the chopper's beam, Ortega caught a glimpse of a fourth man rising to the surface near the aft end of the vessel, one of the divers Omar had brought along to raise the bomb. The water was clear, and Ortega could see some of the netting the diver had just cut free.

Ortega continued to watch as the diver climbed back aboard the small vessel. The diver pulled up his mask and nodded to the other men, and a moment later the tug's operator re-engaged the engine to send the vessel sliding smoothly across the water. The operator looked up and gave the okay sign, letting his boss know that the problem had been corrected.

Ortega looked at his watch, still fuming over the radio message. Five minutes still remained before the Spirit of Aden would sail away. *How dare the Aden's captain give him an ultimatum after he had carried out his end of the deal!* He dismissed the thought, knowing what he would do if the threat was carried out.

Under the searchlight, something in the water caught Ortega's eye just as Fernando was about to take the aircraft out of its hover. Within the circle of light, several objects darted.

Ortega pointed. "Did you see that, Fernando?"

"See what?"

Ortega pointed again, this time angrily. "Down there!"

"I see nothing but water."

A livid scowl came to Ortega's face as he lifted his gaze to bear on the pilot. "Are you blind?" Reaching under his seat, he grabbed hold of an MK3 stored there. Pulling the pin, he hurled it at the water below, the rage within him giving it an extra boost.

"Keep the light trained on the water and hold this position," Ortega growled hotly. "There are dolphins down there! Dolphins with hands! They are the reason the tug keeps breaking down. They foul the props with netting."

Ortega watched as the grenade detonated, the force of it whipping the water beneath them into a frothing mushroom. When the water settled, he saw nothing to give him satisfaction.

"Take us over the tug again!" Ortega yelled. He would be damned if dolphins were going to stop him from getting the remainder of the heroin. Groping under the seat, he grabbed another grenade.

"I thought you wanted live specimens," Fernando said quickly, eyeing his boss as he dipped the Ranger's nose.

Ortega looked over at the freighter, his expression murderous. "That shipment is more important."

The Ranger began to gather speed in an effort to catch the tug.

"Why are we moving so slow?" Ortega complained curtly.

"We'll overshoot the tug if I go any faster," Fernando explained.

"Perhaps I should let Pedro do the flying," snarled Ortega, keeping his eyes trained on the water. "Shine the light out in front of the tug!"

Fernando did as he was told.

On the water below the tug had lost speed, it's driver throwing up his hands in frustration and directing a look of dejection at the aircraft above.

"They fouled her again!" Ortega exploded in disbelief, his manner now making Fernando cringe. The searchlight revealed two dolphins below the waterline. Viciously, Ortega yanked the pin on another grenade, flinging it with all his might down into the ring of light. An incoherent string of ranting profanity left his lips as he awaited the four-second delay.

The sea abruptly bulged off the tug's bow, lifting the boat's keel at a rakish angle and throwing up a plume of spray. The four men aboard her went sprawling to the deck to keep from being tossed into the water. A moment passed before all four looked up in alarm at the chopper hovering overhead. Under the searchlight's glare, there was no mistaking the panic in their eyes.

"Play the light all around the tug!" Ortega roared insanely.

Swinging the light to and fro, Fernando carried out the order.

Ortega's fit of rage escalated further when nothing showed under the beam. His tantrum was interrupted as the radio suddenly came alive with another call from the San Carlo.

"What is it?" Ortega screamed, disregarding radio protocol of any kind.

A short pause ensued before the voice coming through his headphones erupted frantically. "The Aden is leaving! The captain refuses to wait any longer!"

Ortega turned in his seat, ferreting out the freighter's dark bulk on the moonlit sea. Cursing vilely, he felt his anger soar to yet a new level.

- 134 -

Raduyev trotted as quickly as he dared, following the trail that would take him to his objective. Armed with a Kalashnikov he had taken from one of the dead soldiers, he was prepared to take on any resistance encountered. Having familiarized himself with the lay of the land during the past several months, he followed the moonlit footpath that wound its way through the treacherous karst, moving vigilantly and eventually reaching his destination without any major impediments or mishaps. He had left Ternier back at the lighthouse, unmoved by the man's shameful lamentations over the losses he had sustained.

Launching the Rodong was currently his only concern. Now that the H-bomb had been recovered and delivered, he was free to carry out the second phase of the mission. That had been the plan all along anyway, firing off the Rodong shortly after the high-yield nuclear weapon had been safely stowed aboard the Spirit of Aden. It had taken him and his men two months of backbreaking labor to chisel out another of the tunnels near the island's surface in order to make it large enough to accommodate the entire missile delivery system. With an overall length of nearly 12 meters and a diameter of 0.50 meters, the rocket also required a launching carriage that been difficult to erect in the tunnel's limited space. Provided to Iran by way of Pyongyang, North Korea, the rocket was a smaller version of a standard Rodong missile, having been specially modified so that field assembly was possible. Nevertheless, hauling the various parts up from the submarine pen and putting the thing together had required endless hours of gut-wrenching toil.

Moving into an area of dense underbrush, Raduyev lifted several stones to reveal a metal box. He was the only person among his team who had knowledge of the device's location and operation. Inserting a key, he raised the lid on the box to reveal a small console with keypad, each of the keys glowing a soft red. The launch control was wireless, using a microwave pulse to engage the rocket engine and release the locking mechanism on the launching carriage. All that need be done was for him to punch in the 9-digit launch code to send the missile on its way. This particular Rodong had been specifically designed to carry a nuclear warhead with a destructive yield comparable to that used on Hiroshima. The missile would follow a flight path that had been hard-wired into its circuitry, flying a low-level trajectory over the ocean that would give it a limited profile on radar. Only when it neared Miami would it gain altitude to achieve an air burst for optimal effect.

Raduyev spun at the sound of movement behind him, grabbing for the Kalashnikov he had placed on the ground next to him.

"Do not attempt to fire the missile!" a voice scolded harshly.

Raduyev squinted his eyes, staring at the dark figure standing less than three meters away. It was Bashir.

"You are a pox on our people," Raduyev griped bitterly, "but you will foil me no more, for I am sending you to hell where you belong." With those words, he pulled the Kalashnikov's trigger to be rid of Bashir once and for all.

Raduyev's eyes widened when the weapon failed to fire. Cursing, he threw it down and rose to his feet, drawing the Bowie knife he carried rather than the Browning holstered at his side. "I have had enough of you," he hissed hatefully, preparing to leap at his former teammate. But before he could do so, several more figures joined Bashir's steadfast form.

The first tendrils of dawn were beginning to break, and within the gathering light Raduyev perceived a face he had not seen before, though it was similar to that of the accursed dolphin girl who also stood next to Bashir.

"These angels suppress the firing of your weapon, just as they will keep the Rodong from launching," Bashir said calmly.

Raduyev shifted his eyes to the last person to join the trio, and his expression turned even more hateful. "I enjoyed killing your friend, the little Zionist pig," Raduyev taunted, managing to fill his voice with a smugness he did not feel as he stared at the firearm trained on him.

Jake Javolyn stared back with the look of a predator, his eyes the harbingers of death as his finger rested coldly on the Stoker's trigger.

Raduyev gazed down the barrel of the weapon, his expression turning scornful. "You disappoint me, Javolyn. I had always thought you to be a warrior, but now I see you for the coward you truly are."

Javolyn met the challenge, crouching down to pull his K-bar from its scabbard as he set the Stoker aside. "Let's forego the small talk, Yeslam, and get to the thing we both want. Only this time you won't have the opportunity of resorting to your most noteworthy talent, going for your opponent's back when he least expects it."

"No, Jay Jay!" Destiny pleaded. "Don't do this!"

Amphitrite placed a hand on Destiny's shoulder. "The quarrel between these men cannot be avoided, my daughter. To interfere may have disastrous consequences."

Raduyev let go with a mocking laugh. "Yes, do not try to save this man. To do so will only bring Allah's wrath upon you."

Jake stepped in front of Destiny, careful to keep his eyes locked on the Chechen. "Please take your daughter away from here," he requested gruffly.

Raduyev continued to mock, his voice taking on a crazed lilt. "What happens here will not matter. Allah has given his true believers a weapon forged by the very hands of his greatest enemy." He laughed insanely. "I find it humorous that the Great Satan will ultimately be smitten by his own creation."

Something buzzed sharply in the distance, making Raduyev whirl to follow the sound. The noise rose and fell like that of a chainsaw working its way through tough oak. He stared aghast as his eyes fell on the source in the dawn twilight. Two miles out to sea a broken laser beam of red light lanced down on the Aden. He knew what he was seeing, and a feeling of utter failure suddenly took hold of him. The Yemeni freighter was being pelted unmercifully, a hail of deadly rounds raining down upon it. Even from where he stood he could see a portion of the lethal enfilade caroming off the ship's deck and superstructure with incredible ferocity. The tracers abruptly stopped, and in the sky just above the freighter he saw Ortega's chopper turn, coming around for another strafing run.

"This cannot be happening," Raduyev screamed incredulously, but he gathered himself in quickly, placing glowering eyes back on Jake.

An expansive grin spread across Jake's face; he was truly enjoying the Chechen's alarm and he could not resist goading him further. "I see you and your Colombian buddy are having a little lover's spat."

The buzzing started up again. In the distance, the chopper recommenced its attack, sending another stream of tracers angling down on the freighter. The aircraft appeared like a tiny gnat buzzing angrily over a potential host as it poured the full power of its gattling gun into the target below. The broken laser remained focused on the ship for a good four seconds before the gun stopped firing. A flash of bright light suddenly lit up the sea as the Aden's aft section flared with the intensity of an exploding nova.

Jake threw another barb at Raduyev. "Could it be your Allah does not approve of your plan?"

Raduyev turned back to his sworn enemy with savage loathing. "You are a dead man!" Screaming out the words, he lunged, thrusting the Bowie forward with deadly intent.

- 135 -

The explosion knocked the Aden's captain off his feet as though he had been back-kicked by a mule. Stunned though he was, he vaguely sensed the deck of the bridge begin to tilt, and he knew at once that at least one of the rounds had found the concealed explosives contained aboard his ship.

He had picked up the explosives in Kingston, loading them onto the freighter's back deck in three large shipping containers. Each container had been crammed with two hundred packing crates labeled Jamaican rum, half of which were filled with dynamite and aluminum powder. The explosives had been destined for various Iranian-sponsored insurgents operating in Iraq and were to be used in building IEDs, improvised explosive devices aimed at killing American troops.

Dazedly, the captain struggled to his feet, aware that his ship was going down. Lying next to him was the decapitated body of the ship's steersman, pulsing spurts of blood continuing to gush from where the man's neck had been severed. This made it difficult to move along the angled deck, for he kept slipping in the gore as it flowed down the sloped surface. Abruptly, his eyes fell upon another ghastly sight. The shredded corpse of his first mate lay near the rear of the bridge, his body torn apart beyond recognition by shattered plexiglass.

On all sides of him the windows along the bridge had been blown out, and as he grabbed one of the frames for support, he saw several survivors of his crew leap overboard to get clear of the ship. He nearly lost his balance as the freighter began to lean more acutely, and as he glanced astern, he could now see the ship's aft section slipping below the waves.

Drowning at sea had always been his greatest fear, and he wondered why Allah had allowed him to survive both the machine gun fire and the force of the ensuing blast if he was ultimately going to submerge with his ship. Perhaps he was not meant to drown after all. Perhaps God wanted him to live to continue fighting the infidels. Maybe he should make an effort not to perish.

The inane little grin that began to form on his face immediately turned to shock as he reached out to pull himself clear of the doorway. His left arm was gone. Dully he stared at the bloody stump, a short jagged section of upper humerus protruding meekly from his shoulder.

Using what little strength remained within him, he managed to get through the doorway as the deck canted further. The ship was sinking rapidly now and he did not want it to become his final resting place. As water rose up around his knees, he looked back at the nearby island and stared entranced, somehow finding beauty in what he saw. The dawn sun had just cleared the ocean and was bathing the island's flattened plateau in an unearthly golden light, provoking the moisture from the recent rains into a rising mist of silent splendor.

And then something truly glorious caught his eyes. A spectacular rainbow was gathering rapidly within the mist, forming a breathtaking tapestry of vivid hues that bridged the karst jutting from the sea. With his legs beginning to buckle beneath him, he knew he was now too weak to jump clear of the ship. In an effort to comfort himself, he kept his gaze locked on the beautiful image as his head slipped below the water.

- 136 -

Jake was surprised at how fast Yeslam moved. He had never been impressed with the Chechen's speed, having had numerous occasions during Seal training to get a firsthand look at the man's mediocre quickness. But as his nemesis came at him, he saw no hint of the former clumsiness his opponent had once exhibited.

Raduyev slashed out, nearly catching Jake's shoulder with the edge of the blade. Jake sidestepped the frontal attack, circling to his right and opening up some distance between them. With the ease of a juggler, the Chechen tossed the Bowie to his left hand and lunged again, his arm fully extended like that of a graceful fencer. Jake leaned back, parrying the blade away before the tip could rip into his face.

Backing away, Jake noted the demented expression Raduyev wore. The Bowie flashed once more as the Chechen shifted it smoothly back to his right hand. A break in the thicket behind Raduyev gave Jake a clear view of the ocean, and he could now see that the freighter had completely vanished from sight. Here was the distraction he needed that would provide an opening to his enemy's most vulnerable area, that being his ego.

"Your mission has fallen apart," Jake chided. "Your crew neutralized, your ship sinking." He let out a chortle designed to needle. "A befitting end to a terrible leader, wouldn't you say?"

Raduyev's eyes blazed with pent up rage. "An infidel is no match for a true servant of Allah," he hissed, spittle flying from his lips, "one the Almighty sees as his most cherished warrior."

Jake snickered again. "Maybe..." He circled to his left. "And then again, maybe not. But, unfortunately, all I see is a coward standing before me, a man without a shred of honor."

Raduyev's glare deepened into one of the cruelest caricatures Jake had ever seen, and the Chechen began flicking the Bowie rapidly between hands. The blade he wielded was longer than the K-bar by a good four inches.

"After I kill you, these women will become my slaves to do with as I please," Raduyev blustered. Intent on antagonizing Javolyn further, he let his eyes rove obscenely over Destiny and Amphitrite, producing a grin charged with lasciviousness. "I am sure they will give me many nights of pleasure." He feinted to his left at this last provocation, only to leap back to his right to execute a backhanded swipe with the blade's cutting edge. The knife grazed Jake's jumpsuit along the chest, tearing open the fabric.

Raduyev's maneuver provided Jake with the opening he had been looking for. In a flash, he slipped in close to his opponent, digging the K-bar deep into the Chechen's left bicep. Raduyev let out a howl, leaping back in startled amazement at how quickly Jake had been able to penetrate his guard.

"That one's compliments of Tesha," Jake harried in an even tone. "You remember Tesha, don't you?"

The Chechen glanced at his bicep, surprised at the blood. When he looked back at Jake, his eyes revealed a dampening bravado. With his confidence now compromised, he was not so eager to take the offensive.

Jake danced to his right. "And I'm sure you haven't forgotten-" Suddenly lunging forward, he jabbed the K-bar high with blinding speed, only to go low in a blur of motion. He withdrew before the Chechen had a chance to counter, completing the sentence as he did so. "-Captain Sheridan."

Stunned by the swiftness of movement, it took Raduyev a moment to comprehend his right thigh had been stabbed. He howled again as the pain caught up with his surprise.

Jake narrowed his eyes gravely, preparing to inflict more punishment, but the sound of the Bell Ranger's minigun stopped him. Seeing that Raduyev was temporarily hobbled, he risked a peek out to sea. Ortega's chopper was flying low over the water less than a thousand meters away, its weapon blazing furiously as it raked the ocean beneath it.

Standing further back from where Jake stood, Destiny let out a shrill cry. "No!"

Jake winced, bringing his free hand to his head. A sharp sting echoed thunderously at the back of his mind as though his brain had been ripped asunder. Gripped by a sudden bout of nausea, his legs wobbled unsteadily under him.

- 137 -

Ortega looked down at the water in a peeved manner. "I think you could have done a better job," he said angrily, his eyes suddenly shifting to the man sitting in the seat next to him.

"At its highest rate, this type of weapon will automatically kick out of firing mode after a four second burst," Fernando tried explaining. "It's a built-in safety feature to prevent the barrels from melting."

Ortega kept his gaze riveted on the pilot a moment longer before taking inventory of the ocean below. "Your accuracy is what puzzles me. I think you were purposely trying to miss the targets."

Fernando swallowed hard. "I destroyed the freighter. What difference will it make if I failed to hit one of those creatures?"

The Colombian's eyes continued to scan the water. It was possible Fernando might have gotten one of those white dolphins, a smaller one at that. He had seen the tracers kick up a spume close to the creature when it had surfaced, but then the shots had gone wide. He was getting strange vibes from Fernando, reading something in the man's manner to suggest he didn't like doing this.

"Take us back to the ship," Ortega growled hotly.

Fernando nudged the cyclic over, banking the chopper in the direction of the San Carlo. Farther away, two other vessels were moving toward it. Both of its sister ships, the *San Diablo* and *San Pinto* were coming fast to join her.

- 138 -

Destiny saw Jake suddenly reel, fighting for breath. She knew the cause. Her mental link with the dolphins had inexplicably come flickering back, and for one brief instant she had felt Achilles' pain. A round from the helicopter had punctured the young albino's right lung. The impenetrable barrier Achilles had erected earlier had come crashing down with the injury, reopening the strange connection the dolphin shared with his human counterpart.

As if in a dream, Destiny watched as Raduyev limped cautiously toward the man she loved, the Bowie knife clutched firmly in his hand. Inexorably bonded to the pod's youngest member, Jake was feeling the full brunt of Achilles' agony as if it were his own, and it was now obvious to Raduyev that his enemy was caught in the grip of some mysterious seizure.

Without giving it much thought, Destiny picked up the machine gun Jake had set aside on the ground, bringing the barrel to bear on Raduyev before he could use the knife. "Stop!" she cried.

The Chechen halted, surprised to see the weapon trained on him.

Destiny waved the gun. "Get away from him!"

Raduyev turned petitioning eyes to Bashir as Jake took in several ragged breaths. "This girl is no more an angel than I am an infidel," he implored. "If she were truly one of Allah's angels, she would have no use of man-made weapons."

Bashir appeared unmoved by the Chechen's entreaty. "Do not attempt to seek my support, Yeslam. I am only committed to those who are righteous."

Destiny stepped closer to the Chechen, pointing the Stoker threateningly. "Back away!"

Raduyev searched Destiny's face for several seconds more before complying, faltering on his injured leg as he moved backward with a contemptible sneer plastered on his face.

Amphitrite stepped to her daughter's side. "We must hurry if we are to save Achilles."

"Go without me, mother," Destiny said. "I'll stay here with Jay Jay."

Amphitrite seemed reluctant to leave, but Bashir intervened before she could contest the matter. "God go with you, Mother Angel!" he urged. "I will remain here with Destiny." He pointed behind Amphitrite and spoke quickly. "You will find a footpath over there that winds its way down through the thornbush. It will take you to a small ledge where you can dive down into the sea. It is the fastest route to the water."

Anxiety grew on Amphitrite's face as Jake's labored breathing echoed Achilles' distress. She could not delay any longer. "Stay safe, my daughter!" she intoned, turning to take the path behind her at a run.

Destiny moved to Jake's side, continuing to keep the Stoker leveled at Raduyev. Jake had fallen to one knee, his pallor waxen in the light of dawn. Hefting the bulky firearm as best she could with with one arm, she placed a hand on his head, attempting to break the bridge connecting him with the young albino. It was no use. She needed oneness with the others in order to accomplish this, and that had all but deserted her.

Raduyev tittered raucously. "So the mighty Javolyn requires the protection of a woman." He kept up his scornful chortle, continuing to back away slowly, grimacing each time he placed weight on the injured leg.

Bashir suddenly shouted. "Keep away from the-"

Destiny spun to see why Bashir had fallen silent. The Palestinian crashed to the ground in a heap. Before she could grasp what had happened, the Stoker was yanked forcefully from her hands.

Destiny stifled a scream. Ternier loomed above her, his eyes bulging as if they would start from his head. Dangling from his neck was the trinket previously worn by Erzulie, the charm blackened almost beyond recognition.

The Colonel stepped away from Destiny, setting his gaze upon Raduyev. "There is nothing to stop you now," he grunted hoarsely. "Send off the missile!"

Raduyev smiled victoriously, limping the remaining ten feet to the launch control. Within seconds, he punched in the numbers that would fire the Rodong. Completing the task, he looked back at Destiny, his laughter causing shivers to go cascading along her bones.

"How long?" Ternier demanded, his voice cutting into Raduyev's glee like the sharpened edge of a knife.

The Chechen stopped his laughter, his mirth changing over to annoyance. "The Rodong's computer must first go through a pre-launch initiation sequence."

"I care nothing for explanations," Ternier roared. "How long?"

"Three minutes!" Raduyev rasped harshly. His eyes abruptly darted to Javolyn like those of an anaconda ready to feast, and he tested the edge of his Bowie with his thumb. "You can have the girl," he said coldly, "but Javolyn is mine."

- 139 -

As the Bell Ranger headed for the San Carlo's helipad, something made Ortega look back at the sea behind him. "Abort the landing!" he shouted excitedly. "Bring us around!"

Fernando followed the order, banking the chopper hard to port.

Ortega pointed wildly. At least nine albino dolphins were converging on the area of sea where Fernando had last fired the guns. Drawing closer to the creatures, more fins could be seen knifing the water.

The Colombian squinted hard. A huge congregation of gray bottlenose dolphins was now visible. "Fire the gun down into that pack!"

"The gun is empty," Fernando said. "We expended all the rounds."

"Show me!" Ortega demanded, staring over at Fernando suspiciously.

Fernando thumbed the firing button on the cyclic stick. On the chopper's port side, the minigun barrels became blurs of spinning motion, failing to discharge a single round.

Ortega slammed a fist into the control console, his face painted in livid murderous rage.

Fernando spoke quickly, his voice tense as his boss reached for another grenade. "Why kill them when you have the chance to catch the ones with hands. Wouldn't it be better to have the San Diablo and San Pinto deploy their nets?"

Ortega hesitated, giving the suggestion some thought before shaking his head. "No! The white ones are too fast and far too smart to be trapped."

"Look there!" Fernando pointed out hurriedly. "They're keeping a small one from sinking. If they don't swim away, you'll have enough time to surround them." He pointed again at an adjacent area of sea where a furious jumble of whitewater roiled the water. "And you've got tuna as an added bonus."

Ortega fingered the grenade's pull ring as he watched the scene below. The water appeared stained with blood where a group of white dolphins lingered. Within their midst, a smaller one was being kept afloat. "Alright," he finally begrudged reluctantly, placing the grenade back in its box. "Perhaps coming away from here with live specimens is not such a bad idea."

Keying the mike, Ortega hailed the other ships, giving them precise instructions.

Even in the midst of his pain, Achilles heard Amphitrite's urgent call. *Hold on, young one, do not be afraid. We will bring you back to full rejuvenation.*

With his physical existence now fragile and slipping slowly from him, Achilles answered. *I only fear for Jay Jay.*

Your bond with him has become a liability, Amphitrite replied. *Jay Jay has become debilitated by your suffering.*

Achilles felt his body being lifted to the surface. Natalie was supporting him. Coral and Reef were next to her. Nevertheless, he would require either Destiny or her mother to bring the pod's mental energy into full focus. Destiny, he knew, was more adept at this sort of thing than Amphitrite, but something in Destiny's psyche had changed to deflect his sense of her.

And something within himself had also changed, something that was affecting the others as well. He could not explain it. He only knew it was time to take an aggressive stand against the forces confronting his species if they were going to survive and propagate.

They had resources at their disposal with which to fight back. Their very intelligence could be used as a weapon. Through Jay Jay they had learned of the iniquitous human alliances that had come to the island, a brittle union of differing motivations and ideologies held together by threads of greed, power and hate. Driving a wedge of distrust between the parties had been easy enough. Strangely, the whales had willingly lent their support. And now there were other things they could put to good use.

There was heartfelt emotion tied into this new perspective, an emerging side of him he never knew existed. Fully surrendering to this emotion went not without inherent risks, however, for he was vaguely aware of the negative consequences that might come of it. A gleaning of intuition suddenly accompanied his pain, and he immediately understood why he had lost all sense of Destiny. She had fallen prey to the same emotion, and in so doing her purity had been contaminated.

Help me to journey into myself, Achilles cried out, *for that is the only way I can bring Destiny back to us.*

Amphitrite's essence reached out to him. *Always remember to cast away the illusion of separation, little one. Only in unison can we attain the higher self, the very power to manipulate the earth's illusion.*

Comforted by these thoughts, Achilles felt his pain diminish. Before him lay the same rainbow presented to Jay Jay, a thing with no distinct location nor distance. And yet, paradoxically, it gave him direction.

Jake gasped, once again able to breath. The strange debilitation gripping him suddenly vanished as quickly as it had come, and before him he perceived the multi-hued band of light arching away from the darkness.

It was then he became aware of the voice echoing across the cosmos. Achilles was calling out to him. *You must hasten to follow the rainbow, Jay Jay. Merge with it and drink of its energy.*

Sensing the urgency in the words, Jake felt himself catching up to the leading light waves pulsating between galaxies. Without knowing why, he instinctively sensed the thing rushing up from the black void to intercept him even before he recognized the danger. Abruptly, he rolled left, letting the surge of energy carry him beyond the glint.

Coming back to his feet he saw Raduyev before him, the Chechen's face twisted into an emblem of hatred. Thrown off balance by Jake's sudden dodge, the man's eyes bulged in disbelief as his Bowie only met air.

"Kill him already!" Ternier screamed in annoyance, continuing to hold onto Destiny with one hand. "He has no weapon."

Jake found the K-bar to be missing from his hand. His knife lay on the ground near Raduyev's feet.

Emboldened by his unarmed opponent, Raduyev eyed Jake disdainfully, his need to destroy prompting him to ignore his injured leg. "You are weak, infidel," he sneered. He reached down quickly to pick up the K-bar. "Does Allah's chosen one make you tremble so much that you cannot hold onto your weapon?"

Jake circled left, awaiting another lunge by the Chechen. Armed with a blade in each hand, Raduyev was now twice as dangerous. But the Islamist was not so eager to rush in this time, holding back and looking for the right moment to make his move.

"Kill him!" Ternier bellowed impatiently. "Kill him or I will shoot him down from here."

"No!" Destiny cried, suddenly turning on Ternier with liquid eyes and clawing at his face with both hands.

Three times larger than the dimunitive girl, Ternier sent her sprawling to the ground with a vicious backhand. Stunned by the blow, Destiny lay dazed at his feet, blood trickling from her mouth.

Out of the corner of his eye Jake saw what Ternier had done, and in that instant his rage detonated like a megaton bomb. Disregarding Raduyev completely, he bit back a silent oath and leapt at the powerful Haitian before the Colonel had a chance to react. In the span of a millisecond, he exploded across the four meters separating him from Ternier, his legs seemingly energized by something beyond his comprehension. Caught by sheer surprise at the bold move, Ternier's jaw hung agape in frozen astonishment just as the heel of Jake's right foot slammed him full in the face. Tumbled from his feet by the force of the blow, the Colonel still managed to pull back on the Stoker's trigger. Flames belched from the muzzle, stabbing up into Jake's chest.

In that instant, time came to a standstill and a multitude of voices resounded in Jake's head, but the words came to him as one compressed thought rather than a chorus. *Do not let the darkness deceive your senses, Jay Jay, for it will lead you to foolish presumption.* The words were familiar, he had heard them before. Swept along the rainbow's curve, he glimpsed the same dodecahedron he had seen in the dream as the voices continued to indoctrinate. *Unconditional love is the one true component of all reality, Jay Jay. We give it to you freely, enabling you to see beyond the physical deceptions that trick the unenlightened senses. It is your shield of invincibility. You must cast aside all doubts that you can survive this moment.*

Jake sensed the entire pod behind these thoughts, each separate creature merging to join as one unified higher self, and in that instant he fully understood the truth. The power behind all creation could be his if he gave up the illusion of separation.

A sense of exhilaration washed over him at this discovery, immunizing him from the physical and social forces of the universe. It was a state of omnipotence, cleansing and coming easily to him, for he had never let a fear of death govern his actions. It was this state of oneness with the others that freed him, keeping him from presupposing one's separate physical existence to be the ultimate reality. And by consciously living the illusion, he now had the power to manipulate it.

Joined with the others, Jake stared directly into the Stoker's barrel and smiled. Time had stopped, holding back the flame leaping from the muzzle. He could not be touched.

A look of incredulity transcended Ternier's face as he continued to press down on the trigger. "Why will you not die?" he screamed.

"Maybe your aim is off," Jake growled. Stepping in close to where the man lay, he reached down with one hand and tore the firearm from Ternier's grasp. The Colonel offered little resistance, his expression still dumbstruck. Rearing back, Jake came down hard with the weapon, cracking it butt-first into Ternier's forehead and opening a huge gash. Ternier's arms fell limply to each side, his eyes glazed and frozen in a vacant comatose stare.

Whirling back around, Jake locked eyes with Raduyev. The Islamist appeared white as a ghost. "This fantasy of yours to take over the world has become tiresome," he announced calmly, training the Stoker on the Chechen.

Though seemingly still dazed, Destiny rose to stand beside Jake. "He's punched in the launch code to the missile," she fretted. "It will launch in less than three minutes."

Jake stared stonily at his enemy. "I'll only ask you once to stop this missile from firing." In his tone was the unmistakable promise of death.

Raduyev forced a haughty grin. "It is too late for that. Once the code has been fed to the Rodong, it cannot be stopped."

"Then you leave me only one choice."

The Chechen let out a tense, strained laugh. "And what choice is that?" he asked gruffly.

Jake's reply was caustic. "Sending you off to your mentor the devil."

At seeing the look on Jake's face, a rabid animal growl left the Chechen's lips, escalating into a deep throaty rumble. But even before he could spring in a last ditch effort to save himself, Jake turned the Stoker loose. The torrent of bullets flashed across the short space separating the two men and flung Raduyev backwards, nearly cutting him in half.

Destiny looked away as Jake pumped one final burst into the Chechen's fallen corpse. Releasing the trigger, Jake stared down at Raduyev's remains and spat. "Consider your debt to Myers paid in full," he muttered quietly.

A sudden groan caused Jake to look behind him. Destiny was kneeling at Bashir's side, cradling his head as he came around. "Are you able to stand, Bashir?" she asked.

Bashir rubbed the back of his head, attempting to rise on unsteady feet. Destiny rose with him, lending support. "What has happened?" he gasped.

"You were struck from behind," the girl said tenderly, her voice edged with concern. "Do you know how to keep the missile from launching?" she went on hurriedly, knowing time was running out.

Bashir continued to rub his head, shifting his eyes to where the missile control box lay. "Yeslam is the only one who has such knowledge."

Jake quickly interceded. "Where's the missle located?"

The Palestian's eyes fell on Raduyev's riddled body. "About 200 meters from here."

Jake grabbed Destiny by the arm. He had felt the pod's collective mind, now fully aware of what was possible. "You can stop it," he encouraged. "You are the lense through which the others can focus."

Destiny stared back morosely, all traces of the self-assured optimism she had shown him in the past now gone. "Something has happened to me, Jay Jay." Her eyes were wet with moisture, sending forth a frustrated dribbling of tears. "I can't feel the others."

This was not what Jake wanted to hear. Millions of people were about to die.

- 142 -

Destiny affixed Jay Jay with helpless eyes. By falling in love she knew she had compromised herself. The emotion was unyielding in the way it tugged at her, drawing forth a selfishness within her she never knew existed. Her need to prevent Jay Jay's death had caused her to neglect the others. And even worse, she now realized she had broken the cardinal tenet instilled in her by her mother. She had fallen victim to doubt by presuming the future might actually be unalterable. There was a foolish side to presuming, for it had a self-fulfilling power. The painting back in the Gaia cave was the cause of this. She had inadvertently let her mind wander over unfamiliar terrain, an area of the psyche where pessimism abounded. She had become infected with a belief that perhaps Jay Jay's prophesized death was permanently etched into the fabric of space-time, an inevitable occurrence destined to be unpreventable. And it was this that had brought on the fear. With her mind shackled by it, she had lost her sense of the others.

"You've got to try," Jake urged, gently wiping away the tears that marred her face. "Nothing is impossible. You were the one who taught me that."

Destiny stared hard into his eyes. She could see why Achilles had taken to him so readily. In many ways, the two of them were very much alike. Both were fearless, filled with a natural unstoppable energy that sought to challenge danger at every turn, particularly when the danger emanated from some iniquitous source seeking to mete out injustice and misery. And like his bond-mate, the young albino was now determined to fight back, tenaciously lashing out at evil in an effort to rid the earth of such influence.

Bashir stood nearby, watching Destiny closely. "Allah has given you purpose, my angel. With his power behind you, it is not possible for you to fail."

Something within Destiny began to ease as she pondered this, and she realized the threads of fear that had grounded her in the earth's illusion were beginning to break. Letting out a deep breath she relaxed her mind, feeling the last tendrils of dread escape her.

"I know you can do this if you try," Jake reiterated.

"Trying will not be enough, Jay Jay," she said, her tone harboring pessimism. "Doing will be the only thing that matters."

"Then we will do!" Jake declared. "We will do it together."

Destiny felt herself smiling. She was drawing strength from the way he was looking at her.

Turning to gaze out to sea, Destiny realized others had come into the clearing now. Samuel and his mother, Louwanda, had ascended from the caverns below. She recognized other faces. Most belonged to those abducted from Malique, but among them were two that had abetted Raduyev. One was the man with the bloodhound eyes she had seen down in the caverns, the one called Gullu. Kalid was with him.

Jake started, his eyes darkening as they fell on the two bearded men, and he immediately raised the Stoker, prepared to use it once again.

Destiny grabbed his wrist, her grip surprisingly strong. "It's alright, Jay Jay," she assuaged gently. "These men are not a danger."

"You don't understand," he snapped sharply. He pointed the Stoker accusingly at Sherkhan, not daring to take his eyes from the man. "That one cannot be trusted."

Destiny continued to hold his wrist. "Please, Jay Jay."

Sherkhan separated himself from the milling group, moving off to one side of the clearing where no one else stood. Humbly he faced Jake, his arms drooped resignedly at his sides. "I deserve to die," he said softly, sorrowfully. His manner was remorseful, the embodiment of decisive repentance, and he seemed fully prepared for Jake to kill him. "Not only have I betrayed you and your brothers, I have also betrayed Islam."

Jake's frosty glare fell away, changing over into a mystified frown. He felt strangely defused by the man standing before him. Surely such a show could not possibly be contrived. Sherkhan's eyes were pathetically rheumy, holding back a flood of unshed tears, and within them Jake sensed the cloud of tragedy. He turned to Destiny, aware of the depth of empathy gathering on her face as she clutched his wrist beseechingly. The grudge he held for the man suddenly seemed insignificant when weighed against what was currently at stake, a thing of infinitely greater importance.

Slowly he lowered the Stoker, lucidly aware that something within himself had changed, though he couldn't quite pinpoint what it was that now took away his desire for vengeance. Perhaps it had something to do with his interaction with Destiny and the pod, or maybe it was his exposure to their fabulous but cryptic art. By all counts, Sherkhan should pay for his involvement in Myer's death. But within Sherkhan's sorrowful eyes he sensed a crushing despondency, almost as though some terrible calamity had left the man bereft of loved ones, an extortion of the man's very soul that had caused him to do what he had done. In that twinkling of circumspection, something glimmered vibrantly in one of the back corridors of his mind, and he suddenly saw the pathos behind the man's actions. And with this newfound gleaning he was now convinced Sherkhan had undergone the same tranformation as Bashir. The dolphin art affected each person differently, and for some it was able to lift away the shell of the outer persona, revealing the true nature that lay beneath.

Jake met Destiny's earnest stare and gave her a reassuring smile, inwardly ashamed of his brief display of madness. Time was running out. "We've got a missle to stop," he reminded her.

Destiny let go of Jake's wrist and read the faces milling all about her. She had become the focal point of all gazes. Raising her voice, she said, "I'm going to need everyone's help."

"Whatever you ask!" Bashir blurted.

Destiny took a deep breath. "I need everyone to concentrate, to focus your thoughts on one thing."

Those around her began to nod and smile in acquiescence, but it was Bashir who clarified what remained to be said. "A missile is going to launch at any moment, people. We will all carry out God's will by stopping it."

Bashir turned his gaze back to Destiny, presenting her with an encouraging grin. Destiny studied the Palestinian, amazed that he somehow understood what had to be done. Almost at once, a sense of the pod returned, an eager cacophonous buzz resounding in her head.

I am here for you, my daughter.

I, too, Natalie called.

We are with you. It was Coral and Reef.

Our minds will become one, Hermes and Aphrodite intoned.

Let the essence of our thoughts merge into something greater, Apollo and Artemis droned.

Ride my mind and spirit as you ride my back, Hercules rumbled.

As one, all things are possible, echoed Thetis.

We are guardians of the earth's fate, Athena stressed.

And then a twelfth voice nudged her. *Be not without hope, girl, for crystal rain can fall from the darkest clouds.* It was the voice of Jacob. He was reminding her about a passage taken from the writings of Nizami, an ancient Persian poet. There was always hope, even in the darkest hours of adversity.

A multitude of other cetacean voices joined in, soaring into a wondrous heavenly chorus. Like wisps of unyielding love, these various sentiences intertwined and blended, reaching out and latching onto Destiny's central core. Jay Jay was with her, and so was Bashir. Both human and delphine merged, with all distinctions beginning to blur. Slowly, they began to rotate around her, quickly gaining momentum and coalescing into a whirling mass of pure energy.

Intruding its way into this growing collective mind was a growing roar, and in that moment the higher self knew the missile had launched.

In unity with the all, the mind reached out to transcend space and time. Catching a limpid glimpse of her essence at the center of this maelstrom of swirling energy, Destiny's spirit suddenly quailed, gasping out in alarm. Achilles was missing from the whirlpool. And without the young albino, the higher mind, though powerful, would lack sufficient potency to stop the inevitable.

Destiny let out a lamenting cry, unable to focus. *Where are you, my Achilles?* Already she could feel the vortex beginning to dissipate in faltering disarray. Distraught by the mounting fear within her, she called out to him again. *Answer me, Achilles!*

Time hung still as Destiny listened. The roar of the rocket engine clashed discordantly against the rustle of cosmic wind, a foreordained tolling of physical death to those who understood the foreboding sound. Fear was her only enemy now, a thing without form or substance, and yet a formidable antagonist nevertheless. If she let it, fear would bring on the destruction of millions. Failing to conquer it meant doom to innocents. Once again she was letting fear influence her actions. Once again, she was letting it dictate the fate of the world.

No! she screamed out defiantly, but even then she felt restrained, aware that her protest lacked the conviction to snap the chains of dread. The fear assailed her with a sharp insistent tug, storming her very will, and pulled to the very brink of panic she cried out again. *I will not let you rule me!* But she had great difficulty in throwing forth this singular thought and it oozed out of her slowly as though her mind were mired down in a thick slurry of suppressive mud.

In desperation Destiny barely pulled herself free and focused with renewed intensity, more determined than ever to gather in the eddy of swirling energy. And though it stabilized, instinctively she knew it would not be enough.

But the entities within the vortex rallied her, shouting out in one voice, giving her strength. *We love you, Destiny. We love you as we love one another. Love is the greatest power of all, for herein lies the power to create the highest good, the very power of God. Together we are one, a consciousness that cannot be conquered.*

Destiny harkened the words, letting the energy build. And yet she knew it would not be enough. Twelve key entities were now in place, each positioned on a separate plane of the dodecahedron. But a thirteenth would be needed to accomplish fruitation, an entity of absolute purpose. This was something her mother had fathomed long ago from staring into the amulet's crystal, the rule of sacred geometry discovered by the ancients.

A vague presence suddenly entered Destiny's thoughts, a benign splinter of the mind she had often felt from time to time. But now the presence had a face. It was a coffee face, a face that bespoke of the Caribbean. It was a face with wide cheeks and twinkling eyes, a face that teemed with unblemished compassion. All her life she had seen the face, for Jacob had always displayed it in a black-and-white photograph he kept in a glass frame hanging from his cottage wall. It was the face of Esmerelda, Jacob's grandmother, a renowned vaudun priestess.

The face smiled tenderly, radiating a profound kindness. *We have come a long way, my child, and the time is now upon us. Unforeseen circumstances often arise when we stand against evil, sometimes taking those we love on to the next realm of existence.* Esmerelda's spirit sighed deeply, forcing a pinwheel of stars to go spiraling away in the cosmic breeze. *Put your sadness at rest, sweet girl. The Supreme Oneness deems it necessary to intervene. The one you seek is reprieved from moving on, though it is uncertain how long this will last.*

Destiny remained transfixed, trying to find meaning in the words as the face of Esmerelda faded to mist.

And then another spoke in a voice that resonated across infinity. *All that I am is yours,* it said. *Let us create the reality of our choosing.*

Overcome with elation, Destiny recognized the essence behind the voice. Achilles had come to join her. A flame of comprehension suddenly entered her mind. The young albino had sacrificed himself so that Jay Jay could live. And then he had sought refuge somewhere deep inside her, helping her to overcome her fear. Using her as a medium, he had rallied the others into a collective force, allowing Jay Jay to defeat both Ternier and Raduyev.

With Achilles' essence now poised to take them through the dimensional gap, she pressed the cosmic trigger. Almost at once, the maelstrom of coalescing energy imploded, channeling its way through Destiny's being in one explosive, unstoppable surge. And then she knew the missile was no more, its streaking mass vanishing into a singularity on the far side of the universe.

- 143 -

Climbing from the chopper's copilot seat, Ortega stared at the sky above Navassa Island and frowned. He had seen the missile rise up from the island's surface, only to disappear as if it had never existed. He tried to make sense of what he had just witnessed. The thing had literally shrunk in on itself, the roar of its engine suddenly cutting out. Only a vapor trail remained in the morning sky, and now even that was slowly dissipating out over the sea as though the event had never occurred.

No matter, he thought. For whatever reasons, it was really a blessing in disguise the missile had failed. Provoking the Americans would have brought too much scrutiny into this region, especially with Ternier wanting to fuel another civil war in Haiti. Though getting involved with the man called Omar had been a mistake, there was the chance he might actually come away from all this with far more than he had originally envisioned. For it seemed that treasures awaited him at every turn.

Still puzzled by the strange event, Ortega pondered his next move. His first priority was to capture as many of those extraordinary white dolphins as he could lay hands on. Already the seines of all three vessels were being deployed, and it would only be a matter of time before he had a sizeable contingent of specimens caught up in the nets. From his vantage point up on the San Carlo's helipad, he had a clear view of the surrounding sea. Less than two hundred meters from where he stood he could see several of these incredible creatures floating stationary on the surface, including the small one Fernando had nailed from the air. And if his eyes were not deceiving him, he was certain he had spotted a human female riding a gray one.

This time he would make sure the girl stayed captured. Turning, he impaled Fernando with a nasty glare. "I want this bird refueled and ready to go in the next few minutes. Make sure the gun magazine is fully loaded this time."

Assisted by several crewmembers, Fernando avoided meeting Ortega's eyes. "I'm moving as quickly as I can, boss," he said appeasingly.

"A snail moves faster," Ortega admonished sharply, his lips curling cruelly. He watched Fernando closely for the next several minutes, making sure the tasks were carried out.

Ortega shifted his attention to the San Carlo's tug. Though it was now operable again, he had lost yet another crewman. The diver Omar had placed aboard the tug had been the cause of it. At seeing the destruction of the freighter, the diver had turned on the tug's crew, stabbing one of them to death. Luckily, the two remaining men had reacted fast enough to kill the diver before they suffered the same fate.

As he thought about this, his eyes caught sight of bubbles breaking the ocean surface directly off the San Carlo's port side. Probably coming up from the freighter he had sunk.

Disregarding the bubbling water, he entertained himself with visions of all the riches awaiting him. Under the island was a large cache of gold, or so he had been led to believe. And he had not forgotten the stack of boxes Omar had turned over to the Colonel. All of these things he would take for himself once he finished this business with the dolphins.

And then there was the other hoard of gold back in that cove he had raided. He had learned enough from the dolphin hunters to know what those pieces of hardware were used for. The smaller device was a sending unit, while the larger one was a receiver that tracked the coordinates emitted by the sender. He had seen the text message on the receiver, and on it was mention of gold, including the geodetic coordinates of where it could be found. He had plotted those coordinates on a map, discovering them to approximate those given him by Omar when the Islamist had tracked the dolphins back to the Haitian coast. More gold, it seemed, was to be had back in that hidden sanctuary just below Malique.

Ortega smiled greedily at this knowledge. Maybe he would fly to the cove before he stepped foot back on Navassa Island. Certainly the escaped dolphin hunters were on their way there at this moment, and the last thing he wanted was for them to reach the place ahead of him and make off with the stash.

The sound of shouting jarred Ortega from these musings. One of his crewmen had moved to the edge of the helipad and was pointing at the water in alarm. The mild bubbling Ortega had noted a few moments earlier had turned into a gurgling, roiling froth. Only now it had expanded, stretching out in all directions.

Ortega looked on in horror, watching the sea all around him erupt into a churning boil. Bubbles the size of the tug were now breaching the surface close to the San Carlo's hull. He turned sharply. Pedro had come up from below to stand next to him, and on his battered face he could see fright.

"What is happening?" Ortega bellowed.

Pedro shrugged helplessly. "I do not know."

Spray began to explode from the water as the eruption of gas escalated. A half-mile distant, the San Pinto abruptly listed, its bow plunging below the waterline. Further away, the San Diablo began to flounder. Ortega could see foaming white water pouring over its decks, and the tug pulling its seine was now gone from sight.

Never had fear touched Ortega the way it tugged at him now. The sea had become perilous. Here was one reason ships were sometimes reported missing in reasonably calm weather. Such disappearances had happened all over the world since the beginning of recorded history. He was familiar with the theory. Fields of methane hydrates resting on the sea floor were capable of periodically releasing vast quantities of methane gas. When this occurred, the water became saturated with so much dissolved gas that the fluid density was diminished to the point where it would no longer provide buoyancy, and vessels caught in such violent discharges were in danger of sinking without warning. Laboratory experiments had conclusively proved that methane bubbles could cause any normally floatable object to lose its buoyancy, but then again, almost any gas could do this.

The flight deck suddenly lurched violently underfoot, nearly plunging Ortega to the deck below. With his heart skipping several beats, he managed to regain his balance and scramble back into the Bell Ranger's cockpit. He had to get off the ship.

Gripped by panic, Ortega yelled out to Fernando. "Get us airborne!"

Fernando started to climb in from the opposite side, but Pedro yanked him back, striking him hard in the head with a closed fist.

Ortega stared aghast. "What are you doing?" he screamed.

Pedro climbed in next to him and began flicking switches. "I will do the flying!" he said. His tone was gruff and challenging.

Ortega felt his stomach rise up sharply as the ship dropped with startling suddenness. The plunge was short, and the vessel jerked back up as though tied to a huge bungee cord.

Flabbergasted by what was happening, Ortega could only watch as Pedro throttled up the engine. There was no time to reprimand Cardoza's nephew for his show of impudence. Consumed with anxiety, he focused on the whine of the turbine as it powered up for liftoff. All around him, the sea was a raging torrent. Already it had risen up to within ten feet of the flight deck.

With heart-stopping abruptness, the San Carlo dropped again, making Ortega cringe as angry shouts filled the air. Swiveling his head, he was shocked to see crewmen fighting to climb into the back seats. A vicious melee had broken out among the men.

Pulling his pistol, Ortega swung around, fighting against the seat belts and firing at the nearest man. He did not want the weight of additional passengers dragging down the chopper.

The crewman seemed not to notice the stain of blood spreading rapidly across his chest. Driven by terror and adrenaline, he continued to struggle with the others trying to get aboard. Ortega fired again, this time sending a bullet through the man's temple. But as the man fell, two more crewmen hopped over his fallen body in a bid to climb aboard.

Screaming obsenities, Ortega pulled back on the trigger several more times, dropping each man before he could gain entry to the cabin. He was momentarily pinned to his seat as the helicopter suddenly rose. The sensation instantly subsided, and for what seemed like an eternity, the chopper hung jerkily above the deck as though the main rotor could not get enough bite.

Fearful of stalling, Ortega stared down, almost losing control of his bowels at what he saw. Geysers of foaming white water were practically touching the Bell Ranger's skids. The San Carlo was now gone, completely engulfed by a sea of churning froth.

The Girl Who Rode Dolphins

Ortega gritted his teeth, his mind suddenly dredging up one other tidbit of information. Some scientists had theorized that a heavy discharge of a gas less dense than air could bring down planes. And methane, he knew, was one such gas. He could tell the chopper was struggling to stay aloft, unable to get the required lift. And the turbine did not sound right to him, buzzing erratically as though straining to suck in sufficient oxygen to burn fuel. At any moment, the engine could quit. Then the aircraft would drop into the boiling cauldron like a boulder.

Like a man stranded on a gallows, Ortega awaited the inevitable. At any second, the trapdoor beneath his feet would spring open. Like a yo-yo on a string, the chopper bobbed precariously, laboring to remain just beyond the reach of the frothing geysers. Closing his eyes, his mind anchored itself to the wail of the turbine, expecting it to cut out altogether.

Abruptly, the whine of the engine steadied. Suddenly pushed down hard in his seat, the all too familiar sensation made him open his eyes again. They were rising, gaining altitude. Below him, the fountains of foam had flattened. With the discharge of gas now abating, the sea was rapidly calming.

Looking in all directions, Ortega gawked in dismay. All three of his ships were gone.

Wallowing in disbelief, Ortega stared dumbly at the water below as the chopper continued to climb higher. Farther away, the sea remained relatively calm. From his position, he could clearly see the boundaries of the gas eruption. It had only covered an area encompassing his trawlers. But in the midst of this waning effervescence, a small zone had managed to stay undisturbed. And in that zone he could see hundreds of gray forms milling about. Centered among them was a small contingent of albinos.

A gruff voice intruded its way into Ortega's awareness. Swiveling his head, he realized Pedro was speaking to him. "My uncle is going to be very displeased with what has happened," he grunted. On his battered face, Ortega could see the hint of a callous grin.

An image of Cardoza's snarling pet tiger flashed briefly in Ortega's mind, but the anger rising within him quickly supplanted the thought. Dropping his gaze back to the ocean below, he felt the hate fizz up from the pit of his stomach. Though it seemed absurd, he was certain the dolphins were somehow to blame for this recent calamity. "Take us lower!" he hissed, pointing to the heavy congregation of cetaceans off their starboard side. "They did this! I want them all killed!"

Pedro nodded, his manner immediately turning cruel as he nosed the Ranger over.

Uneasily, Ortega watched him manipulate the controls, feeling the chopper respond sluggishly. As a pilot, Pedro was not in the same league as Fernando.

Nevertheless, Pedro was the only option he had at the moment. And unlike Fernando, Pedro had a fervid passion for killing.

As Pedro took the aircraft into a wide, bumpy turn, Ortega glanced in the direction of the old lighthouse jutting above the island. He had an unobstructed view of Navassa's eastern side, and close to the shoreline near the northern end he glimpsed a vessel sitting at anchor.

Ortega frowned darkly. Even from this distance, he was certain he had seen that same vessel before. Yes, it had to be Javolyn's. As soon as he finished with the dolphins, he would have Pedro fly them over there for a closer look. And if the boat was indeed the one used by Javolyn, then he'd destroy it. He had enough firepower at his disposal to obliterate all those who opposed him.

Pedro suddenly yelled, looking below him in confusion. "Where did they go?"

Ortega snapped his eyes back to the area he had last seen the dolphins. The sea was now empty. Angrily, he searched the sea in all directions, whipping his head back and forth before pointing again. "There!" he snarled, motioning furiously at 1 o'clock. "Ahead of us! Rake the water over there!" He was certain he saw fins break the surface. "They cannot escape us."

Pedro jerked the Ranger's nose down, attempting to bring the aircraft into alignment with the sector of ocean Ortega had indicated. And though he saw nothing on the surface that suggested dolphins, he turned the weapon loose. Clumsily, the chopper yawed left, shuddering fiercely as the gattling gun opened up. Added to the drone of the turbine, the sound was deafening. An instant later, a line of spray kicked up on the water directly ahead.

"You're missing the spot," Ortega scolded sharply. With the guns continuing to fire, the Ranger's yaw had worsened, swinging farther to the left.

Ignoring Ortega's admonishment, Pedro held down the trigger.

Ortega screamed. "You fool! You're wasting ammunition!"

Pedro continued to fire until the gun stopped chattering. "The gun is not working," he yelled out in frustration. He let up on the trigger before depressing it again, but the weapon remained silent.

Ortega's fury was rapidly reaching its limit. "Idiot!" he bellowed. "The gun stops firing after four seconds. It requires a few seconds to cool before it will work again."

As the chopper passed over the area fired upon, Ortega looked for signs of a hit. At seeing none, he ordered Pedro to circle around. "Sooner or later, they have to come up for air," he hissed impatiently.

Pedro banked the chopper hard. For the next several minutes, Ortega kept his eyes glued to the ocean, his mood growing progressively darker as the chopper continued to circle. It baffled him that nothing showed on the water below.

With his rage now boiling over, Ortega stared back in the direction of the lighthouse. "Head for that boat and destroy it!" he screamed. "I will at least have some satisfaction."

- 144 -

Mat Daniels studied the helicopter in the distance, the growing buzz of its rotor blades making his heart pound heavily. He had been watching it for the better part of five minutes from Jake's boat, fully aware of its destructive capability. And now it was making a beeline directly for the Avenging Angel, dropping down low in readiness for what he could only assume to be a strafing run.

Knowing they were in deep trouble, he shouted a warning at the top of his lungs. "Everyone take cover!"

Minutes earlier, Hector had set up the M-60 on its swivel mount, and now Mat stood manning the weapon, looking through the shield of plexiglas at the oncoming aircraft. He was quite familiar with the sound of a minigun, and minutes earlier he had seen the chopper rake the sea with a horrendous barrage. He knew he would have only one chance at taking down the helicopter before its awesome gattling gun had the Angel in its sights.

No stranger to such overwhelming odds, Mat pulled back on the sixty's cocking bolt, prepared to defend the vessel as the chopper came closer. It was moving toward him slowly, almost as if those aboard wanted to savor the moment they would unleash the weapon at their command. "It'll truly be a miracle if we survive this," he muttered under his breath.

By nature he was not a religious man, but as he faced down the oncoming aircraft, he began to pray.

- 145 -

Pulled along by Hermes, Jake broke the surface, knowing what was about to happen. Next to him, Destiny sat astride Hercules. The girl appeared incredibly drained from her recent ordeal at stopping the missile, and he intuitively knew she would need time to fully recoup her energies if she was going to undertake a similar feat aimed at negating the danger now closing in on the Angel. But time was a luxury they no longer had.

Jake looked down at the creature towing him. "We're only gonna get one shot at this," he said gravely. "You sure you can do it?"

"I will not fail you, Jay Jay," Hermes twittered back. *"Hold on."*

Jake had just enough time to note the look registering on Destiny's face before his powerful mount pulled him below the surface. "Jay Jay, no-" was all he heard as he was tugged forcefully into the depths. There was no time to debate the issue. And judging from the position of the approaching aircraft, he barely had enough time to attempt what had to be done.

As Hermes descended rapidly, Jake perceived a multitude of gray forms dart out of the way. Without a dive mask, he could not see clearly, but he knew it would not matter anyway. Once he positioned himself, he could even close his eyes.

Hermes suddenly slowed, reaching the nadir of the dive, and Jake released his hold on the albino's dorsal fin. Staring up at the surface, he knew he was deep, perhaps better than 120 feet. But would it be enough?

Keeping his body rigid, he felt Hermes' beak make contact with the soles of his feet. It was now or never.

Hermes took off for the surface, starting the ascent slowly at first to ensure Jake remained balanced. And then Jake felt the dolphin's raw power as the albino accelerated. With his body almost buckling under the explosive surge, Jake strained hard against the pull of the sea, using every muscle in his body to maintain the rigid posture Hermes required.

Gritting his teeth, Jake glimpsed the surface through slitted eyes a split second before becoming airborne. Launched from the water like a guided missle, he could tell Hermes' timing had been perfect. Converging on an intercept point directly above him was Ortega's chopper, its gun still silent as it lined up on its intended target.

Throwing his arms out in front of him, Jake reached for the aircraft's portside skid. He caught it just as the pull of gravity nullified Hermes' boost, and hooking a leg over the tubular skid, he grabbed hold of the rear strut and glanced down. Hermes was just entering the water in a perfect dive sixty feet below him. Still sitting astride Hercules, Destiny stared up at him in horror.

With catlike agility, Jake began to haul himself up into the rear cabin, fully aware that the minigun might be engaged at any second. All the doors on the chopper had been removed, giving him unobstructed access to the back seats. Poking his head up, he could tell the men at the controls were totally focused on the Angel, now less than than 400 feet away.

The man on the right suddenly swiveled his head around, his expression momentarily frozen in stark surprise at seeing another person aboard the aircraft. Jake reacted swiftly, lunging forward with a closed fist before Ortega could shout a warning. Only halfway into the cabin, he was barely able to reach Ortega's face, and the punch landed without any leverage behind it.

Pulling himself into the cabin the remainder of the way, Jake yanked his K-bar from its sheath just as Ortega turned again. Eyes flaming with hatred, the Colombian twisted savagely in his seat, awkwardly extending an arm. Gripped in his hand was a semi-automatic pistol.

Jake slashed out with the knife, slicing deep into Ortega's wrist just as he pulled back on the trigger. The gun exploded an instant before Ortega hollered in pain, and Jake felt something hot singe his scalp.

The aircraft abruptly lurched, then snap-rolled with such violence that Jake was sent headlong toward the opposite side of the cabin. Only his quick reflexes saved him from being flung clear. Catching the starboard door frame with his left hand, he hung suspended by one arm, finding himself looking back into the cabin as the centrifugal force of a nasty left bank stretched his body out laterally. It was then that he saw the pilot's face glaring back at him, and strangely it did not surprise him at all that the man doing the flying was none other than Pedro.

Jake held on tenaciously, his grip rapidly waning as Pedro tried to dislodge him. Ortega leaned to his right, fighting against his seat belt and craning his head out the side door to stare directly into Jake's face, and in his eyes Jake could see the fires of madness burning fervently. Caught by the slipstream of air rushing past, globs of blood from his oozing wrist dribbled back to spatter Jake's cheeks. Still managing to retain possession of the pistol, a cruel smile came to the Colombian's mouth as he shifted the gun to his left hand, angling his arm around the door frame to get a clear bead on his unwanted passenger.

Jake gazed transfixed, his sense of time dramatically slowing as he looked down the barrel of the handgun coming to bear on his face. He had cheated death too many times, and now he knew the bill was finally coming due if he did not let go. Preparing to release his grip, the chopper suddenly bucked hard, and Jake became aware of a white blur falling away beneath him.

Jarred by the impact, Pedro jerked the cyclic back to his right, inadvertently veering the aircraft out of its acute bank. Flung back into the cabin by the sudden shift in inertia, Jake found purchase on the opposite door frame before he could be ejected, the K-bar still gripped firmly in his right hand.

Ortega whipped around in his seat, cursing with rage. With the helicopter now on a straight and level heading, Jake readied himself as the muzzle of Ortega's gun poked from between the seats. Another shot rang out, the sound overlaying the turbine's steady drone. But this time Jake shifted well beyond the path of the bullet. Plowing through the cabin's rear bulkhead, the round entered the engine compartment. A whine of protest immediately erupted from the turbine, escalating quickly into a raucous shriek, and the aircraft began to shudder giddily.

With his ears ringing, Jake sprang forward, jabbing the K-bar into the back of Ortega's gun hand. The Colombian howled shrilly, withdrawing the weapon but still managing to hold onto it.

The chopper snap-rolled rolled to port a second time, catching Jake off balance again. Hurled back to starboard, he again caught the door frame with his free hand. Finding himself in the same position as before, his body hung precariously from the side of the aircraft. More blood spattered his face as Ortega leaned out into the wind to end this standoff. Once more, time seemed to bog down as the Colombian extended the pistol to blow his head off.

Momentarily disregarding the danger, Jake held on, unwilling to let his fingers slide away just yet. Overcome by a strange sense, he looked down. The frozen smile of an albino was directly below him, rising up as if in slow motion. The smile belonged to Achilles.

Almost mesmerized by the sight, Jake watched as the juvenile protracted both arms and reached for Ortega's gun arm. Reaching the apex of his leap, Achilles' jaws parted.

Ortega let out a harsh cry as the jaws closed on his arm. With bulging eyes, he stared as the pistol was ripped from his hand by one of the juvenile's hand-like appendages. He screamed again, his face racked with pain. Bearing the albino's full weight, his limb was nearly wrenched from its socket. Achilles would not let go, and it was only the seat belt that kept Ortega from being torn from the cockpit.

The Ranger bucked several more times, and Jake caught a glimpse of three more albinos as they latched onto the chopper's tubular skids with their wondrous hands. The aircraft dipped precipitously under the combined weight, and it began to plummet rapidly toward the sea.

In desperation, Pedro fought the controls, pulling up hard on the collective and jerking the cyclic to starboard. The shift in G-force was nearly instantaneous, and Jake was able to haul himself back into the cabin, no longer held in the grip of inertia.

Ortega continued to scream. Forced to bear Achilles' full weight by one arm, his body remained bent at an awkward angle as it was stretched halfway out the cockpit.

The juvenile looked up at Jake, reaching out and giving him Ortega's pistol with his free hand. For one meteoric moment, Jake thought to send a bullet into the back of Pedro's head, but Pedro jerked the stick again. Flung to the port-side of the cabin, Jake found himself pitched forward on his belly, his head jutting out the door into the wind. He could feel the chopper coming out of its turn, and as he looked ahead he saw that the aircraft had its nose down and was beginning to line up on the Angel, now less than 40 meters away.

The damaged turbine screeched like a dying animal, making his ears ache. But in that instant the gattling gun's protruding mechanism lay directly before him and he did not hesitate as the barrels suddenly spun. Flames spewed forth as the awesome weapon discharged in a harsh buzz, throwing out a storm of rounds that kicked up a traveling spume of water. Extending the pistol out in front of him, he fired at close to point-blank range and emptied the clip as the racing geyser sped rapidly toward the Angel's bow. The minigun abruptly ground to a halt as parts of the ammo feed leading from the magazine disintegrated. Seized up, the weapon could not fire.

Jake rose up into a crouch and, looking behind him, spotted the thing he had noticed when he had first climbed aboard the chopper. A box of MK3 concussion grenades was strapped to the middle seat. Lifting the cover, he grabbed one of the cardboard cylinders and pulled the pin, letting the spoon pop free. From the front seat, Pedro pivoted his head around to locate Jake, skewering him with a hateful, enraged glare, but at seeing the live grenade being reinserted back in the box, his face turned an ashen white and a look of utter terror filled his eyes. Opening his mouth, he shouted in desperation, but the shriek of the laboring engine made the words indiscernible.

Jake grinned wickedly, giving the panic-stricken pilot a farewell wave of the hand. And with that he leapt clear of the aircraft, knowing the water was only a short distance away. Dropping feet first, he saw all four albinos plunge with him.

Upon hitting the water, Jake surfaced quickly. Eagerly, he looked up at the dying chopper, watching it yaw erratically. On a collision course with Navassa's nearby cliffs, a trail of dense black smoke billowed profusely from its damaged turbine. Frenzied movement within the cockpit could be seen as the helicopter's two occupants fought frantically to jump clear. Pedro nearly succeeded, but he had only fallen less than a meter when the whirlybird erupted in a huge fireball, and he disappeared in the flash of flame. Bits and pieces of the aircraft fell into the sea, while other burning fragments were strewn onto the karst forming Navassa's shoreline.

Satisfied that the threat had been eradicated, Jake turned toward his vessel less than twenty meters away. Mat and a few others were waving to him from the port railing.

"You are unharmed, Jay Jay?"

Jake swung around, seeing Achilles next to him. Grinning from ear to ear, he reached out and rubbed the dolphin's snout affectionately. "Only because of you, my friend." He paused, noticing the small scar on the juvenile's back. The wound was almost fully healed. He had felt the pain of it when the bullet had pierced Achilles' lung. "That makes two I owe you."

Upon rejoining the others aboard the Avenging Angel, Jake was puzzled. Two people were missing. "Where's Zimby and Hennington?" he asked Mat.

Mat shrugged. "Seems they went ashore."

Jake stared at the nearby cliffs, frowning. "What for?"

Mat shrugged again. "The big guy said he had some unfinished business to take care of."

Jake scanned the escarpment rising up from the sea. Deep down, he knew the reason for Zimbola having gone ashore, though he couldn't understand why the broker had accompanied him. Compounding his bewilderment further was the absence of Destiny and her mother once again.

"Seems we got more company," Mat said.

"Huh?" Jake pulled his eyes from the nearby cliffs to stare in the direction Mat was looking. Surrounded by a small cluster of gray dolphins heading toward the Angel, Destiny rode Hercules. Squinting against the sunglare reflected off the water, he discerned three other human forms; two were being supported by several members of the pack while the third was slung across Hercules' back directly in front of Destiny. The girl kept a firm grip on the man, making sure he did not slide off. She still looked exhausted, making Jake wonder if she had anything left within her to revitalize the people she had rescued.

Jake scurried to the rear platform, ready to lend a hand, but Hector, Jacob and Dr. Grahm were already there ahead of him, stooped low to give assistance. Further away, a few albinos were coming on fast to join the girl.

Destiny shouted worriedly. "Do not pull them from the water just yet. I'll need time to resuscitate these men."

Both Grahm and Hector reached out to grab hold of the two closest men while Destiny focused on the one borne by her mount. Jake could see that all three were unconscious. Destiny's charge, however, was missing an arm. A stubborn flow of blood from the severed limb was turning the water red.

Jake studied the men. Two were from the San Carlo, but the one in Destiny's care he did not recognize.

"This one has lost a lot of blood," Destiny said tiredly. "He has other injuries, and its possible he may not survive."

Jake stared fascinated, watching three albinos nuzzling the comatose man's body "I'm sure you'll do your best to keep him alive," he encouraged.

For one brief moment, Destiny stopped her ministrations to gaze up at him. And in that tiny passing of time Jake imagined he was seeing a heavy burden lifted from the girl's soul.

Ternier lifted the blackened charm from around his neck and flung it aside. The ancient trinket was useless to him. Gingerly, he touched his forehead where Javolyn had bashed him, eying his fingertips to see if the bleeding had finally stopped.

Looking around the deserted clearing, his eyes settled once again on Omar's dead body. It was a dismal reminder of what had happened, a stark epitaph to the way his plan had unraveled so quickly. Angered by the sight, he took three maddened steps to the corpse and kicked it savagely in the head.

"Only a truly evil person fights with the dead."

Ternier spun around, shocked to find he was being watched. Zimbola and Hennington stood at the edge of the clearing. He knew at once that it was the big man who had spoken.

"What is it that you want?" Ternier griped angrily, knowing all too well what it was. Out of the corner of his eye, he located the Kalashnikov that had been tossed aside by Omar earlier on. It lay on the ground less than two meters away. Slowly, he began edging toward it.

"Justice!" Zimbola rumbled, his deep bass voice leaving no doubts as to what he had in mind. "We are here to serve justice."

The Colonel sidled closer to the weapon. Rarely had he encountered men larger than himself, and the Jamaican's size intimidated him. "I am a ranking magistrate of the Republic of Haiti. State your business and be done with it."

The giant frowned fiercely, stepping closer. "We are no longer in Haiti."

Ternier leapt for the Kalashnikov. Something akin to a steel vice closed on his wrist as he lifted the weapon, and he found himself staring into eyes filled with loathing.

"You killed Mercades!" Zimbola spat. "And now you will pay for it!"

Ternier gasped, startled by the strength behind the grip. In panic, he lashed out with his other arm, landing a solid blow to the Jamaican's chin and following it up with a knee to the groin.

Zimbola grunted as though pricked by a pin. Shrugging off the blows, he caught the Colonel by the throat to avoid a vicious head-butt. "You will pay," he said in a rumbling snarl.

Barely able to breath, Ternier felt his feet leave the ground, the giant's thumb pressing into his Adam's apple with terrifying force. Knowing he was about to die, he struck out at the face in front of him, fighting to draw breath each time he struck. Something suddenly crunched, an all too familiar sound he had often heard within his torture chambers. It was the sound of cartilage being crushed. But this time it was his own larynx that was collapsing. Horrorified by this one thought, Ternier felt the darkness close in on him like an onrushing black cloud.

Feeling Ternier's body go limp, Zimbola continued to hold him aloft as he walked him over to where the karst dropped off toward the sea. Bellowing like a maddened bull, he heaved the corpse down the steep escarpment, watching it tumble away.

- 148 -

The remainder of the day went by quickly, with Jake finding himself strapped with numerous tasks. As fortune would have it, however, finding Zimbola and Hennington had not been one of them. Both had returned soon after Destiny's revival of the injured men, each hauled back to the Angel by an albino dolphin. Once aboard the sturdy vessel, Zimby's reserved manner was all too evident to Jake, and he did not press him about where he had gone, though he sensed Ternier would no longer be a concern.

Through the efforts of Achilles and the other albinos calculating the effects of wind and drift on a vessel the size of *Relentless*, Jake was able to pinpoint the exact location of Mat's boat, set adrift by Ternier shortly after the Colonel's raid upon the Angel. With Mat riding behind him on the waverunner, Jake covered the fifteen miles of open sea in short order, leaving his friend to pilot *Relentless* back to Navassa by himself. Beforehand, both men had agreed that their vessels would be needed to ferry all those abducted back to Malique.

And then there was the matter of the Islamic terrorists. "We have a problem," Jake found himself saying to Mat.

"Tell me?"

Jake sighed tiredly, the strain of the last 24 hours starting to catch up with him. "I know you have a report to make about what happened out here, but the last thing these dolphins need is Uncle Sam poking his nose around this island."

Perplexity filled Mat's face. "Why is that?"

"Because they're building a refuge directly under this chunk of rock." Jake paused, seeing the surprise in his friend's expression. "There's much more to this than you're aware of."

"I'm listening."

For the next half hour, Jake told Mat everything he knew about the dolphins and their connection with the island. He left nothing out, apprising him of Ternier's scheme and the Islamist plot. Mat's eyes widened appreciably at the mention of their old nemesis, Raduyev, and the Colombian-Jihadist connection, coming alive further at Jake's description of the Chechen's death.

"So you're telling me these creatures used all that hydrogen gas they've been storing to sink those ships." Mat shook his head in wonder. "Incredible!"

Jake assessed his friend closely. Outside the pod and those of his crew, Mat was the only other person he trusted implicitly. "So what's it gonna be, pal? You tell the story to your superiors like it really is and this place is gonna be crawling in military brass. Once they get a whiff of how unique these creatures are, they'll capture as many as they can, using them as military assets. These dolphins don't deserve that."

Mat turned and stared at the island. "God damn you, Jake. You're asking me to ignore my responsibilities. I've got a job to do."

"I know you do, Mat, and you're good at it. But sometimes circumstances get in the way that force us to draw a line in the sand, and in this case it's a line that cannot be straddled." Jake softened his tone. "Which side of that line you going to take?"

Mat threw his hands up in annoyance, then slapped them down hard on the Angel's railing. "Don't press me! I've got to think this out."

Jake knew that tone of voice, realizing he had to back off. A decision like the one he was asking Mat to make was more than just difficult. It might very well change the course of his life. Certainly it would have a major impact on other lives. "I'm going ashore, Mat. I'll show you Raduyev's submarine base if you'd like to see it. I still haven't seen it."

Mat's funk showed a trace of abatement. "I also want to see this dolphin refuge."

Jake smiled. "Whatever you want, buddy."

- 149 -

Led by Destiny, it was nearly midday by the time Jake and Mat reached the cave entrance leading to Raduyev's subterranean base. Having nothing better to do, both Dr. Grahm and Jacob had accompanied them.

"Are the villagers still down there?" Jake asked, adjusting the Stoker's shoulder strap.

"Yes," Destiny said, glancing briefly at the weapon slung over Jake's shoulder. "The danger is long past. Bashir has everything under control."

"And your mother is still with him?"

As if in answer to the question, Amphitrite suddenly emerged from the mouth of the cave.

A loud gasp broke the air behind Jake. "Harriet!"

Jake spun around. Grahm was looking beyond him, staring with his mouth wide open.

For several long seconds, Amphitrite gazed back at the scientist, her face frozen in stoic bewilderment.

"It is you!" Grahm blurted. Overcome with joy, he rushed over to embrace the woman with outstretched arms.

Caught in a fierce hug, Amphitrite continued to appear confused, her arms dangling helplessly at her sides.

The other members of Jake's party stood speechless, captivated by the strange scene unfolding before them.

Grahm relaxed his smothering embrace, holding the woman at arm's length. "It's me, Harriet…It's Franklin." His elation deflated rapidly at seeing Amphitrite's lack of recognition, and within moments his eyes began to mist over. "You don't remember me?" There was an overwhelming crush of emotion in the way the question was spoken.

Amphitrite seemed utterly lost, her manner dull and lifeless as she searched his face. "There…there is a certain familiarity about you," she whispered uncertainly.

Grahm was overwrought with frustration. "I am your husband, Harriet." His words came out in an explosive rush. "You disappeared many years ago. You were reported lost at sea in a hurricane. The sloop you were sailing sank near this island. You were pregnant with our child when it happened." He suddenly paused as he studied her face. "You don't remember, do you?" There was desperation in his voice now.

A pained expression manifested itself in Amphitrite's features, the frustration turning to liquid in her eyes. "There is a blockage to my memory…I…I wish I…" A trickling of tears began to flow down her cheeks.

"It doesn't matter, Harriet," Grahm blurted sympathetically, once more squeezing her tightly to him. "All that matters is I've found you again." He looked down at her face. "The years have been kind to you, my darling. You've hardly aged."

Amphitrite reached up, placing a gentle hand on his forehead. A moment of stillness ensued before a small startled cry left her lips, and she scrutinized his features as if truly seeing him for the very first time. The trickle of tears streaming down her face began to flow more quickly, and she suddenly hugged Grahm with an unrestrained fierceness. "Yes…yes…I see it all clearly now."

Jake read her expression, envisioning the flashbacks currently consuming her mind. Amphitrite was revisiting the past, the portion of her memory that had up to now eluded her.

"You've lived in Haiti all these years?" Grahm murmured in her ear.

"Yes, my darling, but my life has not been without purpose." She shifted sodden orbs to Destiny before turning back to look deeply into Grahm's eyes. "You should rejoice in knowing that Destiny is your daughter."

Destiny stared incredulously. "Father?" She rolled the word off her tongue as though testing the sound of it. For one dizzy and emotionally charged moment she hung back, caught up in all that the word implied before repeating it. "Father!" The word was shouted this time, no longer alien to her.

A touching scene followed as Destiny flew into Grahm's arms. Raining kisses on the girl's cheeks and holding her tightly, the scientist's voice was choked with emotion. "I knew there was something about you from the very first time we met. Oh, my sweet child, you make an old man proud at seeing what a beautiful and courageous young woman you've grown into."

Jake stood back, not wanting to intrude on this tender reunion. As he looked upon the faces of the others, he could not find a dry eye among them. And while Jacob wore a lopsided smile, Jake could not help but notice a trace of sadness in the Haitian's expression as well.

Several minutes passed before Amphitrite finally pulled away from husband and daughter. Turning, she singled out Jake. "I am told you have been searching for something in these waters for some time now, Mr. Javolyn."

"I'd prefer it if you call me Jay Jay."

Amphitrite smiled, her cheeks still wet with moisture. "As you wish, Jay Jay." She pointed to a stack of boxes partially hidden behind a stand of poisonwood trees. "I believe you will find some of the items you've been seeking in those crates over there."

Jake appraised the pile of crates from where he stood. "If those boxes contain what I think they do, I'm not sure I have the right to take them."

Amphitrite's smile became somber. "If you are not the rightful owner, then who?" Releasing a weary sigh, she added, "This is not a matter of choice for you, Jay Jay. The paths our lives take are often guided by a power beyond ourselves, a force far removed from random coincidence. Certain things are meant to happen in order to clear the way for the future and to keep past events from repeating themselves. The lives of all those who stand here have become entwined, coming together for a common purpose. Where mankind goes from here will be determined by the actions we have already taken and the actions we are yet to exercise. Evil takes many guises, and on this day we were able to defeat it, each of us contributing in our own way."

Amphitrite paused, giving Jake a moment to reflect on the things she had just said. "Take possession of the boxes, Jay Jay, and load them aboard your vessel. A higher authority has deemed it necessary that you be entrusted with these things if you are to go on fulfilling your true calling."

"I'll consider it," Jake said awkwardly. "But right now, I need to have a look inside this-"

Jake suddenly lost his tongue. Others were beginning to climb from the mouth of the cave to stand behind Amphitrite. Apparently the remaining villagers kidnapped from Malique were coming up to join her. Several of the newcomers carried boxes similar to the ones stacked at the side of the clearing, and Amphitrite had them place those additional boxes on the pile. The opening to the subterranean cavern was narrow, only allowing the passage of one person at a time.

When the procession of people finally stopped, Jake looked to Amphitrite once again. "Has everyone been accounted for?"

"Two others will be up shortly. Twenty-two people were taken from Malique and three others from a disabled boat. We will require the use of your vessel and that of your friend to take them all back to Haiti. Will that be a problem for you, Jay Jay?"

"None at all." Jake took a quick head count, suddenly aware that Bashir, Sherkhan and the one called Kalid were missing. "As soon as everyone's up, Mat and I will go down there to have a look." As he said this, another Haitian emerged from the cave opening.

"I don't think that will be possible," Amphitrite said. There was apology in her tone.

Mat, who had been standing by in silence, suddenly spoke up. "Why not?"

The ground abruptly rumbled and shook underfoot just as the last person cleared the cave entrance. Less than two seconds later, a cloud of dust spewed from the opening, and Jake realized all the Islamists remained unaccounted for.

Amphitrite stepped away from the cave mouth as the dust began to settle. "An explosive charge has been set off further down, permanently sealing off the tunnel. Access to the cavern is no longer possible."

Jake glanced around sharply, carefully surveying the faces milling all around him one more time just to be certain he hadn't overlooked anyone. "What about Bashir and Raduyev's men? Are they still down there?"

Amphitrite met Jake's eyes, staring back impassively, though her eyes held the glint of mischievous guile. "You have no need to be concerned about them. Their mission is at an end."

"That doesn't mean they're no longer dangerous," Jake objected pointedly. "They have a sub at their disposal."

Destiny interceded. "Bashir is their new leader now, Jay Jay. You have my word that he will not pose a threat to anyone. If anything, the men he commands will now devote their lives to a common good."

"Who is this Bashir?" Mat demanded, staring first at Destiny, then at Jake.

Jake narrowed his eyes wearily, keeping his attention focused on the girl. "What kind of common good?"

"All will soon be revealed."

Jake sighed grumpily, throwing his arms up and rolling his eyes in frustration. It didn't make sense why Destiny continued to remain nebulous and evasive whenever it concerned Bashir.

"Damn!" Mat griped. "Will someone please tell me who this Bashir is?"

Jake tried quelling Mat with a wave of his hand. "Easy, partner. I'll get to the bottom of this." With eyes still clinging to Destiny, he said, "Can I have a word with you in private?"

Everyone stood silent as Destiny followed Jake beyond earshot. "Look," Jake said, "if you say Bashir is not a threat, that's good enough for me. But Mat needs a little more to go on than that. Have you forgotten he works for the U.S. Department of Homeland Security?"

Destiny studied his troubled expression a moment longer. "That's all I can tell you right now, Jay Jay."

"You're placing me in a very awkward position with my friend," Jake grumbled. "As it is, I'm trying to convince him not to report everything that happened at this island. The last thing you want is Uncle Sam probing around here and discovering the extraordinary intelligence of your friends and the refuge they're building."

"I'm sure you'll figure out a way to keep him from doing that. And besides, I can tell Mat is a man of conscience."

Jake was growing annoyed. "Why must you be so vague when it comes to Bashir?"

Destiny's lips curled up in amusement, her eyes provocative and rebellious. "I'm sorry, Jay Jay. I guess I deserve a spanking."

Disarmed by the implication, Jake looked down at her in mock anger. "And I aim to give you one."

The trip back from Navassa went smoothly, with *Relentless* following behind the *Avenging Angel* the whole way. Docking at Malique's main pier, both vessel's shed their passengers quickly. Through the healing powers of the pod, both Emmanuel and Lucette Baptiste were well on their way to full recovery, with virtually all their wounds now fully healed.

With Destiny standing by his side, Jake watched the last two villagers step off his boat. Carried between them was a non-Haitian laid out on a stretcher, the lower half of the man's face shrouded in a dense cluster of coarse dark hair, the stump of his right arm swathed in a thick wrap of white surgical dressing. Clutched tightly in the man's remaining hand was something he refused to relinquish, an object from which the man would not withdraw his eyes.

Jake could not help but smile at what he was seeing. He had since learned the bearded man was the captain of the Yemeni freighter Ortega had destroyed. "If Bashir were still here, he would not be very pleased over the way his painting has been appropriated."

Destiny looked up at him. "I don't think Bashir would have raised a fuss in view of what the painting is doing for the man."

"I still find it amazing how this art is able to free up a person's mind, at least in some people." Jake shook his head as if unwilling to accept what was occurring here. "That man had a key role in a sinister plot aimed at murdering millions of people, and now he's docile as a lamb."

Someone spoke behind Jake. "That is because he did not really accept the ideology he had become snared in."

Jake turned, finding himself staring into Jacob's face. "Have you ever considered using these paintings as a kind of acid test?"

"I assume you mean for gauging a person's mettle," Jacob replied absently, his gaze searching out the crowd gathered near the shore before settling on something. There was bleakness in his eyes.

Jake saw where he was looking, noting that Jacob was watching Amphitrite and Dr. Grahm. Husband and wife were holding hands, talking quietly. "Yeah," Jake responded. "From what I've seen so far, you can use the art to cull out those that are good from the chronically bad."

Jacob turned back to Jake. "I suppose such use might hold some merit, but then we would be playing the part of judge and jury in assessing a person's true temperament." Jacob expelled a prolonged sigh. "The pod has no interest in judging others, Jay Jay."

Jake weighed the words gravely. "Your venture is going to require many more people than you currently have. The last thing you want is ill-intentioned individuals tripping up your plan. Perhaps it would be wise to lay down certain protocols for recruitment."

Jacob brought his eyes back to Amphitrite. "I'll give your idea due consideration."

Jake located the two survivors from the San Carlo. He already knew Fernando and Antonio could be trusted, having seen the way they had reacted to Achilles painting. Both men were standing on the dock next to Mat's boat, engaged in conversation with Chester Hennington. "There's three potential recruits who-"

Destiny tugged sharply on Jake's arm, giving him and Jacob a worried look. "Visitors have come to Gaia, Jay Jay. Hermes and Aphrodite tell me a vessel is anchored just beyond the cove."

"Can they describe it?"

A moment passed as Destiny focused inwardly. "They tell me it's the same vessel you helped the dolphin hunters escape in."

Jake absorbed this information, wondering how Walter McPherson and company had learned about the albino hideaway. But as he thought about it, the answer came to him in a flash.

- 151 -

Walter McPherson's head felt as if it were going to explode as he stared at the strange art hanging against the wall in the small thatched cottage. Never in his life had he felt so ill. Neither Frank Jaffey nor Ben Loomins seemed to notice as he staggered on unsteady legs towards the door. Stepping out into the sunlight, he stumbled down to the water's edge before sinking to his knees and retching harshly. Dumbly, he stared at the slick of bile laid atop the small wavelets lapping gently over the sand as he gasped for air.

"Whatsa matter with you?"

McPherson looked up, seeing Charlie Loomins hovering over him with the small caliber rifle he carried.

"Are you sick?" Charlie asked when McPherson failed to respond.

McPherson managed to stand erect, fighting to bring an icy stare to his features. It was the face of authority developed from more than ten years in the military. "Why aren't you guarding the prisoners?" He turned slightly to glimpse the two people sitting in the sand a short distance away. One was a man, the other a boy.

Charlie acknowledged the captives. "Aw, they're not going anywhere. I don't think they're gonna give us any problems."

McPherson felt his strength beginning to return. "I'll make the decisions around here," he admonished sharply. "There's a pile of gold somewhere around here, and those two probably know where it's hidden."

"I thought we came here for the dolphins," Charlie said weakly.

"We came here for anything of value."

Charlie looked around to observe his surroundings. "Well, so far all I see are trees and water."

McPherson kept his tone in military mode, projecting the voice of command he always used on subordinates. "Henderson has determined this place to be the home of those white dolphins. Sooner or later, they'll come back here, and when they do we'll block off the entrance. But until they do, we'll busy ourselves by finding where the gold is hidden." He drew in air to clear his head. "Now I want you to go over there and keep an eye on them until I figure out our next move."

Charlie turned, shaking his head and muttering to himself as he trudged back toward the captives.

With his temples still throbbing, McPherson watched him go. Breathing deeply, he tried ridding himself of the nausea he was feeling. Even thinking was difficult, and he had to focus hard to collect his thoughts. He couldn't understand why Henderson was not here to meet them. Interrogation of the two prisoners had so far proven useless, with both of them telling him that Henderson had disappeared sometime during the night.

Feeling less nauseous, McPherson let his eyes roam over his pristine surroundings. It almost seemed appropriate that such unusual creatures would reside in such an exotic setting. Henderson had sent a text-message to that delphine-locating device while the unit was still in Jaffey's possession aboard the salvage tug. In the message, Henderson had provided the geodetic coordinates of this cove and inferred the place to be the actual home of Natalie and others of her kind. Henderson had also indicated there was a rich cache of gold situated here, and if McPherson would help him take possession of it, he'd be willing to share it. McPherson had not been privy to this until later, so when Jaffey had offered the Colombians the gold in exchange for their lives, it had come as a great surprise. And it was only after their escape that Jaffy had divulged to him this information, including where the gold could be found.

McPherson let out a curse. He did not like going on a wild goose chase, especially in view of the Colombians who would surely be coming here sooner or later. While being interrogated by them, he had tried withholding information about the dolphins. Oh, he had really tried. He had given them his best bald-faced look of incomprehension and innocence, doing his utmost to deceive them. But the one called Pedro had scared him senseless, and he had ended up spilling most of what he knew. And now that he had time to reflect on it, he felt ashamed that Jaffey and the Loomins brothers had been able to suck up the punishment far better than he, disclosing much less than he had eventually blabbed. At one point he had even lied about the whereabouts of the DBT receiver, but the Colombians had eventually found that too, apparently discovering it during a last minute search of their salvage vessel just before their escape. Unfortunately, the receiver contained a log of all recent transmissions, and it was almost certain his captors would discover Henderson's message.

As McPherson recalled these things, he thought it odd that the leader of his captors was already familiar with this new breed of dolphin. So far as he could tell, the man wanted these creatures even more than he did. But Henderson's revelation concerning a stockpile of gold had added a new twist to the way things were progressing. And if he didn't find it soon, he risked being captured a second time by the men he had escaped.

Something else troubled him. He now knew the identity of the man who had rescued him. Jake Javolyn had been one of the Seal trainees under his watch at the Coronado training facility. At first he had failed to recognize him, and it was only while they were pulling away from the San Carlo in the salvage vessel that it had come to him with jarring clarity. The Colombian boss had even spoken Javolyn's name during his grilling of Ben Loomins, asking the bearded individual standing next to him if Loomins' description of the man was accurate. Fearful for his life, however, he had failed to make the connection. But now it was all flooding back. The bearded one had also been a Seal candidate, a Chechen by the name of Yeslam Raduyev and a classmate of Javolyn's during their stint at the Coronado school. He well remembered the bitter rivalry between the two.

And while it baffled him immensely as to how these former Seals had become involved in all of this, he also realized that it had bought him some time. In sailing away from the San Carlo, he had seen the eruption of flames engulf part of the vessel, and it was this that had emboldened him to come here directly, giving him hope that pursuit by the Colombians would be delayed indefinitely, presumably by the damage the conflagration had caused.

A conflict of emotions gripped him as he pondered these things. His naval career had been under fire for some time now as a result of not heeding Javolyn's allegations concerning Raduyev during their training at Coronado years earlier. Much to his surprise, Javolyn had gone over his head shortly after the incident, sending a formal letter summarizing his concerns up the chain of command. And then he, McPherson, had compounded the problem by explaining away the incident to his superiors as nonsense, describing Javolyn as nothing more than a Muslim hater. On top of that, he had pulled strings with the top brass, insisting that the Chechen be allowed to accompany Javolyn on that fateful Afghan mission, the one in which five members of the Seal team had died, including Myers and Captain Sheridan. His bad judgement had cost him dearly, placing a major obstacle in his path of advancement.

McPherson sucked in another deep breath, looking dismally about him. If only he could capture this new breed of super-intelligent dolphin, his career might be resurrected. But it was really the possibility of gold that interested him even more, assuming the message Henderson had sent him to be true. Finding such treasure would be an absolute godsend. The inheritance he had received after his father had passed away the year before had been far less than he had hoped for. And now the family fortune was all but gone. With a string of bad investments on his part, the lavish lifestyle he had grown accustomed to since birth was now on the brink of bankruptcy. The little money he had left was rapidly disappearing, most of it going toward bribes and down payments aimed at capturing dolphins with hands.

Glancing back at one of the cottages, McPherson stared in annoyance. What were Jaffey and Ben Loomins doing in there?

The angry frown that began to form on his face abruptly changed to bewilderment. Something was buzzing in the distance. Looking up to locate the growing hum, panic suddenly gripped him. Rotor blades were beating the air, their deepening pitch telling him a helicopter was approaching. He stood frozen, his eyes searching the air above. In moments he caught sight of a chopper slipping over the cove's southern ridge.

The chopper abruptly flared, hanging in the sky for a short interval as if those aboard could better study the lush oval-shaped amphitheater beneath them. Moments later, the aircraft dipped lower, the rhythmic flapping of its main rotor growing blatantly louder the closer it came.

McPherson's first impulse was to run, but he realized there was really no place that offered refuge in the oblong confines of the chasm surrounding him. Immobilized by fear, he watched as the aircraft made a slow, almost cautious descent before catching him with a savage down-blast of rotor wash. For a prolonged moment, it hovered ominously over his head before coming to roost further up the beach, its cockpit swinging around to face him just before it touched down. Five bull-necked Latinos spilled from the rear cabin, all of them toting Uzis. Without hesitation, the men rushed at him, their scowling faces showing no signs of friendliness.

Numbed by the intrusion, McPherson could only stand there before being knocked to the ground. Crippled by panic, he found himself looking up the barrel of one of the weapons, its muzzle only inches from his face. Behind the man holding the Uzi, he glimpsed another Latino emerge from the helicopter's co-pilot seat just as the rotors ceased swishing. Unable to pull his eyes away, McPherson stared in awe as the man swaggered closer. Growing up the way he had, he recognized the mien of privilege immediately, for the man seemed to radiate an aura of extreme wealth and power. The Latino came slowly toward him, a man who apparently took pride in his grooming. He was clean-shaven, sporting a shiny crop of jet-black hair punctuated with rich streaks of silver at the sides. His hair was long and neatly trimmed, pulled back austerely into a tightly bound ponytail, with the hint of gel giving it luster.

Chilled with foreboding terror, McPherson gaped dumbly, vaguely wondering how the man was able to wear an expensive, immaculately tailored Armani designer suit in such sweltering heat without sweating.

The impeccably dressed Latino stared down at McPherson as though he were a warden looking at an escaped convict. He seemed satisfied by the fright he was seeing. "My time is very limited," he said. His voice held the inflections of culture and refinement, though his English was tainted with a heavy Spanish accent. He let his eyes linger on McPherson briefly before pivoting his head in all directions to take in the encompassing scenery. "And even more limited is my patience."

The man paused just long enough to let McPherson absorb the underlying threat. "There is a question I have that requires an answer, and you will provide me with this answer without hesitation."

McPherson nodded vigorously, sincerely hoping he would be able to comply. Here was a man used to having his way, and he had no desire to be on the receiving end of more physical punishment. The beating he had suffered at the hands of Pedro continued to haunt him, and from the hooded flat stare the Latino gave him, he instinctively knew the man would bring upon him a penalty far worse than what he had previously endured.

"I am told there exists a treasure trove within this place," the Latino said. "You will tell me where it is."

McPherson spoke quickly, feeling his voice crack under the man's intense strident gaze. "I tried getting that information from the people we found here, but they pretend ignorance. I'm sure they can tell you where it is with the right persuasion."

The Latino's face clouded, and McPherson cringed as though expecting a series of blows to rain down on him. When none came, he risked meeting the eyes of his interrogator, but the man's attention was drawn elsewhere. From the direction of the thatched cottages, one of the man's cohorts was coming back at a brisk trot to join him, rattling something off in Spanish between breaths. Trailing behind him, Ben Loomins and Frank Jaffey were being prodded along by one of the Uzi-wielding gunman.

The Latino nodded gravely, his eyes roaming the cove in all directions once again before settling back on McPherson. "How many people are with you?"

"Three," McPherson blurted. Reading skepticism on the man's face, he quickly added, "Three people are here with me. The other two we found here."

McPherson's captor elicited a faint dubious smile. "What about your vessel? I assume the one anchored beyond this cove belongs to you."

"Yes...two men are aboard her."

"Watch where ya jab that thing," Ben Loomins protested stubbornly, turning to glare at the man prodding him forward. He looked down at McPherson, grumbling in annoyance. "I knew it was a mistake to come here."

The Latino barked several orders in Spanish, and within the span of a minute his henchmen herded over Charlie Loomins and the two people he had been guarding. Singling out Ben Loomins, he pointed to the small inflatable rubber boat sitting on the beach a short distance away. Reverting back to English, he said, "You! You will take this boat out to your vessel and bring back the other two men aboard her. Two of my men will accompany you. If you give them any trouble, they will shoot you and throw you over the side for the sharks."

Ben Loomins sighed loudly, shaking his head as if to say what else could go wrong. "Why does this not surprise me?"

It wasn't until the inflatable, pushed along by its puttering little outboard, was well away from the beach before the Latino leader brought his attention back to his captives. With hardened eyes drifting among them, he glowered menacingly. "We will now have a little discussion regarding the whereabouts of a certain treasure. If any of you attempt to lie, deceive or withhold any information regarding this, you will be taken into the open sea where you will be disemboweled and fed to the sharks."

McPherson shuddered. Instinctively he knew his captor would have no qualms whatsoever in carrying out the threat.

- 152 -

The four men peered down from their concealed position amid dense foliage hugging the chasm's edge. Mat Daniels handed the binoculars to the man on his right. "Recognize anyone besides McPherson and his associates?"

Hennington was still wheezing hard and sweating profusely from the strenuous uphill trek. Physical exertion was something new to him, but Mat admired his determination in keeping pace with the rest of them. Hennington had insisted on coming, offering to help out any way he could. His hands were shaking with fatigue and he had difficulty steadying the glasses as he sighted on the group of people gathered on the beach well below them. The broker of old had undergone a complete metamorphosis, his former flamboyance in dress no longer in evidence. With his trademark fedora now missing and his clothing in tatters, he appeared completely bedraggled and worn. Nevertheless his voice held a calm dignity when he answered.

"The one in the suit is Rafael Cardoza." During his dealings with the Colombians, he had met Cardoza on two previous occasions.

Mat stared over at Jacob. "Is there a way down there without them seeing us?"

Jacob's manner was grave. "Only one place exists where we'll be visible. It's about halfway down."

Mat didn't like the sound of that, but risks were something he had grown used to, especially whenever Jake was part of the picture. Shouldering the weapon he carried, he said, "Then we best get cracking." Keeping his gaze fixed on the Haitian, he rose to his feet. "You have any objections in leading us down there?"

Jacob managed a small smile. "Follow me!" He was still breathing hard as he began to move along the narrow trail that skirted Gaia's rim. He, Mat, Zimbola and Hennington had covered the distance from Malique to the cove at close to an all out run in less than fifteen minutes, and his legs continued to burn from the rather steep uphill hike.

"I hope Jake knows what he's doing," Mat muttered half under his breath. "It just seems like too much of a coincidence those people would come here."

"I do not find it to be coincidental at all," Jacob huffed. "Those tuna trawlers belonged to Cardoza. It is obvious someone aboard those vessels sent off a message about this place shortly before their fleet sank."

"But how'd they know where to go?"

"The explanation is simple. The dolphin hunters provided them with this information."

Following behind Jacob, Mat chewed on this. The more he thought about it, the more it made sense. Hours earlier, Jake had filled him in on the missing details he had not known about the dolphin hunters, one of those details being Walter McPherson's involvement. And through the binoculars, he had definitely recognized McPherson sitting in the sand down there, clearly cowed by Cardoza and his gun-wielding goons.

Mat gritted his teeth in anger. McPherson was a pompous asshole whom he disliked intensely. If it hadn't been for McPherson's meddling influence in the Afghan mission, Myers would still be alive. Under normal circumstances, he would have left McPherson for the wolves, but the fact that Myers' kid was also down there with him put a different spin on things and he'd do whatever it took to keep the boy from getting hurt. He owed Myers at least that much, because if Myers hadn't insisted on taking point back in Afghanistan, it would have been he, himself, who would have fallen victim to Raduyev's treachery.

Another thought entered Mat's thinking, one that didn't add up, and he voiced it to Jacob. "How would the dolphin hunters know about this cove?"

"We had an informant among us," Jacob said, his tone still reflecting his physical weariness.

"Who?"

"One of Dr. Grahm's assistants must have told them about this place."

"If that's true, then how'd he get that information to them."

"He probably found a way through some kind of wireless transmission. Dr. Grahm said that Nicolas Henderson is an electronics genius." Jacob stopped speaking momentarily to catch his breath. "Perhaps Henderson is the traitor."

"But you said Henderson's not down there." Jacob had also gotten a glimpse through the binoculars.

"Either he is hiding or they killed him."

- 153 -

Rafael Cardoza watched the inflatable disappear into the narrow inlet that led to the open sea, his mind dwelling on his nephew's last transmission. Somewhere hidden in this place was a hoard of gold. At least that was what the message had said. Based on some kind of sophisticated hardware hidden under a pillow in Ortega's stateroom, Pedro had discovered information that collaborated the claim of the dolphin hunters.

A dark smile crossed Cardoza's face as he mulled this, for it seemed his instincts not to trust Ortega had been right all along. Placing Pedro aboard the San Carlo was so far proving to be a wise course of action. From the communiqués he had received from Pedro, it appeared as though Ortega had his own agenda going. He was puzzled though. Since the last message, he had not been able to reach his nephew.

Turning, Cardoza let his eyes wander over the five captives forced to sit in the sand. Scowling, his gaze fell on Jeff Parker. "Was it you who sent that text message?"

A blank look befell Parker's expression. "Beg your pardon?"

"My people found an electronic device, some kind of receiver. On it was a set of coordinates showing this location, including a message. The message said gold was hidden here."

The first signs of fear tinged Parker's face, and he looked nervously about. "I...have no idea what you're talking about."

Cardoza eyed his closest gunman, then singled out Phillipe. "Take the boy out into the water and drown him."

The gunman tossed Cardoza his Uzi before yanking Phillipe viciously to his feet. Forcing one of the boy's arms behind his back, he wrestled Phillipe out into the water.

Frank Jaffey spoke up as Phillipe thrashed about fiercely to keep his head from being pushed under. "Let the boy go!" He looked imploringly at Cardoza. "The guy who sent the message isn't here."

"Where is he?"

"I don't know."

Cardoza turned his eyes back to the water. "Drown him!"

"Wait!" Jaffey cried out, speaking as fast as he could. "The one you're looking for is Nick Henderson. He knows where the gold is. He's the one who sent the message. We came here to meet him but he was gone when we got here."

Cardoza nailed Jaffey with a penetrating stare, looking for signs of deception. He was good at reading faces, and from all outward appearances, it looked as though the man was telling the truth. Nevertheless, making an example of one of these people would instill sufficient fear in them to keep them from withholding any more information. And fear was a tool he routinely used in achieving the power he wielded as a Colombian drug lord.

Bringing his gaze back to the water, Cardoza noticed the boy was still putting up an insane struggle. "I said drown him!" he repeated in a deadpan tone.

The man holding Phillipe grinned maliciously, forcing the boy's head below the surface.

Something odd and fleeting touched Cardoza as he watched the order being carried out, almost as though he had been witness to a similar scene here in this setting long ago. But that was absurd, for he knew this was his first visit to this most extraordinary place. Caught in the grip of déjà vu, his mind flitted to his ancestry, a lineage that went all the way back to the Spanish conquistadors. He was familiar with his family history, knowing that a distant relative of his, a bankrupt Spanish nobleman, had been among the first Europeans to sail with Columbus. Coming to this very island seeking to start a new life and replenish a lost fortune, his progenitor had helped eradicate the savages infesting the land, growing exceedingly rich over time. What were they called? Ah, yes, the Tainos.

A strange dawning took hold of Cardoza as he thought about his heritage, and he fantasized that perhaps his ancestor of nobility had killed many of these Tainos in this very place. Yes, perhaps the boy carried a smidgen of Tainos blood in his veins, and now history was repeating itself.

Cardoza smiled cruelly, studying the horror-stricken faces of his captives as they watched what was being done to the boy. The feeling that he had brought about a similar act in this very same place a long time ago was suddenly stronger, and visions of a massacre took hold of his senses.

He was seeing through the eyes of his predecessor, a man who commanded a small army of Spanish soldiers, and the screams of the Tainos being slaughtered in this secluded haven gave him pleasure. Strangely, it seemed all too familiar, a scene perpetuated over and over again in countless dreams he had had as a boy, and now he was reliving it once more. Within this cove his ancestor had found a great hoard of gold, taking it from those he had killed. And it was that gold that had laid the foundation to the family estate, handed down from generation to generation until it had eventually established roots in Colombia.

Instill terror in those around you and then take what you want. Yes, that was the family credo he had firmly embraced, solidly indurated within him by genetics, and one he had taken to heart with a reverent passion. Through his efforts in drug trafficking, the wealth and power of the Cardoza estate had grown dramatically, and he would continue to go on taking from others whenever and wherever the opportunity presented itself. Causing the death of others, it seemed, always led to an increase in wealth, and that was something he constantly hungered for with an insatiable yearning. Wealth equated to power, and power was intoxicating.

Shaking off the visions of past carnage, Cardoza looked at his expensive Rolex watch, knowing his 320-ft. ultramodern yacht would arrive shortly to drop its anchor just beyond the outer reef. Then he would deploy more men, having them scour this hideaway and the surrounding hills until they found the one called Henderson.

Cardoza snapped his head around, following the sound of a small startled cry. Only a ripple of water remained where the drowning was taking place. Completely bewildered, he glanced around sharply to see where his man might have gone.

Setting his eyes back on the fading ripples, Cardoza waited a moment longer. When the man failed to appear, he looked to one of his remaining two gunmen. "What happened to Dominique?"

The gunman stared wide-eyed at the spot where Dominque had been moments earlier. "He slipped and went under."

Cardoza was growing annoyed. "Hand your gun to Raoul, Pablo, and go help him!"

With Raoul keeping his Uzi trained on the captives, Cardoza watched Pablo wade out until he was waist deep in water. A passing storm the night before had stirred up the sea bordering the coastline, leaving the incoming tide pushed into the cove a milky white and effectively masking anything below the surface.

Crouching down until his face was just above the surface, Pablo groped around, willing his hands to make contact with something. Doing this for several seconds, he became increasingly frenzied. This quickly changed to maddened agitation.

"What's going on?" Cardoza demanded.

A mix of astonishment and fright solidified on Pablo's face. "They're gone!" he yelled. "They're both gone."

- 154 -

Mentally linked to Achilles, Jake had a clear picture of Phillipe's plight. The juvenile's biosonar immediately told him what was being done to the boy. Pulled along by the young albino just below the surface, he had slipped unseen into the cove, coming to Phillipe's aid just in the nick of time.

Seething with anger, Jake reached out with his free hand while still gripping Achilles' dorsal fin with the other. Catching the bully unawares, he caught the thug's right ankle and tugged savagely, sweeping him off his feet and dragging him out into deeper water heel-first. Hermes was right behind him with Phillipe in tow, having snatched the boy from the man's grasp. With both dolphins pouring on the speed, they quickly covered the distance back to the cove's inlet where they rose to the surface. From where they now floated, they were beyond the line of sight of those still on the beach.

With Hermes lifting Phillipe's head clear of the water, the boy broke out in a coughing jag, gagging then gasping for air. Using his grip on Achilles for leverage, Jake shifted his hold on the thug, getting a handful of the man's shirt collar where it met the nape of his neck. He continued to keep him under.

The man clawed insanely at the arm restraining him with a strength born of sheer terror. Resolutely, Jake refused to let go, most of his attention focused on Phillipe. Gradually, the boy's breathing steadied.

Only when the thug went limp did Jake pull him to the surface. Another albino swam in to help, and Jake passed his unconscious charge over to Aphrodite.

Satisfied that Phillipe was okay, Jake held on as Achilles dove. Staying submerged, he was wisked rapidly back across the cove. There was still work to be done and he was eager to get on with it.

- 155 -

Cardoza's eyes bulged in disbelief as another of his men disappeared below the surface. Pablo had let out a piercing scream, seemingly fighting against something unseen tugging him under. Tensing with fear, he backed away from the water. When Pablo failed to surface, he pointed his Uzi at McPherson. "You! You are coming with me!"

McPherson sat frozen, his expression ashen.

Cardoza stepped closer and kicked him savagely in the ribs. "Get up!" he roared, all of his previous composure now gone.

Fearful of being shot, McPherson staggered to his feet, his face a mask of pain as Cardoza prodded him toward the helicopter. The chopper's pilot was still aboard, standing by at the controls, and Cardoza motioned for him to crank up the turbine.

Realizing he was the only one among them being led away, McPherson hollered out in panic, his cries of protest competing with the rising whine of the chopper. "I've told you everything I know. The one we found with the boy knows where Henderson is. I'm not the one you want." In desperation, he glanced back at Parker. "Take him!" he begged.

Cardoza looked back at Raoul and gestured, drawing a thumb across his own throat. "Kill him!" he shouted. Raoul nodded back grimly, his gaze momentarily taken from Parker.

Parker reacted swiftly, springing to his feet while Raoul was looking back at Cardoza. In an attempt to save himself, he lunged for Raoul's Uzi, but Raoul knocked him back down before he could get a hand on the weapon. Dazed, Parker found himself looking up into Raoul's maddened eyes, the Uzi aimed at his face. In that instant, Parker knew he was a dead man, his mind reeling in expectation of the hail of heated metal that would take his life. He dropped his gaze in resignation, his eyes coming to rest on Raoul's trigger finger.

Raoul's body jerked. Parker looked back up in surprise, staring into the face of his would-be assassin. The thug's mouth hung open in pained amazement. And then Raoul's head abruptly exploded, and Parker was reminded of something he had once seen. It was the way a watermelon had splattered when he had dropped it from the roof of a building during a prank some years back. Headless, Raoul's body twitched jerkily as it staggered away. Toppling to the ground, it continued to spasm erratically.

Perched on one of the cove's tiered ledges, Mat Daniels stared through the telescopic sight of his SR-25, the target better than two hundred yards distant. The rifle was a sniper's dream, accurate to nine hundred yards, and he had become expert at using such a weapon during his stint in the Seals. He had seen what was about to happen to Parker and had less than a second to react, throwing the rifle to his shoulder and firing in the same movement. The first shot had been too low, catching the man squarely in the chest. Displeased with his aim, he had fired again, this time taking a more deliberate stance and sending the bullet to its intended point of impact. Satisfied with the effort, he watched as Parker rose unsteadily to his feet, safe for the moment. Pivoting the rifle, he sighted on Cardoza, ready to take the drug lord down. The scope was filled with McPherson's frantic image. *Get out of the way, asshole!* he cursed under his breath. McPherson was impeding a clear shot. The way Cardoza was forcing McPherson across the beach, he might end up hitting the Naval captain instead.

Cardoza saw Raoul's head erupt in a pink cloud and instinctively knew the shot had come from somewhere along the ridgeline above him. Almost immediately, his eyes located the source. He could clearly see four men on one of the cove's tiered ledges about midway down, one of them holding a rifle currently pointed in his direction. In desperation, he used McPherson as a shield, hunkering low and keeping a tight grip on him as he wrestled him toward the chopper. Ignoring McPherson's pleas, he shoved him roughly into the aircraft's rear cabin, then followed him in to sit beside him, making sure to keep his captive between him and the unseen sniper. Almost immediately, the chopper rose, climbing two hundred feet straight up before banking hard to starboard. In moments, it cleared the ridgeline overlooking the waterfall and was gone.

Mat lowered his weapon, finding it difficult to suppress a grin. He had to be honest with himself. Saving McPherson had not been very high on his priority list.

With both gunmen now in custody of the dolphins, Jake had Achilles tow him out to the salvage tug. From beneath the surface, he could make out the outline of the small rubber boat tied to the vessel's stern. On his way to the cove, he had seen the small inflatable heading for the tug, two gunmen aboard it with Uzi submachine guns trained on the man steering it.

Jake conveyed his plan to the juvenile. *We'll wait for them to bring the others ashore, Achilles. Then we'll take them by surprise.*

Do not let yourself get shot as I did, Jay Jay.

Jake glanced to his right, seeing Destiny riding Hercules. *You don't have to worry about that. Seals are trained to catch an enemy off guard.*

There may be more danger, Jay Jay. Coral has detected the approach of another vessel. A rotary-winged flying machine similar to the one you destroyed at Navassa has just set down upon it.

Jake gave a mental nod, wrapping his mind around this new development.

Achilles added another thought. *Jacob believes the men we captured belong to the same organization that owns the fishing trawlers we sank.*

Then they've either come for revenge or something else, Jake answered. Projecting his thoughts was becoming automatic now.

A sound from above ended the interplay of thoughts, and instinctively Jake knew the inflatable boat was being boarded again. The tide had changed, improving underwater visibility, and from where Jake hovered below the surface, he could see men climbing down onto the boat's open deck.

Jake waited as the two Uzi-toting gunmen took up positions along the inflatable's bow where they could look back at their three captives. Noting the opportunity, he responded quickly, knowing Achilles was reading his mind. Using the dolphin's backside for support, he pushed off hard with his feet, lunging out of the water and throwing a hand around the throat of each man from behind. Caught completely by surprise, their screams were abruptly squelched as both were pulled backwards into the water. Before they could even comprehend what was happening, Achilles reached out and tugged their weapons away.

Releasing his hold on the men, Jake poked his head above the surface, aware of the bafflement painting Ben Loomins' face.

It took Loomins less than a second to realize who he was staring at. "You again," he muttered, but his tone did not hold the same animosity he had shown Jake before.

Jake found it difficult to withhold a grin. "Yeah, but you could at least say thanks."

Sputtering water, the two gunmen broke the surface, splashing frantically as they struggled to regain the boat.

Jake turned his eyes to the floundering men, then looked back at Loomins. "I can let them climb back aboard if you'd like."

Loomins' countenance clouded. "That's if they're able to do that," he said, waiting for one of the men to raise his head above the inflated gunwale. He let out a grunt as he stomped down hard on the man's head. Though stunned, the man hung on stubbornly, and Loomins had to kick him a second time to make him let go. Knocked senseless, the man fell away, floating momentarily before slipping below the surface. Seeing this, the man's partner treaded water, shifting a fearful gaze from Jake to Loomins.

Loomins eyed the second man contemptuously. "I hope you're a good swimmer, cause there's no way you're getting aboard this boat." He suddenly became aware of Destiny breaching the surface, the large albino bull under her. The man Loomins had knocked cold was slung across the dolphin's back immediately in front of the girl, who kept him from sliding off.

"You should let the sonofabitch drown," Loomins suggested, but to Jake his words lacked conviction.

Jake scanned the sea to the south, quickly spotting the vessel Achilles had warned him about. It was coming on fast, rapidly closing the distance separating it from the salvage tug. The vessel was huge and modern, its sleek hull and superstructure a gleaming white. It was one of those customized mega-yachts fabricated mostly from fiberglass, the kind that only the super-wealthy were able to afford and maintain.

Swinging his gaze back to Destiny, he said, "We better take refuge in the cove." He had no doubts that another fight was brewing, knowing this one would be far more intense and dangerous.

Destiny smiled back serenely. "There's no need to hurry, Jay Jay."

Jake was learning to read the girl well, and on her face he could not detect the slightest hint of alarm.

A loud boom cut through the air, drawing Jake's attention back to the vessel bearing down on them. An expanding spume of water rose from the boat's port side, and upon its deck he could see men scurrying about in confusion. Another explosion followed, this one catching the yacht further back astern.

Jake narrowed his eyes, feeling only mild discomfort from the passing shock waves as they pulsed through the sea. Immersed in water as he was, the blasts might have caused serious injury had the yacht been closer to his present position.

A rush of foaming whitewater a short distance away from the vessel caused him to shift his gaze, and he realized the bow of a submarine was breaking the surface.

"Is that who I think it is?" Jake asked incredulously.

Destiny nodded, continuing to smile. "We now have other friends to join our cause."

Jake kept his eyes trained on the sub as the rest of its hull rose up and stabilized. In moments, the hatch on its conning tower opened and three men flooded out. Even from where he treaded water, he could make out the lines of a shoulder-mounted Stinger missile being brought to bear by one of the men. And then the missile was sent on its way, zipping across the gap separating the sub from its target.

The missile exploded with devastating impact, abruptly turning the whirlybird resting upon the yacht's helipad into a raging inferno.

Holding onto Achilles, Jake scrutinized Destiny appraisingly. "How could Bashir possibly know that boat was a threat?"

"Mother alerted Bashir to the danger before she left the cavern. She had a vision of what was to come." Destiny paused, as if to gauge Jake's reaction. "Bashir and his followers want to devote themselves to protecting the pod."

Jake stared back at the yacht, watching it for the next minute. Severely holed by the sub's torpedoes, its bilges were straining hard to stem the flow of water rushing into its hold. Slowed by the damage, the vessel was making a wide turn, seemingly preparing to head back down the coast.

With the danger now in retreat, Jake looked back at Destiny. "Tell your mother she's an amazing woman," he finally said.

- 157 -

It wasn't until much later in the day that Jake had a moment with Mat. Walking along the water at the northern end of the cove, Jake fixated his long-time friend with a weighty stare. "So what's it gonna be, buddy?"

Mat unleashed a hefty sigh, avoiding Jake's eyes. He looked to the water instead, gazing at the creatures shadowing them. "You're not making this easy for me, ya know."

Jake turned to follow his gaze. "Listen, Mat, whatever decision you make I'll respect. All I can tell you is that within the coming months some incredible things are going to happen. Call it whatever you want, but I can guarantee its going to set the stage for a new phase of history on this planet.

But in order to make that happen, these creatures are going to need help from people like us."

Jake let that sink in before going on. "These creatures are not here to favor any one government or sovereign nation. Their cause is much too pure and noble to pursue a thing like that. In giving them your support, you'll no longer be abetting any arrogant, self-serving politicians or bureaucrats."

Mat practically laughed. "Amen to that."

"You'll be making a difference if you help them, Mat. A huge difference."

"That's all fine and dandy, pal. But ideologies don't pay the bills. What do I do for income?"

Jake could not help but smile. He could tell his friend was beginning to vacillate. "I can guarantee you the pay will be much better than anything the DHS is capable of throwing your way."

Skepticism etched Mat's face. "How's that?"

Jake turned his gaze back to the dolphins. "These creatures are already exceedingly rich. I'm sure they'd be willing to work out an arrangement with you that's more than generous."

Indignation suddenly lit Mat's face. "I'm not some donkey that needs to be coaxed by dangling a juicy carrot, ya know. You're making me out to be some greedy asshole."

"You've got me all wrong, good buddy. Don't forget, I know you way too well to ever think that. And these dolphins will never think any less of you for accepting a lucrative compensation package. Just think of yourself as being a well-paid employee of a budding international corporation. You'll have a compensation package with all types of perks."

Mat paused a moment longer before grinning broadly. "Count me in! With you around, I know things will never be dull."

Later that night, a celebration of sorts took place in Malique. Food and drink were in abundance, and joining the party were faces not indigenous to the tiny coastal fishing village. The atmosphere was jubilant, with wild reggae music filling the air. As if to underscore the festivities, more than two dozen paintings depicting the strange dolphin art were placed in full view for everyone to see.

Now able to walk, the former captain of the Yemeni freighter stared happily at Jacob. "The Koran has an old saying, my friend: 'Saving one life equates to saving the lives of all humanity.'"

Jacob was familiar with the quote. He had read thousands of books, and the Koran was one of them. But he knew the quote was incomplete, for the verse in its full context actually comprised a dire warning, requiring that those who fight against God and his Messengers either be slaughtered, crucified, or their hands and feet be alternately struck off. Earlier in the day he had learned the man's name, and he knew that Abdel believed Destiny, Amphitrite, and the white dolphins to be messengers sent by God. Having now lost an arm, Abdel had shifted his convictions, discarding completely his former allegiance. "What do you plan on doing with your life now?"

Abdel's eyes seemed to gleam with newfound purpose, and he turned them in the direction of Destiny. The girl stood off to one side of the crowd as she talked quietly with the man who had brought him here. "My life is in the hands of Allah's angels. From this day forward, my only wish is to serve them."

Jacob assumed a solemn expression, thankful that men like Bashir and the man standing before him had joined the ranks of sanity. "If that is truly your wish, then perhaps there is a place for you among us. We are in need of people with skills such as yours."

Abdel turned back to Jacob. "It is my understanding that you also serve them."

Jacob held back his amusement. In time, he knew Abdel would come to understand the full context of what fate had led him to. Rather than break the man's illusions, he merely nodded with a smile. Let him draw his own conclusions. "Yes. For a long time now I have served them." *And they me, for they have given my life purpose.*

Jacob looked around, singling out various faces. All about him there was potential. Already he could envision what Fernando and Antonio could provide. And although Dr. Grahmn's presence tended to bring a cloud of sadness to his heart, he knew such sadness would gradually fade in time. There was no disputing the value the scientist would bring to the plan, and he could not deny that having Grahm aboard would only hasten their objectives.

And while Jeff Parker had shown an interest in joining them, Frank Jaffey and the Loomins brothers were another story. They were still mulling Emmanuel's offer. Nicolas Henderson, however, would never be given such an opportunity. The albinos had discovered his body shortly after Bashir had driven off Cardoza and his thugs.

Jay Jay had told him to be wary of Ben Loomins' quick-tempered disposition, but as he observed the man, he could not help but sense a trace of good in him. Perhaps it was possible the dolphin masterpieces had worked their magic on him, permanently defusing any desire within the man to capture dolphins for the sake of profit.

Turning, Jacob located Mat Daniels in animated conversation with Phillipe and the hulking giant, Zimbola. Here was another man with skills similar to Jay Jay's, though he had the impression the former DHS agent's approach to dealing with threats would be a bit more conservative than Achilles' bondmate. Daniels had already accepted the job as Tursiops' head of security, and Jacob knew the man would take the position seriously.

Jacob's eyes suddenly fell upon Chester Hennington. Amphitrite had briefed him on the man's Tainos heritage, and it was this tidbit of information that made Jacob scrutinize the man with far more than a passing interest. Here was an individual they could surely use, a broker with superb negotiating skills according to the things Javolyn had mentioned about him.

Inwardly, Jacob began to smile about such prospects. Months ago, Amphitrite had revealed visions to him. The current cosmic climate was rapidly changing, telling her a nexus was fast approaching. It was now time to move forward at a faster pace, turning their dream into reality. But for this dream to take fruitation, a diverse team of people would be required for the change to take place. It had started with one thought, one voice, and now others were beginning to echo the cause. Expanded by the imagination of others, hope had come fully into view. Yes, the power of visualization was a wonderful, seemingly magical thing, for it could propel an idea into something tangible and real.

Jacob's musings were suddenly interrupted by a sudden cessation of reggae music, and he realized his cousin, Emmanuel, was about to speak. Emmanuel was Tursiops' official spokesman, and he had an announcement to make.

"May I have everyone's attention, please," Emmanuel shouted. He waved everyone in closer to the makeshift dais he was standing upon. Everyone crowded in to hear what was about to be said.

Emmanuel cleared his throat, presenting a huge smile to the crowd. From where Jacob stood Emmanuel seemed to stand taller, with a sure set to his shoulders, so different from the gaunt and withered slouch of his body when they had first carried him aboard the Avenging Angel following his rescue from Ternier's prison. "We are on the verge of great things to come, ladies and gentleman, what future historians might one day call the beginning of a new phase in human history. For those of you who wish employment with this milestone business venture, your skills are most welcome."

Emmanuel paused momentarily to scan the faces before him, then shifted his gaze to the sea behind him. More than two dozen delphine heads poked above the water's surface adjacent to the village's main pier. The dolphins were also listening intently.

Jacob wore a thin smile, knowing most of the things Emmanuel was going to say. The potential sea colony would be the first of its kind ever, the start of a global enterprise with an earth-saving mission, a union of dolphins and humans working in cooperation.

For the next half hour, Jacob sat back and took in the words.

- 159 -

It was not until two days later that Jake had the Angel anchored off the Devil's Horn. As promised, Achilles had led him back to the exact spot where the unusual coral formation in the shape of a sea turtle lay. Uncharacteristically, Zimbola let out a grunt as he pulled the first aluminum case slung by a rope from the water, setting the heavy container down on the deck with a dull clunk.

Seconds later, Jake climbed onto the swim platform, water dripping from his body as he shed his dive gear. "Let's see what we've got," he said.

Using a pair of bolt cutters, Hector snipped off the partially corroded lock.

Jake looked to Destiny, who was already aboard. She wore a quiet smile as she eyed the container. Turning his gaze back to the box, Jake wondered if his search had finally ended. Perhaps his promise to a departed friend would now be satisfied. "Here's hoping," he intoned solemnly.

The cover resisted him as he pulled it back on its hinges. Tugging a little harder, he felt it break free, and he was immediately greeted by the glint of gold in the early morning sunlight. To be sure, he dug his fingers into the mass of coins filling the box. There were hundreds, perhaps even thousands of them. Here was more of the treasure Mercades Myers had pulled up from the depths better than twenty years earlier.

Jake stared up at Zimbola, unable to hide his glee. "I counted twelve more containers down there. I'll go back down and tie off the rope. We'll bring 'em up one at a time."

"You won't have to," Destiny said. As she finished saying this, something bumped heavily onto the swim platform.

Jake looked behind him, spotting Hercules. The dolphin withdrew his hands from another metal container identical to the first. Within moments, several more containers were deposited onto the swim platform as more albinos rose up from below. Having swum the heavy boxes to the surface only reaffirmed the strength of the creatures, for Jake was sure each case weighed better than 300 pounds.

Jake grinned expansively, aware that he now had in his possession most of the treasure Myers' grandfather had previously salvaged from the sea floor.

He found it strange that half of it had come to him as a result of what had happened back at Navassa. Also accompanying that portion of the treasure were bearer bonds that had most likely been stolen from the Haitian national treasury during Baby Doc's reign. As yet, he hadn't taken the time to fully appraise the full worth of the bonds, though he was certain it was well in the tens of millions. These would be be given to Jacob, adding to the monies needed in launching and operating Tursiops Worldwide.

Turning his attention to Phillipe, Jake noted the look of awe reflected in the boy's eyes at seeing the gold. "I've never told you this, Phillipe, but this is your inheritance."

"Huh?"

Jake smiled, amused that Myers' kid didn't have a clue about the promise given his father. He had purposely avoided getting the boy's hopes up until he had actually recovered the treasure.

"Some of this will go toward your formal education. A hefty donation to Harvard should make it easy for you to get accepted without any hassles. Maybe-"

"I want to stay here with you, Jay Jay!" Phillipe looked horrified at the suggestion.

Jake sighed. "I promised your dad if I found the treasure I'd make sure you got a college education."

"I can stay in Gaia and Jacob will teach me."

"We'll talk about this later."

"I want to swim with the dolphins."

Before Jake could reply, the boy dived over the side. Achilles was right there to meet him, and Phillipe grabbed hold of his dorsal fin.

Jake looked helplessly at Destiny. "Kids!"

- 160 -

The feeling was strange to Destiny. An almost tangible force had drawn her deep into the cave behind the waterfall. Irresistably beckoned by it, she sensed its unyielding power. The unseen presence was stronger this time, and instinctively she knew the spirits of the Tainos were calling out to her. Like Hennington, Phillipe also had a trace of Tainos blood flowing through his veins. This she instinctively knew, and she thought it befitting how justice had a way of being served. Some of the wealth the conquistadors had gained at the expense of the people they had all but destroyed had come back full circle to the boy.

But it was the manmade chamber the presence wanted her to see, and she dropped the thought of the boy as she stared up at the ceiling. The mud she had smeared over the painting had fallen away, leaving the artwork fully illuminated under the torchlight, and she now understood that the future had changed, for it was not Jay Jay being mauled by a tiger, but another.

Destiny studied the ancient mural for a long moment before hearing someone emerge onto the landing behind her.

Jake followed her gaze, his eyes clouding in amazement at what he saw. "That's Walter McPherson. He was the one who wanted Natalie."

Destiny turned, her long ebony tresses framing an ivory face in the torchlight, and in her expression Jake could see the immense burden that had been lifted. For one prolonged and giddy moment she just stared at him, not saying anything. And then she dropped the torch, coming at him in wild desperation.

Jake winced. The grip of her arms about his neck was surprisingly fierce as she rose up in search of his mouth. Even more surprising was the feel of her lips as they spread over his, shockingly steamy and moist, and Jake found himself responding with a lusting desire as she melted like wax against him, vaguely wondering if his heart might burst. Afraid he might crush her to dust in his embrace, he finally released her, and for several light-headed seconds thereafter, they clung to each other.

"I love you, Jake Javolyn," she gasped feverishly. "I've loved you from the very first moment I saw you." Her eyes shot to the mural showing Jake firing his guns at the retreating helicopter, and she realized she had loved him long before she had met him.

Jake had difficulty speaking, his throat parched to the brink of closing. "I love you, too," he managed to croak hoarsely, and with an aching hunger that took hold of his very being, he pulled her tightly to him again. The feel of her body against his intoxicated him and he was suddenly electrified with wanting, feeling every nerve within him pulsing with an insatiable yearning. And then they made love, an all-consuming passion that seemed to carry their spirits to the far side of the universe. Caught in its grip, Jake sensed a searing bout of light enfold his soul, something good, eternal and boundless.

Much later, as they strolled hand in hand along the cove's gentle waters, several members of the pod leaped high, seemingly hanging in midair in defiance of gravity as they executed a series of breathtaking acrobatics that bordered on the impossible. But then Jake knew that nothing was impossible.

Destiny stopped and leaned up against him, and Jake sensed the aura of virtue and innocence still clinging to her in spite of their lovemaking. "Oh, Jay Jay, look!" she said breathlessly, pointing. "It's so beautiful."

Jake turned, seeking out the thing that had caught her gaze. The most magnificent rainbow he had ever seen straddled the waterfall. The sun was directly overhead, the light giving stark contrast to the arching hues. He realized a strange quirk of physics must be taking place, for the spray coming off the falls had risen into a golden mist and was interplaying with the sunlight in such a way as to make the individual rills appear like bejeweled necklaces, with each gem coming alive and glinting sharply as the light caught it. Captivated by the sight, he watched as the separate colors pulsed and shimmered as they streaked along their respective bands. And as he followed their paths, he had the impression they were racing to infinity.

He blinked, enraptured even more. The vision was changing, and an instant later he was seeing Achilles' painting all over again, the intricate geometry twisting and snaking and teasing his brain, and he suddenly discovered the underlying lucidity within those brush strokes. *It was the rebirth of hope.*

He blinked once more, then rubbed his eyes to be sure it wasn't some trick of the imagination. The odd display of light had changed yet again, and he realized the face of a Haitian woman was staring down at him, her expression lit up in a benevolent, omnipotent smile, her orbs twinkling like day stars against the milky blue sky. And then the face dissolved, turning back into a dazzling rainbow.

It was an illusion, he knew. From where he stood, it was a thing with no real location nor distance. Nevertheless, he could not refute its existence, for the direction in which it was oriented was palpable, pointing the way to a possible future.

Destiny had also seen the visions, giving a silent thank you as Esmerelda's essence faded into the rainbow. At this moment she felt strangely fulfilled and complete, as though there was nothing missing from her existence, and for the first time in her life she realized she was truly happy and alive. Squeezing Jake's hand, she looked up into his strong face, and in a sudden intuitive flash she knew that he would continue to carry out his one true calling.

And that was to protect.

—

Michael J. Ganas

For all those who are music lovers, the theme song to this novel is called:

ALIVE: Theme To The Girl Who Rode Dolphins

This is available at: www.melissahoneywell.com

About the Author

Michael J. Ganas is a licensed professional engineer and the director of a leading marine engineering firm within the U.S. Following a tour of duty in Vietnam where he served as a helicopter crew chief with the 17th Air Cavalry, he earned a degree in civil engineering from Cornell University. Shortly thereafter, his love of the sea prompted him to pursue a career as a commercial diver, heading a wide array of marine construction projects. This eventually led him into his current occupation, which takes on the challenges of civil engineering in underwater environments. This is his first novel.

Printed in the United States
147059LV00001B/3/P